A plain white envelope caught his attention. . . . There was no return address

Hello David,

I'm the nightmare you seeded many years ago. Guess what? I'm back! And I'm coming to kill you. I'll give you one week's head start. Don't be stupid. If you want any chance at all, you will quit your job now and start running. And do yourself a favor. NEVER look back.

You have such a lovely family. Please say Hi to your exquisite wife, Becky, and those beautiful children, Sumner and Caleb, for me. I'll be by soon enough. It's been a very long wait. And David . . .

Have a Great Day!

See Ya Soon,
An Old Friend

DOWNTICK

DOWNTICK

REGAN C. ASHBAUGH

POCKET **STAR** BOOKS
New York London Toronto Sydney Tokyo Singapore

This book is a work of fiction. Names, characters, places and incidents are products of the author's imagination or are used fictitiously. Any resemblance to actual events or locales or persons living or dead is entirely coincidental.

An *Original* Publication of POCKET BOOKS

A Pocket Star Book published by
POCKET BOOKS, a division of Simon & Schuster Inc.
1230 Avenue of the Americas, New York, NY 10020

Copyright © 1998 by Regan C. Ashbaugh

ISBN: 0-671-01889-2

First Pocket Books printing May 1998

10 9 8 7 6 5 4 3 2 1

POCKET STAR BOOKS and colophon are registered trademarks of Simon & Schuster Inc.

Cover photo by Tai Lam Wong

Printed in the U.S.A.

For Trevor

My Reason for Believing

The Light of My Life

To My Wife, Nancy

Thank you for standing by me
through it all

ACKNOWLEDGMENTS

I am very grateful that there were scores of people who devoted an embarrassing amount of time and effort in helping me create this work. I will undoubtedly leave many out. To them . . . my humblest apologies. But there are a handful whom I can never repay. To them . . . I extend a heartfelt Thank you: Don Bouwens, Dr. Craig Cleaves, Judy Conley, Steve Gifford, Jim Gribbell, Beau Gros, Greg Hanson, Det. Sgt. Tom Joyce, Lt. Fred LaMontagne, Jim Richardson, Robert Yahn, Steve Zanardi.

In particular, I owe a debt of gratitude to four people, my partners in crime, without whose encouragement, dedication, and faith, you would not be holding this work in your hands. To Detective Daniel Young of the City of Portland Police Department—Good friend and staunch believer from day one. What can I say, Danny? Thank you seems woefully insufficient, but . . . Thank you just the same. To my agent, Charlie Peers—part-time coach, part-time shrink, full-time friend. You believed from the outset, and never let me take my eyes off the prize. Thank you for your unending loyalty and faith and for putting up with two years of . . . well . . . you know. To my editor and friend, Tristram "The Slasher" Coburn—Thank you for seeing what others did not and for your tireless efforts on my behalf. You know, and I know, what you've done for this work. Here's to many more. Finally, to my assistant, Jean Gray—As you well know, Jean, I am seldom lost for words, but I am now. I cannot comprehend how you hung in there, even when it appeared most bleak. A truer friend, I never had. I thank you. Trev thanks you. My readers don't know it yet, but they should thank you too.

Regan C. Ashbaugh
September 16, 1997

Impotent hatred is the most horrible of all emotions;
one should hate nobody whom one cannot destroy.

—*Johann Wolfgang von Goethe*

INSANITY'S KALEIDOSCOPE

—⟨⟨⟨—

BOOK 1

Maine woods
Saturday, November 4

It had been twenty years since he'd seen him last, a half dozen or so lifetimes, and it all came down to this. How, he wondered, could a life so blessed turn upside down so fast, so completely?

He knelt in the snow, his heart racing so fast he could feel it pump against his thick chest. Be calm, he thought. Be calm. You can lose it later . . . but if you ever had it together, it better be now. This one's for real.

He told himself to concentrate . . . Think . . . Think. Squatting on his heels, he focused on breathing. Relax, you can do this. You have no choice.

He hid behind the farmer's wall. It was old but solid, pieced together a hundred and fifty, maybe two hundred years ago. It seemed to run forever through the woods, like thousands of others just like it throughout New England. It was handmade of stones, delicately placed one on top of the other, no doubt by a man whose livelihood depended on the vagaries of the weather and the magnanimity of the earth.

And now, this stone wall, old and encrusted with moss, was as dear to him as anything had ever been. He clung to it with his bare hands and listened . . . for something . . . anything. Nothing. Nothing human anyway.

Damn it! I can't sit here on my ass all day. He knew he had to do something—become the more cunning one.

3

He'd swum with the sharks before and could do it again. He *had* to . . . this one last time.

What was that? He cocked his head ever so slightly, squinting his eyes. He listened, trying valiantly to control his breathing. There it was again. A crunch in the snow. A snapping twig? A deer? He was as still as the earth now. Not moving. Not breathing. All he could hear was the falling snow; that calming sound that somehow only Mother Nature has perfected.

Christ! This guy is nuts. Was he close? Did this psycho know where he was hiding? He breathed slowly, afraid the trail of his breath in the bitter cold would give him away. With terror, he realized his legs were going numb, but not from the awkward position in which he sat. They weren't tingly as your arm might be if you'd slept on it funny. No, they weren't tingly numb, they were *numb* numb. He was beginning to freeze—the sweat he'd worked up previously was forming ice on his skin.

Oh my God! It hadn't dawned on him until this moment. The son of a bitch wasn't going to chase him out. He didn't need to. There hadn't been time to dress properly for a night in the woods. He knew he couldn't make it through the night. Not in the snow. Not in Maine. Not in what promised to be one of the nastiest autumn cold fronts to hit northern New England in four decades.

Where the hell were the cops!? They'd been with him just a short while ago.

He groped along the wall on his knees, coming upon a hundred-year-old oak which had begun the slow, arduous task of growing around its rocks. He swung his body around . . . slowly . . . quietly . . . so that he sat, resting with his back to the tree.

With more energy than he thought he had, he began to inch himself up—like an Olympic weight lifter, pushing, straining, clinging to the tree with every inch of his life. Was his nemesis lying in wait, weapon cocked, like a hunter behind a blind? The decision was easy. In fact, there was no decision to make—not if he wanted to live. Only as he turned, slowly peeking around the huge trunk of the tree, did the realization slam into his brain. One of them was going to die. He prayed like hell it would not be he.

—∿∿—

Wall Street, New York
Thursday, October 26

"Goddammit, Bobby! I don't give a shit what the spread is. This client's got eighty thousand shares and he wants out now. Do you understand that? Not yesterday. Not tomorrow. Now! If it moves the market, then it moves the market. This guy would sell his mother to make a buck, and I'm telling you, if he's not in cash sixty seconds from now, you can call and tell him why."

True to form, today was shaping up to be just like any other for David Bridwell Johnson. His friends called him D.B., everyone else called him Mr. Johnson. He was forty-two years old, five feet ten, stocky, with a slight gut. He didn't need to demand respect. It followed him wherever he went.

He was the youngest managing director anyone at his firm could remember . . . and that was saying something. His salary was four hundred thousand dollars a year but his bonus could range from five hundred thousand to well over a million if it was a good year.

He was disciplined. To a fault, some would say behind his back. Driven, smart as they come—and everyone knew it. He loved the Street, as insiders called it, and couldn't dream of doing anything else.

As head of institutional sales for Reardon Haskel, one of the nation's largest investment banking firms, his people worked with some of the best known names and companies in the business—Fidelity, Vanguard, Scudder, Putnam—huge public and private pension funds, not to mention banks, insurance companies and scores of local and foreign governments. It's a job that can kill you—literally—and requires tremendous motivation, skill, and commitment.

David traveled frequently. A typical day might find him eating poached eggs with his department head in Houston, a turkey club in Chicago, and back to New York for an evening managing directors' meeting.

He had two sons—Caleb nine, and Sumner eleven. David felt he was a good father—when he was home. His team had become his surrogate family and he knew it. It bothered him, for he loved his family. But what could he do? Quit it all and teach? He didn't know anything else, and besides, he loved it. Lived for it. Everything's a tradeoff. Would things really be better if he took an easier job, was around more, and was miserable?

Approaching his office, David stopped at his secretary's desk. His voice was distinctive, deep but not loud, authoritative but not overbearing. She'd recognize it anywhere. "Linda, did you get me on that flight to Atlanta tonight? I've got to make that meeting at Coke tomorrow."

A hundred items clouded his mind. It functioned in overdrive now. Before she could answer he was already standing behind the mahogany desk in his office, scanning a dozen phone messages before his flight. "I hate these damned things," he said, adjusting his reading glasses. They usually just hung on his chest.

Linda stood in his doorway. "What things?" she asked.

"These damn glasses."

"You can't read without them, right?" she said, tucking her light-auburn hair behind an ear with her left hand. "You ask me, you should use them more often."

"I know, I know, I just hate giving in to Father Time. It makes me feel so old."

She made a poor-baby face, and walked to the front of his desk. "I moved heaven and hell to get you on a flight tonight, D.B. You think maybe I can get a little more warning next time?"

Linda Barnes had been his secretary for eight years, through four different positions, three chairmen, and two takeovers. She wasn't homely, though not really a looker either. Wholesome came to David's mind as he

6

noticed her floral Liz Claiborne dress for the first time that day. Her slightly outdated Dorothy Hamill haircut only added to the effect.

Linda was thirty-eight years old, married with one child—Mikey. The love of her life. She and her husband lived a bucolic life on Staten Island. Aside from his family, David couldn't think of anyone he trusted more.

"Give me a break," he said, thumbing through the pink slips of paper in his hands. "The bastards moved that pension presentation up a week and some lackey forgot to call us. They're lucky I could rearrange my schedule."

Linda smiled, staring into his turquoise-blue eyes. They embodied a simultaneous intensity and beauty that never ceased to awe her. She loved those eyes. "Somehow I think Coke would make it without you."

David raised an eyebrow. "Very funny. Do me a favor. Call Scotty in LA, tell him I have to move that lunch meeting to next week. I'll call him when I get back."

"Way ahead of you. He can do Friday the tenth, so I already penciled you in. Executive travel is working the ticket switch now."

He winked at her. "You're the best," he said, glancing at his watch.

Linda left, closing the door behind her. David stood for a moment, gathering his thoughts. His office was small and surprisingly drab. Unlike the offices in some industries, offices on Wall Street aren't that big a deal—especially on the trading floors. More often than not, they're on the small side, generally lacking the glamour and pretentiousness one might expect to find. At least on the trading floors. David's office was not much better, but he had put some money into it. The Persian rug at the head of his desk his one attempt at showiness.

What he did have was one hell of a view. From his vantage point he could see up the Hudson River for a mile, scan New Jersey, Staten Island, Ellis Island, the Verrazano Bridge, and the Statue of Liberty. He turned and stood, resting both hands on his window, and looked out. He loved New York, the Street, his job.

David realized he hadn't eaten yet today. He rubbed

his temples, feeling the beginning of a headache. Hunger or tension? He wasn't sure. He turned back to his desk, picked up a pack of Marlboros and lit one with his monogrammed, sterling silver lighter. It was a gift from one of his larger clients for moving a deal out the door when everyone else said it couldn't be done.

He was proud of that lighter. In February of last year, David received a call that would ultimately change the course of his career. A large, multinational chemical company had eyed the acquisition of an adversary for some time. The opposing company's chairman had just died and the board was in turmoil. The time to strike had arrived.

There was just one problem. The market was in the crapper. It was one of those dark and dismal times that visits the Street now and then . . . like a black fog. Until it lifts, you can't give stock away.

No one who works the Street, in no matter what capacity, likes to think of days like that, but everyone knows they're coming . . . just not when. So when times are good, if you're smart, you save, because when times are bad, it's like chewing light bulbs for a living.

But David would hear none of it. He personally flew to see a dozen clients, selling them on the merits of the takeover and the long-term benefits that would accrue to the acquiring company's bottom line, and hence, its stock price. Other, bluer-blood firms told David's client it couldn't be done. Not then. The company would simply have to wait for a more opportune time.

But David took it as a personal mission. A few weeks later, when the deal was done, he sat at his desk sipping a Glenlivet before catching the train home to Connecticut. Linda walked in and said the *Wall Street Journal* was on the phone. They wanted to interview him for their lead story in the next day's paper. He smiled at her—a tired smile—and just nodded.

Where does the time go? "Linda," he said, pressing the intercom key. "Can I see you real quick? I need to wrap up a few things before I catch my plane."

He turned back to the window and saw a tug pulling two heaping barges of trash down the river toward the

Verrazano. He wondered for a moment if they still dumped that stuff out at sea.

"Hi," Linda said dutifully, carrying her day planner under an arm and, to his delight, a Diet Coke and a turkey with Swiss on rye in her hands. "Your timing's good. It's been busy and I know you haven't eaten. I called the deli twenty minutes ago. They just brought it up. Figured you'd want something to eat before your flight."

"You're a mind reader," David said, wearing a big smile. He walked to the front of his desk and lightened her load of his much needed snack. He popped open the Coke, taking a long swig. "Listen, I forgot that Saturday is Caleb's birthday. Could you get him something while I'm gone? Call F.A.O. Schwarz. See if they have one of those Mecha Godzilla sets. Mega Godzilla. Something like that. We were watching the Cartoon Channel the other night and he went bonkers over the commercial. Send up a courier. Have them Fed Ex it to my house. Put it on my card."

She had no problem with such a request. She enjoyed being his right hand. Without her he'd be lost. He knew it, and she did too. Better yet, she knew he knew it. His Christmas bonus said so every year.

David shoved a few items in his jacket pocket. "I've got to get a rough copy of my P and L to Givens before Tuesday's meeting. Where am I staying anyway?"

"The Biltmore."

"All right. Fax me last week's run before you leave. Call the concierge and have it left in my room. Also see if they can bring up some fruit or cheese or something."

"No problem," Linda said, his frenetic pace familiar to her by now. "You know, I'm concerned about that meeting, David. Saperstein wants that mini-institutional desk in the worst way. I can't help but think he's got something up his sleeve."

David stuffed some reports in his briefcase. "Can you get a return flight back to Westchester instead of La Guardia?"

"Did it. Arriving six seventeen. By the way, pick up your tickets at the counter when you get to the airport."

"Good."

"Did you hear what I said?" Linda asked.

He looked up. "Yes, I heard you. He may want it but he isn't going to get it. Not while I'm still breathing. I worked my butt off for two years to make that cash cow what it is," he said, taking a healthy bite of his sandwich, pushing his rear back to keep a glop of mayo from dripping on his tie.

"Any napkins?"

"Sorry," she said smiling.

He walked in that position to his mahogany file cabinet and pulled out a Kleenex.

"What time's my flight?"

"Six fifty. I've got a limo picking you up at quarter of."

"Thanks. Listen. You let me worry about Saperstein. That SOB tries to wrestle that desk from me and it will be the last time he ever takes me on."

"I hope you're right, David. I don't trust him."

"Really?" he said, laughing slightly.

She stared at him, frowning. Was it the light, or was the silver on his temples overtaking his wavy, nut-brown hair? With a slight sense of surprise at the passing of time, Linda noticed that David was graying. Somehow she'd never really noticed it like this before.

"Okay, that's a wrap," he said, wiping his mouth. "Oh, I almost forgot. Have I been getting any weird phone calls lately? Anything out of the ordinary you haven't told me about? Maybe you didn't want to bother me or you forgot?"

"None that I can think of. Why?"

"Nothing big. We've been getting a few weird ones at home lately. Just wondering."

"No, not here, I'm glad to say."

"Good. Music to my ears," David said.

"Probably some kids having fun."

"Yeah." He wasn't sure why, but he had a nagging thought that it was more than that.

"Anything else?" Linda asked.

"Nope. See you Monday."

"You got it. Mikey's got a recital at school tonight. I'm going to rustle that P and L stuff together and head home. He's so nervous. I can't wait to watch him. I really hope he does well."

"He'll be the star of the show. You tell him I said it's okay to have butterflies. I get them every time I make a presentation. Tell him the key is to make sure they're all flying in formation."

Linda laughed. "I will. Have a good trip and get some sleep. You look tired. Oh, and good luck."

"Thanks, I'll need it," David said, stuffing his cigarettes in his jacket pocket.

"Nah, you always knock 'em dead."

David glanced at her and smiled. "See ya."

He smiled as she shut the door.

David felt lucky Linda worked for him. She was very good. He thought of Mikey's recital and his mind drifted toward home. David realized he should call his wife before heading for La Guardia. Walking back to his desk, he took out another Marlboro, lit it, and punched home on his auto dialer.

"Hello. You've reached the Johnsons." David would know the message in his sleep. "Have a great day." Beeeep. "Hi honey. Hi kids. It's Daddy. I'm on my way down to Atlanta. Arriving in Westchester at six seventeen tomorrow night. Don't worry if you can't make it, Becky. I'll grab a cab. See you all then. Beck, I'm staying at the Biltmore. I'll be at Coke the better part of tomorrow. I'll try to call before I catch my flight back. Caleb, I can't wait for Saturday, buddy. Love ya. Bye."

He stood at his window and allowed himself a moment of solitude, dragging deeply on his cigarette. What a filthy habit. David knew he should quit but didn't care. He loved to smoke. At least he didn't do it in front of the kids. Usually he'd sneak a couple in the basement. Often, when he couldn't sleep, he'd go up to his office on the third floor after everyone had gone to bed. He'd read journals, scan trading files, make notes, prepare himself for the war that would be tomorrow. His office was off limits to the kids. He'd smoke like a chimney there.

He grinned as he watched the bluish-gray smoke curl in all directions as it hit the window. *Madness*, he thought. *Oh well, it's better than crack.* Somewhere deep inside though, he frowned. It wasn't the smoking he worried about. It was the booze. When did it start to get out of hand? He really couldn't put a finger on it. What he knew for sure was that he was drinking more than he should.

No rationalization, no excuse seemed to work anymore. He couldn't pour himself a drink without thinking about it. He'd seen a television commercial once for some hotline. It's admonition had never left him. There was a red flag to look for. If you found yourself worrying that you might be hooked, you probably were. David couldn't quite shake his uneasiness.

Some people can nurse a drink until the ice cubes melt. Were they abnormal or was he? Maybe they realized, as he probably would eventually, that booze makes life harder. You say things you shouldn't say, hear other people say things you shouldn't hear, and invariably . . . feel like shit in the morning.

David had once asked his best friend—a recovering alcoholic—what he thought about his drinking. "What do you think, Jonah? Am I an alcoholic?" he asked.

"I don't know, D.B. Is it working for you?" Jonah answered with a question.

Jesus Christ. I ask the guy a simple yes-or-no question and he comes back at me with some Socratic bullshit. "Well, I don't know," he answered instead. "I've got a great job, two beautiful children, a wonderful wife, a winter home, and more money than I know what to do with."

"Well," Jonah answered, "as long as it's working for you."

Now, as he watched the gray smoke swirl up and away from the window, he wondered if it was. He thought now that what he had *really* wanted Jonah to tell him was that yes, in fact, David was one of the worst cases he'd ever seen, and if he didn't seek help soon he would probably lose everything. It would be so much easier if someone— anyone—just told him he had to stop drinking. But it was his little secret and apparently, that wasn't in the cards.

Anyway, David figured it hadn't really hurt yet. Not in a material way. He never drank on the job. No one at work would ever dream he had a drinking problem. In fact, the only time he really drank was at home, after everyone had gone to sleep. He couldn't count the number of times he'd stayed up until the wee hours having just one more.

Suddenly David felt very tired. His eyes were heavy, and for some reason he felt like crying. At times like these he wanted desperately to stop this train he was on and get off, just for a little while, at least until he could find out who he really was—what really mattered to him.

His father was a drinker, though David hadn't realized it until much later in life. He kept a Frigidaire in the garage of their home in Mystic, Connecticut, and always had a beer open while tinkering at his work bench or toiling in the yard. From his earliest childhood, David could remember his father with one type of drink or another. If it wasn't beer on the weekends, it was Manhattans or martinis after work.

To David it just seemed that life and alcohol went hand in hand—like movies and popcorn, barbecues and hamburgers. Booze seemed omnipresent in his formative years. Everyone in his family drank, and more often than not, it seemed family gatherings were nothing more than an excuse to tie one on.

David took his first drink when he was twelve. He and Jonah talked his older brother into buying them a bottle of Smirnoff vodka. "Don't get too fucked up," his brother said, handing him the bottle. "Mom and Dad will kill me."

"Don't worry," David replied. "We can handle it."

His brother laughed. "Wanna bet?"

Asshole, David thought as he and Jonah rode their bikes to the beach. They sat on the rocks of the jetty, mixing the vodka with some orange juice. David would never forget it. The warmth in his belly as it hit home, the sense of finally growing up, like Dad. He felt so cool, so sophisticated. It was as if he'd found the missing link in his life. David and Jonah both vomited that night, an omen David didn't know enough to heed.

Thirty years later he was still drinking and it still made him feel like shit. Somewhere along the way, booze had hooked him. It coursed through his veins, spiraled down his DNA, mocking him at every turn. How did it get so fucked up? At forty-two David had achieved more than most men dream of in their lifetimes, and yet, he still felt lost. He thought now there should have been a sign when he buckled into this roller coaster: Caution! This ride *never* stops.

He turned from the window and stepped to his desk to pour himself a Glenlivet before catching his limo to the airport. After all, his work day was finished. But something inside made him stop. He stood staring at the lower right drawer . . . looking at it . . . almost through it, for the longest time. Deep within he wanted that drink. He began to tremble ever so slightly, caught himself, and for a moment felt scared. Had he become his father? The thought sent spasms down his spine.

"Enough," he mumbled to himself. I'm not going to drink on this trip. I want to feel good when I get back. I want to *really* be there for Cabe's birthday.

He looked at his watch. It was nearly 5:30 P.M. He had to get going. He finished gathering his things, stuffing them haphazardly into his briefcase. He stuffed a few of the more important phone messages in his jacket pocket. Some came from people in the west. He'd return them from his cell phone on the ride to the airport.

He was giving his office a final glance, when his phone rang. He thought for a moment of closing his office door and ignoring it, but noticed the call was on his personal line. Probably Rebecca, or better yet, maybe one of the kids. Putting down his briefcase and his carry-on bag, he ran to the phone.

"Hi," David said.

"David. Ted."

Theodore Hemphill Givens, III, was chairman and chief executive officer of the whole shooting match. He was sixty-one years old, with snow-white hair and piercing green eyes. At six feet seven inches, he towered over almost everyone. He was a man accustomed to getting his way. And while he wasn't dictatorial he exuded the confidence of a Patton.

He also had a list of every managing director's private line and had the annoying habit of calling them with regularity. It was a small thing, just enough to keep everybody on their toes. Not that David didn't respect him. Everyone did. His timing just stank.

"Oh, hi, Ted," David said, rolling his eyes. "I thought you were my wife."

"No such luck."

"I'm running to catch a plane, Ted. What can I do for you?"

"Go. I don't want to make you late. We'll talk when you get back."

David plopped himself on the edge of his desk. "I have a couple of minutes. What's up?"

"Nothing big. I just had an interesting conversation with Harvey Saperstein. Given the nature of the discussion, I thought it only fair I speak with you too. But hey, it can wait. You really should get going. I hear there's a water main break on the FDR and things are backed up to the tunnel. I'll grab you at the meeting Tuesday night."

Shit. "Is there a problem?" he asked, feigning nonchalance.

"No, no. But let's just say I'll be interested to hear your presentation. Listen, you've gotta go. I'll talk to you Tuesday. Have a good trip."

"Okay, boss. See you then," he said with practiced calm.

He stood for a while staring out his window before he realized he was intently listening to a dial tone. "Jesus Christ!" he bellowed to no one and everything, slamming the receiver in its cradle. *I need this like I need TB.*

He glanced longingly at the lower drawer but opted for three ibuprofen tablets in the top drawer instead. He swallowed them with the last of his Coke, walked back to his belongings, looked around, and closed his door as he left. He half walked, half jogged through the trading floor toward the elevators. The cleaning crews were already busy picking up tons of debris from that day's battle.

They seemed oddly incongruous against the backdrop of the most sophisticated trading equipment in the world. Row upon row of quasi cubicles—semicircles really—containing trading screens, quant computers, and banks of telephones. Each trader, David often thought, resembled an astronaut in his space module, surrounded by some of the world's highest-tech gadgetry. The average trading day here exploded in a scene the lay person would think befitting only a Hollywood movie.

There is an unspoken urgency in the traders' work. The tolerance for mistakes on the Street? Exactly zero. One misstep can cost the firm millions, an account, or both. There's a kinetic energy here. Something inexplicable. It settles in your blood and becomes a narcotic in its own right. Billions of dollars are traded just on this floor every day. Sometimes the magnitude of what happened on any given day on Wall Street amazed even David.

David's head swirled. He looked at his watch again. 5:42 P.M. He had to move. He wasn't worried about the limo leaving without him. Hell, they got paid by the hour, they'd sit there all night. It was that damn water main break that Givens had mentioned. He worried now he hadn't given himself enough time.

". . . had an interesting conversation with Harvey Saperstein . . ."

He waited for the elevator, fidgeting with his wedding ring. He had to wait a while because it was the end of the day and every car stopped at nearly every floor, and he was forty-two stories up. Like fleeing rats. He waited interminably until finally, one of the lights dinged red.

When the doors opened he looked inside at the packed elevator as if it were a Tokyo subway. On any other night he would have waited for the next car, but not tonight. Sorry folks. He slowly edged his way in, met by the collective sighs of twelve uncomfortable, impatient rats, anxious to end their day's angst.

". . . Given the nature of the conversation . . ."

After what seemed a week at least, the doors opened

on a huge, ornate foyer. Marble, dark mahogany, and brass were everywhere; the lobby resembled an amphitheater, with real palm trees beneath a hundred-foot, glass-paned dome. The throngs made their way in the direction of the rain forest, while David headed down the back steps toward the side street where all the limos met their rides.

Limo is something of a misnomer. These cars aren't the stretch models that the word brings to mind. Rather, they're almost always Lincoln Town Cars, black, dark blue, or brown, and ubiquitous in southern Manhattan. Companies used them as much for employees' safety as anything else. Sometimes meetings ran late enough that the commuter trains had stopped running altogether. In these instances, a limo would take you all the way home—wherever that was. It's standard operating procedure on the Street.

David stepped outside and was surprised by the cool tingle of the evening air in his lungs. He took one look at the long line of dark Lincolns and immediately realized he'd forgotten to get the limo number from Linda.

"Give me a break," he said aloud and started peeking his head in the passenger side door of the first in line.

"Reardon Haskel. La Guardia?"

"Nope."

He moved to the next. "Reardon Haskel. La Guardia?"

"Sorry, fella."

I can't believe this. There must have been three dozen of them, maybe more. Six minutes later, he hit pay dirt.

"There's a U.S. Grant says you can't get me there for a six fifty flight," David said.

"A man after my own heart," the driver responded, whipping his livery out into the traffic. "Keep it where you can get to it."

"FDR's closed. You're going to have to earn this one."

As the limo began its journey, David leaned his head back, staring at the black velour roof. Givens's words kept resonating in his ears. What the hell could Saperstein possibly have told him that would cause a stir? Had he fabricated something? Did he know something David did not? One big shark tank, he thought.

Worse yet, he worried that perhaps he had underestimated his rival. Had David broken the first rule of battle? Know your enemy. He had read *The Art of War* many times. Sun Tzu would be disappointed. He couldn't allow himself to believe he had made such a mistake.

He'd learned that lesson the hard way, as a senior in college. He and another classmate were vying for an opening as an intern with a large mutual fund company in Boston. David's interview was scheduled for 8:00 A.M. on a Friday morning. He'd gone out with friends the night before, being careful not to overdo it.

He came home early, about 10:30 P.M. only to find a message on the kitchen table from one of his roommates. The gentleman with whom he was scheduled to meet had called. There'd been a death in the family and could they put it off until the following Wednesday?

Shit! What could he do? He'd have to wait. It was only by chance that David learned the caller was his classmate, sabotaging his one chance. He went ballistic, hunting him down in a pub off campus. There were words and some shoving, but friends stepped between them before he unleashed his real fury.

It was his first experience with Machiavellian business ethics, and it would not be his last, but he learned a valuable lesson that day. In business, never let your guard down and *never* underestimate your rivals.

David worried now that somehow he'd missed something, that maybe he had let his guard down. He closed his eyes for several minutes and breathed deeply, trying to think it through. He tried to relax by attempting to figure out which way the driver was going just by feel. He was awakened when his head snapped. Heavy brakes by a man on a mission. He rubbed his eyes vigorously with the knuckles of both forefingers, trying to place himself. He was on the Brooklyn-Queens Expressway. David looked at his watch. It was 6:34 P.M. This guy's good. He might just make it.

He flipped on the reading light attached to the side panel—it was attached to a spring and could be twisted in any direction—and opened his briefcase, frowning at the mess.

He pulled out his mail and ripped off the rubber band, wrapping it around his wrist, scanning the myriad sales pitches and hype. There was some seminar for managers on how to handle difficult employees. A derivitive mortgage bond conference in San Francisco. The AMEX was touting their new SPIDR contract. The Philadelphia Exchange was now trading a new Technology Index Contract. There was a memo from Givens on the revised sexual harassment policy of the firm.

A plain white envelope caught his attention. It was out of the ordinary. A letter addressed to him, typed, with no return address. It definitely piqued his interest. Who could this be? A friend? Rebecca? He wondered who would send him a typed envelope at work with no return address. He put the envelope up to the light. Postmarked Boston. "Huh," he said, sliding his thumb under the flap, tearing it open.

Nothing special, he thought. It was one page, neatly tri-folded on cheap erasable stock, the kind he used for term papers in college. He slipped on his reading glasses and unfolded the letter.

Hello David,

I'm the nightmare you seeded many years ago. Guess what? I'm back! And I'm coming to kill you. I'll give you one week's head start. Don't be stupid. If you want any chance at all, you will quit your job now and start running. And do yourself a favor. NEVER look back.

You have such a lovely family. Please say Hi to your exquisite wife, Becky, and those beautiful children, Sumner and Caleb, for me. I'll be by soon enough. It's been a very long wait. And David . . . Have a Great Day!

See Ya Soon,
An Old Friend

There is no word to adequately describe David's reaction. Incredulous is too calm. Terrified might work. Somehow David knew his whole life had just changed. His eyes widened with alarm as his heart began to thud against his chest. His palms turned gummy with sweat, his scalp burning with tension. A painful flame of bile ignited in his stomach and he could taste acrid, sticky adrenaline racing through the veins in his mouth.

"What airline, mister?" the driver asked.

This had to be a joke. Who did he know that would even attempt humor this sick? He racked his brain. Names, faces came to mind. He'd think momentarily and move on. John? Crazy, but not insane. Shag? No, couldn't be. He made a frantic mental inventory of people, places, conversations, events.

"Hey, mister. Sorry to bother you, but I gotta know what airline."

"What?" David said, looking at his driver in the rearview mirror with glazed eyes.

"What airline?"

"Oh. Uh . . . Delta."

"Spaceshot," the driver whispered to himself.

Two minutes later he yanked the car to the curb, hurriedly making his way to the trunk. He pulled out David's belongings and stood, hand out, an ear-to-ear grin plastered on his face.

David looked at him—through him really—leaning against the trunk.

"You okay, buddy?"

David caught his eyes. "Uh. Yeah . . . I'm fine. Thanks," he said, grabbing his things and turning to go.

"Hey!" the driver yelled.

David turned, confused. The guy wants a tip, he thought. He dropped his bag and reached inside his trousers and fished out a five-dollar bill.

The driver glanced down, then up with a frown. "Thanks, but I was hopin' to see General Grant."

"Oh, excuse me," David said, embarrassed. "I'm sorry, I forgot." He pulled out a fifty and laid it awkwardly in the driver's palm. "My head's not screwed on straight today."

"Yeah," the driver said. Wall Street guys. They'll screw you at every turn.

David made his flight with a couple of minutes to spare, handed his things to the flight attendant, and collapsed in his first class seat, his heart pounding.

"Can I get you something to drink, sir?"

"Oh, um . . . ." Bits and pieces of the last hour's events flitted across his brain. Givens, Saperstein, the note. He didn't want to drink, but he had to have one. Just one. He realized he was trembling and sat on his hands. Even God would understand this one. "How about a vodka martini? Double, please."

"No problem," the flight attendant said. "You look harried, sir. Would you like a warm towel?"

"No, thank you," David said with a wave of his hand.

He took the letter out of his jacket pocket, put on his reading glasses, and read it again. Then again. *Jesus Christ, what do I do?*

All right, now wait a minute. He hadn't gotten where he was by dissolving into panic at the first sign of trouble. He had to think this through. Obviously, some asshole out there was getting his jollies by throwing him for a loop. *Saperstein? The guy's a shark, but come on. . . . It just wouldn't make any sense.* Certainly he wasn't so deranged that he would risk a seven-figure paycheck with a prank like this.

His heart seemed to miss beats. David was stupefied. He tried with desperation to remain calm, think it through. Unless he'd missed something, someone had just threatened his life or his kids' lives or both. His breathing accelerated, causing a sense of dizziness. For a moment he thought he would faint. *Get a grip.*

"Sir?" the flight attendant asked.

She'd been standing there for some time. Hunched over in his seat, elbows on his knees with the letter in his hand, he hadn't noticed her.

"Oh, I'm sorry," he said, leaning back, pulling out the tray for his drink. She placed it on a napkin with the

21

Delta logo on it. He stared at it, the longing rising from deep inside. His desire, his need, was in his gene pool. His craving was involuntary—like breathing. God, he needed that drink. Givens, Saperstein, booze, the letter, Coke, Caleb. The voices and words swam in a riotous frenzy through his brain. He felt nauseated.

David took the drink and belted half of it home before putting it down. He laid his head back, welcoming the tingling heat in his belly. David sat still a few moments before realizing he was going to vomit.

—⁓—

In his entire business life, David could not remember yearning more for a hotel. He had suffered through the flight from La Guardia and thanked God when it was over. The flight attendant knocked on the lavatory door to inform him the captain was requesting all passengers take their seats. He could hear her outside as he clung to the metallic contraption, breathing its chemicals, praying it was a dream.

When he emerged, he was white as a ghost. He tried to ignore the stare from two dozen curious, prying eyes and took his seat. The attendant came over to ask if he needed medical attention.

"No. Must be a twenty-four-hour bug. Just a little queasy is all. I'll be okay."

"Are you sure, sir?"

He was shaking visibly. "Yes. When you can, I'd love a Coke with lots of ice. Oh, and a blanket, please."

"As soon as we're airborne, sir."

"Thank you," he said, leaning back, humiliated, wishing he could just fade away.

Now, in the quiet of his room at the Biltmore, he kicked off his shoes, flung his jacket over one of the chairs, and flopped his racked body on the bed. He was one of the most powerful men at his firm—in control, or so he thought—making deals, closing clients. He was one of a small, quiet cadre of individuals who kept America's corporate behemoths supplied with an uninterrupted flow of capital. He worried just how much all that was about to change.

Let's look at this analytically. What did he know? Someone, for some as yet inexplicable reason, was trying to ruin his career. Whoever it was knew more about David's family than David felt comfortable with. It seemed reasonable to him, at least for now, to believe this was true.

Whoever this wacko was, he knew Rebecca's name, knew his sons' names! Was he an old buddy? Did he know this guy or gal from his past? "And, David . . . Have a great day!" Was that from the answering machine at home? He must be the source of the calls.

What about Saperstein? As improbable as it seemed to him that he could be the source, David decided to confront him on Monday. "That should be fun," he mumbled under his breath. He lay there envisioning the confrontation in his mind, walking through it like a chess match. *What the hell?* Even if it wasn't Saperstein, it couldn't hurt to shake the bastard up a little. Show him his darker side. Make him think twice about whether the mini-institutional desk was really worth the fireworks.

Okay, but what do you know that you can use? The letter was postmarked Boston. That narrowed it down to a manageable million or so. He thought of calling Rebecca, of reading her the letter, but decided against it. It would panic her. Christ, look how he had handled it. Not exactly a paragon of masculinity. No, the letter was postmarked the twenty-fourth. He still had five days. Anyway, he'd be home tomorrow night. They would talk about it then.

He started thinking of the calls he needed to make: internal security, NYPD, maybe the Boston police. He wasn't sure. FBI? They'd probably laugh at him. But then again, maybe not. He wasn't exactly some slouch. Certainly Givens could pull some strings. But what strings? Twenty-four-hour guard on himself, Rebecca, and the kids? Hardly.

Should he quit? Here was a conundrum. *Let's say I do*

quit. Then what? Move? Where to? For how long? No. It was like blackmail. David felt certain that if he gave in to this demand, it would be the first in a string that would be open ended. Running away just didn't appear to be the answer. Hell, he might as well just roll over and die—make it that much easier on the son of a bitch.

He'd dealt with bullies before. Mostly on the corporate level. The best approach was always to call their bluff, bring them out in the open where their nasty, moldy, dark little plans would wither in the light of day. It seemed to David that he didn't have a choice.

But what about the kids? He could hear the calamity of cries from the community, the media, his firm, his in-laws, if he didn't act and something happened.

His head was swimming now. He glanced at the digital clock on his night stand. 10:57 P.M. He had to go on—push this out of his mind—at least long enough to make his meeting with Coke count. *Christ,* he thought, *how am I ever going to do this?*

Dig deep. Relax. Maybe it's just a prank. Nothing big. No harm, no foul. Yeah, well if this is no harm . . . He thought if he ever found out who this asshole was, he was going to sue his ass up one side of Manhattan and down the other. He would make this son of a bitch wish he'd never heard his name. But right now, whoever sent this threat held all the cards. That would change. If David had to, he'd kill him. He'd kill him sure as the sun would rise tomorrow morning. And he wouldn't bat an eye.

This was a side of himself he kept locked deeply in his soul. No one, not even Rebecca, knew of its existence. Occasionally, it bothered him to know in his heart he could kill another human being and feel no remorse. Was that normal? He'd squelch his fear by telling himself it wasn't something he dreamed of or fantasized about. But there'd been times in his life when he knew he could have done it and not even flinched.

Like the time Rebecca called him at his office in tears, fearful of the TV repairman in the playroom downstairs. He'd come on to her and she was frightened. David ran from his office and took a cab all the way home and was waiting when the repairman returned to his store for the day. The confrontation that ensued scared David even now. He knew he could kill. He'd come within a hair's breadth that day. Only providence kept him sane enough to prevent it.

The thought of eradicating this scumbag—of coming out on top—worked miracles on his nerves. David began to feel more in control. He would most likely move Rebecca and the kids to his folks' place in California, at least until this thing blew over or came to a head. Somehow, the thought of death didn't scare him. Strange, he thought, the bigger fear was giving up his job. Oh, he was concerned for his family all right, but he would take care of them.

David lay thinking on the bed. *Let him come.* "Come on you cocksucker. I haven't had a good fight in a while. You don't know who you're messing with," he whispered to himself, staring at the ceiling.

He called the front desk and set a wake-up call for 6:00 A.M., nibbled on some cheese and fruit, and poured himself a ginger ale from the bar. He didn't even want to think about booze right now. If there was a God, he thought maybe the flight was his own personal wake-up call. David figured God most likely carried more weight than he, and he wasn't going to test him twice in one day.

He undressed, hit the light, and tried to think about his meeting at Coke in the morning. He hadn't given the fax Linda sent him as much as a glance. He was drifting off to sleep. *I'll work on it on the flight back.*

The last of the four graves the YMCA employees found were in a row with the other three. David had been allowed to watch and felt he would have an emotional and physical breakdown when he walked around the gravediggers and looked at the partially decomposed face of his nine-year-old son. He screamed at the top of his lungs and felt something in his mind snap.

David sat bolt upright, dripping wet and shaking.

"Jesus Christ!" he said, jerking his body around, sitting on the edge of the bed. *So this is how it's gonna be?* He couldn't remember the last nightmare he'd had. His dreams were odd, like anyone else's—sometimes fraught with danger. But he had never dreamt of the death of one of his children.

David sat there with his elbows on his knees, rubbing his temples with his fingers. *Are we having fun yet?* He shuddered, took a long, deep breath, and walked to the table, pulling out the Marlboros from his jacket pocket. He sat in one of the chairs, elbows on the table, hands clasped together, watching smoke curl up through the dim city lights creeping through the window.

What time was it? He walked back to the night stand and picked up the clock. 3:41 A.M. He felt sick from exhaustion. For a moment, David thought of picking up the run Linda had faxed him and putting together a rough draft for the meeting on Tuesday. He turned back to the table, snuffed his smoke, and lay down in bed. He felt cold now. He pulled the blankets up tight around his neck and lay there, counting bumps in the ceiling.

He desperately needed sleep. For a fleeting moment, he thought of counting sheep and smiled at the sheer silliness of the idea. He toyed with the thought of masturbating but there was too much on his mind.

Sex had always been a good reliever of tension for him. When he and Rebecca first became serious, she was somewhat shy sexually. He was only the third partner she had been with. He'd long since lost track. He took delight in teaching her, showing her, delicately prompting her to higher levels and deeper pleasures.

It wasn't long before they were making love two, maybe three times a day. They experimented, probing every inch of each other's body. As with any relationship, the initial obsession wore off; but sex was still good for them, albeit less frequent. Kids and time saw to that. But still, he missed her and yearned to hold her naked body close to his.

His 6:00 A.M. wake-up call came all too soon. But he was ready to close the largest account of his life. He lay flat on his back, clasping his hands under his head. The morning sun was beginning to shine through his window. He felt relaxed, excited about the opportunity ahead. Closing Coke would sure work as a nice feather in his cap come bonus time. Bonuses were being decided even as he made this trip. If he could close Coke, well, what could he say? He had that Midas touch.

Without warning, like a bombshell, the letter came crashing into his mind—a neutron bomb, oblitering every living thing playing in its recesses. A sense of dread enveloped him. His heart began to race again. He suddenly felt sluggish and heavy. Depression, he thought. This must be what it's like to suffer from that dreaded disease—a constant sense of anxiety, the feeling that your head weighs fifty pounds on your shoulders.

For that one moment, before the letter had come slamming back into his brain, he had been the deal maker again. He remembered what it felt like to be in control, call the shots, have the power. Then, at the snap of a finger, it all evaporated. Like a drop of water on the hood of a car in the middle of August. There one moment and then . . . poof. Gone. Just like that.

David wondered if his mortal enemy, whoever it was, was basking in the delight of knowing he would react this way. Or was he more concrete, not able to enjoy the fruits of his sickness until David actually capitulated. He shuddered with dread.

"Well, asshole, I got my own surprise for you. Ain't no way I'm packing it all up. You'll have to kill me first. Come and get me big boy," he said aloud, trying to convince himself his defiance wasn't spurious.

———

Goodman's secretary made the introductions. "David Johnson, Bob Magdolin."

"Bob," David said smiling, holding out his hand.

"This is Stewart Eisenhart. We all call him Einstein. He's our computer quant king."

"Stewart, hope we get a chance to work with you," David said smiling, extending his hand.

"And this here is my boss, Marty Goodman. I believe you two have met."

"Spoken many times, but never had the pleasure. It's always good to put a name with a face," David said, walking around the conference table, shaking Goodman's hand.

Goodman took it firmly, staring into his eyes. "Good to finally meet you. I've been looking forward to this for a week. I want to see if your people are as good as you say they are."

"We aim to please, Marty."

"That's what I hear."

"Let me know if you need anything," Goodman's secretary said before leaving the room.

Goodman wasted no time. "David, as you know, this firm has had a successful and long-standing relationship with Salomon Brothers dating back to the Nixon administration," he said, standing at the coffee urns, pouring himself a cup of decaf.

He proceeded to explain the circumstances under which David's firm had been given this rare opportunity, stressing that it was early in the process. They were still putting out feelers. Loyalty ran deep at Coke, and they planned to move slowly. The other two men sat on either side of the long mahogany conference table, nodding their heads in agreement.

Marty Goodman was an executive vice-president of Coca-Cola Enterprises, Inc. He was responsible for overseeing the prudent and effective management of one of the largest pension funds in the country. While corporate policy precluded his acting unilaterally, still his vote carried great weight. He knew the markets as well as anyone on the Street and occasionally resented the fact that his income was half that of many younger, less seasoned Wall Street hotshots.

In the final analysis, he was responsible for every aspect of the fund's performance. On a daily basis he monitored beta coefficients of the various segments of the fund. It was his job to see that their respective returns, in the aggregate, were equal to or greater than

28

the various markets as a whole, and that those returns were achieved with less risk.

Each morning at 7:30 A.M., the various heads of the different departments that invested for the fund would meet in the War Room to discuss the previous day's market movements, today's anticipated direction, and to set policy on how best to proceed under that day's prevailing wind.

Harder than it sounds, his job was like threading eight needles at once—for markets are not static. By their very nature they are fluid entities and require the eye of an eagle and the cunning of a fox.

Needless to say, Marty Goodman had both. His was a twenty-five-hour-a-day job. And he did it very well. He was a thirty-six-year veteran and could not imagine working for any firm other than Coke. There was a camaraderie here, an esprit de corps he felt certain could not be duplicated anywhere else. In addition, his stock options alone had made him a millionaire many times over. It would be difficult to find a company whose stock had done as well over the years.

David stood at the head of the table, both hands resting on the back of a chair. Like almost everyone, he had a great deal of respect for Martin Goodman. He didn't dare say a word until Marty had finished. The first rule of good salesmanship is to listen. The second rule is to listen harder.

David's thoughts were interrupted as Goodman finished speaking. "But I fear I'm being rhetorical. I'm sure you know all this."

Goodman finished stirring his coffee and sat down next to Eisenhart, motioning for David to take the chair at the head. Before he did, he walked briskly to the coffee and poured himself a cup, black, as always. He walked back to the head of the table, took off his coat, hung it over the back of the chair, and sat down.

"The point is, you have diligently called me and otherwise courted this firm for the better part of four years now," Goodman continued. "While we here at Coke are big on loyalty, we are even bigger on hard work.

I respect and admire your diligence. You have earned the right to be here."

David glanced at the wall opposite him and noticed an elegantly framed picture of Coke's line of Minute Maid fruit juices and sodas. Sheer curiosity caused him to sneak a nanosecond's glance at the other walls. They, too, were adorned with nicely framed photos of virtually every product and soft drink Coke bottled the world over.

The room was a conference room like any other of the hundreds David had sat in across the country. The product photos aside, it could have been any business in America. Respectable but not ornate. In corporate America, ornate is generally the exclusive domain of the board room. That is where one finds the high-backed wing chairs, the round cherry board tables, chandeliers, crystal, corporate-logo china, and painted portraits of chairmen past.

David found himself watching Goodman's mouth move, wondering what Coke's board room looked like. Caleb would only drink Coke. For some reason he didn't like the taste of Pepsi and could tell the difference in a sip. David was a Pepsi man himself.

Caleb! Oh my God. What was he going to do with Rebecca and the kids? California seemed the logical choice. But what if . . . what if this psycho knew all about him? Where his parents lived, where Rebecca's parents lived. It seemed logical someone so obsessed would do their homework. Maybe California wasn't such a clear-cut choice after all. Maybe he should rent them a place where no one would know or think to look for them.

David felt strangely alone, as if he were a spectator at a play, watching himself perform on stage. His mind felt jumbled. He gripped his pen tightly, feeling the sweat in his palms.

"David?" Goodman asked, looking annoyed.

"Yes?" David answered, cocking his head ever so slightly, raising his eyebrows, as if to say "I'm listening."

Goodman's eyes bored into him. "I asked you a question."

Jesus Christ. You're off to a good start. You just made an asshole of yourself in front of the one man who can make this thing happen.

"I asked you whether or not you regularly conduct computer trading for your Fortune 500 clients and if you recommend that strategy for Coke."

"My apologies, gentlemen. I've had a touch of the flu and I've have had a terrible time of it the last thirty-six hours," David lied through his teeth.

"If you prefer to put this off until another date . . ." Goodman said, looking at his watch.

David was losing him. "No, thank you, Marty. I'm fine. Really. For any other account, I wouldn't have made the trip. This is very important to me and my firm. Please bear with me," David interrupted, knowing he was one slip from the executive version of the bum's rush.

Like all top level executives, Marty Goodman was an extraordinarily busy man and did not suffer fools. Period. If David walked out that door, he would never again return. He knew it. So did Goodman.

"Our analysis indicates that the sheer size of Coke's pension, particularly as it pertains to equities, necessitates . . ."

Before David knew it, the meeting was over. The initial screw-up excepted, David felt he'd done well. He dug deep, mustering all of his emotional strength to stay focused, listen, and concentrate on the here and now.

Goodman rose, followed by the other two. "I want to speak to David alone for a moment," he said—a not-so-subtle signal for the other two men to leave.

"Thank you," Magdolin said, stretching across the corner of the table to shake David's hand.

"Thank you."

"Thanks," Stewart said, following suit.

"Thank you."

Goodman remained standing, watching Magdolin close the door behind him. Oh boy, David thought. This is either going to be really good or really bad. Please don't let it be bad. I just haven't got the strength now.

Goodman walked to the coffee urns again and helped himself to another decaf. "More coffee?" he asked.

David could hear his mother's voice in their Mystic home. "David, I want to speak with you, young man," she would say. He never knew what was coming, how bad a scolding he would get. As he sat, watching Goodman's back, he felt the same disconcerting uncertainty.

"No, thank you."

"Have a seat, Dave. You mind if I call you Dave?"

He hated that name, but this was hardly the place or time to make a stand. "No, please," he said.

"I hope you don't take this the wrong way—"

"Why do I have this uneasy feeling I'm about to get bad news?" David interrupted, suddenly feeling nauseated.

"I wouldn't call it bad," Goodman replied with a grin. "Just fatherly. I've been doing this a long time. I've seen them come, I've seen them go. I have this feeling that something's not right. I don't know why, but I expected a better, tighter presentation than you gave. It's not that it was bad. Just flat. You didn't get where you are by presentations like that. Is there a problem? Anything you think we should know about? I like you, Dave, but I can smell a rat a mile away, and this room stinks. I have absolutely nothing to base this on, and if I'm wrong, then just say so. Call it intuition, but I think that flu crap was just that. I, for one, know that if I'd been after an account this size, this prestigious, I would have stayed focused if I'd had the plague. It just doesn't ring true with me."

"Excuse me?" David said, nearly unbelieving.

"You heard me. I think that flu story was bullshit. I'm going to shoot straight with you," Goodman said, staring into David's eyes. "I believe I can speak for the rest of the crew when I tell you that we have been looking forward to talking to you for some time. I think all of us here were leaning toward Reardon Haskel. I know I was. Speaking only for myself now, today's presentation gave me pause."

David was flabbergasted. He sat there, incredulous,

staring at Goodman's teeth. Had it shown that badly? He thought he'd done pretty well. No shit, this guy had an eagle eye all right.

He tried to speak, but found his lips closed. His mind raced and raced some more. He kept scrolling through responses, one after the other. Nothing came. The milliseconds seemed like minutes as he watched Goodman's eyes scanning him.

He thought of staying with the flu story, but Goodman had seen right through it. He could probably stick with it, but there'd always be that nagging question in Goodman's mind. Oh, he'd be polite, apologize, hope David felt better, and send him on his merry way. But he'd never get this account if he didn't come up with something else, and quick. The truth?

Are you nuts? You can't sit here and tell this man you were just mailed a death threat. But why not? He could write this account off unless he came up with something believable, something from the heart.

"I'm sorry you feel that way, Marty. It's just . . . Well, I . . ." Scroll. Scroll. Holy shit! And people think selling is easy. He could feel his hand moving toward his jacket pocket. "I want to show you something," he said, before he realized the words had left his mouth.

"What is it?" Goodman asked.

"I guess all the pretenses are down now, huh?" David asked, turning to pull the letter from his pocket.

Goodman stared impassively at the side of David's head. "That's a safe assumption."

"All right," David began, taking a deep breath. *Here goes nothing.* "Something happened yesterday that knocked me off my feet. And to be perfectly frank, it supersedes anything we've discussed here today. Don't get me wrong, Marty. There's very little I wouldn't do to get this account and I think you know that. I've busted my ass just to get a chance to be here, and I truly believe, in my gut, that if you go with us, it's a decision you will never regret. But yesterday put everything into perspective for me, real quick."

He slid the letter to a now seated Goodman with his

left hand. David stood and went to pour himself a cup of coffee, staring at a picture of assorted soft drinks on the wall . . . waiting. *I can't believe this is happening. Oh well, it's not as if I'm losing the account.* You can't lose what you never had.

"You got this yesterday?" Goodman asked, following a drawn-out whistle.

"Yes. I was going through my mail on the way to the airport. Let's just say it didn't make my day."

"Man, oh man, I would think not. I can certainly see why your mind wasn't on our little get together this morning."

David sat down in one of the chairs in the middle of the table, turning it slightly so he faced Goodman. "I want this account in the worst way, Marty. But I just can't get that damn letter out of my mind. I don't know what the hell to do."

"Have you told your wife?"

"No. I figured I have four days, and it would just panic her. I want to be there when I show it to her. I owe her that much. I'll be home tonight."

"Four days?"

"I think so," David said. "He said I had a week, and the postmark was the twenty-fourth. Today's the twenty-seventh. If it's for real, that's four days from today."

"Hmmm. Police?" Goodman asked.

"I haven't done shit yet, excuse my French. I've just been trying to figure out what the hell it all means."

"Well, not to sound trite, but I think my dog could figure that out. This *friend* of yours wants your ass hung out to dry."

"Tell me something I don't know," David said, staring into his coffee mug. "What would you do if you got something like that?"

"Well, fortunately, I don't have much experience in matters of this kind."

"Lucky you."

"I suppose the first thing I would do would be to call the FBI."

"I thought of that. But for a stupid letter? They'd probably laugh me out of their office."

Goodman pursed his lips. "Don't be so sure. This is clearly a death threat sent through the US mail. I'm not so sure they'd take it lightly."

David listened, silently nodding his head.

"Well, this certainly explains a lot anyway. I don't envy you, my boy."

"Neither do I," David said.

"I'm trying to think here," Goodman said, as much to himself as to David. "What are your choices? Are you tired of your job? This is a great way out, you know. You might even be able to get a nice severance package."

David shook his head. "Severance or not, I couldn't think of doing anything else. In your life you've never met anyone who loved his job more."

"Except myself, of course," Goodman said, a slight smile picking up a corner of his mouth.

"Of course. Anyway, the way I figure it, if I give in to this demand, where does it stop? He'll own me. Control me like a puppet on a string."

"You're right there. It's hard to figure somebody sick enough to do this would just walk away from the fun. Especially if his victim showed a proclivity to cave quickly."

"That's pretty much how I look at it."

"What about your family?"

"The very thought running through my mind when you caught me in never-neverland. I have no idea. I've got to move them I guess." David put his elbows on the conference table and began massaging his temples. "That will make everyone happy. With the holidays and all coming up. Jesus. What a nightmare. I can't believe this."

"I feel for you, Dave. Let me make a few calls. See what I can find out."

"Listen, Marty, that's very nice of you. But really, this isn't your problem. It's mine. I've taken enough of your time as it is. You want to help me out? Let's do some business. It will be the best decision you've made in a while."

"Always the salesman," Goodman said with a smile.

"Not always. But if I'm not doing it here, now, then

I'm in the wrong job," David said, returning Goodman's smile.

"You've got to get going anyway. As I understand it, Charles has a busy schedule for you today. I think you're meeting with my sector heads at ten, then touring the trading desks at eleven-thirty. We're all getting back together for lunch at twelve-fifteen in the executive dining hall. The big boy wants to meet you."

"You guys do it right."

"It's the only way we know."

They both laughed, Goodman patting David on the back.

"Marty?"

"What?"

"This stays in this room, okay?"

"My lips are sealed."

The rest of the day went well. Just talking to somebody about the letter took a tremendous weight off David's shoulders. He felt sure that any inkling of doubt that had been created in the morning meeting was erased as the day progressed.

He made it to the airport for the 2:50 P.M. flight to Philadelphia. Unfortunately, if you want to fly into Westchester, you almost always have to change planes somewhere along the way.

He thought of calling his parents. Not that he wanted to tell them what was up. He just wanted to hear their voices. Even at forty-two, David could take solace in a quick talk with his parents. They'd slowed some, mellowed in their golden years. His father, miraculously, almost never drank anymore. David couldn't figure that one out. Still, he worried about them. His father's mind wasn't what it used to be. He and his mother had even discussed whether it was the onset of Alzheimer's. David worried whether it was the years of booze catching up to him and wondered if it was a harbinger of things to come for him.

He stepped into a pay phone in the concourse and called home instead.

"Hello?" Rebecca answered.

"Becky, it's me," David said, feeling warmth at the sound of his wife's voice.

"Oh, David . . . thank God you called!"

"What is it, honey?"

"It's Barney. Sumner found him this afternoon hanging from a tree. Someone murdered him, David! The kids are beside themselves. I called the police, but what can they do?"

Holy shit! Someone had killed his dog. "All right," he said, trying desperately to remain calm. "Now listen to me. There's an explanation. I'll tell you all about it when I get in. Try to see if you can get a sitter. Meet me at Westchester at six seventeen."

Rebecca was dumbfounded. "An explanation! How could there *possibly* be an explanation? What in the hell are you talking about?"

She closed her eyes and took a deep breath, her mind pondering a seemingly endless stream of scenarios. David was gone so often. What did she really know about him, what he did while he was away? Was he cheating on her? Could this be the work of a lover scorned? She couldn't imagine it. That just couldn't be an option. *Could it?* God knows they'd had their problems lately. Was David involved in a bad business deal? Maybe gambling debts? As well as Rebecca thought she knew him, it scared her to think he harbored a darker, clandestine side. One she knew nothing about.

She pulled the phone from her ear, flicked her strawberry blond, bob-cut hair with a slight shake of her head. Rebecca didn't hear David's next words. "What?" she asked, audibly annoyed.

"Are you listening to me?" he asked. "Honey, trust me. I promise it will all make sense in a couple of hours. Call Dorothy. See if she can come over and keep you company for a while."

"She's already here," she said curtly. "David, what in the hell is going on? Barney is hanging from a tree and you tell me it will all make sense? Jesus Christ, David."

"Honey, please."

"Please? *Please?* What have you done, David?"

David struggled to quell his anger. "Rebecca, now listen. I haven't done a damn thing. I'll explain when you pick me up."

"God, David, I'm scared."

"Don't be scared, hon. You and the kids are safe. I promise," David said, hoping he wasn't lying. "I'll see you in four hours. I love you."

"I can't wait to have you home."

"I can't wait to get there."

——∽——

Darien, Connecticut, is a small, almost exclusively white, bedroom community of New York. Every day, thousands of people, mostly men, crowd one of three train stations in town, along a two-mile stretch of Metro North's Connecticut commuter line.

Along with its sister towns of New Canaan and Greenwich, Darien is easily one of the wealthiest towns in the United States. Here live some of the most powerful and influential people of our time: diplomats of long standing, chairmen, chief executive officers, chief financial officers, not to mention more than a smattering of the idle rich.

Many members of Darien's two country clubs weren't just rich, they were old money. Hundreds of millions, billions in some cases, passed down through generations, earned in the days of the robber barons or before in steel, railroads, shipping, retailing. In their neighborhoods, they scoffed at the likes of Donald Trump or Warren Buffett. Not that they didn't have the requisite net worth. They just hadn't had it long enough.

Founded in the 1600s by Dutch settlers, Darien was located on Long Island Sound and provided its original inhabitants with a convenient means of shipping and receiving goods. They found it an excellent place to make money. For the most part, today, money is not made there, it just lives there.

The Sound provides some of the most breathtaking views of anywhere in the state. Long, winding, one-lane roads find their way deep into the corners of virtually every peninsula the town has to offer. There are mansions and estates of immense size, with equally immense distrust of anybody from outside.

Ironically, Darien is sandwiched between Stamford and Norwalk, sections of which have some of the ugliest ghettos in the state. A glass wall exists north and south of town. While it's fair to say the town has always been race sensitive, crack and the general disenfranchisement of the underclass have created an even keener awareness and deeply rooted fear.

It was in this environment that Rebecca Johnson found herself spending most of her days, shuttling back and forth between football games, soccer matches, hockey games, birthday parties, PTA meetings and the like. She drove a Range Rover, having lost the battle with David for her first choice, a Toyota Land Cruiser.

There was something about the way Rebecca looked behind the wheel of her Range Rover. Something appealing. More than one man in her neighborhood had thought how lucky a man David Johnson was. She could certainly be labeled attractive, and unbeknownst to her, she was regularly eyed by bored, middle-aged men with a longing their wives would detest.

Not much happens of any real consequence in Darien. There's the occasional fight, a mugging every so often, the usual thefts, B&Es, that sort of thing. But death comes very seldom from anyone's hands other than God's.

The hanging of the Johnson's dog was the talk of the police station. This little prank clearly transgressed the usual line of acceptable delinquent behavior. It was different from your occasional graffiti artist or cherry bomb in the mailbox. There was an inherent malignancy in this act, enough to catch someone's attention—and keep it.

Sumner had run into the house after school on Friday screaming hysterically.

"Mom! Mom! Barney! Hurry, Mom! *Hurry!*"

"My God, Sumner, what is it? What's wrong, honey?" Rebecca screamed down the stairs, throwing her folded laundry on the floor, running two steps at a time.

"Oh, Mom," Sumner sobbed, wrapping his arms around her, holding on tighter than she could ever remember. He trembled uncontrollably in her arms, unable to speak.

"Sumner," Rebecca said, dropping to her knees, taking him by the shoulders. "What's wrong, honey? Tell Mommy."

He shook his head wildly. Terror in his bloodshot eyes. "Barney. Oh, Barney!"

Immediately, Rebecca understood that Barney had probably been hit by a car and braced herself for what was to come. She was surprised when Sumner took her hand and led her to the back door. Her thought processes did a one hundred eighty-degree turn. A dog fight? Had he been maimed? Maybe he had contracted rabies. Some of those raccoons can be deadly.

She was not prepared for what she found. She stood motionless, her hand to her mouth. "Oh, my, God!" She was in a state of shock. Her pastoral, protected life screamed to a halt.

"Sumner, go inside, sweetheart. Mommy'll be right there. Please, sweetheart, do as I say."

She stood for a moment, staring at the lifeless German shepherd hanging from the huge maple in the backyard a good four or five feet off the ground. A tennis ball was shoved down his mouth and his head was slung to one side. She walked up to him, looked at him closely, patted him slowly, and began to cry.

"Barney," she mumbled through a bubble forming on her lips. "Oh, Barn, I'm so sorry. I'm so sorry."

Rebecca felt for a pulse. She tickled him on his inside hind leg. Nothing. Barney was dead. She realized she couldn't get him down without a ladder. The only one big enough to reach the branch was too heavy for her to wield. She thought momentarily of cutting the rope, but the thought of him thumping to the ground like so much ground beef made her heart sink. The police, she thought. I've got to call the police.

It seemed like an eternity. In actuality, the first cruiser pulled up six minutes after her call. The front doorbell

40

rang and Rebecca ran from the TV room, where she had been consoling her son.

"Sumner, honey, Mommy'll be right back, okay?" She left him sitting on the couch almost catatonic, sipping a hot chocolate, watching Bugs Bunny.

Rebecca's older brother had been killed in a motorcycle accident in 1965. She was eleven years old. The shock and the pain almost ruined her parents' marriage—each blaming the other. Inexplicably, she could still hear them fighting as she trotted through the living room on her way to the front door.

"I told you not to let him get a motorcycle," she could hear her mom lecturing her father.

"Sarah, don't start," he'd respond. "We talked about this, remember?"

And the bickering would begin in earnest, neither hearing the pain of the other. Rebecca could still feel the warmth of her flannel pajamas, an adolescent lying curled up in her bed, listening to her parents' incessant quarreling.

She appeared in the open doorway just as the responding officer was pushing the buzzer a second time. The crisp autumn air snipped at her skin as she pulled the front door open, the sudden chill a befuddling contrast to the warmth of her bed so many years ago. "Hello," she said, a slight panic in her voice. "Please, come in, Officer."

He must be new. She didn't recognize him. She wore Levi's and a pink cardigan sweater over a white turtleneck. Her sleeves were scrunched half way up her delicate arms. The policeman noticed a slight quaver in her voice, but found it sensuous nonetheless. Perhaps the quaver made it more so.

"Mrs. Johnson?" the officer inquired.

"Yes. I called a little while ago and spoke to Sergeant Decker."

"Yes, he's my desk sergeant. I was just out on Tokeneke Road. Came as soon as I got the call. I'm Officer Rhodes. Dan Rhodes. I understand someone has killed your dog? Is that correct, ma'am?" he asked, holding his hat in his hands.

41

"Yes, yes," Rebecca said, running the fingers of her right hand over her forehead. "Oh, Officer, I'm just a wreck. I just don't understand it." She stepped aside and motioned him in.

He caught a momentary glimpse of her chest before stepping up to the doorsill. Rhodes followed as Rebecca turned toward the kitchen. "Someone hung it, Mrs. Johnson? Is that correct?"

"Him."

"I'm sorry. Someone hung him, ma'am?"

She leaned now against the counter by the kitchen sink, her arms folded across her chest. "Yes. The bastards."

Rhodes eyed her stricken face. Rebecca's fawn-like hazel eyes were wide with alarm. "What was that, ma'am?" he asked.

"Oh, excuse my language. It's just that Barney's been with us since before my oldest was born. He's absolutely devastated. I'm just so angry. So damn mad. Why would someone do something like this?"

"You said bastards, ma'am. Plural. Do you know who did this? Any reason to believe it was more than one person?"

"Well . . . no. I'm just venting I guess," she answered, turning, suddenly, busying herself rummaging through a cupboard. "Where are my manners?" she said to its contents. "I'm sorry. Would you like a cup of coffee or something? Maybe some hot cocoa?"

Rhodes was a gentleman, yet found himself admiring Rebecca's natural look and delicate curves. She wore no makeup and he found her more striking for it. He watched her buttocks as she stood on tiptoes reaching for something and found himself wondering what her skin smelled like. "No thank you, ma'am. Can I see the dog, Mrs. Johnson?"

"Yes, of course," she said, placing a can of coffee on the stove.

As the two headed toward the back door, the front doorbell rang again. The buzz in the kitchen caused Rebecca to jump slightly. "Excuse me. I'll be right back."

42

Captain Peter Esposito was a twenty-four-year veteran of the Darien police department. His rank was denoted by his white hat. Unlike the rest of his officers, who couldn't dream of living in a town this expensive, Esposito did. Granted, it was on the other side of the tracks, the section of town populated predominantly by working-class Italians: plumbers, electricians, masons, and one cop.

He had bought a tiny two-bedroom bungalow in 1973 for twenty-three thousand dollars, back when homes in Darien were still affordable. The 80s boom put an end to that. He figured he could sell his house for two hundred thousand plus now, and he planned to do just that when he retired.

He stood five feet eight inches, was well built, and had more hair than Rebecca could remember on any man she'd ever seen. She thought for a second that his back must be covered with hair.

"Hi, Mrs. Johnson," he said, as she stood in the open doorway.

"Rebecca, please," she said with a fleeting smile, stepping aside. "Come in."

"All right . . . Rebecca," he said. "I see that Officer Rhodes is here. Have you shown him the dog yet?"

"No, we were just heading outside when you rang the bell."

"Good. Let's all go together," he said, stepping in behind her.

Esposito acknowledged Rhodes standing by the back door. "Dan," he said, stepping into the rustic looking kitchen.

"Cap'n."

"I understand you haven't seen the dog yet. Let's all take a look."

"There he is," Rebecca said, opening the kitchen door and pointing to the tree. She turned away, biting her lower lip. "I think I'll just stay here, if you don't mind, Captain."

Esposito stopped at the door. He spoke softly. "Actually, Mrs. Johnson, I'd like you to join us. I know this is

43

hard for you. But we'll need to ask you a few questions, and it'll save us all time if we can talk while we look things over and cut him down. I'll also need you to comment on any marks or other physical evidence we might find. Tell us if anything looks to be out of the ordinary. We'll need to see what, if anything, occurred during or after the hanging. I'm sorry, ma'am."

She stood with her back to the open door, her left hand on the knob. "Are you just going to cut him down?" she asked Esposito with pleading eyes. "Can't you lower him gently?"

He looked at her momentarily. "Why, yes, ma'am. We can. Do you have a ladder tall enough?"

She showed them to the garage, where the two men retrieved the ladder. Esposito and Rhodes went about their work and spent the better part of an hour and a half at the Johnson home. They were quite sensitive, really, lowering Barney onto a blanket Officer Rhodes had in his cruiser.

Rebecca wanted them to leave Barney with her. Esposito wanted to take him to a vet for an autopsy, check for poison, internal bleeding, things of that nature. Rebecca was heartbroken. She hated the thought of explaining it to the kids. But still, she understood.

The two men asked many questions. Did she know of anyone who had had a run-in with Barney? Barking dog syndrome? Angry neighbors? "What about your husband? Is it possible he rubbed someone the wrong way?" Esposito wanted to know.

To Rebecca's surprise, Captain Esposito called in a detective and a photographer. This type of killing was a bad sign. While none of them knew of the possible connection to David and the note, still, Esposito thought it wise to investigate. Sane people don't do things like this. What was more, Esposito knew that, with very few exceptions, the overwhelming preponderance of violent criminals currently behind bars have at some time or another committed acts of senseless brutality against animals.

Though he didn't tell Rebecca, he knew that Jeffrey

Dahmer kept photos in his apartment of the dog he had tortured, burned, and mutilated. It was very common among society's more frightening, less grounded members. Whoever had done this was someone who needed to be watched.

When the two men finally left, Rebecca called her best friend, Dorothy Entwistle, from across the street. The two women were sitting, drinking hot chocolate at the kitchen table when David called her from Philadelphia.

Rebecca finished her conversation with David, replacing the phone in the cradle on the wall. She stood motionless for a moment, her hand still on the phone.

"Becky? You okay?" Dorothy asked.

"It was David. He's on his way back from Atlanta."

"Did you tell him?"

"Yes. He said he could explain everything. Said he knew why it happened and would explain everything to me tonight."

"Explain?" Dorothy asked, her eyes blinking with incredulity. "What does *that* mean?"

"Don't ask me, Dot. It just doesn't make any sense," Rebecca said, sitting down, a cup of steaming hot chocolate between her palms. Somehow, the aroma and its warmth in her stomach, softened the anxiety she couldn't shake. "Look at me. I'm a mess."

"I don't know, Becky. I think you're holding up pretty darn well. I'd be hysterical. What with the kids and all."

"What do I say to them, Dot? How do you explain something like this to a child?"

Dorothy hesitated for a moment. "Well, I'm not sure there is a good way. Honesty, I suppose. They've got to learn it's a mean world out there. I've always said the drawback to this damned town is that our kids grow up unprepared for the real world. I'll tell you who's got some explaining to do, is that husband of yours. How could he know something like this would happen—might happen—and not say anything to you?"

Rebecca sat silent, staring at the cutting-board island in the middle of the kitchen. "I'm not sure. It doesn't sound like him. The whole mess has me dizzy. I was

45

going to let him grab a cab, but now . . . I think I'd better pick him up. Do you think you could stay, Dot? Watch the kids for a while?"

"Sure. No problem at all. You go and find out what the hell's going on."

"Oh, don't worry about that."

———

On the same day David put his soul on a silver platter to Martin Goodman and Rebecca and the kids' lives took a horrifying change for the worse, Fenton Montague awoke to the sound of two cardinals scuffling in the makeshift bird feeder outside his bedroom window.

Like Shakespeare's Iago, the prototypical personification of evil, some men are cruel and wicked to the very center of their souls. They construct their sickly schemes as much for the artistic pleasure derived from watching them unfold as for the ends to which they lead. They very much enjoy the mental anguish and personal hells they create for their victims. They can feel it, be inside it, shivering with delight at the calamities their victims must endure.

Iago took great pains and pleasure in finally driving Othello to kill his faithful wife. All the while he worked behind the scenes, pulling the strings, directing the players, never satiating his own unimaginable need to witness pain, destruction, and death. Iago took as much, if not more, enjoyment from creating and then watching Othello's mental transformation, as he did from the actual murder of his wife.

This was hard work. Like a creation by a master painter, the sketch had to be drawn and redrawn before any oil could be laid to canvas. Many hours of toiling, of mentally massaging the different possibilities and likely outcomes, needed to be spent. No, this was not work for a layman. Constructing a scheme of evil was itself a work of art. It was too bad, Fenton thought, the average person simply hadn't evolved enough to understand the beauty inherent in such work.

Fenton lived by himself. He didn't like other people.

They were too stupid, too unaware, so self-absorbed, they missed the beauty of life. He fancied himself a nihilist, a follower of the philosophy that denies the basic truths of life. The brainchild of Friedrich Nietzsche, Nihilism teaches that all knowledge, all of mankind's combined intellect—its theories and maxims—are ultimately false.

It was so obvious to him. Why was the average Joe so slow to understand? Why had God imparted to him and him alone this deep-rooted understanding? *So much to do. So little time.* But he reminded himself that the thousand-mile journey must begin with the first step. Wishing for too much too soon was idle. Any great endeavor took time, planning, and hard work.

"Oh, David," he said aloud, leaning over to make his bed. "Are you enjoying yourself now? I hope so. I've dreamt of this for a long, long time. It would be so disappointing if you were to take me lightly. Push me aside. Disregard me. I don't think we'll let that happen again, will we?"

There's a wrinkle. A made bed's no good with wrinkles. He undid the bed and started from scratch. "It's so hard being perfect," he said. He sang as he walked through his sparsely furnished apartment to the bathroom: "The wheels on the bus go round and round, round and round."

Fenton Montague was not a healthy man. The easiest tasks—making a bed, turning off a light, putting away a book—could take ten, fifteen, twenty minutes. It had to be done right, damn it! Life wasn't worth living unless you were going to do it perfectly.

However, these were not his real problems. Fenton also suffered from mental illness—living in the nightmarish underworld commonly referred to as psychosis and split personality disorder. He was often delusional, living in a world in which normal people have no part, of which they have no concept. He suffered periodic breaks from reality. In these moments, he would become his own god, a walking judge and jury of his fellow man. David Johnson didn't know it yet, but his sentence had already been pronounced. Fenton Montague was an obsessed man on a mission. You wouldn't wish him on your worst enemy.

Fenton's preoccupation with perfection was hammered into him when he was a child. His mother would wash his mouth out with soap. Lock him in the closet. Make him eat at the kitchen table naked.

"Fenton," she would say, "there's never time to do it right, but always time to do it over. How many times do I have to tell you?"

"I'm sorry, Mother."

"Sorry doesn't work in this household, mister. Come here now!" she'd scream, standing at the closet, holding open its door.

"Please, Mother. Please? I promise. I promise I'll do it right from now on," he would plead with her. Sobbing. Trembling. Begging.

She eventually created the perfect little boy. He could make a bed, wash a dish, wax a floor, better than your grandmother in her prime. He had become an automaton. Incapable of maintaining sanity in his mother's world, he created one of his own. No one would know the true extent of the wreckage of his mind for some time. Fenton went about his daily life like a zombie, his death instinct forming, growing, mutating all the while.

"The wipers on the bus go swish swish swish, swish swish swish. Oh, the wipers on the bus . . ."

David Johnson stood at the nucleus of his hatred now. In Fenton's mind, David was an insect, a loathsome slug to be crushed under the full weight and fury of his evil and disgust.

Fenton cut himself shaving. The bright crimson flowed unevenly through the textured shaving cream. *I'm going to be your worst nightmare.* "Oh, David. You see what you've made me do? You're really becoming a pain in the ass, you know that?"

—⁂—

"David. Over here," Rebecca said with a wave as her husband entered the airport terminal.

He caught her eye, picked up his pace, and hugged her, dropping his briefcase and carry-on bag.

"Hi, honey. I'm so glad to be home," he said, her lack of reciprocity noticeable.

"Yeah, well, you may not say that in about half an hour. David, what the hell is going on?"

"It's nice to see you too. How was your trip?" David said sarcastically, hurt by her abruptness.

Rebecca was in no mood for pleasantries. "Please, David, not now. I've had the worst day of my life, and you say you know why. I have to know what's going on. Sumner's a wreck, and Cabes isn't much better. This whole thing's a god damned nightmare."

"Come on. Let's go," David said, feeling the weight of events clamping hard in his chest. "I want to get home and see the boys. We'll talk in the car."

They crossed the neon-lit parking lot in silence, their ideal and protected world suddenly coming to a crushing, dramatic halt. Rebecca walked quickly, wondering what her husband could possibly have gotten them into. How could there be an explanation? What insanity was David involved with that could create such an event? She worried about the kids. Especially Sumner.

David walked in longer strides, easily keeping pace with the quicker gait of his wife. He was beginning to feel a different nervousness overcome him now. How should he begin? How would she take the news? Should they tell the kids?

Walking a step behind his wife, David watched the movement of her hips, the same wiggle that had so attracted him when he first set eyes on her twenty years ago. She looked sensual to him this evening. Deep within, he felt a warming ache of desire—an inner longing he knew would not be satisfied anytime soon.

How did it get so fucked up? When they lived together in Boston, it seemed as if the whole world was theirs for the taking. Those were good days. They both attended Boston University. He majored in finance, she in nursing. One night, while Rebecca was training at Mass General, one of her patients died. It was her first death

49

and she was filled with grief—helpless and scared. She sobbed and he held her for the longest time. They talked about it, drank some wine, tossed it about.

Lying in bed, they watched old *Honeymooners* reruns, sharing a joint. The evening ended with the most exquisite lovemaking he had ever experienced. They moved as one, almost switching bodies, each feeling the needs and desires of the other, pleasing one another more than David had thought possible between two human beings. As he crossed the parking lot now with his wife, he wondered whether sex for them would ever be the same.

"Here, you drive," she said, tossing him the keys. He wasn't expecting it. They hit him in the chest, falling to the asphalt. She has a right to be angry, he told himself, bending over to pick them up. This is going to be fun, he thought, unlocking the doors, throwing his stuff in the back seat. He lumbered in, dreading the ride.

David swallowed dryly, acutely aware of the knot tightening in his stomach. "You know, sweetie, I think I might just get that Coke account," he said, avoiding the inevitable.

"I'm glad for you, David. Really I am. But we have to talk about Barney, about what's going on."

His face felt flushed. He yearned for a drink. "You know, I think I learned something today. Sometimes honesty works better than anything. You know, you can put up pretenses—"

"David!"

Silence . . . More silence.

"Look, I know you're mad," David said, staring at the road. "You have reason to be angry. But please don't lash out at me. I'm a victim here too, you know. I loved Barney as much as anybody. I picked him out, remember?"

"I know, David. But why? Why would someone kill him?"

"I don't know for sure. I got a letter at work yesterday. It's in my right front jacket pocket," he said, motioning to the back with his head. "You should read it."

He was quiet while she leaned over the seat, digging for the letter David had now memorized. She pulled herself back, turned on the reading light, and grit her teeth as she read.

She finished in less than a minute. "Oh, God, David. I don't understand. What does it mean?" she asked, looking at her husband. "What does it mean you have a week to quit your job?"

"I don't think you need a degree in nuclear physics to figure it out, do you?"

Rebecca's facial muscles began to twitch, her face growing ashen. For the first time her anger turned to fear. "David, please. Don't be an asshole. Not now."

He glanced at her. "I'm sorry. It's just that I'm scared. I can only assume whoever wrote me that letter also killed Barney. I mean, I don't know for sure, but who else could it be?"

"Jesus, David. What about the kids? What are we going to do?"

"Well, obviously I haven't had a lot of time to think this through. I thought it would be wise to send you and the kids to my folks for a little while, at least until we can get this thing straightened out."

"California? Oh, David. Isn't there some other way? Do you really think we're in danger?"

"Well, I had my doubts, off and on, until you told me about Barney. I don't see we have a hell of a lot of choice right now. Do you? Barney was meant to be a warning, I guess."

They drove in silence for some time, both awash in the emotions of the moment, thinking through their options—the unanswered questions. It just didn't seem possible. One day their lives were normal, and in an instant they had become fugitives, on the run from some unseen enemy whose reasoning and purpose they could only begin to imagine.

"Tomorrow's Cabe's birthday. We can't tell him before then," Becky said, looking out the passenger side window.

"I know. I've thought about it."

"Hell, David, as it is, he and Sumner are basket cases. This is their first brush with death. I don't know what to tell them."

51

"Don't look at me. I don't know what the hell to say to them."

"We can't not tell them, can we? I mean, especially if we have to move for some period of time. They'll need some reason."

"I know," David said.

Rebecca looked at him, her eyes transfixed. "Did you call the police?"

"Not yet. I wanted to talk to you first. I hope you understand why I couldn't tell you over the phone."

Rebecca curled up against her door. "Yes. Thank you."

"Tonight, all I want to do is make myself a drink and curl up in bed and sleep. We'll talk to the police tomorrow."

"Jesus," she said, to no one in particular.

"I've been thinking about that too. A little praying probably wouldn't hurt."

She thought of God. They hadn't been to church in years. "Let's hope he's in a forgiving mood."

David spent that evening consoling Sumner and Caleb. They spoke about what a great companion Barney had been and how they would all miss him. They spoke about good and evil, God and Satan.

Not that David particularly believed in either. He figured there was some kind of a higher power, something greater than himself, but at times like these he always thought whoever he or she was must have one hell of a warped sense of humor. There were so many injustices in the world—so much hunger, poverty and desperation. Sometimes he thought, if there was a God, he wasn't even sure he wanted Him on his team.

Modern Christianity—modern religion for that matter—was not his thing. In fact, the Jesus thing bored him. The incense and rules, bishops and Pope. If Jesus was the Son of God, he felt certain he was watching it all with disdain and disappointment. From what little he could remember from his Sunday school days, Jesus never taught any of that crap.

But David believed even less in Satan. The whole fire and brimstone, horned-creature-with-a-tail yarn was just so much malarkey. But he definitely believed in evil. Whoever pulled those strings he couldn't say, but he felt certain whoever it was had a better handle on their job description than God did.

How could the Bible possibly be true? People living in the bellies of fish. Willing to kill their children for God. That one always baffled him. Weren't the scriptures written forty or fifty years after Jesus's death, at the earliest? David couldn't get a story straight from one Christmas to another. Think how mangled the Bible must have become over the course of time. George Washington and the cherry tree, Abe Lincoln walking a mile to return a penny. Yeah . . . Right.

But the kids needed something. They could understand God and the devil. Even though he told them he didn't think there was a devil, evil did exist. Everywhere. The sooner they learned it, the better off they'd be. Like any parent, he'd like to keep them sheltered from that forever, but that didn't seem possible at the moment. What gnawed at him, but went unspoken, was the very real possibility that it could get worse before it got better.

They talked about getting a new dog. How cool it would be to teach it everything from scratch—watch it grow up. Before they knew it, David told them, they would love it the way they had Barney. Differently, but just as much.

Everywhere David traveled, he always brought something back for them. He tried to ease the pain some by pulling out two City of Atlanta sweatshirts. The kids loved them. But in the end, Barney always came back. Like a bad tooth, you can mask the pain as much as you want, but it will still be there when the salve wears off—especially at night.

He told them as bravely as he could that he would always be there for them, that they could come and talk to him about anything, anytime. Never worry how manly it seems, he said. Everybody has feelings. Every-

53

body cries. They would catch the mean person or people that did this to Barney, and they'd be sorry. You just wait and see. "We're Johnsons, remember?" he told them. "Nobody messes with us," they all said in unison.

He kissed them, told them how much he loved them, and put them to bed. As much as David wanted to make it all go away, he was afraid only time would heal this wound. He wasn't sure how much of it he had left.

The weight in his head was incapacitating. All he wanted to do was sleep. He went to the kitchen and poured himself a large vodka and orange juice— sparingly adding the latter. He walked onto the back deck through the sliding glass door in the dining room, and leaned with his elbows on the railing, staring out at the old maple. Its massive figure broke the dark blue sky. "I'm sorry, Barn," he said, breathing deeply, the crisp November air stinging his lungs. He lit a smoke and just stood there.

"I'm going to kill you, you son of a bitch," he whispered under his breath. "You fuck with me, that's one thing. You fuck with my family . . . I want you to come. I'll be waiting." *Like the Japanese at Pearl Harbor. You've just awakened a sleeping giant.*

He rolled the butt between his finger and thumb until the head fell over the rail, then he pocketed the filter and went inside. He locked the door, making sure to check the broom handle in the runner.

—⁓—

"Hello, Captain," Rebecca said, opening the front door.

"Hi, Mrs. Johnson. It seems like only yesterday," Esposito said with a poor attempt at humor.

"Come in, please."

He stepped in and removed his hat. "Thanks. Gettin' nippy out. Could be a mean one this year."

"I'll tell my husband you're here," she said, trotting up the stairs.

Esposito watched with amusement as Rebecca climbed the stairs. He was struck more by her verve and self-confidence under such trying circumstances, than by her shapely figure. He thought how much fun she would be to take bowling. Self-assured and outgoing. He shook his head slightly, betting that in her single years she had been a great date.

A few moments passed and David appeared at the top of the landing. He wore Top Siders, navy blue corduroys, and a long-sleeved pink polo shirt. He eyed Captain Esposito as he headed down the stairs. Christ, a monkey, he thought.

"Mr. Johnson?"

"Yes. Call me David, please."

"I'm Captain Peter Esposito. Darien police department."

David extended a hand. "Pleasure to meet you, Captain. As you can see, we're preparing for my son's birthday party today. I'm afraid the place is a bit of a zoo."

"Enjoy it while you can, Mr. Johnson. They grow up quick."

"Let's take a walk through the yard. Try not to put a damper on things."

"All right. Let me get my coat." Esposito let himself out, closed the door, and headed back to his cruiser.

"He was one of the two officers I told you about when I called about Barney," Rebecca called out from the kitchen.

"You didn't tell me he was the missing link," David said, walking toward her.

"I know. Handsome, huh?"

The front door opened. Esposito stood in the foyer.

"Let's go in back," David said.

The two men walked through the living and dining rooms, out the sliding glass door, and stood for a while staring at the tree. Neither spoke.

Over the years Esposito had seen his share of wealth. David's house was built in 1907 and though large, it certainly didn't compare to many he had seen. Still, he was impressed by the expansive reach of the back yard. The large maple, planted when the house was built, stood in a row of three at the lip of a slight rise extending the full length of the lawn. Their unfurling branches reached well beyond their trunks, forming nature's version of a long, visually pleasing umbrella.

Esposito stood, his eyes roaming the length of the yard. He noticed things he'd missed in the emotion-filled events of the day before. He eyed the woods beyond, envious of the Johnson's seclusion. He noticed an old barn up on the lip of the hill, to the left of its closest maple. It seemed oddly incongruous, older than the house. He wondered whether the Johnson home had been built to replace an older structure. Maybe the original house had burned.

David lit a cigarette and turned to Esposito. "You know, Captain, I loved that damned dog. I'm going to miss him."

"I know." Esposito leaned on the rail, looking into the woods. "Hell of a thing. Haven't heard back from the vet yet, bein' the weekend and all. Probably won't know much til Monday."

"Doesn't matter. It's not going to bring him back. My kids took it pretty hard. How do you explain something like that?"

"Can't, I s'pose. There's some real wackos out there. People think because this is Darien, we got it cushy. You wouldn't believe the shit I see. Can't imagine what the big city boys go through. This is rough enough, thank you."

David was surprised. "Huh. I wouldn't have guessed."

David had called the Darien police early that morning and spoken briefly to Esposito. "Tell me about this letter you got," he said.

"Not much to it really," David responded, reaching in his back pocket, handing it to Esposito. "Could almost have dismissed it as a prank if it hadn't been for Barney."

Esposito held the folded letter by the top and bottom corners, placing it up to the sun. "Where's the envelope?" he asked.

"In my briefcase."

"Good. I'll need it. How many people have touched this?" he asked.

56

"Fingerprints?" David asked, angry at himself that he hadn't even considered it. "Oh shit, Captain. There are so many fingerprints on that thing, I doubt it would do you much good now. I'm sorry. I wasn't thinking."

"How many people?" Esposito asked again.

"Well, let's see. There's me. I've read it and reread it so many times . . . There's a business colleague. Rebecca. That's it, I think."

Esposito unfolded it, held it on the railing, and read. "Nice guy," he said.

"Oh yeah. A real charmer. I didn't know where I should start, so I thought I'd call you guys first. Maybe talk about some protection for my family or something. I'm not really sure what the hell I want."

"You think this letter and Barney are connected?" Esposito asked, putting the letter in a manila envelope he'd brought with him.

"I would assume so. Wouldn't you?" David asked, a bit nonplussed. "If not, it's one hell of a coincidence, and I don't believe in coincidences. Not this kind anyway."

"I don't assume much in this business, Mr. Johnson. Gets me in trouble. But I have to say, it makes sense, doesn't it?"

"Oh, it makes sense all right. Look, I don't want to seem like an asshole, Captain, but the way I figure it, I've got some psycho after me and my family. We can assume that much. Do you agree?"

"Apparently . . . yes," Esposito answered, taken aback by David's rebuff.

David snuffed his smoke. "All right. You're the cop. What would you do if you got a letter like that?"

"Well, let's see. Strictly off the record now. I guess the first thing I'd do would be to secure my family. Have you thought about that at all? I mean, what you're gonna do with them?"

"Christ, it's all I can think about. My folks live on the West Coast. I thought maybe I'd send them there for a while."

"Do you own a gun, Mr. Johnson?"

"No. Why?"

"You mentioned protection. What kind of protection did you have in mind?"

"Why did you ask if I own a gun?" David asked again. "Do you think I need one?"

"No, I don't. Just wondering, I guess. What kind of protection are you talking about?"

"Hell, I don't know. Can't you guys post an officer at our house for the next week or so?"

Esposito clenched his teeth. A slight clucking sound emerged, the left corner of his mouth pulling back slightly. "I'm not sure. A week's a long time. Budget's tight, you know. Maybe we can work something out for a night or two. I'll have to talk to the chief. But why's it matter? I mean, if you're gonna send them away?"

David didn't answer. *That's a good question.* He felt like a child who wanted it all his way. Was he in denial? He really was going to have to send them away. The very thought saddened him. He would miss them all so desperately. Especially the kids.

Damn it! This is exactly what this son of a bitch wants. He wants to upset my apple cart. I'll be playing right into his sick little hands. But how can I not move them? I really don't have any choice, do I?

Esposito could see David's mind turning. "See my point?" he asked.

"Yes, I see your point," David said, pulling another smoke from the pack. "But isn't that exactly what he wants? I mean, don't you figure that's what he wants me to do? Can't we use them to flush him out or something?"

"Look," Esposito said, shaking his head. "I know it'll be rough, Mr. Johnson. I'm sure just thinking of it makes you sick. It would me. But what are your choices? You can't really be serious about using them as bait, can you? I mean, that's a hell of a risk. One I wouldn't be willing to take. Not until we can find out more about who this asshole is."

"Let's talk about that for a minute. Nothing personal, but I can't imagine the Darien police department is equipped to handle an investigation of this nature, is it?" David asked, sure he knew the answer.

"Well, frankly, this isn't the kind of thing we run into very often. We do get death threats from time to time. As you know, there are some pretty high-profile people in this town. But the threats are usually over the phone. We'll probably call the local postal inspector's office in Stamford and the state police."

Now you're talking. Let's bring in the big guns. David remembered Goodman's comments in Atlanta. "The FBI?" he asked.

"What you've got here is a death threat made through the US mail. What I do know is that anything involving the US mail is generally a federal issue. Problem is, all we got now is a dead dog. No offense."

"None taken," David said, a little stung.

"I'm not sure how seriously they're gonna take all this."

"Well, I tell you what, Captain. It's pretty fucking serious to me and my wife. You talk to any idiot who tries to pawn this off as some joke, I want his name. Got that?"

Esposito turned, leaning his rear against the rail. "Look, I'm not suggesting they're not gonna hop all over it, especially after we had to cut down your dog. I just don't think either one of us knows for sure how many fruitcakes these guys are chasing at any one time. Like I said before, there's certainly no shortage of 'em."

"Let's walk," David said, heading for the stairs at the far end of the deck. As they hit the lawn, walking through crisp, dead leaves, David was reminded he'd have to rake pretty soon. "You mentioned earlier about finding out more about who this guy is."

Esposito wondered where this was going. "Yeah?" he asked.

"How the hell do you do that? I mean, where do you start? Seems to me we got a typed letter with a Boston postmark. How can you possibly find out anything on that information? It's just not enough to go on, is it?"

"You know how many death threats the President gets in the mail every year, Mr. Johnson? The Secret Service tracks virtually every one of them. How do you s'pose they do that? In more cases than not, they don't have anything more to go on that what we've got. Sometimes less."

They walked left, up the slight incline toward the old barn in back. "Sometimes less?" David asked, perplexed. "How could it possibly be less? Unless the damn thing's hand-delivered?"

"I can see you're not a Sherlock Holmes fan."

David looked at Esposito. "Holmes?" he asked, squinting his eyes slightly. His mother was a big Arthur Conan Doyle fan. She always had a Holmes story lying around the house. "Too far-fetched. You can read a whole story and not have a chance to figure out how the hell he knew until the very end. And even then it's some bullshit little thing nobody in their right mind would ever have thought of. Waste of time if you ask me."

"True, but one thing Mr. Holmes knew was his paper. All commercially sold paper has what's known as a watermark. That's the difference in thickness that's imprinted on the paper when it's pressed. You know how, if you put paper up to the light, you can see some kind of an insignia or logo?"

"Yeah?"

"Well, that's a watermark. The Feds got every watermark ever made in their trusty little data banks. Can tell you when it was manufactured, who made it, and who sold it."

Esposito had David's interest now. "You mean to tell me you can tell who sold the paper this guy typed the note on?" he asked, leaning to pull the barn door open.

"Well, yes and no. We might know for a given watermark, from a given area, that it was sold at Staples, Wal-Mart, and Woolworth's, but not at Kmart, Sears, or Office Depot."

"Jesus, Captain, that narrows it down to a few thousand stores. What help could that be?"

"Hey, this isn't rocket science," Esposito said with a flip of his hands. "It takes a lot of man hours. It's painstaking and tedious work. But let's say we start digging into corporate inventory files, we can start to narrow down when that paper was available for sale in different geographic locations and when and where it wasn't."

Maybe these guys aren't so Podunk after all. It really was true what he and Rebecca always told the kids—you can't judge a book by its cover.

"Now, I don't know much about the world of high tech," Esposito continued. "But let's just say our boy used a Hewlett-Packard bubble jet printer. The boys at HP can take a look under a microscope and probably tell you what kind of printer it is, when it was made, and who sold it. Now we go through the same steps as before, cross check, and things start to get narrowed down in a big way."

The two men were standing in the entrance to the old barn, looking into each other's eyes. David went inside and started rummaging through some items in the near corner. "I know I left that bicycle pump around here somewhere. Man, when you got two kids, you can't ever find anything. Got kids, Captain?"

"Three," Esposito said, nodding his head.

"Then you know what I'm talking about."

"Sure do. Goes with the territory, I guess."

"I guess. Go on," David said, still digging.

"Here's where it starts to get tedious. Up to this point, it's been mostly computer shit. Now we got to start going through credit card receipts, daily sales logs, the works. It's not ideal, but it works. I know that for a fact. Just ask the Secret Service."

"Yeah, well that's all fine and dandy," David said, walking to a workbench below an eight-paned window. "But last I checked, I wasn't the President of the United States."

"Like I said, it all depends on how serious they want to get with this thing," Esposito said.

It was pretty obvious David was successful professionally. Esposito figured his two-story Greek Revival home probably had twelve rooms, and from what little he'd seen, none of them lacked for furnishings.

"Look, Mr. Johnson, I don't know what it is you do for a living, but one look around tells me it ain't flippin' burgers. Maybe you know some people. Pull some strings. Like they say, it ain't what you know."

"Here it is," David said, yanking the pump from a pile of junk on the bench. "Yeah. That's some good advice. Believe me, if I can, I will."

"So, are you going to do it?" Esposito asked.

"Do what?"

"Quit your job."

"What would you do?" David asked, turning the tables.

Esposito played with the stubble on his chin. "Boy. That's a tough one. My kids are all grown and the missus died a few years back. I guess I'd tempt fate."

"Okay, but let's assume it's twenty years ago and you had two little ones hanging around. Then what?"

"Hell, I don't know nothin' else but bein' a cop. Like I said earlier, I guess I'd make sure the family was safe, then hope like hell the guy fucked up somewhere along the way, so we could pop him before he popped me."

"You do have a way with words."

"You asked me what I'd do. That's what I'd do."

"Guess what?" David asked, pointing the tire pump at Esposito. "That's exactly what I'm going to do. This asshole's fucked with my family now. I just hope I'm the one who gets a chance to do the popping."

Esposito touched David's shoulder. "Don't go doin' anything stupid, Mr. Johnson. The last thing you want is to go on trial for murder. Even if you're acquitted, it'll screw up your life for years. Doubt it would do much for your career, either."

I've said enough. David figured the safer bet now was to keep to himself just how much he wanted to kill this son of a bitch.

"Yeah, I know you're right," he lied, closing the barn door with a thud. "I'm sure the Feds can handle it just fine." *If they decide to get off their asses.* "Let me ask you, Captain. Do you think this guy's for real, or are we making a mountain out of a molehill?"

"My opinion?" Esposito said, walking beside David back down the incline of the lawn. "You'd better ship the family outta here. At least until we know more."

David nodded his head. "I thought you'd say that."

"I think it's the best advice you'll get all day."

"Okay. So what now, Sherlock?"

"Well, even though it's a long shot, I think I'm gonna try to have the state boys pull some prints off of this thing. Nothing holds prints like paper. It's been cold, but humid. Humidity helps some. I'll need the name of your business colleague who touched it. He probably wouldn't appreciate a SWAT team surrounding his house. I'll need you and Mrs. Johnson to come down to the station to get printed. Hey, if we're lucky, maybe we can pull a latent. On the chance he licked the envelope, I also want to check and see if we can get some DNA from the saliva."

"From an envelope?" David asked.

"Yep, believe it or not. The Feds can help us there, if they decide to help. DNA fingerprinting's fairly new. You watch any of the O.J. trial?"

"Some."

"You ask me, they had him dead to rights. Hell, there just ain't no justice in this world."

"Yeah, well, let's see if we can begin to set the score straight. Starting with me."

They stood on the flagstone patio now. "I'll try like hell. When's the party?"

"One o'clock, I think."

"How 'bout when it's over, you and Mrs. Johnson come down to the station? Let's get the printing out of the way."

"Shit, Captain. Is that really necessary? I work on Wall Street. I got my prints in more data banks than I care to think about."

"Maybe. But still, let's do it anyway. It'll save us time."

"You're the boss," David said, thinking how much more respect he held for Esposito than he had just an hour ago.

"The postmark was the twenty-fourth. That means you have until—" he stopped to think "—Tuesday. I wouldn't waste time if I was you. I'd get on the phone and start makin' reservations and any other plans you got to ASAP."

"What do I tell the kids?"

"Can't help you there, sir. Seems to me you can't hardly lie to them. But then again, maybe you can use the whole episode as an excuse to send everyone away for a while. Pretend it's a vacation to help clear everybody's head. I wish I could help more, but I'm afraid that's not my field. Might want to call a child psychologist or something."

"Okay then. Becky and I will be down sometime this afternoon. Will you be there?"

"Can't say. Ask for Sergeant Walker. He'll be expecting you."

"Then what? Just sit and wait?"

"I'll be back to you as soon as I know anything. I've got a lot of calls to make. I won't let this take a back burner. I promise."

"Thank you. I'll walk you to your car."

"That won't be necessary. I've taken enough of your time as it is. Go and enjoy your son. They do grow up fast."

They shook hands at the gate in an eight-foot hedge separating the patio from the driveway. David headed for the deck, Esposito toward the driveway. David entered the dining room, securing the broom handle again. He dreaded having to act as if everything were okay. Sometimes kids are draining, but then again, that's their beauty. So helpless, so innocent. They always help bring things into perspective, help detour the mind from its day-to-day problems.

Sometimes David thought he'd be okay if they had to live in a cardboard box. As long as they were all together, that was really all that mattered. That they were together—where he could hold them, watch them, hear them. But now. Now . . . even that wasn't going to be possible. He was going to send them all away. He'd be alone with his thoughts, his fears. No ballast. No innocent perspective. He was already desperate for this to end.

"Hey, Dad!" Caleb shouted.

"Coming, buddy," David replied, walking through the

dining room into the kitchen. He suddenly realized he'd forgotten something and bolted to the front door, running down the brick walk, waving his hands at Esposito as he backed out of the driveway.

Esposito didn't see him until he stopped at the end to look for traffic. He pulled back up and opened his window.

"What's up?" he asked.

"I almost forgot," David said. "What about some protection? Think it's possible to get somebody here for the night? He knows where I live, Captain. Who knows what he'll try next."

"I gotta talk to my chief. If there's a problem with it, I'll call you. Otherwise, consider it done."

"You're a good man."

Esposito smiled, rolled up his window, and was gone.

—∽—

Fenton Montague stood at the sink in the kitchen of his apartment. It was an old porcelain double sink with an attached ridged porcelain counter on which he kept a Rubbermaid dish drier. He washed and dried his plate and looked at it under the reflection of the light. *Smudgy*. He took it back to the sink and rewashed it. Dried it again. *Perfect*. For no apparent reason, he laid it in the dish drier.

He was giddy with delight. He felt he knew every move David was making. He was sure he would move Rebecca and the kids. Especially after he hung Barney. "Rise and shine, David," he said.

No doubt he and Rebecca had talked endlessly about their options. Should they move? Where to? For how long? What Fenton knew for sure was that David Bridwell Johnson would not just disappear. He would never quit his job. Fenton was inside his mind now. He could think like David.

"You don't want to give in to me, do you, David? What's the matter? Not used to taking orders? Too bad. Nothing we can't change."

Fenton would have done it differently if he felt David would actually follow through. But he knew him too well. That wouldn't be an option for this victim. He thought for a brief moment how disappointed he would be if David actually threw it all away, folded up his tent and left. He'd have to switch to plan B. But the fear quickly passed.

The driving back and forth from Boston to Connecticut had become tiresome. This commute would have to go. Fenton was packing now. Sparingly. He wouldn't be gone but a few days. He needed gloves, ski mask, a couple of pairs of black pants, and a sweater. Some underwear.

On his last trip down he'd stopped at the Holiday Inn on Post Road, just beyond the Darien border in Norwalk. He rented a room for two nights. Saturday and Sunday. He would not be returning after that. He paid in advance. Cash.

"This old man, he played one, he played nick nack on my thumb, with a nick nack, patty wack, give the dog a bone, this old man came . . ."

Let's see, he thought, neatly pruning a philodendron. By now, David has no doubt contacted the police. New York or Darien? Doesn't matter. They've seen the letter. Death threat via the mail. Definite no, no. They've probably contacted the FBI by now. Maybe the postal police. Maybe both? *The more the merrier.*

The chase was on. "There's many a slip, 'twixt the cup and the lip," he said. He would need to follow his plan meticulously. No deviations. Nothing spontaneous. A thousand things could go wrong and he was lucky if he'd thought of half of them.

David would probably be flying the family out tomorrow. Monday at the latest. It would be just the two of them now. *I love this.* It was a shame it would have to end. Not to worry. This was only half his plan. First things first, though. Too much too soon is never healthy.

He sat down in an aluminum folding chair, his back straight, staring at the only thing adorning his whitewashed walls. A portrait of his mother, sitting at an angle, hands clasped on her lap. An austere, matronly pose, her eyes piercing him with her steely glare.

"You know, dear Mother, my courage and determination are because of you and your training. I would never have been prepared were it not for you."

Fenton ruminated now. His body and mind at one with the anger, the pain and ultimate consequences of his rejection. The day before he first met David and Jonah, Fenton had been fired from yet another job and suffered a horrible row with his mother. He'd spent that night on the street, determined never again to return home. The demons inside him had yet to free themselves, but they were there—slowly, inexorably squirming their way into the twisted gears of his brain. Within forty-eight hours they were to violently explode.

"How could you do this to me, Fenton?" she had screamed. "I worked my tail off to bring you up right. Give you discipline. Teach you right from wrong. But now, look at you. You're an embarrassment to me. Your own uncle has to fire you. Your uncle no less! This is the fifth time this year. All my hard work. All my love, my caring, and look at you . . . you're nothing! A failure. A nobody. You know that? You are not my son anymore. I want you out of my house!"

Fenton was lonely, scared, and broke on the night the three of them met. They befriended him at a local pub. He was nursing a twenty-five-cent draught, David and Jonah were drinking seven and sevens, playing pool. He was hungry and scared. They looked so confident and secure, so healthy and all-American in their ripped jeans, Bean boots, and Izod shirts.

Fenton homed in on the two of them like a moth to light. He needed them so desperately, and a voice whispered in his head that he'd just hit pay dirt. But this was not just any night. This seemingly innocuous jaunt through the dark would set in motion forces that would forever change their lives. Forces that, once unleashed, would prove nearly impossible to stop.

Fenton walked up to the table and laid down a quarter. His true interest was self-preservation, worlds removed from pool. It was his last quarter. His inheritance still dangled on a string. Mother wasn't dead . . . yet. The quarter he laid on the table that night was the biggest bet of his life . . . and it worked. He thought.

As the evening wore on, David and Jonah were sympathetic to his story. They asked him if he had a place to stay and offered him a bed on the third floor of their three-decker. It wasn't much, but it was more than he had. Home was not an option now.

That evening Fenton and his newfound friends stayed up smoking pot, drinking bourbon. In his mind, he had found a home, a bed, someplace to hang his hat, someplace far removed from the wretched dominance of his mother. It was not until the wee hours of the morning, on the second night, that Fenton finally told them.

"Jesus speaks to me," he said. "Every night he comes. We talk. Is there anything you would like me to tell him? Any problem you'd like me to have him take care of for you? It's quite remarkable, really. I'm the luckiest man on earth. He'll be quite pleased you helped me."

David and Jonah exchanged glances. "Let me get this straight," David said. "Are you telling me that you speak to Jesus or Jesus speaks to you?"

"Well, we speak to each other. He usually sits on my bed and we talk for a long time. He's a remarkable man."

Jonah glanced at David. "You mean Jesus comes to you in your mind, or physically comes to you? You know, like the way we're here right now?" he asked.

"Oh no," Fenton answered, feeling important at the interest they both showed. "He doesn't come in my mind. He visits personally. I can touch him."

David and Jonah looked at each other again. The two of them had been best friends since childhood. They knew one another like brothers—maybe better. Words were superfluous. They each knew what the other was thinking.

They left Fenton on the cot in the attic and walked downstairs to their rooms. For the first time since he could remember, Fenton felt safe; his heart almost leapt with cheer at his good fortune. He smiled as he skipped downstairs to use the bathroom. He could hear voices from behind a closed door to one of the rooms. It was David and Jonah. He slid closer, craning his neck to hear. He assumed, correctly, that they were discussing their guest. Fighting off a slight tingle of anxiety, he stood motionless, eager to hear their thoughts. Fenton's heart nearly collapsed as he listened to Jonah speak.

"The guy's nuts, David," Jonah said forcefully.

David was emphatic in his retort. "I'm afraid he's going to slit our throats in the middle of the night. There's no way this psycho spends another night in this house. Period. End of conversation."

Fenton's heart froze; he couldn't believe the words his ears so clearly heard. *They must be joking.*

"I know. But what do we do, D.B.? We can't very well toss him out on his ass. The guy's got nowhere to go. He'll starve."

"Good. One less nut job in the world. He's gone, got it?"

"Maybe we should call his mother," Jonah offered.

Fenton froze with fear. This couldn't be happening. Could it? He found himself wondering if he were twisting in the throes of a nightmare. He was the personification of stealth . . . not moving . . . hardly breathing . . . careful not to move a joint in his body. He dared not let them know that he was privy to their plan.

"I'm not getting involved any more than I already am," David continued. "Tomorrow, we sit him down and just tell him. We make it sound like we did him a favor for a couple of nights but never intended to have it be a long-term thing. We hand him a twenty, wish him luck, and send his sorry ass out the door."

"No arguments here," Jonah answered.

"Good. Then we agree. First thing tomorrow morning."

"Okay. First thing."

"No bullshit, Jonah. I'm serious as a heart attack."

"I know. So am I. The guy scares me. Shit, I won't sleep a wink tonight."

"I don't know about you, but I'm putting a chair under my doorknob. No way I'm going out at the hands of some psycho we let stay under our own roof."

"Good idea. Wake me in the morning."

The following morning, David delivered the bad news. Fenton was hurt but not shocked by their rejection. He had lain awake all night, dreading this moment. His mind tossed to and fro in a hellish soup of fear and rage. More than once he thought of killing them both, but such violence would ultimately be left for the true object of his wrath.

What would he do? Where would he go? Why did they think he was nuts? Jesus did visit him. He thought they liked him, but they were just like Mother. When you think you're safe, they reject you . . . hurt you.

I'll be back. If it's the last thing I ever do, I'll be back. What none of them knew was that Fenton's promise would be many years in the keeping. He would make a detour or two along the way, primarily as a ward of a handful of the state's mental institutions.

Few humans have endured the humiliation Fenton was forced to swallow upon slouching back home that evening. His mother had been merciless, lashing into him with a venomous, spiteful tongue that burned him to his very core. When his mother's verbal tirades were finally through, when there was nothing left for her to rip from what little remained of her son's self-worth, she climbed the stairs and went to bed.

It was all too much. Rejection, heaped upon more rejection, the humiliation and scorn. Fenton was the human embodiment of a walking time bomb. He paced the kitchen for hours, mumbling to himself. It was inevitable, inescapable really. It was only a matter of time, and finally . . . he snapped.

It all seemed a blur, as if he were watching it from outside his body. He could not remember for sure. He thought he recalled holding the pillow over her face, pushing, pushing. With all his strength, pushing . . . brutally detached from her fierce struggle for life's precious air.

Spittle drooled down the corners of his mouth. The muscles in his arms and shoulders were straining, thighs tight, teeth clenched. His eyes bulged, blazing murderously, wild with a fury from deep within.

When it was over, he felt nothing—an emotional vacuum, void of any and all feeling. She must have died in her sleep, he told the police. She was lying there like that when he came in to wake her. There had been an investigation. Some doubts, but no proof. The inheritance would come. He was finally free!

Or so he thought. The psychiatrists appointed to observe him begged to differ. Far from freeing him, the act marked the beginning of a twenty-year ordeal—a hazy kaleidoscope of years in which Fenton found himself shuffled from one hospital to the next, poked, shocked, and prodded like some hapless victim in a bad B horror flick.

Interspersed with an occasional session with a hospital shrink or a chaperoned walk around the grounds, there were many empty hours in which Fenton was left to fence with the demons in his head. But while he may have been insane, he was far from stupid. On the contrary, over the years, Fenton learned two things: how to fake the hell out of the hospital doctors and how deep his vengeful hatred was rooted.

Then, one day, almost as if the system had tired of him, he was set free. The doctors were unanimous in their findings. Fenton was well enough to re-enter society. He had done it! He'd fooled every last one of the sons of bitches. He was given a new suit, a hundred dollars, a pat on the rear, and a wish for good luck. Fenton could hardly contain his joy. As the sun burned through a hazy August morning, the silent hunter walked quietly away; his very being was obsessed with one thought, and one thought only.

Weeks turned into months. Fenton began to fear he would never find David and Jonah. But one day, he was buying a girlie magazine and caught a glimpse of *The Wall Street Journal*. There he was. Plain as day. A sketch of David's face on the front page! The article of which David had been so proud, for which he had toiled so many years, would prove to be the worst mistake he ever made.

Fenton's breathing stopped. For a moment he thought perhaps he was hallucinating. His mind filled with almost orgasmic optimism. He was no longer alone—no longer adrift at sea. *Thank you, God.*

All the pain, all the feelings, came rushing back to him in tidal-wave proportions. Like it was yesterday, he could taste the anger, feel the resentment. Almost as if time had stood still for him, he'd gone back to their place after his release, but naturally, they were gone. They'd long since graduated and begun their lives. Fenton may have lost track of them, but he had never forgotten.

After he'd murdered his mother, his life had spiraled down . . . down . . . down and away. He had been transformed almost overnight into a psychiatric guinea pig, left to the whims and mercies of a never-ending procession of uncompassionate, experimenting, egotistical, self-absorbed shrinks. To his way of thinking, there were exactly two people on the face of the earth to blame.

He always felt in his heart that one day their paths would cross again. He prayed they would. If he was ever so lucky, he would know what to do. He wished his mother were still alive to watch him in action.

He bought the *Journal* instead of *Penthouse,* and took it home to read the story about this shooting star named David Johnson and the deal he had personally made happen. Fenton studied his face and read the story again. And again. And again . . .

—∾∾—

Despite it all, David and Rebecca made every attempt to make Caleb's birthday party a success. There is something about being a parent—no matter how depressed or worried you are, you can hide it for your kids. Caleb had never had so much fun. The kids played a dozen different games, they drank Coke and ate ice cream, cake, and pizza. Among his many gifts were the Mecha Godzilla set and some shirts from his grandparents. There were twelve kids there. It seemed like thirty.

In the midst of the chaos, David stole away to the kitchen, only to be interrupted by Rebecca getting more lemonade. She climbed the steps from the playroom and walked to the refrigerator. She wore penny loafers, khaki pants, and a red and black Pendleton with the sleeves rolled halfway up her arms.

She eyed David skeptically as she opened the refrigerator door. "What ya drinking?" she asked. In her mind she could already hear any one of a dozen bullshit responses her husband would spew forth. She could see through him like a book. Maybe he had them fooled at work, but he wasn't fooling her. Not even close.

What David wanted more than anything, but couldn't say of course, was to be alone with his bottle of vodka. He felt caught, like a kid with his hand in the cookie jar, and resented the guilt she made him feel. "Oh, hi," he said, wearing an elaborately casual expression. "Uh . . . just some orange juice. Needed a moment's peace and quiet."

Rebecca's eyes narrowed with suspicion. *I caught you, okay? Just admit it.* "Just some orange juice?" she asked.

"Yeah, why?"

She crossed her arms. "Why? Because I've known you for twenty years, David. Because I've lived with you for nineteen of those years. Because I'm your wife. That's why. It's only three o'clock. I'm worried about you."

He's lying to my face. Here comes the part where he fesses up, like I'm not supposed to notice he just lied to me.

"I know, I know. Look, I'm sorry, sweetheart. It's just that I'm so stressed is all. I just need a little something to calm me down."

Rebecca didn't answer. She knew her husband better than he knew himself. She knew he had a drinking problem. She knew he knew he had a drinking problem. But the money kept coming in, the sex was good. Just how far should she be willing to rock his boat? She figured it would come to a head sooner or later. She just didn't think it would be now. She was surprised by the anger boiling inside her.

Rebecca's voice was caustic. "Maybe you can join us after you've *calmed down,*" she said, carrying two pitchers of lemonade down the basement steps.

"Rebecca, please don't. Not now."

The selfish son of a bitch. One night when he was out

chasing some big account in Chicago she thought she smelled gas in the house. She couldn't sleep and was reading in bed. She shot upright when she recognized the smell. Rebecca didn't know what to do. Her first thought was to call David. When the call came in to his room, she could hear the music and the laughter. There was clearly a party going on.

"Honey, I'm a thousand miles away. Call the fire department. What the hell do you want me to do?" he said loudly above the din, obviously drunk.

She was furious. "I don't know, David. I guess I mistakenly thought you might care," she said before hanging up. He called back, but she just laid the receiver on the floor, covering it with his pillow.

How many nights had she fed and bathed the kids, mothered them when they were sick, gotten up in the middle of the night when they cried out because they were uncovered and cold, or had a bad dream? How many sleepless nights had she spent reading in bed while her husband drank and partied the night away? Just how high a salary, how nice a lifestyle justifies that?

Rebecca was suddenly full of fury—Barney, the letter, David's absences, his drinking. *What kind of a rug does he think I am?* She turned and came back to the top of the steps. Slowly, but with hardened determination, she put the lemonade down on the floor and closed the door to the playroom. David knew he was in trouble.

"No," she spat. "How 'bout please don't you! Your son is having a birthday party. We're going away for God knows how long and you're up here drinking vodka. If you ask me, I think that's just a little selfish. Don't you?"

David was silent. He didn't know what to say. She was right, of course. But what was he supposed to do? Stop drinking? He felt scared now. Trapped. Like a wild animal in a corner. *Is it working for you, David?* Fear and uncertainty rocked him.

Rebecca stood staring at him, her mouth tightened into a stubborn line. The moment had come. The battle was waged. She would not be deterred. *Admit it. Come on, admit it—you son of a bitch!*

"How long are you going to keep lying to me, David?"
Silence.

"I asked you a question. How long? The rest of your goddamned life?" She wanted desperately to tell him he was a raging alcoholic, but knew that would send him even deeper into his defensive bunker. She just stood there staring at her husband, her face flushing with indignation.

David felt naked. He was holding his drink, the cubes rattling against the glass, betraying his outward calm. He put it down and met her gaze again. He wasn't getting out of this one. He wanted to walk away but knew that would be tantamount to admitting his weakness—a pervasive, inherent illness—one he would rather ignore than face. David's brows furrowed, his eyes haunted with an inner anxiety.

He couldn't do it. Finally, his wall came crashing down around him. All the worries, the games, the lies. He couldn't juggle them in his mind anymore. The letter and Barney had clipped him behind the knees, and in that moment his life seemed to explode into a thousand splintered pieces on the floor. Without warning to himself or his wife, he started to cry.

Rebecca was torn. She wanted him to cry. He should feel like shit, she thought. Not just for this, but for the dozens of other times—family gatherings, Christmases, birthdays, the empty bed at night. Her raising two young boys virtually by herself. Where was he? Where had he been? *Chasing his goddamned career, padding his ego, satisfying his vices.*

But above it all, Rebecca was a good woman, a good wife. Too good. A classic enabler. "David . . . I'm sorry, honey," she said. "It's a bad time for all of us. We'll talk about your drinking when this is all over." She walked to her husband and held him. He wept quietly on her shoulder.

I'm going to have to quit. He realized he was about to lose his best friend in the whole world. But then again, best friends don't turn on you. A mix of grief and freedom filled him.

"I think I'm an alcoholic," he whispered in her ear. Rebecca simultaneously winced with pain and felt the weight of a thousand bricks lifted from her shoulders.

"David, sweetie . . . You are an alcoholic," Rebecca answered softly. "But it's okay. So are millions of others, and they've beat it. They've all done something you've never done. Not until this moment. They all admitted they were alcoholics. You're on your way, honey. Really. You just took the hardest step. I've been praying for you to say those words for years."

He held her tight, not saying a word.

A sense of relief tugged at her heart. "We'll do it together," she said, squeezing him tightly. "I promise. It only gets better from here."

"Dad! Dad!" Caleb said, running into the kitchen from the hall. "Come and look at how this . . . Oh."

"It's okay, sweetie," Rebecca said.

"Come here, buddy," David said, releasing his wife, wiping his eyes with a handkerchief. "Do you mind giving your old man a hug?" he asked.

"Sure," Caleb said, obliging his father, feeling a little uneasy. "What's wrong, Dad?"

"Do you remember, Cabe, how I told you and Sum last night it's okay to cry? That everybody has feelings? Well, Daddy's just having a hard time now. But you know what?"

"What?"

"It's about to get a heck of a lot better. I'm the luckiest dad in the whole world. Come on. Show me that Godzilla set I got you. I bet it's really cool."

"Oh man, you can say that again!" Caleb said, pulling his dad down to the playroom. "Wait till you see . . ."

Rebecca stood for a moment, staring out the window at the old maple. She thought of Barney and fought off tears. No time. She turned, picked up the pitchers, and headed downstairs.

———— ∽ ————

David and Rebecca went to police headquarters as agreed. Sergeant Walker was expecting them and they were in and out in less than a half hour. The biggest deal was washing the ink off their fingers. Even with the special soap the cops provided, it took three washings and more than a little scrubbing.

Shortly after 6:00 P.M., the front doorbell rang.

"I'll get it!" Sumner shouted.

"No!" Rebecca screamed. "I'm sorry, honey," she said, entering the hall from the kitchen, wiping her hands on a dish towel. "I didn't mean to yell so loud. I wasn't sure you could hear me with the dishwasher going. I'm expecting someone. I'll get it."

"Your wish is my command," Sumner said, and sped off toward the den.

Rebecca wished they had one of those peepholes she could look through. She opened the door a crack and saw a police officer illuminated by the porch light.

"Good evening, Officer. Please come in."

"Thank you," he said, taking off his hat as he entered the foyer. "I'm officer Richard Bennett. Darien police. I've been assigned your security detail for the evening, ma'am."

Rebecca opened the door fully. "Make yourself comfortable Officer Bennett," she said. "Let me get my husband."

Bennett watched her hurry down the hallway to the right of the stairs. She turned right in the kitchen and disappeared. He stood in the foyer, craning his neck to get a glimpse of the living room. It was quite large. A huge, expensive-looking Persian rug lay in front of a Victorian-styled fireplace on the inside wall, and he watched briefly as a neglected fire crackled.

Everywhere he looked there was furniture that appeared to be very expensive. Some things just exude money. He didn't know their names or styles, but knew he would never have the resources to buy them.

He glanced quickly at the dining room to his right. It was large, with stained oak floors with a cherry, floral inlay. Between the windows sat two Victorian chairs. They looked ornate—Renaissance Revival saddlebacks actually, though Bennett didn't know it. He wondered if anyone ever sat in them or if they were just for show.

Hearing footsteps rising from the basement, Bennett resumed an indifferent stance.

"Hi, I'm David Johnson. Glad you could make it, Officer," David said, approaching him.

David struck Bennett as quintessentially preppy, with his Top Siders and pink, long-sleeved polo shirt. Bennett noticed a slight cleft in his chin, his white teeth barely showing through a forced, muted smile.

Bennett extended his hand. "Officer Richard Bennett. I've been assigned to watch your premises this evening."

They send me a fucking rookie?

Bennett was actually twenty-nine and a five-year veteran, but he looked twenty-four with his short-cropped hair. "Cap'n tells me you've got some nutcase threatening you."

David put his finger up to his mouth and looked around as if to say, "Quiet. We don't want the kids to know."

Bennett clenched his teeth, mouth slightly open, shrugging his shoulders, indicating he understood.

"Why don't you come up to the study. We can talk more freely there," David said, turning to climb the stairs.

They entered the study and David shut the door, motioning to two chairs occupying a small alcove with a beautifully adorned bay window. "Have a seat over there. Can I get you a cup of coffee or something?"

It would be a long night Bennett thought. He would love a cup of coffee, but didn't want to make David go back downstairs. "No, thank you," he answered, the leather of his duty belt squeaking as he sat.

"How much do you know?" David asked, sitting down in the chair opposite Bennett.

"I don't know for sure, sir. I'll tell you what I do know, and you can fill in the blanks. How's that?"

David nodded his head, listening intently. Bennett finished in a few moments. David was suitably impressed. Esposito hadn't missed a beat and the kid didn't appear to have missed anything in the translation.

"That's pretty much all I know. Did I miss anything?" Bennett asked.

"No. I'd say you pretty much know what I know. So how do we do this?"

"Well, there's not much for you folks to do, really. I'm going to give you a Varda Alarm. It's in my car. If for any reason you need me during the night, just push the button on top. It'll send out a silent signal and I can be in here in a flash."

A Varda Alarm is a brand name radio-frequency signaling device. They are most often used in situations where someone is in fear of bodily harm—a girlfriend or divorcee who is being stalked, for instance, or whose ex has threatened to kill them. All its user has to do is push the button on its top. It automatically signals all units that help is needed and at what address. Since it operates on radio frequency, the intruder doesn't know an alarm has been sent.

A cruiser will hear a repeated message: "Varda One, Varda One, Varda One" transmits across the radio, or "Varda Two" or "Three," depending upon how many a particular force has. The police know where each Varda is located, and can usually have the closest cruisers there in a matter of minutes.

"That simple?"

"Pretty much. All I gotta do now is stay awake."

David stared at him, frowning.

Bennett smiled. "That was a joke. Sorry."

"Oh," David said, pausing a moment before returning the smile, more from relief than at the joke. "I guess my sense of humor leaves a little something to be desired right now."

"I understand," Bennett said, rising from his chair. "I'm going to leave the cruiser parked in the driveway where it can be seen."

"Do you think—" David started to say, then stopped.

"Do I think what?"

"Well, I was just wondering. If you park it out of sight, maybe we'll have a better chance of catching this asshole, should he show up."

"Cap'n Esposito made it pretty clear to me, sir. This was not to be a stealth mission. This detail is to keep off trespassers *before* they get to the house. Those are my orders, sir. I suggest you speak to him if you prefer a different approach."

David was disappointed. He had hoped, on the chance this guy did come tonight, they could catch him and be done with it—finish the whole mess before the weekend ended. He wouldn't have to send Rebecca and the kids away. He could start his sobriety with her help. He would need it.

"I understand," he responded.

"Okay. If there's nothin' else, I guess we'll get started. My shift runs till six tomorrow morning. I'll wake you before I leave."

"Good, although I'll probably be up."

David or Rebecca checked on Officer Bennett a half dozen times that evening, offering him coffee and snacks. Perhaps they weren't aware of it, but subconsciously they wanted to make sure he was still there. No, he hadn't seen or heard anything.

A little before 11:30 P.M., David went out for the last time. He walked down the brick walk to the driveway and saw Officer Bennett's cruiser. Empty. Strangely ill at ease, he walked around the garage toward the rear of the house. He came upon the hedgerow, tall enough to block the sight of anything beyond it. He stood and listened. Nothing. He slowly opened the trellised gate and entered onto the flagstone patio he and Jonah had put in six years ago.

He thought of Jonah for a moment, and how nice it would be to hear his voice. Maybe he should send the family there. Jonah had more land than God, and Maine sure was closer than California. Granted, his house was a little small, but they'd all stayed there before. I'll speak to Rebecca about it, he thought. If she was not against it, he would call and ask him tomorrow. *Sounds like a plan,* he thought to himself, stopping dead in his tracks.

There was a rustling further down the length of the house. Under the deck. He strained his ears to hear. Footsteps. That unmistakable sound of autumn leaves trampled underfoot. He wanted to call out, but didn't dare. He stepped quietly to the side of the house and stood, motionless, listening to the leaves screaming out in the crisp, quiet autumn air.

He could see the beam from a flashlight now. As it approached closer, he could make out the silhouette of Officer Bennett's police cap. David felt like a fool. Worse yet, he thought, how was he going to announce his presence without scaring the living daylights out of the poor guy?

He'd better say something quickly before Bennett's beam shone upon him. The last thing David wanted was to be dropped by a nervous cop in his own backyard.

He cleared his throat. "Officer Bennett?" he called out, as nonchalantly as he could.

David could see the flashlight jump in the night. "Jesus Christ! Mr. Johnson, is that you?"

"Yes."

"You scared the shit out of me."

"Sorry about that."

"What are you doin' back here against the house?"

"I came out to check on you, tell you that we're going to hit the sack. I heard footsteps and panicked, I guess."

"That makes two of us. I was just lookin' around. Makin' sure all the doors and windows are secure. Nothin' out of the ordinary that I can find. Go on to bed. I'll be right here in the morning."

"Okay. Sorry to have startled you," David said, feeling somewhat embarrassed.

"No problem. It's probably the most excitement I'll have all night."

—⁊⁊⁊—

David cringed at the earsplitting noise. The bank alarm was maddening. He didn't know where it came from and he couldn't turn it off. He was locked inside the bank vault, trapped with no escape. They were coming for him now. How could he tell them he was innocent, that the real robbers had locked him in there as a diversion for their own escape. I'm innocent, he pleaded with the police as they manhandled him to the floor. Please don't take me away. I haven't done anything, I tell you. I'm a victim, like the other customers here.

I'm innocent I tell you! He could feel one of the policemen's knees in the small of his back as one of the officers threw the handcuffs on sharply, with a stinging slap. All the while, the alarm wailed loudly. Why won't you believe me? Listen, why would I lock myself . . .

"David? David!" Rebecca said, sitting up in bed shaking him frantically. "David. Get up."

"Wha—What the hell?" he said, rolling over, trying to focus his eyes on his wife. As Rebecca's silhouette against the white ceiling came clearly into view, he jumped to his feet. The smell of smoke was thick and acrid, menacing and unmistakable.

"Becky!" he bellowed, jumping to the bedroom floor, pulling up his corduroys. "Put on clothes. Now! Call the fire department. I'll get the kids."

The wailing of the fire alarms was incessant now. Screaming at the top of their mechanical lungs, *"Fire! Fire! Everybody run for their lives!"*

David's heart was pounding. His mind was thinking a dozen thoughts at once. Caleb, Sumner, Bennett. *Where the hell was Bennett?*

He slipped on his Top Siders, running down the hallway, yelling, "Sumner! Caleb! Get up! Fire!" He entered Sumner's room first. Just in time to see him crawling out of bed. He scavenged wildly through his son's closet, pulling out a pair of Nikes and a coat. "Don't bother getting dressed. Here, put these on and wait in the hall for me. Lie on the floor. Now!"

Caleb met them in the hallway. David ran to his room, retrieved a pair of shoes and a jacket and tossed them at him as he ran by. "Put these on, Cabes. Now. Stay here, at the head of the stairs. Lie down and don't move! Understand? *Do not move!*" David was afraid to have them run outside. He could only imagine what horrors awaited them out there.

He ran back toward the master bedroom slamming into Rebecca as she came out the door. She hit the ground hard. He reached down, grabbed her hand and pulled her up harder. "Come on, let's go."

Smoke was everywhere, thick but not yet overpowering. They all gathered at the top of the stairs for an instant, David saying, "Everybody here? Okay, follow me. Stay low to the ground, breathe lightly and grab the waist of the person in front of you. We're going out the front door. Don't stop for anything."

They were in the foyer in an instant. David pulled the front door open slightly, peeked out, pulled it open all the way and stood in the doorway as his family fled outside.

Caleb went first. When he crossed the doorsill, he took one step and tumbled onto his right side, falling the four steps to the brick walk.

"Caleb!" Rebecca hollered. Then she saw him. She screamed into the night, her hand over her mouth, her body trembling with convulsions. Without hesitation, David scooped Sumner into his arms, stepped over Officer Bennett, and squatted, still holding Sumner, to pick up his younger son. He carried them, one under each arm, down the brick walk toward the driveway. Rebecca was a grown woman. She would have to take care of herself. The kids came first.

Rebecca stood in the doorway as smoke billowed out the front entrance, staring at Bennett.

"Becky! Come on, let's go. Now!"

With a start, she stepped over Bennett's lifeless corpse and broke into a run. When she was next to her husband, he handed Caleb to her without breaking stride. He was still holding Sumner with his left arm.

"We're going to the Entwistle's. They can put us all up for the night."

The Johnson clan scampered quickly down their long drive, directly across the street to their nearest neighbors and Rebecca's best friend. They could hear the fire horn clearly from the fire station, nearly two miles away. Its deep, air compressed wail shattering the stillness of the brisk, New England night.

David pounded forcefully on his neighbor's front door. The porch light came on in a matter of seconds.

William Entwistle opened the door, his wife standing behind him.

"My God, David. Is that your house? We smelt the smoke and just called the fire department, but we didn't know where it was coming from. Please. Please. Come in," he said, opening his front door, standing to one side.

The smell of smoke was pungent in the air.

"You kids must be scared half to death," Dorothy said, stealing a furtive glance at Rebecca, fearful of what she saw.

The kids were whisked off in an instant, the two women instinctively performing their maternal rituals.

"Thank you, Bill. I feel terrible bothering you at this hour," David said, harried and breathless.

"Don't be silly."

David flexed his arms back and forth. They shook with exhaustion from carrying the kids. "We're in a hell of a mess. What has Dot told you? Anything?"

"Just about Barney. I'm sorry, David."

"Yeah, we all are. Well, I can fill you in on the details if you feel like losing sleep. But right now, I need to use your phone."

"Fire department's on their way. I can hear them now."

"I know," David said, thinking it prudent not to mention there was a murdered policeman on his front stoop. "A phone please."

"Sure," Bill Entwistle said, motioning David to the wall phone in the kitchen.

David shook his head slightly. "Listen, I hate to be a pain, Bill, but by any chance, can I use one with a little more privacy?"

"Uh . . . sure. There's one in my study downstairs. Here, let me turn on the lights for you," Bill said, wondering what the hell kind of mess his neighbor was in.

Bill opened the door, flipped on the light, and showed David to his desk phone. "I'll be upstairs," he said, closing the door behind him.

David dialed the police. "This is David Johnson. I live

at thirty-two Woodbury Lane. I need to speak to Captain Esposito immediately."

"We just dispatched a cruiser to your residence, sir. Do you know there is a fire at your house?"

"No shit," David responded, his emotions getting the better of him now. "I must speak to Esposito immediately."

"Captain Esposito is not on duty this evening, sir. Can I help you?"

"Listen to me carefully, Officer. Call him at home. Give him this number," David said, reciting the number on the telephone. "Have him call me back here immediately. Sooner if possible. Believe me, he won't be angry," David said, wondering if he was being foolish not just telling the officer about Bennett.

"Sir?" the cop asked, not sure he had actually heard what he had just heard.

"Jesus Christ. Do it! I'll be waiting," David yelled into the receiver before slamming it in its cradle.

Two minutes later, the phone rang. David picked it up half way through the first ring. He thought it might be the cop calling back. "Hello?"

"David Johnson, please."

"Esposito. It's me. Bennett's dead. We had to walk over his body to get out of our burning house. There's fire trucks coming up the street now, and your duty officer told me he just dispatched a cruiser to my address."

"*Dead?*" Esposito asked, trying to shake the sleep from his brain. "How do you know?"

"I don't know, Captain. Call it intuition. Maybe it was the foot-long gash across his neck that clued me in. I'm not fucking around here anymore! You understand me? If you can't catch this son of a bitch, then I will. When can you get here?"

"I'll be there in fifteen minutes." *Click.*

David sat slumped in the chair, chin to his chest, hands clasped together in his lap. The nightmare of the last forty-eight hours swirled in his head. One psycho can sure ruin your whole day.

"David?" Rebecca asked nervously, poking her head in the door. "Are you all right?"

"How are the kids?" he asked.

"Fine. They're both up in the guest room. They want to see you."

"Okay, I'll be right up. I called Esposito. He'll be here in a few minutes."

"I guess this takes it up a notch or two, doesn't it?" she asked, frightened for her family and her own safety now.

"Just a couple. Honey, tell the kids I'll be right there. Get Bill for me too, would you please?"

A moment later Bill Entwistle entered his office and stood by the open door. David motioned for him to close it. Closing the door, he walked to the side of the desk, crossing his arms over his chest. Entwistle was perplexed. "What's up?" he asked.

"Bill, do you own a gun?" David asked, not moving from his meditative position.

"Yes . . . but—" Bill answered uneasily, raising an eyebrow. "David, what the hell is going on?"

"I'll tell you everything if you really want to know. What's important is that some psycho is stalking my family and wants me dead. I don't know who and I don't know why. That's the God's honest truth. The fact is, I don't have a gun, Bill, and I need one."

Bill knew there was more to this game than met the eye, and he didn't want any part of it. But like it or not, the main character in this play was sitting right in front of him.

"It's registered in my name, David. I don't know all the laws on this stuff, but surely I'll be in deep shit if you end up shooting someone with my gun. I'm assuming so anyway. Don't you think?"

David looked up. "Think? I'll tell you what I think. What I *think* is that someone is trying to kill me and my family. That's what I *think*. What I know is that I'm not going to let it happen. Not if I can help it. I need that gun, Bill."

Bill stood silent, staring at David. His neck was corded, and Bill found himself transfixed by a pulsing vein on its left side. He tried to put himself in his neighbor's shoes. What would he do if someone were trying to kill him and his family? What would he want David to do if he asked him for his gun for protection? He breathed deeply, uncrossed his arms and took a seat in front of his desk, staring at David.

"All right. I've got two guns actually. One's a thirty-eight, the other's a forty-five. I'll make you a deal. I'll show you where they are and unlock the cabinet. Just don't take the thirty-eight. It was my father's. You'll see the ammo. Help yourself. I don't want to know anything more about it. Understand?"

David nodded his head slightly, indicating he understood.

"Also, let's get one thing straight," Entwistle continued. "This conversation never took place. If it ever comes back to me, I'll tell them you stole the gun. Deal?"

"Deal," David said without hesitating. "Where are they?"

Entwistle stood. "Follow me," he said.

—⁂—

It is a common error for people to refer to sociopaths and psychopaths interchangeably. Although the two certainly share many a common trait, by definition, sociopaths enjoy the pain and suffering they cause, but are legally sane. That is, they are grounded in reality. They fully understand the agony and grief that follow their actions. In fact, they are addicted to them, or rather, to the power they create. As important, sociopaths also understand the illegality of their behavior. They just don't give a shit.

On the other hand, technically, Fenton Montague was not sociopathic. Fenton's world was exclusively of his own making. Psychotic, but not sociopathic. He too thrived on the infliction of pain and suffering, but to him, it was God's will. In his world, God's voice was often his sole determiner. He would lie in bed for hours, staring at the ceiling, listening to orders God would bark at him. He would toss . . . turn . . . hum with his palms over his ears. Fenton was not grounded in reality. Not ours anyway.

"Okay, okay," he'd plead, tired and drained. "I've had enough now. Please. I need to sleep."

About the time Jesus stopped visiting, God started speaking with him directly. He was not benevolent. He was often angry. Why was Fenton so lazy? Why was it necessary for him to constantly stay after Fenton? Why couldn't he think of anything for himself? Surely, he was smart enough to realize all the work that needed to be done? How little time he had?

The evening of Bennett's murder, Fenton returned to the Holiday Inn, removed his trench coat and hung it neatly in the closet behind the door. He soaked in the tub now, fully clothed. The clear, warm bath water quickly taking on a dark, crimson hue.

He submerged himself up to his neck, his death instinct in full bloom. The warm water was now completely imbued with Bennett's blood. The sweet smell, the sound of gurgling as Fenton ripped his serrated diver's knife across his throat, not to mention a little piece of something very precious to Linda Barnes he'd already sent David in the mail—as he thought of these things they took on an eroticism that no woman could match. He closed his eyes and realized he had an erection.

Thinking back, he had been surprised but not startled to see the cruiser in the driveway. It was a likelihood that had registered on his immense radar screen of possibilities. Fenton had driven by the Johnson home slowly. He drove several houses further and pulled into the drive of a new home under construction.

He had already been to the Johnson's several times and had actually drawn himself a map of the yard. He entered their property from behind the barn, having literally crawled an eighth of a mile through the woods from their next-door neighbor's yard.

He knelt on his knees, motionless. Waiting. Listening. When he was convinced he was safe, he walked quickly toward the maple from which he'd hung Barney, down the slight incline of the lawn, and onto the flagstone patio. Perhaps the officer had heard the movement of leaves. Good. He waited now with his back to the hedge, next to the trellised gate, on the side with the hinges, holding his knife flat against his stomach.

It had all happened so quickly. Fenton was surprised when it was over. When Bennett appeared through the gate, he had not yet pulled his weapon. Rather, he had his right hand on the butt of his 9mm Glock semiautomatic, still in his unsnapped holster. He held his flashlight firmly in his left hand. Its glow gave him away.

When both his shoulder blades had cleared the gate, Fenton took one step toward him, pulling Bennett's head back and slightly to the left with his left hand, simultaneously bringing his right hand up, slicing the blade of his knife quickly. Deeply.

Fenton didn't know how long Bennett took to die. It couldn't have been long though, for in a matter of seconds the gurgling stopped, replaced only by an endless stream of his life's fluid, flowing into the crevices between the flagstones, glistening in the faint glimmer of the moon.

Fenton wasn't sure that there might not be more than one, although he doubted it. He performed a perfunctory search. Quietly. Quickly. When he was satisfied, he picked Bennett up and proceeded with his plan. *Life's little detours.*

He pulled out a toy suction-cup dart from his jacket pocket, string already attached, and coated it with contact cement. He quickly affixed it to a pane in one of the basement windows he had precut on a previous visit, reached down, unlocked the window, and slipped inside.

Moving quickly now, he was prepared to go back to the barn if necessary, but took a minute to look for anything flammable: paint thinner, maybe turpentine. Bingo! He gathered some laundry, towels, and rags. He looked for a container of some sort. Something large and sturdy enough to contain the fire. He emptied a small metal trash can onto the floor. It would be perfect for his needs. Fenton gathered all his items, throwing in eclectic bits and pieces he felt sure would burn with the most smoke and toxicity. He threw in a ski boot, a basketball, and a box of Hefty trash bags.

Fear was his game. The last thing Fenton wanted was to kill David in his sleep. *That wouldn't be any fun at all now, would it?* When it was all said and done, this would end up being quite innocent, really. But the panic he pictured it would create emboldened him. He could feel the power. The control. He held all the cards now. *When I'm done, David, when I tell you to jump, your only response will be "How high?" You'll realize soon enough, I own you.*

With surprising stealth, he climbed the stairs and placed the garbage can on the Persian rug in the living room. Fenton was filled with exhilaration, almost giddy in anticipation. His mind hummed. "London Bridge is falling down, falling down, falling down . . ." He stood for a moment, gathering his senses, the caustic soup at his feet biting his nostrils.

"Don't let the bed bugs bite," he said, striking a match and tossing it into the container from as far away as he could stand. The roar of the flames was instantaneous. His spine shuddered with excitement. Fenton walked to the kitchen, opened the freezer, and left a little something for David's benefit. He walked down the hall straight to the front door, tacked something to it and quietly left.

—⁓—

Like most small towns throughout America, Darien is serviced by a volunteer fire department. But volunteer and amateur should not be confused. The town is proud of their fire department. They have three stations located in various parts of town, are known to respond quickly and enjoy a reputation of thorough professionalism.

Two tankers were called out and responded to the scene within nine minutes of Rebecca's and the Entwistle's calls. As they approached, they could smell the smoke. Those not otherwise occupied began donning their oxygen tanks and securing their masks.

The lead man recoiled with shock as he approached the front door. "Jesus Christ!" he called out into his mask. "Captain," he yelled, removing his regulator. "You'd better get over here, quick!"

"Holy shit!" Captain Flanagan said, coming upon the scene. "Jackson! Tortelli! Over here, now!"

The two men were at the stoop in seconds, looking at Flanagan for orders. He motioned to the top landing. "Tortelli, you get his legs. Jackson, grab him under the arms. Move! Get him the hell out of here!"

Bennett was removed in an instant.

"Ready?" Flanagan asked. "Okay. Go!" and the hoses were dragged through the front entrance of the Johnson home.

The smoke was still thick. Nothing burns blacker than rubber and plastic. The firefighters were surprised to find it was nothing more than a heap of trash burning in a can in the middle of the living room. The fire was extinguished in short order. Except for some scorching on the ceiling, which required dousing with a hose, it was an awful lot of mayhem for so little actual damage. In fact, as with most fires, the lion's share of damage was caused by smoke and water.

Flanagan stood at the foot of the brick stairs, speaking with Esposito. "Sorry, Pete. We didn't have much of a choice. I figured you'd rather we move him than drag our hoses all over the poor guy."

"Shit, Pat. Anyway you cut it, it's a goddamned nightmare. First I lose one of my own, and then he ends up about as polluted as the Hudson River. This has gotta be one of the messiest crime scenes we'll ever work. Hey, it's not your fault. You did the right thing. From the looks of it, he wasn't killed here anyway. Looks like the perp took him on the patio out back, then moved him here."

"You're shittin' me," Flanagan said. "What the hell's going on here? First, we get a trash can full of rubber burnin' in the living room and then we get a dead cop lyin' on the front stoop. You'd think this was the fuckin' Bronx."

"You wouldn't believe me if I told you."

"Try me," Flanagan said, his curiosity working overtime now.

Both men turned as someone yelled, "Hey, Captain!" from the direction of the driveway. "The state police are here."

"I gotta go, Patty. I'll be seein' ya. Thanks. Hope you can make the Benevolent Ball this year," Esposito said, slapping Flanagan on the back, walking toward the driveway.

"Count on it," Flanagan said, watching his longtime friend walk away.

Esposito reached the drive in time to see two men in suits exiting a large, unmarked Chevrolet Caprice Classic. He walked in their direction, cupping his hands to his mouth for warmth, stopping ten feet in front of the car.

"Captain Esposito?" the taller one asked.

"Yes."

"Are you the commanding officer, sir?"

"That's correct."

"Lieutenant Cedric Halliway, state police homicide," he said, extending a hand. "This is Detective Sergeant Scott Hill."

"Sergeant," Esposito said, taking his hand. "Pleasure's mine."

"Captain, is that one of your men smoking up by the walk?"

"Um . . . shit."

"Please tell him to extinguish his cigarette, *away* from the area, and refrain from smoking on the premises. It's a big enough mess as it is. We don't need ashes or butts not germane to the scene clouding things up."

"Walker!" Esposito yelled, angry and embarrassed. "Swallow that butt! You know better than to be smokin' here. Smoke when you get home."

"Captain, let's take this from the top, okay?" Halliway asked. "Why don't you fill us in while we take a look around."

"The fire boys all done?" Hill asked.

92

"Yeah, just wrapping up. They'll be gone in a couple of minutes."

Cedric Halliway was tall and thin and wore bifocal glasses that gave him the air of an academician. His white hair and pin-like mustache augmented the look. Even if he hadn't known his rank, Esposito would have guessed Halliway the superior officer at a glance. He wore a buttoned tan raincoat and kept his hands inside his pockets. Esposito escorted the two men up the drive and down the walk toward the brick steps.

"Owner of the house is across the street at a neighbor's. Spoke to him briefly after I got things squared away here . . . oh, about a half hour ago. Some Wall Street muckity muck."

"Muckity muck?" Halliway asked. "Can you be more specific than that?"

"Obviously, we'll need to speak to him in more depth. Things have just been a little frantic around here. I believe he works in some sales position for one of the bigger Wall Street firms. Runs the show I think."

They stood at the foot of the stairs, Esposito explaining the situation in which Bennett had been found, his call from David Johnson, and the reason the officer had been moved.

"The firemen moved him over here," he said, pointing to a white sheet on the lawn, silhouetting the unmistakable form of a body. "Other than the sheet, we haven't touched a thing. The ME's on his way now."

"Beautiful," Hill said sarcastically, under his breath.

"You say you believe he was murdered on the back porch?" Halliway asked. "Can you show it to us?"

"Sure. Hey listen, I don't mean to be nosy or anything, but shouldn't you guys be taking notes? You're gonna see an awful lot. Will you remember all of this?"

Halliway laughed to himself. If there was one thing a homicide investigator learned early on, it was to write everything down. In fact, of the many rules governing conduct, numbers one through five were *Don't touch anything.* Six through ten were *Write everything down.*

"Standard operating procedure, Captain," Hill responded. "Generally, when we first come on a scene one of the more critical acts we perform is an initial walk around. Like takin' notes in class. You might miss something important trying to get down what was just said."

"All we want to do now is get a feel. The sights, the sounds, the weather, noises, distances. There'll be plenty of notes before we're through," Halliway added, in his best professorial manner.

While it was true that evil of this magnitude seldom visited his town, still, Esposito told himself he should have known better than to ask that question. It wasn't like this was his first homicide. It must be his nerves, he thought.

"Anyway," Esposito continued, feeling foolish. "Mrs. Johnson calls the department Friday afternoon. Says her dog's been murdered. Some wacko hung him from a tree. I find out later that Mr. Johnson's received a death threat in the mail."

This caught the detectives' attention. They both gave him a glance. Esposito proceeded to fill them in on everything he knew from his conversation with David the previous morning.

"Looks like movin' the family's a foregone conclusion now. Whoever the perp is, he's got a serious bug up his butt over this guy."

"Do you have reason to believe the letter and these incidents are connected?" Hill asked as he and Halliway approached Bennett's body.

"Well, no. Not exactly. I mean we haven't got a match or anything like that. It just seems pretty damned coincidental if you ask me. I'm just assuming."

"Dangerous habit, Captain," Halliway said, lifting the sheet covering Bennett's body, impassively studying the morbid scene beneath. "Scott, see to it his hands are bagged immediately."

"Maybe," Esposito said. "But I'll wax your car if I ain't right on this one."

"Let's see the patio, please," Halliway said, replacing the sheet.

There was a lot of work to be done. First, he'd have to get the photography boys out for a thorough shoot, then the lab technicians. He'd have to mark the location of the body—twice. He'd have to have the body escorted to the morgue, take measurements, draw sketches, rope off the appropriate areas, collect evidence, secure the scene, schedule and attend the autopsy. No question, this was not a lazy man's job.

"Looks like the perp stood here," Esposito said, his face and body now fully illuminated under the klieg lights the police had set up on the patio. "Caught him like this," walking through the motions. "Kid never had a chance. Didn't even have his weapon out."

"I assume these shoe tracks are from the perp exclusively?" Hill asked.

"Well, we . . . um . . . We didn't know it happened here. One of my men stepped right in it before he knew what he'd done. Thank God, he was thinkin' though. Didn't move a muscle. Called for help, and a couple of the fire boys lifted him up. We've already taken his shoes. He was none too happy, I can tell ya."

"Life's like that," Hill replied.

Esposito continued the tour, showing the two men the window pane that had been removed, where they found it (dart removed), and explained what actions they presumed the intruder took prior to the fire.

"Hardly ideal, huh, Scott?" Halliway asked.

Hill shook his head. "I'll say."

"Let's take a look inside," Halliway said, thinking what a field day a defense attorney was going to have with this one. "You say the owner is across the street?" he asked once inside, standing over the black and disfigured trash can.

"Should be. I told him to stay there until we came for him."

"Good. We'll need to speak with him."

—⁓—

David lay on the Entwistle's pullout sofa bed, Rebecca at his side. It was dark and quiet, except for the periodic squawking of police and fire dispatchers breaking the night air. The sound seemed to travel forever, and oddly, David felt embarrassed about what his neighbors were thinking.

Esposito came to the Entwistle's after he got things under control at the Johnson's. He gave David the details of the fire, and explained that it seemed worse than it actually was. It looked like another prank meant more to intimidate than to harm.

"The mind appears to be this guy's game," Esposito had said. "I can tell you from experience, that can get old, real quick."

"It gets older than this?" David asked.

"Look, I got the state police on the way. This one's over our heads. Stay put. Don't go anywhere, understand? They'll want to talk to you."

"I can't wait."

Rebecca twitched through a nervous sleep, mumbling something about the boys. David finally heard the engines pull away, the clear and unmistakable noise of diesel engines drawing softer with every passing second. He closed his eyes and concentrated on his breathing. Nothing lasts forever, he told himself. How and when it ends is the big question.

Atlanta seemed a lifetime ago. It was strange, he thought, how little he cared now whether or not he ever got the Coke account. Funny, the way life has a way of setting priorities for you. He thought of the limo driver, the flight to Atlanta, the presentation, the call to Rebecca, his meeting with Esposito. He had trouble placing everything in its proper chronological order. Had he gotten the letter on Wednesday or Thursday? It seemed as if Barney had been dead over a week. Was Caleb eight or nine?

One thing was certain. It couldn't go on like this for very long. Either he or the son of a bitch who was ruining his life was going to die. Right now, he didn't really care which. He rolled over on his right side and slid both hands underneath his pillow, massaging the cold steel of his newly acquired .45 semiautomatic. He felt a strange mix of fear and exhilaration.

"David," Bill Entwistle said, poking his head through the door. "The state police are here to speak with you."

"Oh, thanks, Bill," David said quietly, dragging himself out of bed. "I'm really sorry to have to put you through all of this. We'll be out in the morning, I promise. Where are they?"

"In the kitchen."

David entered the Entwistle's kitchen still dressed in what he'd put on during the fire, looking every bit as worn and tattered as he felt.

"Mr. Johnson?" Halliway inquired.

"Yes."

Through foggy and tired eyes David knew intuitively that this man knew his stuff. He carried about him a certain coolness—a professional demeanor David could see would be difficult to ruffle. His silver hair aside, David could tell this was not Halliway's first murder.

"I'm Lieutenant Cedric Halliway, Connecticut State Police. This is Detective Sergeant Scott Hill."

"Morning," David said, dreading the thought of spending one minute with these two very serious looking men. He was physically and mentally exhausted and desperately needed sleep. If he were home, he'd have made himself a drink.

"I know this is an inopportune time to discuss the details of this case," Halliway began. "What we'd like to do right now is get some perfunctory questions out of the way, get your input on a couple of key concerns we have, and call it a night. You look like you could use some sleep and I'm sure you've had precious little of it this evening. We'll come back tomorrow after you've had a chance to regroup. Is that acceptable to you?"

"I guess," David said, exhaustion oozing from his pores. "There's been an awful lot going on the last few days. I'm afraid I'm pretty out of it. I'll do my best. But if at all possible, I would appreciate your being brief. I'll help you any way I can tomorrow. Right now, I feel almost sick."

"We understand," Hill said.

Halliway started in. "Captain Esposito told us about

the threat you received. You wouldn't happen to have the letter with you?"

"No. I gave it to him."

"We'll need to see it."

"As I said, Esposito has it."

"Do you have any idea who this person could be?" Halliway asked. "A business associate? Neighbor? Someone you've slighted over the years?" he continued, pressing for any morsel he could find.

"No. Believe me, I've racked my brain. I can't think of anybody who'd do this to me . . . to us."

"What exactly is your line of work, sir?" Hill asked.

David told them as best he could, in layman's terms, with what little energy he had left.

"I don't know all there is to know about Wall Street, Mr. Johnson," Halliway said. "But surely, over the years, you must have made some enemies?"

"Well, yes, I suppose. It's not exactly for the faint of heart. But shit, gentlemen, it just doesn't make any sense. I mean it would be like Michael Jordan deciding he was going to murder someone because he got one of his shots blocked. It goes with the territory. It's hardly a reason for murder."

Halliway scribbled something in his notebook. "As a general rule, Mr. Johnson, strangers just don't do this to other strangers. There's almost always some connection. We'll revisit this tomorrow. I'm afraid it's important."

"We understand that you personally saw Officer Bennett after he was murdered. Is that correct, sir?" Hill asked.

"Yes. We had to walk over him to get out of our house. My wife and kids are going to remem—"

"That may be difficult for your family, Mr. Johnson," Halliway interrupted. "May I suggest some counseling. Particularly for the children."

"Thank you," David said, feeling the deadening pressure of his head on his shoulders. His whole world was imploding in on him; he didn't know how much more he could take.

"I want to show you something. We found it tacked to

the back of your front door. Perhaps you could tell us if it means anything to you," Halliway said, reaching inside his raincoat and pulling out a manila envelope with the note inside. He carefully laid it out on the kitchen counter. He pushed it toward David with the rubber tip of a pencil.

David didn't have his reading glasses. He had to put his face quite close to the note in order to make it out.

The Longest Way Round,
Is The Shortest Way Home.

"That's it?" David asked, still resting on his elbows, craning his head to look at Halliway. "What the fuck does that mean?"

"We were hoping maybe you could tell us," replied Hill.

"Where'd you say you found this?" David asked, wincing slightly.

"Behind your front door."

David felt physically ill. Another minute of this and he thought he would faint. "Look, gentlemen, I'd like to help you. Really I would. But I'm as much in the dark about this thing as you are, and if I don't get some sleep, I'm going to vomit. I'm sorry. Can't we do this tomorrow? Please?"

The two detectives looked at each other.

"Of course," said Halliway. "Just one other thing. Have you made plans for your family?"

"Well, it's all happened so fast. I've thought of a couple of things, but nothing definite. Why?"

"I don't wish to scare you, Mr. Johnson, but I would say we are dealing with a Class A psychopath here. I would make arrangements first thing tomorrow if I were you. It's not only prudent, but would help me sleep a heck of a lot easier," Halliway said, getting up from his kitchen chair, extending a hand to David. "We'll come by tomorrow. Don't rearrange your day. We'll call first."

"Okay."

"Get some sleep. You'll need it."

"Thanks," David said, wondering how he could ever fall asleep now.

———⚬———

There's something about autumn in New England. The summer's activities begin to fade, and a slow, unyielding metamorphosis begins to take place. Fall is a time for dying—beginning ever so slowly—almost imperceptibly.

Sometime in September whole branches transform from lush green to golden shades of yellow, rust, and red. Soon, usually after the first frost, entire trees seem to explode into nature's version of a pyrotechnic show. Pumpkins begin to appear everywhere, on porches, tabletops, store entrances, steps. Their presence ubiquitous, a constant reminder that the dog days have passed, and in their place, the preparations for winter must begin. In the end, as they have for millennia, the trees lose their idyllic beauty. They become cold and barren to sight and touch. The flowers wither, birds fly south, and the grass dies.

As November approaches, a bunker-like mentality begins to settle in. The days grow much shorter, and the holiday season offers only a brief respite from the knowledge of what is to come. After Christmas, a somber, anticipatory mood settles in. The large, white church steeples point to the barren sky, awaiting Mother Nature's expected onslaught.

On Sunday morning, October 29th, David Johnson escorted his family back to their house. Becky and David entered the foyer and immediately went to the living room to inspect the damage, while the kids scampered off to check on their rooms. Rebecca stood in the doorway, her hand over her mouth, using every ounce of energy she had to keep from breaking down.

While only the ceiling had been burned, everything was ruined, covered with a thick, almost sticky silt. The walls, the ceiling, the floors were black with soot. The furniture was unusable, the Persian rug destroyed.

David slid an arm around her waist and stood firmly while Rebecca rested her head on his shoulder. "Oh, David, honey, where do we start?" she asked.

"We don't," he said. "We've got insurance. We're finally going to make some of those changes we've talked so much about. I'm going to get the yellow pages and find somebody who can handle this whole thing from A to Z."

"But we can't live like this until they get to it."

"You're right," David said, turning to his wife. "I'm going to call Jonah and see if he can take you and the kids for a while. He's closer than a brother to me and he and Vickie would love to have you guys for a while. Especially when I tell him the circumstances."

Aware that there was no choice, at least nothing more palatable, Rebecca remained still and silent.

"Honey, that detective from the state police made it clear to me last night. He told me to get you and the kids out of here now. Said we're dealing with a "Class A psycho," I believe were his words. We have to do it, Beck. Today."

"Okay, it'll be good to get away. But you should come, David. There's no telling what will happen to you. Please, sweetheart? I don't want you to stay. Your job's not that important. Not to me anyway."

David held his wife by the shoulders, looking into her eyes. "Look, it's not the job anymore. If I run from this asshole, I'll be running the rest of my life. Believe me, I don't want to stay. I'd love nothing more than to go with you guys. I'll come up every weekend. Promise. It's a hell of a lot more convenient than California or Florida. It's only an hour's flight away."

"I'm scared, David. What if he gets to you, honey? What if he kills you?"

"Now don't start getting paranoid on me," David said, the firmness of his voice masking his fear. "Nothing's going to happen. I promise. I'll have so many cops around me, the President would be jealous."

Rebecca's eyes pleaded. "After what happened to Bennett, somehow that doesn't make me feel any better."

"Now look, I need you strong now, okay? We've got to stop him, Beck. If we don't, where will he strike next? You? The kids? No, this is our only chance. I have to stay here. Everything will work out fine. I promise."

"How can you say that, David?" Rebecca asked, staring at her husband with fear in her eyes. "You don't know what he's thinking, what he's got planned next."

"That may be. What I do know is that he's lost the element of surprise. If he thought he was dealing with a wimp, he's got another thing coming."

"See? That's what scares me. You've changed. You're not Rambo. I'm afraid you're going to try something stupid."

David tapped Becky lightly on the rear a few times. "Come on. We've got work to do. Call Business Express and see if you can get three seats on their next connecting flight to Portland. I'm gonna call Jonah from my office phone. Let's sympathize our watches," David said with a smile, attempting a little humor. "I'll meet you back here in half an hour."

Sympathize our watches. Rebecca always thought that one was so dumb. "How can you make light at a time like this?"

"It's in the blood, honey. I'm a Johnson, remember?"

"I know, I know. Nobody messes with the Johnsons," Rebecca said, smiling herself now.

"That's my girl."

"I love you, David," she said, pecking him on the cheek.

"I love you too, honey. More than you know." He looked at his watch. "I'll see you at eleven forty."

As David walked up the stairs to his third-floor office, he wondered if he would ever see his family again. It was then he realized that Tuesday was Halloween.

—⁂—

Jonah Roberts laughed at the sound of his best friend's voice. "D.B. You sorry sack of shit! How the hell are ya? Vickie and I were just talking about you guys this morning. Thinking we might plan a trip down your way.

It's a great place to visit. I just wouldn't want to live there."

"Look, Jonah. I'm sorry to cut right to the chase, but I'm in some deep shit down here. I really need your help."

"You're serious, right?"

"Jonah, I couldn't be more serious. I know this is going to sound crazy, but I need to send Becky and the kids to stay with you for a while. They're in danger here."

"Danger?" Jonah asked, surprised at the sudden turn in the conversation. "What kind of danger?"

"It's a long story. The Monarch Notes version is this. I got some psycho after me. He's been making threats against me and the family. Friday he murdered Barney and last night he set fire to the house."

"All right, cut the crap," Jonah said, uneasiness in his voice. "This stuff might have been funny in college, but it's lost something with maturity. You're bullshitting me, right?"

David shook his head. "Jonah, I wish I were. I'm telling you, this guy's for real. He's not going to stop until one of us is dead."

"One of who is dead?"

"Either him or me," David said, feeling nervous. Just talking about it seemed to rattle all the skeletons. He thought now that he hadn't had a drink in almost twenty-four hours. He was shaking.

"You're not coming?" Jonah asked, not quite understanding.

"Right. I want to, believe me. But if I run, Jonah, it's never going to stop. Like a schoolyard bully, you know? He'll terrify you every day of your life until you stand up to him. Even if he knocks your teeth out, at least you get it over with."

"A schoolyard bully. Yeah. I know something about that. Shit, man, I don't even know what to say."

"Say they can stay with you. Say that you'd love to have them."

"Don't be an ass. Of course they can stay here. My house is your house. Always has been, always will be.

You know that. We'd love to have them. It's just so weird, is all."

"Tell me about it. Forty-eight hours ago, I was giving the biggest presentation of my life—I think I got the Coke account by the way. Anyway, this psycho sends me a note in the mail. He says he wants me to quit my job and start running or he'll kill me."

"Quit your job and run? What the fuck does that mean?"

"Don't ask me, Jonah."

"Any idea who it is?" Jonah asked.

David doodled something on his desk blotter. "Not a one. Shit, Jonah, you worked the Street long enough to know it's not a popularity contest. But this . . . I mean, hell, we're all making seven figures. Who the hell would mess up a gravy train like that for some personal vendetta? I figure it's got to be someone unrelated to business. Don't ask me who."

"Man, and I was just sitting down to do the Sunday *Times* crossword puzzle. This kind of puts a damper on that."

"Well, trust me, it puts a damper on a lot of things."

"So when are they coming up?"

"I got Becky working on the flight now. Sometime today if we're lucky. I'll call you from the car and give you the specs."

"You got it. You're all family, D.B., you know that. It'll be our pleasure. They can stay as long as they need to. What are you going to do?"

"I'm not sure, to be honest. There's a couple of state police guys assigned to this case. They're coming over sometime today. We'll probably work out more of the details then."

"State police?"

"Yeah, I didn't tell you," David said, closing his eyes. "The guy murdered a cop at our house last night. Slit his throat from here to Hoboken. We all tripped over him running out of the house."

"Jesus Christ, David. I hope you know what the hell you're doing. This guy sounds crazy."

"Oh, he's crazy, all right."

"You see? Yet another reason to live in Maine. Well, listen, you got shit to do. Call me. We'll be here. You plan on coming up at all?"

"Plan to. Who knows what's going to happen, though. Right now, I plan on coming up every weekend."

"You sound as if you think this thing's going to go on for a while."

"Christ, I hope not. But who knows? There aren't exactly rules for this shit."

"No, I guess not. I just hope you catch this asshole. Sounds like a nightmare."

"There's an understatement."

"Well, okay then. Talk to you later. I miss you, buddy."

"I miss you too," David said, truly yearning to see his one true friend.

"Be careful."

"Take it to the bank."

"See ya."

"Bye. Oh . . . and, Jonah?"

"What?"

"Thank you."

—⁓—

That same Sunday, Fenton didn't open his eyes until well past two o'clock in the afternoon. The cleaning lady had unlocked the door and turned on the lights before she realized he was still in bed.

"Oh, excuse me, mister. I'm sorry," she said, scurrying out of the room, closing the door behind her.

Fenton just lay there. Turning on his side, he stared at the drapes that covered the day's glare. Strands of sun peeked through, illuminating dancing dust in the air.

He felt the rush of adrenaline hit him like a shot. He replayed in his mind the events of the prior evening, feeling his knife slice Bennett's flesh with such ease. He had not known the beauty of it. He never realized the sensual pleasure such fury could unleash. He was eager now for the opportunity to take his next victim's life. Once was not enough.

Fenton got out of bed and walked across the floor, locking and chaining his door. This time he hung out the Do Not Disturb sign. It bothered him that he'd forgotten to do it last night. *It's the little things.*

He went to the bathroom where he had placed the Hefty bag containing last night's clothes. He would drop them in a trash bin behind the hotel. He stood at the bathtub, looking at its shining porcelain. He could see no traces of his aquatic celebration last night but would have to buy some ammonia and bleach just to make sure.

He bent at the waist, noticed some hair in the drain, reached down and picked it up between his thumb and forefinger, rolled it in his palms and flushed it. He stood at the toilet, urinated, wiped the rim with some toilet paper and flushed again. There was no way he was going to leave the slightest trace. When he left this room, he would even take his sheets and pillowcases with him.

He stood in front of the mirror now, scratching his genitals. He examined his face closely, looking for any telltale signs of the brief struggle with the cop. He was horrified to see a slight scratch on his left cheek. Where had it come from?

Fenton replayed every second of his encounter with the officer. He thought he remembered the cop reaching back, ever so quickly, ever so slightly, with his left hand. Had he scratched him? Fenton couldn't bring himself to believe it was true. He leaned closer to the mirror, craning his neck to the right, rubbing his left forefinger over the scratch again and again. *It's always something.*

It didn't matter. Even if he had left something the cops could use at the scene, he'd have had his fun with David long before they would be able to do the necessary lab work. Still, he was annoyed at himself. *This is exactly the kind of thing Mother would have abhorred.* "There's never time to do it right, but always time to do it over," she would say. "When are you going to learn to do it right the first time?"

He opted to skip a shave. He wanted to give the area

time to heal. No sense doing anything that would cause blood. Not now, anyway.

Going forward, his every action would be critical. By now David, Rebecca, the police—everyone knew he was to be taken seriously. The authorities would pull out all the stops. The thought of hunting while being hunted aroused him. The excitement grew with each passing hour. Why had he not done something like this before? How could he have lived forty-four years and not known this ecstasy? Why, God, had he had to wait so long to find his calling? He felt cheated. Still, better late than never.

"I have a surprise for you, David," he said, removing the sheets. "This one's right out of left field. You're going to love it."

David had better love it. *This is not easy work, you know?* The countless hours of preparation, thinking and then thinking some more. Fenton had never worked so hard in his life. He felt important. Powerful. In control.

———————

"Honey, could you get that?" David said, reaching into Caleb's closet to pull out some shoes for the trip. "Unless it's the police, tell 'em I'll get back to them."

After Rebecca left to get the phone, Caleb sat on the edge of his bed. "Dad?" he asked, almost bashful.

David turned. "What is it, Cabes?"

"Well . . . I don't understand. I mean . . . Why you can't come with us. It's just that . . . this guy. Why does he want to hurt you? Did you do something bad to him?"

David's heart bled. He brought a couple of pairs of shoes over and laid them on the bed, sitting next to his youngest son. "No, buddy. Daddy didn't do anything to him. I don't even know who he is."

"Then why does he want to hurt you? I don't understand," Caleb asked, his nine-year-old brain fruitlessly, sadly, trying to make sense of the actions of a madman.

"Caleb," David responded in his calmest, fatherly voice. "There is much good in this world. Never forget that. Your mother and I love you and Sumner very, very much. Most people are good. In their heart, Cabes, they are good people. But do you remember what I told you guys after Barney was killed?"

Caleb was looking down at his stocking feet. "I guess so."

"Remember, I told you guys that there was also evil in this world? Do you remember that?"

"Yes."

David laid his hands on Caleb's thigh. "Do you know why Mommy's daddy was never around to see either one of you guys grow up?"

Caleb felt proud knowing the correct answer. "He died, right?"

"That's right. Do you know how he died?"

"No."

"He was killed in a war. He was helping to free people from evil men. Your grandfather was a very brave man, Caleb. He was loved very much. Still is. But sometimes . . . well, sometimes when evil people show up, they have to be stopped. It's not always easy. I want to go to Maine with you and your brother more than anything. But the police want to catch this bad person. They think I can help them do it. What do you think I should do?"

"David," Rebecca said, entering the room. "It's Lieutenant Halliway on the phone. He wants to speak to you."

"Okay, be right there." David looked at his son. "What do you think?"

"I think you should help them," Caleb said, still staring at his feet. "I guess I'm just scared."

"So am I, buddy. So am I. Listen, I'll be right back, okay?" he said, patting his son on the leg. "We'll finish talking then. Here, give me a hug." They hugged each other tightly. "I love you."

"I love you too, Dad."

As David left the room, Rebecca eyed Caleb sitting on the bed, solemn and quiet.

"Caleb? You okay, honey?"

"I'm scared, Mommy."

She sat down next to him, wrapping her arm around his shoulders. "I know, sweetheart. I know."

David picked up the phone in the bedroom. "Hello?"

"Mr. Johnson?" Halliway asked.

"Hi, Lieutenant."

"Hi, Sergeant Hill and I were wondering if now would be a good time to come by." It was not quite the request the words implied.

"Gee, Lieutenant, my wife and I are packing the kids' things right now," David said, not wanting to appear uncooperative. "There's a four fifty flight to Boston out of Westchester. We made reservations this morning."

Maybe it was his paranoia, but he wanted to make sure that both Halliway and Hill understood he really was the victim in all of this. He wanted to make it clear he really did want to help any way he could. But surely they would understand his family came first. Halliway even said so last night.

"I'm glad to hear that," Halliway said. "You're doing the right thing."

"Yeah, well, I wish there was another way. It hurts to think how much I'm going to miss them."

Halliway was silent for a brief moment. "When do you think you'll be back?"

Try not to let your sympathy get in the way of your job, Lieutenant. "Well, it's three o'clock now," David said, looking at his watch. "We'll be leaving in an hour or so. If it's on time, I guess I'll be home around five-thirty. Something like that."

"Good," Halliway responded. "Let's say we meet at your place at six. Does that work for you?"

"Sure. I'll see you then. You know, Lieutenant, I really don't know how much help I can be. I don't have the slightest idea who this wacko is or what his motivation could possibly be."

"Motivation is the easy part, Mr. Johnson. Hatred. Somehow, somewhere, you've given someone reason to feel justified for these actions. I'm not saying they are, mind you. Obviously, they aren't. But in this person's world, they're quite justified. We've got to try to find out why. You're the only person who can help us do that."

"Okay, come on by. You guys want dinner?"

"No, thank you. You go ahead with whatever plans you have. We will have eaten by then."

"All right then, see you at six."

"We'll be there," Halliway said, hanging up.

David pushed the button on the handset, waited for a dial tone and called the Darien police department. "Captain Esposito, please."

A moment later, Esposito was on the phone. "Mr. Johnson. Pete Esposito."

"Hi, Captain. How are you?"

"Fine, thanks. I won't bother asking the same of you. I was going to call you. Lieutenant Halliway told me he suggested that you move your family. I hope you take his advice, Mr. Johnson." Esposito prayed this would be one battle he wouldn't have to fight.

"Yeah, they're catching a flight out of Westchester in a couple of hours."

Esposito was relieved. "Good. Smartest thing you ever did. So what's up?"

"Well, Halliway and his lackey are coming over at six. I really don't know how long they're going to be, but I'd sure like to have some company tonight after they leave, if you know what I mean."

"Already done. In fact, that was the other thing I was going to call you about. We'll have so many men around your house the guy's gonna need an Uzi to get through."

David smiled. "I like to hear that."

"I thought you would. Listen, Halliway called me. Asked if I'd like to be present during your questioning. Have you spoken with him recently?"

"I just hung up with him."

"What time did you say they were coming over?"

"Six."

"I thought I'd come by if you don't mind."

"Mind? Shit, at this point, you can move in. No such thing as too many cops at a time like this."

"Good, I'll see you at six."

"Look forward to it." This time, David made a conscious effort to hang up the phone first.

———————

David and Rebecca had already said their good-byes. They kissed and held, each telling the other how lonely they'd be. She stood now, waiting at the gate leading out to the tarmac. She held two carry-on bags, her coat flung over her right arm. Her purse over her left shoulder. "Come on, boys. Let's not be late. We have to go."

"Just one minute, Beck," David said, squatting, his butt nearly touching the ground. He looked evenly in each of his sons' faces. "Always remember how much I love you both," he said. "This is going to be hard on all of us. But especially your mom. So I want you to be on your best behavior. No fighting, all right? You both need to be big boys while you're away. Okay?"

"Okay," they said in unison.

"I'll be up next weekend. We'll have a blast. And don't you guys worry. The police and I are going to catch this guy, and we'll all be together again sooner than you can say *Gotcha!*"

Rebecca looked at her watch. "David, we have to go."

"Okay, guys, have fun and be good. I'll see you in a week. How 'bout a hug for your daddy the crime stopper?" David said, faking a broad smile.

The three hugged a deep round of heartfelt good-byes, David giving each a good-bye slap on the rump. They jogged to their mother, filed in front of her and were instantly out of sight. Rebecca puckered her lips to her husband. He blew her a kiss and whispered "I love you," before she turned and followed her sons to the waiting airplane.

On the drive home, David realized this was the first moment he'd had to himself since he arrived home from Atlanta. A creeping numbness overcame him as he relived the past three days in his mind. As he relived the circumstances of the past seventy-two hours—conversations, emotions—he was staggered by the turn of events in his life and the rapidity with which they had taken place. He found himself hoping he would wake up—how magnificent it would be if it were all a bad dream. But wishful thinking wasn't going to end this nightmare.

His body screamed for liquor. Every cell told him he would simply die without a drink. He thought for a moment of pulling into a local watering hole on the roadside. Rebecca would never know. No one would ever know. Except himself. He drove on, occupying his mind with thoughts of the police interview that would take place within the hour.

What could he tell them that they didn't already know? Hell, they probably knew more than he did. He just couldn't see what assistance he could possibly provide. And while he understood they had to talk to him, he couldn't help thinking it was all a colossal waste of everyone's time.

David pulled into his driveway at 5:53 P.M. and was mildly surprised to see Esposito's cruiser already there. He drove the long way around it, waved to him, pushed his garage door opener, and pulled in. He lit a smoke, got out of his Range Rover, and walked back to the cruiser.

"Hi, Mr. Johnson," Esposito said, leaning on its left front quarter panel. "Thought I'd get here a few minutes early. Figured maybe you'd want some insight on what to expect this evening."

David dragged hard on his cigarette. "I am a little nervous," he replied, exhaling. "I've never done anything like this before."

"That's what I thought. Most victims are questioned at the scene. Don't have to wait for a formal interview. Their fears don't usually have time to set in."

"You know, Captain, it's funny. I mean, I have that feeling I used to get when my mother made me wait in my room for a spanking from my father. Sounds crazy, I know. It's just how I feel."

"What's so crazy?" Esposito asked, shrugging his shoulders. "These guys represent the ultimate authority. You don't know what to expect or how painful it's gonna be. No . . . it sounds pretty normal to me."

"I just feel so fucking helpless. Like a little kid again. I'm not used to depending on others for help. I like to tackle problems by myself."

"Well, if I were you, I'd thank my lucky stars you got their help on this one. There's no tellin' what this asshole's gonna try next. Believe me, these guys are on your side. They want him as bad as you do now."

"I guess you're right."

"Guess? Listen, a dog is one thing, a cop's another. I wouldn't want these guys after me, I can tell you that much."

"I just don't think I'm going to be able to help much. I don't have a fucking clue who this guy could be. Or even if it is a guy."

"Oh, it's a guy all right," Esposito said. "Unless you know any women who wear size eleven shoes."

"We're getting somewhere now," David said, lighting a new cigarette. "We just narrowed it down to what? A hundred million people?"

"Hey, come on. Remember the conversation we had about the paper? You wouldn't believe the shit these guys can do. Between Interpol, VICAP, NCIC, and DNA analysis. Shit, you're about to witness some real pros in action. I'll be surprised if this guy doesn't end up behind bars. Soon."

"You're speaking my language, that's for sure."

Esposito leaned against the door of the cruiser, looking David in the eyes. "Listen, just tell them what they want to know. If you don't know, just say so. Don't be too anxious to please. Shoot straight. Don't exaggerate, make shit up, or lie. Understand?"

David furrowed his brow. "Why would I lie?" he asked, not sure what Esposito meant.

"I'm not sayin' you'd lie on purpose. It's just that I've interviewed a lot of people over the years. If there's a common denominator that really sticks out, and there's a few, it's that people don't want to disappoint. The police intimidate them. Without knowin' it, they say things that are only half true or leave a little something out so a story sounds better. Understand?"

David nodded.

113

"And they may ask some questions of a personal nature. Things that may not appear germane to the case. Be honest. Believe me, there ain't nothing you can tell these guys they haven't seen before."

"Why are you doing this?" David asked, not able to comprehend why a cop would care enough to give him advice on this subject.

"I just thought it might be helpful. Anyway, anything I can tell you that will help you give us the best information possible is just gonna help us catch this bastard that much sooner. And this is one scumbag I want off the street."

David chuckled once. "You can say that again. Here they are now," he said, poking his chin down the driveway. He looked at his watch. It was 6:05 P.M.

Detective Hill pulled up behind Esposito's cruiser, hit the lights, and turned off the ignition. Lieutenant Halliway got out of the Caprice first, while Hill thumbed through some papers on the front seat.

"Captain, good to see you again," Halliway said, the consummate gentleman.

"Lieutenant. Good to see you."

"Mr. Johnson," he said, extending a hand. "You seem more rested this evening. Sorry we had to bother you last night."

Hill joined the group and shook hands with both men.

"Let's go in," David said, leading the group into the playroom through the garage. "Welcome to Sarajevo, gentlemen," he said, waving his arm out across the room. All four men entered, the smell of burnt rubber was omnipresent. "This is as good a place to meet as any. It's downstairs, so the chairs are still somewhat clean, and the smell's not nearly so bad down here. Please, take a seat."

There was a quiet, simultaneous chorus of thank yous as all four men made themselves comfortable.

"I just got home from the airport. Haven't even had a chance to come inside yet. I don't know about you, but I'd love a cup of coffee. Let me start a pot and I'll be right down. Can I get someone anything?"

"Nothing for me, thank you," Halliway answered, the other two men shaking their heads.

David left up the stairs, butterflies swarming in his stomach. "Let's get in formation," he repeated to himself.

Halliway turned to Esposito and whispered. "Did you talk to him?"

"Yeah."

"You told him what I suggested to you last night?"

"Every last word."

"Good. Thanks."

"No problem," Esposito said.

David came down the stairs a few moments later. "It'll be a few minutes."

"Well, why don't we get started then?" Halliway suggested. "It's going to take long enough as it is, I'm afraid."

David sat on the edge of his chair and clasped his hands. He was nervous. "Okay, shoot," he said.

Sergeant Hill reached for a tape recorder he had laid on the coffee table next to his chair. "We're going to record this, Mr. Johnson, if that's okay with you."

David felt his heart skip. *Just like on TV.* "Sure. If it helps."

Halliway spoke first. "Interview with Mr. David Johnson at his residence. Thirty-two Woodbury Lane. Darien, Connecticut. Sunday evening, October twenty nine. Six thirteen P.M. This is Lieutenant Cedric Halliway. With me are Detective Sergeant Scott Hill, Connecticut State Police Homicide Division, and Captain Peter Esposito, Darien police department.

"Mr. Johnson, would you please give us your full name?"

The interview went on like this for some time. David was asked all the perfunctory questions he hadn't even thought to anticipate: name and address, age, place of birth, nationality, race, educational background, occupation (past and present), places of employment, habits, hobbies, country clubs, associations, what boards he sat on, where he spent his leisure time, business associates, friends, enemies, past or present problems with the law, other legal problems such as bankruptcies or foreclosures.

For over an hour, he answered their questions as best he could. His antagonist hadn't even been mentioned yet. His only break was to get coffee. David rose, feeling tired and cramped. "Gentlemen, I gotta take a leak. I'll be right back. More coffee anyone?"

As he rose, the phone rang. David walked to the corner of the room and plopped himself down in a leather La-Z-Boy. "Hello?"

"David, it's Linda."

"Hi, Linda," he said, frowning. He covered the receiver and mouthed to his guests that it was his secretary. "You sound troubled. Is there something wrong?"

He was not prepared for what followed.

"Oh God, David. It's Mikey. He's been missing since Friday night. We've looked everywhere. My baby! David, someone took my baby! Oh, David. I don't know what we're going to do."

Jesus Christ. This has to be a bad dream. "Oh, Linda. I'm so sorry. Is there anything I can do to help? Money? Connections? Anything. I'll do anything I can. I'm so sorry, Linda."

The three men sat staring at David. He made a face and shrugged his shoulders. When it rains, it pours. *Wait a minute. Oh, my God! It couldn't be.* David was paralyzed with terror. His palms began to sweat, his scalp was searing hot. His heart raced, nearly pounding out of its cavity.

There was a moment's hesitation. "No, thank you, David," Linda said. "We've got the police on it. I don't know what else we can do."

"Nothing, I suppose. I'm sure he'll show up, Linda. I'm just sure of it. You know kids," he said, realizing too late the miserable weakness of his response. In his mind, he was already certain she would never see Mikey again.

David felt like screaming. *This guy is like a metastasized cancer. He's everywhere, wreaking death and havoc. He has to be stopped.* David's mind swirled with a thousand thoughts. He felt lightheaded. His body shook involuntarily from the base of his skull to his toes.

Somehow he felt responsible. But why? How could he have prevented it? How could he have possibly known? His entire life—everything he'd worked twenty years to create—was crashing in on him like the temple at Jerusalem, its huge, solid pillars crumbling to the ground, crushing everyone in its vicinity.

Linda spoke between sobs. "I just wanted to tell you that I won't be in this week. I'm sorry."

"Linda. Please don't be sorry. Take as much time as you need. Don't even think about it. I'll make sure the paychecks are sent to your house. Please tell Tony how sorry I am. Call me with any information, okay?"

"Okay," she said crying. "Pray for him, David."

"I will," he said, wondering just whom he should pray to.

———∾———

The previous Friday evening, Fenton Montague found himself driving north on the Henry Hudson Parkway. The A springs in his '67 Ford Mustang squeaked with every bump. He wore black jeans, black socks, black Reeboks, and a gray T-shirt that read Expect to Win on the front.

He was listening to Jefferson Airplane, singing along with Grace Slick the words to "White Rabbit"—"One pill makes you larger, the other one makes you small, and the ones that Mother gives you, don't do anything at all."

Mikey Barnes lay in the trunk, hog tied, with duct tape over his mouth, wrapped all the way around his head. He had told his parents he would be right back. He just wanted to go to the park at the end of the street to tell his friends he would be out right after dinner and not to leave his basketball there if they left.

Mikey never made it. Fenton could not believe his luck. After seeing the *Journal* article he had moved to New York. He had staked out every aspect of David's life for over a year. He knew what trains he took to and from work. He knew what subways he took. He knew the hours he kept, his way to and from the train station. Rebecca's routine. Where the kids went to school. Their names and birthdates.

Quite by accident really, he learned about Linda and the crucial role she played in David's life. He needed access to David's work environment, and had stayed at a local YMCA boarding room for an entire month while delivering sandwiches for the deli across the street from David's building.

He jumped at any order to be delivered to the Reardon Haskel building. He could remember as if it were yesterday the first time he delivered to the trading floor on which David worked. *Bull's eye!* He would watch, listen, take it all in.

In no time he finagled the deli owner into making David's complex his only run. It would be less time consuming, more efficient, more productive, he could deliver more, quicker. He soaked it all up like a sponge. What started out as nothing more than an attempt to see his nemesis, to watch him on his own turf, had evolved into an opportunity to view his inner workings.

It was in this way Fenton came to understand the relationship between Linda and David. He knew he had struck gold. He just wasn't sure how he could use it. But God hadn't let him down. It was his idea actually. Fenton wished he'd thought of it himself.

Fenton left his Mustang at the ferry terminal on Staten Island one morning and followed Linda Barnes to work. That night he followed her home . . . watching . . . waiting. He wanted Mikey, but never thought he would be hand delivered.

Now, with Mikey in the cold, dark trunk, Fenton shuddered with excitement. He felt as if someone had just handed him a winning lottery ticket. He thought of how helpless the youngster must feel. How terrified. Just as he had felt in the closet. He smiled to himself. There was something about the power, the omnipotence of his being judge and jury. "Guilty!" he screamed aloud. "Sentence . . . death!"

DOWNTICK

Fenton drove for many miles and eventually pulled off the Taconic State Parkway into a secluded area surrounded by woods. It had once been an estate of some robber baron. He wasn't sure what it was used for now. He parked his car at the chain-link fence, pulled out his large wire cutters, dislodged the lock and drove in.

When he finally opened the trunk, Mikey stared at him with wild, horror-filled eyes. Fenton was robotic. Mikey wasn't an innocent little boy who loved strawberry ice cream and loved to watch Sesame Street. He was an object. A means to an end. Any connection between Fenton and rational, civilized behavior had long since withered away.

Fenton reached down, pulled Mikey out of the trunk, and flung him to the ground like a side of meat. He removed the blanket on which Mikey had laid, shook it out, and neatly folded it. He would have to toss it in a trash bin on his way back. He reached further in, unwrapped a Hefty bag, and pulled out a meat cleaver. Fenton toyed with the idea of playing with Mikey for a while—hurting him, watching him squirm. The thought aroused him and an erection began to bulge in his pants.

The idea appealed to him, but maybe another time—another place. Right now, however, there were bigger fish to fry. Nothing spontaneous. *Plan your work and work your plan.* He put his hand in his pants pockets, pulling out two heavy rubber bands.

He picked Mikey up by the knot in back, his hands and feet bleeding now, his stomach scraping rocks. When he found the appropriate spot, he pulled out his pocket knife and untied Mikey's right arm. Mikey squirmed desperately, trying to scream, mucous filling the nostrils of his nose. He couldn't breathe. Fenton sat on Mikey's back, extended his arm and anchored it with his feet. The meat cleaver came down hard and clean on Mikey's right wrist.

Mikey was stung with terror. He began to shake involuntarily, slightly at first, then convulsively, as his eyes rolled up into their sockets. Fenton dragged the boy by the rope around his neck to the edge of a small but steep ravine and sent him flying with one heave. He walked quickly back to Mikey's right hand, held it up for a short while to let the blood drip from it, and carried it back to the Hefty bag from which he had pulled the meat cleaver.

"Oh, David," Fenton said, kneeling in front of his trophy. "First you scorn God and then you scorn me. When will you learn not to bite the hand that feeds you?" He giggled, took off the rubber bands he had put around his wrist, bent all of Mikey's fingers into a fist except the middle finger, and wrapped them tightly with the rubber bands.

He laid the bag in his trunk, Mikey's hand palm-side up, and weighted it with the meat cleaver. He took a couple of bricks and laid them on the middle finger to keep it straight. Soon, he thought, rigor would set in and he would be able to remove the rubber bands. *What a nice little present this will be for the apple of my eye.*

Fenton had a busy day, with Barney in the morning and Mikey in the afternoon. But Mikey was a gift. He hadn't anticipated he would have him so quickly. In fact, he wasn't sure he could have him at all. But fate had intervened yet again. How easy things are when God is on your side. *This should wake 'em up.*

---〰〰〰---

When David hung up the phone, all three men in the playroom sat looking at him. No one said a word. They sat motionless, eyeing him expectantly.

He looked at them, his eyes tearing. "That was my secretary. Her son was abducted Friday. They haven't seen or heard from him since. She and her husband are beside themselves. My heart just bleeds for them. I couldn't even begin to imagine."

"Mr. Johnson, did she say when she saw him last?" Halliway asked, already thinking what David was thinking.

"Not specifically. Just that he left right before dinner. They expected him to come right back."

"When did your son find your dog in the back yard?" Halliway continued.

"Rebecca said it was right after school. Let's see . . . school lets out at two-thirty . . . Probably sometime before three o'clock. Give or take. Why?"

Halliway sat forward. "Well, I can't say for sure. But there appear to be a number of coincidences which have occurred over the last seventy-two hours. Where does your secretary live?"

"Staten Island."

"We know the dog was hung prior to three o'clock," Halliway said, speaking to Hill. "We also know your secretary's son was taken just before dinner. What time does she get off?"

"Five o'clock," David said, sure now he knew where Halliway was headed.

"So, if we say that dinner at her house is around six o'clock, that would leave three to three and a half hours at least for our man to have left here and gone to Staten Island. Certainly enough time, even considering rush-hour traffic."

David rested his forehead on the heels of his palms, his elbows on his knees. "Yeah, I've already thought of that. It looks like this asshole is set on ruining everything that's dear to me in my life. I didn't know what to say to her. Whether I should tell her or not," David said, engulfed in guilt and remorse.

"It's probably best you didn't say anything. We'll need to call the NYPD though. They need to know of the possible connection. Anyway, it'll help our cause if we cooperate, coordinate our efforts, so to speak."

David sat on the edge of the chair, his bladder bursting, not feeling the energy to even get up. He rubbed his temples with his forefingers slowly, deeply.

David's every word carried an undertone of frustration. "Well, guys, let's look at the positive. In a few more days there won't be anyone left in my life for him to screw with."

David rose slowly from his chair, jumping slightly as the front doorbell rang. "I'll get it."

When David disappeared up the steps, Esposito turned to Halliway. "Still wondering if there's a connection, Lieutenant? Ten to one that boy's already dead."

"I'm afraid you're right, Captain. Dealing with someone as deranged as this, we may never find his body," Halliway said, feeling the pressure mount as the clock ticked by.

All three men sat quietly, steeped in their own thoughts of what had just transpired.

"Express Mail," David said to no one in particular, as he walked down the steps carrying a small box. "I didn't know the post office delivered stuff on Sunday, did you?"

"Express Mail does," Esposito added.

"Who's it from?" Hill asked.

"Well, I'm not sure. Let's see," David said, slipping on his reading glasses. "Oh, boy," he said, taking a deep breath.

Halliway was anxious. Bombs hide in little boxes. "What's it say?" he asked.

David shook his head. "It's from You Know Who. Return address, my secretary's home on Staten Island."

"What do you mean You Know Who? Is that how it reads?" Halliway asked.

"That's what it says."

Halliway's breath caught in his throat. "Please put the box down, Mr. Johnson," he ordered sternly.

David laid the box at his feet and sat down. All four men sat staring at it. Halliway rose and knelt in front of Hill, whispering something. They went back and forth for a few moments. Halliway rose, walked to the pool table, reached into the right pocket of his raincoat, and pulled out two latex gloves. He snapped them on as he walked over to the box. Picking it up with the forefinger and thumb of each hand, he walked backwards to his chair and sat down, resting the box on the ottoman.

"Captain," Halliway said, looking directly at Esposito, "Detective Hill is of the opinion this package is most likely not a bomb. Given the nature of the note Mr. Johnson received and the likely psychological makeup of our perp, I tend to agree. My heart says open it, but my brain says call the bomb squad. Before I do, I'd like your thoughts."

"I agree with your assessment," Esposito said, looking at Hill. "Our man's aim is fear and humiliation. It's not in character for him to put an end to his fun before his allotted deadline is up. My guess is whatever's in that box, and God knows I don't want to see it, it's not deadly. Still, I think common sense dictates we should have it looked at."

All three men looked at David now. He looked back and forth between them. *What the hell are you looking at me for?* "Look, if you guys want to know whether or not I think Du Pont's a good buy, I've got an opinion. But if you're looking for my input as to what the hell to do with that box—shit, you might as well ask me to solve the Palestinian issue. Frankly, at this point, I don't give a shit if it blows up the whole god damned house. I say we open the fucking thing and see what we're up against."

The four men waited almost forty-five minutes for the bomb squad to arrive. In short order, they had set up a portable X-ray machine on the pool table. Halliway and the others were ordered to wait in the driveway while they scanned the box. One of the men looked like an old-time photographer as he held his head under a small black curtain, viewing the screen, while the other ran the small box under the X ray.

"Jesus Christ," the man at the screen said.

"What'ya got?" his partner asked.

"Get the Lieutenant, will ya?"

Halliway entered the playroom, leaving the other men in the driveway. He was surprised to see the X-ray machine being packed up.

"Well?" he asked.

The bomb squad technician handed him the box. "This one's all yours," he said, leaving the playroom through the garage.

"Is it safe?" Halliway asked after him.

The man stopped at the door. "Oh, it's safe."

"You're not going to tell me what's in it?"

"Lieutenant, I don't want to be within a mile of here when you open that thing. You wanted to know if it's a bomb, and it's not. Have a good night," and he was gone.

Halliway was more than a little irritated. "Thanks," he said with biting sarcasm. "Can you send the others in on your way out, or is that too much to ask?"

When the others had congregated back in the playroom, Halliway laid the box on the pool table.

"What's in it?" Hill asked.

"Son of a bitch wouldn't tell me."

"This should be beautiful," Hill said.

"Yeah, I can't wait. Here goes," Halliway said, slicing the shipping tape with his penknife. He moved slowly, careful not to disrupt possible prints. They'd have it checked for those first thing tomorrow. He removed the bubble wrapping and stood, staring at the box's contents. He closed his eyes and sighed.

It bothered him that he wasn't more moved. He thought for a fleeting moment of the poor boy and the mental anguish he must have endured. He prayed he was dead before his hand had been amputated. The medical examiner could probably tell them. As he stared into the box, he found himself thinking more of its meaning and possible use in apprehending the sender than anything else. He could not allow himself to feel pain—it would destroy him. This was truly one of life's lonely jobs.

The room fell deadly silent. David wanted to scream, but opted for an innocuous "Well?" instead.

"Scott, would you please take a look at this?" Halliway asked his partner. Hill rose and went to his side, staring at Fenton's little gift.

Esposito was overcome now with curiosity. "Do you mind if I take a look, Lieutenant?" he asked.

"No. Please."

David felt as though he would jump out of his skin. *Jesus Christ! If all you sons of bitches look inside that box and don't tell me what it is, I'm going to kill every last one of you.* "Don't mind me, guys," he said. "I'm just the one he's after."

"Mr. Johnson, it's against my better judgment to show this to you," Halliway said, tapping the pool table with the tips of his fingers. "But under the circumstances, I don't believe we have any choice. Only you can tell us what, if any, meaning it has. But I warn you sir, it's not pretty."

"Look, my whole life's not pretty right now. Whatever the hell it is, let's get it out in the open and talk about it.

Otherwise, I'm afraid I'm going to be lying in the next box you look in."

Halliway rose, bringing the box to David. He wanted him sitting when he saw it.

"Shhit. No!" David closed his eyes, leaned back, and let the tears stream down his cheeks.

—⁂—

Cedric Halliway and Scott Hill had a lot of work ahead of them. They sat at a long, wooden table in a room about fourteen by ten feet, their notebooks opened in front of them. Graph paper with maps of the interior and exterior of the Johnson home were spread over the tabletop. Hill sat holding a yellow legal pad while Halliway paced slowly back and forth, aggressively mouthing a large, unlit cigar. His white button-down shirt was wrinkled, his sleeves rolled halfway up his forearms.

He stopped at the end of the table and removed his glasses. "All right, let's see what we've got—from the beginning. On Tuesday, the twenty-fourth, our man mails a note threatening Johnson's life," he said, rubbing his eyes with his thumb and forefinger, paying special attention to the corners and the bridge of his nose.

"Although it doesn't appear as though it was actually typed," Hill added. "The paper lacks the usual indentations one expects to find with a typewriter, especially at the periods and commas."

"Okay. Task number one. Contact Document Examination. See if they can work their magic and find out what printed this note. Also, compare it with the note tacked to the door."

"No idea how long that will take," Hill replied pessimistically. "They're gonna have to contact HP, IBM, Smith Corona. Who knows how many others."

"That's why they make the big bucks. Tell 'em it's priority one."

"Thank God for computers."

"You said it," Halliway responded, staring now at the yellowing, whitewashed wall of the interrogation room they had requisitioned for the evening. "Okay. Johnson reads the note on his way to Atlanta. Gives it to Goodman down there. Task two. Get Goodman's fingerprints. Put them on file with the Johnsons'. Sometime Friday, our man hangs the dog and hightails it to Staten Island. Task three. Call the vet first thing tomorrow morning. Make sure we get that autopsy report before his morning coffee."

"Do you want to contact the ferry terminal?" Hill asked.

"Put that down the list. We can go that route if we don't get anywhere with what we have. A hundred to one he drove. Hard to kidnap a screaming kid under your arm on a ferry. It's possible, *possible* mind you, that he had a weapon of some sort on the kid. But I'm bettin' he had his car. You?"

"I agree."

The two men walked through each step of their investigation day by day—in some instances, hour by hour. So far, they had used or would need the services of the Connecticut State Police Latent Fingerprint Unit, the Document Examination Unit, the Crime Scene Search Unit, the Photography Unit and the Criminalist Unit.

What started as an apparent prank now involved upwards of two dozen policemen, detectives, scientists, and other technicians from all over the country. When a cop goes down, everything else stops or goes on the back burner. This SOB had to be stopped. Now.

They needed to have the watermark on both notes checked and have a biologist from the Scientific Investigation Bureau run DNA analysis of the blood on Bennett's hands and under his fingernails and also tell them, at least to the nearest common denominator, what type of weapon was used to slash his throat.

A biologist would also need to conduct the necessary tests on Mikey's hand: comparing blood type and any identifying marks. The fingerprint technicians would compare prints lifted from it with something from Mikey's home. Halliway was thankful he wasn't the one who had to explain why the object was being retrieved, or report back to the Barneses what he knew in his heart, the final report's results would be.

In addition, the envelope and stamp would also have to be analyzed for make, prints, and saliva. Contrary to David's initial belief, there was plenty to go on. At least for now. In an odd way, the initial stages of an investigation are often the most hopeful. It's then that virtually every avenue is open. No roads closed. No Dead End signs yet to pop up.

As an investigation wears on and reports begin to filter in, hope sometimes fades to prayer. Other times it blossoms as the road narrows, funneling the hunters through the neck of a bottle toward the eventual apprehension of the unsuspecting felon. Those are the best days, when all the hours and lost sleep—the hoping and prodding—finally lead to pay dirt.

Up to this point almost every aspect of the investigation the two detectives coordinated was out of their control. Their requests were handled by other departments—other people. They needed to be in contact with virtually every department head, forever pushing the envelope of professional conduct and protocol, deftly playing the diplomatic two-step every inch of the way. Needing every report yesterday at the latest, they would coyly nudge here, quietly prod there, while every other investigator from every other division in the state did the same thing. There was more to this game than met the eye. That much was for sure.

It was past 11:00 P.M. when they finally got around to deciding whom they needed to interview personally. While it would be ideal for them to split up and accomplish twice as much in the same period of time, it would not be wise. In fact, it would ultimately slow down the investigation. As each man reported back his initial impressions, they would invariably have to backtrack and re-interview those where a second opinion became necessary.

The two detectives needed to handle every interview together, each knowing when the other was becoming ineffective. Intangibly, viscerally, they would read the personalities of their respective interviewees; one backing off while the other took the floor. You could never tell until the interview process had begun which man's personality would be most useful in extracting the information necessary to move the investigation forward.

Like a comedy duo reading their audience, they could duck and weave, jab and withdraw, without missing a beat, each picking up where the other left off. They knew each other better than they knew their wives—a telepathic tag team performing the art of their profession as well as it could be done.

Halliway sat in the chair opposite Hill. "Johnson mentioned this Saperstein fellow. He seems as good a place to start as any."

"Jesus, Ric, I don't know. Granted, there appears to be motive. There's certainly no love lost between the two. But a white-collar managing director of a huge Wall Street firm? It just doesn't fit. I'll buy lunch for a month if it's him," Hill said, disbelieving.

"Okay, I'll buy that. Then who?" Halliway asked, leaning forward on his elbows, holding his cigar in his clasped hands.

Hill leaned back in his chair, arms crossed at his chest. "Shit, I don't know," he said, looking up at the stained ceiling tiles.

"I'll tell you what. Let's call it a night," Halliway said. "It's not like we don't have plenty of work ahead of us. In the morning we'll contact NYPD and see what they've got on the kidnapping. Maybe somebody'll have a plate or a make. Hey, we might get lucky. Sure would save us a hell of a lot of time."

"You're on," Hill said, standing up for the first time in two hours.

—⁓—

David ran for his life. He could feel the steel blade of the knife rip again and again at the back of his shirt. He could hear the footsteps . . . almost feel Saperstein's breath behind him. Maniacal. Unstoppable.

The headlights from the eighteen-wheeler were directly ahead of him now, but David couldn't stop. The truck bore down on him with unrelenting speed. As it blared its horn at him, he thought it would at least be over now. He could feel its vibration. Deep and menacing, it nearly knocked him off his feet. *Honnnk! Honnnk!*

David awoke with a jolt, sweating from head to toe. His blankets were at the foot of his bed, apparently pushed off by his frantic thrashing. He sat up and realized the alarm clock was going off. *Beep, beep, beep, beep.* He reached over and hit the snooze on the third try. 5:11 A.M. He reached for the blankets and pulled them up over his legs.

His life now had truly become a living hell. David's every waking moment was spent in a crazed combination of fear, hatred, and dread. The only thing that gave him the strength to carry on was the thought of killing this son of a bitch himself. He wanted to look into his eyes and spit in his face.

He visualized his adversary on his knees, begging for mercy. Crying. Sobbing. David envisioned shooting his kneecaps first. He would enjoy watching him squirm, feeling the power over him. The thought was sadistic and it felt good. *He* was in control now.

"Enough!" he cried out, crawling out of bed. David switched off the alarm, put on his robe, and walked to the kitchen to make himself a cup of coffee. He stood at the sink, staring out the window at the outline of the old maples against the blackish-blue sky.

He was scared, not so much from what might happen to him, although clearly that played into his current mental state. What scared him more was his mind. He was changing and he couldn't put a handle on just what it was. But he knew he didn't like it.

The thought of showering, shaving, and dressing for another day of battle weighted his head like lead. David dreaded the very thought of taking the train, fighting the crowds at Grand Central, squeezing onto a crowded subway car. The mere thought of being surrounded by so many people made his heart skip a beat.

He wondered how he could ever acknowledge his

colleagues, perform his duties as if nothing were wrong. Worse yet, he already knew what Linda did not. He felt as though he were carrying the weight of a horrible secret on his shoulders, not able to free himself until it was out. He had never called in sick a day in his life. He wanted to desperately now.

He wanted to cry, but couldn't bring himself to tears. He wanted to drink, but certainly couldn't have one now. The sun wasn't even up yet. But then again . . . why not? Just one. He needed something. The kids were gone. Rebecca was gone. *Look at the enormous pressure I'm under. Anyone in their right mind would understand.* Trying to get sober at a time like this was like trying to tame a lion with a fly swatter. Why bother?

He walked to the liquor cabinet and pulled out a new bottle of Stolichnaya, which he carried to the freezer in his left hand. "Just one," he said aloud. As he reached for the ice tray, he froze. His eyes bulged. The shock was paralyzing.

Perhaps because he hadn't had enough to eat or maybe it was because his nerves were ripped raw; whatever the cause, there was only so much he could take. David was just one man. He could feel the blood rush from his brain and the room begin to spin. He tried vainly to stop himself, but his body's internal mechanisms were already in full throttle. His legs buckled as his body fell limp to the floor, the bottle shattering into a thousand pieces at his feet.

Following the interview with Halliway and Hill, Esposito reviewed David's protection detail with him. He introduced him to Warren McKutcheon, the detail leader, and reviewed how many men there would be, their names, and where they would be stationed. Warren was one hell of a hockey player. Everyone knew him as Skates. David was again given a Varda Alarm, Warren a key to David's house. David was to carry on as if this were any other day.

David had filled them in on his daily routine. He awoke at 5:11 A.M., would be showered, dressed, and shaved by 5:35, and always left the house shortly thereafter. At 5:40 A.M. the following morning, Warren knocked on David's front door. No response. After a few minutes, he let himself in.

"Mr. Johnson. Mr. Johnson," McKutcheon said, lightly slapping the right side of his face. Shards of glass were everywhere. "Wake up, Mr. Johnson. You're going to be late for your train. You were s'pose to have left the house ten minutes ago."

"Jesus Christ, Skates," his partner said. "The guy's tanked out of his mind."

The first thing David noticed upon returning to consciousness was the thick smell of alcohol. He wondered for a moment if he was drunk and braced himself for a hangover. But there was none. It was then he realized McKutcheon was kneeling at his side, looking into his eyes.

"Mr. Johnson, have you been drinking, sir?" Skates asked.

"No. I should be so lucky. What the hell?" David said, sitting up with help from the two police officers.

"What happened?" the other officer inquired.

David had to think for a moment—a whole period of his waking life had been erased from his memory banks. "I was going to ask you the same thing," David said. "That goddamned son of a bitch has invaded every inch of my life. I'm going to kill him. I promise you both, I'm going to kill him with my bare hands!"

"Here, get up, Mr. Johnson," Skates said, helping David to his feet. "What are you talking about, sir? What happened?"

David leaned against the kitchen counter, lowered his head slightly, and pointed to the freezer. "That's what I'm talking about."

McKutcheon looked at the open freezer and noticed a note taped to the ice container. He went over and read it out loud. "'The Lord wants me to tell you D.B., Eat, Drink, and Be Merry, For Tomorrow We Die.'"

Skates's partner whistled out loud. "What the hell did you do to this guy?"

McKutcheon clapped his hands twice. "All right, all right. Come on. We gotta get goin'. Turk, call Esposito and get him out here. Now, Mr. Johnson, obviously you're not gonna make the five fifty. When's the next train?"

"Uh . . . there's a six thirty-two, I think. They may have changed the schedule for the fall, though. I've got to check."

"Please check it and tell me what train you think you can make. We've got three undercover cops at the station right now wondering where the hell we are."

David kept the schedule on the refrigerator with a magnet, courtesy of his local oil company. He walked over and removed it. "I don't have my glasses. Can you read this for me?" he said, handing McKutcheon the schedule, feeling older than his years. "Make sure you're not looking under weekends and holidays."

"If I'm readin' this thing right, it looks like we got a six twenty-one and a six forty-six. Can you make the six twenty-one?" Skates asked.

"What time is it?"

"Almost six."

The thought of rushing around the house like a madman made David anxious. "I'd have to be Superman. Let's shoot for the six forty-six," he said, hoping McKutcheon wasn't going to push the issue.

"Fine. I'll call dispatch and have them relay the delay to our people at the station. Let's move, okay?"

"I'll be ready," David said

Skates turned to follow his partner to the foyer. At the kitchen doorway, he turned. "Mr. Johnson, perhaps this is none of my business, sir, but what were you doing with a bottle of vodka this early in the morning? You're sure you haven't been drinking, sir?"

David was his responsibility, and if he was drunk, Warren damn well wanted to know now. It was hard enough to protect someone coherent—astronomically more difficult if their thinking was impaired.

"It's a long story, Officer. No, I haven't been drinking. And you're right, it's none of your business."

Skates stared at David for a moment, debating whether or not he should explain his reasoning. Declining the opportunity, he turned and walked to the foyer.

Both policemen left the house, Skates shooing away the small crowd of officers that had gathered around the front of the house. "Okay, guys, everything's fine. We roll in half an hour. Be ready."

--~~~--

"Good afternoon, D.B.," one of his salesmen said, poking his head through the partially open door to David's office. "You didn't make the morning meeting, so I thought I'd fill you in on the highlights of the morning Call."

Every morning at 7:30 sharp, the firm's analysts gathered in the auditorium on the top floor of the research department. The Call, as it's known, is broadcast live over the firm's system-wide broadcast network. It's heard live world wide, from London to Tokyo, Chicago to Los Angeles. Yes, the desk in LA is alive and kicking at 4:30 A.M. The Call is also heard in each of the firm's four hundred plus retail branch offices, and highlights of it are recorded and rebroadcast throughout the day as time permits.

"Quickly, please. I'm up to my eyeballs," David said, his heart not in it.

His salesman checked his morning fax. "Okay, Shipman spoke. Said the firm's changed their position on the Fed. Given the Purchasing Manager's numbers out of Chicago and housing starts for September . . ." he proceeded to bring David up to date on the firm's new position on interest rates. Apparently, their outlook for the remainder of the year had turned bearish. They were now betting the Fed was preparing to raise rates.

Higher interest rates are Kryptonite for stocks. Almost always, higher rates mean lower stock prices. It was a bold and newsworthy position David's firm had just taken. One that would no doubt catch the eye of everyone on the Street.

David sat impassively, looking out his window at the Statue of Liberty. "Did you hear me?" his colleague asked.

"Yeah . . . I heard you," David said, indifference in his voice.

"You okay, D.B.?"

"Yeah, just a little preoccupied."

"Well, this is the biggest call we'll make all year. I don't want to sound like an asshole, but you should get preoccupied some other time. We got shit to do. We get out in front of this freight train and we're heroes."

"What else?" David asked, not turning from his view.

He listened to myriad views from some of the firm's leading research analysts—all of which were gloomy. If the firm was right, things were about to get dicey.

"All right," David said, digging deep, making every effort he could muster to perform his duties. Inexplicably, some of his old fire came back. "Conference the desks. Tell them I want them for an eight-thirty call. We got a lot of clients to contact. Have Bernie get Shipman for me. I want him on the line to field questions. Call Bobby and tell him we're going to start moving some stock. Tell him I want to cross as much as we can. Use third markets. Let's see if we can keep this under wraps for a while. I don't want to get in line with every Tom, Dick, and Harry."

"Now you're talkin', boss. What about the quant boys? We'll want to come at our clients with some hedging techniques."

"Good idea. I'll talk to Saperstein myself. I've got some things I need to speak with him about anyway."

Now David's clients were about to witness why he earned seven figures a year. No doubt the job paid well, but then again, very few places demanded upwards of eighteen hours a day, sometimes six or seven days a week. Everything's a tradeoff. Wall Street has a strange way of warping the thought processes. The longer one stays, the harder it is to leave. There's no magnet like money. The hard part is keeping the magnet from becoming a chain.

DOWNTICK

"Close the door on your way out," David said, as his colleague turned to leave. He chuckled to himself. "Good afternoon" is the universal slap to anyone who's not in by 7:00 A.M. It was only 8:10 A.M., but he'd hear about it half a dozen times today. If you're not a morning person, you won't make it on the Street.

GNAWING
FEAR

—⁓—

BOOK 2

David turned and pulled a pack of cigarettes off his desk. It was good to be back, he thought. He slapped the pack against his open palm, lit a cigarette, and tossed the pack haphazardly onto his desk. He stood at his window as he had done a thousand times before.

It was a clear, chilly, breezy autumn day. The sky was a bright blue, with finger clouds moving quickly north through the sky over New Jersey. He stood with his hands against the windowpane, leaning forward, looking down at the river boats. He hadn't thought much about Saperstein since Atlanta, except to mention him to Halliway and Hill. Then, of course, there was that damned dream last night.

"That back-stabbing son of a bitch," he said to the window. David thought whatever move he decided to make now might affect his whole career. Saperstein had clearly gotten Givens's ear. If David went at him defensively, Sap could easily turn it around on him. But if he went after him too aggressively, he could break every taboo of acceptable corporate behavior.

Quiet, clandestine infighting was one thing—it was expected, anticipated, planned for. Open warfare was something else altogether. David could hear Givens's voice. "Just what the hell do you think you're doing, mister? I don't give a shit how much you hate the son of a bitch. In fact, I don't care if he screwed your mother. I

139

will *not* have any managing director of mine acting like Attila the Hun. If you've got a problem with Saperstein, then you damn well better work it out with him like a gentleman! Is that clear?"

But David had learned something in the past few days. Fear works. In fact, it's a remarkable weapon. Hit 'em where they don't expect it. Attack in a manner unplanned for. Anyway, he didn't give a shit anymore. Jonah was right to have moved away from this hellhole. *If I'm lucky, I can get this psycho off my back and think about getting the hell out of here.*

David really did love his job, but it just didn't hold the same importance anymore. He figured Linda would find out about Mikey soon enough and probably never return. It wouldn't be the same without her. He'd make do, but it would be different—not as much fun. His kids needed him now. So did Rebecca. And he needed them.

Without his realizing it, somewhere along the way this damn job had caused him to ignore everything he should have held most dear. With each passing year, he grew more blinded to his own selfishness. Was it the booze? Maybe, but it didn't matter. No more, he thought. It ends now. I don't want to lose what I've got, he thought, but I will not sell my soul to keep it.

David choreographed the conference call with his desks like a seasoned conductor. He pulled nuances from Shipman, getting his unspoken thoughts from the morning call. He explained the consequences of the firm's position to specific people about specific accounts—whom to call first, what to recommend. He told them the quant boys were already fast at work and would be able to offer concrete suggestions by the afternoon.

When David finished he picked up the phone on his console. "Mr. Saperstein's office, may I help you?"

"Alice, it's David. Is Sap in?"

"Yes, but he's in a meeting right now. They should be breaking up before nine. Can I leave a message for him?"

"Why yes, thank you. Tell him I want to see him at nine. Sharp. I'll come there."

"Okay, Mr. Johnson. Anything else?"

"Nope. That'll do it. Thanks."

The elevator doors opened on Harvey Saperstein's floor at three minutes before nine. David wanted to be there on time. He stopped in the men's room, washed and dried his hands, and looked in the mirror. His blue and gold Brooks Brothers regimental tie contrasted sharply with his neatly starched white shirt. He straightened it, looked at his watch, and walked straight to Alice's desk.

"Hello, Alice," he said with a smile, standing in front of her.

"Hi, Mr. Johnson. I'll tell Mr. Saperstein you're here."

She depressed the intercom button. "Mr. Saperstein, Mr. Johnson is here for his nine o'clock appointment."

"Do you always call him Mr. Saperstein, Alice?" David asked, annoyed with Saperstein's pretentiousness.

"Yes, sir."

"How long have you worked for him now?" David asked.

"Six years."

David smiled and nodded his head. *What an asshole,* he thought.

"David. Sorry for the wait," Saperstein said with a smile, emerging from his office. "I was just wrapping up some dictation. You caught me in mid sentence. Please, come in."

Saperstein did not extend a hand to David, which was just as well. David didn't feel like being phony right now anyway. He entered the office, sat in a chair opposite the desk, and lit a cigarette.

"I wish you wouldn't smoke here," Saperstein said.

"Oh, I forgot," David said, feigning concern. "You hate cigarette smoke. Sorry. Got an ashtray?"

"Here, use this," Saperstein said, frowning, handing David a half drank cup of coffee. "So what's this all about? I'm really quite busy."

"Really? Not me. I just went bust at the Monopoly game we got going downstairs, so I thought I'd come up and shoot the breeze."

The game was already afoot. So much for pretense. The two men really did hate each other. Saperstein stared hard at David. "Don't fuck with me, Johnson."

"See, Harvey? Is that any way to treat a guest? I mean, someone really should teach you some manners."

"Your ass is grass, mister. I swear, if it's the last thing—"

"No sir!" David snapped, the words stunning Saperstein. *"Your* ass is grass. Let's get one thing clear. Right here. Right now. You've been fucking around behind my back long enough. I spoke to Givens, asshole. You and I both know what you told him's a sack of shit. Now, you either get off my back, or I will throw you off. Is that clear?"

David hoped Saperstein would take the bait and let slip whatever it was he had actually told Givens. Normally David would never have taken such a risk, but at this moment, he didn't really care.

Saperstein sat, his elbows on the arms of his chair, hands clasped, his forefingers touching his chin. The two men stared at each other, David determined to go blind before he blinked.

Saperstein looked down at his desk, rose, and got himself a cup of coffee, not offering one to David.

"I take mine black," David said.

"Help yourself."

"Don't mind if I do." David rose and walked across the office to the coffee pot.

"What do you want?" Saperstein asked, sitting down at his desk.

"Want?" David asked, raising his eyebrows. "I just told you what I want. You and I both know that *you* want that mini-institutional desk. Why, I can only imagine."

There were thousands of smaller institutional accounts throughout the country—local savings and loans, insurance companies, and banks to name a few. Generally speaking, because of their limited geographic niche they tend to be the domain of the local retail branch. It's at the local level that a broker from a nearby office can usually wield the most leverage. Often times, when the markets went awry, it was the smaller accounts that needed the most hand holding, and clearly the best vantage point from which to do that was at the local level.

From David's point of view, this mini-institutional market was a huge, untapped source of revenue for his team, but for obvious reasons it was a political nightmare from corporate's point of view. David remained undeterred. He pushed and pushed some more, until eventually he became the focus of great disdain throughout the retail branch system. It was but one of many instances where different departments of the same firm found themselves working at loggerheads. The debates at headquarters over the appropriate way to proceed were numerous and turbulent. It was fodder for many an explosive meeting.

Each account was reviewed individually by the powers that be. Sometimes the local broker won out, sometimes David won out. Other times the account was split. It was a bold move that made David many enemies, but he had turned it into a very profitable endeavor for his team. And of course, as always, money talks, bullshit walks.

"Look Johnson, you've stepped on so many toes with this little project of yours it's a wonder you're still here."

"Is that so?" David said, his tone contemptuous. "I appreciate your concern, but last I checked, it wasn't your domain. You didn't get a promotion and keep it a secret did you, Sap?"

Saperstein was quiet for some time. "Anyway," he said, "I believe it could have been handled much more diplomatically. Going in with both guns blasting just didn't make any sense. I told you that from day one. But of course, no one can tell you anything."

"Maybe. But the bottom line is that that desk is one of the most profitable in this firm. I didn't know we did this for our health."

"I'm not so sure it's as profitable as you say. That's why I told Givens I thought you were padding the P and L."

Padding the profit and loss statements! *That's what this was about?* When it came to money, David could be one hell of a prick, but he'd never padded a book in his life.

David could barely keep from jumping his colleague. "Didn't you think it was just a little ballsy to go to

Givens with such an accusation before you approached me? Who died and made you God? Not only do you not have the authority *or* the appropriate information to make such a statement, you also happen to be dead wrong. I've never padded a book in my life, and you know it."

"Do I? Spreads have never been less than they are now. Never. And yet that little baby of yours keeps churning out twenty plus percent growth every year. How the hell do you explain that? Huh? In a market like this? This competitive environment? There's no way. No way."

"I'll show my P and L to anybody who wants to look it. Any time. I have absolutely nothing to hide."

"I see," Saperstein said, getting up to refill his coffee.

David leaned forward on Saperstein's desk. "No, I don't think you do. Listen real carefully now, because I'm only going to say this once. I've worked my balls off to make that desk what it is and every penny of revenue and profit it shows is legit. Come here," he said, bending his forefinger for Saperstein to stand before him. "I want to share something with you."

Saperstein eyed him with disdain. "Screw off."

"No, no . . . trust me, Sap. You'll want to hear this." Saperstein approached slowly. David didn't speak until the two men were close enough for his words to carry the most impact. He spoke slowly. "If you don't tell Givens you were mistaken, that you were operating under inaccurate information and numbers, I will kill you. Is that any clearer?"

"Did you just threaten me?"

David's arms were crossed, resting on Saperstein's desk. He spoke sternly, quietly. "Maybe your hearing's going, asshole. Clean up this mess now or I will make sure you *never* get your year-end bonus. I will kill you sure as the sun's coming up tomorrow morning. Do you understand me?"

"You're history, you know that?" Saperstein said, the veins in his neck pulsating. "When I tell Givens and the other directors what you just said to me, you'll be lucky if you're here next week my friend, much less around for *your* bonus check."

David chuckled. "I will deny we ever had this conversation. Everyone knows you've got a bug up your ass for me. You don't really think anyone's going to believe I came in here and threatened your life, do you? They'll think you're a nut case. You'll be seeing a company mandated shrink for so long, you'll start thinking you are losing your marbles. Don't be a fool, Harvey."

Saperstein sat, resting his hands on his desk, wrapping them around his coffee. He stared into David's eyes, not moving, not speaking a word.

"You had better want that desk in the worst way," David said. "Because if you take it from me, so help me God, I will personally blow your brains out."

Jesus Christ! This guy's out of his mind. Saperstein thought about his options. David was right. No one would ever believe that D.B. Johnson, the firm's brightest shooting star, came into his office and threatened to kill him.

"I don't believe you," Harvey said, calling David's bluff. "You're full of shit, you know that? You're going down, mister."

David reached into his jacket pocket and pulled out the .45 revolver, massaging it in his lap. "It's too bad you can't be more reasonable, Sap. But then again, I'd enjoy seeing your brains splattered from here to Jersey City. Your choice."

David had already thought this part through. If security approached him—and they most certainly would if Saperstein called them—one call to the Connecticut state police would clear up any doubts as to the legitimacy of his carrying a weapon. True, it wasn't his. Yes, he'd taken it from his neighbor. But when the facts became known, who could possibly blame him? No, Sap couldn't win this one. He'd already lost and didn't even know it.

And what if security asked him how Sap knew about the gun? "We spoke this morning on the phone. I told him all about it." You can't prove a negative, David thought. They could never prove anything and most likely wouldn't even try.

Saperstein's eyes bulged out of their sockets. David noticed how ridiculous he looked trying to maintain his cool and act as if everything were normal. "You're insane, you know that?"

David put the gun back in his jacket pocket, patting it. "That's debatable. But in any event, it will just be our little secret. Won't it, Sap?"

Saperstein leaned back in his chair, staring at his nemesis. "Are you seriously telling me you would kill me if I succeeded in taking that desk from you?"

"Sap, I've never been more serious in my life. You know what else? I wouldn't even bat an eye. I'd take you down before you knew what hit you. And you know the best part? No one would ever know I did it. I really hope you're as smart as you act. Time will tell, won't it?"

"Is there anything else?" Saperstein asked as he stood, desperate to get David out of his office.

"As a matter of fact, there is. When are you going to start letting Alice call you by your first name? It's been what, six years? And she's still calling you Mr. Saperstein. A bit pretentious, don't you think?"

"Are you done?" Saperstein asked, thoroughly defeated. How does one fight with a madman? They played by different rules, and what was worse, the rules constantly changed. It was a dangerous game, one that Sap didn't know how to play. Perhaps, he thought, this would be one battle he would back away from.

"There is just one more thing," David said, rising to leave. "It would be most unfortunate if I ever heard about this from anybody. *Ever*. Yourself and security included. Why don't we just pretend it didn't happen. I think that would be best. Don't you?"

Saperstein looked at David through slightly squinted eyes, nodding his head almost imperceptibly.

David stuck out his hand, a big smile on his face. "Friends?"

Saperstein ignored it.

"Have it your way. I'll be seein' ya, Sap," David said, walking out the door.

"Have a great day, Alice. Good to see you again."

"Thank you, Mr. Johnson. Good to see you."

"Call me David."

—⁓—

Autumn's leaves crackled under Fenton's feet as he approached the back of the barn. He had already driven by David's house twice that morning. Nothing. No cruisers. No policemen. He waited in his car at the end of the road early that morning, drinking a cup of coffee, staring at his rearview mirror. He saw David's caravan leaving the driveway and ducked down in his seat. He counted two squad cars and David's Range Rover.

Fenton was fairly certain the house was vacant now, but wanted to be extra sure. No mistakes. After David's protection detail had disappeared he waited half an hour, drove to the train station, and parked his car on a side street. He called a cab, took it several blocks from Woodbury and walked the rest of the way, entering the woods to the right side of David's house.

Fenton's plans called for approaching from the back. Light on his feet, he didn't bother with the roundabout way through the neighbor's backyard as he had done before. Sneaking in behind the barn now, he knelt at its edge, binoculars in hand. He surveyed everything he could. The kitchen window . . . the sliding glass door . . . under the deck . . . the patio. Nothing.

Fenton slowly made his way toward the Johnson home. Maneuvering the slight incline, touching the large maple with his left hand. The only spontaneous action he allowed himself was to walk to the patio where he had killed Bennett. He stood behind the gate, going through the motions with his bare hands, smiling as he slashed the air with his right. The feeling came back to him now. He yearned for more. *Everything in its proper time.*

The right side of David's house was thick with shrubbery and very close to the woods. Located on a slight hill, it was well out of sight from the road. Fenton went to the garage, pulled out a ladder, and set it under the eaves on that side of the house. He carried an eclectic mix of tools in his vest and knapsack—three screwdrivers, a crowbar, a hammer, rope, and nails. He climbed gingerly to the peak and proceeded to pry loose the air vent to the attic. It was larger than most. In fact, its size was what had originally given him the idea.

If there was any part of his plan that worried him, this was it. Not that it mattered. He hadn't come this far only to be sidetracked by a slight miscalculation. When he finally pried the vent free, he tied a thin rope around one of the louvers and lowered it down to the attic floor. With some squirming and acrobatics, he now dangled in the opening, squeezing his thighs as tight as possible. At one point, he thought he wouldn't make it. But just as the fear entered his brain, he was through.

He had done it. He was in! Fenton smiled and stood silent, the acrid smell of burnt rubber still lingered in the air. His heart raced with excitement. He descended the attic stairs, unlocked the kitchen door in back and climbed the ladder again.

He pulled the vent up with the rope, securing it back in its proper place. At least enough to pass the naked eye test. Fenton returned the ladder to the garage exactly as he had found it. He knew the hardest part awaited him. His death instinct in full blossom, he was anxious for more. God, how he needed to kill again. The best was yet to come, but he would have to wait.

Fenton still had plenty to do. He went to the barn and retrieved a red one-gallon container of gasoline, swirling it to check its quantity. *Almost full. Good.* He brought it up to the attic, climbed back down the stairs, and went to David's office. He stopped at the doorway, soaking it all in.

It was a dark room, masculine, but not elegant. There was a large cherry rolltop desk against the far wall. On it sat a telephone console, a computer, stacks of research reports, and a half-full ashtray. In front, swung to one side, was a dark maroon high-back leather chair, the kind with gold tacking around the edges. Against one wall stood a large antique bookcase with Corinthian-style ridged columns on either side and dentil block work adorning the top.

On its shelves stood pictures of the Johnson kids, smiling at the chalet, skis in hand. Smiling for the camera, sailing in some kind of boat, their faces shining brightly in the sun. There was a picture of Rebecca reclining on a log, autumn's brightest colors surrounding her. There were books on sales techniques, the markets, a couple of bestsellers. Sprinkled throughout were some knickknacks and a couple of plants.

Against the opposite wall, between the two windows, hung David's diploma from Boston University. In the corner, opposite the desk was a small table with two university-style chairs pulled up to it, the B.U. insignia on their backs.

Fenton went to the desk, careful not to put anything out of place. He wore latex gloves, the kind a doctor wears. He wanted to make damn sure nothing caught David's eye. In the corner of the desk, underneath the open shelves, sat a Rolodex file. Fenton began thumbing through. "Let your fingers do the walking," he said.

"Let's see. Rubenstein's Jewelers. Robson's Laundry. Ahh, Roberts. Hello, Jonah. Did you miss me? R.R. one sixty one, Harrison, Maine. See ya soon." Fenton copied down the address and phone number and placed the Rolodex back in its original place, carefully flipping it back to the address that had originally shown.

In his mind's eye he could picture Maine. How beautiful it must be this time of year. Must be getting a bit chilly too. Fenton tried to remember when he'd been there last. He stood in the middle of the room staring at the bookshelves, trying to think. *Could it be that he had never been there before?* And then he heard it. A car door slam. Then another.

He jumped to the window, peeking down onto the driveway. It was a light blue Caprice Classic. Must be the staties, he thought, as he ran from the office. He climbed the attic stairs, pulled them up after him and stood motionless. Had he remembered to lock the kitchen door? *Shit!* He couldn't remember. He scolded himself. *Why can't I ever do anything right?*

Perhaps because of television and the print media, the public generally doesn't have a very accurate picture of the job of a homicide investigator. Too often, when they think of a murder investigation, they envision a manhunt—the shrewd sleuth painstakingly assessing the known facts, ferreting out the unnoticed, conducting interviews, all in search of the elusive felon.

While this certainly happens, it is only half the story. For at all times, every homicide investigator's attention is focused on that other, often forgotten truth. It is not enough to catch a murderer if you can't obtain enough evidence to put him behind bars.

More often than not, fairly early in the investigation a seasoned detective will have a pretty good idea who his suspect is. Someone who's been around awhile will usually tell you they're fifty percent home once they know who did it. The actual apprehension may take a good deal longer, while enough facts are gathered to make a case solid enough to stand up in a court of law.

This is the tedious part of the job. The minutiae are always relevant. No matter how immaterial something might seem, it always finds its way into a good detective's notebook. And so it was with Cedric Halliway and Scott Hill. They had spent the better part of six hours at the crime scene on the night Bennett was killed. They sketched the pool of blood in their notebooks, observing the direction of the blood spatter, both at the scene and around the house to the stoop. They measured footprints and shoe types. They made sure Bennett's hands were bagged and that every fingernail was scraped and analyzed. Neighbors had to be interviewed: had they seen any strange cars or individuals? Anything at all? The least significant thing that seemed just a wee bit out of the ordinary?

Seldom had they come upon the scene of a murder as disheveled as this one. If at all possible, a victim should never be moved, certainly not until the medical examiner has released it. Bennett had been moved not once but twice.

The site of this murder was any investigator's nightmare, polluted almost beyond compare, with numerous footprints, smoke, ash, and water. There was no doubt these facts would hamper the investigation. The two men would have to rely more heavily on the reports they waited so anxiously to get.

"There's no sign of a struggle," Halliway said to his partner, who was stooping at the hedges, observing blood spatter patterns for a second time. "There's no apparent evidence of a scuffle. No sole or heel marks. The blood is undisturbed, except where the perp walked through it."

"Probably carrying Bennett in his arms, from the impression of the sneaker marks on the flagstone and walkway," Hill added.

The two men reenacted the bloody scene of early Sunday morning as they envisioned it happening.

"All right, the perp is standing here," Hill said. "It tells me three things. One, the gate opens this way, so our man knew to wait here so Bennett wouldn't see him. Two, he was obviously lying in wait. It was clearly premeditated. Three, he's smart. He staked out the premises enough to know the gate opened this way."

"Maybe, but how do we know he hadn't just gone through the gate to get to this spot?" Halliway wanted to know. "Maybe that's the first time he saw it."

"Even if he did, it's still premeditated. He came through, saw which way the gate opened, and waited."

"Okay, but smart? I'm from Missouri on this one."

"Not just smart, Ric. Smart and cold as an ice cube. Look at the blood spatters on the gate. You can tell by the general lack of them, that he waited until Bennett had cleared that gate. No. I tell ya, Ric, he knew to wait here and knew to wait until Bennett was clear. He was thinking—patient, calculated."

Halliway checked his notes. "The M.E. says his throat was slashed from left to right. So we know he's right-handed."

"Yeah, and no prints anywhere, so we know he wore gloves."

"All right. The M.E. says that due to the nature of the wound, Bennett would have died in a minute, probably less. Our man waits . . . lets him bleed like a stuck pig.

Once Bennett shows no sign of life, he picks him up, probably cradle-like," Halliway said, holding out his arms, palms up. "And carries him through the gate, around the drive, and along the walk, and lays him at the foot of the stoop. There would have been more blood if he'd carried him over his shoulders."

"Yep. And the only footprints are when he's carrying Bennett away," Hill said, pointing to the footprints. "Which means he stood there, Ric. He stood there, and watched him die. I'm makin' book. He's smart and ice cold."

"I'll buy it. He's no wimp either. I mean, he takes down a cop without so much as a shot fired, much less a struggle, then carries him around the house. Doesn't drag him, mind you, but carries him. You know how heavy dead weight is."

"Sure do. Bennett weighed one eighty-seven. And one eighty-seven dead is a shitload heavier than one eighty-seven alive."

It is true what they say about dead weight. If you lift a person while they're breathing, then lift the same person when they're dead, there's a marked difference. No one's fully explained it. It's just a fact of life—so to speak.

Halliway walked toward the basement window. "Okay. He comes back here, avoids the pool of blood, and removes the windowpane. No telling when he cut it. He reaches in, unlatches the window and slides down to the basement. There's blood all over the bottom of the window, so he must have gone in feet first, stomach up."

"I didn't get so much as a thread from that window. I wonder if our boy was wearing some kind of nylon or rubber suit," Hill wondered aloud.

"Maybe," Halliway interjected, "but he obviously wiped it down. Probably checked it and the bottom sash for loose threads."

"See? The boy's smart."

Halliway nodded, lost in thought. "Yes, and sick."

"The worst kind."

The pager on Halliway's belt beeped. He removed it and jotted down the phone number in his notebook. "It's the M.E. Maybe we got a break."

"Man, I hope so. We ain't got nothin' here."

Halliway walked back to the cruiser, dialed the number on his car phone and waited. "Dr. Reichman, speaking."

"Hi, Irving. It's me. What ya got? Tell me it's something good. We could use a break."

"Do you remember during the autopsy I mentioned to you the contents under one of the nails appeared to be somewhat different than the rest?"

"Yes?" Halliway asked, his adrenaline beginning to pump.

"Well, we lucked out really. The manner in which the officer fell was quite fortuitous. His hands were remarkably clean. Do you remember I pointed that out to you?"

"Yes, I remember," he responded, losing patience. "What do you have, Irving?"

"Well, it's not much. But it appears that Officer Bennett has someone else's blood under his middle finger. It will take a while to run DNA analysis, but we definitely have a blood group. Quite rare really. It's type AB with an Rh negative factor."

"And its significance?"

"Simply put, only eight to ten percent of the US population has blood type AB. Everybody has an Rh factor, either positive or negative, but you rarely find a negative factor with type AB blood.

Halliway gave Hill a thumbs up. "Excellent work, Irving. You never cease to amaze."

"Thank you. All in a day's work."

————⁃⁓⁓⁓⁃————

The New York state police and the Connecticut state police agreed to cooperate in aspects relating to David's transportation to and from work. As head of the investigation, Halliway decided early on that riding the subway was impractical. There were too many people, too close together to effectively protect David in the event his attacker came at him there.

However, for two reasons, he agreed to let David ride the commuter train. First, David could actually get a seat, and with Metro North's help, space could be made available to surround David with cops who could pass for any other commuter. Second, since trains ran on a particular line, and arrived at or left Grand Central at predetermined times, it seemed logical that if his attacker chose his commute to go after him, he would choose the train for his attack. Grand Central offered him a better opportunity to know where David would be, and when.

The last thing Halliway wanted was to break David's schedule too much. He wanted to give the perp the illusion of control, a false sense that everything would be as he had planned. Taking David out of circulation more than necessary would not give him the opportunity to carry out his threat. David would be kept a prisoner and the perp would walk the streets that much longer. Without putting David in unnecessary harm, Halliway preferred to give his man just enough rope to hang himself.

As agreed, David called Trooper Daniel Trowbridge of the New York state police from his office when he had finished his day's work. David was ashamed to admit that, though paradoxical, he was glad a police officer had been killed. It was the only reason he was getting so much attention. It was tragic of course, but when you got right down to it, David was still alive and the only reason the police were spending so many man-hours was because they wanted to catch Bennett's killer. David was secretly thankful.

"Officer Trowbridge," David called out into his speaker phone, staring out his office window. "I'm ready now. I'll be downstairs in ten minutes."

"Trooper, please," Trowbridge said.

"What?"

State cops are weird about being called Officer. "It's Trooper Trowbridge."

David made a face. "Whatever."

"Please stay there, Mr. Johnson. Trooper Rivera and I will come get you. You're on the forty-second floor, correct?"

"Yes, but is that really necessary?" David said. He was

clearly agitated. "It's going to be quite an embarrassment being escorted out of my building by two policemen."

"I'm sorry, Mr. Johnson, but those are my orders. Anyway," Trowbridge said, rolling his eyes at his partner, "we're not in uniform. We're each wearing suits. No one will ever know."

David breathed deeply. "All right. Forty-second floor. I'll meet you at the elevators in ten minutes."

"Please stay in your office, Mr. Johnson. We will meet you there."

"Jesus. All right, all right. My office. Ten minutes."

David hit the button on his phone and stood, smoking a Marlboro, looking at the lights of New Jersey. For some strange reason, he thought of George Steinbrenner and wondered whether or not he would ever move the Yankees there.

He could see the golden torch of the Statue of Liberty burning brightly in the dark. What a beautiful job they had done restoring her. He thought how nice it would be to visit her again. He hadn't been since he was a kid. It was odd, he thought, how people came from all over the world just to see her and yet she had become nothing more than a hood ornament in his panoramic view.

He tried to think of how he would keep himself from drinking tonight when he got home. He would have to try and find a way. He realized he hadn't had a drink now since the flight to Atlanta. In fact, he had gone without one now longer than he could remember. *Before college, maybe?* He wasn't sure.

What David did know was that this mess he was in had in some ironic way caused him to begin his sobriety. He didn't want to screw it up now. He had come close this morning, but even then his tormentor had won out, miraculously keeping him from the bottle. "Thank you . . . I guess," he said aloud.

"Mr. Johnson?" Trowbridge said, standing in his office doorway.

David turned with a start. "Christ. You scared the shit out of me. You guys ready? Let's get out of here."

"What exactly do you do here?" Trooper Rivera

wanted to know. "Is this where I see everyone standing around screamin' and waving things on the news?"

"No. That's what we call the pits. Those are usually where futures contracts are traded. You know? Sugar, coffee, pork bellies. You can find those here at the New York Mercantile Exchange, or in Chicago at the Chicago Mercantile Exchange or the Chicago Board of Options Exchange. We call it the C-bow. You know, for the letters, CBOE?"

"Yeah, I always wanted to ask someone about that," Rivera said, as the three men turned the corner to the elevator bank. "Do they really trade pork bellies? I mean, who the hell would buy and sell pork bellies? It sounds stupid if you ask me."

"You ever eat ham, Trooper?" David asked, always happy to discuss his domain. "Or bacon? You wouldn't think it was so stupid if you had two thousand head of swine you were looking to sell. A cattle farmer can hedge all or some of his herd through the futures markets by locking himself in a certain price. There's any number of things that can wipe someone out in that business, but at least they can control the price risk. That's how they hedge their bets. I can tell you for a fact, some of the smartest traders alive wear overalls and drive tractors for a living."

David strayed a little. "Stay close, Mr. Johnson. Between the two of us, please," Trowbridge said. He was obviously in charge.

One of the elevator bells rang and the doors slid open. Trowbridge motioned for Rivera to take a look. He walked two doors down and motioned for the other two men to follow. When they were in the elevator, Trowbridge stood against one of the doors preventing it from closing and faced the other elevators, calling someone on his walkie-talkie. He stepped inside and let the doors close.

"We'll have a straight shot down. We coordinated with building security," he said, looking at David. "No stops for this baby."

In no time they were at lobby level. Trowbridge stood

in front of David as the doors opened. Rivera stepped out and looked around. "All clear," he said.

"Mr. Johnson, please stay between us, sir. I'll be in front, Trooper Rivera will be in back. Let's go. Car's to the left."

David found himself wondering if the President went through this everywhere he went. *This could get very old.*

"David!" someone called out. Trowbridge swung around, his right hand under his jacket, while Rivera slammed David against the wall with his body.

"David, what's going on here?" Ted Givens asked. "Are you okay?"

"It's all right, gentlemen," David said, his adrenaline pumping wildly. "This is the chairman of the board." David's face was flushed with embarrassment.

"David?" Givens asked, approaching closer. "Who are these two men?"

"Ted, good to see you," David said, breaking free from the wall, hoping the whole scene didn't look as ridiculous as he felt. "I meant to call you. With our shift in stance on the Fed today, I've been busier than a one-armed paperhanger," he said, extending a hand now.

"What's going on?" Givens asked again, shaking David's hand but looking over his shoulder at the two men standing behind him.

"Ted, you wouldn't believe me if I told you. Long story short, someone has been threatening me and my family. Becky and the kids moved away yesterday. These gentlemen are from the state police. Providing me with protection until we can catch the bastard."

"Threatening you?" Givens asked, somewhat perplexed. "I don't understand."

"Well, neither do I. But believe me, Ted, it's for real. Whoever it is, murdered our dog and nearly burnt down my house," David said, deciding not to mention Bennett. "I meant to call and tell you. It started right after we spoke last week. I haven't had two seconds to look at my numbers. I'm afraid I'm going to have to put off my presentation tomorrow night. I'm sorry, Ted. But it's just been a nightmare."

"Don't you worry about that, my boy. Just make sure the family's all right. Do you need anything from us? If so, just name it and you've got it."

"No. Thanks anyway, Ted. I think we got it under control. At least as much as one can expect."

"Doesn't matter anyway, David. I spoke to Saperstein this afternoon. Says he was mistaken about what he told me last week. He was looking at the wrong numbers. Apologized every which way from Sunday."

"What did he tell you anyway, Ted?" David wanted to know, testing whether or not it was all about the P and L.

"You know," Givens said, resting his hand on David's shoulder. "Some things are better left unsaid. Let's just say that I have the utmost faith in you. Always have. Funny, but I really don't like that fellow. Too stuck-up for my tastes."

David smiled softly, remaining quiet. Sometimes silence is more powerful than words.

"Well anyway, you two gentlemen make sure you look after this man. He's the next chairman of this company. We'd like him to make us some more money before he goes." Givens laughed, slapping David on the back. "Anything you need, David. Just say the word."

"Thank you, Ted. That means a lot."

"Limo's waiting," Givens said. "I've got to go. Nice seeing you, David. Gentlemen." Like that, he was gone. When Theodore Givens said he had to catch a limo, he meant a real limo.

"So that was the big cheese, huh?" Rivera asked.

"In the flesh."

"What do you think he's good for a year?" Rivera asked.

"You wouldn't want to know," David said, slipping in between his escorts.

"Come on . . . A million? Two?"

"Jorge, would you cut the shit?" Trowbridge said.

David laughed. "Let's just say you're a little low."

Rivera whistled. One of those long, drawn-out whistles that says, "Wow, you've got to be kidding me."

David smiled. *If you only knew.*

They arrived in front of Grand Central Station on 42nd Street at 7:36 P.M. Yellow cabs were ubiquitous, and horns and sounds of the city were everywhere. David had a 7:53 train to catch.

The two state policemen stepped out of the car and opened the passenger door on the sidewalk side. They were met by two other troopers dressed in full uniform. David felt like a convict being transported to the Federal penitentiary.

They walked briskly through the front doors in box formation. *Just get me to my train.* The public address system blared overhead. "Eight oh one to Poughkeepsie now departing track forty-seven . . . Due to a track fire, the seven fifty-nine to White Plains now moved to track twenty-five on the lower level." David and his entourage moved quickly into the main foyer.

No matter how many times David entered this room, its sheer size and beauty continued to impress him. Begun in 1903 and finished in 1913, when everyone traveled by train, it was designed to inspire wonder and reverence. The huge marble structure was decorated with ornate handrails; the hundred-foot ceiling had the constellations painted on it, tiny electric lights marking every major star. Grand Central was an example of architectural times gone by, when money was no object and buildings were works of art. Its aged elegance stands in stark contrast to the high-tech gismos and Madison Avenue advertising plastered throughout. But David always thought that it carried a grace about it no amount of modern tinkering could erase.

"Hang on guys," David said. "I got to look and see what track we're leaving from."

David stood, surveying a departure screen. "Okay, track thirty-seven. This way," he said, pointing to his right.

The four men took him to the middle car and handed him over to one of four Connecticut state policemen who would be his silent company back to Darien.

"Thank you, gentlemen," one of them said. "Any problems?"

Trowbridge shook his head. "Not a one."

"Good. See you tomorrow." The New York state police detail turned and left.

"Mr. Johnson, I'm Trooper Roderick Longdon, Connecticut State Police. The four of us are your detail. Please follow me, sir," Longdon said, leading David to five empty seats. "Please sit here," he said, pointing to a seat by the window. David didn't know it, but these three adjoining windows had been mirrored from the outside. You could see out but you couldn't see in. Longdon sat next to David, the other three fanned out in seats behind and in front of him.

So as not to draw attention to themselves, the troopers took their seats and pretended to read various newspapers and magazines. Longdon handed David a *New York Post* and whispered, "Just act normal. Enjoy the paper. We'll get you there in one piece. Promise."

David smiled slightly, not sure whether or not he had just been patronized. "Mind if I sleep?" he asked Longdon.

"Be my guest."

David closed his eyes, leaned his head against the window, and concentrated on his breathing. He pictured Rebecca's nude body and imagined making love to her . . . squeezing her flesh . . . feeling her hair . . . smelling her body. He realized it had been a week at least since they last made love, and began to feel that familiar warmth of yearning in his groin. He laid the paper on his lap, self-conscious about the erection forming in his pants.

Jonah Roberts and his wife Victoria lived on eighty acres of farmland and woods in a small house that Jonah had built with his own hands. The house sat on top of a small hill, the entire south side composed of triple-paned windows. There was a nice size kitchen, half the length of the house, a living room with a wood stove, and a small, step-up bathroom with only the necessities. Off the small entranceway on the east side of the house was a fourteen-by-twelve-foot bedroom. Off the living room, on the west side was a guest room, small but comfortable. Caleb and Sumner slept there. Rebecca slept on the pullout sofa in the living room.

By choice, they had no cable or satellite dish. In fact, with an antenna from the junkyard, they only received a handful of local stations, and some of them were fuzzy. They used well water, and made their own cheese, butter and cream. Their barn was the larger, more important structure on the Roberts property.

In it they stalled their swine, dairy and meat cattle, and horses. The animals could survive virtually any temperature, and had witnessed nights as bitter as thirty below zero, but the wind is their real enemy. No animal can survive the harsh, windy, winter nights, except the sheep with their thick blankets of wool. A night can feel as cold as fifty or sixty below when the wind kicks in.

They had moved to the small rural town of Harrison, Maine, five years earlier. Jonah, a successful investment banker in his own right, had made a small fortune in real estate in the eighties. His high six-figure salary, combined with several million in real estate gains, had afforded him the opportunity to leave the maniacal hustle and bustle of the Street and find his roots and a saner life in Maine.

Childless by choice, Jonah and Victoria Roberts loved their new life. There was something romantic and wholesome for both of them in calving a newborn in the wee hours of the morning, nursing an ailing member of the herd back to health, or even in putting a sickly horse to sleep.

There had been three of the latter over the years. The first, Jonah shot in the head in the back pasture. Vickie stayed inside, crying quietly to herself, unable to witness one of the facts of life on the farm. It had shaken Jonah. From that moment on, he vowed he would never do it again. The other two were felled by the vet via injection. While it may sound cruel, death on the farm is every bit as real as it is anywhere else. If Jonah only knew.

Rebecca Johnson and the Robertses sat now at their kitchen table looking out over the riding ring and the jumping course sloping down a pasture behind it.

"It just doesn't make any sense, Becky," Victoria said, handing Rebecca a cup of hot cider. "Who would possibly do this to you?"

"I don't know, Vickie. David and I have racked our brains. We've gone through just about every person we've ever met. We just can't figure it out. It's like the *Twilight Zone*."

"I've told David for years to get out of that hellhole," Jonah said, watching the kids play in a pile of wood chips next to an old blue Ford tractor. Maybe now, he'll listen to me."

"It's not that easy, Jonah. I mean, what if he does quit and we all move away? What if we just pack it all in and move to Florida . . . here . . . any place for that matter? Who's to say he won't follow us? Ruin whatever lives we start, no matter where it is?"

"Surely, Beck, you can't be considering continuing as you always have?" Jonah asked. "If nothing else this has to have thrown a little reality into David's list of priorities? Hasn't it?"

"Well, ironically, it may just have gotten him sober. In the midst of all this he admitted to me he was an alcoholic."

Jonah pursed his lips. "Well, there's a start. You know I speak from experience when I say that booze can ruin everything."

"I know, believe me. You should be grateful you were able to kick it, Jonah. You've been a different person since you stopped drinking. Nicer, more patient."

"Generally, less of an asshole," Vickie said, smiling at Jonah.

"Very funny," Jonah said. "Listen, Becky, I'm as grateful as they come. I thank God every day for giving me a second chance at life. But I won't lie to you. It was very difficult. Lots of bumps in the road."

"There's an understatement," Vickie added, getting up to refill her cup of cider.

"Are you done?" Jonah asked his wife, half sarcastic. "Sometimes, I wonder how I stay sober, living with you."

"Oh, oh. Below the belt, Jonah," Becky said, laughing.

"No seriously. Any time David needs help staying away from the bottle, have him call me. I'll drop everything. It's the least one drunk can do for another. Almost a responsibility, really."

Jonah had been a recovering alcoholic for almost seven years. Every drunk remembers their last drink, or if they can't, at least their last drunk. It was the winter of 1988, the night of his team's Christmas Party. That evening proved to be his wake-up call. What is it they say? Alcohol is the two-by-four God uses to get your attention.

He'd gotten his fair share of DWIs, blackouts, embarrassments. But nothing ever hit him the way that night did. Security found him in a stall in the ladies room, his pants around his ankles, urine all over the floor. It was almost 3:00 A.M.

Victoria was wild with worry. She had called the police to report her husband missing after making several embarrassing calls to see if his other cronies had made it home. One by one, groggy and drunk, they told her when they got home and where they had seen her husband last.

Jonah hadn't taken a drink since. The reality of that evening hit him like a blow to the groin, and he was shaken to realize that he was more than a social drinker gone overboard. He was a full-fledged drunk. The classic functioning alcoholic. Barely.

Rebecca was taken by his offer. "Thank you, Jonah. You're such a doll," she said.

"You know how we feel about both of you," Vickie added. "We hate to see you going through this."

"Well, I just pray it ends soon. That they catch this maniac and we can have our lives back." Rebecca stared out the window now, watching Sumner throw wood chips all over Caleb's head.

The two kids were having a ball, but she knew the

novelty would wear off soon enough. She and David had removed them from school until the storm blew over, but she feared the first time one of them asked to go home. What would she tell them? What if all this just went on and on? She felt slightly nauseated and very scared. She prayed that David would be okay.

"I can't thank you enough. Really. It's so nice of you to let us stay here. I don't know what to say."

"Don't be silly," Vickie said. "You've always been family and you know it. It'll be just like old times. We'll have a blast."

Rebecca smiled at her. They had been best friends since college. It was one of those rare occurrences. All four of them were like brothers and sisters. Still she longed for home . . . for David. She felt a yearning in her stomach for her old life. Her heart tightened. As happy as she was to be here, this was still going to be hell.

———————

Fenton Montague stood motionless in the middle of the Johnsons' attic. For the first time he felt a tinge of fear. His carefully laid plan had not included the mutability of the human mind. Stuck alone, blind to the outside world, he would need to carefully harvest an inner peace. Like a deer in a field who thinks it hears something, he cocked his head, barely breathing, listening for voices, car doors, footsteps, anything. But he heard nothing.

From up here how would he know when the coast was clear? How would he know when the cops had left? He strained his eyes to the opposite side of the attic. There, at the peak of the roof, was another vent. This one overlooked the driveway. In front of it were dozens of cardboard boxes, chests, rugs, and a hundred other knickknacks a family gathers over the course of time.

Like a golfer eyeing a putt from the spot where the ball lay, over every inch of the green to the hole, Fenton viewed his approach to the vent from where he stood. He felt fairly confident he could work his way to the last quarter or so of the distance without making any notice-able noise. But once he stood at the end of the carpet remnants, which he recognized from David's office, he wasn't sure how he would make it the rest of the way. *Get there, then worry about it.*

He remembered when he was a boy, his father would take him rabbit hunting. "Always step heel first. Then let the rest of your foot down slowly," he would say. Fenton felt sad at the thought of his father. Always a calming influence on his mother, he promised Fenton he would always look after him, that he would always protect him. No matter what.

But then one winter, he died of brain cancer. And that was that. Something in Fenton's mother snapped. She became more rageful, more uncontrollable, inclined toward sudden bursts of anger and tirades. His father had lied to him. He was an innocent young boy, helpless at the hands of a merciless, demented, and overbearing mother. The night he died, Fenton never felt so scared. So alone. He cried until he thought his eyes would bleed.

His father died on November 4, 1959. Shortly there-after, his mother began locking Fenton in the closet, forever haranguing him for his imperfections. It was in the closet Fenton learned to soothe himself by singing.

He hummed to himself now, "Oh, the old gray mare, she ain't what she used to be, ain't what she used to be . . ." *Be careful.* He mustn't screw this up or else all his planning, all his years of dreaming, would evaporate in an instant. He shuddered at the thought of getting this close to his dream and having it taken from him by someone who didn't know what he knew—who hadn't shared in his pain . . . his rejection.

Rejection! He stopped in his tracks. He could feel it. The sense of humiliation. The longing for approval that was ruthlessly yanked from his grasp every time he thought he might finally become just another guy. No. God worked in mysterious ways, and it was all necessary to save Fenton for his final calling. He prayed he did the job well. "I'll show you, Mother. You'll see. I'm not the failure you think I am."

He stepped slowly. The heels of his Reeboks followed dutifully by their soles. One after the other. Slowly . . . methodically. He maneuvered around a mound of old hockey equipment and stood at the foot of a pile of boxes. How could he possibly move them without being heard? Did he dare climb them? Too risky.

Then he heard a car door slam. Then another. A motor started. *They're leaving.* He held his breath and listened. The motor ran for some time and Fenton realized he needed to breathe. He inhaled deeply, slowly, quietly— becoming lightheaded. He put both hands on a box and held his head down. *Finally.* He heard the car begin to pull away, and listened until he could hear it no more.

Quickly but silently, he made his way back to the steps, pushing down the attic door, creating a few inches' gap from which he listened intently. Convinced he was alone now, he found an old broom handle and pushed the door completely down, measuring the distance from the opening to the floor. He had to get busy. He hadn't planned on the interruption. Reaching inside his vest he pulled out a nylon rope ladder which he hung to within a foot of the floor of the hall.

He pulled out two sixteen-penny nails and hammered them into the two-by-four framing above the attic opening, just wide enough to accommodate the nylon rope. Fenton removed his knife, cut off the extra rope and tied two tight knots around each nail. Stepping on the ladder with one foot first, then the other, he pushed with all his weight, then rechecked his knots for any give. There was none. These would work perfectly.

Next, he moved the attic door down, then up. Then down, then up again. Listening for spots that creaked. He pulled out a tiny can of 3-In-1 oil and gently worked those areas he felt were a problem. *I hope you appreciate this, David. I wouldn't do this for just anyone.* Satisfied it was as quiet as he could make it, he pulled out a rag and wiped down the treated areas. No dripping oil on the hall rug. Someone might notice.

Fenton climbed down the ladder and went to the kitchen, checking the door to see if it was locked. Good.

He was better than he thought. He really should give himself more credit, he thought. He put his hand up the sleeve of his sweatshirt to keep from leaving prints, opened the freezer door and took out an ice cube, sucking on it longingly. He was thirsty. With his hand still in his sleeve he opened a cupboard, took out a large glass, poured himself some water and drank two glasses full. He put the glass in his vest. He would need something to piss in during the night.

Fenton went to the bathroom, sat on the toilet and urinated. He flushed, went to the mirror and looked at himself. He smiled and felt aroused by the fun he had planned.

"There is no pleasure, without pain," he said.

Like so much in life, a good police investigation is mostly hard work and dead ends, sprinkled with an occasional stroke of good luck. Lieutenant Cedric Halliway and Detective Sergeant Scott Hill were about to receive one of the latter, though they wouldn't recognize its entire significance. Not immediately.

It's said that opportunity knocks but once, and even then, sometimes very quietly. Those more observant and patient tend to be the ones capable of noticing it for what it is, then running like hell with it when it shows. How many millions of opportunities come knocking every day only to be passed up or swept aside because their potential benefactor was too tired, in a bad mood, not observant, or otherwise preoccupied? But a good cop? They may miss opportunities in their day-to-day lives like the rest of us, but seldom does one get by undetected if it relates to a case.

Pete Esposito was sitting with his feet on his desk when he called the Connecticut state police, trying to reach Lieutenant Halliway. He was reviewing an NFL schedule, attempting to figure out who the Giants were playing on Sunday. He was disappointed to see it was

San Francisco. There was a day that would have been one hell of a game, he thought. What a difference a few years makes.

"Captain, Lieutenant Halliway is in the field at the moment. Can I take a message for him, or would you prefer I put you through to his voice mail?"

"Um . . ." Esposito was thinking. How important was this new information anyway? He was pretty sure he'd hit some kind of pay dirt. "Voice mail would be fine. Thank you."

Esposito waited impatiently for Halliway's taped message to end. "Lieutenant, this is Captain Esposito. We've got something here I think you'll want to know about. Could be nothing, but then again, I'm not sure. Call me at the station. If I'm not here, have dispatch ring me. I'm on till eight. If you get back to me after then, please call me at home. The desk sergeant has my number. Thanks."

Pete Esposito laid the phone in its receiver and sat back in his chair, hands clasped across his stomach. It was just a little too coincidental. Or was it? Maybe he was reaching. He wanted this son of a bitch in the worst way. He'd already decided he would spend the rest of his life tracking him down if that's what it took. No one—but no one—was going to kill one of his men and walk away from it.

He sat up straight in his chair, picked up the phone, and called the vet. "Doctor Yallow, please."

In less than a minute, Dr. Bernard T. Yallow, D.V.M., picked up the phone. "Hello, Pete. I'm sorry I didn't get back to you sooner, but I've been up to my—"

"What ya got, Bernie? Anything?" Esposito interrupted.

"Well, yes and no."

"Come on, Bernie. What the hell does that mean?"

"Captain," the desk sergeant said, poking his head around the doorway, "there's a Lieutenant Halliway on the phone from the state police. Says he's returning your call."

"Listen, Bernie. I gotta get back to you. Sorry," he said, hanging up. He pushed the blinking button on his console. "Lieutenant, thanks for getting back to me so soon."

"No problem. I just called in to check my messages. What do you have, Captain? Make it some good news."

"Well, I think I may be able to oblige. This morning our protection detail escorted Johnson to the train station. We had two cruisers. One in front and the other behind. Anyway, one of my men happened to notice a car at the end of Johnson's street. Appeared to be empty, but the Mass plates caught his attention. He jotted the number down on a whim."

Good thinking. "Is that so?"

"Yep. You know, I was thinking, with the letter postmarked Boston and everything, might be worth pursuing. I wanted to get a few men out there to start askin' around, but I wasn't sure how you'd want to proceed."

"Hmmm. Interesting. All right, tell you what. Send your men out. Speak to the neighbors. Find out if anyone had visitors from Massachusetts over the weekend."

"You got it," Esposito said, feeling the excitement rise within him.

"What time is it now?" Halliway asked mechanically.

"Almost four thirty."

"Why don't we meet at the station at seven? Do you think you'll have had enough time to find out anything by then?"

"God, I hope that's enough. See you here at seven."

"Good. See you then."

"Lieutenant, there is one other thing," Esposito said, saving the best for last.

"Yes?"

"My head man on the detail went back to the spot where the car was parked after he'd put Johnson on the train. The road drops a bit there. Collects all the dirt and mud that flows down the street. Seems he found a pretty good sneaker print in it."

Halliway felt a twinge of excitement himself. You just never know. "Really?" he asked.

Esposito felt like a kid on Christmas morning. "Really. Know what else?"

"Let me guess," Halliway mused, seeing it coming. "It's a Reebok."

"Lieutenant, you're a regular Kreskin."

Halliway could feel it now. That one moment in an investigation when everything turns. "Captain, have that print plastered. Now. We don't want to lose it—"

No rookie here, sir. "Way ahead of you, Lieutenant. Sent someone out as soon as he called. Got it here at the station now."

"Excellent work. We'll need to have the lab compare it to what we have from Johnson's patio."

"Ten to one it's a fit."

"Let's hope so. See you tonight," Halliway said, hanging up. Halliway turned to Hill. "You know what, Scott?" he said, hanging up the car phone, "I think we just got our first break."

"Let's hear it," Hill said, his mouth full of the last two bites of a Filet 'o Fish sandwich.

After his conversation with Halliway, Captain Esposito walked quickly through the detective squad room. "Dicky, Conklin," he said, motioning to the two men to follow him. "Meet me in the interrogation room, ASAP."

The men had no sooner taken their seats then Esposito began. "Gentlemen, we got a possible break in Bennett's case."

"Yes!" Conklin yelled.

Esposito filled the two men in on the conversation he'd just had, paying special attention to the seven o'clock deadline. They pulled out a detailed map of Woodbury and decided on six houses they would interview first. If whoever was in that car wasn't visiting someone in those six homes, it was difficult for them to imagine he'd have parked where he did. Even the six they chose was pushing it. These homes weren't exactly next to one another. Esposito told them to work individually. They had limited time before Halliway and Hill were due to arrive.

"Don't let anything pass. Friends, relatives, colleagues. Did any salesmen show up? Poll takers? Anybody they don't know from around here. Did they see the car? Did they recognize it? Did they see who was driving it? The works."

"What kind of car is it?" someone asked.

"Mass motor registry says it's a red Mustang. 1967. Fairly unusual. That'll help. Registered to a Fenton Montague. Newberry Street, Boston. Anything else?"

"Yeah, this Montague guy. What's he look like?" Conklin asked.

"Pretty nondescript, I'm afraid. Caucasian. Five ten. Blue eyes. Brown hair. No distinguishing marks or glasses. Like fifty million other white guys, unfortunately. Any other questions?"

Both men shook their heads.

"Good. Don't forget. Seven o'clock. If at all possible, report back here. Otherwise, call in with anything you've got before then. Okay? Go."

—⁂—

Officer Warren McKutcheon and his protection team waited while the train emptied of people. He sent one of his men to speak with the conductor to hold the train until the platform emptied and the switch in detail could be completed.

Though David had kept his eyes shut the entire ride, he hadn't gotten a wink of sleep. His mind was racing, too jumbled for sleep. The letter, Barney, the fire, Rebecca and the kids, the gun he had in his jacket pocket, Saperstein. He even thought about Coca-Cola and Goodman for the first time that day. How much longer could he put up with this?

What if the guy just disappears? What if he gets spooked by all the police and decides to try his luck another time? How long will the police protect me? How long can I expect Becky and the kids to stay away? Certainly we'll all be at risk if we eventually went about our normal lives, waiting for this psycho to return like a bad cold in winter. Should I sell the house and move? Where to? David had a knot deep inside his stomach, a clump of anxiety, as if he were at the very top of a roller coaster about to begin its descent.

Skates smiled at David. "Mr. Johnson. Good to see you, sir."

"Honey, I'm home," David said, attempting humor but sounding more fatigued and desperate.

McKutcheon had a few words with Longdon of the Connecticut state police, then turned to David, who was still seated. "If you'd follow me, Mr. Johnson, we're going to leave the train at this exit."

David was humiliated. The other commuters were staring at all of them now, trying to figure out exactly what was happening. When he rose, he felt their eyes burning into his back. He reached up, grabbed his briefcase and coat from the overhead rack, and followed McKutcheon out the forward door, consciously avoiding eye contact with anyone.

David was met on the platform outside by two uniformed officers and escorted down the steps to the parking lot. He had handed the keys to the Range Rover to Officer McKutcheon before he got on the train in the morning. It was already running, sandwiched between two Darien police cruisers. It had been watched all day—Halliway's idea. Once down the steps, they walked him to his waiting car in a triangle formation.

David was beginning to feel like a caged animal. He hadn't had time to stop and look at the sky or feel the relentless approach of winter. McKutcheon stood at the driver's side door. David walked to the passenger side door and opened it as McKutcheon lumbered behind the steering wheel. David lingered. Breathing the crisp fall air.

"Mr. Johnson," McKutcheon said through the open passenger door, leaning across the front seat. "Please get in, sir. There's no telling what might happen with you standing out there like that."

David took one last, quick breath and got in the Rover. "I'll tell you, Officer, I know you guys are trying to keep me safe. And I appreciate it. Really, I do. But I have to say, I don't know how long I can stand to be shuffled to and fro like some kind of prisoner. I feel like I'm the convict."

"I know, Mr. Johnson," Skates responded, truly feeling sympathetic for his charge.

"Could you please call me David?"

"Sure thing, sir. You know, you're the true definition of a victim. Your life's been turned upside down and right now you don't have a life. I feel for you. I mean that. But we got no choice. Not until we either catch this maniac or tomorrow comes and goes and nothing happens."

David felt his heart tighten and miss a beat. "What if nothing happens by tomorrow?" he asked, scared to hear that he might be left to fend for himself—waiting, looking over his shoulder, jumping at every sound or quick movement he encountered for the rest of his life. He knew deep within he couldn't live like that for very long. Something would have to give. And soon.

"Well, I can't rightly say. I'm pretty much a cog in this wheel. Do what I'm told, ya know? I guess the powers that be get together and discuss how best to approach it once we cross that bridge. A lot can happen between now and then. Let's just try to focus on the here and now."

The protection detail used a secured tactical channel. It would be very difficult for the average Joe to listen in.

"Team Green to Team Red. We're ready to roll," McKutcheon said.

"Roger that, Green."

"Team Blue. You ready?"

"That's a Roger."

"Okay, let's roll."

David stared out the window, watching downtown Darien whiz by. Some time passed before he spoke. "This is unfucking believable. You know that, don't you? In my wildest dreams, I would never have thought this would happen to me. To anyone. I keep thinking I'm dreaming. That I'm going to wake up and this whole thing will have been some kind of a horrible nightmare."

Skates spoke to the windshield, both hands on the wheel. "It's a nightmare all right. It just ain't no dream."

David shook his head. "I know, I know."

The convoy pulled into the Johnson driveway at 9:27

P.M. David was surprised to see a cruiser already in the driveway. *Jesus Christ!* What could his neighbors possibly be thinking? He must be the talk of the entire neighborhood. The whole goddamned town for that matter. He was filled with an odd mix of fear, anger, and abject humiliation. *It just keeps getting worse.*

Pete Esposito was waiting in his cruiser, the overhead light on, writing some notes to himself on the case. As he saw the headlights of the convoy approach, he closed his notebook, pocketed his pen, turned off the light, and got out to stand at the side of his cruiser.

He watched as the lead cruiser pulled up behind him. McKutcheon drove ahead, flipping the automatic garage door opener, pulling into David's garage. Esposito was filled with electricity but didn't let on.

He walked into the driveway, extending his hand. "Mr. Johnson, how ya holdin' up?" he asked.

"Never better, Pete. I tell you, I'm having the time of my fucking life. Really. You should try it some time."

Esposito remained silent for a few moments, preferring to let the anger and sarcasm dissipate in the evening air. "I need to talk to you. Can we go inside?"

"Do you have something?" David asked, stopping as if struck in the face. "You do, don't you?" he asked, not sure he wanted to hear what would come next.

In a scene reminiscent of Robinson Crusoe, David felt the panic rise from his bowels to his brain. Crusoe, stranded on his tiny mound of sand, wanted more than anything else to see another human being, to be able to talk to someone. Anyone. At least that's what he thought. Until that dreadful day when he saw footprints on the beach on the far side of the island. Suddenly, and without warning, he panicked at the mere thought that he was no longer alone.

And now here David stood—his only prayer to catch this psycho—about to be confronted with news of his attacker. He wasn't sure how he knew, but he did. He could feel it, and he froze at the idea that they might be getting close.

"Can we go inside?" Esposito said, ignoring David's question.

"Sure. Come in," David said, leading the way into the playroom.

David leaned against the pool table. Esposito pulled up a chair, took off his hat and laid it in his lap.

Esposito looked at David for a moment. "David, does the name Fenton Montague mean anything to you?"

David thought for a moment, staring back. His jaw finally dropped as he gawked at Esposito in disbelief. He was incredulous. "Fenton Montague?" he asked. "You're joking, right? I mean . . . I met him twenty years ago in Boston. I was still in college. Why?"

"Well, long story short, one of our men took the number off a car with Mass plates as you left for the station this morning. He didn't think much of it at the time. It was parked at the end of your road. He went back to check it out after you got on the train and found a sneaker print in the mud. Looks like we got a match with those found on your patio in Officer Bennett's blood."

"No shit?" David asked, feeling an odd sense of surprise and fear. "Fenton Montague? I can't believe it. You really think it's him?"

Esposito shrugged his shoulders slightly. "Don't know. Wanted to run the name by you first. Sounds like there's some connection."

"Connection? I . . . I don't know if you can call it that."

"But you know him?" Esposito wanted to know.

"Well, not really. No, I can't say I *know* him. But I met him long enough to know he's out of his mind."

"If he is, in fact, our man, that's a slight understatement. Feel like filling me in?"

"Well, there's not much to tell really. Shit, this was ages ago." David cocked his head, staring into space. "Well . . . let's see. One night my best friend and I were . . ."

—⁓—

It was very early Tuesday morning, October 31st, when Lieutenant Cedric Halliway and Detective Sergeant Scott Hill found themselves anxiously discussing the new break in the case over a somewhat hurried and edgy breakfast. Something inside both men told them they had just begun the homeward stretch.

"We got him, Ric," Hill said, punching the air with his fist, his mouth full of a ham and cheese omelet.

Halliway remained impassive. "Well, we know who he is anyway. Now we've got to find him," he said, making every attempt to conceal his excitement, from himself, as well as his partner.

"Oh, come on, Ric. I know you better than that," Hill said, smiling at his partner. "You can't pretend you're not just a little excited. Save the act for home."

"Let's just make darn sure we do everything by the book. I mean *everything*. We need to keep a tight leash on every player in this game now. This is one bastard I couldn't stand to see walk."

There was no question in their minds they had found their man. But it's a big country. Both men knew a felon can survive on the lam for years. Some are never caught. And even if they are, convictions are often harder to achieve than the public thinks. The two detectives were still a long way from home.

Both men fell silent as the waitress approached. "More coffee?" she asked.

"Yes, please," Hill answered for both men. "Make mine decaf."

Halliway waited for her to leave. "I've been in touch with Mass Registry of Motor Vehicles. They should be faxing a photo of Montague to the station as we speak."

"We've got to get into his place, Ric."

"Let's talk to Johnson first," Halliway said, taking a sip of his steaming hot coffee. "We'll drive up when we finish with him. We can spend the whole day and night there if need be. In the meantime, let's get in touch with the Mass state police. I want an eye on that apartment. We'll send them a fax after we speak with them. I want to know the second anyone fitting his description shows up."

"You think he's still living there? I mean, he's been

awful busy down here. Doesn't fit that he's driving back and forth."

Halliway was playing with his fruit cup now. Two things affected his appetite—nerves and excitement. Right now, he had a healthy dose of each. "I agree, but we don't have any choice," he said.

"I can't wait to snag this son of a bitch," Hill said, buttering an English muffin.

Halliway was silent. He prayed they'd catch him.

"You know, time's an issue here, Ric. It's Tuesday morning. If our boy's true to his word, he acts today. Sometime. I don't know what's going through Johnson's head, but he's got to be jumping out of his skin. You think? Hell, if I were in his shoes, I know I would be."

Halliway looked at his watch. "Let's see, it's a little after six now. We probably should have talked with him last night, but he begged me to put it off. Told me he already told Esposito everything he knows. I shouldn't let my feelings get in the way, but I feel sorry for the man. Figured it couldn't hurt to wait until everyone had a good night's sleep."

"Maybe you and me, but I don't think Johnson did much sleepin' last night. Still, you did the right thing. I would have done the same," Hill added, nodding his head.

"I told him we'd be by before seven. We should get going."

Hill motioned for the waitress, scribbling in his palm. "The sooner the better," he said.

The two state police detectives pulled into the Johnson driveway at 6:49 A.M. David sat in his office, his hands wrapped around a mug of black coffee. He stared blankly at the cubbyholes of his desk, taking in nothing. He was tired. What little sleep he'd gotten was interrupted by the most bizarre nightmares. He had showered and shaved by 4:30 A.M. and spent the last two hours trying to work on his profit and loss statement—an exercise in futility.

He looked out his window at the sound of the car pulling up his driveway. "Christ," he said. There were four of them. It looked like a drug bust. Would he ever have some explaining to do when this was all over. He could only imagine the rumors floating around the neighborhood. He had to laugh. With all that was happening, why he would even bother worrying about that now, he couldn't imagine.

David looked at the pictures of his family on the bookshelf. They'd been gone less than two days, and he was already sick with loneliness. He had called them from the office last night before leaving. It was wonderful to hear the kids. He missed the TV blaring, the fighting, the constant buzz of activity present in a house with children. It seemed so quiet. He wished he didn't have to be alone.

The thought of sneaking a swift drink flitted across his brain, but he decided against it. Not that the idea faded quickly. In fact, David toyed with it for some time, almost as if his admitting he was an alcoholic gave him the green light to drink in the morning. But that was a slippery slope, and as big as his problems were, he thought it best not to exacerbate things.

David picked up the phone on his desk and called Jonah's. "Come on, come on," he said, tapping his foot as the phone rang and rang. "Hi. You've reached the Roberts residence. We're unable to answer your call right now . . ." David didn't hear the rest. Only the beep woke him out of his daydream.

"Hey guys! It's Daddy," he said, faking his most enthusiastic voice. "I miss you and love you all. I can't wait to see you this weekend. Check and see if there's a hockey game. We'll all go. It'll be great. Jonah, this part of the message is for your ears only. Please listen carefully," David said, pausing for effect. "The police think they know who this wacko is. We've both met him, Jonah. If they're right, you need to call me as soon as possible. It's very important. Call me. Can't wait to see you. Bye."

Pete Esposito met Halliway and Hill in the driveway. He had been waiting since 6:30, and was in the middle of talking to Skates when they came up. "I want three men around this house all day today, Skates. No one comes up that driveway. Clear? Make sure someone's in back and in front at all times. If anyone has to take a shit, make damn sure they're replaced *before* going inside. Got it?"

"Clear as a bell, Cap."

"Tonight's Halloween. Who knows what's gonna be going on in the streets tonight. Block the drive with a cruiser as soon as Johnson leaves this morning. I don't want any kids up here."

"You got it."

"Anything out of the ordinary, I want a call immediately."

"Good morning, gentlemen," Halliway interrupted, extending a hand to Esposito.

"See you later, Cap. I got a dozen things to do," Skates said, smiling at the two men as he left.

"Thanks, Skates. Call me if you see anything," Esposito said to his man, nodding a hello to Halliway and Hill. "Lieutenant, Sergeant, good to see you."

"Thanks for getting here so early," Halliway said, getting right to the point. "I think your presence will be helpful. Particularly if you can interject when you think he's inadvertently left something out, or is telling it differently than he told you last night. What we learn here today could be of grave importance. Not only to the investigation, but hopefully to the conviction. We need everything."

"Roger," Esposito said.

David rose as the doorbell rang. "Here we go again," he mumbled as he went downstairs to answer the front door.

Halliway wore his calmest smile. "Mr. Johnson. Good morning, sir. We're sorry to have to interrupt your workday like this. I hope you understand."

"Of course. Come in, please."

The house was a disaster zone. David, caught in the grip of his Kafkaesque world, hadn't lifted a finger to clean a thing, save for removing the burned-out garbage can to the garage. While the stink had lessened with the passing of a few days, the house still harbored the unmistakable smell of smoke.

"I'm sorry for the mess, gentlemen. It wasn't exactly of my own making. We can talk in the playroom or in my office."

"Whichever is more comfortable for you, sir," Halliway said.

"Well, the office would be different for you guys, I guess. Let's try that."

"Lead the way," Esposito said, as the three men followed David up the steps to his office.

"Let me just grab a chair from the bedroom," David said, detouring to the master bedroom to retrieve one from the alcove. "All set," he said, returning with a chair under one arm and his coffee in his free hand.

The men climbed the last set of stairs to David's office. He sat in his leather chair, swiveling around to face the room. He left the other men to fend for themselves. "As I told you last night, Lieutenant, the Captain here knows just about everything I can remember about this Montague fellow. It wasn't as if we were friends or anything."

"Apparently not," Halliway said with the faintest of grins. "We'll try to make this as brief as possible. However, given the nature of the investigation and the seriousness of the crimes we believe this man has committed, I'm sure you understand the necessity to review this in the utmost detail. Being a businessman you're surely aware how things tend to get lost in the translation. It's simply too important for us to depend on Captain Esposito's version of what he thought he heard you say last night."

What? No tape recorder? "I understand fully. If it'll help you to catch this psycho, you can take all day. I'll help any way I can."

"Thank you. We appreciate your cooperation."

"We're going to tape this, just like last time, if you don't mind, Mr. Johnson," Hill added, pulling the small recorder from his jacket pocket.

Of course. David nodded his head, indicating it was all right with him.

"Mr. Johnson, I'm aware that we are going to ask you questions you may already have answered. If I could ask you, please, to pretend this is the first time you have heard these questions, it will be most helpful. Just take your time. Try to answer everything as fully as possible. Don't leave anything out, no matter how trivial it may seem. Okay?"

"Okay. Shoot," David said, his hands clasped in his lap.

David recounted, in the most accurate detail he could remember, the evening he and Jonah first encountered Fenton Montague. It was a long time ago. He had trouble with many of the more specific questions Halliway and Hill posed.

. . . "No, I'm sorry. I just don't recall if he had a limp or any peculiar characteristics. Perhaps the fact that I don't remember indicates he didn't. I just can't be sure. .

. . . "No, I don't recall if he said anything about military experience.

. . . "Again, to the best of my recollection, there's no memory of his mentioning weapons of any type. I think I'd remember if he showed us one. I'm pretty sure he didn't.

. . . "Yes, I think it would be accurate to describe his response as one of disappointment. I mean, I don't know what he expected from us. Apparently a hell of a lot more than we gave. I do know he had nowhere to go. We gave him twenty bucks.

. . . "That's a good question. Let me think about that for a minute . . . Well, I suppose that's partly true. We didn't really feel guilty, but on the other hand, we certainly didn't have to give him any money. Yeah, I guess if I'm honest with myself, I'd have to admit perhaps I felt we were being a little harsh. In hindsight, the very fact that we gave him some money probably indicates that we felt somewhat bad. But look, gentlemen, we didn't owe this guy anything. Shit, he was lucky to get a warm bed for a couple of nights."

It went on like this for over two hours; David was unable to believe that anything that happened the two nights Fenton had spent with them, or even the morning David told him to leave, could possibly have led anyone to this type of behavior. He kept thinking it must be some wild coincidence. In his mind he simply couldn't find any justification.

"Captain," Officer McKutcheon said, walking into the office, "I thought you'd like to know that we just located Montague's car. It's on a side street by the train station."

———

Fenton was acutely aware of the presence of people in the house. He had heard the cars pull up the driveway, the smattering of slamming doors, the doorbell, footsteps, voices. He was remarkably focused, and therefore, remarkably calm. He'd thought about this from every conceivable angle. Try as they might, the authorities simply could not out-think him on this one.

He peeled a banana he'd brought in his knapsack, marveling at its beauty. It even came with its own handle. God truly was an extraordinary individual. *I could never have thought of such a thing.* Fenton sat in the lotus position on a small wool blanket. he took small bites, chewing each one thoroughly.

This is beautiful. He was at a disadvantage now and he knew it. From the moment he entered David's house, he would be operating strictly on feel and assumptions. But the mere fact that he could pull the strings, direct this play, and not even be in the theater—the mere thought of his brilliance gave him goose bumps.

He was disappointed to think he'd planned this better than they could play the game. His parking by the train station was a stroke of genius. He wondered how many men they would use for David's commute and day at work. *A dozen? Probably more.* They would be looking everywhere but here.

But what if they hadn't noticed it? Could it be possible he had planned this diversion so well, only to have it go for naught? He didn't like this part of his plan. The not knowing was the hardest part. Not that it mattered. He would win either way. But it certainly took some of the fun out of it, just thinking they were missing the full joy of the ride. He had planned this a long time, and hated to think it was time poorly spent.

Of course, if they had found it, he knew the nature of the game would change radically. They would know who he was now. But that would be a little too little, a little too late. He was where he needed to be now. Nothing they learned from this moment on would be of any consequence to him.

In his mind's eye, he could see the detectives debating the meaning of finding his car where they did. Had he already taken a train into the city? Did this mean it was likely the attack would occur there? Would he be waiting at Grand Central? There were so many variables, they would be running around like the Keystone Kops trying to figure out what it meant, and how to handle it. *Just a little gas in the fire. You ain't seen nothin' yet.*

He knew what happened to sports teams that looked beyond their next, weaker opponent, toward the bigger game the following week. Fenton reminded himself he would be foolish to think about Jonah now. But he knew in his heart that David was the weaker prey. He hid behind his money and prestige. The simple fact was that his hands didn't have any calluses. Fenton knew that David didn't know how to fight. Behind his starched white shirts, Brooks Brothers ties, and money, there stood an emotional weakling. He was sure of it. Quick to give in. Easily tormented. Easily crushed.

Jonah, on the other hand, was different. He had left it all behind. Fenton tried to think what Harrison would be like. What was Jonah doing there? Not high finance, that was for sure. Fenton thought back to the night the three of them met. Both men drank heavily. David seemed rougher. A more shoot-from-the-hip personality. Jonah seemed more cerebral, even then.

Fenton was so excited to have found friends. He wanted desperately to show them what a neat person he was. His heart raced as he sat, thinking back to that moment in time when he felt his life had a chance to change for the better. Mother had never allowed him to have friends. None ever came to his house, and he was never allowed to visit anyone's home. Ever.

Fenton was socially stunted. He wasn't sure how to act, what to say. But they had talked to him! They bought him drinks. They invited him into their home. "Thank you, God," he remembered saying to himself. For once, Lady Luck was shining on him. He was going to make the best of it.

They could never know the trauma they had caused him. That morning, as David spoke, delivering the news Fenton knew was coming, he could only see David's mouth moving. When it was done and the words had been spoken, he retreated into himself. He fought the rejection. "I thought we were friends," he wanted to say. He was filled with pain. "Why don't you like me?" he wanted to ask. But it didn't matter. Like every other person in his life, they too had let him down.

David had tormented him. "This Jesus thing," he said. "I'm sorry, Fenton, but Jesus doesn't just come visit, and even if he did, Jesus wouldn't like it here. Look, we're not religious in this house. It would be best if you found a place more to your way of thinking. Nothing personal. Really. It's just not going to be a good fit."

But Fenton felt sure that at the first sign of danger, Jonah would take a stand. His conquest would require greater skill and more patience. *Oh well . . . constant dripping wears away the stone.*

He heard footsteps now. People talking in the hall. His mind said, "Go check it out, see if you can hear what they're saying." His soul said, "Sit right where you are, Fenton. It doesn't matter what they say, what they think they know. You have all the power." He finished his banana, tucking the peel behind a box to his right.

He closed his eyes, laid his hands in his lap, palms up, and sang to himself. In his mind. "I'm a lumberjack and I'm okay. I sleep all night and I work all day. Oh, I'm a lumberjack, and I'm okay . . ." He could see the darkness. Feel the fear. He was in the closet now. A scared, naked, nine-year-old boy. He felt the memory envelop him, fear shuddering down his spine. His body shook involuntarily for a moment, as his central nervous system performed its exorcism. His toes tingled.

His eyes still closed, Fenton could feel the warmth overtaking him. Back in time. The tears stopped flowing from the child in the closet. They were replaced instead, by the world to which he clung for his sanity. He leaned back and could hear his mother leave the room, shutting the door behind her. He was safe now. He would wait . . . still . . . quiet. Lost in a world he alone had created. And only he knew.

—⁓—

David sat in his office at work, smoking a cigarette, staring out his window. The morning commute had been a nightmare. He felt like Adolf Eichmann being escorted through the streets of Tel Aviv—fearful at every turn that someone would come out of the woodwork to murder him. This whole thing was quickly becoming untenable.

He thought perhaps he should have gone to Maine with Rebecca and the kids. There was no way he could keep this up much longer. For that matter, there was no way the police would keep this up much longer. He felt a deep quiver go down his spine, shaking his body with surprising fury. David extinguished his cigarette in his ashtray and sat with his elbows on his thighs, massaging his temples.

He wanted to call Linda, but wasn't sure it was the right thing to do. Certainly under different circumstances he would have picked up the phone in an instant. But he knew more than she did. How could he possibly call her, inquire about Mikey when he already knew he was dead? How could he carry on the conversation under those circumstances? The whole scenario would be surreal.

But certainly she would expect him to call. If, on the outside chance she did come back to work, how could he ever explain to her why he hadn't called? If he told her the truth, she'd probably blame him for the rest of her life. *Maybe. Shit, I don't know.*

It was becoming increasingly difficult to hide the fact

that something was going on. Say what you will about Wall Street, one thing's a given: the people who work there aren't dumb. Linda was out, David had been late two days in a row. No one could remember when that had happened before. And now there were strange men hanging in and around his office and around the trading floor. Something was up, and for once, the rumors weren't nearly as bad as the facts.

"Trooper Trowbridge," David said, without looking up. "Is it really necessary for you to stand here in my office all day? Surely, he's not going to just walk in here and start blasting away."

"Orders, sir."

"Jesus Christ. Orders. Look, I've got twenty people under me out there, none of whom has ever seen anyone stand in my office for more than half an hour at a time. This is going to become a problem. They already know something's up."

"Mr. Johnson, something is up, sir. At the risk of sounding rude, I would think you'd prefer to have it this way than to have us just pack up and go home."

David turned to look out his window. "I never said I wanted you guys to go home. But isn't there some kind of a happy medium?"

"I don't know what to say, sir. You have a maniac after you who's already shown he doesn't mind killing. It's just impossible for us to know when or where he'll show. If it's that much of a problem, I s'pose you can speak to my commanding officer."

David wanted to scream. He was losing his grip. The events of the past few days had begun to wreak devastation with his psyche. He didn't know which way was up any longer, completely out of the loop on all events affecting his life. Not only did he not have control over Montague, he felt as if he had effectively lost control of his ability to breathe without permission. He was trapped in his new, warped world, and felt every ounce of its suffocating hold. David preferred to die than live this way.

"Look, I can't take it any longer. Enough's enough. If

he comes, he comes. If he kills me, he kills me. At this point, I really don't give a shit. Let's just call the whole damned thing off. I'll fend for myself."

Trowbridge looked at David. *He just doesn't get it.* "I'm afraid it's not that simple, sir. This psycho killed a police officer. Even if I wanted to leave you alone, I couldn't."

"What are you telling me?" David asked, plopping himself into his chair, feeling defeated. "If I told you to leave . . . that I didn't want protection any longer . . . called the top brass and told them to forget the whole goddamned thing, you wouldn't do it?"

"I'm afraid that's right, sir," Trowbridge said, re-crossing his legs. "Frankly, at this point we're more interested in catching him than we are in protecting you. Now, *please,* don't misunderstand me. We want to keep you safe, but I'm sure you know that's not the only reason we're doing this."

"The thought's crossed my mind."

"Well, your mind isn't playing tricks on you."

David rose from his chair, opened his front desk drawer, and swallowed three ibuprofen tablets dry. "Well ain't that fucking grand? How long do we do this for? What if he doesn't come after me as he said he would? Is this just an open-ended thing?"

"I can't say, sir. That's a decision to be made at higher levels. Listen," Trowbridge said, checking to see that the door to David's office was fully closed, "I can't even begin to imagine what your life is like right now—"

"Life?" David asked with a sarcastic laugh. "That's a good one."

Trowbridge hesitated for a moment, attempting to appear sympathetic. "We need your help, Mr. Johnson. I'm no shrink, but please, sir, try and relax. I know this sounds stupid, but maybe you can breathe deep. Close your eyes. That kind of thing."

"Give me a fucking break, will you? I need this like I need AIDS. I'm not closing my eyes and I'm not going to breathe deep."

"I'm sorry you feel that way. I'm trying to help. We

ain't goin' away, Mr. Johnson. At least not today. So you might as well try and find a way to deal with it. That's all I'm sayin'."

David exhaled, his shoulders drooping. "Look, I'm sorry. It's just that . . . shit, I don't know. Shit!" he thundered, loud enough to be heard outside his office. Several people glanced in his direction. David lowered his voice. "I mean, my whole goddamn life has become some kind of a *Twilight Zone* episode. I just can't believe this is happening to me. Sometimes I think I'm going to snap. Can we just go home now? There's no way I'm going to get shit done here today."

"Well, I don't know. I'll need to call headquarters. It's a little early. They may not want you breaking your normal schedule."

"Oh, that's great. Listen, while you're at it, ask them when it would be okay for me to take a dump, all right?"

Winter comes early to the state of Maine. Most years, the first significant snowfall occurs before Thanksgiving. This particular year didn't look to be any different. There's an old wives' tale that says the bushier the squirrels' tails grow in the fall, the worse the winter will be. While Jonah was not really a believer in old wives' tales, he was pretty sure the squirrels looked thicker than usual this season.

On this Halloween day, the sky was a dull gray, locking in a dampness that, when coupled with the cold Canadian air from the north, found its way right to the marrow of your bones. They were all riding horses, Caleb on top of Allycrocker with Jonah, and Sumner on top of Caractacus with Victoria. Thomas Jefferson was Jonah's favorite figure from the American Revolution, and it was in his honor that he named his two favorite Arabian horses after Jefferson's. Rebecca rode alone atop an older mare Jonah had jokingly named Equity.

Rebecca had been a wreck all night. The anxiety of what would happen the following day was unshakable. It was inescapable, like the insufferable humidity of a hot summer day. She could not escape it, nor release herself from its grasp. The fear was pervasive—present in her every waking thought.

Despite the unrelenting panic she felt, there would be no rest for Rebecca Johnson. She still had motherly duties to perform. She had to discipline her children, see to their baths, their meals, and their well-being. That, in and of itself, was exhausting work, but with the added burden of fearing for her husband's life and the safety of her own, her maternal obligations took on a weight she could hardly bear. She loved her children dearly, but there were times she felt all she wanted to do was curl up in a ball and wait in bed for the nightmare to cease.

When she spoke to David last evening she told him that Jonah and Vickie thought it would be a good idea to get out of the house. She told David they'd suggested a day trip to Peaks Island. The kids would love the ferry ride, they could eat lunch at the local restaurant on the island, and have dinner in Portland before heading back for the night.

"David, honey," Becky said to her husband. "I don't know what to do. It just seems wrong to be out all day, knowing that you . . . knowing you're going through such hell."

David was adamant. "Becky, I think it's a great idea. What can you do from Maine anyway? Believe me, sweetie, I got more cops around me than the Pope. I'm beginning to think this whole thing was a stupid idea to begin with. Christ, even if he tries, he'll never get to me. Believe me, I'm safer than you and the kids. Go. Have a good time."

"Really? They're really giving you protection?"

"Protection? Honey, it's crazy. I never have less than four or five cops around me at any one time. I can't even breathe. It'll just make me all the crazier knowing that I'm down here going through this crap and you're up there just sitting by the phone all day. Please go. I can at least live vicariously."

Rebecca was unconvinced. "You really think I should?" she asked. "It just doesn't feel right."

"Nothing would make me happier. Really. Please go

and try to enjoy yourself. Trust me. Nothing's going to happen down here. Not unless the guy's got an atom bomb."

"I'll go if you say it'll make you happier. I don't know how much fun I'll have."

"Try. For me."

There were many acres of woods on Jonah's property. In his free time, he spent countless hours clearing bridle paths through which he and Victoria would eventually ride for hours. Through the woods, about a half mile in, just over the crest of a small rise, there was a long rock wall, behind which was a clearing. This marked the back forty of his parents' farm. He'd spent many a glorious summer there as a young boy. At least that's how he viewed it now.

It was here Jonah learned how to ride a horse and drive a tractor. On those very pastures, Jonah's father taught him how to bale hay. It was hard, thankless work that took place every summer, right in the thick of the stickiest, steamiest, dog days of the season. The misery of the chore only exacerbated by the need for jeans and a long-sleeved flannel shirt, buttoned all the way to the neck. Nothing itches like baled hay.

Jonah remembered how he hated to bale. His father would wake him early in the morning. "Jonah, come play with me, son." It was a siren song from which Jonah used to pray he could break free. But his father loved to bale. There was something cathartic in it for him. Something that soothed his tight, urban-wound nerves.

Now, thirty years later, Jonah looked back on those days with longing. He wished he could see his father again. Tell him how much he loved him, how thankful he was for all he had taught him. In his younger, more heady drinking days, he wished his father could have lived to see his success. But the need to fulfill his ego lessened with time—and sobriety. Now, Jonah only longed to be half the man his father was. He worried now and then that he was failing.

"Let's stop here," Jonah said, getting off his horse, reaching up and grabbing Caleb under the arms, hoisting him to the ground. "You see this bridge here? I built it myself."

The kids ran back over the bridge, jumping up and down on it, marveling at its uncompromising construction.

"You built this yourself, Uncle Jonah?" Caleb asked.

"Yep. Even designed it myself."

"Cool!" Sumner chimed in. "How long'd it take ya?"

"I started it two years ago in June. Didn't finish until the end of that summer."

"Man! This thing'll be here forever," Caleb added.

"Hope so," Jonah responded, pride evident in his voice.

Rebecca shimmied her horse next to Caractacus. "They never grow up, do they?"

Vickie looked at her and smiled. "No, not really. There's always a little boy inside, isn't there? But you know, I've never seen Jonah have more fun than when he was building that stupid bridge."

"God, I wish David would walk away from it, Vickie. Just like Jonah. We never see him. He's so married to that damn job. Sometimes . . . I just want to scream. His kids are growing up without him. I've done all I can do."

"Do you still love him?" Victoria asked, watching Jonah and the kids scamper all over the bridge.

"Caleb, honey, be careful, please," Becky called out, watching her children like a hawk. "I think so, yes. You know, there's a lot of water under the bridge. I think if he kept drinking and working . . . I don't know. I've thought of leaving him. But the kids would be devastated."

Victoria Roberts sat quietly on her horse. She felt for her best friend. Rebecca was the hapless victim of a workaholic functioning alcoholic. Vickie had been there. There wasn't a thing Becky was feeling she hadn't felt herself. Her heart was heavy with sadness at the life in which she saw Rebecca trapped. The saddest thing of all was that only David could do anything about it.

"Maybe you should try Al-Anon. You need someone to confide in, Becky. Someone to share your pain with."

"Mom!" Caleb screamed. "Come here. Come on. Look at this. It's so cool."

"I'll be right there, sweetie! Hang on one sec!" she yelled in his direction, then finished her thoughts with Victoria. "He's admitted he's an alcoholic. He knows he has to stop. I'm praying things will get better."

"Just don't be naive, Becky. Jonah used to tell me some of the sayings he heard at AA meetings. One of them was Fake it til you make it. He says it means that many times, once someone gives up booze, their life tends to get worse before it gets better. It's like having the flu. You can lie in bed for hours feeling like crap, but you don't begin to feel better till after you vomit."

Becky's heart sank. She sat impassively, not betraying the fear in her heart. "But it gets better, right?"

"Oh, it definitely gets better. Just don't expect miracles. Sobriety is a slow, painful process. It's not an event."

"Mommy! Come on, Mom! Look how cool this stream is. I can see fish in it. Come here!"

"I'm coming! Hold your horses," she said, looking at Vickie. "Motherhood calls."

As Rebecca dismounted, she realized for the first time that she was jealous of her friend. Victoria had the perfect life—not to mention a sober husband. How often appearances deceive. At first glance, who in their right mind would ever think Rebecca Johnson was not the happiest woman alive?

She handed her reins to Victoria and jogged with fake enthusiasm to the bridge. Victoria eyed her, thinking perhaps she and Jonah had made a mistake not having children. Something about them was so angelic . . . so innocent. Though she would never admit it, she was sometimes bored with her rural, rustic life. Certainly there must be more to it than churning butter and milking cows.

They had gotten out early that morning, a thick frost covering the grass in the pastures. After Rebecca had spent a suitable length of time eyeing the bridge and looking at fish, Jonah decided they had better get going.

"Okay, let's get back," he said. "We have a big day ahead of us. You guys ever been on a ferry before?"

———∾———

It was after 5:30 P.M. on Halloween day when the green light came for David to head home. He normally left later than that, but through channels, Halliway was informed of David's mental state, and felt that forcing him to wait any longer would be tantamount to cruel and unusual punishment. He could only imagine what was going through his mind.

David and Trowbridge decided it simply wasn't feasible for them to sit there all day, that it would be acceptable for them to walk the trading floor. David had spent the last two hours touring Trowbridge through his love in life, and ironically, realized afterwards that it was the most relaxing two hours he'd experienced since Thursday.

There was something about the frenetic energy—the responsibility and huge sums at stake—that juiced him. David was made for his job. He wished it could go on forever. But in the back of his mind he knew it would never be the same again.

"These are the firm's bond trading desks," he said to Trowbridge, waving his hand across an area of the huge room. In an average week, we will trade a few trillion dollars through here."

Trowbridge wore a dubious expression. "Trillion?" he asked.

"With a capital T."

"Man. That's unbelievable," Trowbridge said, shaking his head.

"It's pretty well compartmentalized. Those boys over there, near the far corner, they trade primarily government agency bonds. We just call them agencies. Freddie Macs, Sallie Maes, Ginnie Maes, all sorts of bonds morally backed by the US government, but not issued by them."

"What's a Sallie Mae?" Trowbridge wanted to know.

"That's a nickname for the Student Loan Marketing Association. Ever get a school loan?" David asked.

"Yeah."

"Well, your loan was most likely grouped with hundreds of others of its kind and pooled into a bond that ends up getting traded a thousand times over through dozens of places just like this."

"No shit?"

"No shit."

And so it went for the better chunk of the afternoon. David explained to his protector the ins and outs of the various trading desks cramped in rows and cubicles on the football-sized trading floor.

"I'll be damned," Trowbridge responded to some tidbit of information he'd never even thought of before.

"Neat, huh?" David asked.

"Man, I'll say. What do they do over there?" Trowbridge asked, pointing to the opposite side of the floor. Though he hadn't forgotten his reason for being there, still, he was thoroughly enjoying himself. There aren't many people who get to see the inside of the capitalist system at work. Yet, every person on that floor would have dropped their jaw if they'd caught a glimpse of Trowbridge's loaded .357 Magnum or his leather extra-ammunition pouch.

"Those guys there trade zero coupon bonds," David responded.

"Zero what?"

David could have given tours of his world all day long. He hadn't thought about the mess of his life once the entire time. The tour was a godsend. He desperately needed the break from reality.

"Listen, this is great," Trowbridge interrupted. "I could do this for a week. Really. But I should call in."

Reality. Trowbridge's comments stung David. "Oh yeah," David said, feeling his heart grow heavy again. "Sorry, I get carried away."

"Hey, don't be sorry. That was real fun. I can see why you like it."

When they finally received the okay to leave, David felt oddly at ease. Like the naughty boy who's been ordered to wait in his room for two hours for his father to come deliver the spanking: at some point you just want him to enter. Not because you like the punishment, but because in time, the wait becomes the more painful.

"Maybe this whole thing will finally come to an end." David said optimistically.

"Let's hope so."

"Do you think he'll come after me in Grand Central?"

"I really couldn't say, sir," Trowbridge answered non-committally. As he thought about the question, what he really wanted to say was, "I sure as hell hope not."

There was a very real danger present—quite possibly lethal, and both men knew it. After Fenton's car was found, there was tangible reason to believe he might make his attempt in Grand Central. Despite their brave facade, both knew there was a good chance either of them could be killed tonight. Whether you work on Wall Street or for the state police, that's a fear you never get used to.

As David's detail approached Grand Central, everyone was quiet. The fear of the unknown gripping each man differently, with no one escaping the common denominator. David almost wished Fenton would show himself, Jack Ruby style. He really didn't care if he was successful or not. At least it would be over. And anyway, in Dallas, the cops weren't expecting it. You could hardly say that tonight.

By contrast, to a man, the New York state police detail assigned to protect David hoped like hell they could get him on that train and be done with it. No one wanted a shoot-out. If this wacko was going to come out of the woodwork, let him do it on Connecticut's time.

When the handoff was complete Trowbridge and the other troopers turned and walked away. "Thank God," one of them said.

———⁓———

It's a three hour drive from Darien, Connecticut, to Boston, Massachusetts. Halliway and Hill had finished questioning David just before 9:30 A.M., and were on I-

95 north by 9:45. As usual, Hill drove. Halliway used the car phone as they passed one turn-of-the-century industrial town after the other. In the frenzy of activity the veterinarian had been almost completely forgotten. Once they'd learned the killer's identity, priorities had quickly changed. Still, Halliway felt he should speak with the vet. Perhaps he might have something . . . anything . . . that would shed more light on the situation, or at least assist in an eventual prosecution.

He looked up Yallow's number in his notebook, and dialed. He turned to Hill as he waited for Yallow to come to the phone. "Scott, did you remember to call the Mass state police? I don't want to hang around for the landlord to let us into his apartment. I want to make sure he's there waiting, with key in hand."

"Yeah, I spoke to Druckman before we left Johnson's place. Said to—"

Halliway stopped him mid sentence by putting his left forefinger in the air. "Good morning, Doctor. I apologize for not getting to you sooner. Especially given the fact we had you drop everything to perform that autopsy first thing yesterday."

"No problem, Lieutenant," Yallow responded. "Always a pleasure to help."

"I'm interested if you found anything that might assist us in the investigation of Officer Bennett's murder," Halliway said, not letting on they already knew who it was. The fewer people who knew that the better off they would be. "Anything at all? If it doesn't help us catch him, anything you can provide might help us put him away when we do."

"Well, like I was telling Captain Esposito yesterday, yes and no. The cause of death was asphyxiation by hanging. No doubt about that. The neck wasn't broken—"

"Was not?" Halliway asked.

"Correct. I'm afraid the poor dog died slowly. There was the usual V bruise around the neck one might expect to find with any hanging victim, animal or human. Due to arterial pressure, there were many small areas of compartmentalized bleeding. We call them petechiae.

They were numerous in quantity and varied in size. Primarily in and around the moist areas of the face, the lips, inside the mouth, the eyelids. Where you'd normally expect to find them."

Halliway wished Yallow would just get to the point. He'd seen death many times over the years, more often than the man he was speaking to. "Anything that would help us determine the killer?" he asked. "Fingerprints? Foreign blood? Something of that nature?"

"No, I'm afraid not. As for cause of death, it was clean. There were no subdural hematomas, or anything else for that matter, that would cause me to believe the dog had been beaten or otherwise mishandled. I'm afraid your man didn't leave a scrap of biological evidence."

"Toxicology results?"

"We came up empty there too. Of course, there are an awful lot of toxins out there, Lieutenant. But I have a lab here and tested for the usual suspects with what my facilities can handle here, arsenic, cyanide, chloral hydrate, ethanol, carbon monoxide. Nothing. I'm afraid if you want to find out more than that you may have to wait a few weeks."

"No, that's all right. Dead end, uh?" Halliway asked, not really disappointed. He might have been more so, had he not believed they'd already identified the killer. For a fleeting moment, he hoped they weren't after the wrong man.

Yallow responded to Halliway's question. "As for the body, yes. However, I did find something under the collar which I assume you'll find of some importance."

Halliway's interest in the conversation suddenly rejuvenated. "Really? What's that?"

"Well, as you know, it's customary in all autopsies to describe clothing worn by the deceased. Generally, in the case of domestic animals, this is limited to . . ."

Halliway had witnessed more autopsies than Doctor Yallow had probably performed. *It's only a dog.* "What did you find, Doctor?"

"Well, neatly taped to the inside of the collar was a small note. It reads—hang on, I've got it here somewhere—Here it is. Let's see, can't see anything without my glasses."

Hill looked at Halliway with a slightly quizzical, what-the-hell-is-going-on face.

"Let's see, 'You must lose a fly to catch a trout.'"

Halliway squinted. "Anything else?"

"No, I'm afraid not."

"Is it handwritten or typed?"

"Typed."

"Doctor, would you be kind enough to put that in a paper bag? I'll have an officer come by to pick it up."

"Of course. I'm sorry I couldn't be of more help."

"On the contrary, Doctor. You've been most helpful. Thank you again."

"What the hell was that all about?" Hill asked, turning to Halliway as he hung up the phone.

"Well, it seems Mr. Montague has more than a passing interest in proverbs."

"Oh yeah? What'd he find?"

"He found a note taped inside the collar. Something like, You must lose your fly to catch a trout."

"No shit?"

"It's what the man said, or something to that effect."

"Inside the collar? How the hell'd he do that?" Hill asked.

"Must have waited for the dog to die first. At least pass out. Then put it there. That, or he has a heck of a way with animals."

"You see, Ric? What'd I tell ya? Cool as a cucumber. This guy's scary."

"I know."

—⁂—

Officer Warren McKutcheon listened intently to the message transmitting through his ear plug. "Green, ready," came the word from one of his men.

"Roger that, Green," Skates answered. "Blue? You in position?" he asked into the mouthpiece wrapping around his cheek.

"Roger. Blue, all set."

"Skates!" one of his men yelled from the driveway. "It's Esposito!"

Officer McKutcheon strode across the sloping front lawn toward his cruiser, noticing one of his men in an evergreen across the lawn. He spoke quietly into his mouthpiece again. "Red, make sure you're deep enough into that thing. Use those branches to your advantage."

"Roger that."

"Ten-three, Cap'n. What's up?" Skates asked, picking the microphone up off the front seat.

"Just checking in. How you makin' out?"

"All squared away here. An earthworm's not gettin' in here tonight. Not unnoticed anyhow."

"Good. Listen, get everyone in position and get out of sight. If our man's ever gonna show, he's not going to do it if the place looks like the Maginot Line."

"Just gettin' ready to head to the train station. Everyone's set. Supposed to rain—hard. Could be a bitch."

"Them's the breaks," Esposito said. "Now go."

"Yellow? You read me?" Skates asked, returning to the task at hand.

"Yellow. In position."

"Stay put in that barn. Our boy likes the back. Better than even odds, if he comes tonight, he comes your way."

"I can only pray he does."

"Okay, boys. Let's roll. We got a train to catch," Skates said to the officers loitering near their cruisers in the driveway. "This is Rainbow. We're rolling. If everything goes according to plan, we'll be back here in half an hour. Stay put and stay quiet."

"What time's his train due in?" one of the men in the driveway asked.

"Seven thirty-four. Let's go."

"Roll 'em, roll 'em, roll 'em," somebody sang, as they all got in their cruisers and backed out of the Johnson driveway.

"Trooper Longdon," Skates said, by way of a hello to the Connecticut state policeman, as the doors to the Metro-North train opened.

Longdon nodded. "Officer McKutcheon."

"I take it there weren't any problems?"

"Not a hitch."

"That's the way we like it," Skates said, walking toward David. "Mr. Johnson. You know the routine. Follow me, sir."

David was now an official prisoner of his own life. What had started as an apparent sick little joke had now evolved into a living nightmare—a web of fear, uncertainty, and protective measures that affected everything he did. He was almost numb.

Let's see . . . my family's gone. Barney's dead. My house is destroyed. Mikey's dead. Bennett's dead. My every waking move is monitored by scores of men. I get it now. I'm having a nervous breakdown. God damn you, Fenton Montague! You are the human version of the Ebola virus. Everything you touch dies! There can be no peace in my life until you die too. If it's the last thing I ever do, I will not rest until I personally see you laid six feet under. He laughed aloud.

"What was that, sir?" McKutcheon asked.

"What?"

"You just laughed," McKutcheon said, looking at David.

"I did?"

"Something funny?"

"Yeah. The whole fucking thing. Don't you think?"

Skates glanced at one of the other men in the protective diamond and raised his eyebrows. "Mr. Johnson, I'm sorry to do this," Skates said, placing David in his Range Rover. "But could I ask you to lie on the seat for a moment? I'll be right back."

"Sure thing," David said, staring out the windshield, not moving from his upright position.

Skates jogged to the lead cruiser. "Jimmy, get on the horn. Tell dispatch we need a doctor. I'm worried the pressure may be gettin' to him. Let's just take the precaution. Have him meet us at the Johnsons'."

The ride home was quiet and uneventful. Neither David nor Skates spoke a word the whole trip. Skates occasionally turned to look at David, trying to discern his mental state. It was a tough read. David sat still in the seat—not moving, not speaking, staring straight ahead.

Something in David had become the killer now. He dreamed of the pleasure he'd feel in ripping the life from Mr. Fenton Montague. David envisioned him on his knees, begging for mercy . . . crying. David's heart raced as he pictured the bullet entering Fenton's forehead, blowing a grapefruit-size hole out the back of his head.

The small indiscretion with his laughter, and the attention it brought, caused him discomfort and unwanted attention. He was careful now, as he played Fenton's murder out a dozen times in his mind, not to give himself away. He didn't smile or move his lips as he softly and secretively massaged the revolver in his right outside jacket pocket.

I will wait, he thought. *For as long as it takes, I'll wait. So you think I'm a puppet whose strings you can pull at will? No . . . You will come and I will be prepared for you. Perhaps, Fenton, you misjudge me? I'm not quite the lightweight you believe I am. Come on, big boy. I'm waiting.*

As the Range Rover entered Woodbury, the two escort cruisers drove past, leaving Skates and David to themselves. There was plenty of help neatly hidden away at home. They pulled into the driveway just before 7:50 P.M. David was surprised to see an ambulance parked in front of his house.

"You guys expecting the worst?" he asked.

"Just a precaution, Mr. Johnson. I thought it wouldn't be a bad idea to have a doctor take a look at you—"

"What the fuck for?"

"You've been under a great deal of stress lately and well . . . frankly, I thought maybe you might want a tranquilizer or something."

David laughed. "Tranquilizer, huh? Shit, McKutcheon, you don't need to send an ambulance out here to give me a fucking tranquilizer. I've got the best stocked medicine cabinet in the state."

As Skates pulled into the garage, he turned and looked seriously at David. "Listen to me, Mr. Johnson. I can't tell you what to do—"

"Damn right you can't," David interrupted.

Skates closed his eyes and inhaled. "Truth is, I'm concerned about you. Nothing personal. I think a nightmare like this could put any one of us over the edge."

"I am not over the edge, god damnit!"

Skates put his hands out, trying to calm David's emotions. "I didn't say you were. All I'm saying is it can't hurt to have someone look you over. Maybe they can give you something. Might help you to relax. You know? Get a good night's sleep."

"I could use one of those."

"I'm sure. We need you alert tomorrow. It's not going to help any of us if we're protecting a zombie. Just talk to them. I don't even know what they're gonna recommend, if anything. But whatever it is, if you don't feel like doin' it, then fine. You're a big boy. Let's just see what they have to say."

David was defiant. "Whatever. I don't give a shit. Maybe they can knock me out. I won't have to think about any of this crap until tomorrow."

"Yeah . . . well, doubtful."

"Hey, a man can dream, can't he?"

—◦◦◦—

Like a prizefighter waiting in his locker room before the title bout, Fenton's adrenaline began to pump. Tonight was the night. All his waiting, watching, planning—it would all be worth it after tonight.

He was focused now. There were no thoughts of Maine—of Jonah. He played every move in his mind over and over again. His only true concern was that in his haste to secure a clean escape, he would be unable to enjoy David's death. He wanted to savor the pain . . . the fear . . . the anguish. He wanted to watch him bleed—taste his blood. However, there appeared little chance of that tonight. The more he dallied, the greater the chance of capture. Fenton thought he'd go insane if he were caught, unable to complete his task. He wondered what insanity was like.

It must be cold outside. He wrapped the wool blanket around him. Fenton sat in the lotus position—quiet, still, emotionless. He breathed through his nose, his eyes closed. He was going through the actions he would take on this night, virtually step by step.

He was aware of activity around him though he wasn't sure what it was. He could hear car engines periodically throughout the day, doors closing, voices, walkie-talkies. At one point, a few hours ago, he'd been startled to hear footsteps on the roof. *Are they on to me? Did they somehow know?* But they passed. He chastised himself for even doubting.

Without warning, he twitched his face to fight back tears. He was in his mother's kitchen now. He was eight, maybe nine years old. They sat opposite each other, eating their dinner quietly. Fenton was afraid with every bite he took. He painstakingly tried to eat quietly, not wanting to rattle his silverware on the plate. His napkin was squarely in his lap. He dared not ask for seconds or more milk or to have his mother pass him anything. He would eat exactly what he was given. Nothing less. Nothing more.

"Fenton, I thought I told you to make your bed this morning," his mother said out of nowhere.

He looked up at her, his face growing drawn and pinched. "I did, Mother."

"You did, did you? Go take a look and come back here."

He left the kitchen as directed, went to his bedroom, and stood in the doorway looking at his bed. It was made. He knew he'd made it. He walked closer, looking it over. He didn't see anything wrong.

"I did make it, Mother. I just looked," he said, taking his seat at the kitchen table.

Fenton's mother stood, rage forming in her eyes. "Come with me, young man," she said, walking from the kitchen to his bedroom. She stood at the foot of his bed and pointed. "That, Fenton, is what we call a wrinkle. Do you see it?"

Oh God! Please, God. "Yes."

"You see it now but didn't see it this morning?" she asked, her arms crossed over her chest.

"Well . . . I . . . I was late for school, and I—"

"Don't talk back to me young man! Who do you think you are?"

He started to cry. Nothing infuriated his mother more than tears. He tried to hold back. With all his might, he tried. "It's so small, Mother. I must have missed it. I'm sorry," he said softly, hanging his head.

"Sorry? That's all you have to say? You're sorry? Look at me when I'm talking to you."

He looked up, a lone tear streaming down his right cheek. He was defeated now. There would be no escaping her wrath.

"Take off your clothes!" she roared.

"Mother, please . . . Please don't."

"Now!"

When he finally stood naked in front of her, she looked him up and down. "What do you think I should do, Fenton?"

He stood with his hands at his sides. He didn't dare cover his genitals. "I don't know, Mother," he said despondently, his head hanging on his chest.

"What was that? I didn't hear you."

He hesitated. "I should be put in the closet."

"Really?" she asked sarcastically. "Not tonight, Fenton. I believe you truly are sorry. You see the error of your ways, don't you?"

"Oh yes, Mother," he said, feeling a glimmer of hope. "I promise. I'll never do it again. Never."

"Promises are like pie crust, Fenton. They are made to be broken. Lie down," she said sternly. "You will sleep there tonight. And I don't want to see a blanket on you when I come in here in the morning."

Fenton shook his head quickly and opened his eyes. Tears poured down his face. He looked around the attic as if to check and see if anyone had just witnessed his past. He wiped his eyes and cheeks with the blanket and took a deep breath.

"David," he whispered. "You were my friend. I

needed you. Trusted you. And you threw me out like
yesterday's garbage. *Now* you are my enemy. Tonight,
you die."

———

On Newberry Street in Boston, Scott Hill pulled the
Caprice up behind a double-parked Massachusetts state
police cruiser. He pulled out his cruiser's Connecticut
state police identification shield and laid it on the
dashboard. Halliway sat motionless for a short while,
taking in the neighborhood. Like a dry sponge, he soaked
up its ethnic makeup, socioeconomic characteristics, the
makes of cars lining the street, and the general upkeep of
the Victorian-era row houses.

He observed that this was a nice neighborhood.
Quaint. Old. He guessed it dated back to the mid to
latter part of the 1800s. Though it was daylight now,
Halliway could envision the street at night. The old-
fashioned looking street lamps enhanced the Victorian
feel. In his mind, he could easily picture what Newberry
Street looked like one hundred years ago. In fact, with
the exception of the cars and the paved streets, the
neighborhood probably had not changed much.

When Halliway had visually satisfied himself, he took
a few notes, got out of the car, and joined Detective Hill
at the foot of Fenton's stoop. He noticed there were still
wrought-iron scrapers and rings in the granite steps,
remnants of a bygone era when people scraped their
boots after hitching their horses.

Hill was busy speaking with a Massachusetts state
trooper. Halliway approached in silence. "I've got the
warrant here, Ric," Hill said to Halliway as he joined the
conversation. "Trooper Whitaker here was nice enough
to bring it along."

"Thank you," Halliway said, extending a hand. "Lieutenant Cedric Halliway, Connecticut state police."

Halliway was thirty years his senior. Something about
him reminded Whitaker of his grandfather. "Hi, Lieutenant. Nice to meet you," the trooper said. "Lincoln
Whitaker. Just call me Linc. Actually, that warrant is

your copy. As you know, we need the original to file with the courts."

"I understand," Halliway responded.

"So, your partner here tells me we got ourselves a real psycho on the loose."

"It appears so. Are you joining us in the search?"

"Yes, if it's just the same with you. The boys at HQ get a little antsy when we start crossing state lines."

"I understand, believe me. If I could just ask you this favor? Please don't touch anything until we've had a chance to look it over. You understand, I'm sure."

"You bet. This is strictly protocol, Lieutenant. The place is all yours. I don't plan on touchin' anything. But if you need a hand, just holler. Deal?"

"Deal. Where's the landlord?" Halliway asked, annoyance creeping into his voice.

"Already come and gone. You know these guys. Wasn't interested in sticking around. Said just to close the door behind us. It locks automatically."

Halliway looked skyward as the first drop of rain hit the meaty part of his left hand. "Let's do it. No sense getting wet."

"Follow me," Whitaker said, taking the granite steps two at a time.

Fenton's apartment was on the third floor. As they climbed the stairs, Hill was struck by the ornate banister. "They don't make 'em like this anymore."

"Right." Whitaker added. "This whole Back Bay section is nice. I'd love to live here if I didn't have kids."

"How many do you have?" Halliway asked, his breathing growing more labored as they ascended the flights of steps.

"Three. Five, seven, and eleven. Best thing that ever happened to me. You?"

"Two. Twenty-seven and thirty. Got two grandkids."

"Hey. Congratulations."

"Thanks," Halliway added quietly as they approached the third-floor landing, not bothering to offer that one of them was mentally retarded. The thought of his precious granddaughter made his heart grow heavy, and while the other two men couldn't see them, his eyes assumed a wounded look. He would never get over it. Get used to it, yes. Get over it, never. His heart bled for his daughter and her husband.

"Apartment twelve," Whitaker said to no one in particular, standing aside as he pushed the door open. "Call me if you need me."

Hill entered the apartment first. He stepped inside a few feet and stopped. Halliway followed. The two men stood side by side, their tan raincoats touching one another. They'd done this many times before. Instinct took over now.

"What do you think, Scott?"

"Neat, isn't he?" Hill answered.

Halliway looked around. "My wife would be jealous."

Walking in the direction of the living room, he clasped his hands behind his back and soaked it all in. There were plants everywhere. All kinds of plants—hanging plants, viney plants, bushy plants, and small trees.

He thought of the story his kids used to love, *Where the Wild Things Are*. The lead character, a boy named Max, is sent to his bedroom by his mother. While there, his imagination takes over and his entire room turns into a jungle. Fenton's apartment was startlingly similar.

Halliway walked to the bay window overlooking Newberry Street and took in the view. On the sill were various items of gardening paraphernalia: a pair of trimmers, Miracle-Gro, sprayers, a watering can. He took a step closer and leaned down. On the edge of the sill sat a small frame containing a saying handwritten in calligraphy. He tilted his head down slightly, using the upper part of his bifocals, and read aloud. "Genius Is An Infinite Capacity For Taking Pains."

"What'd ya say, Ric?" Hill called out from the bathroom.

"Nothing."

Halliway had said something, of course, but Hill knew that nothing meant nothing we have to talk about now. He knew all too well they'd get to everything before they were through. Whatever it was, Hill would see it before their day was done.

Halliway turned and walked slowly toward the bedroom, observing everything he passed. He stopped and looked around. It dawned on him now that there was nothing on the walls. Not one thing. Not a picture, map, painting, poster. *Nothing*. Not just here, but in the entire apartment. *Odd*. He didn't think he'd ever seen that before.

Walking down the hall he stopped outside the bathroom. "Anything interesting?" he asked his partner.

"I'll say. Take a look at this," Hill said, stepping back and pointing to the open cabinet beneath the sink.

Halliway stepped in, knelt down slowly in a squatting position, and peeked inside. "Well, I'll be. Scott, call Mr. Johnson. Now. Tell him not to eat anything in his house that's not in a can, or that he didn't just buy."

"On it."

Halliway snapped on a pair of surgical gloves, reached inside the cabinet, and pulled out a small, dark brown glass container of strychnine. He had seen a case of strychnine poisoning some years back. A lawyer who fancied himself a weekend chemist had left a container within reach down in his basement. He found his six-year-old son that night, lying contorted on the middle of the cement floor.

Of all the poisons, strychnine is by far the most brutal. Its victims suffer from violent, wild convulsions. It feeds off the adenosine triphosphate in the body's muscle tissue and causes fierce, violent seizures. Almost always, its victims die with their eyes wide open, their face convulsed in a grotesque and tortured grimace. Cause of death—sheer exhaustion and asphyxiation.

Halliway unscrewed the top. It had been opened. The lab could tell him how much had been used. No doubt the manufacturer could help with that also. There was no telling what Fenton had done with it, where he had used it, or what his plans for it were. God only knew where he got it. Halliway was worried. A container of strychnine was ominous in any home. In Fenton's home . . . Halliway began to realize the possibilities. They were unthinkable.

He already knew Fenton to be dangerous. Now the early tugging of real fear began to gnaw at him. *How sick was this man? Had he killed before? Was Bennett his first? If so, did he like it?* Halliway hated to admit it, but he was beginning to realize just how smart their current prey was. A psychotic personality with an above average IQ and a proclivity for murder . . . he closed his eyes and shook his head.

"I called him at the office, but they didn't know where he was," Hill said, returning to the bathroom door. "I left a message on his answering machine at home and called Esposito. He'll get word to him."

"Good. You know, Scott, this opens up a Pandora's box for us. If we don't catch this psycho . . . and soon . . . we could be in it deeper than we ever imagined."

"I know."

Halliway rose, closed the cabinet, and walked to the kitchen, setting the strychnine container on the table. The kitchen set was strictly 1950s—the two chairs aluminum with red plastic cushions ripping at the sides, the table a worn, speckled Formica.

He stood in the middle of the kitchen looking all around him. Other than its striking cleanliness, nothing seemed particularly out of the ordinary. A Lucite-encased Lord's Prayer with a small magnet on its back was stuck to the refrigerator. Halliway walked over and pulled open the door, surprised to find it completely empty. Of food, anyway.

"Scott," he called out. "Come here for a moment."

Hill appeared a few seconds later, entering the kitchen from the hallway. "What ya got?"

"Take a look at this," Halliway said, holding the refrigerator door open.

Detective Hill walked over to the refrigerator, his eyes resting on the note hanging from the top shelf. He read aloud. "Judge not, that ye be not judged."

"Seems we've got a religious zealot on our hands," Halliway stated, closing the refrigerator door.

"Yeah, I'm sure God is proud," Hill said. "Well, this answers one question. Unfortunately."

"What's that?"

"He's not comin' back."

"It appears not," Halliway said, his voice a lifeless monotone. "Damn. I was hoping this would be our chance . . . if we would just keep our eyes on this place long enough, he'd eventually show up. But it sure seems like he was expecting us."

"I wonder how he knew we'd be on to him?" Hill asked, looking at Halliway.

Both men answered simultaneously. "The car."

"It doesn't make sense, Ric. You mean to tell me he meant for us to find that car?"

"I don't know," Halliway said. "You think maybe the car was a ruse?"

"Man, this guy's got more twists than a Hitchcock movie."

Halliway looked at his partner. "Nice analogy."

Hill shrugged his shoulders. "Hey, what can I tell ya?"

"Well, if he didn't know we'd find his car, then how else do you explain how he knew we'd come here?"

"Christ, I don't know, Ric. I don't know what to make out of this guy. One thing's for sure though."

"What?" Halliway asked.

"We're gonna have to track him down the hard way."

"Yep. Feelin' lucky, Scott?"

———— ⚉ ————

David ripped the thermometer from his mouth. "Look, this is ridiculous. I don't have a god damned fever! What I have is a psychotic killer on my ass. You guys are treating me like some schoolboy, and what I need more than anything right now is a good, stiff drink. You wouldn't happen to have one of those in your little black bag there, would you, Doc?"

"Mr. Johnson, we talked about this," McKutcheon said. "Please, just let the man do his thing and he'll leave. Promise."

"Jesus Christ! Every one of you here knows I don't have a fucking fever. What is this anyway? Some kind of a legal cover-your-ass thing? Look, I'm not going to sue anyone, okay?"

"Have it your way, sir," the EMT said, wrapping the

plastic thermometer in its package and stuffing it into his coat.

"All right . . . obviously, you're on edge," the attending physician said. "If you'd like, I can give you something to calm you. Something that might help you sleep."

David looked at him. "I've got a medicine cabinet full of Valium and Xanax. You got something better than that in your magic bag there?"

"Well, without getting too technical, I was thinking of something a little stronger. Something more along the lines of Halcion. Ever take one?"

"No, but I'm always game," David said, smiling.

"Well, I can give you a couple. If you want them, of course."

"Of course," David said with biting sarcasm.

"Mr. Johnson," Skates interjected. "Please don't bite the guy's head off. These gentlemen are here at my request, and for your benefit. Give 'em a break, will ya?"

"Okay, okay. I'm sorry . . . What's your name?" David asked the physician.

"Thomson. Doctor Arthur Thomson."

"Look, Doc, I don't mean anything personal. It's just that . . . oh, forget it," David said, with a wave of his left hand. "Even I'm getting sick of talking about it. What do you have that won't make me feel like a zombie in the morning? It is true, I could use a good night's sleep."

The four men sat in the playroom, listening to Thomson explain the effects of different drugs to David—their relative pros and cons. He explained that ideally, he'd prefer not to give him anything at all. That sometimes a hot bath and a glass of warm milk were as effective as anything he could offer. But he was also sympathetic. He understood there were times in everyone's life when a little extra something can help. They decided on Halcion.

"Take two of these a half hour or so prior to retiring for the evening. You should sleep like a baby. But I must warn you, sir. You cannot drink if you take them. Do you understand me?"

"Alcohol, right?"

"That's correct. Alcohol interacts very strongly with

this medication. You mentioned a stiff drink earlier. I recommend that you take either one or the other. But *please* don't take both. Is that clear?"

"All right," David lied. He'd simultaneously drunk more booze and taken more barbiturates in his life than he cared to remember. David smiled. *You obviously don't understand, gentlemen. I'm a trained professional.*

McKutcheon saw both men to the door.

"Doctor," David said across the room.

"Yes?" Thomson said, turning back.

"Thanks."

"You're welcome. Good luck."

David watched McKutcheon close the door and walk back into the room. "Well, what now?" he asked.

"I hope you're not pissed, Mr. Johnson. I thought you could use some help."

"Shit, McKutcheon. I'm not pissed. Thanks for caring. I mean it."

"You're welcome. Just don't drink if you take them."

"Yeah, yeah," David said, smiling at McKutcheon. "Seriously. What do we do now?"

"Well, what do you usually do?"

David felt the weight of sadness overtake him. The things he usually did couldn't be done now. They were in Maine. "Well . . . let's see. I'm not used to having the house all to myself. Damn place is a pigsty."

"Maybe you could clean up some," McKutcheon offered.

"Nah, screw it," David said, flipping his hands toward McKutcheon. "I called someone from the office today. Said they could get started on Friday. I'm not touching a damned thing. Hey . . . I know. I think the Rangers are playing the Canadiens tonight."

"There you go," McKutcheon said, opening his hands, palms up, indicating the problem was solved.

"Want to stay and watch the game with me?" David asked.

"I'd love to. Hockey's my favorite sport. Thought I died and went to heaven when they won the Cup a few years back. But I got to get goin'. The detail outside's my responsibility."

"Is anybody going to stay inside this evening?" David asked.

"Wasn't in the plan. I don't think a fly's getting close to your place tonight. But still, if you want, we can probably arrange it."

"Thanks anyway," David said, not sure whether or not it would make him feel more comfortable or more of a coward. "You really think he'll try something tonight?"

"Can't say, sir," McKutcheon said. "Can I ask you a question, though?"

"Sure. What?"

"Have you thought of quitting your job and moving away?"

David laughed heartily, gallantly hiding his inner anxiety. "Officer, wild horses couldn't get me to quit my job. What do you think pays the mortgage? Why? You think I should have?"

"No, just curious."

"You guys got a pool going or something?"

"No, no, no. Not at all," McKutcheon said. *Man, this guy doesn't quit.* "Just wonderin' is all. Now, don't forget your Varda Alarm. Anything happens you think we should know about, you hit that button. We'll be in here before your finger's off the thing."

"Roger."

McKutcheon chuckled to himself at David's little joke, the corner of his mouth turning up ever so slightly. "All right then. I'm gone. See you in the morning. Remember what the doctor said," he warned, closing the door behind him as he entered the garage.

David leaned back in his chair and closed his eyes. He sat there for some time thinking about McKutcheon. *Nice guy.* He'd have to remember him somehow when this whole thing was over. Maybe tickets to a Ranger game. His firm had great seats. David was always turning them down. *I bet he'd like that.*

This whole thing was so surreal to him. There just didn't seem any way someone, no matter how crazy, was going to try to break into his house tonight. In his wildest imagination, he could not believe that Fenton was that dumb. David didn't exactly have a criminal mind, and even *he* would know better than to try something *that* stupid.

Maybe David only felt this way because he had the benefit of knowing the men were out there. Maybe if Fenton actually did show up, he'd follow through with whatever his plan was *after* he saw that the house was unprotected. But even that seemed crazy to him. Surely Fenton would be suspicious of that very fact. *Wouldn't he?* Surely he'd expect *someone* to be around the house—even if he couldn't see them. Finding no one would only make him suspicious. *Wouldn't it?* David knew it would him. *Oh well. The guy's off his rocker. Who the hell knows how his mind works?*

David leaned back in his chair and closed his eyes.

"Mr. Johnson! Mr. Johnson! We got 'im sir! We got the weasel!"

"Yes!" David cried out, raising his hand into the air, the weight of a thousand bricks lifted from his shoulders. "Let me see the son of a bitch, can you?"

"Better than that, sir," McKutcheon said. "Here, take my gun. Me and the boys have been talkin'. Thought you'd like to shoot him a couple of times."

"Oh man, I love you guys. Can I hurt him first?" David asked.

"Of course! Wouldn't be any fun if we couldn't watch him squirm."

As David reached for McKutcheon's gun, Skates peeled off his face . . . and there . . . standing right in front of him, was Fenton Montague.

"Gotcha!" he said to David, his face beaming a maniacal smile.

"No!" David yelled.

He woke with a jolt, sitting straight up in his chair— his eyes as wide as quarters, sweat dripping down his face and the sides of his ribs. He looked around the room, snapping his head from side to side. He realized he needed to breathe.

David leaned back in his chair again and focused on regaining his breathing pattern. He felt lightheaded; he closed his eyes and dropped his chin to his chest.

"Holy shit," he said aloud. "Much more of this, and I'm not going to make it."

He looked at his watch. It was almost 9:30. Damn it! He had wanted to speak to the kids. They'd probably be in bed by now. He walked over to the La-Z-Boy, sat on an arm and picked up the phone to call Jonah. "Let's see," he said, "Two oh seven four four eight. No, wait. Four four nine. No, wait, eight . . ." *Shit! I got to go upstairs.*

David put the phone in its receiver and headed up to his office to get Jonah's phone number.

— ⁂ —

Caleb and Sumner Johnson were having the time of their lives. More surprisingly, all things considered, Rebecca was, too. Desperately in need of emotional relief, she threw herself into the events of the day. It gave her great joy, and much needed diversion, to see her children having such fun.

Naturally, she thought of David. She called his office once but was told he was not on the trading floor. She left a message that she was thinking of him, that she loved him, and was looking forward to speaking with him that evening. But just the thought that he was around the office somewhere, doing his thing, made her feel more comfortable. Everything was still all right.

Jonah Roberts and the crew jammed into his Toyota Land Cruiser for the hour plus drive to Portland. The key to staying comfortable in New England's changing climate is to layer. They brought a couple of carry bags full of clothing—sweatshirts, coats, gloves, ski hats, and a couple of Thermoses of coffee. As the saying goes, if you don't like the weather in New England, just wait ten minutes.

Jonah heard it was going to rain later that day in Boston, which meant they would most likely be getting it sometime near evening. Though the skies were overcast, he felt they would probably have the better part of the day before their festivities were interrupted.

They planned on catching a ferry to Peaks in time for lunch at Jones Landing. There was one at 11:47 A.M., but that still left them with over two hours to kill. Portland is an old and beautiful town with a seafaring tradition dating back three hundred years. There are many things to do and see, but Jonah thought he knew just the destination for the kids.

"Hey, I know. You guys want to see New Hampshire?" he asked, looking in the rearview mirror.

"Yeah!" Sumner said.

"Sure!" Caleb chimed in.

Victoria turned sideways, looking at her husband. "That's a long drive, hon," she said.

"I thought we were going to Portland," Rebecca said.

"We are. I thought the kids would like the Observatory, Vic."

"Oh, Jonah, that's a great idea," Vickie said, her eyes lighting up. "They'll love it."

The Portland Observatory was built in the early 1800s to facilitate the burgeoning shipping trade, and in its day it was a marvel of high-tech gadgetry. Resting on top of Munjoy Hill, it rises several stories. For many years it was the tallest structure in the state. On a clear day one can easily see Mount Washington and the White Mountain Range in New Hampshire. Jonah hoped the overcast skies wouldn't make a liar out of him.

Ultimately, it didn't matter. The Observatory had been closed for good, deemed unsafe for public use. Everyone was disappointed. Jonah in particular. He knew the kids would have loved it, what with its winding stairway that narrowed precipitously as it rose, the huge, hand-hewn beams, and unbeatable view—not to mention a great look at the Aegis missile cruiser dry docked at Bath Iron Works for repair. But it was moot now.

The five of them opted for the Children's Museum in Portland instead—a well run and sizable concern, especially for a town of Portland's size. Many say it's better than Boston's. The kids had a blast jumping around, meeting new friends, exploring, touching, and feeling everything. They left with about forty-five minutes to spare and drove toward the ferry terminal stopping at the Eastern Promenade along the way.

Portland is shaped like a saddle. The rises on either side are called the Eastern and Western Promenades. Portlanders just call them Proms. The Eastern Prom offers a beautiful view of the islands dotting Casco Bay and Fort Gorges, built in the 1800s over a twenty-year span and never used. Jonah dropped quarters in the public telescopes and dropped back, letting the kids scan the scenery.

They drove to the terminal with twenty minutes to spare and pulled the car in line. "We get to take the car over?" Sumner asked.

"Yeah, cool, huh?" Jonah said.

"I'll say."

"Won't the boat sink?" Caleb asked, as the adults chuckled to themselves.

Once the car was snugly in place, they all got out and walked to the decks above, Rebecca and Vickie taking seats in the heated interior while Jonah took the kids to the upper deck.

"They must be exhausting," Vickie said to her friend.

"The kids?" Rebecca asked, looking at her friend. "Like you can't imagine. I don't know how people have more than two. Sometimes I think of having another, but then the very thought of it makes me tired."

"They're darling though. You're very lucky."

"Yeah, they are. Thanks. I love them more than I ever thought I could love anything. Sometimes though . . . I wish . . . I just wish I could have my own life."

"Do you and David ever get away?"

"Since the kids were born I don't need all the fingers on one hand to count the number of times we've gotten away . . . just the two of us. I guess I'm just tired."

"A little trip wouldn't hurt, you know. Just the two of you. Maybe you could rediscover each other. You could leave the kids here. We'd love it."

Rebecca laughed. "You'd want to kill me after two days."

"No, really. It's a treat for us. Sometimes I wish we'd

had kids," Vickie said, staring out the window. "Oh, well . . . too late now. I'm almost forty-three."

"Don't be so sure, Vickie. Medical technology's advanced a good deal."

"I know, but it doesn't matter now anyway. Jonah got a vasectomy last year."

"Oh," Becky said, a little disappointed. "You can always adopt."

"I've thought about it, believe me. But Jonah's pretty adamant. He really doesn't want kids. Says he knows himself. It just wouldn't be for him. He gets annoyed when I bring it up. Says we agreed on this a long time ago. Feels like I'm blindsiding him or something."

"How long have you been feeling this way?"

"Just in the last couple of years, I guess. Funny thing is, Jonah loves having kids around."

"Yeah, I can tell," Rebecca said, smiling.

"What makes it fun, he says, is that he knows they're going to leave."

Rebecca chuckled.

Victoria took out a Kleenex from her jacket pocket and blew her nose. "Would you do it again?" she asked.

"Have kids? Well . . ." Rebecca was quiet for a moment. "I don't know if that's the right question. I mean, I love them so much. They add a whole new dimension to your life. But . . . I guess a better question is whether I would have married David and had kids. The combination has been pretty draining. I guess I never thought I was going to raise my children by myself."

"He's really not around much, is he?"

"Oh, you know how it goes, Vickie. Jonah played that game for a long time."

"Yes, he did," Vickie replied, a tone of painful memories permeating her voice.

"I think David loves me and the kids, I just don't know what he's running from. The same thing that makes him drink, I guess."

"You think he really might quit?"

Rebecca clasped her hands together. "God, I hope so. I really do."

"Don't let what I said this morning worry you. It's

worth it. Believe me. Life gets so much better. Sometimes though . . . well, not all marriages make it through."

"How do you mean?" Rebecca asked, her face betraying a touch of worry.

"Jonah says a lot of times the dynamics of a relationship change so dramatically after one or both spouses stop drinking, they realize they just don't have that much in common anymore."

Rebecca sat quietly, looking out at the beautiful scenery of autumn in Maine. She wasn't sure she cared, but she knew the kids would never get over it. They adored their father. Maybe because they got so little of him. She *would* miss him though.

Was it the sex? She wasn't sure. She knew that if they split up, it would be a long time before she would feel comfortable making love with another man—especially the way she did with David. But she could do without. Maybe she had gotten lazy. He was a great provider. Money was never an issue. The kids never wanted for anything. Neither did she, for that matter.

The grass is always greener. Yes, she could leave. Probably get a pretty good settlement in the process. But would she be happier, or would she simply be trading one set of problems for another? The easy way out was seldom the best way out. No . . . she would stick it out. She wasn't going to back out now, just before they had a shot at a better life.

"I do love him, Vickie. There's been a lot of pain. A lot of hurt. But I do love him still."

"Good. Then work with him. Stay by his side. He'll need you now."

"That's the frustrating thing. It seems as if all I've ever done is give to him. The thought that I have to give even more now . . . that I'll have to be even more understanding . . . when I'm the one who could use the nurturing, I guess it just makes me angry."

"Well, I don't know if you can have it both ways. I mean, if you stop giving, will he get sober? Maybe it's the price you'll need to pay for a lifetime of sanity."

Rebecca rummaged through her purse, pulling out a

gumdrop. "Well, when this whole thing is over, he and I are going away. Just the two of us."

"Good idea. You think he'll go?"

"He won't have a choice," Rebecca said.

"Well, this crap you're going through now won't go on much longer. I'm sure of it. It just can't."

"I hope not, Vickie. I mean . . . this is just crazy. You know, it's a funny thing."

"What?" Vickie asked, looking at her friend.

"I can't wait to see the schmuck."

"That's a good sign, don't you think?"

They laughed until they cried.

———∽∽∽———

Fenton squatted, wadding the used toilet paper into the freezer bag in which he had just defecated. He zipped it shut and laid it quietly under some draperies behind a box to his left. He slowly sipped a small can of orange juice he had brought in his knapsack. He didn't want food in his stomach now. Juice would do just fine. For the activities he had planned this evening, all the blood must flow to his brain, not his stomach.

His watch read almost midnight. He still had a few more hours to go. Fenton wanted to strike in the early morning, but still hadn't decided exactly when. He felt pretty sure it should be some time between two and three.

Fenton was disappointed he was letting his emotions get the better of him. Try as he might, he was having more and more difficulty relaxing. He moved his head from side to side, stretching his neck muscles. This was exhausting work. He knew the wait would be the least enjoyable part of his plan, but he hadn't known just how difficult it would become in the waning hours.

He needed to get blood to his unused muscles. He rose slowly, placing his hands on his hips, and leaned generously from one side to the other. He didn't bounce from side to side, but rather, leaned until he felt his muscles stretch, then pushed just a little harder until his synapses signaled his muscles were still alive.

220

Fenton put his hands over his head, reaching as far to the ceiling as he could, then laid them on his head. He turned his torso, looking behind him, straining to one side as far as he could without severe discomfort. Again, same routine, opposite side—stretching in a given direction until it began to hurt, then pushing just a little more.

He needed to work his legs, but that would be trickier. Up until now he'd done everything from a stationary position. He never moved his feet. But to work his legs he would have to lie down. He needed to be very careful. Fenton flattened the blanket on which he stood and slowly, carefully, sat down with his legs straight out in front of him. He laid his torso quietly to the floor until he was flat on his back.

Fenton realized he was enjoying himself just a bit too much. The slightest creak could give him away. While he was keenly aware of any noises he made, still, he felt uneasy about getting too absorbed in the invigoration of putting his body to work. He lay motionless for some time staring at the underside of the roof. He listened, but all he heard was the beating of his heart. Its pace was faster now.

It was chilly. *Upper thirties, maybe forty.* He could see his breath. When he had satisfied his muscles' need for oxygen he rolled onto his left side, pulling the blanket over him. He didn't fear falling asleep. There was too much adrenaline for that. Besides, he had slept over eight hours during the day. He curled up into a ball and stared at the eaves in front of him. It was dark, but his eyes had grown accustomed. By now he knew every inch of his new home.

Fenton was filled with excitement. The sheer joy of the hunt would soon be replaced by the final climax. There was something sensual in his task. He tried to feel it . . . be with it, but it escaped his grasp. This feeling, almost a tingling from within, was something he couldn't pinpoint. It was ephemeral—there, but not there.

It didn't bother him. In fact, he enjoyed it. But he wanted the control. That was the fun of it. Something deep within was tugging at his internal strings, calling his shots. He wondered for a moment whether or not that something was really him. He thought it strange that while he could control it all on the outside, something was controlling him from the inside. Forces deep in his psyche. Forces he could not understand and wasn't sure he wanted to meet.

Was it God? Was God speaking to him via his sixth sense? "Lord," he whispered, "I have come to do your bidding. I pray you give me the strength I'll need to succeed."

Some time passed and Fenton suddenly became unbearably cold. He began to shiver. First in his bowels and stomach, he could feel his innards begin to cramp. Soon it was uncontrollable, forcing him to bite on the blanket to keep his teeth from chattering. It was almost too much. Was panic setting in? He didn't know, but he had to move. If he waited much longer, he felt he would die.

He looked at his watch, holding his left arm still with his right hand. The fluorescent hands read 1:32. He sat upright, letting the blanket fall from his shoulders. He pivoted on his behind so he could reach his knapsack, and pulled out his knife, holding it in his right hand, feeling its cold, hard steel with his left. He had purchased it specifically for this task. A regular knife would never do, but a diver's knife will cut through most anything. Certainly someone's neck.

He laid the knife at his knees, sat on his heels, clasped his hands and prayed. "Our Father, who art in Heaven, hallowed be Thy name . . ." When he was done, he crossed himself, looked skyward, and winked.

"Many are called, but few are chosen," he whispered. "It is time," he said, placing the knife between his teeth.

It was 3:30 P.M. on Halloween day when Lieutenant Cedric Halliway put the container to his lips and took his last sip of egg drop soup. Trooper Whitaker knew of a Chinese takeout nearby, and was nice enough to offer to get everyone lunch. Instead, deciding to stay with protocol, Halliway asked that he stay on the scene. Sergeant Hill went to pick it up.

DOWNTICK

Hill ordered a Diet Coke, fried dumplings, won ton soup, pork fried rice, and a broccoli and beef entree. He ate with a plastic fork. Halliway ordered tea, egg drop soup, and steamed vegetables with tofu. He ate with chopsticks.

There was something about eating with chopsticks that fostered a more cerebral quality in him. One had to think, each move a little more labored, just a touch more difficult. It wasn't second nature or robotic. Consequently, it demanded a more methodical and deliberate mind-set. Halliway felt it gave him a sense of order in a disorderly world.

Hill chewed a dumpling. "I've torn the bedroom inside out," he said.

"Anything?"

"Not really. Either our boy took a lot with him, or he lived a pretty sparse existence. A pair of loafers, a few shirts, pants, a pair of gloves. A handful of books on gardening and plants. No photos or journals. A *Penthouse* magazine. I did retrieve some hair samples from the floor under the bed. Sheets were gone. I've bagged the pillow for saliva comparisons. Strange though. There was something hung above his bed. It's not there now, just a nail in the wall."

"Hmm," Halliway mused.

"You?" Hill asked, munching on his last dumpling.

"Pretty much the same. Nothing of real interest. I've been through every book on his shelf. Plants, Jesus, Scriptures, that sort of thing. Nothing under the rugs or cushions. Nothing in the planters."

Halliway and Hill knew exactly what they were looking for. They kept a keen eye out for anything bloodstained—clothes, towels, weapons. They were particularly interested in clothing. In most instances, sadistic killers save little relics from the people they have murdered. The police call them trophies.

To a killer, particularly the serial killer, trophies act as a reminder of their moments of triumph over another living being. They fondle them, sleep with them, masturbate on them or with them. A killer can use a trophy to

223

relive his triumph time and again, thus tiding him over
until the next conquest.

The two men had no way of knowing whether or not
Fenton had come back to his apartment after he murdered Mikey or Bennett, but it was their best shot. They
hoped to find something . . . anything . . . that would tie
him to either one or both of those murders.

They were already running Fenton's transgressions
through VICAP—the FBI's Violent Criminal Apprehension Program. Upon request, every police department in
the United States and Canada can access its data base.
Unfortunately, neck slashing is a relatively common
occurrence. It certainly doesn't happen every day, but
often enough not to stick out. It is seldom, however, that
an amputated hand is sent through the US mail.

The program is essentially a clearinghouse of violent
criminal behavior. If other law enforcement agencies
anywhere in North America were working on cases with
similar characteristics, VICAP would flag them. If you
were looking for someone or had apprehended someone
with a particularly violent MO, VICAP was where you'd
want to start. Depending on the similarities in the cases,
a department might fly a detective out to talk to the
defendant or compare notes with the arresting officers.
Many previously unsolved cases had been closed this
way.

Halliway and Hill were also looking for the printer.
They hoped that somewhere in that apartment Fenton
had a printer that matched the various notes connected
with this case. If they could find it they would be a lot
closer to conviction. So far though, they'd come up
empty.

Halliway wiped his mouth with a napkin, folded it,
and put it in the paperboard soup container. "All right.
It's twenty of four. Why don't you tackle the guest room.
I'll take the kitchen," he said to his partner.

"Okay, boss, see you in a while," Hill said as he rose
from the table.

The kitchen was bare bones to say the least. The
silverware drawer had one of those Rubbermaid plastic
dividers in it. There were one knife, one spoon, one fork,

a can opener, and a bottle opener. The utensil drawer held more items, but not by much.

Halliway pulled up a chair and stood on it, looking through the cabinets. They contained a minimum of nourishment. On the second shelf was an assortment of store brand soups, canned vegetables, pastas, and beans. The lower shelf held a box of Shredded Wheat, some granola, a plastic bag of long grain wild rice, and an onion. That was it. He opened the cereal boxes and looked inside.

Halliway carefully put his right foot on the counter and pulled himself up to get a look on top. Nothing. Not even dust. He stepped back down, replaced the chair, and knelt in front of the cabinet under the sink.

"My, oh my," he said.

Here, there appeared to be every detergent ever made. Murphy's oil soap, 409, Fantastik, Mr. Clean, Spic and Span, Pine-Sol, ammonia, bleach, scrub brushes, rags, and sponges.

For the better part of an hour, Halliway meticulously went about his search—one cabinet at a time, one item at a time. When he was done he stood in the middle of the kitchen looking for anything he might have missed. He did a mental inventory of shelves, cabinets, and drawers. He'd gotten to them all. Satisfied there was nothing else there, he turned and walked down the hall to join Hill.

"Hey," he said, announcing his presence. "Anything?"

"Shit, Ric, what a colossal waste of time. There's nothing here. Nothing I can find anyhow. You're welcome to look, if you want."

"No. I'm sure I couldn't do any better."

"So what now, kemo sabe?" Hill asked.

Halliway walked back to the doorway, and looked down the hall just in time to see Whitaker enter the bathroom. He walked to its door and rapped twice with his right knuckle.

"Need something?" Whitaker asked.

"Yes."

"Name it."

"Do you have the landlord's phone number?"

225

"Sure do."

"Good. Can you get him on the line? I'd like to speak with him."

"One landlord, coming up," Whitaker said, zipping up his pants.

Hill had followed his partner into the hall and was almost run over when Halliway turned to join him in the guest room. "Care to fill me in?" he asked.

"We need to look at the storage bin."

"It's our last hope," Hill said.

"You're not kidding. If we come up empty there I don't know what the hell we're going to do."

"Lieutenant!" Whitaker called from the kitchen. "I got 'im."

"Good. I'll be right there," Halliway called down the hall, turning to look at Hill. "Keep your fingers crossed."

He strode to the kitchen and took the phone from Whitaker, putting the palm of his hand over the mouthpiece. "What's his name?" he whispered to Whitaker.

"Rothstein."

"Mr. Rothstein?" Halliway said, introducing himself. He wasted no time getting to the point. "As you know, sir, we have reason to believe Mr. Montague may have some connection to an investigation we're conducting."

"Yes, I'm aware of that."

"We've been unsuccessful in our search of the apartment, and we need to search Mr. Montague's storage area if he has one. By any chance do your tenants in this building have access to storage bins? Either on premises or off?"

Rothstein hesitated. "Yes . . . they do. In the basement."

The warrant had been written in such a way as to allow a search of any areas or encumbrances used outside of the apartment for storage—personal or communal. No matter how bad the crime, how vicious the suspect, if the warrant doesn't specifically state it, it can't be searched. Halliway and Hill had thought this one through.

"Would it be possible for you to show them to us?" Halliway asked.

"You do have a warrant for all this, right? I could get my ass sued up and down both sides of Comm Ave for this."

"Of course, sir. We can show it to you if you'd like."

"So you want me to come up there now, I suppose?" Rothstein asked, slight annoyance in his voice.

Halliway was in no mood for diplomacy. "Yes," he said. "Immediately, if not sooner."

Halliway heard Rothstein breathe deeply. "All right. I live in Brookline. It'll take me twenty minutes or so. I'll leave now."

"Good. We'll be waiting. And Mr. Rothstein?"

"What?"

"Don't forget your keys."

The same afternoon Halliway and Hill were conducting the search of Fenton's apartment, two New York City police detectives pulled into the driveway of Anthony and Linda Barnes. The driver mentioned to his partner that he'd just seen someone spread the venetian blinds and look out the window.

"Well, they know we're here. I wonder if they know why," Detective Aniello Spignorelli said to his partner, stepping out of the cruiser and tucking his raincoat tightly around his neck. "I hate this. I've done it a thousand times, and it never gets easier."

"You want me to tell 'em?" his partner asked.

"Yeah, would ya? I just don't have it in me today."

"Okay, but let's just get it over with," Detective Richard Moore said, walking to the front door.

The door opened as they rang the bell. "Mr. Barnes. Good afternoon, sir," Moore said. "Can we come in?"

Over the past seventy-two hours, Tony and Linda Barnes had come to know these two men better than they wanted. A spurt of adrenaline coursed through Barnes's veins. "Gentlemen," he said.

"Can we come in?" Moore asked again.

"Please. I'm sorry. Come in. It's miserable out."

227

"Thank you."

The two detectives stood in the small foyer, removing their raincoats, folding them over their arms. It was a small gesture but lent an air of hominess. If they imparted the news they had to deliver without even bothering to remove their coats, it would seem cold, almost as if they were planning on leaving immediately thereafter. They wanted to give the impression they would stay as long as needed. Of course, neither one hoped it would be long.

Barnes felt heat rushing to his face. "Here, let me take those," he said. "Do you have any news? Anything at all? Our lives have been on hold since Friday. We can't sleep, eat . . . all we do is stare at the walls," he said, speaking into the hall closet as he hung up their coats.

"Is Mrs. Barnes here, sir?" Detective Spignorelli asked.

Barnes grimaced. "Yes. Why?" he asked, turning around. "Something's wrong, isn't it?"

The two detectives looked at each other.

"Isn't it?" Barnes demanded.

"Mr. Barnes, can we take a seat in here?" Moore asked, motioning to the living room. For news like this, you always want them sitting down.

"Oh, my God," Barnes said, in pain, his hands balled into tight fists. "Mikey's dead isn't he? *Isn't he? Tell me!"*

Linda Barnes walked into the foyer from the kitchen, wiping her hands on a kitchen towel. "Tony, what is it?" she asked, looking at her husband's face.

There is never an easy way to do this. The best rule of thumb is to just get it out and let the grieving process begin. There was no way Moore was going to have it his way, so they all stood awkwardly in the foyer. His partner tried to move everyone toward the living room. *We shouldn't do this here.*

Inexplicably, Moore started talking. "Mikey has not been found yet," he began. "However, I'm terribly sorry to have to tell you this, but the Connecticut state police have conclusively identified an amputated hand as belonging to your son."

In one of those cruel ironies of life, decorum dictated he wait a few seconds for the shock to settle in. Linda Barnes wailed from somewhere deep within her, collapsing to the ground, striking her head against the corner of the bottom wooden stair. Nothing bleeds like the head. In a matter of seconds, before anyone had an opportunity to react, a pool of blood was forming under her right cheek.

"Jesus Christ!" Tony Barnes screamed, running to his wife, pitifully trying to wipe away blood with the dish towel. Both detectives operated on pure instinct at the sight of the growing pool of crimson. Spignorelli ran to Linda's aid, kneeling on the tiled floor, turning her body over. He wasn't really thinking now. He yanked the kitchen towel from Barnes's hand and began wiping away blood from her forehead.

Moore was at her feet. "It's too awkward here," he said. "Let's get her out in the middle where there's more room."

Moore took her legs while Spignorelli took her under her arms. "Mr. Barnes, go and get two bath towels and a couple of washcloths. Oh, and a bucket of warm water!" he yelled after him, as Barnes turned the corner into the kitchen.

"Shit, I can't fuckin' believe this," Spignorelli said to his partner, trying desperately to find the cut.

"There," Moore said. "Just below her hairline," pointing to the spot.

It had caught her just right. An inch and a half gash revealed itself as Spignorelli vainly attempted to wipe away the flow of blood. He found the spot, wadded the towel on it and pressed down hard. She'd be okay, at least physically, but the cut would probably require stitches.

"Spig, we should call an ambulance," Moore said, rising to make the call.

Anthony Barnes returned, water spilling as he jogged, holding the bucket in his right hand, the towels bunched together in his left.

Detective Spignorelli lifted Linda's head. "Here, fold

one of those up and put it under her." The open space between her head and the floor made it obvious what he meant. "You got those washcloths? Give 'em to me."

Anthony Barnes felt nauseated. He had just received the most horrible news any parent could imagine and now he had to physically fight off vomiting as he watched his wife bleed profusely, her blood smeared all over the shiny, tiled foyer floor. His head began to spin. He needed to brace himself on something. Anything. He leaned against the entrance to the living room, letting his body slide down the molding until his knees were at his chin.

Spignorelli wanted to keep Tony Barnes busy. "Mr. Barnes, I need you now," he said. "Your wife's lost some blood. We need to keep her warm. Do you have any blankets?"

Anthony Barnes stared catatonically, just nodding his head.

"Get one please," Spignorelli requested, watching Barnes squat. "Mr. Barnes! I said get a blanket. Now!"

Detective Moore returned from the kitchen. "They're on their way," he said.

Spignorelli was sitting flat on his shins, Linda Barnes out cold in his hands. He looked up at his partner and motioned with his head to her husband. "Dick, see if you can get a blanket from the bedroom. We need to keep her warm."

Jesus, where did this thing go wrong? Moore walked over to Mr. Barnes, knelt down beside him, and inched him up slowly until he was standing. "Mr. Barnes, where do you keep your blankets? We need them for your wife."

Tears were streaming down Barnes's face. He looked Moore in the eye, forcing the detective to look away. The anguish was too stark, too real, too poignant. "I'm sorry," Barnes babbled, almost incoherently. "It's just too much."

Spignorelli had lost patience. "Screw him, Dick! Just grab one from the bedroom."

As Moore left the foyer to hunt for blankets, Barnes

turned his head to Spignorelli. "Mikey's hand. How did they find it?" he asked.

"Let's just get your wife squared away first, okay? I promise we'll tell you everything we know so far."

"I asked you how they found it?"

"Mr. Barnes, look at me, sir," Spignorelli pleaded. "You're wife is lying in my arms, bleeding like a stuck pig. I'm doing the best I can here, and you're not exactly helpin' much. Please, sir. Let's do this later. Now's not the time."

"There's nothing else I can do for her," Barnes said, his voice an unsettling monotone. "You want me to hold her head, I will. You've already called an ambulance. Now tell me how you found his hand."

Spignorelli closed his eyes and inhaled deeply. *Okay asshole, you asked for it.* "It was mailed to someone in Connecticut." As annoyed as he was, still, he thought it best to leave out the details. At least for now.

"Connecticut?" Barnes asked, "Why? Who lives there?"

This was getting dangerously close now. Spignorelli had to think fast. He thought of liability. He thought of Barnes's mental state. There was no way he could tell him it was his wife's boss. Certainly not now.

"Here," Moore said, jogging down the hall, holding a blanket outstretched in his right hand.

Spignorelli lifted the towel ever so slowly, peeking underneath to see if the bleeding had stopped. "I think I hear the ambulance, Dick. Go out and flag it down, will ya?"

Spignorelli glanced up at Mr. Barnes. He needed to take the offensive. Barnes had become monomaniacal. He would push this line of questioning until he dropped.

"Mr. Barnes, I want to stress that we have not found your son's body," Spignorelli said, the whole scene strikingly surreal. "There is still every likelihood he is still alive," he lied, wishing he hadn't spoken those last words. But he needed to divert Barnes's attention. Maybe throwing him a bone might work.

It did. "Bullshit! What d'you think? I'm an idiot? How

could he stay alive under those circumstances? Look at the trouble you've had with my wife, and she's just got a cut on her forehead."

Spignorelli sensed that Barnes was coming out of it now. He seemed a little more grounded—less loosely wound. The siren from the ambulance was deafening. Then it stopped. He knew help would arrive in a matter of seconds. *Good.* His legs were going numb.

Out of nowhere, Barnes asked again. "Who lives in Connecticut?"

They'd have to talk about it anyway. It wasn't like it was something that could be avoided. Knowing his shift as medic would end momentarily gave him strength.

"Your wife's boss, sir. It was mailed to Mr. Johnson."

"Johnson? What kind of bullshit is he—I'll kill him."

"You may have to get in line."

David Johnson reclined, feet up, in his La-Z-Boy, holding a bottle of Glenlivet between his legs. His body craved alcohol; its cells had been denied their life fluid for five days. Like a newborn in the night, his nerves screamed to be heard . . . starving . . . begging him to give in. He put the bottle down on the floor to his left, popped the chair to its upright position, and walked to the middle of the floor. He stood there, staring at the bottle, running both hands through his hair. A sudden chill shook his body involuntarily.

"Shit," he said. He went to the bottle, picked it up, and unscrewed the top. He sniffed it longingly, swirled it around some, and sniffed it again. He palmed the cap in his left hand and walked to the pool table, setting the scotch down on it.

He leaned with both hands on the pool table. "So what's it gonna be, boy?" he said aloud. He didn't *want* to drink. This was not a matter of not wanting to. Hell, he would have quit a long time ago if it were that simple. This transcended want. This was about need. Like a fish needs water. Like fire needs oxygen. *How am I ever going to get out of this?*

DOWNTICK

David removed his hands from the table and held them out in front of him. They were trembling. He locked his fingers behind his neck, closed his eyes, and took deep breaths. The bottle was his lighthouse, announcing shore and safety—and danger. It beckoned him. He could smell it in the air. He put the top to his lips and licked it, but not much booze makes its way to the underside of a bottle cap.

The sense of urgency was overwhelming, invading his soul. His heart fluttered with palpitations. David felt frightened as he fell to his knees, tears welling in his eyes. He felt strangely disembodied, as if he were watching himself suffer. He clasped his hands in his lap and rocked slowly back and forth.

What was there left for him now? His family had been chased from his house; he was alone—hunted and scared. His entire life had been turned upside down as if caught in the vortex of a giant twister that was sucking him down with tremendous force. *One neverending, god damned downtick.* Like a plummeting stock from which all the buyers have backed away.

David sat back on his rear and brought his feet out in front of him, pulling his knees to his chest. He looked at his feet and realized he was still wearing his wing-tips. *Christ! I'm still in my suit.*

"All right," he said with despair, breathing deeply. "You've handled some of the biggest deals on the Street. You deal in billions of dollars every day. You can do this. You can do this. You can do this." Like a mantra, he repeated it over and over to himself, rocking like a child. He desperately wanted to pray, but didn't know how.

"God . . ." he started, rising to his knees. *This is ridiculous. Get undressed. Maybe take a shower. All right, here's the deal. Call Rebecca. Take a warm bath. Get something to eat. If you still have to have it when you're done, then that will be it. You can start your sobriety another day. When things are better. When you have your family back. When this asshole is caught.*

David stood again, straightening his arms, resting his palms on the pool table. He was aware that he was sweating. *Must be detox.* He didn't move, as perspiration dribbled down his sides, tickling him in an unpleasant way. He patted his forehead with his sleeve, his blue shirt darkening where it had absorbed the moisture.

He pulled out the piece of paper from his shirt pocket on which he'd written Jonah's phone number, went back to the La-Z-Boy, and sat down, pulling the phone onto his lap.

Victoria Roberts answered the phone. "Hello?"

His voice felt shaky, but sounded fine. "Hello, Vickie?"

"David! Oh, David. Becky will be so happy you called. How are you?" she asked.

"Snug as a bug. No sign of him yet."

"Oh, it's so good to hear your voice. We've thought about you all day."

"Well, here I am," David said, feigning calm. "Down in the jungle, fighting for truth, justice, and the American way. How have the kids been?" David asked.

"They're so adorable, David. You and Becky are really quite lucky."

David smiled. "Thanks, Vickie. They are pretty cute, if I do say so myself. Is Jonah around?"

Jonah? "Uh . . . sure. See you soon."

"Bye, Vic."

Rebecca and Jonah were standing in the kitchen, listening to Vickie's conversation. Becky was smiling. She took a few steps forward as Vickie ended the conversation, extending the phone out toward them. "He wants Jonah," she said, shrugging her shoulders to her best friend.

Rebecca furrowed her eyebrows and took a seat at the kitchen table. Jonah glanced at her, feeling a little embarrassed. He took the phone from his wife and leaned against the kitchen sink.

"Hey, what's up, bud? You decide to pack it in down there, or what?"

"Jonah, did you get my message?" David asked, uncharacteristically moving right to the point.

Jonah felt pain at the obvious toll this whole ordeal was taking on the Johnson family. "No, I haven't checked the machine. We just got home a short while ago. The kids wanted to see a hockey game. We lucked out. The Pirates were in town. Why?"

"Does the name Fenton Montague ring a bell with you?"

Jonah didn't speak for a few seconds. *Fenton Montague?* "You don't mean that wacko we shacked up in Boston? How could I forget?"

"It's him, Jonah."

Jonah was shocked. "Montague? You gotta be shitting me? How do you know?"

Victoria and Rebecca exchanged glances.

"Well, it's not a hundred percent yet, but that's who the cops told me they think it is," David continued.

"What makes them think so?" Jonah asked.

"They are working on it now. I'll probably know something more certain tomorrow, maybe the day after."

Jonah ruminated on the events of those two nights twenty years ago. He wasn't sure what to make of what he'd just heard. *What does it mean? David wasn't the only one who'd thrown Fenton out.* "Did they give a reason why?" he asked.

"Who?"

Jonah closed his eyes in exasperation. "The cops."

"Oh . . . hey look, you know what I do. Shit, I told the cops everything I could remember. We only met him that once, right?"

"Yeah, that I know of."

Rebecca was listening to Jonah's end of the conversation with a keen ear. She was worried. Something was wrong. *This better not be one of those things they keep just to themselves.* She felt a pit in her stomach, as if an internal trap door had just flung open. The relative calm brought about by the events of the day was sucked from her now, as if by a vacuum. Victoria pretended to busy herself with a batch of fresh cider, listening intently to every word.

"Jonah?" David asked.

"Yes?"

"If the cops are right, we've both got problems. You know that, don't you?"

"David, I just can't believe that," Jonah said, moving into the living room, turning his back to the two women in the kitchen. "There's got to be more to it than meets the eye. I mean . . . shit, David, it just doesn't make any sense, does it?"

"Hey, welcome to my world," David said, suddenly feeling guilty at dragging his friend into the middle of this mess. "Look, Jonah, I'm not saying that I *know* anything. Maybe he doesn't even remember you. But I had to tell you, don't you think? I'd sure as hell want to know if the shoe were on the other foot."

Jonah felt a trace of fear. No matter how close the friend, how terrible the problem, how truly bad you feel for someone else's circumstance—still, there's always that little voice in the recess of the mind that says, Thank God it's not me. In one minute Jonah had been transformed from sympathetic observer to fearful player. Suddenly, his life had lost a good measure of its tranquility.

Jonah pulled the phone cord with his left hand, walking further into the living room. "I haven't gotten any notes or anything," he said, half whispering.

"Anything strange been going on at all? Phone calls? Anything like that?" David asked.

"No. Nothing. Anyway, we're unlisted. How the hell could he ever find us?"

Victoria watched her husband sit down in a chair in the far corner of the other room. This looked ominous. She laid down her wooden spoon, covered the pot, and walked to the edge of the kitchen, just close enough to hear what Jonah was saying. She heard his last line clearly. The words shot through her like an arrow, her adrenal glands jumping into action. She wasn't sure what it meant, but she knew it wasn't good.

"Vickie?" Rebecca called from the kitchen table. "What is it?"

Victoria put up her right hand, signaling for quiet. She turned her head halfway, offering Rebecca a profile, her finger to her pursed lips, shaking her head ever so slightly. Rebecca rose from the table and joined her friend by the wood stove. She didn't say a word.

"Well, all right then. We'll see you this weekend," she heard Jonah say as he rose and turned around, a frown on his face. "I'll put her on."

He walked back toward the kitchen, handed the phone to Rebecca, and sat at the kitchen table. Victoria followed and sat opposite him. "Honey, what is it? What's wrong?" she asked.

Jonah told her what David had said, explaining the events that had occurred in Boston so many years ago. "I don't know what to do," he said.

When David finished speaking with Rebecca, he hung up the phone and closed his eyes, the phone still resting in his lap. It was almost 10:30. He had to get something to eat. He rose, walked to the pool table, and replaced the top to the scotch bottle.

McKutcheon had relayed Esposito's warning about the strychnine. David stood in the kitchen trying to decide what he'd like. He really didn't have an appetite but had learned long ago that you have to eat. Some people eat more when their anxiety level is high. David had always been just the opposite. He remembered a lengthy litigation he'd been involved in once. During that period he lost over twenty pounds, and had learned then to eat something no matter how bad he felt. Eventually, lack of food only makes matters worse.

He pulled out a small frozen chicken pie. He set the oven to three seventy-five, placed it on the rack, looked at his watch, and went upstairs to the master bedroom.

Forty minutes. Just enough time for a bath. He removed the gun from his jacket and placed it on the bed. David emptied his pockets, placing his change and bills in their usual spot on the dresser and the Halcion tablets on the counter in the bathroom. He figured he'd take them just before he got in bed to read. He hung up his suit and threw his socks and underwear in the hamper. *Shit, I've got to do my own laundry.*

He ran the water extra hot, and sat down on the stool with a copy of *BusinessWeek* as the tub filled beside him. It took him a while to fully submerge himself in the water, but once in, it was better than he had imagined. He couldn't remember the last time he'd taken a bath.

As he lay there, David realized he wanted a cigarette. He got up and ran, dripping wet, to his nightstand, grabbing his Marlboros and a lighter. There were some advantages to bachelorhood—Rebecca would have killed him if she had seen him do that.

A half an hour later the knots of his muscles seemed to loosen slightly. David stepped from the tub and dried himself vigorously. He threw on a pair of sweats, a T-shirt that read Panama Canal Yacht Club, and his slippers. He went to the bed, retrieved his gun, and walked over to his nightstand. He placed it next to the Varda Alarm the police had given him.

David thought for a moment, if for some crazy reason he needed to use it, a response sure wouldn't take long tonight. But it was really kind of wasted on him. No one could be safer than he was right now. *Hey, every little bit helps. Even if it just helps me feel better.*

It was 11:15. David went downstairs, poured himself a glass of milk, and checked the chicken pie. He remembered his father would occasionally put a shot of bourbon in his milk. Ironically, the thought disgusted him. It looked as if he was going to make it, at least through the night.

The pie was golden brown on top, the sides just beginning to drip onto the aluminum foil on the bottom oven shelf. He actually felt hungry now.

The rain pounded against the kitchen window. David felt bad for the cops outside, but soothed himself by thinking they probably didn't feel bad for him when one of his people lost an account. He figured they wanted to become cops. No one put a gun to their head.

He set himself a place at the table, trying hard to keep some semblance of normality. He chuckled to himself at the attempt. His house was a wreck, his family gone, some psycho was on the loose with David's name printed on his forehead, and here he sat trying to pretend everything was okay.

He finished his meal quickly. Once he got a bite or two inside him, he was disappointed he hadn't cooked two, but he finished what he had, eating straight out of the aluminum container. He rinsed his things, laid them in the sink, and threw out the container. Stopping at the garbage, he reached back in, pulled out the aluminum bowl, washed it and put it in the recycling bin. His kids always chided him for not recycling. It was everybody's responsibility, they said. Boy, how things had changed since he was in school.

He made a quick tour of the house, checking windows and doors, making sure they were locked. He checked the broom handle in the sliding glass door. Standing there, he wondered if he could see anything outside. There were no lights on now save the forty-watt bulb above the stove. David pulled back the curtains slightly and put his nose up against the water-marked glass, cupping his hands to the window as he looked in all directions. Nothing. Wherever they were, they were hidden for the night.

"It's almost midnight," he said quietly to himself. "You better get your ass to bed." He walked back through the kitchen and stopped at the entrance to the foyer. He stared at the doorway to the steps leading to the playroom. In his mind he could see that scotch bottle just sitting there on the pool table. He thought of Dr. Thomson and his admonitions . . . of Becky . . . the kids . . . of Jonah.

It was a siren song, and he knew it. *You've made it this far. One more night's not going to kill you.* He practically ran up the stairs, afraid the bottle's pull might win out.

David always slept nude. Walking to the bathroom, he threw his clothes over the chair in the corner, took both Halcion tablets with a full glass of water, urinated, hit the light, and crawled into bed. He decided not to set his alarm. "Screw it," he said. *I'll wake up when I wake up. I need the sleep.*

David was a Tom Clancy fan. He'd heard good things about his latest thriller and bought it the weekend before the nightmare started. Now would be as good a time as any to begin reading it. He rolled over, flipped on his light and picked up the book. Propping his body up on his and Rebecca's pillows, he hoped he could escape for a while.

Shortly after 1:30, David was awakened by a noise. He

wasn't sure what it was, but it didn't matter. Clancy's novel lay on his chest. David was so tired, he felt he could sleep for a week if given the chance. He tossed the book on the floor, reached up, flipped off the light, and rolled over on his left side, dead to the world.

———∞———

Cedric Halliway stood at the window of Fenton's apartment. Looking down over Newberry Street, he watched the rain come down in sheets. Sergeant Hill and Trooper Whitaker sat at the kitchen table discussing the case. Halliway thought back to his younger days, when he was a rookie on the force. That was thirty years ago.

He and his wife, Rose, had a lot of dreams then. Their second child had just been born. Their first had suffered complications at birth and died in its third week. After April's death, things were never the same. He was never the same. Always reserved, he simply withdrew into his shell even more.

The two of them were thrilled at the arrival of their newborn. It was a chance for revival, a new lease on life. They named her Hope. He and Rose doted on their baby daughter. Times were tough then. There never seemed to be enough money to make ends meet. For years they barely got by, surviving paycheck to paycheck—his hours long and unorthodox. Those were difficult years on his wife and on their marriage. But they stuck it out. They had not planned to have more children, but three years later, Rose told Cedric she was pregnant again.

They were to have their first boy. They named him Jacob. Halliway tried to remember the exact sequence of events. His memory was still good, honed as it was by years of detective work. Still, it was a long time ago. If he remembered correctly, he thought that somewhere around the time Jake started to walk, he had applied for the opening in the homicide unit.

When he got the position Rose was ecstatic. In the early years, she worried about him constantly. A state trooper on the road at all hours of the night—stopping strangers, approaching dark, unlit cars. She'd always had a vivid imagination. It was not a helpful trait on those many nights she spent alone. The life of a homicide investigator was entirely different—difficult in its own way, but in her mind, not nearly as dangerous.

As the kids grew their lives fell into a tranquil, if not boring routine. Halliway didn't suffer from wanderlust. Boring was just fine with him. In fact, he liked it that way. When the kids entered middle school Rose took a job as a receptionist at a local law firm. She worked there still.

Together they planned for retirement, always putting away a little something out of each paycheck. They talked of the things they would do with their free time— the grandchildren, the places they would take them, the stories they would read to them. The day Hope gave birth to his granddaughter was the happiest of his life. The day she called to tell them she'd been diagnosed as mentally retarded, he thought he would die.

Halliway stood at the window now, watching the rain wash over the street in torrents, amused by people scrambling to and from their cars, scurrying down the street, fighting with their umbrellas. He felt tired. With all that had happened in his life—the joy and the sorrow—one thing remained constant. The psychos never went away.

Like pod people, they seemed to reproduce at an astonishing rate. There were times he felt he was moving a mountain with a spoon. But he loved his work. Someone had to do it, and there was still nothing quite like the thrill of the hunt. Even after all these years.

As he watched the street below, he saw a dark blue Lincoln Continental pull up behind his cruiser. He turned toward the kitchen. "Trooper Whitaker. What kind of car does Rothstein drive?" he asked.

"Lincoln . . . I think."

Halliway walked to the front door, picking up his raincoat and hat along the way. "He's here, gentlemen. Let's go," he said, walking out of Fenton's apartment.

The trio met Herbert Rothstein as he hit the first landing. "Mr. Rothstein?" Halliway asked, making the perfunctory introductions.

"Gentlemen," Rothstein said firmly.

"We would like to see Mr. Montague's storage bin, if that's possible."

"Of course. Like I said, they're in the basement. We need to go back down."

Everyone followed him down the stairs to a doorway under the first rise of steps. Rothstein unlocked it with a key. "All my tenants have a key to this door. The laundry machines are down here."

"How many people live in this building?" Hill asked, standing at the back of the small crowd.

"Well, let me think. I own six buildings. There's fourteen units in this building, I think. Probably twenty people. Something like that. Careful, gentlemen," Rothstein said, opening the door. "The steps are old and there's not much headroom."

Rothstein flipped on the light and stood to the side as they all filed down the steps one man at a time. "The bins are this way," he said. "You know, this is very new to me. I don't know what you believe Fenton to be involved in, but I just hope you're mistaken."

"Any particular reason you say that?" Halliway asked.

"Well, he's always been such a good tenant. Never a problem. Always pays his rent on time. Always. He's clean. Takes care of the place. It's hard to find tenants like him."

"You can say that again," Hill said under his breath from the back.

"Did you say something, Sergeant?" Rothstein asked.

"No. Nothing."

"I don't mean to pry, you understand," he started, "but do you mind if I ask what you're looking for? I mean, what is it exactly you believe him to be guilty of?"

"I'm sorry, sir," Halliway said. "We really can't comment on that. I hope you'll understand."

"Oh, of course. I shouldn't have asked. Just being nosy. But you have to admit, it's not every day I do this for the state police. It must be something big."

"Could you show us to his bin, sir?" Halliway asked politely.

Rothstein was used to being in control. He was a wealthy man, highly respected in his community. He took good care of his tenants. There weren't many landlords like him left in Boston.

"You know, I probably should take a look at that search warrant of yours. I've never had to do this before. I want to make sure I cover all the bases."

Halliway inhaled deeply but quietly. The man was within his rights. He understood, but just wanted to get on with it. "Trooper Whitaker?" he said, stepping aside to let him pass.

Whitaker took a couple of steps forward, reaching into his back pocket, pulling out the search warrant. "Here it is, sir."

"Can I take it?" Rothstein asked.

Whitaker looked at Halliway. "It's his building," he answered.

This guy's no dummy. Halliway knew why Rothstein wanted to see it. If he couldn't find out what he wanted to know from the police, then he'd just have a look at the search warrant. *Too bad. You're going to be disappointed.*

Rothstein wouldn't find anything of particular interest in the warrant. They were designed that way. Generally, warrants are five pages long, but the only pages police are obligated to show are the first two. The affidavit, explaining the reason for the warrant and any specifics the police may be looking for, is never attached. What if the person they showed it to was involved? One look at the warrant and they'd know what the cops knew. This way the only information they'd have was what areas were to be searched.

Rothstein took the warrant, brought it underneath a fluorescent bulb hanging to his left, and began to read. He looked let down. "Is this it?" he asked.

Sorry, old man. "That's it," Halliway answered, declining to elaborate.

"I don't know why, but I thought search warrants were longer than this."

"They are," Halliway responded.

Rothstein looked at him. "So where's the rest of it?"

Enough of this bullshit. You lost, okay? "That's all the law requires us to show, sir. Please . . . the storage bins?"

"Of course, of course," Rothstein said, handing the warrant back to Whitaker. "Let's see, I haven't been down here in a while. I believe it's this one over here."

He counted to himself as he walked along the bins to his left. "Twelve. Here we go, gentlemen. Now for the hard part. I haven't opened one of these in years."

He fiddled with his keys for a while, incorrectly guessing on his first two tries. Halliway removed his glasses, rubbing his eyes as he struggled for patience.

"Ah, here we go," Rothstein said. He jiggled the key a little in the York padlock and the gate to Fenton's bin swung slowly open.

"Thank you, sir," Halliway said. "We won't be needing your services any longer. You're free to leave if you wish."

"If you don't mind, I'd just as soon stay. It's not every day you get a chance to see the police in action."

Halliway looked at Hill. *Why am I not surprised?* It was Rothstein's building. They couldn't very well kick him out. "If you wish, but please, sir, if I could ask you to stay over here, I would appreciate it," Halliway said, motioning to a spot out of the way.

"Oh, certainly," Rothstein said.

Halliway and Hill began removing Fenton's belongings one item at a time. Mercifully, his bin was only half full. They were relieved when they saw Rothstein stop at this one. Some of the others were packed to the top.

About twenty minutes into the process Rothstein excused himself. "Well, I should be going. Please put everything back when you're done," he said.

"Okay. Thanks again," Hill said, busily digging through some boxes.

Halliway said nothing. He was in no mood for placating Rothstein's inquisitiveness. He waited a few moments until he was sure they were alone. "Got too boring for him, huh?"

"I'm surprised he lasted this long," Hill said.

Whitaker laughed.

"Well, well, well," Halliway said. "What have we here?"

"Find something?" Hill asked.

"It's a Hewlett-Packard LaserJet II box. Not empty either."

Halliway pulled it out and set it on the ground next to the other items. All three policemen gathered around as Halliway peeled off the tape that fastened the box. When it was fully open, they stood there, taking turns looking inside.

"And the fat lady sings," Hill said.

—⁓—

Rebecca, Jonah, and Victoria sat at the kitchen table discussing David's conversation with Jonah. Jonah was not one to worry unnecessarily. He'd learned through the years that worry seldom gets you anywhere and almost always does more harm than good.

Jonah had been sober seven years now and learned that there is only so much in one's life you can control. Let go, let God, was Jonah's motto now. He was not particularly religious, but he most certainly believed in God—a power greater than himself.

Even recovering alcoholics will periodically yearn to drink. After years of sobriety, occasionally something would happen in Jonah's life that would bring back the desire, like a burn victim who can't stop playing with fire. Alcohol, in any form, was Jonah's Achilles' heel. He simply could not drink. But as he sat with the two most important women in his life, holding a mug of hot cider, he wished he could have one. *Just one.* Just enough to take the edge off.

He was faintly aware of someone talking. A distant voice . . . unintelligible . . . like one of Charlie Brown's parents.

"Earth to Jonah," Victoria said.

He snapped to as if from a trance. "What?" he asked.

"David said he thinks we're safe here," Rebecca said. "I asked if you agreed with him?"

Jonah thought for a moment, chewing his lower lip. "I

think so. I mean, this guy's not exactly the stealth terrorist. He thrives on fear. That's his power trip. No . . . We'd know it if he'd set his sights on us. That's what David thinks, and I agree."

Vickie shook her head. "It just seems so crazy. That he would want to kill David because of something that happened twenty years ago. There's got to be something else. Don't you think?"

Jonah turned up the palms of his hands. "That's what I told David."

"You think it's possible David pissed this guy off some other time?" Becky asked. "Some Wall Street deal or something? Something he's not aware of? The Boston connection just seems like too much of a wild coincidence."

"Could be," Jonah responded. "Wild coincidence wouldn't begin to describe it though. David sure as hell doesn't remember anything like that. Not that he knows of anyhow."

"Well, if it was Boston," Vickie added, "I mean . . . shit, Jonah. David didn't act alone. You kicked him out too."

Jonah stood. He'd had enough. "Look," he said, walking to the stove to refill his cider. "This isn't healthy, Vickie. Becky and the kids came up here to get away from all this crap. We have absolutely *no* reason to think he has any plans for me, much less knows where the hell I live."

"So what do we do?" Vickie asked.

Jonah's voice was biting. "What do you mean, what do we do? Christ, Vickie, what do you think we should do? Move? Come on. Enough's enough. This is stupid and I'm not going to play anymore. I already told you, he doesn't know where we live, and even if he did, we'd know he was coming *way* in advance. Now, stop it. Both of you."

"Listen here, Jonah Roberts," Rebecca said. "My husband is down there, a virtual prisoner in his own life. God only knows how scared he is. He doesn't let on, but I know him. Who wouldn't be? He calls here and tells us the cops think the guy hunting him is the same guy you did the same thing to. So don't tell me this is stupid. I'd like to see you not care if the situation were reversed."

Rebecca's anger caused some tension at the table, but the three of them were like family. Everyone sat quiet for a while sipping their cider. Jonah finally broke the silence.

"Look, Becky, I'm sorry. I'm not trying to play it down, but I really do think we're all just borrowing trouble. He hasn't even tried to touch David yet. Shit, the police will probably catch this asshole long before he even thinks to look for me."

"Are you crazy?" Rebecca asked. "The bastard killed a cop on our front steps! That's not exactly mind games . . . is it?"

Jonah dropped his head and rubbed his temples with his fingers. He'd forgotten about that. *Just a minor oversight.* Maybe he *was* trying to live in denial. Maybe they were in danger. But what were his options?

"Do you think you should leave?" he asked Rebecca. "Maybe you and the kids should go to your folks' place."

"I asked David that," Rebecca answered. "He doesn't think it's necessary but said he'd think about it. Said we'd talk about it more tomorrow. He told me he wants me to be wherever I feel the kids are safest, but he didn't think we'd be any safer than where we are. At least not now. The cops will probably have more on this Montague guy tomorrow, and we should look at what they find and then decide."

"Well, that sounds like a plan to me. Now listen, I want you both to look at me. This is important," Jonah said, hesitating for a moment, assuring their full attention. "I really don't think we have anything to worry about. I mean that. I'm not just bullshitting you either. Let's not forget who he'd be after, okay? It's not like I'm some disinterested party. If I'm not worried, then you shouldn't be either. Okay?"

"Okay," they both answered.

"Good. Promise?"

"Yes."

"All right, it's almost midnight. We should get to bed. I promised the kids we'd clear some of the woods

247

tomorrow. Something tells me they're not going to let us sleep in."

Rebecca looked up at the clock on the wooden post in the kitchen. "I had no idea it was so late," she said, yawning. "I'm exhausted."

Victoria took everyone's mugs and walked to the sink. Rebecca followed and began washing them. "Leave 'em, Beck. We'll get them in the morning."

"All right. Since you put it like that," she said, smiling at Vickie.

Vickie turned and gave Rebecca a hug. "Good night," she said. "Everything's going to be all right. I just know it."

"I hope so, Vickie. I can't wait for it to be over."

"I know. It'll end. Sooner than you think."

"From your mouth to God's ears."

"See you in the morning," Jonah said, pecking Rebecca on the cheek as he walked to the bathroom.

Jonah made it into bed first. Victoria pulled off her sweater, exposing her naked bosom. She went to the closet and hung it up, still wearing her jeans. Jonah watched her from the cool sheets of their bed. The heat from the wood stove never seemed to fully make it to the bedroom, and a constant chill hung in the air. Victoria's nipples were hard. The sight of her breasts still excited him, even after all these years.

"Come here," he said lovingly.

"It's cold. Hang on."

She slipped off her jeans, folded them over the chair, slipped on her flannel nightgown, and crawled into bed. She hunched her shoulders and shook a little bit. "Brrrr. Warm me up. My feet are freezing."

They cuddled like two spoons. Jonah slipped his hand under her nightgown, sliding it up to one of her breasts, cupping it with his warmth. He nibbled her ear and ran his tongue along the base of her neck.

"You still turn me on, you know that?" he whispered in her ear.

"I do, do I?"

"Uh, huh," he said, sliding his hand down her stomach, placing the palm of his hand firmly over the mound of her pubic hair.

Victoria turned and found Jonah's lips in the darkness. They kissed softly in the night. A yearning sparked from somewhere within, firing waves of heat into her belly. She longed to have him inside her. She reached down, pulled up her nightgown, threw her leg over him, and guided him into her. They lay like that for some time . . . barely moving . . . exploring each other with their tongues . . . feeling the safety of each other's warmth.

"I love you, Jonah Roberts," she whispered in his ear.

He reached down and grabbed her buttocks, pulling her tightly to him. They began to move slowly in rhythm with one another.

"I love you too."

—∽∽—

Early in the morning on Wednesday, November 1st, Fenton Montague sat motionless on the attic floor. After a time, he quietly rolled up his blanket and tied it to the underside of his knapsack. He put his baggie inside another and stored it snugly in one of the side pockets. He took out a tennis ball and shoved it in his right front pocket, put away the can of orange juice, looked around for other belongings or trash, and slowly . . . quietly . . . carried his knapsack to the boxes he'd piled up under the attic vent.

He had formed a makeshift staircase with some of the sturdier boxes on Monday afternoon, and now he could easily climb them to the vent above. Fenton stood at the foot of the staircase, straining his eyes to see above him. A second nylon ladder lay on the top box, ready for use, attached to studs in the wall just like the first down below.

He walked back to the spot from which he'd come, studying it in the dark of the night. He smiled. He was ready now. The hard part was over. He had earned some fun and games.

Fenton picked up the mop handle he'd found a few days earlier and took the few steps necessary to reach the attic entrance. He straddled it now, one foot on either side. The steps lay folded up in front of him. He reached down and grabbed the rope he had attached to the bottom stair and held it in his hands. He put both hands on the mop handle and placed it in the second to last rung, pushing down and away, as if casting a boat from shore with an oar.

He needed to push hard at first, which was difficult because he also wanted to go slowly. As the door finally opened, a few inches at first, and then a foot or more, a sense of unbearable excitement fluttered his stomach. *We'll see who's in control now, won't we, David?*

The door glided smoothly, without a squeak, but no matter how carefully he might have planned it, still it was impossible to make it completely quiet. He pushed a few inches at a time, stopping occasionally to listen. Gaining confidence that the door was moving freely, he pulled the rope taut, against the direction of his push.

This part was important. He had thought it through a hundred times. He needed something to push the door down, but at the same time he needed some way to keep it from slamming open. The opposing forces of the push of the handle and the pull of the rope were working exactly as he'd planned.

The angle of the door grew steeper. The further down it went the more firmly he pulled against it with the rope, until finally the mop handle would move no more. *Perfect.* He laid the handle on the plywood floor next to him, picked up the nylon ladder, and slid it down to the floor below. He could feel the warmth of the house rise to meet his face. He liked it.

Ever so slowly, one methodical step at a time, he positioned himself to climb down the ladder. It's astounding how quiet one can be with the proper determination and the required patience. Fenton didn't fear the ladder's strength. He'd checked it already. The less he had on his mind right now, the better. Slowly . . . he began the descent of death.

When Fenton was firmly planted on the runner in the

hallway, he stood for several minutes. He wanted to collect his thoughts, absorb his surroundings, let his eyes adjust to the new light. There was no way for him to know who, besides David, was in the house. In fact, there was no way for him to know that David was in the house. *Some things have to be left to fate.* He leaned against the wall, breathing deeply but slowly through his mouth.

He began the long journey down the hall, past the staircase, toward David's bedroom. He crawled on all fours, his right side touching the wall, his knife in his right hand. When he reached the doorway to the bedroom, he stopped. He knelt there on all fours like a wild animal on the prowl . . . looking . . . smelling . . . listening. He wasn't human now, completely transformed into a perfect killing machine.

He'd rehearsed this over and over in his mind. Like a highly trained athlete, he knew every move he would make. What he didn't know was that his prey was wounded. The horrifying realization that you are about to die, and the strength that accompanies it, would be fatally diluted in David's case by the medication now flowing freely through his veins. It would be easy. *Too easy.*

As if in combat, Fenton crawled on his belly to the foot of David's bed, staying low . . . out of sight in case he wakened. He could hear David snoring. Slowly, with great effort, he moved inches at a time. He was so close. He could taste the blood in his mouth. As he came around the corner of the bed, he stopped again. He didn't breathe . . . didn't move. *You're mine now, asshole.*

Fenton's eyes were level with the nightstand now. He didn't know what the little box with the button on top was, but he knew a pistol when he saw one. *David, I'm disappointed in you.* Fenton picked up the .45 revolver off the nightstand, stretched his upper torso slowly back, and stuck the gun under his belt at the small of his back. *Just like the cops.* He pulled the tennis ball from his pocket, palming it in his left hand.

He could hear David's labored snoring. He was in the

deepest of sleep. Fenton slowly rose to his knees, arranging the knife comfortably in his hands. Using every muscle in his upper legs, he pushed up without the use of his hands, standing now above his prey. He watched him for several moments.

To David, the whole thing seemed a hallucination. He could feel Saperstein breathing on him, the cold steel of the gun he'd taken from David resting firmly on his Adam's apple. It was so real, so lifelike. "You're mine now, asshole," Sap was saying. David could feel the heat from his breath on his face. He swatted the air above him with the back of his hand to push it away, but he hit Saperstein's arm.

Saperstein's arm? David's mind flowed in and out of thoughts, worries, fears. "Don't fuck with me," he said, but Saperstein kept calling his name. Whispering in his ear. David could feel his breath hit his eardrum. He turned his head a couple of times, but the gun pushed harder, it's cold steel pressing into his flesh. David's eyes began to flutter.

Fenton's erection strained to free itself from his pants. *Oh, this is beautiful.* "Daaa-vid," he whispered closely to his ear. "Oh, Daaa-vid."

David opened his drugged eyes, the reality of the moment incomprehensible to him. Still in a dream, he closed his eyes hard, squinting comically in the process. When he opened them again, the horror of his dream became the reality of his life. He fought the Halcion for some semblance of his known world. *This could not be happening.* He was still a nonbeliever.

In the flash of a second, Fenton straddled David on either side, beneath the blankets. His knees firmly wedged at his side. Only David's right hand was free. He was trapped, immobilized, as if in a straitjacket. His eyes bulged with fear. He tried to say something but found himself choking on a tennis ball shoved firmly in his mouth.

It was all too much. He wasn't capable of fighting off the drugs, comprehending the horror of the moment *and* Fenton's presence at the same time. In a final, desperate act to save his life, he reached for the nightstand. He was in the middle of his bed; it was hopelessly out of reach.

He flung his right fist wildly at Fenton's smiling face, but the attempt was futile from the start. Given the circumstances, there could be no strength behind the gesture. He couldn't pull his elbow behind him for velocity, making his attempt feeble at best. It's eerie what the eyes give away. Fenton could see the pathetic swing coming while David was still thinking about it. He caught David's wrist in midair, and in a swift, firm movement slid it under his left knee. The battle was complete.

Fenton stroked David's sweaty hair with his left hand, holding the knife firmly against his throat with his right. Fenton could feel the stiff body beneath him. Every muscle straining for freedom, but afraid to move. The fear in David's eyes filled Fenton with a sense of masculinity—with power and control. He stared into them for the longest time, watching them flit from side to side in the dim light of the night.

"David, I needed you. I wanted to be your friend. I thanked God I found you. I would have done anything for you. *Anything.*"

David's face was glazed with shock. He tried desperately to free himself. Fenton grabbed his hair and yanked his head down into the pillow. "Don't even fucking move, asshole," he said, "or I'll slit your throat clean through. Do you understand me? This is not your play anymore. This is my play, and I'm the star."

David was having difficulty breathing through his nose. He struggled for oxygen. Every time he would attempt to suck in Fenton let more weight down on his chest. He was suffocating.

"What's the matter, D.B.? Can't breathe?"

David's eyes pleaded with Fenton. *Please! I can't breathe. I'm going to die.* Every cell in his body struggled for life, but the Halcion fought him at every turn. He thought of Caleb and Sumner. The innocence of their voices played in his mind.

Fenton smiled maniacally. "Don't worry. You'll pass

out before you die. Tell me, David. Did you ever think of quitting?"

David closed his eyes, relaxing his body somewhat. There was nothing he could do. He had lost.

Fenton yanked his hair again, forcing David's eyes open. "I'll ask you *one more time*. Did you ever think of quitting?"

In an act of surprising defiance, even to him, David widened his eyes, stared straight into Fenton's, and shook his head firmly back and forth. *Go ahead. You can kill me, but you will* never *control me.* He knew he would die now and desperately wanted to spit in Fenton's face. More than anything he wanted to tell him to go to hell. His sheer helplessness only added to the overwhelming desire to go out the winner.

"I didn't think you would. You're stupid, you know that?"

David heaved for breath, his heart beating madly to pump what little oxygen it could get to his body. The sweat dripped from his forehead. His mind whirled, twisting in a violent eddy, fighting battles on several fronts. His brain screamed at him in a crazed yearning for life.

Without warning, Fenton decided not to push his luck. There were battles to wage. "You know what?" he asked.

David stared at him, the terror coming now from suffocation, not from Fenton.

"Death is the Great Leveler."

David saw Rebecca's face, smiling at him in the distance.

Fenton pulled the serrated side of his diver's knife with all his strength from one side of David's neck to the other. It cut deep and clean, blood spraying everywhere, as if his endless struggle for air had built an inhuman pressure inside David's veins. Fenton sat there, his mouth open, feeling the release inside his pants.

He sliced again and again as hard as he could, the specially designed knife making relatively quick work of the bone and cartilage of David's spine. Fenton could feel the warmth, the sensual ecstasy flowing through his body. When the feeling had passed he realized David's head had rolled sideways on the pillow. He picked it up by the hair, still straddling the body, and cut what remaining strands of nerve tissue and muscle kept David's head attached.

"David, we could have been friends," Fenton said, holding up David's head, staring into his lifeless eyes. "Why did you mock me? Why were you so quick to judge me? Didn't you know you were my savior? My Christ on earth?" Fenton spit in his face. "Fuck you, David. Mr. High and Mighty, with all your money and power. A lot of good it did you, huh? Huh, Mr. Hotshot?"

Fenton carried David's head quietly to the top of the stairs. He laid it there as a housewarming gift to whoever would be the one lucky enough to be first inside.

"Good-bye, David," he said, carefully propping it up so that it rested on the floor against the top post of the banister. "Say hello to God for me."

Fenton climbed the nylon ladder, went back to the attic and retrieved the container of gasoline. He lowered it to the floor with some rope and climbed back downstairs. He poured it over David's body, his bed, and the floor, stopping in the doorway to soak the entrance.

He went back to the bed, pulled a sheet over his hand, and picked up the phone. He dialed 911.

"Darien fire department. What is your emergency?"

"Thirty-two Woodbury Lane. Hurry. Please, hurry," he whispered, as if choking on smoke.

He replaced the phone, looked at the bedside clock on David's nightstand and waited. In less than a minute the signal blared from the horns on top of the station house in town. The police would also be informed. It wouldn't be long before all hell would break loose.

Fenton decided to test fate, filled as he was now with a sense of invulnerability. He waited one more minute, walked to the doorway, and lit a wooden match. He stood as far back as he could and tossed it into the room. The fireball threw heat at his back as he quietly walked to the nylon ladder leading to the attic. He climbed it quickly, pulling it up after him, dislodging it from the nails. He lay down on his stomach, reached down with his right arm, and grabbed one of the steps, pulling them up, folding them as they rose. He lay there, holding the attic door open a foot or so, and waited for something to happen.

He didn't have to wait long. In a matter of seconds he could hear voices outside. Someone was yelling, *"Fire! Fire!"* When he heard the front door open, he released his pressure on the steps, letting the springs close them quietly. He rose, walked to his knapsack, stuffed in the nylon ladder, and climbed the boxes to the vent.

This part of the attic was farthest away from David's room. They would no doubt search every inch of the house for him. It would probably be a while before someone thought to look in the attic, and even that was assuming the fire didn't spread too rapidly. He grabbed the rope he had tied to the vent, pushed on it firmly, and let it slowly down to the ground.

Fenton stuck his head out the opening, looking in all directions for signs of movement. Nothing. Everyone had congregated in front. Fire is a great distracter. He thought he could hear the first of the fire trucks now. He held his knapsack out the opening and let it fall to the grass, throwing the nylon ladder out after it. Fenton crawled out the opening feet first, stomach down. He was surprised to find he made it through a little easier this time. He hadn't counted on that. He wondered for a moment just how much weight he'd lost in the last few days.

Fenton climbed down the ladder, grabbed his knapsack, and took off through the woods. He never looked back. *So far, so good.*

—∞—

Shortly before 3:00 A.M. on the morning after Halloween, Austin F. Prescot, II headed for home in his Audi A8. By any measure he was legally drunk. Making certain to follow the speed limits, he conscientiously set his speed control two miles under the posted limit. He drove cautiously, both hands on the wheel, his left eye closed to keep the center dividing line from multiplying on him.

At fifty two, he was a bit thick around the waist, but felt he still carried it well in a suit. He was the chief operating officer of a major pharmaceutical company headquartered in Manhattan and stood a good chance at the top spot when the current CEO retired two years from now.

As Austin pulled off the second Darien exit of I-95, he made every attempt to concentrate on his driving. A car on the road at this hour of night will attract the attention of the police quicker than just about anything he could think of. He drove slowly, but not too slowly, down the Post Road, through the center of town. Past the Darien Sport Shop, the one movie theater, a family-owned grocery, a pizzeria. He turned right just before the railroad trestle.

He passed Ernie's, feeling a touch disappointed as he realized it was too late for him to pop in for a nightcap. He had gone to the Rangers game that night with a few colleagues. The Canadiens were always a good game, and this one was no different. Afterwards he and another drinker from the office decided to have a few pops at a local pub on 33rd Street. Drinkers always know who the other drinkers are. They ferret each other out like singles at a couples' dance.

Without planning it, he stayed well past the time he had promised himself he would leave. He was flying to London in the morning and would not be in the office the rest of the week. With no responsibilities at headquarters and several hours of flight time to recover, he was handed a rare opportunity to let go, and he took it.

He squinted at the road now, thinking he was really too old to be doing this. He just didn't have the stamina anymore. Austin wondered why he didn't stop, and dreaded the thought of waking up in the morning. He reached into his glove compartment, took out a bottle of extra strength Excedrin, and swallowed three caplets dry.

Austin could see headlights in his rearview mirror. They were behind him a bit, but closing the gap. His heart began to beat faster and his palms began to sweat. A wave of paranoia rushed over him. He decided to do something he'd never done before.

In his mind he tried to figure the distance between the approaching car and himself. A quarter mile, he figured. There was enough time. He was too close to home. There was too much at stake. He felt certain it was the right thing to do. He turned right onto a road that was not his, drove for fifteen seconds or so, pulled over to the side of the street, shut off his lights, and got out of his car. *Now try to prove I was driving under the influence, Officer.*

He stood at the hood of his car—the crisp, damp air chilling him to the bone. He had already decided he would hide if he saw headlights make the turn. He stood . . . watching . . . waiting. He was holding his breath now as he saw the lights approaching on the street up ahead. He was ready.

The car raced by, and in a moment it was dark and quiet. He dropped his head and laughed to himself. *This can't be normal, can it?* He breathed deeply, trying to regain his composure. Prescot decided this was one of life's events best not shared with anyone else. He looked up at the sky, the dark blue clouds breaking up now, slightly illuminated by a half moon off to the west.

What was that odor? He breathed again, smelling it clearly now. *Smoke.* Somewhere close, there was a fire. In the stillness of the night he stood motionless and listened. He could hear the unmistakable sound of radio transmissions. *Emergency vehicles. Holy shit! I got to get out of here.* He walked back to the driver's side, got in his car, turned on his lights, and pulled away.

Austin did a three-point turn, anxious to get home, desperate now for the safety of his bed. Like a soldier crawling the last twenty yards to his bunker, he was very close, yet there was much that could happen between here and there. He didn't dare relax until he pulled into his driveway.

Prescot almost didn't see him. "What the hell?" he

said, slamming on his brakes. The man in front of him was waving his arms furiously, obviously hurt. Austin put the car in park and stepped out, putting one foot on the pavement.

"Are you okay? Jesus, I nearly ran you over."

"Hospital. Please. Hosp—" the man said, collapsing on the road in front of him.

"Shit," Prescot uttered in despair as he ran to the man's aid. *I should never have taken this turn.*

"Here, let me help you to the car."

———

"W̲ould somebody *please* tell me how the fuck this happened!" Warren McKutcheon screamed as he fumbled at the front door with his key. "I can't see a goddamned thing! Dickie! Get a light over here. Now!"

Officer Richard Newhouse was already behind him. "Here," he said.

"Detail! Roll! Roll! Roll! Let's move! Now!" McKutcheon screamed into his mike as he kicked open the door, standing to one side lest flames leap from behind it. "Come on!" he said to Newhouse. "Let's go!"

Newhouse grabbed his jacket. "Skates! We can't go in there," he yelled over the roar of the flames within.

"He's my responsibility, Dickie! I got to get him."

Newhouse clung to Skates by the collar of his jacket. The two men stood practically nose to nose. *"Listen to me! You'll die in there.* Skates, you can't go. I don't know what the fuck's goin' on, but if Johnson were alive, he'd be out by now. If he's not out now he's dead."

"You don't know that," McKutcheon said, frantically trying to pull free from Newhouse's grip. "He could be suffocating in his room while we're sittin' here yankin' our puds! You want to stay, then stay. I'm goin' in."

By now, the other officers had gathered at the altercation in front of the Johnson home. "He's right, Skates," someone said. "You're not equipped. You'll never come out alive."

Newhouse held McKutcheon firmly, fearing what he'd

do if he let go. "Even if you make it through the flames you'll never get through the smoke. You'll pass out before you get upstairs."

McKutcheon attempted again to yank free from Newhouse's hold. *"Jesus Christ! He's dyin' in there, Dickie! He's dying!"*

"Skates, listen to me! He's already dead. Look at that, will you?" Newhouse said, pointing up at the raging conflagration with his left hand, holding McKutcheon with his right. "Look at it!" he screamed again. "He's dead, man. Got it? *D E A D, dead.* Nothing you can do is going to change that. You go in there and get killed, I swear to God, I will *never* forgive you. *Never!*"

The sirens were clearly audible now in the tranquil night air. There were two, maybe three engines.

"Someone get to dispatch," Newhouse barked. "Tell those guys this one's for real. Have their masks and tanks on."

Skates stood there, helpless. He knew Newhouse was right. He would never make it. Not in a million years. It would be suicide. The heat became unbearable as the fire worked its way down the hall, flames shooting down the staircase. They had to back away. Skates was filled with grief. He couldn't understand how this could have happened. There just wasn't any way.

Had Johnson committed suicide? Had he set the fire? Had he decided enough was enough? Had he decided to end this nightmare on his terms? He must have. *Who else could it have been?* Was it some type of explosion? Couldn't be. *From the bedroom?* It didn't fit. McKutcheon's mind was jumbled. He couldn't talk any longer.

He squatted, his elbows on his knees, his head in his hands. He began crying, heaving deep, sobbing breaths. He had been charged with keeping this man safe. David Johnson was his responsibility, and now he lay roasting like some pig at a July Fourth picnic. Skates simply couldn't take it.

As if a distant background noise, he could faintly hear the sirens as the fire trucks pulled up the Johnson driveway and out into the street. The sound of diesel engines roared behind him. He could hear someone mumbling orders, men yelling, the fire roaring. He was lost deep in the grief of his failure. They would need to take him away.

Newhouse knelt next to McKutcheon, laying an arm around his shoulders. "Skates, Skates," he said, failing to get his attention. "Listen to me. You couldn't have done more. Hear me? You did everything you possibly could."

McKutcheon was inconsolable.

"Skates, listen, buddy. We gotta move now, okay? The fire boys are here. We gotta get out of their way, Skates. Come on, let me help you up."

When Newhouse had safely removed McKutcheon from the line of action he turned to one of his colleagues. "Spats, do me a favor. Get an ambulance up here. Skates is gonna need some help. I've never seen him like this."

"Got it."

The fire captain gave his orders firmly, loudly, deftly. He ordered his men, outfitted in full fire-fighting protective gear, to search downstairs. They looked for any human, living or otherwise. Upstairs was out of the question, at least for the time being. Two other teams worked the flames, one from the front door up the staircase, the other from the lawn through the master bedroom window. The entire west wing of the house was a raging inferno now. They'd save it in the sense that it wouldn't burn to the ground, but it would be a long, long time before anyone lived there. It would never again be the Johnsons.

In time, the flames receded enough for the attack team at the door to begin their way up the stairs. They fought the flames valiantly, expertly. It couldn't have been done better. They worked the steps, the walls, the ceilings with the nozzle, spraying in a wide arc, beating back their nemesis with trained precision. Sweat streamed down their masked faces, the clothes beneath their protective layers were soaking wet.

The second man on the hose nearly jumped from his boots. "Holy shit!" he said, barely audible through the noise and his air mask.

261

"What?" the other responded, looking in the direction of his partner's gloved, pointed finger. He had to lean forward, barely able to discern what it was through the intense smoke. "Jesus, Joseph, and Mary! I got the hose!" he yelled. "Go get Flanagan!"

David's head was partly scorched. The powerful stream of water from the fire hose had moved it from its original position. It lay on one ear a few yards down the hall, resting against the wall, where it had been propelled by the initial blast of water.

Flanagan and the fireman who initially saw David's head climbed through the melee to the top of the steps. The fireman pointing it out to Flanagan before joining his partner on the hose.

Flanagan had to lean over to see it through the smoke. He looked at it with disgust. "Jesus Christ! I never want to see this house again as long as I live."

Fire is loud. It roared in the bedroom. Captain Flanagan struggled to be heard through his mask. He walked closer to his men, who were now fully involved with the fire, and leaned toward them as he spoke. "All right! Forget it! Let's knock this sucker down so the cops can get in here! If there's a head, there's a body, so keep your eyes peeled!" Not that it mattered, the smoke was too thick.

Flanagan didn't want to just leave it there, but he knew better than to touch it. He climbed back down the stairs, twisted off the regulator from his mask, and walked toward the small crowd of police huddled on the front lawn.

"Who's in charge here?" he asked.

Newhouse traded glances with a couple of the men. McKutcheon was clearly in no shape to deal with anything at the moment. "I am," he said, stepping forward.

Flanagan didn't recognize him. "Officer, I'm Captain Patrick Flanagan. May I speak with you for a moment please?"

Flanagan wasn't sure just how many people should know about the decapitation. He correctly assumed that, as with most ongoing investigations, the fewer people privy to the facts the better. He figured he'd let the authorities decide who should and shouldn't know. No need to tell everyone at once.

"Of course," Newhouse responded, walking with Flanagan a few yards away.

Captain Flanagan stopped, letting Newhouse take a few steps past him. When Newhouse turned Flanagan spoke quietly, his back to the other officers.

"I'm sorry, I didn't catch your name," Flanagan said, removing his helmet and air mask.

"Oh . . . Newhouse, sir. Richard Newhouse."

"Listen, Richard. One of my men just called me upstairs. I, uh . . . I don't know how to say this really. But . . . well . . . there's a decapitated head lying in the hall upstairs."

"A head?" Newhouse asked quietly.

"Yes. I'm not sure whose. Could be Johnson's. It's partly burned and it's very smoky up there. Visibility's bad to say the least. But once we got her knocked down, I think Captain Esposito should see it."

"You can say that again. I had dispatch call him. He should have been here by now."

"Good."

"Jesus. Are you sure it's a head?" Newhouse asked.

Flanagan looked at him. "Trust me, Richard."

—∞—

Cedric Halliway found not only Fenton's printer but also an opened package of paper stuffed neatly in the back of Fenton's storage bin. He had hoped to find both. One without the other would not be nearly as powerful in court.

He and Hill finished in the basement a little after 8:00 P.M. They neatly wrapped and secured the fruits of their search in the back seat of their cruiser, bid Whitaker good-bye, and left Boston a half hour later. They grabbed a quick bite for the road at the Roy Rogers on the Mass Pike and were back at headquarters just before 11:30 P.M. on Halloween night.

Rose was asleep when he arrived home. Halliway was exhausted. He couldn't put in the same hours he once did, not without repercussions. He and Hill had both been burning the candle at both ends. Even warring armies have to rest. Halliway looked forward to a good night's sleep. He undressed in the guest room, neatly laying his suit on the bed. He went to the bathroom, closed the door, tossed his socks and underwear in the hamper, and splashed hot water on his face.

There were times that being in the world of the criminally insane—handling their belongings, thinking their thoughts, touching their underside—made him feel dirty. In these instances he would shower for half an hour, just standing under the steaming hot water, purifying himself of the sickness of the world in which he toiled. But there wasn't time for that tonight. He didn't feel dirty. He felt tired.

He took his robe from the back of the bathroom door, put it on, and looked at himself in the mirror. Halliway knew he really should think about packing it in. He'd gone about as far as he was going to go in his career. But retirement scared him. *What would he do with himself?* Yes, he and Rose had made many wonderful plans, but that was all talk. Action is easy to verbalize when you know you don't have to do it. He could feel Father Time closing in on him. *Let me just catch this scumbag. Then I'll re-evaluate.*

The digital clock on his nightstand read 12:47 when he finally crawled into bed. He pulled the sheets and blankets out from underneath his wife, wrapped himself in them, and lay on his right side, staring at the wall. He remembered he had to get the snow blower in for repair this weekend. It was his last conscious thought before sleep.

Rose Halliway jumped up from a deep sleep at the sound of the phone piercing the tranquillity of the night.

"Hello?" she said, clearing her throat.

Captain Esposito felt uncomfortable. "I'm sorry to bother you at this hour of the night, Mrs. Halliway. Is your husband there?"

She wasn't sure. He hadn't been when she went to

sleep. She looked over and laid the telephone between the two of them on the bed, placing her head back on her pillow. *You'd think I'd get used to this.* "Honey, it's for you. Ric," she said, nudging him slightly.

Halliway moaned, craving sleep. His body desperately fought his attempt to open his eyes. It begged him for more.

She pushed him a little harder. "Honey, it's Captain Esposito. Ric, come on. He's waiting for you."

"Oh, God," he mumbled, rubbing his forehead. He felt nauseated. "What time is it?" he asked. His clock read 3:14. "All right, all right," he said, running his hands down his face, pulling down his cheeks and the corners of his mouth.

He picked up the phone from the bed. "Hello, Pete." *This better be good.*

"Hi, Ric. I hate to bother you this early in the morning. I just got out of bed myself."

"No bother," Halliway lied. "Goes with the territory. What's up?"

"He got 'im, Ric. Don't ask me how, but Johnson's dead as a doornail."

Halliway sprang up, pulling his legs out from under the sheets, bringing them over the edge of the bed. "What? How could—"

"He cut his damned head off. We found it lying in the hall. Just about burned the whole fucking place down, too. It's a mess, Ric. You best get out here."

Halliway was stunned. "But I thought you had his place covered?"

"We did. Believe me, no one, I mean *no one,* entered that house. Not tonight."

Halliway dragged his left hand through his hair. "Shit!"

Rose turned her head now, resting her hands under her pillow. Over the years, there had been hundreds of calls in the night, but it wasn't often she saw her husband respond like this.

"All right, I'll be there as soon as I can. Did you call Hill?"

"No. Wanted to speak to you first."

"I'll call him. Stay put," he said, lying back down, replacing the receiver in its cradle.

"Honey?" Rose asked. "What is it? What happened?"

Halliway closed his eyes, drawing a deep breath. "David Johnson. He's dead. Somehow the son of a bitch got to him."

Rose closed her eyes. "I'm sorry," she said.

"He's got a wife and two little kids," Halliway said, the balls of his hands resting in the sockets of his eyes. "Jesus, I want this guy. Look, hon, I gotta go. I'm sorry. I'll call when I get the chance."

He leaned over and kissed her on the cheek. "Love you," he said.

"Love you too," Rose said, her head buried in the pillow.

He sat on the edge of the bed, his forehead resting in his hands. "Boy, I'll tell ya. This isn't getting any easier."

"You don't have to keep doing it," his wife said from the warmth of their bed. "It's time we started to think about enjoying ourselves. Before it's too late."

"I know, I know," he said, wiping the corners of his mouth with his thumb and forefinger. "Let me close this one, then we'll talk."

She'd heard it all before. He'd said that the case before this and the case before that. It was in his blood, she knew. There was nothing she could say. She lay there silent, watching her husband dress in the darkness of their room. She wasn't mad or hurt, just disappointed.

Halliway threw on a pair of khaki pants, loafers, and a turtleneck sweater and left the room, closing the door behind him. He walked to the kitchen, stopping at the wall telephone to call his partner. He hated to do it. He knew how lousy he felt. *I'm twelve years older. If I can do it, he can too.* God knew it wouldn't be the first time, although he couldn't remember the last time he was this exhausted.

"Hello?" Mrs. Hill asked, fumbling with the phone.

"Hello, Patrice, it's Ric. Sorry to wake you. Is Scott there?"

"Um . . . yeah. Just a sec, Ric."

He could hear mumbles coming across the line. He

thought he must feel exactly as Esposito had only a few moments earlier.

"What?" Hill said, his voice betraying sheer exhaustion.

"Hi, Scott. What ya doin'?" Halliway asked mischievously.

Hill had heard his partner ask him this a hundred times before. "Nothin' much. Just sittin' here hoping you'd call."

"Good. Get dressed."

"What's up?" Hill asked.

"Esposito just called me. It's Johnson. He's dead. Took his head clean off."

Hill bolted upright in bed. "What? But I thought—"

"Already been through this, Scott. Come on, get dressed. I'll be by in twenty minutes."

"Man. Tell you what, Ric. You handle this one yourself. I'll make it up to you next time."

"Yeah, that'll work. See you in twenty minutes."

"Yeah, yeah. I'll be here."

Halliway didn't pull into Hill's driveway. He waited in front of the mailbox, engine running, instead. Hill was out of his house in a matter of seconds, approaching Halliway's car with a travel mug of instant coffee in each hand. The two men shot the bull for a while. All focus with no breaks will kill you, snap your nerves, or both.

"I don't know about you, but I feel refreshed. Couldn't have slept another minute," Hill said, handing his partner a coffee.

"Thanks," Halliway said, pulling the car out into the street. "When this one's over, I'm gettin' away. Just Rose and me. Maybe some bed and breakfast somewhere. Maybe Canada."

Hill snickered. "Nice and warm there this time of year."

"All right then, how 'bout the Keys?"

"Now you're talkin'. Could I tag along? You wouldn't notice me. I promise."

"Right. In your dreams," Halliway said, sipping his coffee.

They drove in silence for a while, Hill leaning his head

back on the headrest. His eyes were closed. "So, what the hell happened? I thought they had that place sealed tight."

"So did I," Halliway said. "Esposito said no one made it near the place. Not tonight, anyway."

"Well, *someone* did. You said he took his head off? You mean that literally?"

"Yep," Halliway said, nodding his head. "Esposito said they found it lying in the hall."

"Oh, that's beautiful. How the hell are we going to explain this one to the brass?"

"I'm not sure yet. Maybe you can do that."

"Yeah, right. And you're takin' me to the Keys."

Halliway smiled, watching his headlights break the morning darkness. "I've been thinking," he said.

"Oh, oh."

"Esposito swears that no one came in or out last night. But if no one went in, then how do you suppose he got to Johnson?"

Hill thought a moment. "I've been asking myself the same thing since you called. It's pretty obvious, I think. Either he dug a tunnel to his house or he was already in the house. I'm not sure which theory I believe yet," he added, making an attempt at comic relief.

Halliway's mouth formed a dry line. He turned to Hill. "Could it be possible the perp hid in his house for the last few days?" he asked in a disbelieving tone. "We've had the thing covered since Monday. Where was he?"

"Where would you hide if you wanted to stay in a house undetected?" Hill asked.

"There's only two places."

"Right," said Hill. "The basement and the attic."

Halliway thought aloud. "Would you hide in the basement? People use them all the time. Laundry, tools, storage. When's the last time you were up in your attic?"

"Pretty much my thoughts exactly."

"You mean to tell me that son of a bitch hid in the attic for the last two days?" Halliway asked. "I can't believe that. Can you?"

"Like I said, Ric. Smart. Smart *and* cold."

"Christ, Scott, we got to stop this guy."

"There's an understatement."

Halliway had retrieved Jonah's address and phone number from David's Rolodex file in his office. He didn't dare call. This was news that protocol dictated should be delivered in person. He would make the request from the phone in his cruiser. He spoke to a Sergeant Thibodeau at the Maine state police.

"I'm working on an investigation down here involving a very much at-large murderer. He's killed three people that we know of, one of them a police officer. I need to ask an unfortunate favor."

The word unfortunate caught Thibodeau's ear. He frowned, seeing it coming. "We'll do it if we can," he said.

"His last victim was killed early this morning. We believe his wife and children are staying at a friend's house in Harrison. I'm sorry to have to ask this of you, but we need you to send someone out to inform the family of his death."

"So we get the fun part, huh?"

"I'm afraid so."

"Where exactly in Harrison?"

"I can't really say. The address I have here is a rural box number. I can give you that."

"Shoot," Thibodeau said.

Halliway gave his counterpart what information he had on Jonah—the rural box number, the telephone number, his name.

"What was the victim's name?" Thibodeau asked.

"David Johnson."

"And his wife's?"

"Rebecca."

"Okay, Lieutenant. Consider it done. What do you want us to tell her? Anything specific?"

Halliway thought the less said now, the better. "Not really. I suppose you should ask if she has a preference of funeral homes, religious rites, things of that nature. Also, tell her I'd appreciate it if she stays where she is. The house was destroyed by fire. They can't come home."

"You want us to tell her that?"

It was going to be shock enough, he thought. "Probably not, you think?"

"Probably not."

"I agree. Just tell her I said to stay where she is. Have her call me at any one of the following numbers and leave a message. I will be back to her immediately. I can be reached at . . ."

Halliway thanked Thibodeau for his cooperation and apologized one last time for the inconvenience. As he sat holding the phone, it dawned on him for the first time that he and Scott needed to seriously discuss arranging some kind of protection for the Robertses and their guests.

Thibodeau hung up the phone and sat quietly for a few moments. He was located in Augusta so he couldn't do it. Thank God. He called the barracks located closest to Harrison, in Gray. He spoke to an old buddy, Thomas Cyr. He relayed his conversation with Halliway, giving him what information he had, explaining the dos and don'ts as Halliway had instructed.

"You know where that is?" Thibodeau asked.

"We'll find it. Well, I guess I should do this one," Cyr said. "I hate doin' this."

"Don't we all."

Captain Cyr called the Post Office in Harrison and got the street address of the Roberts's home. He put on his hat and coat and walked out to his cruiser, dreading the chore in front of him. Telling a spouse or close family member of a relative's death is always painful—its difficulty is only compounded when the cause of death is murder. There simply is no good way to do it. Every cop on earth dreads it.

It was just after 8:00 on Wednesday morning, November 1, when Captain Thomas Cyr's light-blue Maine state police cruiser pulled up the long incline of the

Roberts's property. As he drove to the crest in front of the house he could see two people on horses in the field below the riding ring. He wasn't sure they had seen him yet.

He got out of the car, put on his hat, gave the house a quick once-over, and looked in the direction of the horses. He wasn't sure, but he thought they both looked like women and wondered if one of them was Johnson's wife. He half hoped they'd see him, so he wouldn't have to make the walk. Not that he was lazy. He just thought if they came to him they could all go inside. *That would be better. You always want them sitting down.* But it didn't appear he was going to be that lucky.

Cyr adjusted his holster, his 9mm Sig Sauer 225 having shifted uncomfortably during the twenty-minute ride. He could hear a chain saw from somewhere off in the direction of the woods, and started for the field, noticing the two riders looking in his direction. *Maybe they saw me.* He stood and waited. They had stopped moving now and were sitting still on their mounts.

Victoria Roberts was the first to notice the cruiser. Her breath caught in her throat. *Oh God. Please don't make it bad news.* She pulled the reins on Caractacus and brought him to a halt. Rebecca saw her friend come to a stop and looked first at Vickie, then in the direction in which she stared. Becky's face seemed to pale, as if all the blood was draining from it. Her entire body froze. Her temples began to throb as she felt the sweat of her palms in her riding gloves.

"Oh, my God," she said quietly to herself, pulling Allycrocker up beside her friend. "Vickie, what do you think it means?"

"I don't know, Becky. Maybe they caught him," Vickie said, not believing her response.

"Vickie, I think I'm going to be sick."

"Maybe it's good news. Let's go see what he's got to say."

"I hope you're right," Rebecca said quietly.

So do I.

Captain Cyr could see the two riders approaching

now. He lumbered slowly back toward the house, wanting to be close enough so that a suggestion to go inside would seem the obvious choice. If he met them fifty yards from home, it would be awkward at best.

The two women trotted at first, both watching for any telltale sign on the trooper's face as they got closer. Neither one spoke. Rebecca thought she would pass out from the suspense. As she approached, the butterflies in her stomach nearly fluttered out of her mouth. She didn't like what she saw. The trooper wasn't smiling. It was like getting a letter of rejection; once you've read "We're sorry to inform you . . ." you don't need to read any further. The rest is just filler.

Captain Cyr removed his hat in an old-fashioned gesture of chivalry. "Morning, ladies," he said.

"Morning," Victoria said, pulling Caractacus to a stop in front of the cruiser. Rebecca was silent.

"Is either one of you Victoria Roberts?" Cyr asked.

Rebecca shook with relief. *Thank God. It doesn't have anything to do with me.*

"I am," Vickie responded.

Cyr turned to Becky. "Are you Rebecca Johnson?" he asked.

Oh, God! Rebecca's heart hammered against her ribs, then seemed to stop altogether. She nodded her head slowly, terrified of what she was about to hear.

"Mrs. Roberts, do you mind if we talk inside? Maybe the two of you could tie up your horses."

Cyr had done this many times before. In most cases it was a car accident, though occasionally there was a fatal snowmobile accident or a logging death. He'd only had to inform a family member of murder once in his fourteen years. His palms were wet.

Rebecca just stared at him. "Is something wrong?" Victoria asked.

"I'm afraid so," Cyr said, walking up the steps to the house, pushing the issue now. He really didn't want the woman on a horse when he told her that her husband had been murdered.

Victoria dismounted, tying Caractacus to a tree. Her

mouth was dry. "Come on, Becky," she said. "Let me help you down."

Rebecca started to shake. Her mind began to play tricks on her. A thousand scenarios whipped through her brain. *Maybe David had been hurt. Maybe kidnapped.* She could hear the chain saw whining in the distance. She thought of Caleb and Sumner. *If David was dead, how would they ever deal with it?*

When the two women had dismounted, and it became obvious they intended to go inside, Cyr walked back down the steps and offered to help Rebecca.

"Here, let me get that," he said.

"Thank you," Victoria said, handing him Allycrocker's reins.

"Why don't you take her inside, Mrs. Roberts," Cyr said quietly to Vickie. "I'll be right there."

Vickie helped Rebecca up the steps to her home while Cyr tied Allycrocker's reins to the tree and stood at the front of his cruiser. He took a deep breath. He hated doing this. He'd lost both his parents, and even though both had died of natural causes, he felt he knew how painful this would be for her.

When he entered the kitchen the two women were sitting at the kitchen table holding hands. He took a seat, laid his hat on the table, and looked Rebecca in the eyes.

Rebecca spoke her first words since coming in from the field. "He's dead, isn't he?" she asked.

Cyr felt that split second of angst, that moment of God-like awe when you know the news you carry is going to ruin someone's life. "Yes, ma'am. I'm sorry to have to tell you this, but your husband was murdered last night in your residence."

Victoria knelt at her best friend's side, holding her tight, letting her tears of grief cascade onto her sweater.

"I'm sorry, Becky," she whispered. "I'm so terribly sorry."

"My deepest sympathies, ma'am," Cyr added, certain Becky hadn't heard a word.

Victoria turned her head in Cyr's direction. "Thank you, Officer," she said. "We need to be alone now."

"I understand, ma'am. There is just one more thing," he said, reaching into his coat pocket, pulling out a slip of paper. "I'm s'posed to tell her that Lieutenant Halliway wants her and the children to stay here for the time being. When she feels up to it, she is to call him at either one of these numbers and leave a message," he said, pushing the phone numbers across the kitchen table. "He has your number. He'll return her call immediately."

"Anything else?" Victoria asked.

"No, ma'am. That's it."

Victoria hugged her friend firmly. "Thank you. Please shut the door on your way out."

He could feel Rebecca's grief. "I will," he said, replacing his hat. "Again, my sympathies, ma'am."

—⁂—

Fenton Montague stumbled toward Prescot's Audi. His benefactor's arms were wrapped around him, keeping him steady. Austin Prescot wanted desperately just to get home. He wished now he'd driven straight there. Instead, he was stuck helping out a stranger. And while he didn't have any choice, he wished he would just go away.

Prescot helped him into the passenger side of his car. "You've got blood all over you," he said. "What the hell happened?"

Fenton collapsed into the front seat, feigning exhaustion. "Hospital, please," he said, in a quiet, raspy voice.

Austin Prescot closed the passenger side door and walked around the front of his car to the driver's side. Fenton watched him in the glare of the headlights through one open eye. *Not a bad choice. Just about my size.*

Prescot was aghast. *What the hell am I going to do with this guy?* The nearest hospital was in Stamford or Norwalk. He couldn't very well drive him there. Christ. He was worried about making it the last few blocks home. He couldn't take him to the police. Talk about walking into the lion's den. He wasn't sure exactly what to do as he plopped into the driver's seat and put his car in drive. It wouldn't matter.

Fenton leaned over and stuck David's .45 harshly in Prescot's ear.

"What the fuck?"

"Drive, asshole," he said.

The reality of the moment took a few seconds to soak into Prescot's brain. *What have I done?* Prescot's mind played out the last few minutes with brutal clarity now. *How could I screw up like this? One minute from home, and now I'm going to die.*

"Please don't hurt me," he blubbered.

"Shut up!" Fenton yelled, pushing the gun harder into the side of his head. "I said drive."

"Look, I'll give you my money, my wallet, my car. Just please, *please* don't kill me!" he begged, tears beginning to form.

Fenton pushed hard, forcing Prescot's head sharply to one side. The cops would be swarming this area any minute. "If you don't get the hell out of here in the next three seconds, I'm gonna decorate your window there with your brains. Now drive!"

Prescot shook uncontrollably. "Oh, God. Oh, God," he kept mumbling. He put his foot on the gas, not sure where to go.

"Get on ninety five south," Fenton ordered.

"Where are we going?" Prescot asked, hopelessly dazed with fear.

"Hey! You don't talk, got that? I talk. You drive."

They drove in silence for the next twenty minutes, Prescot sniffling from time to time. He desperately needed to relieve himself but dared not say a word. He thought his bladder would burst. Eventually his mind became his worst enemy. *How long can I go on? I can't drive forever. I've got to take a piss!* Urine began leaking out, wetting his suit pants. He squeezed his thighs with all his might, his mind in desperate fear, his bodily need to urinate almost making him vomit.

"Get off here," Fenton said.

They took the Port Chester exit. Fenton directed Prescot through the center of town, eventually ordering him to turn onto King Street. They drove for several miles, Fenton's silence maddening . . . deafening.

"Left," he said. A short while later, "Left," again.

They were in the guest parking lot of Pepsi Cola's Westchester offices.

"Get out," Fenton ordered, pushing his gun deeply into the side of Prescot's head.

"Strip."

"But I'll freeze."

"Strip!"

Suddenly, Austin Prescot had had enough. "No," he said, looking straight into Fenton's eyes. "If you're going to kill me, then kill me. But I will not be your dog. Fuck you!"

Fenton's rage erupted from deep within. *Do you know who I am? I own you, mister. No one says no to me. No one!* He walked a step or two away from Prescot, just enough for him to put down his guard ever so slightly. Without warning Fenton turned and struck him sharply on the temple with the butt of his gun. Prescot fell limp, urinating on the pavement as he lay in a clump on the ground.

Fenton undressed him. He took everything: his rings, watch, glasses, socks, and underwear. Standing now in the clothes soaked with David Johnson's blood, he leaned down, put the .45 to Prescot's left temple and stopped. *No . . . every little thing matters. One shot fired in anger could screw up the whole plan. I can't do anything to attract the cops.*

He went to the car, reached into his knapsack, and pulled out his knife. He wished he could spend more time with this asshole, but first things first. He leaned down, grabbed Prescot's hair, lifted his head up, and quickly jerked the serrated edge of the blade across his throat. He stood there a moment, watching the fountain of blood form a pool on the blackened asphalt. *No time. Gotta go.*

"See ya 'round, asshole," he said.

He threw his bloodstained clothing into a pile in the back of Prescot's Audi and quickly changed. Fenton wished Prescot hadn't pissed his pants. Instead of putting them on, he cranked up the heater and laid them to dry on the floor beneath the warm flow of air. It was almost 4:30.

The car was still running. Fenton got in, adjusted the seat, and pulled out into the road, making sure to use his blinker. He continued north on King Street and took the Merritt Parkway south. He wanted to make sure he put the cops off the trail as long as possible. New Jersey would be a good place to start.

As the Merritt turned into the Hutchinson River Parkway, Fenton took it to the Cross County Parkway, hooked up with the Saw Mill River Parkway in Yonkers, and headed for the George Washington Bridge via the Henry Hudson Parkway. Tri-staters just call it the GW.

Fort Lee, New Jersey, is the first city one comes to on the Jersey side of the George Washington Bridge. Fenton had his own money but was pleased to see that Prescot had left him over three hundred dollars in his wallet. When he hit Fort Lee he pulled into a Mobil station, put on Prescot's pants, filled the Audi with Super, and began to look for food. It was just past 6:00 A.M. now.

He pulled off the turnpike, drove into a McDonald's, and ordered two breakfast burritos, two hash browns, a large coffee, and two containers of orange juice. He was starving. He also asked for a glass of water and extra napkins.

Fenton pulled over to the parking space farthest away from the restaurant and ate his meal with ravenous delight. Like a wild animal devouring its prey, he took large bites, chewing each aggressively. Periodically looking up, his eyes darted from side to side. He checked his rear- and side-view mirrors for signs of passersby.

When he had finished eating, he adjusted the rearview mirror downward, looking at himself for the first time in several days. Not pretty. He wet a napkin and began the process of grooming himself as best he could. He wiped dirt, sweat, and blood from his neck and face, scrubbed his hands and under his arms. His image in the mirror reflected the beginnings of a thick beard. *Good. I'll need it.*

He continued down the main thoroughfare, fortuitously finding a twenty-four-hour drugstore. He parked in the parking lot, checked himself in the mirror one last time, and went in. He purchased nail clippers, underwear, socks, toothpaste, toothbrush, a razor, shaving cream, and a pair of sunglasses.

When he reached the counter he laid out his things, consciously avoiding eye contact with the cashier. She made a perfunctory attempt at small talk, but abandoned it quickly. Fenton was hardly a paragon of amiability. Her chatter made him nervous. He didn't like people. "Thanks," he said, as he picked up his bag and left.

Fenton walked to the Audi, took his knapsack out of the trunk, and walked to a pay phone near a now dark liquor store. He was confident that while some of the more industrious employees of Pepsi Cola had probably started to arrive for work, they would undoubtedly bypass the visitor's parking lot. Still, soon enough someone would find Prescot's body and the search would be on. It wouldn't take long for the police to make the connection once they identified the victim and where he lived. Fenton thought it wise to get as far away from Prescot's car as possible.

Fenton called a cab, and thirty minutes later was paying cash for a single, nonsmoking room at the Clinton Inn in Tenafly, New Jersey. He took the elevator to the second floor and walked the length of the corridor to his room next to the ice machine. Unlocking the door, he threw his knapsack and bag on the bed, ripped off his clothes, and immediately started the shower.

As the water ran, steaming up the bathroom, he emptied his Walgreens bag onto the bed and grabbed the razor, shaving cream, and scissors. He brought them back to his makeshift sauna, tossed them on the counter, and stepped into the shower for a much needed escape.

Fenton stood under a stream of water as hot as he could tolerate for the better part of twenty minutes. *God, does this feel good.* He finished, dried himself, put the razor and the shaving cream in the shower, wrapped a towel around himself and stood at the foggy mirror anxious to begin his transformation.

Leaning over the sink he began clipping his hair as far down to his scalp as he could without cutting himself. He felt around with his left hand, occasionally finding a missed clump. Satisfied he'd gotten all he could with the scissors, he turned the shower back on, stepped inside, and rinsed his head under its steaming jets.

Fenton lathered his scalp thoroughly with soap, then applied a generous layer of shaving cream to one side of his head. Feeling with his fingers he began to shave in short, even strokes. He would need to repeat this process two more times.

Standing in the shower he could feel every wrinkle on his scalp for the first time in his life. When finally he could feel nothing but skin, he turned the shower off, toweled down, and viewed himself in the mirror above his dresser. *Not bad. Not bad at all.* He had kept his beard but shaved his head. Once he added the sunglasses, the metamorphosis seemed almost miraculous. He hardly recognized himself. He walked to the side of the bed and literally fell onto it. The clock on his nightstand read 8:02.

—✦—

The previous evening's storm had ushered in a cold front from the north. On Wednesday, November 1st, the sky was clear and blue, rinsed pure by its heavy downpour. The trees' bright autumn leaves rustled calmly in a cold breeze sweeping in behind the front.

It was just before 7:30 A.M. when a visitor to PepsiCo reported seeing Prescot's body in the upper-level parking lot. The guard inside the foyer of the main building removed his walkie-talkie from its holder and called headquarters. "Dunston to base. Over."

"This is base, Dunston. What is your situation? Over."

"We need a unit to check out the visitor's parking lot. I've got a woman here who says she just found a dead body lying in it. Over."

"Dunston. Did you say a dead body? Confirm. Over."

"Affirmative. Dead. As in lack of life. Over."

"Visitor's parking lot? Over."

"Affirmative."

Pepsi security responded immediately. A white Jeep with the Pepsi logo on its hood and PepsiCo Security printed on the doors, pulled up to the visitor's parking lot less than two minutes after Dunston's call.

"Holy shit!" the security man said. He got back in his Jeep, sitting sideways, and pulled the mike off its cradle on the front of the dash.

"Heinrecker to base. Over."

"This is base. What ya got? Over."

"Base, we have a Caucasian male. Nude. Fifty, fifty-five. His throat's been slashed. Better call the police. Over."

"His throat's slashed? Repeat. Over."

"Affirmative. Get the cops here. Hurry."

"Heinrecker. Are you sure he's dead? Did you check for a pulse? Over."

"Spence, trust me on this one. This guy's had his last Pepsi. Over."

"Roger that. Calling the police now. Stay there. Rope off the area. Over."

"Roger."

"Heinrecker?"

"What?"

"No one in or out, got it? Including you. Stay put. Over."

"Roger that."

Three New York state police cruisers responded to the scene within seven minutes of one another. With remarkable efficiency they cordoned off the area, set up barricades, and directed traffic until detectives and the state medical examiner could arrive.

"What do we got?" the M.E. asked the detective in charge, ducking under the yellow plastic ribbon marked Police Line Do Not Cross.

Lieutenant Harry Rideman answered. "Not a hell of a lot, I'm afraid, Doc. No clothes, no jewelry, no car. Throat's been slit from ear to ear. Got a couple of footprints in the blood, though."

"Barefoot or shoes?" the M.E. asked.

Rideman understood the thinking behind the question. He knew the importance of this find. It could be their only lead. At least for now. An ex-smoker, Rideman characteristically picked at his teeth with a toothpick. "Looks like sneakers. Don't look new, either."

From an investigator's standpoint, worn shoes are always better. Everyone's shoes wear differently. They can be as useful as fingerprints.

The medical examiner had arrived last. Technicians were already busy collecting blood samples and taking photographs from every conceivable angle of the scene and its surroundings, the footprints, as well as close-ups of the body.

A technician was working on the softer, hairless parts of Prescot's body with strips of photographic paper. Methodically, but with artistic skill, he clamped individual sheets down, one at a time, on his abdomen, buttocks, inside wrists, and the under parts of his upper arms.

There was always a shot they could lift a print from one of these areas, assuming it had been left sometime after 9:00 or 10:00 P.M. Anything north of ten hours begins to push the envelope. Areas of the body with hair other than peach fuzz won't yield a usable print. But the technician had seen enough corpses to have a pretty good idea. He figured this one for six hours, maybe less. With one this fresh, the M.E. could tell them within half an hour, give or take.

There were many things the detectives at the scene were hoping the medical examiner could clarify for them, not least of which was time of death. The M.E. snapped on a pair of rubber gloves and began his examination, performing some perfunctory visual and physical checks first. When he finished, he began checking the body for signs of rigor mortis.

Like so much else in nature, the laws of rigor follow a pattern. Rigor is caused when the body's muscles lose the source of energy they require for contraction. Adenosine triphosphate, or ATP for short, normally dissipates fully in a corpse after about four hours. The muscles' lack of ATP causes rigidity and stiffness, which is only mitigated by the onset of decomposition.

Rigor normally begins within two to six hours and is complete within a similar time span. Muscle rigidity occurs in the face and jaws first, moving to the upper extremities, torso, and lower extremities in that order. Many variables play upon the timing of its arrival, among them the weather, the victim's fitness and weight, and physical activity just prior to death. Heat accelerates the rigor process. Cold retards it.

In reality, rigor mortis is one of the least reliable means of ascertaining time of death. There are other, far more accurate scientific methods, such as those associated with the relatively new field of forensic entomology, the study of insects associated with death.

The unmistakable death scent common to all corpses draws flies by the thousands. Insects follow very predictable laws of nature, and it is unusual indeed when flies are not laying eggs on a corpse within an hour after death. Within twelve hours, maggots hatch and begin feeding on the flesh. Within forty-eight hours, spiders, mites, and millipedes arrive to feast on the orgy of bugs at the scene.

The M.E. could clearly see fly larvae in Prescot's nose, eyes, and mouth. He looked up at Rideman standing above him, watching him twiddle his handlebar mustache. "Did you check with the weather people yet?" he asked.

"Yep. Said the front pushed through sometime after two-thirty last night."

"What was the low last night?"

"Got down to forty in the city. You got to figure three, maybe four degrees colder out here."

The M.E. checked his watch. It was almost 9:15.

"Well?" Lieutenant Rideman asked.

The M.E. knew exactly what he wanted. "Well, what?" he asked, playing ornery.

"Did he tell you who's gonna win in the fifth at Belmont? Come on, Doc. You know what I'm lookin' for."

"I won't be able to say for sure until I get him back to the lab."

"Yeah, yeah, I've never heard that one before. Come on. Placate me. Take a guess."

Time of death is far more difficult to pin down than most people realize. It is as much an art as a science; the examiner's experience is as large a determinant as anything.

The M.E. stood up, snapping off his latex gloves. "Well, he blanches on his back, and that's how we found him, so we know he hasn't been moved. Lividity's not fixed, so we can assume less than four hours, anyway. Judging from the lack of rigidity of the large muscle groups, the weather, and the fact his body temperature is about five or six degrees below normal, I'm guessing three to four hours."

"So sometime between four-thirty and five-thirty, right?"

"Roughly. You'll have to wait for a better number. I'll need to run some tests. Anyway, Harry, you know rigor isn't all it's cracked up to be. There are too many variables. That's the best I can do for now. Sorry."

"That works, Doc. Thanks."

Rideman's partner joined them. "Harry. Just got word from headquarters. FBI says NCIC shows an Austin Prescot was reported missing this morning. Computer says the wife states he never made it home last night."

Contrary to the impression given in the media, there's an extraordinary amount of cooperation between the FBI and local law enforcement. They are seldom involved in the turf war that television and the movies are apt to depict. Like VICAP, the National Crime Information Computer, or NCIC, is a national data base run by the FBI. It's available, free of charge, to every law enforcement agency in the United States, Canada, and Puerto Rico. Professionals just call it the Computer.

NCIC holds a record of every police stop conducted in the country, where a computerized license check has been requested, as well as all the be-on-the-look-out-fors, and any other information police departments across the country either want to find out or want to share. All inquiries go through the mammoth central computer in Washington, D.C. Local agencies can contact NCIC and have teletypes sent to all departments on a national level or on a specific geographic basis.

When a police officer stops you on a routine traffic stop and goes back to his cruiser, he's not checking with motor vehicles to see if your car is stolen. He's running your name and plates through NCIC. On-line, real time, and extremely powerful—it's a great way to track some-one down.

What Rideman's partner had just said didn't make sense to him. Prescot had been missing for twelve hours, max. Rideman squinted his eyes slightly. "It hasn't even been twenty-four hours. What's he doing in the Compu-ter?"

"Apparently, he's the second in command at some large drug company. Had a big business trip to London and missed his flight. I guess the responding officer thought that was enough."

"It would be for me. Anybody else missing in the last twenty-four hours?" Rideman asked.

"Computer comes up clean. At least since Monday."

"Where's she live?"

His partner checked his notes. "Darien."

"Sin City, huh? Name?"

"Rita. Rita Prescot."

"Call her, Oscar. Tell her we're short on details, but we still need to speak with her. Ask her to stick around for the next hour or so. Looks like we're takin' a trip across state lines."

SHATTERED
SLEEP

—⚬—

BOOK 3

Scott Hill sat down at the table in the interrogation room he and Halliway had commandeered for the Montague case. He slid a cup of coffee across the table to his partner, pulled out a pack of Camel filters and lit one.

"I thought you quit," Halliway said.

"I did," Hill responded, blowing smoke toward the ceiling.

"Oh."

"This son of a bitch has gotten under my skin, Ric. I just can't seem to relax anymore."

"Careful, Scott. Don't get too close. It'll kill you."

"I know, I know. Sounds like you and Pat went to the same school."

"She's giving you good advice."

"I want this guy, Ric," Hill said, staring into Halliway's owlish, bronze eyes. "I want him bad."

The round clock on the wall read 8:17. Lieutenant Halliway and Sergeant Hill had spent over three hours at the Johnson residence subsequent to the fire. David's torso was hopelessly burned. There was little they could know until an autopsy was performed, and given the severe damage to his body, even that would prove less helpful than usual. One thing was certain. Someone had cut David's head off with a knife.

"All right, what have we got?" Halliway asked, pushing his files to the side, laying a yellow legal pad in front of him.

Hill began the litany. "Well, there's Bennett. Throat slashed. We got the kid. Hand hacked off. Body not found. Most likely dead."

Halliway looked up at Hill over his glasses, his eyes saying it all.

"All right, he's dead. Happy?"

Halliway frowned. They both knew he was dead. Over time you become immune to death, but the children always linger in your mind. Halliway didn't like it any more than Hill, but it was what it was, and no amount of wishful thinking was going to change it. There was an uneasy moment of silence.

"Next," Halliway responded.

"There's Johnson. Decapitated. There's the Reebok footprint in the blood on the patio that matches the one found at the end of the road. We know Fenton and David had come in contact in the past. Circumstances not exactly rosy. We know Fenton's car was seen on Johnson's street Monday morning."

"What time was that again?" Halliway asked.

"About . . . let's see," Hill responded, referring to his notes. "Around six-thirty in the morning."

Halliway was fixed in concentration. His eyes were closed. "Keep going."

"Fenton's car was found near the train station. We've got five notes. The note he sent Johnson. The one from the back of the door. The one from the freezer. The note Yellow found on the dog, and the note in Fenton's fridge in his apartment . . ."

Halliway interrupted. "Document Examination should be back to us shortly with the results on the printer and the paper. There sure as hell better be a match."

"Don't even think it, Ric."

"What do we know about this guy's psyche? What makes him tick?"

"That's the tallest order of all," Hill said, exhaling cigarette smoke. "Tryin' to get information out of a hospital is like pulling a molar from an alligator. I've been in touch with Bridgewater State, St. E's, Mass General, and MacLean. They aren't givin' up anything. They say we can sue 'em if we want, they'll still win. Client records are confidential. Period."

"What about your friend?" Halliway wanted to know.

Hill dropped his butt in the bottom of his Styrofoam coffee container.

Halliway disapproved. "Pretty."

"Don't start, Ric. I've already got a wife. Anyway, I called Rhonda this morning. Says she'd like to help us . . . if she can. Said she'll see what she can do. She's pretty sure she doesn't have access to that information, but thinks she knows someone who does."

"How many psych hospitals are there in Boston anyway?"

"Jesus, Ric, there's so many hospitals in Boston, just thinkin' about it gives me angina. I told her to start at those four. If she doesn't get anything there . . . well, we'll cross that bridge when we get to it."

"All right. So Montague goes to Johnson's home sometime Monday morning. Had to have been after they escorted him to the station. He was still out and about in his car early that morning."

"Or so we think," Hill added.

"The Reebok prints say so," Halliway continued, finishing his coffee. "Anyway, he climbs up the ladder to the vent in David's attic. I got the print boys running whatever they can find on it right now. With any luck, we'll hear back from them sometime today. He settles in and waits until early this morning to strike."

"How could he do it, Ric? I mean, there's no sign he took a shit or even a piss. He's got to be incredibly focused."

"Obsessed is a better word."

Hill was flipping through his notes. "What time did Esposito say they sent a man over there anyway? I don't think I've got that in here."

"Umm . . ." Halliway hesitated, scanning his notebook. "Around noon, I think. Make a note to ask him. So, let's say you're in the house of the guy you want to murder. What do you do?"

Hill was thinking when the desk sergeant knocked on the door and poked his head in. "Sorry to bother you, gentlemen. Lieutenant, there's a Captain Esposito on the line. Says it's urgent."

Halliway looked at Hill, rising from the table. "Thank you, Sergeant." He rolled down his sleeves, buttoning them as he got to the door. "Let's hope it's good news," he said, as he walked out of sight.

"Captain, what ya got?" Halliway asked, picking up the phone.

"I just had an interesting call from a Lieutenant Rideman with the New York state police. You know him?"

"Heard of him."

"Oh. Well, anyway, he tells me he's investigating a slicing. Up at Pepsi in Westchester. Says the victim came up missing on the Computer. Asked if I wanted to be present when he questioned the wife, seeing as how it's our jurisdiction and all."

"What did you tell him?" he asked, wishing Esposito would get to the point.

"I'm heading there right now. Guess where the guy lives?"

You're killing me, Pete. "I have no idea, Captain."

"One block from Johnson's home."

That caught his attention. "Interesting," Halliway said.

"When they found him he was stripped nude. Throat slashed ear to ear. No car. Nothin'. You think it's possible our man carjacked him or something? Used his car to escape?"

"Could be. Call me as soon as it's over. I'll be here for the next few hours. If I'm out leave a message on my voice mail. You could have something here, Pete. Make sure you get the make and year of the victim's car."

"You got it. Talk to you when it's over."

Halliway walked back into the interrogation room carrying two fresh coffees.

"Anything?" Hill asked.

"Looks like our boy's on a bit of a spree."

———

$\mathbf{R}$ebecca Johnson sat at her friend's kitchen table, looking out over the riding ring and the pasture beyond. Her eyes were red and moist, her face ashen. Her insides felt as if a cold fist was closing slowly over her heart. She held a crumpled Kleenex in her right hand, occasionally dabbing her eyes.

She stared through a blurry haze at the wall of trees beyond the fields. Many of them had begun to lose their leaves, but there were still holdouts, bright red and yellow against an ever-broadening backdrop of gray. She drew an eerie strength from the knowledge that they had been there before she was born and would be there after she died.

Victoria put a cup of hot cocoa on the table in front of her and took a seat. She spoke quietly, looking out the window. "Becky, Officer Cyr said that Lieutenant Halliway wants you to call him." She slid a piece of paper out into the middle of the table. "He left two numbers for you."

"I just don't have the strength now, Vickie. I will in a while. Promise."

"When are you going to tell the kids?" Vickie asked.

Rebecca dropped her head, tears running down her cheeks. "Oh God, Vickie. What am I going to tell them? How do I explain something like this to two young children? They're just going to die."

Victoria's chest felt heavy, tears forming in her eyes. "There is no good way, Becky," she said, laying her hand on her friend's arm. "All of you are going to have to grieve in your own way. I guess the sooner that begins, the sooner you can all get on with your lives."

"I can't even think. I don't know who to call or what to do. I don't even know what insurance company David used. I don't think I'm going to make it, Vickie."

"Jonah's still in the woods with the kids. You want me to go get them?" Vickie asked.

Rebecca was torn. She knew what she had to tell them would forever change their lives. The kids didn't know it yet, but they were enjoying their last carefree moments on earth. One part of her brain told her to prolong it as long as she could. For them. The other part said she needed to get this over with. She needed to share her grief with her children.

She looked up at Vickie solemnly. "Would you?" she asked.

"Of course. Will you be okay here by yourself?"

Rebecca remained quiet, nodding her head.

Victoria rose, walked to the coat hooks on the rough-hewn wooden wall next to the door and put on her coat. She stood with her hand on the knob, looking at her friend. "I'll be right back," she said.

Rebecca yearned for sleep. She felt like crawling into bed and curling up into a fetal position. She tried to think of what to tell her children. They would know something was terribly wrong the moment they saw her. Should she sit them at the kitchen table? Should she take them into the bedroom? Should Jonah and Vickie be present? She was adrift in a sea of emotions.

Rebecca turned her eyes to the large picture window on the side of the house, watching Victoria walk briskly by the pile of wood chips used for the horses' stalls. She felt such sorrow for her children. Very shortly, life would never again be the same for them. She wished there was some way, any way, she could shield them from the inevitable pain.

Her body heaved, but tears would come no more. A body only has so many. Rebecca watched Victoria's body diminish in size as she scampered down the field, approaching the entrance to the trail in the woods. She could faintly hear the whirring of Jonah's chain saw from somewhere deep in its interior. She stared through hazy eyes as Vickie disappeared.

She didn't know if she could do this. Her heart beat quickly, her palms were wet, her face twisted in anguish. A short while after Vickie entered the woods Rebecca realized she wasn't breathing. She closed her eyes and inhaled deeply. Her body shuddered, a quiver shooting down her spine. Then it happened. Silence. Jonah had turned off the chain saw. Vickie was telling Jonah of his best friend's murder.

The floodgates had opened through which the tears that passed could never again be put back in their place. She watched the entrance to the trail now with unbearable anxiety, seconds feeling like hours. When finally she saw Caleb and Sumner come bounding playfully out into the pasture, a sob burst out her mouth. She leaned over the table gripping her knees with her hands. She tried to pray.

"Oh, God, please. Please give me strength."

The tops of her thighs began to hit the underside of the table as her legs twitched up and down uncontrollably. *Here they come. They're running. They're happy.* Caleb ran up the wood chip pile followed by his brother. Jonah and Vickie walked hand in hand, tagging a short distance behind.

Rebecca felt as though she would pass out. She watched as if on a big-screen television the final seconds of tranquillity her children would know for a long, long time. She could hear one, then both of her sons' feet bounding up the outside steps. In a last ditch effort to avert sudden collapse, she shot up from the table and walked to the living room. *Please, God. Give me strength.*

"Mom!" Caleb shouted, running into the kitchen. "You won't believe how much wood we moved today. We started a whole new trail. Uncle Jonah says—" He stopped mid sentence as his mother turned around, standing in the middle of the living room.

"Mom? What's wrong?" he asked.

Sumner, out of breath, joined him at his side. "What is it, Mom?" he asked.

Jonah and Victoria stood by the kitchen table, watching, their arms wrapped tightly around each other. Jonah had tears in his eyes. He wasn't sure what to do. Maybe the presence of a man would lend an air of normality. But then again, maybe this was something the Johnsons should share alone.

"Boys, Mommy needs to talk with you," Rebecca said,

digging deep. "Come here please. Sit on the couch so we can talk."

Caleb was scared. He began to cry. Sumner, being two years older, tried heroically to act in control. Both boys approached slowly, sitting on the edge of the couch. Rebecca knelt in front of them. Instinctively, Jonah stepped forward. He stood now by the fireplace. He didn't know what the spatial rules were at a time like this, but he desperately wanted to help. He just wasn't sure he should . . . or could. Victoria sat motionless at the kitchen table, staring outside. She couldn't bear to look. She closed her eyes tightly as Rebecca began to speak.

"Caleb, Sumner," she started, the pause interminable. "I have to tell you something. But before I do, I want you both to know that I will always be here for you. Okay? I will always love you. Always."

Jonah looked down, clenching his right fist to his mouth. His left arm wrapped tightly around his chest. Both boys were crying now. In a primordial attempt to maintain sanity, Rebecca's mind disengaged as she began to speak. She was watching herself tell her children the unimaginable.

"Daddy is . . . your Daddy is dead."

Theodore Givens's secretary knocked once on the door to his office before poking her head in. "Ted, there's a Lieutenant Cedric Halliway on the phone for you. From the Connecticut state police. Says it's important."

Ted Givens was drinking a cup of coffee, the *Wall Street Journal* spread out on his desk. He gazed at her with a quizzical look, a kind of what-the-hell-does-he-want-with-me? look. "Put him through," he said.

He swiveled in his chair as he picked up the phone, watching the Staten Island ferry dock at its terminal. "Ted Givens speaking."

"Good morning, Mr. Givens. I'm Lieutenant Cedric Halliway of the Connecticut state police."

"Good morning, Lieutenant. May I help you?"

"I'm afraid not, sir. I've called with a bit of bad news."

Theodore Givens, III, lived in Summit, New Jersey, certainly one of the wealthiest towns in the tri-state area. It wouldn't be unthinkable that terrorists or kidnappers had taken his wife. But this gentleman was from the Connecticut state police, not the New Jersey state police. Givens wasn't immediately worried for his family's safety, although the thought certainly crossed his mind.

"Yes? What is it, Lieutenant?"

"Well, sir . . . I've called to tell you that David Johnson was murdered last night. In his home."

The news rocked Givens. He shot upright. "Murdered?"

"Yes, I'm afraid so, sir."

"Oh, my God," he said, drawing out the words. "Who? Why?"

"Unfortunately, sir, I'm somewhat limited as to what I can tell you, given the ongoing nature of the investigation. Let's just say we feel we have a very good lead and are doing everything in our power to apprehend the perpetrator, even as we speak."

"Jesus Christ. I can't believe it, Lieutenant. Are you sure?" Givens asked rhetorically. "He was one of our brightest young men. This firm will miss him greatly."

"I'm sure of it, sir. I'm sorry to have to bother you so early in the morning with news of this nature. But I felt a courtesy call was in order."

"Yes, thank you, Lieutenant. Have you spoken to Mrs. Johnson yet?"

"No, not yet. She and the children are out of town. I'm expecting to hear from her shortly."

"You mean, they don't know?"

"They've been informed, sir." Halliway changed the subject. "Is there anything you'd like me to tell her?"

"Uh . . . yes, there is," Givens said, pausing to think. He had to say something. "Please extend my deepest sympathies to her on behalf of myself and the firm. Tell her if there is anything she needs . . . anything at all . . . she is to call me without hesitation. Understand?"

"Yes, sir. I'm sure she'll be appreciative."

"Lieutenant?"

"Yes, sir?"

"Catch the son of a bitch who did this. Whatever the cost. If your budget won't allow you to perform any task you think will be useful in his apprehension, I want to know about it. I will personally pay whatever it takes to put this cocksucker behind bars. Is that clear?"

"Yes, sir. Thank you."

"Do you know anything about the funeral arrangements, Lieutenant? Place? Time?"

"No, not yet. I can let you know when I hear something, if you'd like."

"Yes, I'd appreciate that."

"I'll let you know as soon as I find out anything. I'm sorry, Mr. Givens, but I really must be going. Thank you for your time."

Givens was afraid he'd hang up. "Lieutenant?" he asked quickly.

"Yes?"

"Have you seen many murders before?"

If you only knew. "More than I can count," Halliway said.

"Maybe you can help me. I mean, what do I tell everyone? I'm not quite sure I know the etiquette here. You know . . . how to handle this properly."

"I don't know if I can help you there, sir. I've had to tell a lot of people some pretty bad news over the years. It never gets easier. I guess the best advice I can give you is to be up front. Encourage discussion. Do you have a psychiatrist or psychologist on the payroll?"

"This is Wall Street, Lieutenant. We put their children through college."

"Well, I might suggest you speak to him or her first. You might also want to make them available for individual counseling to any of your employees who feel they might need it. I'm afraid I can't be much more help than that."

"No, that's good advice. Thank you."

"You're welcome. I have to go."

"Of course, Lieutenant. Thank you for calling."

Ted Givens hung up the phone, staring blankly at the

Journal. Suddenly, none of it seemed that important anymore. He was suddenly aware of the fragility of life, how we all take it for granted until we see firsthand how quickly it can be snatched from us.

He pushed the intercom button on his console. "Kathryn, I need to call an emergency managing directors meeting. Please have everyone meet in the conference room at ten o'clock, sharp."

"Will do. Do you want me to call catering?"

"Just have them bring plenty of coffee. It shouldn't take long."

"Okay. Ten o'clock."

Givens reached for a Macanudo from a box on his desk. He carefully clipped the end, throwing it in the wastebasket. He leaned back in his chair, turning the cigar several times in his mouth, and lit it with his lighter. Plumes of grayish-blue smoke rose into the air.

He was contemplative. "David, if you can hear me, I just want you to know you were one of the very best. I was proud to have you on my team." Givens held the cigar skyward. "This is for you, my man. I know how much you enjoyed a good smoke. I promise I will look after your wife and children. You have my word. You will be missed."

Tears formed in the corners of his eyes. He took out his handkerchief and wiped them. Ironic, how no amount of money, no amount of power, can ever fully shield someone from the vicissitudes of life. Givens rose and walked to his window, staring at the Statue of Liberty. *No golf this weekend.* Instead, he decided, he would visit the Beauty in the harbor.

—⁓—

There are many factors that cause the brain dysfunction known as psychosis. The list includes forces endemic to the individual and exogenous or external determinants. Certainly chief among these are interpersonal and family relationships.

By definition, the psychotic suffers from, at best, a seriously distorted sense of reality, at worst, a total break with it. The perceptual and cognitive processes have become so impaired that psychotics are left virtual prisoners within their own world.

While it is true that some who suffer from this unspeakable psychological impairment may have auditory hallucinations, memory lapses, or difficulty in the use of everyday language, it is not true that they are never in touch with reality.

On the contrary, over the past century there have been hundreds of cases in which people enduring its wrath have moved freely to and from the world we label as real, often times not remembering actions performed while in the throes of their alter, hellish netherworld.

Around 11:00 A.M. on the morning of November 1st, Fenton Montague awoke from his fitful nap. He was still nude, lying on top of the covers of his bed at the Clinton Inn. Though he was cold, his body was covered with sweat. He brought the palm of his right hand to his forehead to wipe back his hair, stopping in mid motion. His fingers open, he patted his scalp. *My hair! Where is my hair?* The sudden beating in his chest scared him. He rose, walked to the bathroom, turned on the light, and stood frozen in front of the mirror. *Jesus . . . please. Not again.*

Fenton didn't recognize himself. He was immobilized with fear. He stood staring, arms wrapped around his chest. *What have I done?* With incapacitating horror, the events of the past few days hit him with seismic fury.

Individually, but as if all part of a single event, each of his murders returned to his mind. He was there now as he slit Bennett's throat. He could see it, hear it, feel it. He could feel his own body melt as he saw Mikey's pleading eyes—their saucer-shaped stare piercing his brain. He felt the hatred and fear of David's eyes as he slashed again and again, severing his spinal cord. He could see the fountain of blood—taste its metallic stickiness.

Fenton sat on the toilet, an overwhelming nausea ripping at his intestines. He heaved dry once from deep within his gut, spun around, and gripped the sides of the bowl, viciously purging his McDonald's breakfast. Soon there was nothing left, yet his body would not stop. His stomach heaved violently, again and again. Fenton gripped the bowl tighter with each onslaught, grimacing from pain the body feels when it purges but has nothing left to offer. Finally—just when he thought he might pass out—as suddenly as it started, it stopped.

He knelt at the toilet, strings of spittle and blood hanging from his mouth. He was spent. There was no energy left. He tried to stand but was unable to. Fenton crawled slowly to the tub, reached inside, and turned on the bath. He rested the side of his head on the cold porcelain, staring at the knobs as he adjusted the temperature with his left hand. When it was filled he crawled in, submerging himself in its warmth.

He thought for a moment of drowning himself. Oh, God, he pleaded. *What is wrong with me? Why don't you leave me alone. Please. I just want to be left alone.* He lay there for a long time, his ears submerged, just the openings of his nose peeking through the still bath water. He wished he would die.

As the water began to cool, it provided less and less safety. Eventually he yearned for bed. Stepping out, he turned on the red heat lamp in the ceiling and dried himself slowly with a towel. There was something about the heat. It made him feel safe. Like a fetus in the womb.

Walking from the bathroom, Fenton suddenly realized he didn't know where he was. He walked to the television console and looked at the propaganda one finds at every hotel. He knew he was in a hotel, but didn't know which one and didn't know where. He walked back to the nightstand, picked up a pad of paper, and read the address and phone number on the bottom. *Tenafly, New Jersey? What the hell am I doing in Tenafly, New Jersey?*

Fenton put on a clean pair of underwear, remembering now his shopping spree and the young Walgreens cashier. He walked to the door, opening it just enough to put the Do Not Disturb sign out. He walked back to the bed and crawled in, wrapping the blankets tightly around him.

He thought about the prior evening, shuddering as he felt David's spine give way under his relentless attack.

He remembered climbing out of the house and stopping a car. *Oh, God. The man in the Audi!* He'd forgotten about him until just now. He remembered driving to PepsiCo, killing him, and taking his car.

Fenton panicked for a moment, not sure where he'd left it. For a moment he feared it sat outside in the parking lot. Now he remembered what he was doing here. He'd taken a cab. He was safe. He had to put them off the trail. He didn't want them to think he was heading for Jonah's.

Jonah! Oh, my God, Jonah! Please God, he prayed, closing his eyes. *I want to stop. Please help me stop. I don't want to kill anymore.* He opened his eyes, staring at the popcorn ceiling. He pondered his situation for quite some time, his soul deeply punishing him for his deeds. His stomach hurt. He held the covers tightly around his neck. More than anything, Fenton wanted to just fade away. To be no more.

He felt scared, alone, and extremely tired. What was he going to do? He couldn't very well just go about his life as if nothing had happened. He thought of taking a bus home, but remembered with disgust that he'd burned that bridge, too. *God, Fenton, what have you done?*

For a moment he thought of turning himself in. *Let's just end this nightmare now. I can't live like this. More people will die. I have to stop myself. Maybe I can get some help.* But he had already been shuttled to and from more psychiatric hospitals than he could remember. *And look how much good that's done for me.* No, he felt certain if the police got their hands on him they would surely execute him. He feared death. He just couldn't do it. He didn't have the courage. Surrender was not an option.

He began to shake, fearful of who he was and what he would become again. He felt as though he were the only living thing in the universe—alone, destined to live out his nightmare to its conclusion. Whatever that was.

Without warning, his eyes filled with tears. He clung to his bedcovers as they streamed down his cheeks. He pressed his lips tightly together, vainly attempting to keep them from trembling. The battle was fruitless from the beginning. Fenton began to sob. The tears poured down his face, soaking the sheets at his neck. He tried to stop but his body had demons to purge. *Don't fight it.* Inevitably, he surrendered to the emotional onslaught. He'd never cried so hard in his life. Well, maybe once. Eventually he fell asleep.

When he awoke, the clock on the nightstand read 12:37 P.M. He reached for the phone and called Connecticut information. He lay on his left side staring at the wall, the phone by his side. He had made his decision. In a moment filled with trepidation and fear, he dialed the number.

"Connecticut state police. May I help you?"

"Yes, can you connect me to whoever is in charge of the Johnson murder. In Darien."

"That would be CID, homicide. One moment please."

A detective answered the phone. "Yes, who is in charge of the Johnson murder case?" Fenton asked. "I need to speak with him."

There was a moment of awkward silence. "That would be Lieutenant Halliway. One minute, sir. I'll see if he's in."

Fenton hung up the phone and waited a few minutes. His breath quickened, his pulse roared in his ears. He dialed again.

"Connecticut state police. May I help you?"

"Yes, Lieutenant Halliway please."

—⁓—

On the morning of Wednesday, November 1st, Oscar Stephenson and Lieutenant Harry Rideman drove their unmarked dark-blue New York state police cruiser slowly into the lane marked Private Drive. No Trespassing. The digital clock on the dash read 9:03 A.M.

The air was filled with a unique odor, something akin to rotting salt water. As the two detectives drove further they came upon a neatly cemented rock wall about three feet high, stretching the entire length of the right side of the meandering, one-lane road. Beyond it the muddy flats of one of Long Island Sound's inlets were clearly visible.

It was low tide. The sea water had retreated, leaving nothing now but surface plants wilting on the glistening mud, patiently awaiting the faithful return of their aquatic life support system. The mud threw off a pungent smell, almost like waste water, but not quite. It seemed oddly incongruous—out of place in a neighborhood so clearly reeking of wealth.

Across the inlet large older homes sat majestically on their acre or two of paradise. They carried a certain elegance. Most of them dating back to the early 1900s through the twenties. They were more reminiscent of the era of *The Great Gatsby* than many of today's more modern, airy structures. Some might call them mansions.

There was a certain architectural style prevalent in this peninsular section of Darien distinguished by the use of stone, brick, and wrought iron fences. The entire area evoked memories of a different historical era. The frequent use of urns and statues only augmented the feel.

"Can you believe this, Harry?" Stephenson asked. "I can't believe people actually live like this. Makes me feel about three inches tall."

Lieutenant Rideman was philosophical. "These people got the same problems as the rest of us. Probably more. Money can't buy happiness."

Stephenson wore a you-don't-expect-me-to-believe-that grin. "I'll tell you what," he said. "You give me the choice between bein' miserable and broke or miserable and filthy rich, I'll take the bucks every time." He leaned over his steering wheel, peering out his windshield. "What was that address again?"

Rideman checked his notebook. "Thirteen."

Stephenson was looking at two ivied stone pillars on either side of a driveway. A gargoyle sat atop each. "Thirteen. Here we are. I hope we're dressed okay."

Rideman smiled, twirling his mustache. "You feeling up to it today?" he asked his partner, hoping he'd offer to break the news.

"Hey, I did the last two," his partner said. "You can do this one."

It was worth the try. "Okay," he said, as Stephenson drove up the winding cobblestone drive.

The fingerprint technicians had run Prescot's prints through the computer and come up with a match. The lab had radioed the results on their drive up. Rideman thought for a moment how many times he'd done this. He couldn't count. After a while, they all seemed to melt together. But it was always tough, always a drain. He dreaded the task before him. As if preparing for a game, he closed his eyes and took a deep breath, steeling himself for what was to come.

Eventually they came to the top of a small rise, the driveway taking them to the right side of the three-story English Tudor home. Ivy had taken root and crawled freely up the sides and around the windows. The drive looped at the end. Stephenson followed it, parking the cruiser behind Esposito's under the portico attached to the side of the house.

"Call in. I'll go knock," Rideman said, getting out the passenger side door. He pulled back on a door knocker in the shape of a gothic-looking lion's head, and made contact four times against the nail-studded wooden door. He stepped back, waiting. A little time passed and he stepped forward to knock again when he heard movement inside.

The door opened. Rideman was surprised at the elegance of the woman standing before him. She was five foot seven, maybe eight, and he guessed she was in her mid fifties. She wore dark blue corduroys, white Asics sneakers, and a knit white and pink sweater with rose-buds scattered across the front. She'd obviously been crying.

"Mrs. Prescot?"

"Yes."

Stephenson joined him at the door as he spoke. "I'm Lieutenant Harry Rideman, New York state police homicide. This is my partner, Oscar Stephenson."

"Ma'am," Stephenson said, dipping his head slightly.

"Good morning, gentlemen. Please, come in."

"Thank you," they said in unison.

It was immediately obvious to both men that Rita Prescot, while worried sick, was completely oblivious to the fact that her husband was dead. Rideman dreaded the job before him.

It wasn't just the natural anxiety any normal human would suffer before imparting such horrible news. There was more to it than that. For he knew that when someone turns up murdered, the primary suspect is almost always a spouse, lover, or immediate family member. At least initially. To rule that out is folly. Rideman would want to talk to Rita Prescot at some length, searching for nuances. Discrepancies. Telltale signs.

He also knew Mrs. Prescot would want information—anything that would help empower her in her time of grief. Rideman would need to walk a thin line. He would need to surreptitiously probe, while simultaneously maintaining the all-important air of sympathetic messenger. It was an acquired skill—emotionally draining to say the least—something a good detective can do with his eyes closed.

The more money a victim had, the closer his family would be scrutinized. But this case was unique. After investigating a few hundred murders, a good homicide detective gets an early feel for what is and isn't probable. More often than not, the likely scenarios are apparent early on.

In all his years Rideman couldn't remember a single case of a wife slitting the throat of her husband. Women don't seem to kill that way, at least not by themselves. He'd seen plenty of shootings. He'd even seen poison and some drownings. And yes, he'd seen his share of stabbings, but never the throat. Still, right now everyone was a suspect. It wouldn't be the first time a woman had hired someone to murder her husband.

Even though he viscerally felt Rita Prescot was not involved, still, this early in the investigation he wanted to keep as many facts from her as he reasonably could. At least for now. Not until they had an opportunity to check bank records, brokerage accounts, life insurance policies, the will. There were still too many unanswered questions.

Captain Esposito had already arrived and was waiting for the two men in the sun room of the Prescot home. Everyone took a seat, an uneasy silence enveloping the room. Rideman wasted no time, wanting to get the worst part over with as quickly as possible. After the bare minimum of pleasantries, he informed Mrs. Prescot of her husband's death.

She took the news with more dignity than he had seen many wives exhibit over the years. She was clearly stunned, visibly trembling, as tears rolled freely down her cheeks. For Rita Prescot, the grieving process had just begun. Unbeknownst to the three cops sitting in that room, the investigation into her husband's murder was nearer to closure than they realized.

At one point, Rita Prescot excused herself, ostensibly to visit the bathroom. Rideman knew she most likely needed to let it all out. In her absence, Esposito rose and walked over to Rideman. "You mentioned to her that you had some things to go on. Mind elaborating?" he asked. "There could be a connection between your boy and someone we're after here."

"Really?" Rideman asked, surprised to hear it.

"Yeah. Last night we had a murder just a block from here. More than one, actually," he said with the wave of a hand. "It's a long story. Bottom line is, we believe the perp set out on foot. We're thinkin' maybe he carjacked Prescot on his way home."

"I'll be damned."

"Something else too. He's a throat slasher."

Rideman pushed his lower lip outward. "Well, we got a couple of sneaker prints in the victim's blood. Other than that we don't have a hell of a lot, to be honest."

Esposito's eyebrows rose. "No shit? It may be more than you think. We got two sets of prints we believe belong to him. Looks like we need to do a little comparing."

"Looks that way, doesn't it?"

—◆—

All shoe manufacturers in the country submit information to the FBI laboratories in Washington, D.C. with every change in tread pattern to their sneakers. Similarly, tire manufacturers regularly submit new tread designs. In this way, law enforcement computer data banks are kept up to date. Very few people have access to this information.

The Connecticut state police and the New York state police had already ascertained the year and make of the Reebok prints they had found at the various locations. What was important now was to make a definitive link between those found at the scene of Prescot's murder and those found around David's house and in the street.

Rideman thought now of Esposito's comments. He felt a revitalization at the information pertaining to the Reebok prints the Connecticut boys had found. He had foreseen a long and tedious investigation. Beginning with practically nothing, he envisioned countless hours of painstaking research, phone calls, and interviews. Followed by more of the same. The job can often be boring, particularly in the early stages, before things heat up as the suspect list narrows.

But now, suddenly he had been handed an unexpected and much welcome break. If New York and Connecticut were searching for the same man, it was quite possible that much of the legwork had already been done. He and Stephenson could join the hunt midway.

Feeling somewhat uplifted, he called the Connecticut state police. Rideman asked for Halliway and was put on hold. He checked his fingernails as he waited, holding the phone to his ear with his shoulder, picking at one of his cuticles.

"Good afternoon, Lieutenant. Cedric Halliway."

"Hi, Lieutenant. Harry Rideman, New York state police, homicide. I understand from a Captain Esposito of the Darien police department that the two of us may be looking for the same man."

306

"Yes, he called me a short while ago. I understand you found some Reebok prints at your scene this morning."

"That's correct. I was worried it wasn't much to go on until he and I spoke this morning. Suddenly, I'm feeling more upbeat."

"We're pretty much in the preliminary stages at this point," Halliway said. "It looks as though we just made our first definitive link between him and the three murders we've been investigating. My partner and I have been over every inch of his apartment. Apparently he's fond of proverbs. He's left five of them at various scenes. We found a printer and some paper in his storage bin. Our document people just informed me we got ourselves a match."

"So you know who the perp is?"

"We believe so, yes. A Fenton Montague. Lives in Boston."

Rideman was pleased. This might be easier than he'd thought. "Listen, Lieutenant. I'd like to send over a technician to make some comparisons. See if it's the same guy."

"Makes sense to me. The man you'll want to speak to is Stanley Tau. He's the best I've ever seen."

"Great. I'll have one of our guys call him. What have you got anyway?"

"Well . . . we've got three sneaker prints. Two in blood on some flagstone, and a cast of one we found in some mud at the end of the street where one of the victims lived. They're all fairly clear. A good technician should have no problem with them."

"They match?"

"Like two peas in a pod."

Every sole of every shoe in the world, no matter how nondescript when new, will take on special characteristics as it's worn. Some people walk on the outside of their feet, while others walk on the inside. The longer the shoe is worn, the more telling the wear becomes, until finally, a seasoned evidence technician can tell with virtual certainty that two separate prints came from the same shoe.

"I understand your man's a slasher?" Rideman asked.

"You can say that again. Let me fill you in on something, Harry. This guy is bad news. I mean *bad*, with a capital B. If we don't catch him, and soon, I can guarantee you we haven't seen our last."

"Well, obviously, Cedric—"

"Call me Ric."

"All right, Ric. Obviously we're going to need to cooperate. No sense reinventing the wheel every time we think we're on to something."

The two men traded home, work, pager, and cell phone numbers. They agreed that daily communication was essential, and set a time of day they could most likely be reached. Unfortunately for both, it was when they were at home.

Halliway noticed the other light blinking on his telephone console. "Harry, can you hold a moment? I've got another call."

"Sure thing."

Halliway put Rideman on hold and hit the button for his other call. "CID. Homicide. Lieutenant Halliway speaking."

"Lieutenant Halliway?"

"Yes."

"This is Fenton Montague. I believe you are looking for me."

Halliway stood, waving his free arm wildly back and forth, desperately trying to get someone's . . . anyone's . . . attention. Everyone was busy at their own work. In desperation, he picked up a book on abnormal behavior lying on his desk and tossed it across the room. It landed with a loud thud. Both detectives in the room looked up, startled. Halliway's eyes were full of frantic desire. He turned the forefinger of his right hand round and round, indicating he needed a trace. One of the men ran out of the room.

He didn't dare put Fenton on hold. Rideman would have to wait. He could feel the adrenaline pump through his body. "Why would we be looking for you, Mr. Montague?"

The cat and mouse game had begun.

"Cut the bullshit, Lieutenant. I hate to be patronized."

Halliway's brain raced, thinking of ways to stall. "Well, how do you think we should proceed from here?"

"Listen, I don't have much time."

Here comes the part where he tells me he doesn't want to be traced.

"I know you'll try to trace this, but please, don't waste your time. I may be crazy, but I'm not stupid."

Really? "No. But you would agree, would you not, Mr. Montague, that you are in need of psychiatric help? We can help you."

There was a menacing tone to Fenton's laughter. "There's a good one. But really, Lieutenant, keep your day job. It's not that funny. Tell me, this help you speak of, would that be before or after you fry my brains in the electric chair?"

"No one wants to kill you, Mr. Montague. I'm not going to lie to you. Of course we want you apprehended. Get you off the street before you kill again. That is our job, is it not? Certainly you can't begrudge us that?"

"Listen, enough of this crap. I have something I want you to know. I don't want to kill again. Believe me. I can't help it, Lieutenant. The voices. They come when I'm not expecting them. God tells me what to do. When I become him, I don't know what I'm doing."

"When you become who, Mr. Montague?"

"Don't call me Mister," Fenton said, turned off by Halliway's mock deference. "Look, I'm not an idiot. You can be as nice to me as you want, but you and I both know you'd just as soon drop me with your forty-five as see me go to trial."

"No, that's not true," Halliway lied, straining to see any sign that the trace had been started. "You need help. We can provide that for you."

Fenton glanced at the clock on his nightstand. It had been almost a minute now. He figured it would have taken them at least that long just to begin the trace.

"I've got to go. I'm sorry. Really I am. I hope you understand. Please don't hate me."

Halliway could feel him slipping away. "Wait. Don't go. One more question."

"Quickly, Lieutenant."

"Do you know who you'll kill next?"

"Yes . . . if the voices come again."

"Please, Mr. Montague. I beg you. Help us help you. Tell me, so we can stop you before it happens again. We won't hurt you. I promise."

Fenton laughed before hanging up. "Right."

———~~~———

Early in the morning of Thursday, November 2nd, Officer Cornell Jackson of the Fort Lee police department was patrolling the parking lot of the Walgreens Drugstore that Fenton had visited nearly twenty-four hours before. The fluorescent hands on his watch read 4:07.

He drove slowly by the various stores in the strip mall looking for the usual signs of something amiss. He shone his searchlight through their windows, checking for movement, lights that normally weren't on, or anything else that seemed out of the ordinary.

When he finished, he swung his cruiser slowly around and began a perfunctory drive through the nearly abandoned parking lot. Strange, he thought. Hadn't he seen that same Audi parked in the same spot when he drove through here yesterday? He might normally have paid it little attention. After all, the drugstore was open twenty-four hours. It could belong to an employee. But the Connecticut plates stood out—they clearly said otherwise.

He pulled his cruiser next to the driver's side door and got out to have a look. He walked around the trunk of his car, approaching the Audi from the rear. He shone his flashlight inside, slowly walking up to the driver's side window. Nothing. Jackson took a few steps forward, shining his light on the seat, the dash, and the floor in front. The car was empty. But something wasn't right. He could see dark smears of something on various parts of the car's interior. Was it blood? And anyway, who leaves an expensive out-of-state car just sitting in the lot of a not-so-great neighborhood for so long?

Jackson copied the plate number on his notepad and walked directly to his cruiser. He sat sideways on the front seat, side door still open, and pulled the microphone from the radio on the dash.

"Dispatch, this is one eighteen. Requesting a twenty-eight on Connecticut plate number Paul, Frank, Edward, double Z, zero, two."

Dispatch responded immediately. "Roger that, one eighteen. Running a twenty-eight on a Connecticut plate Paul, Frank, Edward, double Z, zero, two."

"Affirmative."

Jackson sat in his car looking at the sky beyond the apartment buildings across the street. It was still dark but had begun to carry that faint, scarlet-blue hue—the early harbinger of dawn. Jackson sat impassively, waiting. A few minutes later dispatch responded.

"One eighteen. NCIC comes up positive for the vehicle in question. Is it a green Audi A8?"

Jackson sat with a heel on the runner, resting the mike on his knee. "That's affirmative."

"One eighteen, please wait for further instructions."

The Fort Lee police dispatcher called in a detective from the squad room. "Nate, Cornell Jackson just requested a license check for a vehicle with Connecticut plates. The Computer reports the owner was found murdered this morning in Westchester County. Can you inform Darien and check with New York? See how they want the car handled?"

Nate Bridgman took the slip of paper containing the requisite information and left the room to make his calls. His first was to the Darien police. He wanted to confirm the accuracy of the teletype before sending New York scurrying like so many cockroaches in the light. Several calls later, after ascertaining the case was Lieutenant Rideman's, Bridgman called the New York state police.

Predictably, New York dispatch informed Bridgman that Rideman was at home. Probably out like a light, he thought. He had to stop and think a minute. Finding the car was important, but was it important enough to get the poor guy out of bed. Well, he thought, if I'm going to err it isn't going to be because I didn't tell him. He thought what he'd want if this were his investigation. If he were in charge, he'd definitely want to get his hands on that car. ASAP.

"I need to speak with him. It's important."

"If you give me your number, I can contact him and have him call you."

"Thank you," Bridgman said, giving the detective his number. "I know it's early, but I'm quite certain he'll want to know what I've got. Tell him it's relating to the Prescot murder."

"I'll make the call now. How long will you be at this number?"

"As long as it takes."

Approximately eight minutes later, Harry Rideman called back.

"Lieutenant Rideman. Thank you for getting back to me so soon. I'm sorry to wake you at this hour, sir, but I thought you'd want to know we just located Austin Prescot's car."

"Where?" Rideman asked.

"Here in Fort Lee, in the parking lot of an all-night drugstore."

"Do you have a man with it now?"

"Yes, sir."

"Good. Here's what I want you to do. Secure the vehicle. Can you impound it someplace safe?"

"Yes. We normally use the garage at headquarters."

"Good. Have it towed there. Do not touch *anything.*"

"Roger. Do you want our lab people to take a look at it?"

Rideman thought about that one for a minute. He knew his people were good. He didn't know about Fort Lee's.

"No, not right now. Let's just get it impounded. I'll be back to you shortly with instructions."

"Good enough, sir. I'll be waiting."

"Thank you, Sergeant. Good work."

Rideman set about making a pot of coffee before

starting what would surely be a long day. He walked to his study, retrieved his notebook, and carried it back to the kitchen table. His wife and kids were still sleeping. *Who isn't at four-thirty in the morning?* He listened to the coffee percolate as he jotted down the time and subject of his conversation with Sergeant Bridgman.

If Halliway was correct and there was a connection between Prescot's murder and the ones in Darien, they had a very sick boy on their hands. The sooner they got him off the street the better. He felt sure if they didn't catch him soon, there would undoubtedly be other, related murders to investigate.

Rideman wore a gray Nike sweatsuit. He rose, poured himself a cup of coffee, and sat back down at the kitchen table. He set his coffee down and turned sideways with his elbows on his knees, lost in thought. The thumb and fingertips of each hand pushed against one another, steeple like, resting on his mustache. The early morning hours were always his best. It was then his head was clearest—he had the most energy and the fewest distractions. His best thinking often came just before the sun rose.

He pulled his chair up to the table and brought his coffee to his lips with both hands. In these quiet, early-morning moments, he could nearly transform himself—becoming one with his prey—thinking their thoughts, feeling their feelings, anticipating their next move.

Rideman thought now of the conversation with Fenton that Halliway had told him about. He wasn't sure what, exactly, they were dealing with. A paranoid schizophrenic possibly? Fenton didn't appear to fit the stereotypical description of a sociopath. The mere fact that he heard voices told him that. There was clearly some level of psychosis. But what brought it on? What made him need to kill? Fenton himself said he didn't want to. *It never ends.*

He wasn't sure what to do about the car. He didn't know that Fort Lee's technicians weren't good, but he wasn't sure he wanted to take the chance. If he sent his own technicians down to work over the car it would be an unspoken insult. Even though he would never acknowledge his doubts, everyone would know. On the other hand, evidence they might secure from the Audi could be critical to putting Montague away. Did he dare jeopardize that for the sake of a few bruised egos?

I just can't risk it. This is too important. They'll get over it. They're big boys. He rose, walked to the phone on the kitchen wall, and dialed the number Sergeant Bridgman had given him. As the phone rang he wondered for a moment if he was making the right decision. As fast as the doubt came, it disappeared. He knew he was doing the right thing.

"Fort Lee Police. Sergeant Bridgman."

"Morning, Sergeant. Lieutenant Rideman here."

"Oh, yes. Hello, Lieutenant. Any decisions?"

"Yes, Sergeant. Please keep the car impounded in your garage. We'll be sending a team of technicians down to work on it sometime this morning."

There was a brief pause. They both knew what the other was thinking. "Okay, she'll be waitin' here."

"Sergeant?" Rideman started, wanting to explain.

"Yes, Lieutenant."

"Forget it. Nothing important."

—⁓—

At Rebecca's request, Victoria Roberts called Lieutenant Halliway for her on Wednesday morning, November 1st. She informed him that Becky was having a difficult time dealing with her grief and that of her children.

"Lieutenant, Becky wants to know if it'd be okay if she called you later today. I don't think she's up to it right now," Vickie said.

Halliway had seen his share of pain. He understood. Still he wished Rebecca had called. He needed to speak with her. "Of course, I fully understand. Tell her, please, to leave a message if I'm not available. I will get back to her as soon as possible. It is important that I speak with her."

"I will," Vickie said, needing a few answers herself. "Lieutenant? Can I ask you a question?"

"Sure."

"I don't know how to say this exactly, but . . . well, do you think Fenton killed David because of what happened in Boston twenty years ago? I mean, it just seems so crazy to me."

"Mrs. Roberts, crazy is the operative word here. We haven't found any other connection. Certainly Mr. Johnson couldn't think of one. He swore he never saw him again after that. Not that he knew of, anyway."

Victoria sighed deeply. "It's just that . . . well, Jonah was part of it too, you know?"

"Yes, Mrs. Roberts, I'm aware of that. We need to remember that we are dealing with a deranged man. There's just no way we can superimpose our rationality on a mind this seriously impaired."

"Do you believe that means Jonah is in danger also?"

Ah, the sixty-four-thousand-dollar question. "I can't say for sure, ma'am. What I do know is we need to operate under that assumption. I left a message on your machine to have you or your husband call me. Didn't you get it? I'd hoped to discuss this very thing."

"No, Lieutenant. I'm sorry. There's been so much going on. Neither one of us has checked our messages. We probably had the kids out with the animals. They're very cathartic, you know?"

"That's what I understand," Halliway responded. "In any event, we've formed a tactical team, and are in the process of discussing possible scenarios as we speak. We've been in contact with the Maine state police. They're aware of the situation and will be posting surveillance of your property. Frankly, I'm hoping he shows. It will probably be our best opportunity to catch him quickly."

Halliway's words stung her. Until now she and Jonah had been observers. Granted, the nightmare was close to home, but still it wasn't theirs. That had just changed. "But didn't you think that about David? And look what happened to him," Vickie said.

"Mrs. Roberts, I don't want to say there were mistakes made in our protection of Mr. Johnson because I truly don't believe that to be the case. However, having said that, I also believe we now have the benefit of hindsight.

There now exist certain known facts we simply weren't aware of the first time around."

Victoria pulled the phone to the living room and sat on the hearth by the wood stove. "Well, would you advise us to leave? Maybe move to a different state or town? At least until you get a better handle on this guy?"

Rebecca sat at the kitchen table, watching Jonah throw rocks with the kids outside, eavesdropping on Victoria's conversation. It all sounded frighteningly familiar. No one can possibly know what it's like until they've gone through it.

Halliway remained quiet for a few moments. He and Hill had discussed this. "No, Mrs. Roberts. My personal opinion is that you are as safe there as you will be anywhere else in the country. You know the terrain so to speak. He doesn't."

"True. But I'm not sure I feel comfortable knowing that he knows where my terrain is."

Halliway scribbled something on a notepad. "That's understandable," he said. "But I don't see that moving changes much. Wherever you move, you will then be as stationary as you are now. And the picture becomes more cloudy every time we need to coordinate with a new police department in whatever locale you choose. We'll be much more effective if we can work exclusively with just one agency."

Vickie was frightened. She could smell the cookies in the oven beginning to burn and rose to get them. She stopped when she saw that Rebecca had beaten her to it.

"Well, maybe," she said. "But doesn't it make sense to find a police department in a town where he doesn't know we live?"

Halliway was becoming a bit concerned. If she and Jonah were seriously considering moving as an option, the entire investigation could be derailed. If they wanted to start running, there was no telling how long it could go on. Anyway, he thought, there's no way to know that Montague knows where you live, much less cares.

"Look, ma'am, this is a free country. I can't force you to do anything. You can pack up and leave tomorrow if you choose. But there's no telling how cooperative or uncooperative the new force will be. Maine is committed to helping us catch Montague. In my book that's a major plus. Also it's worth mentioning that at least for now, we don't have any reason to believe he has plans for you or your husband, or even that he knows where you live."

Vickie watched Rebecca watch her. "Still Lieutenant, it just seems to me that we're sitting ducks."

Halliway found himself having to defend his point of view. "All right, Mrs. Roberts. Let's play your scenario through. For argument's sake, let's say you and your husband move to Casper, Wyoming. You move in and I call local law enforcement. Or you call them, or we both call them. Whatever. We tell them we want protection. We explain what's happened, why we're requesting it. That's pretty much how you see it happening, is it not, Mrs. Roberts?"

"Yes."

"Okay, so let me ask you this. How do you think they're going to react when we tell them the reason you moved there is so he wouldn't know where you are? Right off the bat, it seems to me you're worse off. If I ran that department I can guarantee you I wouldn't post men outside your house. Not under those circumstances. I mean, you've admitted yourself he doesn't know you're there, right? Now, maybe I drive a cruiser by a little more often, but that's about it. The public doesn't understand the tight budgets most departments are under, Mrs. Roberts. There's no way I could justify twenty-four, maybe twenty-five dollars an hour for every cop on a detail like that. No . . . if you ask me, ma'am, you leave and you'll be walking into uncharted and unprotected waters."

Vickie was quiet. She hadn't thought of any of this. "So what do we do then? Just sit around like we're under house arrest?"

"We're working on a plan right now. We've got a conference call scheduled for later this afternoon with the Maine state police. Either myself or someone from their department will be contacting you once we've had a chance to figure it all out. But I know this much for sure, there'll be at least one man stationed inside and outside your house beginning this evening. Assuming that's okay."

"Gee, I don't know, Lieutenant. Let me think about it."

An awkward silence ensued.

"That was a joke, Lieutenant," Vickie said. "Of course it's okay. The sooner the better. We've still got the Johnson family here."

"I'm aware of that also. Same rules apply. We don't know who he's after. Everyone starts splitting up and I foresee more trouble than we've already got. You'll all be safest right there. That's my professional opinion."

"Safety in numbers, right?"

"Something like that," Halliway said, worried that maybe he hadn't explained himself very well.

Immediately following his conversation with Halliway, Fenton Montague dressed, threw what few belongings he had into his knapsack, and called a cab. Before leaving the room he urinated in the toilet, stopping to look at himself in the bathroom mirror one last time. *I can't even recognize myself.* He adjusted his sunglasses, straightened his tie, and walked out of his room. He didn't bother with his phone bill at the front desk. He thought about it though, laughing to himself. Given the circumstances, somehow it just didn't seem that important.

Fenton wasn't worried Connecticut had traced his call. He used *67 before dialing—Bell Atlantic's Caller ID block. Fenton reasoned they might have gotten as close as the state of origin, but figured it was next to impossible they could have gotten more than that. But you just never know. Maybe they lucked out and narrowed it down to Bergen County. God forbid that had happened. Things could get sticky.

It wouldn't be long before the Audi was located, and

Fenton could only imagine how quickly the heat would rise after that. He thought it best he say good-bye to New Jersey. No sense creating problems he could just as easily avoid.

He thought of having the cabbie drop him off at the bus station, but a wave of paranoia began to overtake him. He needed to get over the GW Bridge. Now. He told the driver to take him to the Port Authority.

"Are you sure?" the cabbie asked. "It won't be cheap."

"Maybe my English isn't good enough?" Fenton responded.

The cabbie shrugged his shoulders. "You're the man."

Fenton kept his *New York Times* in front of his face the entire trip. He wasn't interested in getting pegged by some two-bit taxi driver. He couldn't find anything on David's murder, or Prescot's. They'd occurred after the evening run. He was disappointed—not because he wanted to revel in his accomplishments. He was out of that world now. But he did want to know everything he could to help him stay ahead of the law. The slightest nuance might help him. He'd have to wait.

"Port Authority," the cabbie said, pulling up to the curb. "That'll be sixty-three dollars and twenty-eight cents."

Fenton got out of the cab, walked to the window, and handed the driver a hundred-dollar bill. He walked away, never making eye contact. He explored the area for a while, the pulse of the city once again an astonishment to him. There was nothing about Boston that equaled this, and Boston wasn't exactly Cedar Rapids.

At its busiest, Boston still maintains a small-city feel. The downtown streets are narrower, the buildings older. What he witnessed around him now was chaos on a galactic scale. Hundreds of yellow cabs lined the street like a Jackson Pollock painting. The din of horns and sirens pierced his ears. People everywhere. Thousands of them. Tens of thousands of them. People were pushing carts of clothes up and down the street, completely oblivious to the mayhem surrounding them.

He hadn't been to Manhattan since his reconnaissance

on David, and though it wasn't that long ago, the electricity in the air stunned him like a blow to the solar plexus. He stood in awe for several minutes, finally brought back to reality by the stench of a homeless man asking him for a buck.

Fenton was in no mood for philanthropy. *Don't you know what they'll do to me if they find me?* "Fuck off," he said, barely giving the man a glance.

Turning north on Seventh Avenue, he found a clothing store and paid cash for a sweater, a pair of Nikes, some sweat pants and a baseball cap to cover his bald head. Fenton was ready now. The activity around him was mesmerizing, although he wasn't sure if he liked it or not. Another bum approached him. Fenton physically pushed him out of the way. There was an in-your-face quality about this city. *That,* he didn't like. It was time to leave.

Fenton was famished. Walking south to the Port Authority, Fenton stopped along the way to buy a falafel and a knish from a street vendor. He swallowed the knish in a few bites and was wrestling with his falafel as he approached the entrance to the bus station. Stopping to finish, he noticed two of New York's finest talking to each other just outside a set of doors. Like a deer eyeing humans in the woods, he stopped dead in his tracks. A wave of panic struck him at his first sight of the law since the murders.

Fenton ditched his wrappers in a trash can, wiped his face haphazardly with a napkin, and walked in, as far away from the cops as he could. The crowds seemed to converge on him now, their crushing onslaught filling him with fear and anxiety. He felt naked amongst the throng and wanted desperately to get away. Entering the building, he realized for the first time that he didn't have anywhere to go.

There was too much activity around him. He needed to think. He leaned against the wall, wrapping his arms around his knapsack, watching the crowds scurry past. He tried to focus on his breathing. *In deeply, through the nose. Exhale. In deeply . . .* Closing his eyes, he envisioned different parts of the country. He could see himself drinking a piña colada under an umbrella in Florida, or basking in the midnight glow as he strolled the Vegas Strip.

But he didn't know these areas. It would be hard enough to run as it was. He imagined it would be exponentially harder in cities and towns with which he was not familiar. No, he thought, he'd stay in New England. People forget how small the original colonies are. Particularly New England. It's small and easy to get from one city to the next.

He knew it well—its states, counties, and towns. It would be easier to hide. He knew what towns had bus service and what towns didn't. He knew where the trains ran and where they didn't. He could stay hidden forever in that little corner of the world. Of this, he was confident.

But he was undecided where in New England he should head. He thought of Boston, but that was a little too close to the hornet's nest for his liking. He thought of Hartford, then Providence, but settled on Portsmouth, New Hampshire. Amtrak service doesn't run north of Boston. He'd need to take a bus.

It was almost 2:00 P.M. His bus didn't leave for over an hour. He squatted, leaning his back against a wall, and waited. Fenton held his knapsack tightly to his chest, certain that everyone's eyes were on him. He watched people talking, wondering if they were talking about him. Did they know who he was and what he had done?

Waiting patiently, listening to the public address system overhead announce arrivals and departures, his eyes darted about maniacally. He cautiously surveyed all activity around him, mindful of anything out of the ordinary—a stare that lasted too long, someone pointing in his direction, people walking toward him.

He understood now that this game was going to require a different kind of planning, a different level of emotional energy. His feet firmly rooted in reality now, he wasn't sure how long he could keep it up. *As long as it takes. As long as it takes.*

But something was tugging at him, knocking on the door of his subconscious. He felt a loneliness settling in. A deep, insidious dread began materializing in the base of his bowels, working its way up his central nervous system. It settled firmly in his cranium. He knew he would never again be able to relax. For the rest of his life he would be looking over his shoulder . . . wondering . . . worrying. David must have felt this way.

And something was missing now, also. Remorse. Fenton was aware of what he'd done, but was far more interested in his own self-preservation. He thought about it, and was hardly proud, but things were too jumbled—too out of sync for him to get a true handle on his emotional inventory. *Maybe after I've settled down.* Maybe then, it would hit home.

He thought briefly of Halliway's comments on the telephone. Maybe he should turn himself in. Had the detective meant what he said? Maybe they *could* help him. Fenton's body shook as his spine quivered, transmitting an electric tingle down his back and arms. He wasn't sure where he would live or how he would make a living. A profound foreboding embraced him as he tried to think of the next forty years of his life. *One day at a time. One day at a time.*

Glancing at his watch, Fenton was surprised to see how much time had passed. It was almost 3:00 P.M. He rose and walked quickly toward the bus platforms, his palms sweating profusely. The crushing throngs had become physically and emotionally unbearable. *You're almost there. Stay tight.* Reading the signs denoting each bus's destination he found the one to Portsmouth, got in line, and waited to give the driver his ticket. He eyed the dark windows of the bus with longing, fearing he would never get inside.

───※───

Procedure dictates that homicide detectives attend the autopsy of the murder victim whose case they are investigating. Characteristically, Cedric Halliway arrived early for David's on Wednesday afternoon. He had witnessed scores of autopsies in his career. Some detectives never get used to them, but Halliway didn't have that problem. It was a necessary part of the job—one he neither looked forward to nor dreaded.

But there was something about David's that ate at him. Perhaps it was the fact he'd been decapitated and burned beyond recognition, but Halliway doubted that was the reason. He felt more certain it was because he felt he had failed him. David had placed his trust in his handling of the whole affair.

Perhaps he should have kept better tabs on what Esposito was doing—the directions the protection detail was receiving. Somehow, some way, the number one rule of fortification had been broken. Run a thorough sweep of the inside first. Somewhere along the line, Halliway began to feel that he alone was responsible for David's death.

He puffed on an unlit cigar, watching the incinerated remains of what had been David Johnson's torso lie lifeless on the shiny, stainless-steel slab. *How could I have missed it? How could I have not thought of the attic?* It was so obvious now. He felt like a fool.

Normally there would be many questions he hoped an autopsy could answer. But not this time. Perhaps because he already had most of the answers, he was annoyed that he had to watch this one. He already knew the cause of death. Because the head was not burned like the body, it had obviously been removed prior to the fire. He knew the fatal wound. He knew the type of weapon. He even knew the approximate time of death. Sometimes it was helpful to know how long the victim had lived after the fatal wound. But there wasn't much mystery there. You don't live long after your head's been cut off. If Halliway had needed further answers, he would have been disappointed. There was so much the medical examiner would never be able to tell him, not with a body like this.

When the autopsy was over Halliway drove back to headquarters in his Caprice. He drove with both front

323

windows down, lost in a world of his own, letting the cool afternoon air rush around him. He thought of Rebecca and her kids, miserable at the pain they must be feeling. He thought of Fenton and his sick, twisted mind. He could feel the pressure of his .45 in his shoulder holster. *You were right, Fenton. I'd like nothing more than to drop you where you stand.*

"I'm going to find you, Fenton Montague," he said aloud, inaudible over the swirling air. "You can run, but you can't hide. One day soon you're going to screw up, make the slightest mistake. And I'm going to be there. Your obituary will be my swan song."

He walked into the squad room, removing his messages from his pigeonhole. He stood there, flipping through the pink slips of paper. There were calls from *The New York Times, Hartford Courant, Darien News,* and the *Boston Globe.* Esposito had called. There was a call from the fingerprint lab, as well as from Document Examination. But it was the call from Rebecca Johnson that caught his eye.

He walked over to his desk. It was neater than the rest of his colleagues'. He sat down, put his feet up, and dialed her number.

"Hello?" Jonah answered.

"Good afternoon. Mr. Roberts?"

"Yes."

"This is Lieutenant Halliway from the Connecticut state police."

"Oh, yes. Hi, Lieutenant."

Halliway was marking the time of his call in the notebook resting on his knees, the phone cradled between his left shoulder and his ear. He acknowledged the wave of one of his colleagues with a slight rise of his chin. "I spoke at some length with your wife earlier today. Did she tell you?"

"Yes, Lieutenant, we spoke about it. And I agree with you. We'd just be renting trouble to move this show on the road," Jonah said, taking out a container of milk from the refrigerator.

Halliway felt reassured. "Good. We're still finalizing

some of the particulars. It shouldn't be long now before we have a definite plan. Thank you for bearing with us."

"I understand, Lieutenant," Jonah said, pouring himself a glass of milk. "I'm sure you're quite busy."

Halliway smiled. "That's a fair statement, Mr. Roberts. I'm returning Mrs. Johnson's call. Is she in?"

Jonah looked out the side window toward the barn. "No, but I can get her. I think she's in the barn with Vickie and the kids."

"If it wouldn't be too much trouble."

Jonah left for the barn. "Hey, guys," he said to the boys, approaching Rebecca in the barn. "Becky, Lieutenant Halliway is on the phone. He wants to speak with you. You want me to tell him I couldn't find you?"

Becky put her hand on Jonah's arm. "You're such a doll. No, I probably should speak with him. I can't avoid it forever."

"Caleb, Sumner, come here a sec. I want to show you something," she heard Jonah say as she walked toward the house.

Rebecca climbed the steps, her gait heavy and slow. She entered the kitchen, eyeing the telephone lying on the table. She sat down, took a long, deep breath, closed her eyes, and picked it up.

"Hi, Lieutenant," she said, trying her best not to sound overwrought.

"Hi, Mrs. Johnson," Halliway said. He didn't want to mention the murder. After all, they both knew why he was calling. But he wasn't sure it was proper etiquette to ignore it either. "Please accept my sincerest sympathies, Mrs. Johnson. My heart goes out to you and your children. I know this is an extremely difficult time for all of you."

Becky tightened her lips, fighting back tears. "Thank you, Lieutenant. I appreciate that."

"Mrs. Johnson, first let me start by saying I wish I could be there to do this in person. I apologize for having to do this over the phone. I hope you understand."

"Of course, Lieutenant. You have your hands full down there, I'm sure."

Halliway began, ignoring her comment. "There are some pressing issues I'm afraid we need to resolve. Do you think you're strong enough to discuss them now?"

Her eyes looked haunted by an inner pain. Her soul felt as if it were etched with sorrow. But there was no turning back now. "Yes, Lieutenant. Thank you for asking."

"Do you know whether your husband wanted to be buried or cremated, ma'am?"

Rebecca shut her eyes tightly, fighting back tears. "He always said he wanted to be cremated, Lieutenant. He used to joke that if there was a God, he didn't want to be underground when he came looking for him."

Halliway found humor in that, but continued impassively. "We just finished the autopsy and we need to take him to a funeral home. Do you have a preference, Mrs. Johnson?"

"We never really discussed that. Churchill's, I suppose."

"You'll need to contact them, Mrs. Johnson. There will be questions pertaining to cost and the type of service you desire. I'm afraid I can't be of much help in that regard."

"I understand," she said, resting her forehead in her left hand.

"Do you plan on having a service, Mrs. Johnson?"

"I've given that a lot of thought, Lieutenant. For me, I think I'd rather not. But I think the kids will need some closure. I guess the answer is yes."

"Then I trust, from your comments, that you and the children plan on attending?"

"Yes."

Halliway asked the question to which he really needed the answer. "Do you know if Mr. and Mrs. Roberts also plan to attend?"

"We talked about that last night. I know they'd like to . . . if you think it's okay."

Halliway was quiet for a bit. "Well, frankly . . . it's not ideal. I'm sure you understand why I say that. I think under the circumstances, any service will be difficult. But having Mr. Roberts there will most certainly add to the difficulty. Then again, I understand the need to have a service, and his desire to be there."

"I know he said he'd be heartsick if he couldn't attend."

"How would you feel if he didn't?" Halliway asked.

"Fine, I guess. David, Jonah, and I . . . we went way back together. I know how much he loved David. Whether he comes or not is irrelevant. At least to me."

"Well, if you truly feel that way, I may try to speak with him. See if we can convince him to stay in Maine," Halliway said, feeling a little unsure of his ground.

Rebecca sat back in her chair, wrapping her free arm around her chest. "I trust you, Lieutenant. If you think it's best that Jonah not go, I'll certainly understand. Though I can't speak for Jonah."

"Well, I suppose I'll have to worry about that."

She really didn't care one way or the other. Her children's father was dead and nothing Jonah, Halliway, or anyone else did, would ever change that. "Good luck," she said.

A moment of silence passed, unnoticed at first. "Mrs. Johnson, there are a few other things, if that's okay?"

Why stop now, Lieutenant? "Please. Continue," she said.

Halliway really didn't want to discuss this, but he'd be damned if he was going to let her find out in the paper, or through the grapevine. "Well, I don't know if you know the manner of your husband's death. As painful as this is, we need to talk about it."

Rebecca squeezed her arm tightly around her chest, her thighs pushing against each other. She knew this was coming.

"An officer from the Maine state police came this morning. He didn't tell me any details. Just that . . ." She paused, pressing her lips together tightly, squeezing her eyes, trying to keep from breaking down. "He just said that David had been murdered."

"Yes," Halliway said softly. "Sometime early this morning. We believe the murderer hid in the attic of your home. There's evidence to—"

Rebecca was speechless, feeling anger for the first

time. "The attic?" she asked, her voice betraying her utter bewilderment. "How the hell did he get in the attic? Weren't your men watching the house?"

Here we go. Halliway could see himself named as a defendant in a wrongful death suit. "I know it's difficult to hear, ma'am, but—"

"Difficult to hear, Lieutenant?" Rebecca interrupted with biting sarcasm. "No. Having a stranger tell me that my husband has been murdered was difficult to hear. I'd say having you tell me the man who did it was waiting inside our home . . . I think impossible would be a better word, Lieutenant. That's *impossible* for me to hear."

It is what it is. This was one of those times in life where no amount of ducking or weaving was going to make it better. Sugar coating this one simply couldn't be done.

"The Darien police posted a man outside your home shortly after noon on Monday. The only explanation is that Mr. Montague must have entered your residence sometime before that. I will tell you, I think it was handled as well as it could have been. There was *no way* we could know he would wait up there that long."

"Really?" Rebecca asked sharply.

Halliway tried his best to remain unperturbed. *Let's move on. We haven't even gotten to the bad part yet.* "I'm sorry, Mrs. Johnson. I'll lose sleep over that decision for a long time to come. But in our defense, ma'am, I have to say you have the benefit of hindsight. If I had to do it over again and didn't know anything different from what I knew then, I'd make the same decision. In this profession you can only go by your experience. In my thirty years I've never seen anything like it. I'm afraid none of us have. There's not much more I can say, except I'm truly sorry."

Becky was quiet for a long time.

Halliway thought perhaps she'd hung up. "Mrs. Johnson?"

"Yes?"

God I hate this! "There's something else, ma'am. I'm afraid it's not going to be pleasant to hear."

Rebecca trembled at the thought of what was to come.

"Do I need to hear this, Lieutenant? Do I have to be put through more?"

Halliway really didn't know how best to do this. "Well, if you want, I suppose we can wait until you come down for the service. I don't see any harm in that."

How can I possibly sleep now? No one can hear a statement like that and just walk away. *You don't expect me to hang up now do you?* "No, Lieutenant, I'll need to know sooner or later. Just say it."

Halliway was drained. "Perhaps it would be best if we waited until we were face to face. I'm not sure we should discuss this over the phone."

Rebecca leaned forward, her free hand pulling the elbow of her phone arm tightly to her side. She rocked slightly back and forth, the emotional pain crushing her with its weight. "What, Lieutenant? Discuss what?"

"Mrs. Johnson—"

"Just say it!"

"Your husband was decapitated."

———— ∾ ————

Apart from the note in Fenton's refrigerator, there was still no definitive proof that he had killed anyone. Even the note in the refrigerator only alluded to his killing. Yes, he'd called Halliway, but the call had been made to the phone on his desk. Since it didn't come through 911, it wasn't recorded. On the witness stand it would be Halliway's word against his. No prosecutor in the country would take a case to court with just that.

True, Halliway had found Fenton's printer and paper in his storage bin, but any defense attorney worth their salt could wriggle out of that one. Halliway could hear it now.

"Is it true, Mr. Montague, that the paper used to leave those notes, and the printer used to print them, were found in your possession?"

"Objection! Your honor, neither of those pieces of evidence the State is so quick to jump on were found in my client's possession. They were in his storage bin, in the basement of his apartment building. He's already testified he lent them to a friend of his for several weeks before the events in question took place."

"Sustained. ladies and gentlemen of the jury. You are to disregard any mention of the printer or paper found in Mr. Montague's apartment storage area. Madam prosecutor, I will not warn you again. You are not to mention . . ."

No. Finding Fenton Montague was going to be hard enough. Putting him behind bars could prove to be infinitely more difficult.

The day after Rebecca Johnson spoke with Lieutenant Halliway about her husband's murder, a dark blue van pulled into the Fort Lee police department parking lot. It had the words New York State Police Mobile Crime Scene Unit printed in two lines across each side.

Lieutenant Rideman had called his head evidence technician after his conversation with Sergeant Bridgman of the Fort Lee police department. The technician called a colleague with the Connecticut state police. The two state police evidence technicians stepped now from the van and began walking toward the station house. One of them was Robert Phillips from New York. The other was Stanley Tau from Connecticut. The two had met before, and had even worked a previous case together. The proximity of their states necessitated an ongoing coordination of efforts. Their paths crossed most recently when Phillips called Tau about the Reebok imprints. In fact, he was the first person Phillips called after hearing from Rideman of the Audi in Fort Lee.

It became obvious almost immediately that the respective sets of prints the two agencies had in their possession were indisputably from the same sneaker. From that moment on, both men decided they would make every attempt to coordinate their activities in this case. Now, they approached the desk sergeant, showed him their official identification tags, and asked to speak with Sergeant Nate Bridgman.

"Have a seat, fellas. I'll tell him you're here."

A short while later Bridgman appeared, walking down the stairs. Neither man knew who he was or what he looked like, but they made the connection as he approached. He was smiling, his hand outstretched.

Bridgman took Tau's hand first. "Nate Bridgman, Fort Lee police."

"Nate, Stanley Tau. Pleasure to meet you."

"Bob Phillips, Nate. A pleasure."

"You guys want some coffee or something?"

Tau let Phillips speak. It was legally his investigation. "No, thank you," he said. "I think we'd just as soon get started, if you don't mind."

"Knock yourselves out," Bridgman said, his face forming an it-don't-matter-to-me expression. "Here, let me show you to the garage."

The three men stood now at the trunk of the Audi. "She's all yours," Bridgman said. "Take as much time as you need. If you want to get a bite to eat later, stop up. I know a great deli a few blocks from here. Best pastrami I've ever tasted."

Phillips looked at Tau, smiling. "We may just take you up on that."

It was almost 10:00 A.M. You can never tell for sure, but Tau figured four, maybe five hours, and they'd be gone. Then he looked inside. He let out a long whistle. "Man, Bob, you see the blood in this thing?"

Phillips shook his head in disgust. "Yeah. Looks like we got our work cut out for us. Tell you what. Why don't you shoot. I'll start gettin' the stuff ready."

An evidence technician's job is very demanding. Their every move is examined and re-examined in a court of law as much as, and probably more than the activities of anyone else involved in a murder investigation. Each procedure must be calculated, thought out, methodical. A good technician moves with extreme caution, recording every step immediately after it's made. They must *never* leave *anything* to memory.

Tau began photographing the vehicle. He used two different cameras and consequently took minutely accurate notes of each shot. He spent over an hour taking pictures of the Audi—from behind, the front, the sides, the inside. A typical shot took several minutes. He would stand back a few feet, focus in on the object or area in question, set and reset his camera, and take his picture. The typical accompanying description read something like this:

Roll 1. Exposure 12. November 2. Audi A8.
Inside of right passenger side door. Taken from
kneeling position. Four feet back. Canon AE1.
Kodak Ektachrome. ASA 50 f-22 @ 1/90 sec.
With strobe.

Each exposure was annotated immediately after being shot. As Tau finished with a particular section of the car, Phillips started in with fingerprinting and blood scrapings. Each piece of evidence was individually wrapped or bagged, then numbered and described. It was slow, often tedious work.

After the inside of the car was thoroughly photographed, Phillips and Tau began employing the art of lifting latent prints from the car. There is no poetic license in the use of the "art". Lifting fingerprints from a crime scene is no easy task. It requires patience, a steady hand, an almost encyclopedic reservoir of knowledge and a healthy level of experience.

There were several different types of surfaces on which they had to work. There were smooth, nonporous surfaces such as the glass and chrome and rough, porous surfaces such as the leather and wood grain. Depending on the type of surface involved, the prints found on any one of them needed to be handled in a specific manner.

The two men went about the business of securing every print in the car. Contrary to what one might think, the single best place to find latents in a car is not the steering wheel. Prints there get piled up—one on top of the other—until finally they become an indecipherable mass of smudges. A good technician knows the first place to look for prints in any vehicle is the rearview mirror. Tau checked there first.

Working in unison, they seldom spoke during this part of their probe. Diligently finding, viewing, dusting, and finally lifting each print one at a time. Minutes became hours. They would search a particular section of the car, viewing it from several different angles with a flashlight. Often latent prints become quite patent if shone in the right light at the right angle.

There are three major sweat glands in the human body each of which secretes different organic and inorganic substances in differing amounts: the eccrine glands, the sebaceous glands, and the apocrine glands. Some finger-printing techniques are specific to a particular com-pound, while others act to show only the oily and greasy components of a print.

Tau and Phillips worked each set of prints in a particular order, since failing to lift one via one method might negate the ability to lift it via another. Early on, they debated whether or not to use super glue. With this process, fumes from the glue interact with varying compounds of the print, eventually forming a beautiful—and very liftable—thick, white print.

But this would entail the car being sealed shut, and since they obviously couldn't be in the car while the glue's toxic fumes worked their magic, they'd have to make sure they had performed every task possible before putting the procedure to work.

Super gluing a car makes every print in it come to life. The actual process can take up to two full days, though there are a couple of different ways to speed it along. But you either super glue or lift prints via more traditional means; the two are mutually exclusive. Time was an issue however, and there didn't appear to be any need wasting it lifting prints manually if they planned to use super glue. However, early on, it was readily apparent that there was no shortage of liftable prints. The two technicians decided most anything they could lift via the gluing process could also be done manually. This car was loaded, it wasn't like they were desperate for a print.

Phillips had already called for a locksmith. He had just left shortly before the two men finished with the inside of the Audi. It was time to turn their attention to the trunk. Tau prepared his Canon for the requisite photos once it was opened.

"Bet ya it's empty," Phillips said to his colleague.

"Empty, as in empty?" Tau asked. "Or empty as in nothing useful to the case?"

"Nothing useful."

Tau thought a minute, looking at his watch. It was almost 2:00 P.M. He was starving.

"You're on," he said. "Loser buys lunch."

Phillips smiled. "Good, I'm broke." He lifted the trunk.

"Well, well, well," Tau said, looking at the pile of bloody clothes and Reebok sneakers lying inside. "That pastrami is tastin' pretty good already."

———※———

"It's a definite match," Lieutenant Halliway said to a seated Dectective Hill, as he entered their now-too-familiar interrogation room at headquarters. "We got him dead to rights. I just hung up with Stanley. Says he's one hundred percent sure. The prints on the Audi match those found in Fenton's Mustang at the train station and the ones found in his apartment. And listen to this. They found Fenton's clothes and Reeboks in the trunk."

Hill was scribbling something in his notebook. Halliway's last statement caught his attention. *"The* Reeboks?" he asked, looking up.

Halliway nodded his head. *"The* Reeboks," he said, taking a seat opposite Hill. "Stan's been working with Phillips from New York. Says the two of them definitely agree. The Reeboks found in Prescot's Audi match the prints found at the scene at Pepsi, and the ones we found here."

"How 'bout the blood?" Hill asked.

"They're running it now. Apparently there was so much of it, it's going to take a while to determine whose is whose. I got them looking for David's as well as Prescot's. The crime lab will let us know as soon as they have something. They're running some mitochondrial DNA tests. Could take several days."

Hill smirked, shaking his head slightly. "Boy, just when you need it most."

"Let's just hope Johnson's blood is there. If not, we

still come up empty with Montague as a suspect in his murder," Halliway said.

Hill leaned back in his chair. "Yeah, but not Bennett. His sneaker prints were all over that patio."

"True," Halliway said, putting his feet up on the table. "But a good lawyer could raise a credible defense that they weren't his shoes. Or at least he wasn't in them when the prints were left. He borrowed them, found them, better yet, lost them, and somebody else picked them up. I'd feel better if we found it on his clothing. They found hair samples on the shirt. Biology's running analysis now to see if it matches the hair we found in his bedroom."

Hill seemed a bit nonplussed. "Come on, Ric. What jury's gonna buy that? I'd like to see his lawyer explain how the hell those Reeboks ended up in Bennett's blood on Johnson's patio."

"Hey, I got two words for you. O.J. The more we can nail him down, the better off we are. You just can't tell with a jury. You know that, Scott. Can't you hear it now? Some hot shot attorney's gonna tell that jury that the same guy who killed Bennett killed Prescot. That's why the sneaker prints match. 'But my client has already testified the Reeboks the police found were not his shoes.' It's a defense lawyer's wet dream, Scott."

Hill got up to stretch his back. "Well, maybe. I mean, I see your point. But why can't we just compare the Reeboks' wear to the wear of the other shoes we found in his closet?"

"We can," Halliway said, finishing his argument. "But how many other people in America wear their shoes down the same way? A quarter million? Half million? Even if it's just ten thousand. It's more circumstantial than I'm comfortable with."

"Yeah, maybe. But—"

"But nothing," Halliway interrupted. "I'll feel better if we find Johnson's blood on Montague's clothing. Then I'd like to see his lawyer explain away how we found his hair on the same shirt."

"Can't argue with you there. Let's keep our fingers crossed," Hill said, lighting a smoke.

Halliway sat up, reaching for the pager vibrating on his belt. He wrote down the number and looked up at Hill. "What ya got from your contact up in Boston?"

"Well, I spoke with her this morning. She said it's tougher than we might think. Apparently these damn hospital records are sealed like Fort Knox. She did find somebody who got us a hit, though. Looks like Fenton spent the better part of the past two decades at Bridgewater State."

Halliway sat on the edge of his chair, preparing to leave to return his call. "Aah, nothing like contacts," he said. "So what do we know?"

Hill picked his notebook up off the table. "Well, I don't know all there is to know about this stuff. But it sounds like we got one sick boy on our hands."

"Really? I'm shocked," Halliway said. "Anything specific?

Hill flipped through pages of his notebook. "This may take a few minutes."

"Let's hear it."

"Okay . . . here goes." Hill rose, deciding to pace. "Apparently, Fenton's mother died under questionable circumstances in 1978. In the end, no charges were filed. Investigators apparently couldn't get enough to make anything stick. But Fenton was remanded for a time for a court-ordered psychiatric evaluation. From what I could glean from the conversation, over the years Montague's been diagnosed with any number of diseases of the brain. I think my contact called them brain dysfunctions."

"There's a surprise."

Hill smiled. "Just wait. I didn't know people could even be this screwed up. At different times he's been diagnosed as suffering from psychotic depression, paranoid schizophrenia, bi-polar disorder, and just plain old psychosis."

Halliway closed his eyes, raised his eyebrows and shook his head. "That's it? A mere rookie."

"Well, I tell ya, Ric, this guy's gone through the wringer. Whatever the hell he suffers from, paranoia appears to be paramount," Hill said, running his right forerfinger over the pages of his notebook. "Here we go. Apparently paranoid behavior can occur in just about anyone. Sometimes brought on by stress. But in most of us, it usually passes. Someone suffering from a true case though, may often have other abnormal brain disorders. But not always. The most typical accompanying disorder is schizophrenia."

"Schizophrenics hear voices, right?" Halliway asked. "Do you know?"

"I didn't, but I do now. Not all schizophrenics halluci- nate, but some suffer from audio and/or visual hallucina- tions."

"That certainly explains my conversation with him on the phone. Hearing from God and all," Halliway said, rubbing the back of his neck. "Go on."

"Ironically, it appears that in most cases people who suffer from this disease are seldom violent. What they really want to do is crawl into a cave and be left alone. I think those were her words," Hill said, scanning his notes. "Yeah, here it is. 'Crawl into a cave.' Anyway, our boy underwent several episodes of what she called ECT or electronconvulsive therapy. We know it as electro- shock therapy. From what her contact could gather, after these treatments, Fenton would apparently suffer severe periods of memory loss for long periods of time. So in an attempt to circumvent this side effect, they tried various antipsychotic medication."

"Like what? You mean like tranquilizers?" Halliway asked.

"No. I asked the same thing. She told me some of these drugs do have a tranquilizer component, but they're really designed to work with the individual cells on the neuron level."

"I see," Halliway said, in his best Freudian accent, pulling on an imaginary goatee. "Please continue, Doc- tor Hill."

"Okay, so these antipsychotic drugs apparently affect the . . ." Hill stopped to find the word in his notes. "The dopaminergic system in the body. They act to block the body's dopamine receptors. Please don't ask me, Ric," he said, looking up at Halliway. "I don't have a clue. I don't know how, I don't even know if the docs know how, but the drugs seem to mitigate what she called the environmental bombardment these people suffer from. It offers a type of perceptual filter. A means of making the world a less scary place in which to live."

Halliway leaned forward, putting his elbows on the table, cupping his chin with his thumbs. "You mean to tell me that Montague's scared?" he asked.

"I'm no shrink, but that's the picture I got. If I'm reading all this right, I think the guy's scared out of his wits."

"I'll be damned," Halliway said, pushing his lower lip out. "So these drugs, what are they? Did she think Fenton was still using them?"

Hill sat down, laying his notebook on the table, pausing long enough to light another cigarette. He thumbed through his notebook again, resting his finger on the spot.

"I guess the big drug companies are always making breakthroughs in this area. There's a group of drugs in the . . ."—he stopped to scan his notes again—" . . . phenothiazine family. The older ones, such as Thorazine—"

"Our good friend, Thorazine," Halliway interrupted.

"Yeah, well, from what I understand, Thorazine can have some pretty nasty side effects. The big breakthrough after it was Haldol. Now though, I guess they have a newer family of antipsychotic agents. Ever hear of Clozaril?"

"Son of a bitch," Halliway said.

"What?"

Halliway stood. "You know what? We may have just stumbled on a way to find our man. If he calls again, we need to beg him to take his medication. It's safe to assume he's not taking any now, right?"

"Yeah," Hill said, nodding his head. "That's a safe bet. Our contact couldn't imagine he'd be doin' all this if he were still on the stuff. Apparently one of the major benefits of Clozaril is its ability to mitigate audio hallucinations."

"Well, I guess we can assume he's not taking it then.

All right, here's how I see it. We beg him to get some. Tell him we'll get him a prescription somehow. I don't know yet. I've got to think it through—"

"That's not the best part though," Hill interrupted, flipping pages of his notebook.

Halliway raised an eyebrow.

"Ready for this?" Hill asked. "Anyone on Clozaril must be registered with the Clozaril National Registry in New Jersey."

Halliway was visibly excited. "You mean to tell me there's a national clearinghouse that tracks users of this stuff?"

"Yep."

"Somehow, Scott, we've got to get him to a pharmacy. If he calls again and we can get him to buy some, we can find him. I can feel it."

Hill was doubtful. "Now all we have to do is get him to buy some."

Halliway shrugged his shoulders. "Piece of cake."

━━∽━━

Fenton's trip south had thrown everyone for a loop. Halliway told Lieutenant Rideman he was almost certain Fenton would head for Maine. Suddenly though, with the discovery of the Audi in New Jersey, virtually the entire eastern seaboard was up for grabs. Certainly Maine was appearing less likely.

At this point in the investigation, Halliway and Rideman were in constant contact. There was so many things that had to be done, their effects clearly had to be coordinated. Both men, being consummate professionals, would see every chore through. Cooperation now was vital. It would be an extraordinary waste of time if they busied themselves with tasks the other had already completed.

By agreement, Halliway ran an off-line search through NCIC in Washington. With a date of birth and a Social Security number he could cross reference virtually every stop made by every police officer in the country. He ran Fenton's vitals as well as Prescot's. Maybe they'd luck out. Maybe Fenton was using Prescot's license and ID instead of his own. If he'd been stopped in Anchorage, Alaska, or Ontario, Canada, and presented either one of them to a police officer, the Computer would pick it up.

They also agreed that Halliway would handle all communication with Maine. If there was something they wanted checked or run through a computer there, he was the contact. He had an Attempt-to-Locate teletype on Fenton Montague sent to all Maine law enforcement agencies. The wire described Fenton's last known appearance, general build, and height. It explained he was wanted in connection with at least four homicides, one of them Capital murder. He was armed and extremely dangerous.

The words *Capital murder* always stand out to a police officer. Like a word printed in red in the middle of a book, it focuses the eyes and screams for attention. Fenton Montague had killed a cop. Every law enforcement officer, everywhere in the country, wanted him now.

Halliway needed to anticipate all possible tracks Fenton might make if he made his way to Maine. He had spent the better part of Thursday morning making phone calls. A good cop always has a stable of steady contacts. They cultivate them slowly, over time. They are always interested in the quality, not the quantity, of the information.

The first thing Halliway did was to contact what he called his oldies but goodies. He contacted a woman he'd used for years at Social Security. It's strictly against policy for anyone at Social Security to provide information of any kind to the police. For any reason. A good contact at Social Security is worth its weight in gold. It's an excellent means to track someone.

"Hello, Betty," Halliway said.

He was an old and trusted friend. She could have lost her job, or worse, any number of times with the information she had provided him over the years. But she was a true ally of the police, helping keep the scum off the streets in any way she could.

Any person applying for virtually any social service needs to show a valid Social Security number. Thanks to Betty's help, if Fenton applied for food stamps, unemployment insurance, housing assistance, or any number of other government subsidies, under his or Prescot's Social Security number, it was now set to be flagged.

Next, Halliway called his long-standing contact at the Department of Motor Vehicles. Thank God for cars. More perps get caught because of them. He explained the situation as briefly as he could. The fewer details the better. For both parties concerned.

Once again, if Fenton tried to register a car under either one of the names Halliway thought he might use, there'd be bells and whistles aplenty. Cedric Halliway would know about it within the hour.

New Jersey was Lieutenant Rideman's responsibility. Why did Fenton drive to New Jersey? Did he know someone there? Was he planning on murdering someone there? Did he have family in the state? Had he gone to school there? Was it just a spurious attempt to throw the cops off track?

There were many questions to which they needed answers, and there was only one way to get them. This part of the job often seemed like paving a road with a butter knife. Call after call. Question after question. Hour after hour. It was monotonous, tiresome, and almost always fruitless. But you just never knew. All you need is one break. Just one.

Rideman called vital statistics in Trenton first. Identifying himself, he made sure to get a supervisor, someone who could spend a good deal of time with him. He wanted to know if Fenton had ever been married or divorced in the state, how many children had been born in the last twenty-five years with the last name Montague. He checked to see if Fenton had any brothers or sisters in the state. Perhaps his father lived there. People on the lam will sometimes head for home, at least for a short time, knowing it's more difficult for family to turn them in.

Next he checked with the state Worker's Compensation Board. Had anyone in the state of New Jersey with Fenton's name ever filed a worker's comp claim? The hours went by, one call melting into the next.

He called the bursar's office of every college in the state, both private and public. Had anyone by the name of Fenton Montague attended their university in the last twenty-five years?

Like Halliway, Rideman too had a lengthy list of contacts. He called his at DMV, seeing to it that if anyone using the name Fenton Montague or Austin Prescot attempted to register a vehicle anywhere in the state of New Jersey, he was to be contacted immediately.

For Rideman, the whole process was sheer torture. When he was done he stood and stretched his body to keep from falling asleep. He looked at the clock. Almost six hours had passed. He and Halliway had agreed to contact each other after they were through. Halliway let Rideman call him. His list was longer. He knew he'd finish last. They both knew it.

Rideman dialed Halliway's direct line. He rested a cup of coffee on his right knee, his feet on his desk, looking every bit as tired as he felt. "Ric, it's Harry."

"Hi, Harry. Finished?" Halliway asked.

"Yeah, pretty much. One big, fat zero. Not even a nibble. For the life of me, if there's a reason he went to New Jersey, I don't know what the hell it is."

"Why do *you* think he went?"

"Honestly?"

"No, lie to me."

"I think he's trying to throw us off the trail. He doesn't have any ties to that state. None that I could find anyway."

Halliway thought for a minute. "That's what I think too."

"So what do you suggest?"

"I'm not sure," Halliway said, turning to sit on the edge of his desk. "I feel helpless just waiting. But I don't know what else we can do."

"Did you run an Attempt-to--Locate?" Rideman asked.

"I called the Maine state police. Should be done by now."

"Maine only?"

"Yes."

Rideman finished his coffee, throwing his Styrofoam cup in the trash can behind him. "I'll run one through NCIC. This guy could be anywhere."

Halliway had the nagging notion they were up against an above-average prey. "You think it's possible he went to the metropolitan area to catch a plane? Leave the country?"

"Good question. I thought of that. But why wouldn't he have just parked at the airport? It would have taken us days, maybe weeks, to find the car there."

Halliway tried to think it through. "I don't know. Maybe he doesn't want us to know he's abroad."

Rideman squinted his eyes slightly, the sudden thought that they'd missed something frightening him. "Ric, did you call Interpol?"

"No. Did you?"

"Shit. Do you know if Prescot had his passport on him?"

"No. I'll call his wife and find out," Halliway said, urgency in his voice. "You start with his name and info. I'll be back to you ASAP."

Rideman hung his head, disappointed they had let this escape them. "If he's left the country, Ric, we got to stop him before he gets out of whatever airport he's flyin' to."

"I'm afraid we're a bit late on that one."

"If there's a God in heaven, Ric, please let him still be in the country."

"A God in heaven," Halliway repeated. "I wonder what Bennett, Johnson, and Prescot think about that now?"

––⁓––

At 6:00 A.M. on Thursday, November 2nd, Jonah Roberts crawled out of bed and sat at his computer in the corner of his bedroom. Vickie was sound asleep. This was his time to review his portfolios. He checked the markets on his Bloomberg Information System. A relative newcomer to the financial information world, Bloomberg had become a real player, competing head to head with Reuters and the Dow Jones News Service. Jonah liked its presentation better.

He browsed through news reports on the various companies whose stock he owned, making notes periodically on something that caught his eye. He felt certain the Fed was going to raise interest rates soon and wanted to make sure he adjusted his portfolio accordingly. He made a note to himself to place a sell order on his General Motors and Ford holdings before the market opened.

He read the numbers on his screen, checking results in London, Paris, Frankfurt, and Tokyo. If the economy here was heating up that could only be good news for the foreign markets. As much as they might hate to admit it, they still catch cold when we sneeze.

He quickly scanned the market closings on various bellwether bonds—primarily the ten- and thirty-year treasurys. He checked the spot price of gold in London and the closing price in New York. He looked at the dollar's close against the major world currencies—the yen, the pound, the franc—carefully writing in his notebook those items that piqued his interest or that he felt were cause for alarm.

You can leave the Street, but the Street never leaves you. It was a genetic thing, Jonah was convinced. You either have it in your blood or you don't. Also-rans get eaten for breakfast on Wall Street. Like the old poker saying goes: If you've been in the game for half an hour and you don't know who the patsy is, you're it.

For the first time in a long time Jonah was scared. He kept thinking it couldn't be possible. It didn't seem real that David was dead. Certainly he hadn't been killed because of some insignificant event in Boston over twenty years ago. There must be something else, he kept telling himself. Something David and the police must have missed.

What had been his best friend's nightmare, which he watched from afar, was now suddenly his. He hadn't given it all up and come to Maine to live like this—a prisoner in his own house. Jonah turned off the computer, slipped on his robe, and left the bedroom to make a pot of coffee. As he entered the kitchen, the sight of a strange man sitting at the table nearly sent him into cardiac arrest.

"Good morning, Mr. Roberts," the state trooper said, looking over his shoulder.

Jonah's heart caught in his throat, stopping somewhere just south of his Adam's apple. "Jesus, you scared me half to death," Jonah said, grabbing a wooden post for support.

"Sorry about that. Did you forget I was here?" Trooper William Martin asked.

"Yeah, I forgot all right. I just about had a heart attack."

"Well, you can relax now," Martin said, rising from his chair. "Get used to it. We may be here for a while."

Jonah walked into the kitchen, trying to pretend everything was normal. "How long you think you're going to need to be here?" he asked, uncomfortable at the intrusion into his life.

"Can't say, sir. As long as it takes I guess. Or until word comes from on high to scrap the detail."

Jonah put his finger to his mouth, motioning to Rebecca sleeping on the fold-out couch in the living room. "As long as it takes to do what?" Jonah inquired in a whisper.

Martin matched Jonah's tone of voice. "Catch the psycho that's after you."

"Do you know he's after me? Last I heard, we didn't even know for sure that was the case."

"Well, we don't, I guess. But from what I can tell, the boys in Connecticut think it's a pretty good bet."

Jonah poured heaping spoonfuls of coffee into the filter, trying his best to act nonchalant. "I can't imagine he'd be crazy enough to even try. He'd have to know he'd be caught."

Martin leaned against the wooden post, his arms crossed. "There's no telling with these people, Mr. Roberts. They don't think like you and me."

Jonah plugged the coffee maker in and took a seat at the kitchen table. Martin joined him.

"What exactly do you guys have out there?" Jonah asked, motioning to the pastures beyond.

"In what way, sir?"

"I mean what kind of surveillance do you have around the house?"

"Well . . . let's see. There's me. There'll be two of us rotating on in-house duty. The other man relieves me at eight. There's two men outside, one in the hay loft in the barn. He's got a straight view down your driveway. Another one in a duck blind just behind the riding ring. Did a good job with it too. You'd never know it's there if you didn't know to look for it. And then there's two men in cruisers, one at each entrance to your road."

"Jesus, how long can you keep that up?" Jonah asked, rising to get two mugs from the cupboard. "That's got to cost a fortune."

"I don't know. S'pose that's for the big boys to figure out. It certainly isn't up to me."

"What if he doesn't show for a week or two? When do you think they'll re-evaluate?"

Martin thought about Jonah's question for a short while. "Well, I don't know the budget the way they do. But I'd guess if nothing happens in a week or so, they'll probably pare us back some. I'm not sure it's black or white. Surveillance or no surveillance. There'll probably be someone lookin' over the place for a while. It's just a matter of how many."

Jonah poured two cups of coffee and brought them to the table, sliding one in front of Trooper Martin. The two men sipped quietly, Jonah cupping his mug with both hands, staring out the window. He caught a glimpse of the duck blind. To his mind it stuck out like a sore thumb. After all, this was his property. He knew every inch of it in his sleep.

Jonah turned his gaze to Martin. "What time did you

get here last night? I was at a selectmen's meeting. Didn't get home until after eleven. I forgot all about you when I came out here this morning."

Martin hesitated, swallowing a mouthful of coffee. "I came on duty at eight."

Jonah was quiet for a while, as if lost in some deep recess of his mind. "I remember when I was a kid. We had just moved to a new town in Massachusetts. Being the new kid on the block, I didn't know a soul. One day, this kid I'd seen around—he was scruffy looking, hung in a rough group—he comes up to me and tells me the leader of their gang wants to beat me to a pulp."

Martin sipped his coffee. "Kids are brutal, aren't they?"

"Yeah, ain't that the truth? So he tells me I better be careful—watch my ass. Shit, even now I get goose bumps thinking about it. So naturally, I'm scared to death. I'm thinking these guys are the toughest, meanest things going. I couldn't eat, couldn't sleep. I hung out in classrooms after school until well after all the kids had gone home, looking, watching to see if they were around. When I'd finally convice myself the coast was clear, I'd sneak out of the side entrance to the school and run all the way home. It had to have been two miles."

"How old were you?" Martin asked.

"'Bout eleven, I guess," Jonah said, looking toward the ceiling. "So one night, my father comes into my room and sits on the edge of my bed. I can remember it as if it happened last night. God, I miss him. He was quite a man. Your father still alive?"

"No, died in Nam. I was ten years old. The saddest day of my life."

"I'm sorry."

Martin took another swig of his coffee, waving haphazardly with his free hand. "Hey, that was a long time ago."

"But you still feel the feelings, don't you?"

"Like it happened yesterday."

Jonah rose and brought the coffeepot to the table, setting it on a trivet. He was silent for a few moments.

"That's what this is like for me. I remember Dad handed me a glass of warm milk and stroked my hair as he spoke to me. I felt so safe in his presence. You know what he told me?"

Martin shook his head. He was truly interested in Jonah's story.

"He told me men don't run. That as scared as I was, I was going to have to confront my nemesis. I can't remember his exact words now. Oddly though, I do remember bits and pieces. He told me I had to put an end to it. That I couldn't live my life like that. It must have been painful for him and my mother to watch me go through such misery. I do remember he asked me, 'What's the worst thing that can happen?' I remember crying. God, I was scared. I think I answered something like 'I would get beat up.' Something like that. He said, 'That's right. Maybe you even lose a few teeth. But it will be over, Jonah. You won't have to worry about him any more.'"

Morning entertainment. Martin hadn't counted on this. "What'd you do?"

"I can still taste the fear," Jonah said, closing his eyes, reliving that time in his life. "The next day, after school, I stood at the side entrance of the school, trying to catch my breath. I could see them. I remember shaking as I walked to the corner where they always hung out. They were always standing there. Smoking cigarettes. I swear, I didn't think I'd make it. My heart beat so fast I thought I was going to faint. I walked across the street and went right up to him. He was so much bigger than the others. I remember he had a scruffy beard. He didn't go to our school. He was a junior in high school, I think. He towered over me. I remember thinking how I would fight him, that being smaller was sometimes an advantage. I said, 'I hear you want to beat me up. I don't want to fight, but if we have to, then let's get it over with.' You know what he did?"

Martin was mesmerized. "What? Did he hit you?" he asked.

"No. He laughed. He looked at me like, Who the hell

348

are you? He said he didn't want to beat me up. I remember him saying. 'You're joking, right? Don't bother me.' He told me to go home. I can remember walking away, hearing them all laughing as I left."

"That was it?" Martin asked.

"That was it. All that worrying. All those wasted emotions. And he didn't even know who the hell I was. I learned a life lesson that day. It's the same with this Montague guy. I wish I could face him, be done with it. Have it end one way or another. I promised myself I would never live in fear again, and here I am, living in fear. It runs against everything I've become."

Martin leaned forward, speaking quietly, "There's one difference, though. This guy's for real. He follows through on his threats."

"I know," Jonah said, pouring himself some more coffee. "You think he'll come?" he asked.

Martin shrugged. "No way to tell. Maybe tomorrow. Maybe next month. Maybe never."

"So we just sit and wait?" Jonah asked, shaking his head. "I'd rather die."

Martin looked Jonah in the eyes. "Careful what you wish for, Mr. Roberts."

—◈—

Fenton Montague stepped off the bus in Portsmouth, New Hamshire, just before 10:30 P.M. Wednesday night. These episodic forays into nothingness were extraordinarily tiring and taking their toll on his emotional and physical state. On the ride up he tried to think of when he'd last been out so long. He really couldn't remember. Up until now, he had always been in some hospital when they came. And when he was locked up, he was on his medication.

He couldn't remember exactly when he had let his Clozaril prescription run out. He thought he remembered it being shortly before he saw David's face on the front page of the *Wall Street Journal*. But he wasn't sure. His thoughts had become more jumbled since then. He knew he was turning dangerous—too dangerous. Just before leaving Boston, something inside made him go for a white blood cell count for his Clozaril prescription.

What he did know was that if he could, he would have to put an end to this madness. When Fenton was lucid he could discern right from wrong. He didn't want to kill anymore. Not if he could stop it.

The police would have a dragnet out for him the size of Jupiter. There was no place on earth he'd be safe, no place he could hide for very long. He knew he would have to keep on the move. *No rest for the wicked.*

Carrying nothing but his knapsack and the sweater on his back, he walked the streets of Portsmouth. Such a beautiful town. Fenton felt he would like it here—for as long as he stayed anyway. The city's fathers had long ago seen dollar signs in the preservation of its colonial heritage. Gas lights illuminated the narrow city streets, where whole sections looked as they had two hundred, three hundred years before.

Portsmouth, New Hampshire, is truly one of New England's treasures. The first settlers landed in 1623, soon dispersing to areas west and south. Portsmouth's next settlers were the land-hungry travelers of the *Pied Cow,* setting foot on the west bank of the Piscataqua in 1630. They came seeking religious freedom and a better way of life. Not unlike Fenton Montague.

In the 1600s and 1700s, Portsmouth was the seat of the acting provincial government, and as such, became a major political and economic hub of New England. Like so many other New England towns, its history is deeply rooted in the seafaring tradition of that time. It became a vital link between the colonies, Great Britain, and the West Indies.

Consequently, many of its winding, narrow streets are lined with old colonial structures, as well as with ornate houses built by the wealthy merchant class or well-to-do sea captains. Buildings of Federal and Georgian architectural design seemingly line every thoroughfare. It was more beautiful than Boston, Fenton thought. Certainly more quaint.

He was cold. He would need a jacket. Winter in this

part of the country is different from winter in New York or New Jersey. It gets much colder much earlier. For some reason Fenton felt it was unseasonably cold for this time of year. It felt more like December than early November.

Except in Boston and a few of the larger metropolitan cities, cabs don't cruise the streets of towns in New England. Even if they did, there are just too few of them for you to be lucky enough to catch one while waiting on a street corner. Any Yankee knows you almost always have to call.

Fenton walked east on State Street, passing various shops and restaurants along the way. Eventually, he passed a pub filled with people. He stopped just long enough to get its name and stepped inside. Its hominess and warmth almost compensated for his discomfort at the crowd of people and the grayish-blue plumes of tobacco smoke. Walking to the back, he looked up a taxi company in the telephone directory. Ten minutes later Fenton stepped into the back of a black and white cab.

"Where to, mister?" the cabbie asked.

"The cheapest motel in town."

The cabbie spoke to Fenton, looking in the rearview mirror. "The absolute cheapest? Or just someplace reasonable?"

"Someplace reasonably cheap," Fenton responded.

"Good. I wouldn't send my next-door neighbor to the cheapest place. Anyway, I hate that son of a bitch."

Fenton smiled a patronizing smile. In a few short minutes he was tossing the cabbie a five-dollar bill through the window.

"Have a good night," the cabbie said, looking at the bill.

"Yep."

It was a local place, obviously owned by the same people who lived there. The neon light outside read Colonial Pines Motel in fluorescent green handwriting. Under that hung a much smaller sign that read Vacancy and another one under that read Cable TV. It was nice enough—one of those long, V-shaped, single-story motels familiar to virtually any traveller across the nation.

Fenton walked into the door marked Office, stepped up to the counter, and rang the bell. He could see the dull blue glow of a television from the partially open door to the room behind. A woman in her mid fifties came out to greet him. Her hair was in curlers and she had a worn robe over her red flannel pajamas.

"Need a room, darlin'?" she asked, stepping up to the counter.

I'm not your darling, bitch. "Yes. Please."

She reached below the counter, pulling out a pad for Fenton to fill out his name and address. "How many nights?"

"Just one, I think. Will there be a problem if I decide to stay a few more?"

"This time of year? Honey, you can stay till spring. All the leaf peepers have left. October's one of our best times. All the city folk comin' up to see the foliage and all. No, I'm afraid it slows some for the next few months."

"Good. How much?" Fenton asked.

"That will be twenty-nine-ninety-five. Here," she said, sliding the pad toward him and laying a pen on top of it. "Fill this out. I'll get your key. You want something close or farther away?"

"Wherever it's most quiet."

"Room fourteen. You'll like it. Just got a new bed too."

Fenton filled out the form using a fictitious name and address and slid it back toward the woman along with two twenty-dollar bills.

"Thank you," Fenton said.

"Thank you," the owner said, handing Fenton his key. "Check out's eleven in the mornin'."

He turned to leave, stopping as he got to the door. "By the way, could you tell me where the nearest pharmacy is?" he said as he turned.

"Three blocks that way," she said, pointing. "Take a left at the bicycle shop and you'll see a little mall. There's a Rite Aid in there. Opens at eight."

"Thank you. Good night."

"G'night."

Fenton took a long, steamy shower, trying to cleanse himself of the wickedness within. He scrubbed every inch of his body roughly with soap, rinsed, and scrubbed again. When he finished he sat on the toilet seat cover, one towel over his head, the other around his waist. He inhaled deeply, taking in the hot, moist air . . . cleansing his lungs. He dried, crawled into bed, and didn't move until the next morning.

He awoke to the most terrifying sound he'd ever heard. Someone was knocking at his door! He lay there for some time, not responding, exploring exits in his mind. Fear gripped his innards. Finally, he spoke.

"Yes?"

"Sir? It's almost eleven. I need to clean the room."

Fenton put his hand to his chest.

"Oh, God, I'm terribly sorry," he said, getting up and opening the door a crack. "Give me ten minutes. I've never slept so soundly."

"Take your time. I'll do number three first."

Fenton peeked outside the chained door, glimpsing the same woman who'd helped him last night. She had a *Boston Globe* folded on the top of her cleaning cart.

"Would you?" he asked. "Thanks so much. I'm sorry." She started to walk away. "Is that today's paper?"

"Yeah. More death and mayhem. Wouldn't buy it except for the ponies."

Fenton unchained his door, reaching his hand out. "Could I bother you to see it? I'll leave it right here when I'm done. Promise."

"Help yourself."

"Thanks," he said, taking the paper from her outstretched hand.

He closed the door, chained it, and brought the paper back to bed with him. Nervously, he sat up straight and unfolded it flat on the blankets. There were the usual headlines: some particularly nasty IRA bombing. In Boston, with its large Irish population, that's always pretty big news. An article down the left side on the federal budget impasse. He scanned the page furiously with his eyes, his heart stopping when he saw it. There, on the right, in the middle of the paper, was his picture.

The caption read: "Police Hunt Boston Man, 41, In Slaying of Policeman, Three Others."

Somehow, until now, he had thought it might go away. After all, not much had seemed to change in his life. He came and went as he pleased. No one stopped him. No one seemed to care. He kept having these fanciful thoughts that maybe, if he could just avoid capture long enough, the whole thing might just blow over. The police would move onto bigger and better things, occupying themselves with more promising cases that were easier to solve. Better public relations.

The sight of his face on the front page of the *Globe* filled him with an odd mix of awe and shock. The newspaper item hit him with the impact of a blow to the head. Fenton suddenly froze, stunned with fear. He felt a flash of fever-pitched heat at his temples as he realized that all the events of the last few days were not only vividly remembered, but that overnight he had become one of America's most wanted fugitives. What he hadn't realized, at least until this moment, was that there was nothing bigger. He was about as big as it got.

Okay . . . wait. Wait, wait, wait. Who are you?

"Fenton," he heard someone say.

"What?" *No, wait. I'm not ready yet. Please. Oh, God please. Okay, okay. All right. You're all right.* "Got to get to the pharmacy. Got to get to the pharmacy."

Struggling with every ounce of energy he could dig from anywhere, in every cell of his body, he fought. *Got to call Dr. Rosenstern.* He frantically turned to the phone and dialed Boston information. He was changing again. He couldn't stop it. *Oh, God! Please, God. I don't want to. Not yet. Give me a chance. I can . . .*

"Bridgewater State Hospital. Hurry."

"Hold for that number please."

With incredible focus, Fenton dialed the number to Bridgewater State. *Come on, come on. Answer.*

He could hear the voices clearly now. "Fenton?"

"Wait!" Fenton screamed out loud. "Please wait!"

"Bridgewater State Hospital. How may I connect your call?"

"Dr. Rosenstern please," Fenton responded in a near-panicked voice.

"One moment please."

Again, the voice. "F-e-n-t-o-n. You're disappointing me."

"No!"

The woman from the motel was knocking on his door now. "Sir? Are you okay?"

"Wait!" Fenton demanded of the demons in his head. "Do you hear me? You are going to wait!"

The motel owner was startled. Something wasn't right. She put her ear to the door, thinking her guest was in some kind of danger. Was someone hurting him? She couldn't be sure. She strained to hear the conversation. Whatever was happening inside his room, he was screaming.

"Dr. Rosenstern's office. May I help you?"

"Oh, God! This is Fenton Montague. I must speak with Dr. Rosenstern. Now!"

"Mr. Montague, Dr. Rosenstern is doing rounds now. I can have him call you if—"

"I must speak to him now! It's an emergency. I'm going to kill again. Please help me."

Again the voice. "Fenton! Fenton Montague. Listen to me! I want you now."

"Wait just one moment please, Mr. Montague. I'll page him for you."

"Page him? *Page* him? I can't wait that long. I have to—" *What was that?* He heard someone running by his window. It was too late.

The motel owner had no sooner heard the words, This is Fenton Montague, than she was off and running toward the office. She had read the paper. She recognized the name. Now that she thought about it, she recognized the face. Yes, he didn't have hair, but it was him. She was sure of it now. Locking herself in the room behind the front counter, she frantically dialed 911.

"Portsmouth Police. What is your emergency?"

"Fenton Montague. I have Fenton Montague!" the

355

owner whispered hysterically into the phone. "The man on the front page of the—"

Every law enforcement officer in New England knew who Fenton Montague was by now. "Woooah, ma'am. Slow down. What do you mean you *have* Fenton Montague?"

"My name is Shirley Pines. I own the Colonial Pines Motel. He's here! He's screaming in his room. Please hurry. I know it's him."

"Okay, ma'am. Listen to me. Get as far away as you can. Now. Do not attempt to talk to him or stop him. I'll get cruisers rolling immediately. Now go!"

Shirley didn't even bother hanging up. She was gone before the dispatcher realized he hadn't gotten Fenton's room number.

—⚡—

Shortly after noon on Thursday, November 2nd, Rebecca Johnson began packing her children's things for the trip back to Darien. David's funeral service had been scheduled for 10:00 A.M. Saturday morning. It promised to be quite a circus.

Rebecca's mind juggled a hundred scenarios as she folded her kids' underwear and socks into her suitcase, preparing for the trip south. The thought of re-entering the house in which she and David had spent so many years terrified her. She wasn't sure she could do it. She wasn't sure it was even wise. But in her own way, like the kids, she needed closure. Tears filled her eyes as she packed, eventually streaming down her cheeks. She continued packing, resigned to the fact that her life would be full of a great deal of pain for a long time to come.

"Want some company?" Vickie asked, sticking her head through the open door to the boys' bedroom.

"Sure."

Vickie felt concerned as she saw her friend's tears. "You okay?" she asked.

Becky could hear the crackling of the fire in the wood stove as Vickie came into the bedroom. Its rustic song was a stark contrast to the pain flaming in the emptiness of her heart.

"I'll be okay," she said, placing socks in a suitcase. "You know better than anyone that David and I had our problems. In my own way, I loved him very much. I will miss him dearly. But more than anything, my heart breaks when I think of the kids. They worshipped him, Vickie. They had so little of him. They soaked up every minute of him like a dry sponge. I'm so afraid they'll never be the same. That I've lost my little darlings forever."

"Oh, Becky. I'm so sorry," Victoria said, taking her friend in her arms. The two women stood like that for several minutes, tears streaming down their cheeks.

Bones are always stronger at the break. What doesn't kill you, makes you stronger.

Through her sobs, Becky spoke into her best friend's shoulder. "How can I ever replace him, Vickie? I'm a woman. They need a father."

Victoria held Rebecca tightly. "You can't replace him, Becky. You shouldn't try. I know how this will sound, but in time, the pain will heal. The boys . . . they'll grow up, fall in love, provide you with beautiful grandchildren. The three of you will grow so much closer."

Rebecca didn't hear. "What am I going to do, Vickie? Where will we go?"

"Here, let's sit down," Vickie said, gently nudging Rebecca to the edge of the bed. The two sat side by side. Becky hugged her friend as if she were a life preserver in the open ocean. Her head was buried in Vickie's chest.

"Jonah's good at times of crisis," Vickie said. "Through the years, he's learned little sayings in the Program. They help him keep his head on straight. Right now, Becky, you have to keep your mind on the here and now. Don't borrow trouble. You don't know what the future will bring. Jonah has a favorite saying: If you want to make God laugh, tell him your plans. I think you got to do this one day at a time, Beck. Don't project. It'll overwhelm you."

Rebecca sat up straight, sniffling. She wiped her nose

and mouth slowly with the back of her hand, vainly attempting to regroup.

"Where are the boys?" she asked.

"They're out in the woods with Jonah. They need him now. You know what a calming influence he is."

"God, I know," Becky said. "You're so lucky, Vickie."

Victoria chuckled slightly. "Funny, I think the same of you."

"Me? Why?"

"Oh, I don't know. You seem so strong . . . so together. You have two beautiful children. They'll be such nice young men. I guess I'm envious sometimes. It's always greener, isn't it?"

"Yeah," Becky said, the hint of a laugh forcing its way out of her mouth.

"Come on, I'll help you. Let's finish up and get out of here. I think a nice, long walk would do us both some good. Won't be much longer and we won't be able to until April. Not without snowshoes."

Rebecca handed Vickie clothing, which she neatly packed into her friend's suitcase. "The boys will be all right, Becky. Really, they will."

"I pray you're right. I'm just heartbroken for them. How do you think they'll handle the funeral?"

"The same way we all will. It's a process. They'll cry. They'll grieve. It'll be painful. But, I really think that's healthy. The more they can get out now, the better. You know, Becky, I know a good child psychologist in Bridgton. The schools around here use him a lot. It might be good for all of you to go."

Rebecca refolded a pair of Caleb's cords. "I've been thinking about that. When we get back, maybe you can give me his name. I'd like to get the kids started as soon as possible. I think it would be healthy for them."

"I'll call him tonight. He and his wife are friends of ours. I'll see if he can rearrange his schedule to fit you in. I'm sure he'll bend over backwards to help if he can."

Becky finished handing Victoria the last item of clothing she felt her kids would need and sat down on the edge of the bed opposite her friend. She stared at Vickie now.

"How's Jonah feel about not going?" she asked.

"He's not happy about it. I think he put up quite a stink with that Lieutenant. The only thing that made him decide to stay was that he told Jonah there was a chance his presence would put us all in danger. Jonah just doesn't want to be responsible for that. He told me that as much as he wants to go, it would be selfish to put everyone else in jeopardy."

Rebecca pursed her lips. "He must be sick."

"Yeah, well, everything's relative, isn't it? I'm sure David will understand."

Rebecca smiled. "David would be proud of him."

When Vickie finished packing everything neatly, she sat down on the opposite bed. She rested her elbows on her knees, cupping her chin in her hands.

"Have you decided whether or not you're going to go in the house?" she asked.

"Yes, I need to do it, Vickie. There're too many memories. Too much family history. I just can't walk away from it all. I think seeing it one last time will be my closure on David's death."

"It will be very painful."

"I know. I'm scared. Will you come with me?" Rebecca asked.

Vickie looked up at her. "Of course. We'll do it together. It'll be good for both of us."

"Anyway," Becky continued, "I want to get some photo albums, a few mementos. Assuming they're not destroyed."

"What are you going to do with the furniture?"

"Give it to the Salvation Army, I guess. I don't want it. It's probably such a mess, I don't know if they'll take it. I want a few pieces. Things that have been in the family for a while. I'll probably have them shipped up here. Put in storage. The rest . . . I wouldn't even want to keep. Even if it's not ruined. Too many memories."

"You're going to have it shipped up here?" Victoria asked.

"Yeah. I've been thinking, Vickie. You're the closest thing to a sister I have in the whole world. I want to be close to you now. Would you mind if the kids and I moved up here? I don't know where exactly. Portland maybe. We'll find some place. I just don't want to be alone."

"Oh, Becky, I'd love it. We'll have so much fun. It'll be like old times. What about the boys though? Have you talked with them?"

"No, not yet. I suppose I won't do it if they're really against it. But we need to start fresh. I think they'll love the idea of being close to Jonah. We'll see. One day at a time, right?"

"Right. Come on, let's take that walk."

They walked into the kitchen, passing Trooper Martin's replacement sitting at the kitchen table. "We're going to take a walk. We'll be back shortly," Vickie said.

"Okay, ma'am. I'd tag along, but my orders are to stay here. You may want to check with one of the men outside. Let them know what you're doing. I think they'll want to keep an eye on you both."

As they grabbed their coats and walked outside, the women looked wide-eyed at each other. Like two little girls, "Tag along?" they mouthed to each other.

"You know, Vickie," Rebecca said, as they walked toward the barn to inform the trooper in the hayloft of their plans. "Both of our folks are flying in tomorrow. I'm so nervous. I haven't seen David's parents for a year. This whole trip's going to be a nightmare."

"Maybe," Vickie said, taking her friend's hand. "But the whole trip's not going to happen all at once. Remember, the journey is home."

Rebecca squinted her eyes slightly, not sure she understood. "The journey is home. What's that mean?"

"The journey is home? Well, it means you should live in the moment. Don't be looking too far down the road. Imagine someone hurrying to get somewhere, passing hundreds of beautiful rose bushes along the way. She doesn't stop once to smell any of them. All the while she is thinking, I've got to get home. I've got to get home. Just before she comes over the rise in the hill . . . just before she's going to get a glimpse of her house, a car comes over the hill and runs her over. She never even gets home, and she missed all those beautiful flowers along the way. The journey is home. That's my motto."

"The journey is home. I like that," Rebecca said. "I'll have to try and remember it. Too bad I'm not passing a lot of rose bushes right now."

Victoria put her arm around Rebecca's shoulders, hugging her body tightly. "You will, Becky. You will."

—⁓—

Three Portsmouth police and two New Hampshire state police cruisers pulled up to the Colonial Pines Motel within four minutes of each other. They spread out along the length of the V-shaped motel. No one would leave any of those rooms now without walking right into a gauntlet.

The first officer to arrive opened his door and knelt behind it, holding his semiautomatic toward the sky with both hands. He held that position until the second unit arrived, pulling up in front of the room closest to the office.

"Did you get a room number?" the first officer called out, as his colleague assumed the same position.

"No, did you?"

"Shit. Keep an eye out. I'll call."

The first state police unit pulled up just as the officer was crawling onto his front seat to call dispatch.

"Dispatch, this is thirty-seven."

"Ten three, thirty-seven," the dispatcher responded.

"We have units arriving at the motel now. Do you know what room he's located in?"

"Negative, thirty-seven. Couldn't catch it before the owner slipped away."

The officer hung his head, holding the mike in his hand. *Of course.* "Roger that, dispatch."

The state police trooper yelled out. "You boys got a room number?"

"Negative!" the first officer yelled to the sky above. "We're gonna to have to search room to room!"

"That's beautiful," the state cop mumbled to himself.

As the second state police cruiser pulled up his colleague cried out. "Tommy! Drive to the office and get the keys. We don't have a room number."

The state cop responded with a nod of his head. He checked the office and the room behind the counter, slowly entering each, his 9 mm double-action, Sig Sauer 225 semiautomatic cocked up at the wrists. When he was satisfied they were vacant, he reappeared with the master key ring.

Kneeling, he crawled under the window to the first room and waited. The fourth and fifth cars pulled up simultaneously, the last, a Portsmouth police cruiser, at the far end of the V, in front of room fourteen.

One of his colleagues called out to him. "Dutch! We don't have a room number! We need to go room to room! Stay put! Keep an eye out on the other rooms!"

With the other thirteen rooms being watched, the four police officers began the task of entering and searching each—one at a time. They stood on either side of each door. One officer knocked while they all waited for a response. The last thing they needed was to drop an innocent guest.

"Police! Open the door!" If there was no response, the officer with keys, still kneeling, would reach over and unlock the door. This is one of those moments in a cop's life when he knows it can all end in a second. One moment he's just cruising along, passing the hours until his shift is over, and in the next, his life can be taken from him in the blinding flash of an instant. Their collective adrenaline ran wild.

This wasn't Rambo. They didn't just charge in. No sense walking into a fusillade of bullets. The element of surprise had long since been lost. The cop closest to the door's hinges stood with his back to the wall, pushing it open with his right hand. He'd take a quick peek inside before pulling back his head. At his nod, the other two closest to the doorknob, would turn quickly toward the inside, one standing, the other kneeling, both holding their weapons straight out.

When finally they came to the last room, their hearts were pumping overtime. It would be some time before any one of them came down from this call. It was now or never. Like a game of Russian roulette: with each passing room they knew they were getting closer to the bullet in the chamber. Finally, after five clicks, you know what the next pull of the trigger offers. The fifth officer had joined them now. They were going to catch this son of a bitch.

A sense of disappointment and dread filled each man as they opened the door to the empty room, searched every inch, and realized he'd gotten away.

"Shit!" one of them said.

"Where's the owner?" another one asked.

One of the officers ran to his cruiser. "Dispatch, this is fourteen. The motel's been searched top to bottom. He's gone. There's no one here. Can you advise us of the owner's ten twenty?"

"Negative, fourteen."

"Do you know if she had a car?"

"Negative."

Jesus, give me something. "All right, what's her name?"

"Shirley Pines," dispatch responded.

"Dispatch, she had to leave here somehow. Run a Shirley Pines through DMV. Let's get the make and year of her vehicle. We need an all points on that car now."

"Ten four, fourteen. Running DMV now. Will respond."

The Portsmouth police officer sat in his cruiser, holding his mike. His legs hung out the door. He was joined by his two colleagues.

"We were so fuckin' close," one of them said. "I can't believe the son of a bitch slipped us."

"He can't be but a few miles from here," the other one said.

The officer holding the mike spoke. "I know, but with every passing minute he gets farther and farther away. We got to get a make on her car. I got a feeling he's either in it with her or in it by himself. Either way, we find the car we find him."

The radio crackled as dispatch responded. "Unit fourteen. DMV has a make on Pines's vehicle."

"Ten three."

"A dark green Crown Victoria. Nineteen seventy-nine. New Hampshire license, Paul, Ida, Nora, Edward, Sam."

"Roger that," he said, repeating the plate number.

"Affirmative, fourteen."

"Thanks. Dispatch, put me through to Chief Vaughn."

"Ten four. One moment."

The dispatcher told her colleague to hold the board while she went to get Portsmouth's chief of police. A moment later, Vaughn picked up the phone. "Who is it?" Vaughn asked the dispatcher.

"Stivers, sir."

"Stive, Vaughn here. What ya got?" the chief asked, taking his dispatcher's chair in front of the microphone on the counter.

"He's gone, sir. Not a sign of him or the owner. I think it's possible he could have her car. We ran DMV. Got a make, year, and license. He's in town, sir. I can feel him. We can get 'im if we're quick."

"And lucky," Vaughn added. "All right, good work. I'll get the specs from dispatch and run a teletype. Keep your eyes peeled."

"Don't worry, Chief."

Vaughn left instructions with his dispatcher and left to speak with his teletype operator. The hunt was on.

The dispatcher sat back down in front of the large bank of blinking lights. "All units. Be on the lookout for . . ."

———m———

Shirley Pines had no sooner ended her conversation with the Portsmouth police dispatcher, when she grabbed her purse and was out the door, climbing into her 1979 Crown Victoria. It wasn't until she was finally seated behind the steering wheel that she took a long, deep breath. Frenzied, she dug through her purse, finding her keys. Her hands shook violently as she tried to put them in the ignition. Finally, after several tries, she met with success. She whipped her car in reverse and threw it in drive before she had even come to a stop. Thank God! She knew she was safe now.

Slowing, she turned on her left blinker, letting oncoming traffic pass her. She wet her pants as the icy feel of cold steel stuck in the base of her neck.

"Go straight," Fenton said, rising from the floor in back.

Fear is a powerful motivator. It may not work in the long run, but Fenton didn't care about the long run, or the short run for that matter. What he cared about more than anything was the here and now. He sat in the back seat behind Shirley Pines, voicing instructions to his captive. He didn't bother keeping David's gun on her. She'd already been told he would blow her brains out if she so much as peeked in the rearview mirror.

"What's your name?" Fenton asked.

Pines was whimpering, not ingratiating herself with her passenger. She jumped in her seat as he asked again, this time more forcefully.

"I asked you your name!" he bellowed.

"Shirley," Pines said, through sobs.

Fenton was smiling now. Reality as he had known it less than an hour ago was now a thing of the past. "You know what, Shirley?"

"Please don't hurt me. You can have anything. My money, my—"

"Shut up! And stop crying. You're startin' to bug the shit out of me. We're going to play by some simple rules here, Shirley . . . Okay?"

Silence.

"Okay?"

As instructed, she held both hands on the steering wheel. Fenton didn't want her giving anyone signals he couldn't see. Her arms shook uncontrollably. He loved this part, the moments before he killed his hapless victims, when they turned into masses of blubbering, begging fools.

He hadn't killed a woman yet. Well . . . his mother didn't really count. The tension and fear in the car filled him with a sense of sexual excitement, his mind envisioning a dozen different scenes. Over and over, he pictured what he'd do to her if only he had the time. His desire to make her scream—to hurt her, to make her beg—was overwhelming. This is what had been missing. *Why haven't I thought of this before?* What he needed was women.

I'll do Jonah and then I'll do the wives. He was disappointed he hadn't done Rebecca first. He'd certainly had the chance. More than once he had followed her around Darien. How much fun that would have been. That tight little ass. Those soft, pleading, hazel eyes. Think of the pain it would have caused David. *Oh well. Live and learn.*

"Did you call the police?" Fenton asked.

Shirley bravely shook her head, desperately keeping sobs of terror to herself. Tears streamed down her face. She had trouble seeing the road.

"Boo!" Fenton said, laughing as Shirley literally jumped off the seat. "Shirley? When I talk to you, you answer me. That's rule number one. Got it?"

"Yes."

"Good. You learn quick. See that gas station? Turn in there."

She didn't know how she could survive—being so close to humanity, so close to salvation—and not being able to cry out for help. She practiced pleading with her eyes. *Oh God. Someone notice me. Please! Someone notice.*

As she made the turn, Fenton gave her instructions. "See that blue Cherokee?" he asked.

"Yes."

"That was very good, Shirley," Fenton said with a smile. "Pull up behind it."

She did as she was told, trying with all her might to keep her arms still. Fenton leaned forward, his lips at the back of her right ear. "Do you believe in God, Shirley?"

She was practically catatonic now. "Yes," she responded, her voice barely audible.

I can't have some lonely bitch telling the cops what I look like now, Fenton thought. No sir. That just won't do. He adjusted his baseball cap and shoved his gun under his belt at the small of his back. He reached inside his knapsack and pulled out his knife—the same one with which he had killed three men.

"Well then, this is your lucky day," he whispered to her, smelling her hair. "You not only don't have to spend a little play time with me, but you get to meet your maker."

She tried desperately not to hear him. Shirley stared straight ahead, her eyes closed. Fenton's last words stung her ears. Get to meet my maker? But they registered too late. He pulled the knife up from his side and placed it quickly to her throat.

"Bye-bye, Shirley," he said, pulling her head back by the hair, ripping the knife's razor-like serrated edge deeply through her neck. The windshield splattered red, blood dripping from the rearview mirror.

Hardly anyone takes their keys out of the ignition when they pay for gas. Fenton figured he could tour the country this way if he wanted—stealing one car after another until hell froze over. The Cherokee's owner had just gone inside to pay for his fillup. What a moron.

Fenton turned to look at his ex-captive now, hunched over in the front seat. He pursed his lips, sending her a mock kiss, and climbed inside his newfound wheels. Turning the ignition, he was gone as quickly as he had appeared, a floating cloud of dust and dirt in front of the Crown Victoria, the last remnant of his presence there. That . . . and a slumping, bloodied, Shirley Pines.

Fenton took US Route 1 over the Piscataqua River toward Kittery, Maine, the radio bellowing at a deafening pitch. As he drove the height of the Memorial Bridge, he was surprised by the size of the sprawling complex known as the Portsmouth Naval Ship Yard, which is a bit of a misnomer, as it is located on the Maine side of the border. He'd never seen it before. Rolling cranes and giant water towers with ten-foot letters that read U.S. Navy were visible beside huge terminals, hangars, and dozens of older brick buildings. Here is where the Atlantic nuclear submarine fleet goes for overhaul and repair. Everything is done under the cover of a roof. American anti-reconnaissance at its best. It was a neat sight. He was glad he'd gone this way.

Fenton was no longer afraid; his brain now functioned

like a well-oiled machine. Thinking several moves into the future, he played out the most important chess match of his life. At the rotary in Kittery, he followed signs to I-95 north, tapping his thumbs and fingers on the steering wheel, listening to Mick and the Stones play one of his favorites, "Sympathy for the Devil." He sang aloud. "Please allow me to introduce myself. I'm a man of wealth and taste."

As he drove, he kept a keen eye on the clock. He figured he knew within a matter of a few minutes how long he had to ditch his newest acquisition. Though he was suffering another psychotic break, his alter-personality was not oblivious to the powers that hunted him. While he didn't know the minutiae of all the technology at their disposal, what he did know was that they were a force to be reckoned with. He could not afford to take them lightly, for as sure as the sun will rise tomorrow morning, they'd snag him—like a fox being chased on the hunt.

His eyes were like wide-reaching radar, seeing far ahead of him and even farther behind. He knew he was vulnerable now. He would need to seek shelter. Come in from the cold. He was too visible this way, and he didn't like it. He needed to think.

Fenton turned off the radio and concentrated on the task at hand. He could probably travel for days like this, stealing one car after another, but he knew he would eventually trip up. Sooner or later, there wouldn't be a gas station, or it would be empty. In time, if he kept pushing his luck, it would run out on him.

What he needed was a car. His own car. Something he could use freely. Something that could act as his wings, not his shackles. Slowing to sixty miles an hour, he rummaged through the Cherokee's glove compartment, looking for a map of Maine. Finding one, he unfolded it in front of the steering wheel, looking up at the road and then down to the map in equal parts. He was at a disadvantage. As familiar as he was with New England, somehow Maine had escaped him over the years. He was relatively unfamiliar with the state.

More than anything, what Fenton wanted was to get

off the main roads—out of the crowds—to melt into the unspoiled landscape of rural Maine. He would need to stay someplace, preferably for a week or two, while he had time to formulate his attack. Events had been dictating the pace. Fenton knew he desperately needed to turn it around. He was the director of this play. He needed to regain control.

Fenton took Exit 2 off the Maine Turnpike and traveled north-northwest on Route 109 toward Sanford. He hoped to find a used car lot there. As he drove, the furious pace of the past hour or so caught up with him. He realized he was squeezing the steering wheel, breathing more quickly than he would like. He rolled down the windows, followed the posted speed limit signs, and tried to take in the beautiful scenery of the trip.

He passed old farmhouses and barns. They seemed two hundred years old. They probably were. He saw dairy cattle grazing, acres and acres of farm land and pastures—even recently harvested corn fields. He passed a beautiful large white Grange Hall and was reminded of a dying part of America's rural past. He was surprised by Maine's agrarian landscape.

Fenton felt more at ease now. Pulling into town, he passed huge old brick mills; as usual, abutting the river in town. He had become so immersed in the rural beauty, he nearly forgot he needed to dump the Cherokee. He was pushing it now. One mistake and it would all be over. *No Jonah. No justice.*

He pulled into the parking lot of a local drugstore, thinking he could ask the owner where a car lot might be. He'd emptied his bank account before leaving Boston. He figured he still had ten, maybe eleven thousand dollars. All in cash. All in his knapsack.

As Fenton entered the drugstore, a voice spoke to him. He was shocked at first, taken off guard by its sudden appearance. The voices usually came when he was idle: sleeping, napping, sitting around the apartment. He couldn't remember them coming when his mind was so focused—of a single purpose.

The voice seared his brain like a part of his inner soul that was desperately trying to keep him from the worst of himself. "Your Thorazine, Fenton. Don't forget your Thorazine. You're here. Do it." The voices were loud. They wanted his attention. They had it. *Ironic, though. I don't take Thorazine. I take Clozaril.* He walked to the pharmacy counter in the back of the store and stood silent for a few moments, waiting while the pharmacist finished filling a prescription. The pharmacist eventually looked up, embarrassed to have made his customer wait.

"I'm sorry, sir. Can I help you?"

"Yes. I hate to bother you with this, but I'm in a bit of a jam," Fenton began. "I lost my prescription, and I'm afraid that without it . . . well, without it, let's just say I'm afraid."

Here we go, the pharmacist thought. Another druggie coming up with any lie he can to score some dope. "What is the prescription for?" he asked.

"Clozaril," Fenton answered.

Immediately, the pharmacist understood his customer was for real. Addicts don't make up lies for Clozaril or Haldol, or any other phenothiazines for that matter. It would be like working a scam for insulin. The scam artists were almost always looking for some kind of benzodiazepine like Valium or Xanax or synthetic opiates like Percocet or Vicodin.

"I understand," the pharmacist said sympathetically. "What is your doctor's name? I can look him up on my computer and get him on the phone."

Fenton needed to make a decision. In seconds, his mind tossed about the ramifications of what he was about to do. He'd already pressed his luck once by calling Rosenstern from the motel. Surely, if Fenton spoke to him, told him where he was, it would jeopardize his freedom. But it was almost one o'clock. Fenton knew that Rosenstern would be at lunch. Better yet, the shrink that covered for him always rubber-stamped everything. Fenton doubted he would even catch his name. It was definitely a calculated risk, but he had to take the chance.

"Doctor Rosenstern," Fenton said, speaking much lower now. "He's at Bridgewater State in Mass."

"I'm sorry, sir," the pharmacist said, tilting his ear

ever so slightly toward Fenton. "I didn't hear that. Where is he?"

"Bridgewater State. In Massachusetts."

The pieces were falling together quickly for the pharmacist now. What stood in front of him was a former patient of a state psychiatric hospital, and he was looking for Clozaril. The pharmacist felt a little ill at ease. He knew that in most cases, someone on Clozaril would be relatively harmless—at least to people other than themselves. But there's only so much modern medicine can do for certain people. At some point, mental illness crosses a line. The pharmacist hoped the unfortunate man in front of him wasn't yet on the other side.

"Well, let's see," he said, pulling out one of several yellow pages from underneath his counter. "Bridgewater . . . Bridgewater. Here we go. Bridgewater State Hospital."

He dialed the number and waited, the moment filled with an uneasy silence. The two men made eye contact. The pharmacist smiled. Fenton did not. Fenton watched the pharmacist, the seconds seeming like hours. Finally, he began to speak.

"Yes. Can you connect me to Doctor Rosenstern please?" The pharmacist smiled again, the wait interminable. "Yes, this is Henry Strutweiller, of Strutweiller's Pharmacy in Sanford, Maine. Is Doctor Rosenstern available?"

He looked at Fenton. "I'm on hold," he said. "As I'm sure you know, sir, I'll need an okay'd white blood cell count before I can fill a Clozaril prescription."

Clozaril cannot be prescribed once a patient's count drops below thirty. A white blood cell count can be ordered at any major hospital or any of a dozen private labs in a major metropolitan area. If a patient passes, clearance is only good for a week. Fenton had just made the deadline, having been tested the previous Friday before leaving Boston.

"I understand. I've got one here," he said, reaching inside his pants pocket.

Fenton turned as he heard the cow bell above the front door jingle. His internal organs ceased functioning as he watched a Maine state trooper approach him. He was trapped. The cop moved closer. He was between Fenton and the door. His fight or flight instinct jumped into overdrive. His sweat glands pumped perspiration as adrenaline seeped into every cell in his body. His mouth became dry, his skull nothing more than armature for the clay of his face.

He waited . . . watching but not watching, trying to appear disinterested. He looked outside, keeping an eye on every move, every step the cop took. When the trooper reached the counter, he had a bottle of Pepsi and a pack of Camels in his hands. He smiled at Fenton. Fenton smiled back.

"I left my wallet in the car," Fenton said to the pharmacist. "I'll be right back."

The pharmacist nodded, holding the phone between his chin and shoulder, ringing up the cop's purchase. "Bob, haven't seen you around lately," he said.

"Been on vacation the past two weeks, Henry. Good to be back, though. Florida's okay, but still, there's nothing like Maine."

Fenton turned the ignition of the Cherokee and backed out. In the ultimate irony, the Maine state police cruiser had pulled up right next to him. The cop must have just been coming on duty, maybe driving to his barracks. Whatever the reason, he hadn't put two and two together. That Cherokee was more than just a stolen car. It was a stolen car driven by Fenton Montague. Every cop in New England was looking for it by now.

That was a bit too close for comfort. I've got to dump this car. He drove a short way and was relieved to see a row of multicolored plastic triangular strips blowing in the slight breeze. He could read the sign now as he drew closer. Stew's Used Cars & Auto Body. He drove past, parked in the lot behind a Dunkin' Donuts, grabbed his knapsack, and walked the block and a half back to the used-car lot.

At about the same time, Doctor Rosenstern picked up the phone with Henry Strutweiller. "Doctor Rosenstern speaking."

"Yes, Doctor, I have a man here who says he's a

patient of yours. Apparently, he's lost his Clozaril prescription. Says his last count was Friday. If you'd be kind enough to check the lab, I'll be happy to help him."

Rosenstern was rigid, almost cold. "What was your name again?" he asked.

"Strutweiller. Henry Strutweiller. I own the—"

"Listen to me, Strutweiller. Is the man there now?" Rosenstern asked.

Strutweiller was a little put off. "Well . . . actually, no. He left to get his wallet. Why?"

"Can you tell me what this man looks like?" Rosenstern asked.

What the hell? "Well, let's see. Caucasian. Mid forties. Medium build. Five tenish."

"Did he have a Boston accent?"

"Yes."

Rosenstern was firm and resolute. He spoke without delay. "Strutweiller, call the police. Call them now. I believe the man you just saw is Fenton Montague."

"Fenton Montague? Should I know that name? . . . Oh, you mean the man all over the news?"

"Yes. Call the cops. Now! Then call me back."

"Bob!" Strutweiller yelled, throwing the phone in its cradle, running out of the store to catch the Maine state trooper. For a horrifying moment, he had visions of Montague coming back into the store. How would he ever be able to act normal? If Montague suspected him, he'd kill him for sure. He ran out the door just in time to see the trooper's cruiser pulling away.

"Bob!" he screamed. "Bob!"

Too late. He was gone. No doubt lost in the world you create before suffering re-entry at work after a relaxing vacation.

"Shit!" Strutweiller said, jogging back into his store. He ran to the phone and dialed the Maine state police. The Sanford police certainly weren't going to handle this one. "Yes, this is Henry Strutweiller of Sanford. I just had Fenton Montague in my store. Hurry. He's in town."

"The Fenton Montague, sir?"

"Christ," he answered, uncharacteristically annoyed.

"How many of them are you looking for? Come on, we're wasting time!"

—∽∿∽—

"Scott!" Lieutenant Halliway yelled down the hall from their makeshift command post in the interrogation room. "We got a make on him!"

Hill looked up as he heard Halliway call his name, dropping the file he was holding on his desk as the words his partner spoke registered in his brain.

"Yes!" he said, clenching his fist. He ran down the hall, slapping Halliway's shoulders as he slowed at the door, walking inside. "Today's our day, Ric. I knew it when I woke up this morning. I could just feel it. I got to remember to buy a lottery ticket. Lady Luck doesn't come knockin' that often."

"Here's what we got," Halliway said, holding his arms out in front of him. "Christ, look at this, will ya? I got goose bumps. All right . . . he leaves the motel in the owner's car. Slashes her throat at the gas station, takes the Cherokee, and that's where we lose him, right?"

Come on, come on. "Right?" he answered.

Halliway stood, incapable of sitting right now. "Okay. So apparently he drives to Maine. Stops in some town called Sanford." He turned the map lying across the table so it faced his partner. "Right . . . here," he said, pointing.

"Come on, Ric, you're killing me. Where is he now?"

"I just got off the phone with the Maine state police. They recovered the stolen Cherokee. He's got to be in the area somewhere. They want to know how we want them to proceed."

Hill looked up at Halliway, concern etched on his face. "We got to be *real* careful here, Ric. We lose him now, and everyone's morale is gonna dive. We gotta make sure we do everything right."

"Okay, so how do you want to handle this? They're waiting for my call," Halliway said, leaning with the sole of his right foot up against the wall.

"We need to get out a teletype," Hill said.

"Right. I figure we send one to the Maine state police and the Sanford police, if they got 'em. Let's be sure and get one to the county sheriff, just to make sure."

"What about these other little towns?" Hill asked, bending over the map. "Alfred? Emery Mills? Waterboro? They seem so small. I can't believe they have police departments."

"We're gonna find out. I'll get it all when I call the Maine boys back. Meantime, we need a door-to-door search. Every motel, every hotel, every boarding house and restaurant. He's there Scott, and we're gonna find him."

"What the hell is he doin' in Sanford, Maine?" Hill asked.

"I can only guess he's going after Jonah. The detective I spoke to told me the man who called them was a pharmacist. Owns some local shop in town. He said . . . are you ready for this? Fenton was asking to get a Clozaril prescription filled."

"You're shittin' me."

"Nope. Actually, he didn't have a prescription. He had the pharmacist call his psychiatrist at Bridgewater. That's how the pharmacist made the ident. Apparently, his shrink—" Halliway stopped to refer to his notes, "a Doctor Rosenstern, tipped him off as to who he was."

Hill scrunched his face slightly. "How the hell did he know? He must have a thousand patients that take that stuff."

"Yeah, that's what I thought. The Maine boys spoke to him. Apparently Fenton tried to reach him earlier in the afternoon and identified himself to his secretary. I guess the Doc put two and two together."

Hill steepled his fingers against his chin. "I'll be damned."

"See? I told you we'd hit it with the scrips," Halliway said.

"Yeah, you called that one, all right. Okay, so how do you want the teletype to read? We gotta make tracks."

"I've already got something down," Halliway said, flipping a page in his notebook. "How's this? 'Urgent!!' I added two exclamation points for effect. 'Be on the lookout for a Fenton Montague. Five feet ten inches tall, stocky build. Possible beard. Possible shaved head. Last seen at Strutweiller's Pharmacy in Sanford, Maine. Wanted by Connecticut state police, New York state police and New Hampshire state police on five murder charges. One of them a law-enforcement officer. Believed to be on foot. He is armed and *extremely* dangerous. Approach with caution. If apprehended, pay particular attention for any knives or sharp instruments. They are needed for evidentiary purposes.'"

Halliway looked up at his partner. "Well?" he asked.

"Sounds good. You left two things out. Don't forget to add that he's Caucasian and you may want to put in his last known vehicle. You never know what might tip the scales."

"Good," Halliway said. "Can't believe I forgot that. All right . . . what else?"

"How 'bout roadblocks?" Hill asked.

Halliway shrugged his shoulders. "For what? We don't know what he's driving. If he's driving. He could be running through the woods for all we know."

"All right then, how 'bout at least a surveillance detail on all the major roads leading out of the area."

"Better yet," Halliway said, pulling up a chair opposite his partner, "let's see if we can get Technical Service to run us a set of computer-generated photos. One with hair and a beard, the other shaven with a beard. We can fax it up there and have it in every cruiser in the state within a few hours."

Hill exhaled smoke rings toward the ceiling, his hands folded behind his head. "I don't know, Ric. Seems like a long shot to me. A man can travel a long way in a few hours. Shit, by the time they get 'em, he could be in New York. I don't think we got the time. We've gotta take a few chances. Let's just set up some surveillance posts," Hill said, referring to the map in front of him. "We can't cover every road, but then again, maybe he's afraid to get too off the beaten path. Maybe he's thinkin' he'll stick out like a sore thumb if he's the only one on the road. Look, let's get some people on . . ." he paused to view

376

the map again, "two-oh-two north, two-oh-two south, one-eleven east and four south. It can't hurt."

Halliway pulled the map around, surveying his options. "Okay," he said, looking up at Hill. "But what the hell are we having them look for? We can't very well tell them to be on the lookout for suspicious looking men."

"Why not?" Hill asked. "This guy's running for his life, right? He can feel the heat all around him. He's pumped, Ric. There's no telling what he might do. Hell, he's already carjacked before. Why wouldn't he do it again? Tell them to look for bald men. Tell them to look for men with beards. Hell, I don't know."

"Men with beards? In Maine?" Halliway asked. "Christ, Scott, I figure half the men up there have beards."

Hill chuckled. "What the hell makes you say that?" he asked.

"Well . . . shit, Scott. I don't know. It's Maine. I guess I just figure half of them are lumberjacks or fishermen or some such thing."

"Yeah, they probably have to drive to Boston to see a dentist. Hey, that reminds me," Hill interjected. "How do you compliment someone from Maine?"

Halliway could always count on his partner to break the tension. When you least expected it, he'd throw out a one liner. Nothing big. Always just enough to keep everyone sane. "Please, Scott, not now," Halliway said with a smile. "I don't know. How do you compliment someone from Maine?"

"Nice tooth."

Halliway rubbed his forehead. "Unbelievable," he said, his chest heaving ever so slightly with a chuckle that never quite made it out. "Are you done?"

"I say we do it, Ric. We've gotten luckier."

"All right, I'll tell 'em. What else?" Halliway asked.

"We should at least fax them up his driver's license photo."

"On it. Anything else?"

"I'm not sure. You run the teletype. Let me think. If we've missed somethin', I'll think of it while you're out."

"Okay, be right back," Halliway said, leaving the door to the room open as he left.

Hill sat silent for a moment. He smiled. "Lumberjacks and fishermen," he said aloud. *Boy, do Mainers get a bum rap.* He scribbled on the yellow legal pad in front of him. Drawing a line down the middle, he spelled out the words To Do and Done above each column. In bullet form, he wrote down all the things he and Halliway had just discussed.

Turning his attention to the To Do list, he scribbled down the word Roadblocks, stopped to think for a moment, and picked up one of the three phones that had been installed on the table in front of him. He dialed a Connecticut operator, explained the nature of his call, and asked to be patched directly through to Maine information.

Hill got the numbers of the Sanford police and the York County Sheriff's Department. A good cop doesn't just rely on his teletype, not for something this important. Hill followed up the teletype Halliway was sending with a call to each department chief. He wanted to make sure they were aware it was coming and that the information was disseminated to all units as quickly as possible.

Halliway walked back into the room in time to hear the end of Hill's conversation with the York County Sheriff's Department. "He is extremely dangerous, Sheriff. Under no circumstances are your men to take him lightly . . . Yes, that's correct . . . Okay, thank you," he said, hanging up.

"Who was that?" Halliway asked.

"The county sheriff. I wanted to make sure we followed up the teletype with a call to each department."

"Good thinking. I thought of that on my way back here."

"Yeah, sure," Hill said with a mischievous smile. "So what now? We wait, don't we?"

There comes a time in most investigations of this nature when a detective realizes he's done about all there is to do. Even with all the high-tech equipment, the computers, the contacts, the dragnets—eventually waiting becomes the only alternative. It's always the hardest part.

"That's about it, I think. I don't know what else we can do," Halliway responded.

"You know, Ric, I just had a terrible thought. What if they get in a firefight and one of them kills him. We'll never even get to slap cuffs on him."

"Don't even think it, Scott."

———

As usual, Jonah Roberts awoke early on Friday morning. He didn't need to set an alarm. He'd been getting up with the sun for so many years, his body was programmed by now. He lay on his left side, the cocoon of his bed warm and safe. For the first time in a long time, he didn't feel like getting up.

He turned, expecting to feel Victoria's warm body. He wasn't interested in making love. He thought they might just talk for a while. But she was gone. *Probably taking a shower*. He knew she wanted to get an early start to Darien. If they left by 7:00 A.M., they'd probably make it there around 1:00 P.M., give or take.

He lay on his back, looking at the wooden beams of his ceiling. He wondered what life would be like without Victoria. He dearly loved her. She was his reason for living. Through thick and thin, she'd been there for him, during his worst drinking years—the blackouts, the vomiting, the embarrassments. The very fact he had found her—that she hung in there through it all—made him feel certain there was a God.

Every alcoholic reaches a bottom in their life and learns the rule of holes the hard way. It's very simple really. When you find yourself in one, stop digging. Some use the bottom as the impetus to begin crawling out of the hole they've dug, while others just keep on digging. Victoria had been instrumental in helping Jonah climb out of his.

He got up, slipped on his robe, and went to his computer. As he sat there staring at the blank screen, he realized he just didn't care. The markets' daily gyrations didn't matter to him now. AT&T, Coca Cola, General Electric, McDonald's. They'd all be there tomorrow morning. And the morning after that. And the morning after that. He wasn't so sure about himself.

He walked out the door, now fully expecting to see his new uniformed house guest. "Good morning," he said to Trooper Martin.

"Morning."

Rebecca's fold-out bed was already put away. He could hear the shower running.

"Where is everyone?" he asked.

"Well, your wife's in the bathroom. Mrs. Johnson went out to the car. Said she'd be right back."

Jonah nodded his head and walked to the bathroom to urinate. Passing the kids' room, he noticed their door was still closed. The bathroom was open in design, with no ceiling, just eight foot walls all around. A wool Sioux Indian blanket he bought out West hung on a rod. It was the only door.

The sight of it made him think of David. "Jesus Christ, Jonah," he remembered David saying on one of his trips up. "You got more money than God, you'd think you could afford a fuckin' door."

Jonah always loved it when David came up. It was fun watching him decompress. "Hey, we came up here to get away from all that pretentious shit. The blanket works just fine."

"Since when is a door pretentious?" David asked. "You know, I think all this clean air and woods crap has gone to your head."

"I hope so," Jonah answered.

He finished at the toilet, hung up his robe and let his pajama bottoms fall to the floor. Poking his head into the shower, he watched as Victoria washed her hair. She hung her head back, running her fingers through it from the base of the skull up. He eyed the suds of the shampoo as it flowed over her breasts, past her navel, and through her pubic hair. Her glistening body arched delicately under the streaming water. He yearned to hold her.

He pulled his head out and waited a minute or so for her to finish rinsing. He didn't want the first thing she saw when she opened her eyes to be a head sticking through the shower curtain.

"Vickie," he said a touch louder than normal to be heard over the flowing water.

"What?" she answered.

"Good morning."

"Morning."

Pulling the curtain back, he stepped inside the shower with his wife. She stood so the water hit her first, spraying him with more of a mist than anything else. He was cold. His nipples hardened. Jonah never understood why people thought taking showers with someone else was so romantic. To his mind, someone was always going to be uncomfortable.

"Hi," Vickie said, pulling back her shoulder length, sandy-brown hair with both hands.

"Hi, hon," he said, putting his hands around her waist.

They stood like that for a short while, the water streaming over each of them. He was melancholy, desperately wishing he could make the trip south with Vickie. He knew he would miss her more than ever the next few days.

Vickie ran her fingers along Jonah's back, lightly probing the crack of his buttocks with her fingers, not sure exactly what she was starting . . . or why. She knew how to turn him on, but wasn't sure she wanted to start. This was hardly the time. Yet there was something about the moment—the odd sense of sadness, the anxiety. She needed release.

Jonah wasn't thinking of sex either. There was too much going on, too much tension in the air. Not to mention a policeman in the kitchen. But there was something about the moment, the very need for stealth, that warmed his loins. He was surprised when blood began flowing to his organ.

She took him in her hands and began stroking him gently.

"What are you doing?" he whispered in Vickie's ear.

"Shhh. Let's just enjoy each other," she whispered back.

381

Lowering Jonah to the floor of the shower, she slowly guided him inside her. He lay with his shoulders against the head of the tub, water spraying down on Vickie's back. He cupped his palms lightly over her wet breasts, their firmness exciting him as if it were the first time. They moved slowly, quietly. Vickie gripped her hamstrings, straining her neck toward the ceiling, rhythmically moving her pelvis in tandem with her husband's. The need for quiet and secrecy only added to the clandestine pleasure.

When finally they both released, Vickie lay down on Jonah's chest. She realized now that her knees were killing her. She listened quietly for voices or noises from outside. She thought she heard Becky say something. She worried just how quiet they had been, and even wondered if that much quiet hadn't stood out by itself.

"Do you think they heard us?" she whispered in Jonah's ear.

"I hope so."

"Oh, stop it," she said, rising to one knee. *At least the cleanup is easy.*

They both rose, quietly holding each other's bodies in the warm stream of water. "I've got to get going," she said. "Becky wanted to leave by seven-thirty."

"Better hurry," Jonah said, lightly patting his wife's behind as she stepped out of the shower.

Jonah always shaved in the shower. He did it by feel. He couldn't remember the last time he'd used a mirror. He finished shaving and stepped out, drying himself quickly. He wanted to help pack the car. Throwing on his pajamas and robe, he stepped out of the bathroom just in time to see both boys walking out of their bedroom, still dressed in their Mighty Morphin Power Rangers pajamas. Their hair was laughably disheveled. Becky called it bed head.

Jonah stood at the bathroom door. "Hey guys," he said.

"Hi, Uncle Jonah," they said in unison, the sleep not yet out of their voices. Caleb yawned.

"Can I use the bathroom, Uncle Jonah?" Sumner asked, walking toward him.

"Sure."

"Hurry up. I got to go too," Caleb said.

"You can go together. You know how to cross swords?" Jonah asked.

"Jonah!" Vickie barked, sitting on the fold-out couch, leaning over to tie her Bean boots.

The boys seemed lethargic, their usual spunkiness gone. Jonah didn't know what to do, what to say. Opting for silence, he stood in front of the wood stove, watching Sumner close the wool blanket behind him. His brother waited outside.

He looked at Vickie. "What's the matter with that? I used to do it with my brother all the time."

"You're impossible," she said, getting up, walking to the kitchen.

"What?" Jonah asked, perplexed and a little angry.

Much to their annoyance, Becky made the boys shower. She folded their pajamas and put them in a travel bag, laying out their clothes on their beds. When the boys finished, they dressed in the bedroom. The two women were outside at the car, getting things ready for the long trip south.

Jonah made a pot of coffee for everyone. Trooper Martin approached him and leaned back against the kitchen counter.

"You know," he said quietly, taking sides. "I used to cross swords with my brothers all the time too. I thought it was a blast."

"It is," Jonah said, shrugging his shoulders. "Hey, what do women know?"

"Beats me."

"Jonah, can you check the tire pressure before we go?" Vickie said to her husband, coming in from outside. "I think the right front is low."

"Sure."

Becky walked in behind her. "Caleb, Sumner, you guys almost ready? We got to get goin'. We're late already." Nothing. "Kids?" she called out.

When they didn't answer, she walked to the bedroom to check on them. She put her hand to her mouth as she opened the door, her heart shattering with agony at the sight of her two young sons sitting on the edge of a bed, crying softly in each other's arms.

Becky knelt in front of them. "Oh, God, kids. I'm so sorry. Here," she said, holding out her arms to her children. "Let me hold you. I love you so much."

As if making a leap from a floating log to a lifeboat, they each grabbed their mother, clinging to her like Velcro. A piece of her died that day as they sobbed on her bosom. Life would never again be the same.

Trooper Martin approached, wanting to offer some help with the luggage. "Mrs. Johnson?" he said, coming to the door.

Her eyes pleaded as she looked up at him. "Oh, I'm terribly sorry, ma'am. Forgive me," he said, closing the door behind him.

Martin stood with his back to the door, running his hand through his hair. Every once in a while, you see something you know will never fade from your memory. He trotted outside, joining Vickie and Jonah at the car.

"Mr. and Mrs. Roberts, I don't know if I should say anything, but Mrs. Johnson's in there holding her children like there's no tomorrow. They're both sobbing. I thought you might want to know."

Vickie and Jonah looked at each other. "Why don't you go in, Jonah? The boys could use you right now."

"You sure?" he asked, not wanting to interfere. "I don't know what to say," he said.

"Ask Becky if the boys could use you now."

He felt unsure. "Okay," he answered, in that tone of voice that says, If you really think I should.

As Jonah left to go inside, Vickie turned to see a Maine state police cruiser pulling up the driveway. She glanced at Martin, a quizzical look on her face.

"Your escort, ma'am," Martin said.

Vickie pushed a suitcase to one side of the back of the car. "Escort? Is that really necessary?"

"Just to the New Hampshire border. From there you should be okay."

"God, I hope so," she said, folding her arms across her chest.

Martin was cool, professionally distant. He kept his hands in his pockets. "Well, like we discussed last night, we know he's in the state, ma'am. It's just a precaution."

"The kids are gonna be scared out of their wits."

"It'll be behind you. I just wouldn't tell 'em," he said, scratching the top of his scalp. He hoped he didn't sound too aloof. "They may never notice it."

"Yes, I s'pose that's not bad advice. Can you tell him to wait at the end of the road? Follow in behind us there?"

"All right, I think we can do that."

"Good. I'm gonna check inside. Be right back."

Vickie half walked half jogged back to the house. As she entered, she saw Rebecca leaning against the refrigerator, her arms wrapped tightly around her chest. She was fighting back tears.

"Becky? You gonna be okay?"

Becky remained silent. She just nodded her head, avoiding words. She knew that to talk, to open her mouth, would bring the inevitable sobs. She fought with all her energy to remain strong.

Vickie looked at the bedroom. The door was closed. She trusted Jonah to do the right thing. He was good in times of crisis. The worse the circumstances, the stronger he became. At least that's how it came off.

"Is Jonah with the boys?" she asked.

Becky nodded her head.

"Do you think they can travel, Beck? We really should get going."

Becky squeezed her lips together as hard as she could. Vickie could see this was killing her. *The journey is home. The journey is home.*

Vickie approached her friend. "Come here," she said softly, taking her into her arms. They held each other, neither speaking. Words were superfluous now. There was nothing anyone could say.

Trooper Martin came into the kitchen from the cold, catching the two women embracing. *Jesus Christ. This place is a morgue.* He stepped back outside and walked toward the barn.

The two women released each other as they heard the

bedroom door open and smiled as they watched Jonah walk out of the room holding each child by the hand.

"We're ready now, right guys?"

"Right," they said.

"Okay, go get your jackets. I'll meet you out at the car. Remember what I said."

The three adults watched the two angels scamper through the kitchen. They looked as cute as ever reaching up to the hooks and pulling down their coats.

"What did you tell them?" Rebecca asked when the boys had left the house.

"Trade secret. We made a solemn promise we wouldn't share it."

"So," Vickie asked. "What'd you tell them?"

"Hey, it's a secret, okay?" Jonah said, smiling.

"Don't you guys ever grow up?" his wife asked.

"Not if we can help it," he said, feeling better as he heard Rebecca chuckle for the first time all day. "Listen, Becky," Jonah said, walking to his friend, taking her shoulders in his hands. He looked her in the eyes. "I want you to know how much I wish I could go. I know you know that. My thoughts and prayers will be with you all weekend. Remember to tell David how much I love him."

They embraced. Jonah stroked Rebecca's hair, tears forming in his eyes. "All right, this isn't going to get any easier. You guys got to get out of here, before I break down, too. Remember to call me," he said, as they all walked toward the side door.

When they were at the car, the boys were already inside, buckled up and ready for the trip. "Look at this, will you?" Becky said, approaching the car. "What did you say to them?"

"Not on your life," Jonah said. "Now, did you get everything? Wallets? Money? Purses?"

"Yep," Vickie answered. "Already walked through twice."

Jonah walked up to Vickie, pecking her on the lips. "All right, drive carefully. And don't forget to call." He peeked his head inside the driver's side door and winked at the boys. "You guys gonna be all right?" he asked.

They both nodded.

"That's my boys. Remember how much I love you. I'll see you when you get back."

"Bye," Caleb said.

"Bye, Uncle Jonah," Sumner said.

"See ya soon," Jonah said, stepping back outside. "Okay, honey, I'll see you on Sunday. I'll miss you."

"I'll miss you too," Victoria said.

"Thanks for everything, Jonah. You're a godsend," Becky said, blowing him a kiss as she got into the passenger seat.

He waited for Vickie to get inside, closed the door for her, and watched as they pulled out of the driveway. Jonah waved, blowing a kiss as they disappeared down the incline. He was already lonely. A sense of longing tugged at his heart.

On Thursday afternoon, Fenton Montague paid $1,700 cash for a 1986 black Bonneville. In Maine, you don't need to register a car at the time you buy it. The dealer gives you temporary plates and you register it at DMV. You do however, need to produce proof of insurance. Not surprisingly, Fenton had taken Austin Prescot's from his Audi.

He pulled out of the lot, stopping at the road for oncoming traffic. He looked east, then west. A clear and foreboding omen approached from the west as he watched two Maine state police cruisers drawing near, lights flashing, their sirens piercing the rural calm of a windy but otherwise tranquil day.

There was about them a menacing look, their headlights flashing back and forth, back and forth. Through Fenton's eyes, they seemed to have a mind of their own. Modern dragons—slayers of evil, on a mission. He knew their mission was to slay him.

He waited, holding his breath as they drew nearer. A sigh of relief shook his body as they went screaming by. Fenton thought it had gotten far too hot, far too quickly, around Sanford, Maine. There was heat everywhere. He needed to get away—*now*—lie low for a while and let the ruckus die down some. Allow the focus of the hunt to tire and move elsewhere.

He knew now was not the time to attack. Whether he could see them or not, Fenton knew Jonah's place would be swarming with police. He hated to concede them the game. But still, he thought it better to flood the turret and save the ship. They may have taken this battle, but he knew in his heart he would take the war. *Don't rush it. You've come this far. You've waited this long. A little while longer won't kill you.*

What Fenton needed was a place to hole up for a few weeks, someplace relatively safe where he could formulate his plan. But where? He didn't know this state. Should he head for Portland? That was probably cosmopolitan enough. He could melt into the woodwork there. But wouldn't that be the first place they'd look?

Maybe he'd be better off picking a place more out of the ordinary. A little more off the beaten track. There seemed to be no shortage of places like that here. He wondered for a moment how many others for whom the law had other plans opted to make their homes in the rural backwaters of Maine.

What he did know was, by reputation, northern New Englanders are a distrustful lot. Notoriously slow to take to newcomers, they have a traditional wariness of people from "away." He could choose any one of a few hundred towns from Hiram to Lynchville, from Hebron to Fryeburg. But wouldn't that cause more talk in town than he wanted? He could hear it now. Everyone from the local package store owner to the town librarian would be talking about the new guy in town. No . . . that would be inviting trouble. He opted for Portland.

He connected up with Route 111 and headed east toward I-95. Maybe the YMCA there took residents. It would be a perfect place to hide for a day or two. At least until he got his bearings—had a chance to talk to some locals about quiet places to stay.

Fortuitously, the Portland Y had one available room. Fenton parked in the lot and entered from the High Street side. In an act of rebellious egotism, Fenton paid cash for two nights, registering under the name Austin Bennett. *Catch me if you can.* He walked the stairs to his room, dropped off his knapsack, and lay down on the bed, testing it for comfort. He went to the bathroom to splash water on his face, noticing for the first time the stubble of his hair growing back. He would need to shave again. *On second thought, I'll let it grow. A little bit of growth might not stand out quite so much.*

He locked his door behind him and left for a walk around town. It was cold. His sweater was not nearly enough protection for the sub-freezing windchill whipping through the city's streets. *Boy, the weather changes quickly here.* He stopped at a Goodwill retail store and paid sixteen dollars for a winter coat and a winter hat. He was pleased with himself. *Not a bad deal.*

Over the years Fenton had heard much about Portland. Read much about Portland, actually, it's rustic, seaport feel, cobblestone streets, and many restaurants. He walked up toward Congress Street, the main thoroughfare traversing the city. As he passed the Maine Historical Society he stepped in to see if he could get a map.

The woman behind the counter was helpful but talkative. The last thing Fenton wanted was conversation. *I don't need a friend, lady, I need a map.* All he wanted to do was get away. He took several pieces of literature on the city and left.

As he walked, Fenton liked what he saw, but at heart, he wasn't all that interested. He was still the hunted. Every cop on every street corner would be looking for him. He wore his jacket collar up, making sure to wear his sunglasses and his newly purchased hat. He'd already dumped the baseball cap, figuring, correctly, that wearing it now he would too closely match his last known description.

Reviewing his map, he was intrigued to see there were islands in the bay—islands on which people lived and commuted to and from work on ferries. Portland's version of the commuter train. It appealed to him. Maybe that would be a good place to hide.

A twinge of excitement filled him. He thought he

might just have found his destination. He picked up his pace, walking undeterred to the Municipal Ferry Terminal. Stepping inside, he approached the ticket window.

The man was looking down, stamping consecutive forms one after the other. Fenton cleared his throat. "Excuse me, sir. I'm looking for a place I might relax for a while. Get away from it all. I'm in the process of finishing a book and need as few distractions as possible."

The man eyed him. "Yeah?"

"Well, I'm new to the area. Do you think one of the islands you service might be a good choice?"

"For peace and quiet?" the man asked.

"Yes. Somewhere where I won't be bothered."

"Mister, you could die on some of those islands and no one'd know it till spring."

"Really? That's exactly what I need. Where would I go to rent a place?"

"There's a ferry to Peaks," he said, looking at his watch. "Leaves at 3:45. Once off the dock, if you walk up the hill a mite you'll see a real estate office on your left. They'll be glad to help you."

"Great. Thanks," Fenton said with a smile. He feigned leaving, but turned back. "Oh, I almost forgot. Is Peaks Island a part of Portland?"

"Yep."

"I'm afraid someone may have stolen my wallet. I can't find it anywhere. Is there a police station there where I can file a claim?"

"Police? On Peaks?" the man said, chuckling. "Mister, the cars out there don't even have license plates. Hell, they only got one constable, and he only works the busy months. No, I'm afraid if you want to file something with the cops you better do it here. You won't find much help out there."

Perfect. "That's too bad. All right, thanks again," he said, taking a ferry schedule and walking out of the terminal.

So it was settled. He would move to Peaks Island for a few weeks. Let the pressure die down some. With any luck, maybe the cops would lose interest, think he'd left the state. He had to assume they were all over Jonah's place. If he waited long enough maybe they'd start to pare down his protection. Remove it entirely if he let enough time pass. Like everyone else, police departments only have so much money.

Fenton was filled with defiance, his mind swirling with grandiose arrogance. *This is my play, gentlemen. Nice try, but we do this at my speed. I call the shots. Not you. You haven't figured it out yet, have you? I can run rings around you assholes. Why fight me? Look how much good it did David. Spend your time on something more productive. Find some drug pushers or petty thieves—someone you can more easily match wits with. Trust me, gentlemen. The world's a better place with one less scumbag around.*

He would move to Peaks first thing tomorrow. He still had a few things he needed to do. On his way back to the Y Fenton stopped at a gourmet food store in the Old Port. He bought a pound of fresh brownies—marbled chocolate. He also bought a bottle of wine. The wine was for him. The brownies weren't. This was like taking candy from a baby. He needed to celebrate.

———

Befitting its independent nature, the state of Maine hangs all by itself off the eastern seaboard of the United States. Consequently, it gets darker much earlier than in other parts of the country. By mid to late December, it's virtually dark by 4:00 P.M. Early November is not quite as harsh. But still, it was nearly 5:00 P.M. on this Friday afternoon, and the moon could hardly wait any longer.

Jonah Roberts had emptied the horses' stalls with a dung shovel and found himself racing against the setting sun to spread the soiled wood chips out along one of the back pastures. He bounced in his seat as the old Ford tractor sputtered along, pulling the spreader behind it. Having performed this chore a thousand times before, Jonah had learned it took about two years for the chips to fully biodegrade and become a part of the soil.

The sun was well behind the line of trees to the west

when the spreader finally emptied the last of its load. Jonah stopped the tractor, got off, and pulled a broom out of a hollow metal pole in the corner of the spreader. Standing inside the spreader he quickly brushed away the larger chunks left behind.

By luck really, he happened to catch sight of a hawk circling the skies overhead. They were such majestic birds. In a few more minutes Jonah wouldn't have been able to see it. Hawks are migratory, and Jonah knew it would probably be the last one he'd see until spring. He stood motionless in the spreader . . . quiet . . . alone with his thoughts. He laid both hands on the top of the broom handle, enjoying the purplish-crimson of the evening's dusk.

Up until a day or so ago his life had truly been a dream come true. He had more money than he would ever need, a wife whom he cherished, a house he had built with his own hands, and eighty acres of land in the most beautiful state in the Union. If God had created the earth, Jonah thought he must have done Maine on his best day. As he stood watching the outline of the trees against the darkening sky, he couldn't help worrying that fate would intervene and prevent him from enjoying it much longer.

He smiled as he thought of what a local dairy farmer had said to him shortly after he moved to the area. Jonah was interested in purchasing a used tractor the farmer had for sale. Walking around it, kicking the tires so to speak, he asked the farmer if he'd lived in Maine his whole life. "Nope . . . not yet," the old man replied calmly, as if discussing the weather.

Sergeant Francis Cunningham, the head of Jonah's protection detail, sat quietly in Jonah's hayloft squinting into his binoculars. As he stared out into the fields, he could barely make Jonah out against the backdrop of the trees. Dressed as he was in jeans and a blue flannel shirt, only Jonah's skin stood in contrast to the enfolding dark. And since he wore gloves and a Boston Red Sox hat, there was precious little of that.

Cunningham scanned the edge of the woods where the pastures melted into trees. Realizing how ridiculous it was to struggle to see like this, he switched to his night vision goggles. Jonah and the tractor stood out as clear as day now. The heat emanating from them made an easy mark for the goggles' infrared eyes.

All the officers in the detail wore microphones on their shoulders like the ones worn by the Secret Service. Each had a small wire leading to a plug placed firmly in one ear.

The trooper in the hayloft spoke into his mike. "Switching to night vision goggles."

"Roger that," came the different replies.

The officer who had replaced Martin that morning stood at the windows on the south side of the Roberts home. He too watched Jonah in the field through his night vision goggles. He spoke to the window, holding his goggles firmly to his head. "Fran?" he inquired of his sergeant in the barn.

"Ten three."

"You see that movement in the woods? About fifty yards to the left of Mr. Roberts?"

Cunningham took a moment to zero his sights in on it. Something was moving just in front of the trees in the same pasture as Jonah. He could feel his adrenaline begin to pump. "Yep, clear as day."

The man in the duck blind could hear the conversation. He was closest to the action. "Stick, you see it?" Fran asked him.

"Yeah. Spotted it right after you two started talkin'. It appears to be headed in Roberts's direction. How do you want to handle it?" Trooper Peter Stickney asked.

"Okay," Fran said, "here's what we do. I'll get a scope on him. Stick, you approach from Roberts's side. Get him to lie in that spreader if you can. Tell him not to move until you say it's okay. I'm not takin' any chances though. One false move from that son of—"

"Wait a minute, wait a minute," Stickney interrupted. "Jesus Christ, it's a fucking deer."

"You're shittin' me?" Fran asked, staring through his

goggles. Stick was right. It must have been grazing. They hadn't been able to make out the body outline until it raised its head. "Christ. All right, everyone, false alarm. Back on watch. Sorry about that. Good eyes, gentlemen."

When it became too dark to see, Jonah slowly made his way back to the house, pulling the tractor up to a spot next to the wood chip pile. *It's cold. This could be one hell of a winter.* He gave his horses fresh water, tied wool blankets over them, closed up the barn and went inside.

"You missed it," Trooper George Spowart said to Jonah as he walked into the living room. "We thought we had a bead on him while you were down there. About fifty yards to your left. Had the whole group jumpin'."

Jonah's heart skipped. Couldn't have been that big a deal, he figured. Everyone still seemed safely tucked away in their spots. Just the same, Spowart's comment took him off guard. "On who?" he asked.

"Fran had a scope on him and everything."

"On who?" Jonah asked impatiently, wondering why Spowart kept using the word him. "Who was it?"

"A friggin' deer. Can you believe that?"

Jonah's shoulders dropped. He hadn't realized how much tension had built up inside him. "Tell Fran he should have dropped him. It is the season. Would have made for a nice dinner tomorrow. I could have made you guys venison burgers."

It was almost 6:00 P.M. now. Jonah had successfully passed one day alone. He took off his flannel shirt, laying it over the brick wall behind the wood stove, and retrieved the trash from the bin in the kitchen. He leaned down, opened the stove, and stoked it with the garbage. In the cold months he and Vickie burned virtually everything that wasn't recyclable. After he'd nearly emptied the garbage pail, he threw in a couple of small, split logs, positioning them with a thick, leather-gloved hand.

He pulled up a rocker and laid his feet on the brick hearth at the foot of the stove. Sitting now in his T-shirt, he wiggled his toes as he spoke to Spowart. "You know, George, my wife and I never had kids. Every once in a while I wonder if we made a mistake. You got kids?" he asked.

"Yep. Six," Spowart said, standing by the brick wall.

"Six?" Jonah asked, unable to comprehend what that would be like. "Look, I don't mean to pry or anything, but how do you afford that? I mean . . . I'm sure your job pays well and all. But six kids?"

Nothing grabs people's attention like talking about their lives. Spowart sat down by the stove. "The wife and I, we've always been pretty good with a buck, and we just love kids, I guess. It's all a matter of where your priorities lie."

Jonah never understood why anyone would have so many. It always struck him as a little selfish. It wasn't like the world didn't have enough people. Jonah let go a long whistle. "I guess so. But still, six sounds unmanageable. How do you spend quality time with them all?"

"Oh, we get by. The kids know they're loved. The wife works, so that helps some."

Jonah shook his head, deciding that Spowart was definitely on a different planet than he. There was no sense continuing the conversation along these lines. The two men were of different worlds.

"So what's the latest on Montague?" he asked, changing subjects.

"Last I heard they'd spotted him in Sanford. Of course, I've been here all day. Somethin' new could have come up. But they haven't caught him yet, that's for sure."

Jonah stared at the glow of fire through the windows of the stove door. "Do they think he's still in Sanford?"

"Couldn't say," Spowart responded, shrugging his shoulders. "If he is, they'll find 'im."

"And if he's not?" Jonah asked.

"Could be anywhere I s'pose."

"You think he's still in Maine?"

"Your guess is as good as mine. If I had to bet, I'd say yes."

Jonah sat still for a while. As much as he hated to admit it, he thought he agreed with his house guest.

"You're probably right," he continued. "But it seems to me the longer you keep half the force out there, the longer it's going to keep him away. I've been thinking it might make more sense to have one, maybe two of you here. That's it. He's never gonna show with so many men around."

Spowart pulled his knees up to his chest. "Yeah, could be. But it didn't seem to help your friend much."

"But that was different," Jonah said, stung by the indifference in Spowart's comment.

"How so?"

"Well, I mean, up until that point the cops didn't know what they were dealing with. He's got to know you're on to him now. That you know how capable *and* warped he is."

"Okay, so let's say we pull everyone off but me. He's not going to know that. You wouldn't know anyone's here from walkin' up the driveway. Doesn't seem to me it matters whether there's just one of us or twenty. Perception's reality."

Jonah hadn't thought of that. He sat quiet for a bit, thinking through Spowart's last comments. "David was my closest friend," he finally said. "I loved him like a brother. But he and I are different in many ways. I just can't sit here waiting to be killed. I've got to do something. *Anything.* One way or the other, I just want all this shit to end."

"What are you gonna do?" Spowart asked.

"Shit, I don't know. I've been thinking about that."

"It's a big state, Mr. Roberts. You can't very well go lookin' for him."

Jonah was preparing to respond when the phone rang. "Hang on a sec," he said, getting up to answer it.

"Hello?"

"Jonah Roberts?" the man asked.

"Yes. Who's calling?" Jonah asked, watching Spowart look at him.

Fenton had found himself at a convenience store and just couldn't pass up the chance for a little fun and games. "Hi, Jonah. It's me. I just wanted to tell you that all the cops in the world can't protect you, old buddy."

"What cops?" Jonah asked defiantly, pointing madly at the phone, trying to indicate to Spowart who was on the line. "I'm all by my lonesome. Just waiting for your ass."

"Really? That's so *manly,* Jonah. I knew you'd be the tougher one. David was such a layup."

Jonah was suddenly filled with fury. "Go *fuck* yourself, asshole."

Fenton clicked his tongue three times. "Tch, tch, tch. That kind of anger won't help you much when the battle comes, Jonah. Emotions just get in the way."

Spowart had run out of the house. Jonah could only assume he didn't want to be heard on his microphone and had gone to the barn to tell Fran. "Where are you, you son of a bitch?" Jonah asked, his voice filled with disdain. "Let's get it on. Right now. Tell me where you are. We'll go at it, man to man. I'll take your fucking head off with my bare hands."

Fenton laughed. "Jonah?"

"What?"

"Before I'm finished with you, you'll beg me to take your head off."

Then he hung up.

———

Cedric Halliway rubbed the back of his neck vigorously with his left hand. It was 3:30 in the afternoon, Thursday, November 2nd. Scott Hill sat, his feet perched up on the table. His eyes were closed as he smoked his cigarette, blowing smoke rings toward the ceiling. The two men were exhausted. They'd done everything they could think of—called in every favor, spoken to every contact, had conference calls and interviews, read lab reports, attended autopsies, conducted searches. There simply was no more to be done. All they could do now was hope Fenton made a mistake.

"Shit!" Halliway said, jumping to his feet. "You know what? I forgot to inform Jonah's detail of the strychnine hazard. Did you do it?" he asked Hill.

Hill shook his head. "Slipped my mind."

"We gotta make sure we let someone up there know."

"I'll add it to the list," Hill said, scribbling in his notebook.

Halliway was dumbfounded—incensed by Fenton's arrogance. Oh, he was smart all right. Maybe *too* smart. "A strength stretched too far becomes a weakness," he said under his breath.

Hill looked at him. "What'd you say?"

Halliway waved it off. "Nothing."

"No, really. What'd you just say?"

"I said a strength stretched too far becomes a weakness."

"That's it!" Hill said, suddenly standing.

"What? What's it?"

"Look, Ric. I can't believe we didn't think of this before. The guy's obsessed right? I mean, he's really monomaniacal. Let's beat him at his own game."

Halliway was interested. "I'm listening."

"You got to figure he's watching TV. At the very least, he's reading about himself in the paper, right?"

"That would fit the MO of a scumbag like this. It's the only thing they've got in their miserable little lives that makes 'em feel like anything."

"And this is war, right?" Hill asked.

Halliway nodded his head. "As close as it gets."

"One hint, Ric. It's one of the most powerful weapons enemies use against one another, but it's not a weapon per se. I mean . . . it doesn't kill anyone."

Halliway shrugged, closing his eyelids, stretching them down with his fingers. "Christ, Scott, I don't know."

"Think."

"All right, all right," Halliway said, not really interested in playing this game. "It's not really a weapon but it's powerful and enemies use it against each other in war."

"Right."

Halliway thought a moment. What the hell was Scott talking about? "Wait a minute," he said, his eyes lighting up. "Son of a bitch. Disinformation."

"Right," Hill said, pointing at him with a finger and thumb, as if pointing a gun. "We should be using the radio and television and newspapers to our advantage. Let's make him think Jonah has refused all help. Hell, we can't force him to let us stay on his property, right? Let's get word out that he's acted against all advice. That he's stubborn as a mule and isn't gonna change his life for anyone."

"It just might work," Halliway said, curling down his lower lip. "It's not like he's going to forget about Jonah. He's gonna go after him eventually. Let's tip the scales. I like it, Scott. We might be able to move this thing up a bit. You think he'll buy it, though? Might sound too much like a trap."

"Maybe," Hill said, putting his feet down, pulling up to the table. "But what if we arrange it so it comes out like a scoop. Some hotshot reporter for AP or some local rag cites unidentified sources. We can have it start out as a trickle and let it gain steam as other people in the media pick up the story."

"Listen, at this point, I'll try anything," Halliway said, throwing up his hands. "What we've done so far sure as hell hasn't worked. Where do you want to start?"

"What's the big newspaper in southern Maine?" Hill asked.

"You're asking me?"

Hill picked up one of the phones on the table and dialed Maine information. The operator had the answer. He jotted the number she gave him on a yellow legal pad.

"The *Portland Press Herald,*" he said, putting the phone in its cradle.

"All right," Halliway said. "We need to do this right. No sense pissing everybody off if we don't have to."

"What ya have in mind?" Hill asked.

"I was thinking it might be smart . . . politically . . . if we let the local police know what we're up to."

Hill was adamant. "No way," he said, shaking his head vigorously back and forth. "Look, Ric. As it is we're gonna have five, maybe six people in on it. We've got to call the president or chairman, or whoever the hell runs the thing. There's the reporter, whoever that ends up being. Not to mention any other poor slugs they think they've got to talk to. And anyway, we're gonna need to talk to the state police. It's not like we won't have informed local law enforcement. People can't keep secrets, Ric. You know that. The fewer people that know about this, the better. It already leaks like a sieve, and we haven't even started yet."

"Okay, I'll buy that. So now we got to think of a story. How do you want it to read?" Halliway asked. "I say we just jot down what we want it to contain and let the reporter work his magic."

"How 'bout that criminal psychologist the department uses from time to time? Let's run it by him too. See what he thinks will push Montague's buttons," Hill said.

"Good one. Call him."

The two men spent over an hour discussing various pros and cons of the doctor's input. When finally, they had a list of a dozen or so particulars they wanted to be sure the article contained, Halliway picked up a phone and called the newspaper.

Halliway asked to speak to the office of the president, a Mr. Ralph Gossimer. Once transferred, he explained who he was to Gossimer's secretary, the general nature of the call, and that it was urgent police business. Otherwise he left out the juicier details. A few moments passed before Gossimer picked up the phone.

"Ralph Gossimer speaking."

"Mr. Gossimer. Good afternoon, sir. This is Lieutenant Cedric Halliway. I'm a homicide detective with the Connecticut state police."

This didn't happen every day. "Yes, Lieutenant. What can I do for you?"

"Well, sir . . . my partner and I are in a bit of a quandary, and we believe you might be able to help us."

That comment caught his attention. *How can I possibly be of help to two homicide detectives from Connecticut?* "I'm always glad to help the police, Lieutenant. I'll do what I can. What is it you need?"

"I'd like my partner to join us. Do you mind if I put this call on speaker?"

"Certainly. Be my guest."

Halliway hit the speaker phone button. "Mr. Gossimer, I have Detective Sergeant Scott Hill on the line with us," Halliway said.

"Good afternoon, Sergeant," Gossimer said.

Hill leaned forward to be heard. "Mr. Gossimer, thank you for your time, sir."

"So, what's up?"

"You're familiar with the Fenton Montague investigation I assume?" Halliway asked.

"Sure am. Last I heard he was up here somewhere. That's big news in this neck of the woods."

"Yes . . . well, sir," Halliway continued, thinking it was about to get bigger. "Sergeant Hill and I have been heading the investigation from the get-go. We were wondering if we could ask you a small favor?"

Just after 11:30 A.M. on Friday, Fenton finished wrapping his brownies in a small tin container he'd bought at the gourmet shop in Portland's Old Port. He used a brown shopping bag and masking tape. Throwing his scraps in the garbage he packed what few belongings he had neatly into his knapsack and left the YMCA for the last time.

Fenton drove his Bonneville north on 295 to Freeport, Maine. Like a student driver taking his test, he followed every speed limit, used his blinkers religiously, and came to full stops at stop signs. As he drove off the exit and began inching his way down Main Street, he was appalled at the throngs of people.

In addition to being the town in which L.L. Bean is headquartered, Freeport also happens to be one of two major outlet centers in the state, the other being Kittery, just north of the New Hampshire border. Kittery gets most of the traffic from York County, New Hampshire, and points south. Freeport gets just about everyone else.

Nothing brings out early Christmas shoppers like cold weather and snow. This day would be no different. The local weather service was calling for an afternoon high in the low to mid twenties, with light snow expected later in the evening and continuing through Saturday. Even for northern New England, a snow storm of any magnitude so early in the season is quite unusual. Six to eight inches was expected. It had everyone abuzz.

Fenton bought a *Maine Gazetteer,* a detailed map of every road, hill, lake, and mountain in the state, broken into seventy different grids. He scanned the page containing Freeport and found a cemetery located on West Street. He turned right off Main, momentarily caught off guard by the sight of three Freeport police cars lined side by side next to a brick building on the corner. Making the turn, he realized he had just passed Freeport's police headquarters. He accelerated slightly and drove the short distance down the hill to Woodlawn Cemetery. He stopped for a short while, long enough to give it a good looking over.

Perfect. Just the right touch of age. From the road at least, it looked old, bordering on decrepit. Cut-granite pillars flanked a wrought-iron gate that hung open, off kilter just enough to lend a touch of New England charm. Its white wooden fence was decaying in spots, and whole sections had begun composting in the ground. There was a look about it that suggested to the passerby that whatever lay beyond, it was not a place of renewal.

Fenton did a three-point turn and headed back up to Main, driving its entire length, up one side and down the other. He looked for a place to park, but there wasn't an empty spot in sight. Annoyed, he finally pulled the Bonneville into a satellite lot a short distance down the hill, in front of L.L. Bean's Factory Store. He checked his *Gazetteer* and walked to the Freeport post office, a block down from Bean's. He carried a very special package and wanted to make sure it got out that day. He also wanted a postmark other than Portland.

"I need this to get to Harrison no later than tomorrow," he said to the postal clerk standing behind the counter.

"Shouldn't be a problem," the man said, taking the small box from Fenton's hands. "But I s'pose if you want to make doubly sure, you should send it overnight."

"Overnight it is," Fenton answered.

"You know, you could drive it there quicker," the clerk added.

"Who's got the time?"

"I hear ya there."

Fenton paid the extra cost for overnight delivery, looked at his watch, and walked the block or so back to Bean's. He wasn't sure when, but he knew he'd be visiting Jonah's soon enough. He envisioned the assault might well require a good deal of time in the woods, and wanted to make damn sure he had a pair of insulated winter boots and a warm pair of gloves. If Fenton wanted clothing to help keep him warm, there was no better place on earth to look than L.L. Bean.

Bean's is a rarity in American business. Open twenty-four hours a day, three hundred and sixty-five days a year, the privately held corporation prides itself on a tradition of quality and an unwavering belief in the often used but seldom practiced slogan, the customer is always right. This corporate mantra has served the Bean family exceedingly well. Since the company's revenues are in excess of $1.2 billion, it's hard to argue with their strategy.

Fenton felt squeamish among the throngs of people. In a certain sense, the hordes filled him with a feeling of safety. Like a needle in a haystack, he could blend right in, becoming one with the crowd. But on another, very real level, their sheer presence and numbers caused him great angst: an anxiety bordering on sheer panic. He craved solitude.

Conscious of everything around him, he moved quickly toward the store. He stopped to look at the various display windows on the outside. There were five in all. Some offered lifelike scenes of nature. Others exhibited various product lines in a natural setting. There were ducks and pheasant, all stuffed of course, in various stages of movement. In another window there were some foxes. The white one caught Fenton's eye. He hadn't known there was such a thing.

Entering the massive store he stopped for a moment to catch his bearings. To his right, on a level below, he could see a half dozen pitched tents in various colors and sizes. There were sleeping bags, some good to thirty degrees below zero. There were snowshoes, ice picks, ropes, spikes, ice houses—virtually anything one could need to survive an extended stay in the elements.

Walking further, he found himself staring at a standing, six-foot-high, stuffed black bear—the University of Maine's mascot. Walking a ways to his left he was surprised to discover a pond in the middle of the store. He didn't give it much thought until he stopped at the landing and looked down. It was then he realized it was filled with live trout. This show of nature—a living, breathing display of God's handiwork—in the middle of this huge moneymaking machine filled him with a sense of excitement. Fenton stood, staring at the fish. He yearned for the woods.

He climbed another smaller set of steps toward the footwear department, and came upon a large section filled with benches. They were packed with people. Associates scurried back and forth to the stockroom, ferreting out people's sizes and styles.

Fenton stopped, surveying the scene. It was hardly the ideal environment for him to make his purchase, but they had what he needed. He could see them clear as day, hanging on the wall. He would have to suffer through it. Something to his right caught his eye. A man was sitting off to the side, patiently waiting for his wife. His face was hidden behind that day's *Press Herald*. The front page was clearly visible.

The article was positioned in the left column, its headline in relatively large, black print. Fenton could read it easily. He stopped breathing as the words stung his eyes. Police Thwarted As Harrison Man Refuses Protection. *Is the paper telling the truth? Is Jonah, in fact, waiting all alone for me to come?* It couldn't be true. The cops wouldn't allow it. They'd make him accept their presence. *Wouldn't they? Could they?*

Fenton's mind raced with possibilities. How could he move to Peaks and let things cool down if there was a chance he could take Jonah now? In an inexplicable moment of sensory hallucination, his taste buds watered

with the memory of the sweet sensation of David's blood
as he relived the excitement he experienced in overpowering him. The sensual beauty. The power. The oneness
with God. The sense of duty fulfilled as he slashed again
and again through the muscle and sinew of David's
spine. His pants had already begun to bulge before he
realized he desperately needed to be alone.

Running to the bathroom just beyond the man with
the paper, he thought he might faint as he waited for a
stall. *What are they doing in there? Come on, come on.*
Finally, a door opened, and Fenton nearly ran over the
man ahead of him in his rush to get inside.

"Jesus Christ, mister," the man said.

Fenton was in no mood for fools. "Fuck off," he said
from behind the door.

"Nice guy," the man said to someone in line as he left.
"I can get that kind of treatment back home in
Brooklyn."

The desire was back now. In all the excitement of the
past thirty-six hours the cops had nearly, if only tempo-
rarily, extinguished his death instinct. But that was then.
This was now. He had to get his hands on today's paper.
He had to know if the article was indeed about Jonah.
How did the reporter know what he knew? Certainly it
wasn't common knowledge.

Fenton sat on the toilet, his hands on his knees, his
back arched. He craned his neck to look at the ceiling,
taking long, deep breaths. He could feel the sexual
arousal as his mind watched Shirley Pines melt before
him. He wished only that Jonah was a woman. But there
was plenty of time for fun later. *Business comes first.* He
completed the release he so desperately craved, his body
shuddering with excitement at the thought of Jonah's
conquest. He breathed deeply for some time, re-focusing
his mind.

*All right, you're here. Get what you need. You'll only
have to come back for it later.* Fenton couldn't think of a
worse scenario than driving all the way out to Jonah's,
finding that it was, indeed, his for the taking, then having
to come all the way back here to get what he needed. And
if not Bean's, then someplace else. Someplace away from

his nemesis. Fenton knew himself—knew how his own mind worked. If he got to Harrison and homed in on Jonah, it would be nearly impossible for him to break away. *Do it now while you've got the chance. Time and tide wait for no man.*

He took a seat, waiting patiently on the bench. His hat and sunglasses were still on, his winter coat pulled up around his neck. An associate spoke to him as he passed with three boxes of boots in his arms.

"Be right with you, sir."

The employee finally sat in front of him on one of those padded stools, ubiquitous in every shoe store in America. "What can I help you with?"

"I'd like a pair of those Hi-Tecs," Fenton said, pointing to the wall. "Ten and a half D."

"That's easy enough. Do you want to see anything else?"

"How long does it take to get to Harrison from here?" Fenton asked.

"You can't get there from here," the salesman responded with a smile, unable to pass up the old joke.

Fenton stared at him blankly.

Not one for conversation, the salesman thought. He saw all kinds. "Well, let's see," he said, thinking for a moment. "Back roads? Probably an hour and a half. Maybe longer, depending on whether or not you get stuck behind a logging truck."

"So if I left now I could be there before noon?"

The salesman smiled. "Oh, definitely. Unless you're walking."

Fenton stared at the man seated in front of him through his opaque glasses. *Just get the fuckin' boots.* "I'll take the Hi-Tecs and a pair of wool socks."

On Friday afternoon, Cedric Halliway sat on the edge of the conference table in the interrogation room. His feet were crossed as he leaned on his arms, cupping the table's edge with his hands. He was staring at a huge map of Maine he and Hill had hung up on the wall. Little pins with different colored round heads jutted out in various positions around the southern part of the state. A string of green denoted Fenton's assumed or possible routes of travel, red marked spots where he had been seen or was reported to have been seen.

Sightings are always a problem in investigations of this nature. Not that most people mean to do harm, although there never seems to be a shortage of those who do. But people also want to help. Unfortunately, there are plenty who ache for something important in their lives: the aged, mentally impaired, bored, stoned. They see what they want to see in a desperate attempt to bring meaning and excitement to their lives. The two detectives had combed through almost two dozen reported sightings. Through various means, including more than a little intuition, they had ruled out all but five.

A pin with a yellow triangle on it marked Jonah's residence. Both men assumed Fenton would head there eventually. They believed in their hearts this was truly a situation where all roads led to Rome. The problem was that the Cherokee had been found and there were no reports of stolen cars in the Sanford area. How was Fenton getting around? By what means had he managed to escape the watchful eyes of every cop in the state? Surely, if one of them had spotted him walking the streets they would have taken notice. But there had been no reports of anything out of the ordinary. No carjackings. No trespassers. No vagrants. No bumps in the night.

The answer came shortly after 8:00 A.M. Friday morning with a phone call to Halliway's home. Even with all the excitement and mayhem involved in coordinating the dragnet to snag Fenton, the police had managed to prioritize their efforts—checking motels, restaurants, boarding houses, and truck stops first. There were only so many cops and a lot of ground to cover.

Certainly, matters could have been expedited had the Cherokee been found sooner. But several hours had passed before the police discovered it in the back parking lot of the Dunkin' Donuts. By that time nightfall was upon them. Most of the local businesses along Route 202 had already closed for the night. It was becoming painfully clear they had missed him, that somehow, despite all their efforts, Fenton had eluded them yet again. Frustration and embarrassment began to set in.

As morning broke and the various establishments opened for business, the police swarmed over the area. Working in teams of two they interviewed every store and business owner within a mile of the Cherokee. It was shortly before 8:00 A.M. on Friday when they found the answer to their questions.

The owner of the used-car lot thought he recognized the man in the photo the police showed him. It was the chin that gave him away, he said. More than any other feature he felt certain his chin betrayed him. He was pretty sure of himself.

"It's hard to say for sure, Officer. I mean, he wore a baseball cap and sunglasses. But the face looks pretty familiar," the owner told the two state troopers.

"Can you tell me if he had an accent?" one of them asked.

"Well, let me think," the owner said. "Yeah. Yeah, he did, now that I think of it. I'd guess somewheres around Boston. It was slight, but still pretty recognizable."

The owner gave the police all the information he could about the car he sold Fenton, its vehicle identification number, the make, year, color. Distinguishing marks such as whether or not it had whitewalls, rust spots, bumper stickers, vinyl roof, or any detailing.

When the two cops finished, all hell broke loose. The troopers immediately informed their superiors of the hit; they, in turn, sent out a region-wide NCIC teletype. The captain of the local barracks in Kennebunk phoned his superior in Augusta, who immediately phoned Halliway in Connecticut. The first call Halliway made was to his partner. The second was to Lieutenant Rideman.

"Harry, it's Ric. Listen, we got a hit on Montague. He bought a car in Maine. I think Scott and I are going up. Figured I'd ask if you wanted to join us."

"Shit, Ric, I'd love to. Thanks for the call, but I can't. I'm workin' a double slaying down here and there's no way I can break away."

"Yeah, I read about that," Halliway said. "Some mob hit."

"Not sure yet. Could be. Anyway, do me a favor will ya, Ric? Snag this son of a bitch."

"Count on it, Harry. Count on it."

Sergeant Hill was seated on the opposite side of the table from Halliway. He inhaled deeply on a Camel, exhaling slowly. His feet rested on the chair next to him.

"A black, nineteen eighty-six Bonneville with white detailing, Ric," Hill said, between puffs. "How hard can that be to find? Every cop in the state's looking for it. It's only a matter of time now. Today's the day we nail him. I can feel it."

Halliway stared at the map, speaking to it. "I'm not so sure, Scott. How do we know he's still driving the thing? He's proven so far he's no dope. Somehow, I just don't think it's going to be that easy. It's already what? Two thirty? And still no word. You'd think somebody would have seen something by now."

"Hey, we're due for a break. The net's closin' in on him, Ric. Anyway, maybe he's resting somewhere. Hasn't been out in it since yesterday."

Halliway wasn't as sure. "Maybe, but I've been thinkin'. We need to station lookouts on the roads leading to Harrison," he said, jumping down off the table, looking closer at the map. "There's only three ways in or out of town, thirty-five north, and one seventeen from the east or west. That's it. That's a manageable number. We'd be able to see him coming a mile away. Let him get inside the net, then close it tight. One house at a time, if we have to."

Hill had his doubts. By any stretch of the imagination, this would prove a difficult sell. Lookouts and road-blocks aren't free. "We don't know the state police will go for it. Sanford was one thing. We knew he was there. This is something different altogether. It's pure speculation, Ric. Hell, they've already got half a dozen men lookin' over Jonah's farm in one capacity or another. I can't imagine their budget's any better than ours. I'm wondering how much they can afford to put into this thing."

"I know he's going there, Scott. This is our best chance. Let's call them and set it up. If they balk, then I'm calling Givens. See if he's willin' to foot the bill. The man's got to be worth millions. He personally told me to let him know if we needed anything. We'll see if the man's true to his word or just full of shit."

"Certainly worth a try. God knows we got nothin' to lose."

"If they spot him, I pray like hell he doesn't end up gettin' blown away. I swear I'd die an angry man if we don't get to introduce ourselves."

Halliway looked at Hill for the first time the entire conversation. "They got to catch him first. No sense worrying over things we can't control."

"I hate that saying. People use it all the time and it drives me nuts. When's the last time you were able to do it? I worry about stuff I can't control all the time. I think everyone does."

"Not everyone. Maybe that's why you picked up smoking again."

Hill patted the pack of Camels in his shirt pocket. "Yeah, well as soon as this thing's over, I'm quitting again. Filthy habit. Wish I'd never started."

"That makes two of us."

"Very funny."

The two men smiled, each lost in his own thoughts. They were quiet for some time. They were so close they could taste it. And yet they both knew how far away they really were. Anything could happen. Maybe Fenton would never show. Maybe he'd just fade into the woodwork somewhere, never to be heard from again. There were a hundred things that could go wrong.

Hill lit another smoke, flicking the match in his right hand, and tossing it toward the ashtray. He missed. "What do you think Fenton has in store for Jonah?"

"I don't know," Halliway responded. "Makes you wonder though, doesn't it? I mean, the fact that he's gone up there even though he knows we've got to be on to him."

"Jonah told the cops he heard three blasts from a large boat when Fenton called him. Had to have been by the water somewhere," Hill said.

"Look at that state, will you?" Hill said, pointing to the map. "There's got to be hundreds of miles of coastline. I just don't see how that helps us any. He could have been anywhere."

"Yeah, well let's just hope he sees today's paper. He could be anywhere now, but I got a hunch if he sees that paper, he'll be in Harrison soon enough."

Halliway spoke as he pulled up a chair. "Maybe that's the hook we can use. See if that doesn't help us present a case to the Maine boys for putting together some lookouts."

"This waiting is killing me, Ric. I want this son of a bitch. If we get this close," Hill said, his forefinger and thumb a half inch apart, "and he walks . . . I don't even want to think about it."

"All right, we're not doing any good just sitting here yankin' each other. Get on the hooter to the Maine state police. See if you can get them to look at things our way. Hell, for all we know, they'll be happy to do it."

"Okay," Hill said doubtfully, watching his partner put on his jacket. "Where're you going?"

"I'm gonna go see the chief. I can't sit around here any longer. I'm goin' crazy. We need to be there, Scott. If we leave now, we can be there before nine. You got a travel bag with you?"

"Always," Hill responded.

"Good. We're gonna get him, Scott. Soon. I can feel it."

Hill gave his partner a thumbs up. "That's the best idea I've heard in a week."

—⌘—

Fenton sat in his car, the heater running, scanning his *Gazetteer*. The clerk at Bean's was right. You really couldn't get there from here. Not without taking a handful of tiny little back roads with which he was not familiar and had no desire to explore. Yet he hated the thought of losing all the time it would take to backtrack to Portland and head for Harrison from there.

He decided to compromise. He'd head south on 295 to Yarmouth. From there he could take Route 115 through Gray, all the way to North Windham. Ironically, Gray holds the nearest state police barracks to Harrison. It was almost 2:00 P.M. when Fenton pulled his Bonneville out of the parking lot in Freeport.

The sky was overcast. A deep, brooding cloud cover settled overhead, locking in a moisture that, when coupled with the cold, was chilling to the marrow. Anyone who has ever lived in snowy areas for any period of time knows what it means to smell snow. It's a certain something, impossible to describe, but real nonetheless. Fenton drove with his windows fully down. He could smell it in the air. He thought he could see the sky spit an occasional flake. It could serve as the perfect cover if the opportunity truly did present itself.

He exited 295 and looped onto 115 west making certain to follow the speed limits. *Don't get sloppy now. You've got all the time in the world.* He drove through Yarmouth, impressed with its quaintness. The numerous white church steeples, large white farmhouses and the small village green all looked like something out of a Norman Rockwell painting. It was quintessential New England. There was also money here. He could tell by the size of the homes and the make of the cars on the road.

But in short order he was driving through some of the most rural country he'd seen in a long time. He'd noticed something unusual about Maine. You didn't need to drive far from any city or town before the landscape took on an entirely different feel. In a matter of minutes, large, two-story homes with five bedrooms and a Volvo or Saab in the driveway gave way to dairy cattle and acres of spent corn rows surrounded by woods. This was a new phenomenon for him. One he liked very much.

Once in Gray he stayed on Route 115 south before hooking up with Route 302 in North Windham. As far as he could tell from his map, from there it was pretty much a straight shot up the west side of Sebago Lake and then on to Harrison. He'd been on the road a little over half an hour, and figured he had just about a half hour to go. He turned right and drove through North Windham. The town contained a depressing but omnipresent mix of America's most recognizable chain stores. They seemed a scourge upon the land.

There were Wendy's, McDonald's, Burger King, Wal-Mart, Dairy Queen, Dunkin' Donuts, Kentucky Fried Chicken. He thought for a moment how poorly the city's leaders had planned its growth. Out here in what was clearly some of the most beautiful scenery in the world, there stood this mini Vegas Strip, screaming neon advertising in his face. He was profoundly disappointed. *How could anyone have let this happen?*

As if to redirect his thoughts Fenton flipped on the radio, scanning the band for something he could rock to. He was pumped now, his adrenaline flowing freely. A smile crossed his face as he heard Jimmy Hendrix's "All Along the Watchtower" roar across the airwaves. He hit the volume full force. It was perfect for his needs. His toes began to tingle as the rousing beat energized his soul.

It was then he decided that if given the chance today, he would grab it. Tomorrow at the latest. There had been too much excitement, too much stimulation for him just to crawl into a hole and wait. The need for death and dying was back. His need, his all-consuming desire for power and control—for pleasure and pain—kept charging at him, pulling at his psyche, pounding in his heart, heating his loins. Revenge would be his. There could be no turning back now. Not if there weren't any cops. He prayed the paper was right. Fenton hated the thought of retreat, of having to turn back.

As he continued north, he soon was out of the mini strip mall that was North Windham and began to eye, once again, the beauty that is Maine. A huge lake appeared on his left. He was taken by its sheer size and beauty. It was an enormous body of water.

413

Not only does Sebago Lake serve as Portland's sole source of water, it also offers residents and visitors alike myriad opportunities for both summer and winter fun. Fenton's mind wandered back to the trout in the pond at Bean's. He wondered now whether they knew they were captives, whether they yearned for a home this large. Or were they too dumb to know the difference?

Entering Naples, Fenton continued on Route 302 west of Long Lake. He was halfway around it when he realized he should have shot straight up 35 on the east side. It was too late now. He passed signs that warned of moose crossing and falling ice and snow. There were signs with arrows announcing the way to such hamlets as Sandy Creek, Fryeburg, Brownfield, and Hiram. He was entering a more rural environment. The homes on the side of the road, the lack of people, and the endless scenes of beauty told him so.

He entered Bridgton and was once again taken with the small-town feel—the old farmhouses, the huge homes, the ever-present Civil War monument in the rotary. At one point he glimpsed Long Lake as he slowed his car to wind through town. The water was still, mirror-like, reflecting what color was left on the trees. He could imagine hordes of people in the summer coming up for a breath of fresh air from such places as New Jersey, New York, and Massachusetts. Natives call them rusticators, a twist on their pursuit of the rustic life, if only for a week.

Looping around the top of the lake out of Bridgton, he stopped in a small variety store in Harrison to ask directions to town hall. The sign outside read Village Market. He stepped inside thinking he would get a sandwich. But the smell of pizza changed his mind. He bought a small container of Minute Maid orange juice and two pepperoni slices.

There was one other thing Fenton still needed. All he had from the address he took from David's Rolodex was a rural route number. He needed a street address. He would need to move very carefully here. He was close. Too close. He could almost feel the heat. A stranger in town . . . asking questions. In small-town New England, that always raises an eyebrow.

"Hi," Fenton said, walking into the store, sporting his warmest smile. "Excuse me, but I need to make a local call. Would you happen to have a phone book by any chance?"

The owner was talking to a farmer. The two men appeared to be discussing local politics as best Fenton could make out. Something about a bond issue to line the local dump.

"Sure," the owner said, reaching below the counter. "You can use this phone here if you're not long. I'm expectin' a call from the missus."

"No, thanks. I won't bother you. The pay phone outside'll be fine."

"Suit yourself."

Fenton carried the phone book outside, leaned against the white clapboard of the building, and looked up Jonah's address. There it was. Clear as day. Jonah Roberts. Edes Falls Road. He looked patiently through the pages, running his finger down the street addresses. He needed to find someone, anyone else, who lived on that road. It was fortunate that Harrison was such a small town. In less than a minute he had two names. He put a quarter in the phone and pretended to make a call. Confident enough time had passed, he hung up, returned the phone book to the store's owner, and thanked him.

"Find it?" the owner asked, taking back the book.

"Yep, now I just got to get there," Fenton said. He knew he'd made a mistake as the words left his mouth. *Shhhit!*

"Where you headed?" the owner asked.

In a burst of anguish Fenton knew he was trapped. What could he say? He didn't know any other roads to name but the one he'd just looked up. He couldn't ignore the question. Certainly that wouldn't go unnoticed. His mind raced for an answer. There couldn't be any doubt everyone in town knew Jonah's predicament. If Fenton told him the name of the road, the man would immediately notice the coincidence—Fenton would have. He hesitated, thinking through a response, the pause just long enough to stand out. The owner was looking at him. So was the farmer. Fenton's face tingled. He probably would have killed either one had they been alone.

"You know where you're headed, right?" the owner asked.

"Oh, yeah, that's not the problem," Fenton responded. "Could you tell me how to get to town hall?" he asked, desperately hoping to change the subject.

"Who ya tryin' to find anyway?" the owner asked.

Fenton could feel the hair on the back of his neck stand up. "The Thompsons," he said, recalling one of the two names he'd just looked up. "You know 'em?"

Fenton watched the two men exchange glances. "Sure do. Everybody in these parts knows the Thompsons," the owner said.

The damage was done. No harm in asking now. "Can you get there from here?" Fenton inquired, applying a nonchalant smile.

"Well, let's see. Your best bet is to take . . ."

When the owner finished giving him directions Fenton thanked him and stopped at the door on his way out. "Oh, I almost forgot. How *do* I get to town hall?" he asked again.

"Couldn't be any closer. That's it right there," the man said, pointing across the street. "Although this is a pretty small town, mister. Not much of a town hall, I'm afraid. Locals here just call it the town office."

"That's it?" Fenton asked, looking across the street.

"That's it. Like I said. It's a small town."

Fenton was disappointed. He would have preferred to get farther away from the two men in the store. Out of sight, out of mind. For a moment he toyed with the idea of leaving and coming back later. He tried to think of just how damaging the events of the last minute had been. Did he have reason to worry? Had he caused undue concern? There was no way he could know for sure. Local townsfolk are always such a difficult read.

Might as well do it now. It would look even more suspicious if he left and then came back. Fenton decided it would be better if he acted as if he didn't have anything to hide. He knew he'd need to keep his antennae up, though. He left the store and drove across the street, parking his car in the small lot behind the town office.

He walked inside and was met with a friendly hello from the woman behind the counter.

"Can I help you?" she asked.

"Yes. Would it be possible for me to see the tax map for the town of Harrison?" Fenton asked.

"Sure. Any particular part?"

"Edes Falls Road."

"Have a seat," the woman said, motioning to a table and chair in the corner of the sparse municipal office. "I'll bring it over."

He watched her enter an adjacent room. It contained a podium draped on either side by the American and Maine State flags. On the floor in front were rows of chairs all facing forward. Fenton figured it must be where the selectmen met. He watched her walk to a stand in the back corner of the room and pull off a huge book. It looked a hundred and fifty years old. It probably was.

Fenton sat at the wooden chair and table. They looked worn, maybe from the turn of the century, maybe a little later. He watched the Village Market from his seat. He could almost see directly into the store. He decided he'd leave if he saw the owner pick up the phone. But wasn't the man expecting a call? Fenton fretted. How would he know the difference? Well, he'd just keep an eye out. If he were lucky, he could get what he needed before it became an issue. His mind tossed about various possibilities. Just what were his options anyway?

"Here it is," the town clerk said, laying the old thick book on the table in front of him. She had marked the page that would be of interest to him and flipped it over to the sheet of paper she'd stuck in as a marker. "This is it, here."

"Thank you," Fenton responded, looking up at her briefly.

"Are you from around here?" she asked, the typical New England way of telling a stranger he'd been spotted.

417

People! What a pain in the ass. Everywhere he went there were people. Asking questions. Giving him looks. *Why can't they just mind their own business?* He was on to her act. He knew what she knew and knew that she knew it when she asked him. Wherever there were people, there were games. Oh, how he hated the games. Fenton felt ill at ease. He was too close to the hornet's nest. He was pushing his luck and he knew it. He needed to find some inner reservoir of self-control, to remain the gentleman. He was so close, he couldn't screw it up now. She would have died if she could have read his mind.

"No," he answered, "I'm thinking of buying a farm and a friend of mine told me there were a few for sale in the area. Just interested in what I'd be lookin' at in taxes is all. They get ya comin' and goin', don't they?" he asked with a smile.

"You can say that again," the clerk said, walking back to her seat. "Let me know if you need anything."

"Thanks."

His blood ran cold as he studied the tax map in front of him. Jonah owned eighty acres of premium real estate on the top of a small hill. Fenton could see that a farmhouse with twelve acres of land abutted his property on the west side. That would be a perfect place from which to enter and check things out. He just had to figure out a way to get into the woods from that side without being noticed. He wasn't worried. He always found a way.

Looking for the owner of the smaller farm, Fenton's shoulders shook with panic. Jonah owned that one too! But which house did he live in? Was it the farm or the house on the hill? *Shit!*

He stared out the window, looking at the owner of the store behind his counter. Fenton was deep in thought. How should he handle this? How far could he push without being noticed? Had he already crossed that line and didn't even know it? After a few moments, he smiled. He thought he had just the question to do it.

"Excuse me, ma'am," he said, motioning with his right hand held halfway up. "I'm a bit confused. Can you help me for a second?"

"What do you need?" she asked, walking toward him.

"There must be some mistake. I thought this property here was for sale," he said, pointing to the smaller farm. "But if I'm reading this right it's owned by this Roberts fella. Is he selling the whole thing or just the farm?"

The clerk pursed her lips, placing her hands on the table, leaning forward. "Hmmm, that's Jonah's place. I don't think he'd be selling everything. In fact, I'm surprised he's sellin' the farm. He must have just put it up. Been in the family forever. I knew his grandfather. Been empty for years though. Ever since his father died. I can call and ask," she offered, standing up straight.

"No, that won't be necessary," Fenton said, with a wave of his hand. "But thanks anyway. I was hoping for something larger. You wouldn't know of any places around that have, oh . . . twenty, maybe twenty-five acres, would you?"

The clerk thought for a moment. "No, none that I can think of. There's a real estate office just down the street a ways. You can check with them. Called McGilicutty's Realty. You can't miss it."

"Thanks, I think I'll give them a visit," Fenton said, closing the book and handing it to the woman.

"It's an old red barn about a quarter mile down the road," she said, pointing to her right.

"Okay, thanks again," Fenton said, opening the door to leave.

Fenton backed up his Bonneville, preparing to pull out of the lot, when he hit the brakes. His car was still hidden from the road, but their speed caught his eye. He was suddenly struck by a strange sense of déjà vu as he somberly watched two Maine state police cruisers whip by in the road below him. The only difference between now and Sanford was they didn't have their lights flashing. But Fenton knew that whether the dragon was spitting fire or not, it spelled danger just the same.

—⚋—

"Look, Sergeant, I want to help, but I don't have the authority to order something like that," the captain of

419

the Gray barracks was telling Scott Hill when Cedric Halliway re-entered the interrogation room.

"Captain, can you hold on for one moment?" Hill asked, seeing his partner walk back in the room. "Ric, I got the local barracks commander on the phone. Says he can't authorize such a use of manpower on pure intuition."

"Put him on speaker," Halliway said.

"Captain Perkins, I've got my partner here," Hill said. "He'd like to join us. Mind if I put you on speaker?"

"Be my guest," Perkins said.

"Good afternoon, Captain. I'm Lieutenant Cedric Halliway."

"Good afternoon, Lieutenant. As I was telling your partner, we just don't have the manpower to put up a lookout or roadblock, or whatever it is you men want. We've got nothing to go on, and it's not like we don't already have men at Roberts's place. I do that, and I'm lookin' at a dozen men at least. At twenty-five bucks an hour, I just can't justify it. Even if I had the available manpower. And anyway, I've got hundreds of square miles to cover here. This isn't the only wacko on the loose."

"That may be so, Captain," Halliway responded, "But he's the only wacko on the loose who we know is in your area and who has killed one of our own."

Perkins spoke defiantly. "Look, if he shows up at Roberts's residence, we got him sure as shootin'—"

"And if he doesn't, Captain?" Halliway interrupted, determined not to let this chance slip away. "Tests the waters? Smells the heat and decides to boogie? Our way we have a chance. Your way we don't. Can I ask what it is you're concerned about, Captain? Is it your superiors?"

"Damn right. I take that many men off their patrol to sit and wait for some car that may or may not show . . . I better be able to show something for it when the bill comes in."

Halliway thought he'd try an appeal to his ego. Everybody has one. "And if you catch him, Captain? You're the hero, right?" he asked.

There was a pause on the other end. *Works every time.* "Look, gentlemen, I want to help you, really. But I've already got six men tied up in this mess."

"All right, what if we offer to pay for it?" Halliway asked, watching Hill mouth, 'Are you nuts?' "We've got the okay."

Hill's jaw dropped. *Who the hell have you been talking to?*

"Well, that's a horse of a different color. What's your budget?" Perkins asked.

"Whatever it takes," Halliway said with amusement in his eyes, watching his partner's chin nearly flop to his chest.

"Let me make a few calls. I'll be back to you shortly."

"How shortly?" Halliway asked.

"Twenty minutes. Tops."

"We'll be here," he said, hitting the disconnect button.

"Have you gone mad?" Hill asked, the second he heard the line disconnect. "The chief's gonna shit his pants over this."

"He's never gonna know about it. After I spoke to him about going to Maine—we got the nod by the way. We'll leave as soon as we hear back from Perkins. You got everything you need, right?"

Hill nodded.

"Anyway, after I spoke to him I took the liberty of calling Givens. Explained our situation, and before I could even ask, he offered to pay whatever it costs. Out of his own pocket. Said he'd put a hundred K in an escrow account today. We can draw it down as we need. There's only one stipulation."

"So, he really did it? Let me guess. He wants the press from it, right?"

Halliway shook his head. "Wrong, mister cynic. It has to remain anonymous. No one is to know it came from him. It's our little secret. I told him I thought we could handle that."

Hill narrowed his eyes speculatively. "You're joking, right?" He couldn't believe what he'd just heard. "No one does that."

"Givens just did."

"Well I'll be damned. Now there's a good man, Ric. God doesn't make too many of those. Shit, in that case let's call out the National Guard. We can lay it on so thick he'll have to walk over us just to get out of that damn state."

"We're gonna lay it on thick all right. But I don't want to tell Perkins where it came from. Anonymous or not. Better he thinks . . . better they all think we paid for it down here. They'll never do it if they know the funds came from a private source. Breaks every rule in the book."

Hill tilted his face and smiled. "No shit. That's a little sneaky, Ric. You sly dog. I didn't know you had it in you. Guess you can afford to push the envelope when you're starin' retirement in the face."

"Hey, life's a crapshoot," Halliway said. "Now let's get ready to roll. Where's your stuff? I'll get it to the car. You wait here for Perkins's call."

"Hangin' in my locker downstairs. Did you make reservations somewhere?"

"No. Tell Perkins we're coming up. Ask him the best place to stay."

"Ric, what if he wants something in writing? Doubt if he's gonna put his job on the line on just our word."

"Tell him we can do one better than that. We can bring a cashier's check for ten grand to start. More, if he needs it. Money talks."

"And bullshit walks," Hill chimed in.

Perkins called back less than a half hour later. "Okay guys, you're on."

"Thank you, Captain," Halliway said, sighing audibly with relief. "Let's do it."

Just before 3:30 P.M. Halliway and Hill were on the Merritt Parkway heading north for Maine. As darkness fell, Hill looped onto I-495 outside of Worcester and pulled over to the side of the road. Halliway was out cold. He hated to wake him but he needed sleep himself. They were still an easy three and a half hours from

Harrison. At this rate they wouldn't get there until after 10:00 P.M. He turned on the radio, leaned back, and waited for his partner to stir.

"Rise and shine," he said, resting on the headrest, staring at the ceiling.

"Where are we?" Halliway asked, wiping dribble off his chin.

Hill turned his head sideways. "You look so cute with spit dripping off your face."

"Funny," Halliway said shaking off sleep, feeling mildly embarrassed. "Where are we?"

"Half hour outside of Worcester. You looked so snug there, I just didn't have the heart to wake you."

"Hey listen, if it really bothers you, feel free to drive the rest of the way."

Hill opened his door, turning toward Halliway. "Yeah, that's a good idea. Wish I'd thought of it."

"All right, out of the way, Mario," Halliway said, shooing Hill off the seat with a hand.

Halliway scooted over, buckling himself in. Hill opened the passenger side door and slumped into the warm seat. He stared straight ahead. "You know, Ric, I've never shot my weapon on duty. Pulled it a couple of times, but never shot it. I don't know what I'd like more. Puttin' a hole right between this scumbag's eyes, or sending him away for the rest of his life."

Halliway placed his foot on the brake, pulling the shift into drive. "Wish we could do both," he said.

—⁂—

Friday had been uneventful for Jonah Roberts and his detail. After all his arguments failed, he finally agreed to let the police do his grocery shopping for him. He gave one of the men a short list of items to pick up. He only needed enough for the three of them in the house, plus whatever he'd bring out periodically for the other men: an occasional sandwich, a Thermos of coffee, some crackers and cheese, a baggie full of cookies.

That afternoon, Jonah had given the trooper a short

list and a fifty-dollar bill. Among the items he needed were coffee, milk, toilet paper, aspirin, orange juice, donuts, bread, cheese, and cold cuts. He also asked the trooper to bring him back a *Press Herald*. He wanted to read the article the police had constructed.

It must have been convincing. There were close to a dozen telephone messages on his machine, all from friends and neighbors exhorting him to reconsider. He didn't have the heart to call and lie to them. The truth was definitely out of the question—at least for now. He opted to ignore them.

Jonah sat in his rocker opposite the wood stove, warming his stocking feet on the hearth. Trooper George Spowart sipped a cup of coffee at the kitchen table, staring out the picture window in front of him, contemplating the low gray clouds barely visible against the evening sky as they slowly rolled in from the south.

"I can't believe it's gonna snow," he said to the window.

"I've lived in the Northeast my whole life. Don't think I can remember them calling for this much quite this early. Even out here."

"It's gonna be an awful long winter. You ski, Mr. Roberts?" Spowart asked.

Jonah was quiet for a while. He wasn't listening. "Do you think Fenton's going to take the bait?" he asked.

Spowart rose, carrying his cup of coffee to the fold-out couch. "I hope so," he said, taking a seat. "I'd love nothing more than to drop the son of a bitch where he stands."

"Don't do that," Jonah said, tying his boots. "That'd be too good for him. I want to see his sorry ass rot in a pen somewhere for the rest of his friggin' life. Anyway, if someone's going to blow the bastard's head off, it's going to be me."

Spowart looked at Jonah. "You would do that?"

Jonah turned the chair to face Spowart. "What? Kill him?" he asked. "In a New York second. I pray for the chance."

Spowart understood, but still he was a cop. "Don't go doin' anything stupid, Mr. Roberts. Not that you're ever gonna get the chance. But if you do, you'd better make sure it's in self-defense. Murder is murder. If you drop him in cold blood, I don't know that the D.A. would have any choice but to file charges against you. Probably not murder one, but still enough to make you wish you'd thought twice."

"Taking this cocksucker out would be doing society a favor," Jonah said. "Society would thank me."

"Maybe, but that don't mean they won't arrest you first. It'd be a shame after all this if you ended up in jail."

Jonah rose to put a few more logs in the wood stove. "I don't get it. This asshole has more rights than I do. You can take it to the bank this is the only country in the world that would arrest a man under those circumstances. Shit, the guy's murdered a cop, not to mention my best friend. Not to mention the kid and those two other poor souls."

"Those would be the charges, yeah. But he hasn't been convicted yet," Spowart responded.

Jonah felt anger. "Convicted? *Jesus Christ!* You guys know it's him. Everybody knows it's him. You mean to tell me there's a possibility the guy could go on trial and walk away from all this? I'm telling you . . . I'd snap."

"No, he probably won't walk. My guess, he'll be found legally insane. Incapable of standing trial. Probably be remanded to some psych hospital for the criminally insane. You know? Like the guy who shot Reagan."

Jonah walked to the kitchen to get a cup of coffee. "Incapable of standing trial, my ass," he said from the kitchen counter. "He's been smart enough to kill all those people and elude you guys for a week. Oh, he's capable all right."

"Well, if and when the time comes, that won't be for you or me to decide. That's what courts are for."

"Courts," Jonah said disdainfully, sitting back down in his rocker. "You mean the kind where justice is done. Like in the O.J. trial?"

"Look, it's not a perfect system. I'll be the first to admit that. Listen . . . Mr. Roberts . . . I don't mean any disrespect. Really, I don't. But if you don't mind me sayin' so, you're soundin' mighty bitter." Spowart put out his hands as if to stop Jonah from interrupting him. "Now don't get me wrong. I don't blame you for bein' pissed. I would be too. Hell, I am. He killed a cop, remember? But if the police went around killin' every perp we arrested 'cause we knew they were guilty or 'cause we hated them, I'm sure you'd agree that could get pretty scary, pretty damn quick."

Jonah sipped his coffee. If there was one trait he'd learned, it was to listen. And not just remaining silent until the other person stopped talking so he could spew forth his beliefs—but really listening. Somewhere along the way, he'd learned there was a huge difference between hearing someone and listening to them. He didn't feel attacked, nor did he feel that he needed to defend his ego. He didn't take Martin's comments personally. In fact, he was impressed with his levelheadedness.

There was silence for a while. Trooper Spowart began to feel uneasy, worried that he'd pushed Jonah too far— hadn't shown the requisite empathy. But still, the law's the law. It can't be changed for every Tom, Dick, and Harry that feels they've got a grudge to settle.

"You think I sound bitter, huh?" Jonah asked.

Spowart didn't respond. *This could get nasty.*

"I'm sitting here thinking about what you just said," Jonah continued. "I guess you're right. I don't know if bitter's the word or just plain angry. I think I'm more pissed off than bitter. But either way, your point's well made. I need to give your comments some thought. It takes a big man to be able to look beyond all that's happened. Be willing to let the law take over. I guess I'm not sure I'm that big."

"You're bigger than you think, Mr. Roberts," Spowart responded. "And if it makes you feel any better, I think you're a good man. I'm glad to have met you."

Jonah smiled. "Thank you. That's nice to hear."

"Nice has nothing to do with it. It's the truth."

"Well, it's all moot anyway. If he does show up, you guys'll have him shackled and stuffed in a cruiser before I even know he's here." Jonah smiled. "Unfortunately," he added with a smile, for humor.

Jonah made them a small bowl of salad with cheese

and beans and a large pot of coffee. Trooper Spowart set the table for two, watching the season's inaugural snow flakes begin sputtering from the sky.

"I don't know, Spowart," Jonah said, placing the bowl of salad down on the kitchen table. "You must have a picture of your captain doin' a sheep in the back forty or something to pull this part of the detail. The other guys must hate you."

Spowart eyed him quizzically. "How do you mean?"

"I mean, you're in here snug as a bug, getting ready to sit down to a nice meal, and your friends out there are freezing their gonads off munching on God knows what."

"We drew straws to see who got it. My lucky day, I guess."

"I'll say. It's cold as a witch's tit out there."

"It all works out. I've done my share of the freezing before, trust me," Spowart said, pouring them both coffee.

"How come you guys don't rotate?"

Spowart took a seat, tucking a napkin into his collar. "We discussed it. Decided for continuity's sake to keep everyone in the same spot. 'Specially as it pertains to you. We figured it was going to be hard enough on you and your family as it is. This way lends some kind of stability to your life."

"Such as it is," Jonah interjected.

Spowart smiled. "Such as it is. Anyway, we didn't think it fair to have a different person marching in and out of here every twelve hours. We figured the same face might lend an air of normalcy to an otherwise crazy situation."

"You guys really discussed that?" Jonah asked, pouring them both a glass of milk.

"Yep. Surprised?"

Jonah shrugged his shoulders. "Yeah . . . I guess. It just seems odd you guys would give a shit."

"Well, to be perfectly frank, Mr. Roberts, we didn't do it just for you. Nice as we are." Spowart smiled. "We wanted everyone to get familiar with their station. No sense havin' me new to the barn, learning all the angles and routines of the woods, on a night when he might come. This way, everyone's pretty well settled in. They know what they're looking for and'll notice something that doesn't fit."

The conversation went on like this for some time. They talked about Fenton and the observation teams, the article in the paper, the likelihood of its working, and what the cops would do if they caught him. Jonah was particularly keen on this last subject. He wanted to hear it all, from the time they spotted him to the time they got him down to the barracks.

When they finished their meal the two men cleared the table. Jonah washed the dishes. Spowart dried.

"Thanks, Mr. Roberts. That hit the spot," Spowart said, pouring himself another cup of coffee and sitting back down at the table. He looked at his watch. "Well, another hour and a half and I'm headin' home. Don't hang around here on my account. If you got somethin' to do, go ahead."

"Thanks, I think I'll go to the bedroom. I've got some reading to catch up on," Jonah said.

"See you tomorrow."

"Let's hope not."

Spowart had to toss that one about for a moment. He finally got it. "We should be so lucky, huh?"

Jonah smiled and retired to the bedroom, closing the door behind him. He sat at his computer, flipped on the terminal, and waited as it booted up. He thought for a minute of the project he'd started in the woods earlier that afternoon. He and Vickie had long talked of clearing a bridle path that looped around the northeast corner of the property. There were some beautiful woods through there. Somehow a forest of birches had grown in the middle of the dense woods, and they had discussed more than once how nice it would be to have a path to take the horses through it.

But it meant he'd have to build another bridge. He and an escort had spent a few hours in the woods earlier in the day, walking the loop by foot, deciding on its optimum placement. He stopped now and then to cut down an occasional dead tree with his Poulan chain saw.

He wanted to fell as few live trees as possible. This would be no small undertaking. The loop would probably be the better part of a mile long, maybe longer.

This time of year the fallen leaves hid a lot. He would stop and scan the area, feeling for rocks and water by kicking through the undergrowth with a boot. He marked it out with red plastic ribbons, which he wrapped around trees. Tomorrow he'd start out by the stream to see if he couldn't get some logs laid across it to facilitate his crossing. Jonah figured he could use some of the logs he'd cut today. He looked forward to it. He needed to keep his mind busy. Vickie would be thrilled he'd started.

Jonah scanned his portfolio again. He knew the Federal Reserve was scheduled to meet for the autumn session the following Tuesday and Wednesday, and he was certain they were set to raise rates. He could smell it. His contacts on the Street told him it was a seventy-five–twenty-five chance. Maybe even higher.

The market apparently thought so too. The Dow had dropped over three hundred points while he was toiling in the woods. He pulled out his notebook and scribbled some thoughts on different methods of protecting his portfolio. He was somewhat excited actually. Good traders can make money in any market environment. He didn't much care if it rose or dropped or by how much. What he wanted more than anything was movement. Any movement—in any direction.

When he was done he shut off his computer, reviewed his notes, and laid them out on his desk to remind him to call his broker first thing Monday. Then he crawled into bed and hit the lights. The clock on his nightstand read 8:58 P.M. He was exhausted. He looked forward to a good night's sleep.

—⁓—

The same Friday afternoon that Jonah worked in the woods, Fenton drove west out of Harrison on Dawes Hill Road, toward Hobbs Hill. The electric thermometer-clock he passed at the local Bethel Savings Bank said the temperature was twenty-six degrees. The occasional flake of snow that hit his windshield earlier was replaced now by more meaningful flurries. The sky could hardly hold back any longer. It wasn't quite snowing, but Fenton noticed it was definitely more than just a spit now.

Inland Maine is always colder than the coast and the foliage shows it. The lion's share of the trees had lost their leaves, or at least their color, by now. Hundreds of thousands of acres of birch, maple, beech, and oak stood starkly barren against the constant green of pine, hemlock, and spruce. They seemed like a huge, gray carpet, God's welcome mat for the pure white snow that was to come.

Fenton drove around the area, passing farmhouses that were well over a century old. Some closer to two. There were intermittent, large modern dwellings built on the ridge overlooking the lake. Obviously out of place, they had no doubt been built by out-of-staters seeking refuge from the rigors and garbage of modern society.

He traveled up Dawes Hill taking in the scenery. This particular route took him on a steep ascent, eventually leading to a ridge upon which stood two lonely homes with a wide, panoramic view of the valley below. From this perch he turned right onto Maple Ridge Road. Periodically, he passed a pickup truck pulled off to the side of the road. They were always tucked neatly into the woods and they were always empty. He didn't know just what to make of it. You sure as hell didn't see something like that in Massachusetts. Not the part he hailed from anyway.

The road began to veer right ever so slightly. Fenton remembered from the tax map that the road to Jonah's family farmhouse would be coming up soon on his right. He paused at the intersection, eyeing the one-room schoolhouse on the corner, and made the turn. He drove with the car's heat on high. Try as he might, he couldn't get warm. There was a chill residing inside him he couldn't seem to shake. He was so close his body shivered, savoring the thrill of the hunt. He could practically hear Jonah's voice echoing through the woods.

There it was! Majestic in its rustic age and beauty. *It must be two hundred years old,* he thought, as he pulled the Bonneville into the dirt semicircle that looped in front of the Roberts property. Actually, it was older. White clapboards covered the farmhouse's sides, and while many older farmhouses have working shutters, this one had none. The farmhouse, though comfortable looking, had a utilitarian quality. At a glance, it spoke volumes—nothing wasted, everything for a purpose. The roof sagged in the middle from age and the windows and doors had shifted crookedly from years of settling.

By New England standards, the house itself was relatively small; its two stories were not quite a square, but barely a rectangle. Attached to it was a long, single-story clapboard-covered structure connecting the house to the barn. It was obviously as old as the house and had no doubt contained the privy in times gone by. If the original owners had been lucky it was a three holer.

The farm was like so many others of its day: the real effort, time, and space were spent on the moneymaker—the barn. Fenton stepped from his Bonneville and leaned on its roof, eyeing every feature of the large building. It sat sideways, facing the house. Three large, four-paned windows sagged along its side. It was unpainted. Raw, hand-hewn, weather-beaten boards drooped, cracked, and split all along its exterior. Throughout the country people pay a king's ransom for authentic wood of this type. It was certainly worth more razed than standing. At least monetarily.

The barn had two huge, swinging wooden doors held shut by an old two-by-four pushed through two wooden loops. Above them was an opening now covered with wood. Fenton imagined days when bales of hay were stored up there. He pictured the farmer tossing a few down every day or so in winter to feed his cattle. Above the opening, a long, hand-hewn eight-by-eight jutted out a good five feet. No doubt it was the joist used to lift the bales for storage after haying season. The top was adorned with an ornate, octagonal cupola. At its very top stood a weathervane—quintessential New England rooster quivering in the wind.

Fenton sat back down in the front seat of his car. He picked up his *Gazetteer* from the seat next to him and looked up Harrison in the Index of Cities, Towns and Villages. Turning to the grid containing Harrison, he picked a toothpick he'd taken from the Village Market out of the ashtray. He used it to measure distance on the map's key and crudely estimated how far he was from Edes Falls Road. He figured three quarters, maybe a mile at the most.

Jonah was here. Fenton could feel him. He got out of his car and began a slow, tedious inspection of the premises. He walked to the window closest to him at the corner of the house. Putting his hands to the glass, he peered inside. There was some furniture, although it was hardly lavish. The house appeared to have been picked through. The best of its previous belongings were undoubtedly sitting nicely in Jonah's place across the way.

Fenton's lips curled in disgust as he vilified his prey. *So that's how it goes, Jonah? The old man dies and you take his boots? You're scum, you know that?*

Fenton checked the front door, trying the doorknob, hoping it would be unlocked. No luck. He looked in the mudroom. Nothing. He walked back around the north side of the house, stopping periodically to look in any window he thought might offer a view of a room he had not yet seen.

A stiff breeze picked up from the west. Fenton felt chilled as it whipped its way around the house. On the side of the house where he now stood, he was only a few yards from the woods. He could hear the trees rustle in the wind, their frozen limbs rasping against each other— a discordant and constant scraping that was the only noise in an otherwise humbling, quiet afternoon.

Fenton stepped around the back of the farmhouse, walking briskly, stuffing his hands in his pockets to shield them from the cold and falling snow. How difficult life must have been for people back then. Nothing came easy. Every little thing was a daylong chore. Washing clothes, cutting firewood, baling hay, making meals—it must have seemed that life was one tedious and endless job.

And yet, the thought of the Puritanical work ethic, the tight-knit family, the firm and unwavering belief in God—all these things appealed to Fenton. He thought he would have liked to live on this farm in its heyday. That was what life was meant to be like.

He stood on the back porch facing away from the house. If he'd read his map correctly, from this vantage point a clear day would offer a beautiful view of New Hampshire's White Mountains and Mount Washington. With great interest he eyed the acres of pasture that lay ahead of him and the dense woods beyond. The frozen ground flowed down and away at a slight grade, like a playground slide. Fenton could feel it beckoning him to his nemesis's farm. He was in Jonah's world now.

Fenton stood for the longest time, eyeing the woods that lay before him. He began to walk down the slight incline toward the edge of the woods. He passed a seventy-year-old Pa-Pec silager, a rusted tractor that had to have dated from the thirties, an old baler, and various and sundry other artifacts of the farm's agrarian past. Studying the woods, as if determining in his mind the path of least resistance, he looked as deeply into them as he could, one tree at a time.

Suddenly, out of nowhere, a thunderous clap echoed from a point beyond. Fenton was gripped with horror at the unmistakable sound of a rifle shot ringing out from the woods somewhere to his right. It was followed immediately by a second shot, a short pause, and then another. With speed that surprised him, Fenton darted to the stoop, squatting against the old house. Was someone shooting at him? Had Jonah anticipated his movements? Had he been lying in wait, praying for this moment?

Fenton sat motionless for a long time, waiting for something to happen. He thought perhaps he was out of sight now. Maybe whoever had taken the shots couldn't see him, squatting as he was in a ball against the house. He feared moving lest he be spotted again. He sat

433

motionless, his back against the old clapboarding of the house, his hands wrapped around his knees. He had left the jacket and gloves he bought at Bean's in the car. His hands felt brittle, the wind hurting them at its very touch.

How long can I sit like this? He knew he'd have to move eventually. Certainly, if he were the unwitting prey of some armed man, he would have sought a new vantage point by now. He would have tried to hit him again. The clouds were thick and low, the swirling snow gaining momentum. It would be at least an hour before dark. He couldn't wait that long.

In a move resembling that of a jungle cat, he leapt to his right, tumbled once over his shoulder, came to his feet, and ran wildly around the corner of the house and along its side. He didn't breathe until he came to the front of the house. He reached the corner, and unconsciously, instinctively, gripped it tight, swinging himself around. His arms were outstretched as if he were crucified to the clapboards of the front of the house.

When he caught his breath he ran for the car, turned the key, and whipped the Bonneville into drive, spinning dirt and rocks into the air. His heart beat wildly as he tried to breathe in something approaching a normal pattern. Driving around the slight bend, back toward Dawes Hill, Fenton saw a man in a bright orange hat, bright orange vest, and camouflage winter pants putting something into the back of his pickup. Fenton slowed to a crawl, rolling down his window.

"Hi," he offered with a smile. "I see a lot of trucks parked along the side of the road. What ya guys doin', anyway?"

The man looked at Fenton for a moment, not sure he had heard the question correctly. "Doin'?" the man asked.

"Yeah, why're they parked out here on the side of the road?"

Must be from away, the hunter thought. "Deer hunting. Season started Wednesday."

Of course! Now it made sense. "Oh," Fenton said, embarrassed. "Any luck?"

"Nah. Almost though. Got a couple of shots off on a mighty big cruncher. I'll never see a rack like that again. Oh, well. Tomorrow's another day. You live 'round here?" the hunter asked rhetorically.

"Just visiting," Fenton said.

No shit. "I'd stay out of the woods if I were you."

Fenton smiled and drove away. He laughed out loud. *How could I be such a fool? These are the things careful planning prevents.* He laughed, more out of relief than humor. He was anything but pleased with himself. He thought for a moment he really should rent that place on Peaks. Take his time. Think this out. But he was so close. Inside his soul he yearned for the taste of Jonah's blood. He could practically reach out and touch him. He felt like a man just released from prison who's told he can look at the whore but can't touch her—waiting just didn't seem possible.

He drove slowly back up Maple Ridge Road, the sky darkening with each passing minute. He thought he would stop in town, get something to eat. Nothing big. It would probably be smart if he stopped at the other store he'd seen. He thought he remembered seeing the name Gas 'n More. Maybe they'd have a sandwich and some chips. If he was lucky they'd have one of those rotisserie displays where he could get himself a few pieces of chicken, a slice of pizza, or maybe a burrito.

He thought it best not to loiter. He'd grab something quick and eat it in the car on his way out of town. He'd stop for the night at one of the motels he'd noticed on his way up. Preferably one out of the way. He needed to think through his movements now. It would be best if he approached Jonah's in the early morning hours anyway. Now was not the time. Not only were there hunters in the woods, but the sun had set. Besides, he hadn't thought out his plan yet.

He pulled into one of the diagonal slots on the road in front of the store, slipping on his jacket as he walked toward the old front door. It was from here he'd placed his call to Jonah. When he had finished, he smiled and pushed open the door slowly, only to catch the owner and two men in line eye him when the cow bell rang above the door. Fenton smiled and was pleased to see they had a small deli case. Maybe he'd get a turkey sandwich. He waited patiently, surveying the produce for sale.

Fenton's eardrums rang as the conversation he couldn't help overhearing pierced the store's calm

"No shit?" the owner asked one of the men. "When did you see them?"

"Not more than five minutes ago. Was just coming back from Doc McIntyre's place in Bridgton. Had to slow to a crawl just to get by."

"Sheriff or state police?" asked the other man.

"Troopers."

The owner was leaning over the counter. He glanced at Fenton. "Be right with you, mister," he said.

Fenton nodded his head.

"Did you ask 'em what they was lookin' for?" the owner asked.

"I'll tell ya, Shep, when you got two state troopers lookin' in either side of your car, you don't ask questions. You just keep right on crawlin'."

The second man lowered his voice a bit. Fenton had to strain to hear. "Bet anything, it has something to do with that flatlander from Boston everybody's been looking for."

"You really think he's here?" the owner asked.

The first man shrugged. "If he is, I hope he's lost out in those woods. A man can get some turned around out there."

"If he's in those woods," the second one added, "a few nights out there's gonna seem longer than a hard winter. Wonder if he'd know how to dress for Maine?"

"*I* wonder if they're on any other roads?" the owner asked.

"The troopers? Yeah . . . I just saw Charlie down at Dunlevy's. Was checkin' up on his mother up in Buckfield. Told me he passed 'em comin' in on one seventeen."

"Jesus, they got it closed right up, don't they?" the owner said.

"They must know somethin'," the second man said.

"Ayuh," the first man continued. "If he's smart, he'll hole himself up someplace dark and not come out till spring."

The owner started making his way down his side of the counter toward Fenton. "Listen boys," he said, "I got a customer. Let me know if you hear anything new. This could get kind of excitin'." He stood opposite Fenton now, wiping his hands on his apron. "What'll you have, mister?"

—⁓—

On Saturday, November 4th, Jonah was surprised to learn he'd slept more than twelve hours. He never did that. He lay in bed rubbing sleep from his eyes, aware of the erection beneath his sheets, his body's defense against urinating in bed. He crawled out, slipped on his pajama bottoms, and wrapped his robe around him. He walked to the bathroom, self-conscious of the lump sticking out from underneath the robe.

Trooper George Spowart was sitting at the kitchen table. "You again?" Jonah said to Spowart's back, as he walked toward the kitchen.

Spowart was drinking a cup of coffee. "Mornin'," he said, staring out the window. "Déjà vu all over again, huh? It's like I never left. Was late too. Damn car wouldn't start. Cunningham's gonna rip me a new one for missing the morning shift change meeting."

"Sounds rough," Jonah said jokingly. "You mean to tell me Martin's been here and left?"

"Yep," Spowart said, turning to look at Jonah. "You must've been one tired camper."

"Tired's not the word for it," Jonah said, turning the corner, relieved to have his back to Spowart now. "I can't remember the last time I slept twelve hours," he called out from the bathroom. "I guess I needed it."

"I hear we've got some roadblocks set up around town," Spowart said between sips.

"Really?" Jonah responded, spraying endlessly onto the bowl's porcelain. "You think they'll accomplish anything?"

"Anybody's guess," Spowart called out. "Sure can't hurt."

"I'm surprised you guys can afford all this. Last I heard your budget was cut up in Augusta. Wasn't it?"

"Yeah, sure was. Rumor has it the Connecticut boys are paying for it."

"No shit?" Jonah asked, feeling a thousand times better, turning the corner from the living room.

George turned in his chair to look at Jonah. "That's what I hear."

"Man, they want him bad, huh?"

"We all want him bad, Mr. Roberts."

"Yeah, but they're putting their money where their mouths are."

Spowart raised an eyebrow, waving his hand at the expanse of the farm. "Hey . . . we're not exactly free, you know."

Jonah poured himself a cup of coffee and joined the policeman at the kitchen table. "I'm sorry. I didn't mean it like that. You guys have been great. There's no way I can ever repay you for being here when we needed you. No offense, okay?"

"None taken," Spowart said, staring back out the window.

"So what makes them want to put up roadblocks all of the sudden? Do they know something we don't?" Jonah asked.

"I guess they got a make on his car. They must figure there's at least a fifty-fifty chance he'll be comin' here sooner or later. If they know what he's drivin', the chances are pretty good they can snag him."

"From your mouth to God's ears," Jonah said, clasping his hands together in mock prayer.

Spowart shrugged his head and flipped his fingers open. "Crazier things have happened."

Jonah pulled his chair out at an angle and crossed his legs. "When'd they set 'em up?" he asked, holding his coffee with both hands on his robed knee.

"Sometime yesterday afternoon."

Jonah was quiet for a while. He prayed the roadblocks worked, wanting desperately for this nightmare to end.

He was a virtual prisoner in his own house; his forays into the woods had quickly become his only escape from the relentless monotony of the wait.

"I'm gonna throw together some grub," Jonah said, standing up. "Want anything?"

"No, thanks. I ate at home. On second thought," Spowart added after a short pause, "a glass of orange juice would be nice."

"One orange juice coming up. Hold the mayo."

Spowart smiled. "Mr. Roberts, mind if I ask you a personal question?"

"Depends."

"I know it's none of my business, it's just that I've never had a detail quite like this . . . you know, had an opportunity to get to know someone over the course of several days. Other than a partner, of course. I guess I'm just curious."

"What? Curious about what?" Jonah asked, turning to look at Spowart.

"Did you and the missus ever have any kids?"

Jonah smiled. *This guy and kids!* "No. By design."

Spowart eyed Jonah. "Ever wish you'd had some?"

That was a legitimate question. Jonah turned, placing his rear against the sink, both palms leaning on the counter. "I guess every once in a long while I wonder what it would have been like. But really, George, I'm just not a kid kind of guy."

"How do you know if you never had any?"

"I don't know. I think it's more a matter of knowing whether or not you really want them. That was a feeling I just never had. Kind of tough to shove 'em back in the burner once they're out and crying and you know you've made a mistake. I guess it wasn't an experiment I felt safe trying."

Spowart placed his elbows on the kitchen table, holding his coffee in both hands. He stared out the window, not speaking a word.

"Why do I get this feeling you think I've made some kind of a terrible mistake?" Jonah asked.

"Oh no, I don't think that. Really, I don't," Spowart said, shaking his head. "I guess I just can't understand someone not wanting to have kids, is all. It's not a mindset I can comprehend."

"Well, it runs both ways. I can't imagine someone having as many as you. The very thought just blows me away."

"It takes all kinds, I guess, huh?"

"That's what makes markets."

Spowart gave Jonah a quizzical look. "Guess so. Whatever the hell that means."

Jonah looked at the clock on the stove. It was past 11:00 A.M. He slid his eggs out onto a plate with a spatula, pulled out his English muffins, and brought them to the table.

"That's what makes markets?" Jonah asked.

"Yeah. What the hell does that mean?"

"Oh, it's just a Wall Street saying. I guess it just means that not everyone likes the same stocks. You know . . . different strokes for different folks."

"Oh."

Jonah sat down. "I got to get going," he said, taking a mouthful of eggs. "I want to start cutting a trail today. Surprise Vickie when she gets home."

"It's snowin' out."

"Best time to be with nature," Jonah said.

"Wall Street really did twist your mind."

"Hey, what am I gonna do? Sit here playing gin rummy with you all day?"

Jonah finished his breakfast, changed into his work clothes in the bedroom, and brought his Bean boots out to the living room. He sat in the rocker, lacing them on.

"Mail should have come by now. I think I'm gonna run down and get it, then get started. That's okay, right?"

"You're just going to the end of the driveway?" Spowart asked.

"Yep, be right back."

Jonah retrieved the mail from his mailbox on the road. It hung from a log he had balanced on a boulder at the end of his driveway. A large rock sat on the other end for balance. He always thought it was kind of neat.

He walked gingerly back up the incline to the farm,

careful of the snow beneath his feet. He shook the small box wrapped in brown paper. There was something loose in it. Return address, Cemetery, West Street, Freeport, Maine. *What is this? Some kind of a joke?* He tried to think of who he knew who lived in Freeport. Who would send him something with a cemetery as a return address? Only one person came to mind. His curiosity worked overtime. What the hell could it be?

Jonah walked into the living room from the door on the east side of the house, pulled out a small pocketknife, and started cutting open the package before he even reached the kitchen table. When he finished ripping it open, he instinctively threw the wrapping into the wood stove and opened the tin of brownies. There was no note, no letter, no card. Nothing. Who were they from? He couldn't help but think of Fenton. *But why would Fenton send me brownies from Freeport? Certainly, he'd have put something inside, just to let me know they were from him. It just didn't make any sense.* He couldn't figure it out. *Maybe a bad joke from one of Vickie's friends?*

Jonah looked around for Spowart. He was nowhere to be seen. He called out his name, thinking he might be in the bathroom. *Must have gone out to see one of the guys.* He looked in the direction of the duck blind but didn't see him there. He was probably either in the barn or out back for a smoke.

Jonah couldn't begrudge him that. He figured this detail was probably pretty boring for all of them. A part of him hoped it would stay that way. Another part prayed that all hell would break loose so he could put this terrible chapter of his life behind him.

Jonah stared at the brownies for a moment, not able to figure out who had sent them or why. He wasn't hungry anyway. He'd just finished breakfast. Not that he would have eaten them if he were. He shrugged his shoulders, replaced the lid, and laid the container on the kitchen counter. *If Fenton is trying to intimidate me with brownies . . . he's crazier than I thought.*

He put on his jacket and gloves and left the house, walking to the toolshed inside the barn. He grabbed his chain saw and an ax and walked them to the loader attached to the back of his tractor, then grabbed a can of gas and a small container of oil and brought them back to the tractor too. Jonah walked back toward the barn, stopping at the ladder to the hayloft.

"Hello!" he called out, looking up the wooden ladder. He wasn't sure who was up there today. "Is Spowart up there with you?" he asked as a head poked out from the opening.

"Nope. Why?"

"I just wanted to show him something. He must be out back. When you see him, tell him there's something on the kitchen counter I want to show him, will ya?"

"Hang on a sec," the trooper said, his head disappearing from sight. Jonah could hear him saying something. "He could have his mike out. Things start to hurt after a while," the cop said, poking his head back in the opening. "I'll make sure he gets the message."

"Thanks," Jonah said, walking toward the tractor. He couldn't wait to get into the woods and put all this crap out of his mind.

Naples, Maine, lies at the southern tip of Long Lake, just at the western mouth of the Bay of Naples. Locals call it Brandy Pond. Cedric Halliway and Scott Hill drove the three plus hours there Friday night from their stop on 495, just outside Marlborough, Massachusetts. They pulled into the small parking lot of a quaint country inn—the Augustus Bove House. The clock on the dashboard of the Caprice read 9:47 P.M.

The two men were weak from exhaustion. They'd been running virtually nonstop since Bennett's murder early Sunday morning. That seemed like a year ago now. Halliway checked in while Hill sat on a chair in the small, quaint foyer. When Halliway finished he walked over to his partner. Hill's legs were crossed, his right ankle resting on his left knee. He was already asleep; his head was back at an angle, snoring awkwardly.

Halliway kicked the sole of his foot. "Come on Sleeping Beauty," he said, rousing him from his nap. "Rise and shine."

They had adjoining rooms on the second floor overlooking the lake. There was no elevator. Reluctantly, the two men trudged up the stairs.

When they reached their rooms, Halliway stopped. "What time you want to get up tomorrow?" he asked his partner.

"How 'bout noon," Hill replied.

"That works," Halliway responded, standing in the hall of the hundred-and-fifty-year-old inn. "Do you have a second choice?"

Hill stood at his door, his long travel bag slung over his shoulder. "Well, we're gonna need to catch up with the state police in the morning. We'll need a bite, first. How 'bout eight?"

"Seven-thirty," Halliway said.

"Jesus, no rest for the weary. Okay, meet you in the foyer at eight."

THE
NIGHTMARE
SINGS

—◦◦◦—

BOOK 4

Saturday morning, Halliway and Hill met in the foyer as planned, a few minutes after 8:00 A.M. Both men had passed out the previous evening as soon as their heads hit the pillow. It was the first full night's sleep either one had gotten in a week. They felt refreshed, ready for a long day's work. Hill was famished.

The inn was a bed and breakfast, so both men took seats at an old-fashioned table against the wall, anxiously anticipating their morning meal. The table was covered with an embroidered white-and-pink tablecloth and decorated with one red carnation in a Victorian vase. They both ordered coffee. Hill ordered the bacon and cheese omelet special, Halliway a bowl of fruit salad and a scone.

"A scone, Ric?" Hill said snidely. "Living on the edge?"

"I called the state police," Halliway said, ignoring Hill's dig. "They're going to send a cruiser by at nine. A Captain Boyd."

"Whose car you wanna take?"

"I s'pose his. I couldn't find my way to the ocean from here. Any problem with that?"

"Fine with me."

They ate mostly in silence. Only an occasional inquiry followed by a brief conversation broke the serenity of the meal.

"How do you want to start?" Hill asked at one point, slapping jelly on his toast.

Halliway shrugged his shoulders. "I figure we head for Harrison. Let's start asking around. You got the photos?" he asked.

"Right here," Hill answered, patting a small gym bag.

"Good. I've been trying to think of places he may have stopped in. I've got a few in mind. Any ideas?"

"Restaurants, for one," Hill said with a full mouth. "If there are any. Maybe convenience stores. How many places can there be?"

"Not many, I assume. Boyd will help us in that regard, I'm sure."

When they finished, both men went up to their rooms to brush their teeth, relieve themselves, check their weapons and ammunition pouches, and generally gather their thoughts for the day ahead.

Halliway knocked on Hill's door a few minutes before 9:00 A.M. "It's almost nine, Scott. You ready?"

Hill came out and locked his door behind him. "Today's the day, Ric. I've got that feeling."

"So do I," Halliway responded.

"You know, that's the first time you've seemed sure this entire investigation. Now that's a good sign."

"We'll see."

They walked down the stairs together, stepping out onto the front porch just as Boyd was turning his Maine state police cruiser into the small lot from the road. Halliway looked across at the lake. In an instant he began to understand the beauty of Maine. The Augustus Bove House stands directly at the mouth of the lake, overlooking its entire length. The site was breathtaking, something he didn't see much of in Connecticut. He looked at his watch. 8:59.

Boyd pulled into one of the seven parking spots cut into the side of the inn's lawn and got out of his car, leaving it running for the heat. He waited at the foot of the brick walk, brushing snow back and forth with his boots. Halliway and Hill walked gingerly down the steps, mindful of slipping, meeting up with Boyd at the edge of the lawn.

"Captain Boyd," Halliway said, his hand extended. "Lieutenant Cedric Halliway, Connecticut state police."

Except for the gray in Halliway's hair, for some strange reason, the two men reminded Boyd of Abbott and Costello. "Lieutenant, pleasure to meet you. You must be Sergeant Hill?" he asked, taking Scott's hand.

"Captain," Hill said.

"Call me Tom," Boyd said.

"Good enough, Tom," Halliway said. "Call me Ric. This is my partner, Scott."

"Nice view, huh?" Boyd asked, turning to look down the lake.

"I'll say," Hill responded.

"This place here," Boyd continued, motioning toward the house, "it's been an institution in Naples for a hundred and fifty years. Old man Bove used to be quite the mover and shaker in his day."

"He sure had a good eye for location," Halliway said.

"Any trouble finding it?" Boyd asked.

"Nah," Hill chimed in. "Other than the fact we were both hallucinating by the time we got here."

Boyd laughed. "Yeah, long drive from Connecticut."

"No shit," Hill said.

"How'd you sleep?"

"Like a log," Halliway said, Hill nodding agreement.

"So, I'm your appointed chauffeur. How do you want to start?" Boyd asked. "You eat yet?"

Hill patted his belly. "Yeah. She serves a great breakfast in there," motioning to the inn with his thumb. "Pretty good, too."

"Okay. Let's roll."

The three men climbed inside the cruiser. Halliway took the front seat next to Boyd, Hill took the back.

"Buckle up, gentlemen. It's the law," Boyd said, grinning at Halliway. "My orders are to take you anywhere you want to go, Lieutenant. No questions asked. Your call."

"Do you have a map?" Halliway asked.

"Do I have a map?" Boyd asked jokingly, pulling out a *Gazetteer* from under his seat. "Best map of Maine made anywhere. DeLorme Mapping makes them out of Freeport. This is the first year they've offered them topographically, though. Nice touch, I think. What section?" he asked, opening it in his lap.

"Let's start with where we are now."

"Naples. That's map four," Boyd said, handing it to Halliway. He leaned over, pointing out the town with his right hand. "This here is Long Lake. Bridgton is here. Harrison is on the northern tip of the lake . . . here. You can get there one of two ways. One seventeen through Bridgton on the west side, or a straight shot up thirty-five on the east side.

"West side, east side," Hill added with a smile from the back. "Sounds like we're in Manhattan."

"Hardly," Boyd said.

"We'd like to start asking around," Halliway said, looking up through the windshield. "Makes sense to me to start at the center and move outwards from there. You think, Scott?"

"Sounds like a plan."

"Take us to Harrison, James," Halliway said, smiling.

"Harrison, Maine. Next stop."

Boyd opted to cut across the mouth of the lake and take 35 north. They rode a short distance in silence, as the two visitors took in the scenery.

"You been to Maine before, Scott?" Boyd asked, looking at Hill in the rearview mirror.

"No. Looks like I've been missing something."

"You, Ric?"

"Not since I was a kid."

"What have you guys been doin' your whole lives? Like the sign says when you enter the state: Welcome to Maine. The way life should be. When you guys are done here you won't want to go back."

Hill looked out his window. "That depends on whether or not we have this scumbag with us."

"Speaking of scumbags," Boyd said. "What's the story with this guy anyway? Care to fill me in?"

"I'm afraid, Tom, what we have here is a deinstitutionalized maniac," Halliway said to his window before turning to Boyd. "Spent a good deal of his life in Bridgewater. Should never have been let out. Looks like he hasn't been taking his medication, and he's just slipped off the deep end. And I'm talking *really* deep."

"That's what I understand. Killed a cop down in Connecticut, is that right?"

"Yes," Halliway answered. "An officer from Darien."

"And that was just a start," Hill added.

"And so now you think he's gonna end up in Harrison because of this Roberts fella?" Boyd asked.

"Yes," Halliway said.

Boyd drove with both hands on the wheel. "Why now?" he asked, lifting his right hand. "I mean, what makes you think he'll show up now and not a week or a month from now?"

Halliway looked at Boyd. "Can you keep a secret?"

"Sure."

"Did you happen to read the article in the *Portland Press Herald* the other day? The one about how Roberts had refused protection?"

"Yeah . . . but it didn't make any sense to me. I mean, I know it's not true. We must have three or four guys on his property."

"Well, the paper did us a little favor."

"No shit," Boyd said. He looked at Halliway with a broad smile on his face. "You mean to tell me you planted that story? Whose brilliant idea was that?"

"Say hello to Mr. Disinformation," Halliway said, pointing to the back seat with his left thumb.

Hill raised his right palm, just enough to acknowledge Boyd's glance into the rearview mirror. "Pure genius, Scott. These guys always want to read about themselves. I'd bet a million bucks there's no way he missed it."

"We're hoping so," Hill added from the back. "At least get him snooping around some."

"How small is Harrison?" Halliway asked.

"This time of year? Maybe four thousand people. Summertime, you get all the rusticators from Mass. That number probably triples."

"Well, we thought we could start with all the usual places he might have entered. You know, restaurants, convenience stores, gas stations."

"That shouldn't be hard. There's only one gas station.

Two stores. You got Gas 'n More and the Village Market for convenience stores, and the Clay Pot and the Cogswheel House for restaurants. Only the Cogswheel's open year round. Other than that, there's not much really. Not in November. Most of the town is located in a building called The Block. There's a bank, video store, antique shop. Nearby is a realty office and the town office."

"Any police?" Halliway asked.

"No," Boyd said with a chuckle. "In the past, I know the selectmen have hired a part-time officer for the summer months. But not this time of year."

Boyd stopped at the roadblock just long enough to chat briefly with a colleague. He introduced Halliway and Hill, asked a few questions, and continued north.

"They've been out since about three o'clock yesterday. If your man shows up in that Bonneville, he's history."

"Any roads not covered?" Halliway asked.

"Not a one."

The trio was quiet for the rest of the drive, Halliway and Hill both lost in thought.

"Thar she blows," Boyd said, pulling into the town center.

Hill was surprised. "So this is Harrison, Maine. Smaller than I thought. What do people do for work here?"

Boyd thought a moment. "Oh, you've got quite a mix really. Some cottage industry stuff. Tourism, obviously. There's some knitting mills around, the electric company. There's also a few apple orchards and dairy farms. Believe it or not, there's some very big money in this town. One guy has his own airstrip."

There is just the one intersection in town, where Route 35 meets Route 117. The town office stood on the right, just behind the small village square, where an American flag flew on a flagpole and three monuments formed a semicircle honoring the brave men and women who served their country in both World Wars, Korea, and Vietnam.

Opposite the square stood The Block, a large brick structure two stories tall, with a clock tower in the middle. To its left was an old flagstone library, built in the shape of a circle. Adjoining it on the right was the Clay Pot, and just down the road on the left, on the north shore of the lake, was the Gas 'n More. Opposite that was the Cogswheel House.

"Why don't we park this thing somewhere," Halliway said. "Get out and start askin' around. Let's have those photos, Scott."

"Photos, photos," he said, rummaging through his bag. "Okay, all set."

"Good. Captain, you're free to stay here, or join us if you wish."

Lieutenant Boyd knew better. *Not quite, gentlemen.* "Why don't we all go together. You might be more successful if I go with you. Locals here are a bit distrustful of strangers. I think they might tend to remember more if a Maine cop is with you."

"You know the place better than we do," Halliway said, taking a photo from Hill and opening his door.

"A whole 'nother world," Hill said.

"Nice corner of it, too."

"I'm sure," Halliway said, turning around to look at Boyd. "Although I'm not so sure I'd feel that way in January."

"Yeah, it gets mighty cold."

"How cold is cold?" Hill asked.

"On a cold day you can get highs around zero, minus five . . . something like that."

"Highs? As in that's as warm as it's going to get?"

Boyd opened his door. "Yep."

Hill whistled. "Man, that's cold. Why do people live here?"

"I'm sure they'd want to ask you the same thing about Connecticut."

The three men stood outside the cruiser. Halliway and Hill scanned the tiny hamlet of downtown Harrison. It wasn't much by their standards, but locals called it home.

"I s'pose this is as good a place to start as any," Halliway said, motioning toward the Village Market. "It's right here."

"Let me go in first," Boyd said.

Halliway waved his hand toward the store's door. "After you."

"Good morning," Captain Boyd said to the owner as he stepped through the door, removing his hat.

The owner was filling the sliding door refrigerator with a fresh case of Diet Pepsi. He looked up, not acting the least bit surprised at the sight of the three men entering his store. "Mornin'," he said. "Can I help you?"

"Are you the owner?" Boyd asked.

"Sure am," the man said, sliding the glass door shut, leaving half the case still unpacked. He approached the three men standing by the cash register. "Since seventy-three. Name's Atchison. Mirle Atchison. What can I do for you, Officer?"

"Mr. Atchison, I'm sure you've read in the papers about the fugitive from Boston that's been eluding the police for the past week."

"You mean that psycho who killed them people down in Connecticut?" he asked, glancing at Halliway and Hill. "Sure have. It's the talk of the town."

The moment's glance didn't go unnoticed. Boyd introduced his two companions. Pleasantries were exchanged all around before Boyd started in again. "We have reason to believe he may have visited here in the last forty-eight hours. I was wondering if you'd be kind enough to look at some photos for us?"

Atchison walked around the counter. "I knew you fellas was up to something. Can't get in or out of this town without a passport. Sure, let's have a look," he said, removing a MegaBucks lottery-ticket holder from the counter for room.

Hill stepped forward, laying four photos on the counter. Two were of Fenton, the other two of convicts long since jailed. If this had been a medical experiment, they'd be considered placebos.

Atchison studied them at some length, spending a good deal of time on each. "I don't recognize either one of these here," he said, handing the two placebos back.

So far he'd passed.

He picked up one of the two remaining photos,

holding it close to his face. After a short while he replaced it on the counter and picked up the other one, following the same procedure.

"Geez, gentlemen. If you ask me, these two are the same man."

"You're correct, Mr. Atchison," Halliway said. "Does he look familiar?"

Atchison couldn't believe that Fenton Montague had been in his store. *Don't tell me I actually spoke to him?* "Well, yes he does. If I'm not mistaken, I think he was in here yesterday."

"Can you tell us what he wanted?" Boyd asked.

"Yeah . . . Was askin' directions. Wanted a phone book. You're not telling me that's him, are ya?"

"A phone book?" Hill asked, evading Atchison's question. "What'd he do with it?"

"Took it outside. Made a few calls, I think. Wasn't gone long."

"You said he was asking directions. Can you tell us where to?" Boyd asked.

"Sure. Said he was here to see the Thompsons out to Edes Falls Road. I remember 'cause Bert Spire was in. We both looked at each other. Thought it kind of odd. Hell, the Thompsons both eighty-five if they're a day over fifty. Don't think they've had a visitor in ten years. Not from away."

"How'd you know he was from away?" Hill asked.

Atchison gave him a You're-joking-me-right? look.

"Do you know if he went to see them?" Boyd asked, writing something in his notebook.

"Couldn't say, Officer. Sorry."

"This man," Halliway continued. "Can you tell us what he looked like?"

Atchison motioned his head to the photos lying on the counter. "You got two pictures of him right there. Shit, I was only a few feet from the guy. He's not the one you're after, is he?"

"Anything you noticed that's more up to date?" Boyd asked. "You know . . . hair length, beard, clothes, that type of thing?"

"Well," Atchison said, looking at the ceiling, pulling

on his chin. "Let's see . . . he had a hat on. Didn't look like he had much hair underneath. Course, you can never tell these days. Could have been up in a ponytail, I guess. But it looked like he had it cropped pretty close. Like he was in the Marines or something."

Halliway and Hill looked at one another. He had shaved his head. "Anything else?" Hill asked.

"Yeah. Had a bit of a beard growin'. Maybe a week old. Something like that. But that nose and chin. They kind of stick in my mind."

"Did you notice anything else?" Halliway asked. "Anything at all. Even if you think it's unimportant, we'd like to know about it."

Atchison pushed out his chin, pursing his lips outward. "He wore sunglasses. Wanted to know where the town offices were."

"Did you tell him?"

"Of course. Didn't think there was any reason not to."

"Even though you thought it odd he was asking about the Thompsons?" Hill inquired.

Uh, oh. Boyd knew that kind of question could quickly turn an ally into an enemy. They'd have to move a lot slower than that. "What Detective Hill is trying to say . . ."

Atchison was visibly annoyed. Certainly less direct. "I know what he's tryin' to say, and I don't like it one bit. Look, Officer," he said, pointing to Hill, "I mind my own business, hear? I don't know that he's not a grandson or somethin'. Maybe looking to buy the place, for all I know. The thought that some psycho's walkin' around town sure as hell wasn't a concern on my radar screen. I didn't know until just now you guys thought he was up here."

Boyd was trying desperately to bring the conversation around now. "I'm sure what Detective Hill meant was . . ."

"He can speak for himself, sir," Atchison said, his voice an octave lower. "He's a grown boy. What were you implying, Officer?"

Hill was quick on his feet. "I'm sorry if I insulted you. That wasn't my intention. Really. I was just trying to get a handle on how out of the ordinary you thought a visitor to the Thompsons was. If you didn't call the police, you must have thought it was okay."

Atchison looked at Hill in silence for a moment. It could go either way now. Halliway could see they were about to lose him if they hadn't already. He had to wrest control from Atchison. "What did he want at town hall? Did he say?" he asked, pretending everything was okay.

Now Atchison was on the defensive. If he let his hurt pride get in the way and refused to answer the question, he'd look petty. Atchison closed his eyes momentarily. "No, he didn't say. But I know he went there. Bert and I saw him drive over."

The interview was Halliway's now. Hill had effectively been removed from the process. "You saw his car?" he asked.

"Yep."

"By any chance, do you remember what make?"

Atchison couldn't quite let it go. "You know," he said, looking at Hill. "I would have called the police if I'd thought something bad was afoot. Not much happens here to put you in that mindset."

"I understand, sir. Looks like a beautiful town," Hill said, becoming extra gracious. "I'd like to bring my family back some day."

Atchison smiled, feeling sufficiently redeemed. "Of course, Officer. We love tourists here. I'll even give you the nickel tour."

"Do you remember what kind of car he drove?" Halliway asked again.

"Something black. Older model. Early eighties, maybe? Temporary plates, I remember that."

"Can you think of any particulars, Mr. Atchison? It's important. If you saw it again, how would you recognize it? Was it American? GM, Ford, Chrysler? Maybe foreign?"

"Olds, I think. I can't be sure."

"Can you remember the model?"

457

Atchison kind of bobbed his head, moving his shoulders slightly. He was thinking. "You know . . . if I had to bet, I'd say it was a Bonneville."

"But you can't be sure?"

"Not a hundred percent. I only looked at it for a short bit. Had a customer come in."

"So you saw him go in town hall?" Halliway asked.

"Well, not exactly. I mean, I assume he did. He parked in the lot right behind."

"Who's the town clerk?" Halliway asked, hoping he'd used the right terminology.

"Town clerk? That'd be Mavis Fornier. Been workin' there as long as I can remember."

"Is it open on Saturday?"

"No, but you can call her at home. Her husband's some sick. I'm pretty sure she'd be around."

"Do you have her number?"

"Well, no. But it's in the book," he said, reaching under the counter. He flipped through, running his finger down a page. "Let's see . . . Fornier, Fornier. Here ya go. Fornier. Zeke and Mavis."

Halliway took the book from Atchison and copied the number down in his notebook. "Seventy-two Carsley Road. Is that far from here?"

Atchison shrugged his shoulders. "Ten minutes, maybe. Depending on how fast you drive."

"Can you tell us how to get there?"

"I know where it is," Boyd said.

Halliway handed the phone book back to the owner. "Mr. Atchison, you've been most helpful. Thank you very much, sir."

"My pleasure."

Hill tried to make amends. He went to the refrigerator, pulled out three Diet Pepsis, and brought them to the counter.

"Thank you, Mr. Atchison. I'll take these and a couple of MegaBucks tickets."

"Any particular numbers?"

"Do you have machine picks?"

"Sure."

"Let the machine decide."

Atchison reached down to the ground and retrieved the MegaBucks ticket holder, replacing it on the counter. He pushed some buttons on the green lottery machine behind him and out popped two square, pink and white tickets.

"Here ya go," he said, handing Hill his tickets. "Sodas are on the house."

"No, thank you, but I couldn't. I'd like to pay," Hill said, shaking his head.

"All right, that'll be four thirteen, with the tickets."

Hill handed him a five. Atchison rang it up and gave him back his change. "Feeling lucky today, Officer?"

"You could say that."

— ⁀⁀⁀ —

On Friday night, as darkness descended over the trees and farmhouses of the tiny hamlet of Harrison, Maine, Fenton Montague was becoming increasingly aware of his precarious hold on freedom. The ever-tightening grip of the law was fast becoming a choke hold. The police were frustrated because the madman they sought was always a step or two ahead of them, and Fenton became more and more furious as he realized they were always only a step or two behind. There was no margin for error in this game.

If Fenton was the hare, the cops were the tortoise— slowly and methodically dropping the dragnet in place. The strong arm of the Maine state police had begun a steady and relentless squeeze. The grip was constantly tightening, until through sheer numbers and force, the scum would finally begin to ooze from between its fingers. Fenton knew now he'd be spending the night in Harrison.

Drunk driving roadblocks are not uncommon in the state of Maine, but the lookouts the state police set up weren't quite like that. They were more to slow traffic than to stop it, designed to allow the troopers a good look at the vehicles and their occupants. The roadblocks operated in teams of two. One cruiser facing in at an angle, toward the middle of the road, the other doing the same from the opposite side. They were spaced about fifteen yards apart, just enough to let traffic squeeze through.

Four teams set up camp. One west of the bridge, at the northern tip of Long Lake, just beyond where Routes 35 and 117 connect. Another just north of Carsley Road on Route 35. One just east of where Route 121 connects with Route 117, and the last just south of the Maple Ridge fork on Edes Falls. If you were going to Harrison you'd have to pass through them. Unless you turned around. And there's hardly a better way to say come and get me.

Fenton was far from pleased. *How can they possibly know I'm here?* They were unstoppable—relentless in their pursuit. When would they quit? Give it up for better prospects? *Don't they realize they can't catch me?* And yet, with each passing minute Fenton could feel the suffocating hold growing tighter and tighter.

Could it be possible he wouldn't get out of this one? No problem, he thought. He looked at his *Gazetteer.* A half day's trek through the woods, a mile and a half, maybe two, and he'd come upon Bolsters Mills Road. He'd be past them and on his merry way—halfway to Albany before they even realized he was gone.

But still, just knowing they sat in teams only minutes from where he was now, on roads all around him—the very thought drove him wild with anger. *I'll show every one of you bastards.* "You think your petty little games will catch me?" he roared as he drove down Maple Ridge Road. *So you think you're going to snag me, do you? Shackle me? Cage me like some wild animal? Strap me tight in your electric chair? Don't hold your breath, gentlemen. You haven't seen anything yet.*

Up until now it had all been business. He hadn't even started having fun yet. No one would deprive him of that. *No one!* "I will not allow it!" he bellowed at the top of his lungs, his knuckles white as he gripped the steering wheel.

Although it had not been part of his hastily impro-vised plan, it was obvious now he would need to spend the night in the farmhouse. Fenton approached the abandoned small white schoolhouse on the corner of Carsley and Maple Ridge for the second time that evening, slowing as he turned right. He allowed himself a moment's worry that events were dictating his actions. Slowly at first, almost imperceptibly, he was losing control. Other people—invisible forces—were beginning to intrude on his play.

More than once in the last few hours he'd been taken by surprise. His temples pounded with rage as he felt the strings of his marionette pulled from his grasp. Only one at first . . . then another . . . and another. At this rate he'd be dancing to their tune in no time—a thought that drove him wild. He needed to get the job done and get out. Far away from here.

As he approached the farmhouse yet again, he could barely discern the silhouette of hills surrounding Harrison through the dark gray clouds hanging low over the small valley. The hills were a mile away, maybe less. If the day were clear he knew he'd be able to see the stately, snow-covered peak of Mount Washington. He'd heard it lost its snow sometime in August only to gain it back again sometime in September. Winter must be a bitch in this neck of the woods.

A few hours ago he had sped away in fear of his life; now he pulled into the dirt loop in front of Jonah's family farm, confident that he was safe. He wasted no time, making it priority one to ditch his car. The barn would be ideal. Fenton drove the Bonneville to within a few yards of the large wooden doors and got out. He pulled the weathered two-by-four from its slots and threw it to the ground, swinging both doors open with all his might, their weight at first hindering, then finally accelerating the process.

"Shit!" Fenton said, as he stood looking into the depths of the dark building. He fumbled around, finally finding a light switch. One sixty-watt bulb buzzed on, hanging from a wire a few rafters in. Nothing had driven in or out of here for years.

Directly in front of him, five feet or so beyond the opening, stood a small, makeshift workbench. On it lay the motor of some antiquated piece of farm machinery.

Its useful days had no doubt passed with the last World War. It was corroded with a thick layer of rust and covered with barn dust and spider webs. Fenton figured it had to weigh several hundred pounds.

Everywhere he looked there were relics of the farm's busy and varied past. Items of all sizes, cras, and usefulness filled every nook and cranny. Fenton wasn't sure just how to remove the motor, but he knew he couldn't do it unless he cleared some of the other debris first.

He thought for a moment of entering from the other side of the barn, and slowly made his way through the maze to check it out. He had hoped this way might be easier, but that dream was dashed when he stepped over an old brass bed and opened one of the rear barn doors just wide enough to look out.

Below him was a ten-foot drop. He was puzzled at first, but it made sense as he thought about it. This was the end of the barn the muckrakers used when clearing the evening's dung from the stalls.

Fenton stood staring at two wooden toboggans lying side by side, leaning against a five-foot pile of old wooden doors. His mind wavered momentarily, and he suddenly saw himself standing in a dairy barn just outside Pittsfield, Massachusetts. His father had taken him there as a young boy to visit an old army buddy of his.

He remembered those times now with longing. Those were good days. He felt an aching in his heart at the thought of his father. He loved him dearly. Too bad he had lied to him, up and died, as if his son didn't matter. Fenton knew from that moment on he could never trust anyone again. The remaining years of life with his mother became a living, torturous hell that in time, only heightened his sense of isolation and fear.

The thought of her as he stood alone in the dark, damp, cold barn brought memories of the closet slamming into his brain. His head snapped as he remembered kneeling in it, desperately needing to go to the bathroom, crying out loudly as he strained to keep it inside him.

"Mother!" he screamed, squeezing his thighs together,

rocking back and forth. "Please, Mother, I won't do it again. I promise! Pleeease," he begged. "I have to go to the bathroom!"

The helpless boy's body heaved as he started to sob. Tears streamed down his face as urine seeped down his legs. Slowly at first, quickly becoming a tidal wave as his mind resigned itself to the fact that he would spend yet another evening in the closet for his misdeeds.

Alone and helpless in the barn, he stood deathly still as a sense of dread overtook him. He looked down at his pants, the sense of warmth enveloping his legs. Fenton realized he'd wet himself. His eyes bulged with fury. He nearly fell several times as he scrambled over and around the piles of debris that lay between him and the opening of the barn. His breathing was labored, his movements awkward, as he struggled desperately to free himself from the confines of his past.

He fought frantically to escape. But he was like a circus elephant, trained from birth that escape is impossible by having a leg chained to a post—eventually it doesn't even try to escape, whether or not a chain is attached. Its young mind was indelibly imprinted with what can and cannot be done. Fenton was lost somewhere between fighting to free himself from the barn and feeling he couldn't move more than a few feet in any direction. His desperate attempt to reach the far door and his mind's indelible imprint of the closet were at ferocious odds. He thought he might faint as he reached the motor at the far end of the barn. Scurrying past it, he stumbled clumsily toward the front of the Bonneville, falling face down in the accumulating snow.

Fenton rose to his knees, wiping the cold from his face, and stood for several minutes, resting his hands on the warm hood of the car. He breathed deeply, his eyes closed. He felt lightheaded from the battle that continued in his psyche.

When finally he felt together enough to stand, he put his hands on his head and walked to the side of the house. Reaching the back, he sat on the edge of the porch, his feet dangling off the side. Fenton sat for a bit thinking of ways to move the motor in the barn, staring into the woods that would eventually bring him to his salvation.

He was almost home now. His obsessive desire for ultimate victory—for the last laugh—lit sparklers in the inner lobes of his brain. He was nearly giddy with the knowledge that by this time tomorrow night, he, Fenton Montague, would have delivered the final blow. That revenge would finally be his . . . to savor . . . to embrace . . . to bring closure to the humiliation—no, the *ruination*—this smug farmer had brought about.

One more night. Just one more night. Break into the farmhouse, snuggle up and stay warm—and above all, get some sleep. Tomorrow promised to be a busy day.

—∾—

On Saturday, November 4th, Jonah drove his tractor slowly through the snow, down the pasture to his east, toward the opening leading to the main trail. He was caught off guard by the sight of someone out of the corner of his eye. He turned to see Trooper Stickney following him, rifle in hand, his semiautomatic strapped to his side.

Jonah stopped at the entrance to the woods, letting Stickney catch up. *Which one's this?* There were too many cops. He couldn't get all their names straight.

"What's up?" he asked, as Stickney approached, slowing his gait.

"Nothin'," he said, standing at the side of the tractor now. "Sergeant Cunningham asked me to escort you."

Jonah rolled his eyes. "Look, what's your name again?"

"Stickney. Peter Stickney."

"Look, Trooper Stickney, I don't want you guys to think I don't appreciate what you're doing for me. I really mean that. But I got to be able to have some time to myself. I'm going nuts stuck here like some prisoner."

Stickney raised his free hand. "Hey, I understand. Knock yourself out. I'll hang back. You won't even know I'm here."

"There's nothing in there but a mile of woods. You guys don't think you're being just a little paranoid?"

"Mr. Roberts, all I know is our job is to protect you, and we can't very well do that if we can't see you."

Jonah breathed deep. "I know, I know. But I stand a better chance of getting attacked by a bear than by Montague in there," he said, waving his hand toward the woods.

"Good. Then we both got nothin' to worry about."

"So this isn't negotiable, is it?"

Stickney shook his head slowly. "No, sir. It's not."

The fight left Jonah. He hung his head in realization that this was his new life. He was learning to hate it.

"All right, you know how to use a chain saw?"

"Sure do."

"Well, you might as well help out if you're going to just stand there staring at me."

"I don't know that I should do that, sir. I can move some wood if you'd like. But I think whatever I do probably shouldn't require more focus than that. I do have a job to do. Shame, too. I love this stuff."

"What stuff?"

"You know. Workin' in the woods, clearing deadwood, hauling logs. I got a camp up to Jackman. I'm always out there doin' something."

"Climb in," Jonah said, motioning to the loader behind him.

Jonah drove the tractor down the trail feeling oddly out of sorts. When would he ever be alone again? About an eighth of a mile in, just over the bridge, Jonah cut the engine. They gathered the items from the loader and cut left into the woods, ducking branches and stepping over fallen trees. They spoke about the snow, the upcoming winter, the Celtics, anything but Fenton. Stickney was determined not to be the first to bring him up.

Shortly after Jonah and Stickney began toiling in the woods, Trooper Spowart took a final puff of his cigarette and flicked it into the snow-covered brush behind Jonah's house. He took these breaks seldom, always in daylight, and always when Jonah was elsewhere on the farm. He never strayed more than a few yards and always kept his position so that he could see the driveway.

Walking back along the west side of the house, farthest from the barn, he took the snow-covered wooden steps up to the small landing outside the door. He stood still for a moment, brushed the snow off the railing, and leaned against it watching the flakes fall through the trees. He reminded himself to get his snow blower tuned. He had a feeling it would be a hell of a winter.

He was in no rush to go inside. The first snow of the season was always special for him, marking in his mind the beginning of a new chapter in the lives of his children. He smiled as he pictured dozens of different size snow boots sitting neatly placed, side by side on the floor of his mud room at home. His kids loved winter as much as they loved summer.

They skied, played hockey, built snowmen, had snowball fights, and sledded the whole season through. They also meant he had his own personal shoveling crew. That was one of the many advantages of having kids. He'd have to remember to tell Jonah that when he came back inside.

Spowart lit another cigarette with his lighter, dragging the smoke deeply into his lungs, its warmth a comforting contrast to the cold outside. Inhaling, he could hear the sound of the chain saw off in the distance. It would idle for long periods of time, then rev to a fever pitch. He wondered what it would be like to have that much free time. To be able to work in the woods whenever he felt like it. Jonah Roberts was a lucky man, or at least he would be again when this psycho was out of his life.

Flicking his butt into the woods, Spowart exhaled until he could tell the difference between what was smoke and what was his breath against the cold winter air. He replaced his earplug, flung open the door, and stood on the rug, brushing snow from his shoulders. He removed his hat and hung it on a wooden peg next to the door, standing silently, staring at the interior of Jonah's quiet, modest home. Spowart's shoulders fell as he sighed, thinking just how boring this detail was becoming. He was happy not to be outside, but still, sitting around a house all day, day in and day out, can get a little monotonous.

He walked into the kitchen to pour himself a cup of coffee and spotted the round, metal canister on the kitchen counter. He and Jonah agreed that anything in the house was his. The only rule was to pick up after himself.

"Help yourself," Jonah had said. "I just don't want to see a mess in the sink. That's all I ask."

Spowart pried open the lid of the container and was pleasantly surprised to see an untouched pile of marble brownies staring up at him.

"Hmmm," he said, pouring his coffee to the rim. "A man can get fat on this job."

He pulled one off the top, replaced the lid and sat at the kitchen table, laying his treat on a napkin. "George?" he heard Trooper Cunningham say through his earpiece.

Spowart broke his brownie in half, dunking a piece in his coffee. "What?" he responded, taking a large, satisfying bite. The chocolate and cream-cheese marble melting in his mouth.

Like the rest of the men on the detail, Cunningham wore a mike on his shoulder. He had to press a button on its side before speaking into it. "Mr. Roberts wanted me to tell you to take a look at something he left on the kitchen counter. He seemed a bit perplexed."

"Did he say what it was?" Spowart asked.

"Negative. Just that he wanted to show it to you. I got the feeling it was somewhat out of the ordinary."

"Okay, thanks, Fran. I'll take a look."

A few minutes passed as Spowart rose to check the kitchen counters. Nothing seemed out of place. In fact, the only thing new were the brownies. He sat back down, finished dunking his brownie, and licked his fingers when he was through.

"Man, that's too good," he said, rising to top off his coffee and help himself to another brownie. "One more," he said aloud, sitting back down at the kitchen table.

Five minutes or so had passed since Cunningham had

last spoken to his colleague. "George," he said, turning his head to speak into the mike on his shoulder. "Find anything?"

No response.

"George?"

No response.

"Spowart. Acknowledge."

Silence.

"Spowart!" Cunningham yelled, becoming a little uneasy. "Shit! These fuckin' mikes."

He climbed down the ladder from the hayloft in the barn, dropped to the cement floor in the barn with both feet, and quickly walked to the steps leading to the door on the east side of Jonah's house. He opened the door and pulled his gun as he heard something in the kitchen smash to pieces.

He could clearly hear someone moaning in agony. He thought of calling out, but decided stealth was the better approach. He made his way quickly to the corner of the kitchen, holding his Browning M1935 Hi-Power semiautomatic up in the air with both hands. He knelt and peeked quickly around the corner.

"Jesus Christ!" he yelled, replacing his gun in its holster, running to the aid of his colleague.

Spowart was writhing on the floor, bleeding from cuts from a thousand pieces of glass and porcelain. He had pulled the dish rack off the counter in a desperate attempt to grab something before going down. His body was racked now with the involuntary contractions of every muscle in his body. His legs and arms flailed wildly, as his head banged repeatedly against the floor, his stomach and chest heaving surreally up and down.

Spowart's back began to arch until only his feet and head were on the floor. His face was contorted in a hideous death grimace.

"George!" he screamed, running to his side. "Jesus Christ, George! What happened?" he asked, trying desperately to get some information.

Cunningham tried in vain to get Spowart's body to relax. He tried holding his arms, then his legs, then he tried pushing his torso back down. This was way over his head. Whatever was going on here was beyond anything he'd ever seen. He was at a loss, but knew with certainty there was nothing he could do to help.

The microphones and headsets the troopers were using were set to a tactical channel that could only be heard by the men on the detail. They sure as hell couldn't help. What he needed was a cruiser, but there wasn't one in the driveway. The other detail had taken it when they switched shifts. For a split second he thought of running to one of the cruisers at the end of the road, but immediately realized how futile an effort that would be. He pulled his radio off his belt and radioed the barracks in Gray.

"Spencer, it's Fran," he said hurriedly. "Spowart's down, Spence. I need a ten fourteen now. Radio one of the cars out on the street. We got to get him to a hospital now, Spence!"

"Fran, what do you mean Spowart's down?" the desk sergeant asked.

In a terrorizing moment of fear, Cunningham remembered that Spowart had been late this morning and had missed the morning shift change. *He didn't hear about the strychnine!* "Call a car, Spence. *Now!* There's no perp. I'll explain later. I think he's been poisoned."

The desk sergeant contacted both cars on the radio, and in less than a minute a cruiser came reeling up the driveway, slamming to a stop. Its lights were flashing but, as per orders, it approached in silence. The trooper flew out of his car, leaving his door open, and took the steps to the house two at a time.

"Holy shit!" he said, catching sight of the mess, running to Spowart's side. "What the hell's goin' on?" he asked Cunningham with disbelief.

"Come on, help me get him to the car. We got to get him to Bridgton ASAP. I don't know if he's going to make it."

The two men struggled mightily to control their spastic patient. It took no small effort to master Spowart's flailing appendages, to say nothing of ignoring his screams. They ran him down the steps, Cunningham nearly falling as they hit the ground.

"There's nothing we can do, Bob," Cunningham said. "Just throw him in."

Cunningham held his shoulders while his colleague opened the rear door, ran around to the other side, opened that door, and crawled inside on the back seat. Lying on his stomach he leaned over toward the ground and grabbed Spowart's feet. His angle was such that he couldn't pull hard enough. He lacked the leverage to get his feet on the seat.

"Shit!" he yelled, as he stepped out the door, grabbed Spowart's feet and tossed them up on the seat. He ran back around the cruiser, crawled in and prepared to pull.

"Here," he said. "I got 'im. Ready?"

"Yeah."

"Okay, push!"

The other entrance to Edes Falls Road was farther away. The second cruiser pulled up just as Cunningham was pushing with every ounce of his strength, while his colleague pulled Spowart across the back seat. Cunningham crawled in back with his stricken friend, wiping the sweaty hair from his forehead, trying to prevent him from choking on his tongue.

"Hank, watch the farm," Cunningham told the second trooper.

The new arrival was dumbstruck, the whole thing so shocking and surreal as to make him momentarily lose conscious thought. "What the fuck happened?" he asked.

"Later. Come on, Bob! Move!" Cunningham said.

The trooper called dispatch as he spun around in the driveway. "Spence, it's Smitty. Call Bridgton Hospital. Tell them we're bringing in a state trooper. He's suffering spasms like I've never seen. Tell 'em his arms and legs are flailing and his torso's arched. Also, call Augusta, have them fax Spowart's medical files ASAP. He's bad, Spence."

"Ten four. I'm on it."

The cruiser barely slowed as it came to the end of the drive. The trooper sped to the top of the hill, took a right on Zekelo Road and was doing seventy-five in a matter of seconds. His siren wailed now.

———

It was past 1:00 P.M. on Saturday afternoon, and though it was cold and snowing, Trooper Peter Stickney had still worked up a sweat helping Jonah lug dead trees from various parts of the woods to the stream. As discussed, he didn't use the chain saw, but he felt awkward just standing there watching Jonah work. In his heart Stickney knew Jonah was right. Nothing was going to happen out here. What a pain in the ass this detail was. He couldn't wait for it to end.

Stickney waited for a moment's lull with the chain saw. Jonah wore ear protectors, so he had to approach him to be heard. Jonah was hunched over a log, clearing snow from its bark. He jumped as Stickney tapped him on the shoulder.

"Jesus!"

"Sorry, Mr. Roberts. Listen, I can't hear a thing with that chain saw going and being down in this ravine. I really should check in. Why don't you take a break and come up with me? Just a few minutes, so I can check in."

Jonah gave him a look. "Come on, Stickney," he said. "You're killin' me. We've been out here now for what, two hours? It's not like we've had to beat back psychos. Just let me work. Go check in and come back. What could possibly happen?"

"You're not going to make this easy, are you?"

"Christ, Stickney. You know as well as I do this is a fucking waste of your time. Now go check in, or whatever the hell you got to do, and come back. I'm not going anywhere."

Stickney looked at Jonah for a long time. He knew he shouldn't leave him alone. On the other hand he also believed what Jonah was saying. Anyway, he couldn't very well force Jonah to come. "All right, but don't go anywhere. I want you right here when I come back."

"Yes, Trooper Stickney," Jonah said, imitating a six-year-old.

Stickney took off through the thick woods, looking back occasionally until it was fruitless to try any longer.

In a short while he came to the main trail and depressed his mike to report in. He could hear Jonah's chain saw whirring in the woods.

"Fran, it's Stick. Acknowledge."

Nothing.

"Fran, it's Stick, do you read me?"

Silence.

"Shit," Stickney said, as he took off toward the pastures. Was he too far away to be heard?

As he approached the opening in the woods leading toward the pastures beyond, he stopped and depressed his microphone again. "Fran, this is Stick. Acknowledge."

More silence.

He removed the battery pack from the bottom of his radio. A red flashing light indicated his batteries were dead. *Shit.* He'd plugged them into the recharger last night before he'd gone to bed. Maybe there was dust on the connection or maybe his cat had unplugged it. It wouldn't be the first time. Whatever the reason, his radio was dead. He'd have to check in on foot.

He tried one last time. "Spowart, this is Stick." He started up toward the pasture, stopping as he saw the light-blue state police cruiser in the driveway. "What the hell?" he said aloud, picking up his pace.

As he came up the small hill, he could see Trooper Henry Fairchild standing in front of the barn.

"Hank!" Stickney called out.

Fairchild was surprised to hear his name called. He looked in the direction of the voice. "Stick, is that you? What the hell are you doin' down there?"

"What am I doing down here?" Stickney asked, trotting up the pasture. "What are you doing up there?" Stickney passed the wood chip pile and approached Fairchild, shaking his hand. "What the hell's goin' on? Where is everybody?"

"There's no one here but me. What are you doing up here?"

"I went to check in, but my fuckin' battery pack is dead. Where is everyone?" he asked, looking around.

"They took George to the hospital."

Stickney flinched. "Hospital? Why?"

"You don't know?"

"Know what?"

"Where's Roberts?" Fairchild asked.

"Know what, Hank?"

"Well, I don't know much. Fran radioed Spence. He called me and Bob and told us to hustle our butts up here. All I know is that when I got here, Fran and Bob were shovin' George in the cruiser. Christ, Stick, he looked like a zombie."

"George?"

"Yeah, George. His arms and legs were flailin', his back was arched. They couldn't even get him in the car."

"Jesus Christ," Stickney said, concern lining the ridges of his brow. The chain saw must have blocked out the sirens. "What happened?"

"Don't know. They hightailed it out of here, though. Goin' to Bridgton, I think. They were afraid they were gonna lose him."

"Lose him? What do you mean, *lose* him?"

"I mean, he looked like he was dyin'. The scariest thing I ever saw. I tell ya, I've never seen anything like that before. Not ever. He was in some fuckin' kind of pain."

"Shit. So what are you doin' here?" Stickney asked.

"Fran told me to keep an eye on the store. So that's what I'm doin'. Is Roberts down there in the woods?"

"Yeah."

"Is anyone with him?"

"I got to call Spence. Find out what he knows. Have you spoken to him?"

Fairchild shook his head. "No."

"I can't fuckin' believe this!" Stickney said, pounding his fist against the barn door. "What could have happened?"

"Search me. I think I heard one of them mention poison."

"Poison? But how?"

"Shit, Stick, how the hell do I know? I mean, I've spent the last few days sittin' in a cruiser at the end of the road. Next thing I know, I'm responding to a ten seventy-four from Spence, and now I'm standin' here talking to you. If you want to know more, you'd better call Spence."

"That's what I'm doin' right now," Stickney said, taking the steps to the house two at a time.

"I'll join ya."

Stickney walked to the telephone hanging on a wooden post in the kitchen and dialed the barracks. Police radios are not for conversational purposes.

"Maine state police, can I—"

"Spence, it's Stick. What the hell's goin' on with George? Any news?"

"Nothin' yet. Fran called in. Said the doctors had him in emergency. That's all I know."

"Do they know what it is?"

"Not yet."

"Damn."

"Careful, Stick," Spencer said. Ask any cop. Swearing over the radio is one of the surest ways to get suspended without pay.

Stickney breathed deep. He hated letting his emotions control his reason. "Yeah, yeah . . . I hear you. Thanks, Spencer. Let us know if you get any information."

"I'll call if I hear anything."

"Thanks, Spence. Hank's here with a cruiser. Contact him. My radio's out."

"Ten four."

Stickney hung up the phone and stood motionless for a few seconds, his hands on his hips.

"Anything?" Fairchild asked.

"Nothing. He's in emergency. That's all we know. Shit!" he said with a slight snap of his head. "I can't believe this."

"You want me to go down with Mr. Roberts?" Fairchild asked.

"Give it a rest, Hank!"

"Hey, don't take it out on me. We got a job to do is all."

Stickney leaned against the post, rubbing his temples. "I'm sorry, Hank. I didn't mean to blow up at you. It's just this Spowart thing has me all shook up. I wasn't going to let him out of my sight but just a minute or two, until I saw your cruiser in the driveway and knew something was wrong."

"Hey, Stick, he's my friend too. You're not the only one who's upset."

"I know, I know. I'm sorry. I just feel like we should hang by the phone until we know something."

"Well, why don't you go back down. If I hear anything, I'll let you know."

"Shit, Hank, you couldn't even find us down there."

"All I got to do is follow the sound of the chain saw."

"Chain saw," Stickney said, tilting his head like a dog who's heard something. "I don't hear it. Do you?" he asked his colleague.

Hank listened for a moment, walking to the side door and opening it. "Nothing. It's quiet."

"God! I hate to go down there at a time like this," Stickney said. "What I really want to do is go to the hospital."

"You know you can't do that, Stick."

"Yeah, I know. But this wait's gonna kill me."

"I'll let you know as soon as I hear something."

"All right, I'm goin' down. Come get me if you hear anything. I want to be the first person you tell if you get a call. Got it?"

"Promise."

"Good. You religious, Hank?"

"How do you mean?"

"I mean, do you believe in God?"

"Yeah, I guess."

"Well, stop guessing and start praying. George needs our help right now."

"I'll do my best."

"So will I," Stickney said, straddling the door sill, one foot on the outside deck. "Let's just hope it's good enough."

On Saturday morning, Fenton awoke on a bed, curled into a ball, wrapped tightly in an old and pilly US Army blanket he'd found in the farmhouse's hall closet. The morning air was cold and crisp. He could see his breath clearly against the outline of the dark brick fireplace facing him from the opposite wall. He lay still for a few moments, gathering his bearings, realizing he had to piss like a racehorse. The previous few days must have taken more out of him than he'd thought. His watch read 11:13 A.M.

Fenton walked out to the back deck and urinated off to one side. He re-entered the farmhouse, grabbing an apple from his knapsack, and sat in a beaten, worn-out rocker, pulling his legs up lotus-style under him. It was too early yet to proceed. He would need to wait a few more hours still. Fenton wanted to make his move with the setting sun.

He closed his eyes, chewing his apple slowly, humming the tune in his head. "Three blind mice. Three blind mice . . ." If the newspaper was correct, and Jonah was alone on his farm, today would be his crowning salvation. Oh, how sweet . . . how beautiful it would be to walk away the champion—to melt into the woods one last time, knowing in his heart that he had taken an eye for an eye. One lost life for another. He could fade away, knowing forevermore that his accounts were finally settled.

Time seemed foreign to Fenton now—lost as he was in his meditative world. "See how they run. See how they run . . ." What was time anyway, but some quantification of the beating of one's own heart? Would time cease to exist once he had silenced Jonah's? The minutes floated by and accumulated into hours, as he dreamed of his imminent success, warming himself through meditation and sheer will power, slowing his heart to a paltry thirty-six beats a minute.

"They all went after the farmer's wife, who cut off their tails with a carving knife. See how they run. See how they run." Fenton was unsure just how much time had passed before the sound registered fully in his brain. What was it? Eyes still closed, he cocked his head slightly, listening to the on again, off again whir of a small engine. It seemed to emanate from somewhere deep in the woods beyond . . . wafting up toward him . . . drifting up the pastures behind the farmhouse.

Like a bat in the black of night, Fenton zeroed in on the melodious sound. Someone was out there with a chain saw, and he felt certain he knew who it was. There would never be a better time. He smiled at the image of what was to come.

There wasn't time for thought and logistics. It was anybody's guess how much longer Jonah would stay in the woods. Fenton rose and walked over to his knapsack, pulling out his knife. He was filled with an odd sense of anxiety now. God had offered up Jonah to him sooner than he had anticipated. Like an internal video machine, Fenton's mind played through scenarios as he sat on the floor, lacing up his new Bean boots.

He reached over and slid his knapsack closer, removing the vest he had used when he climbed into David's attic. He put the .45 revolver into one of its pockets and emptied a container of bullets into the pocket underneath. He placed his knife into its sheath and strapped his belt through its loop.

Fenton stood in the small living room, patting himself, trying to think of anything he had missed. He laughed aloud at the thought of making Jonah eat the brownies. Even if Jonah had thrown them out, which was likely, still Fenton figured they would be in the trash. Strychnine poisoning is such a horrible way to die. Yet, in his mind, the sheer joy of watching his prey's agony could never approach the pain Jonah had caused him so many years ago.

He slid on his lined, deerskin gloves, and walked out of the farmhouse for the last time. He didn't worry about the tracks in the snow. They'd be covered soon enough. There'd be no sign he'd ever been there. Not from the outside anyway.

Fenton walked quickly down the pasture ahead, the hum of the chain saw stroking his eardrums clearly now. This time, Fenton would not turn back, but rather continued on a straight course. He passed the old Pa-Pec silager and various other pieces of rusted, outdated farm machinery—the line of gray timber growing slowly larger as he worked his way down the slight grade of the abandoned fields. There was no protection from the elements out here, and, as if to prove the point, a prewinter wind whipped snow painfully in his face.

He continued his downward trek, the farmhouse growing smaller in the distance behind him. There were several acres of pasture. Fenton figured it would take him ten or fifteen minutes to traverse it. The ground was uneven and more than once he almost fell. He walked quickly but steadily, watching for holes and rocks in the snow-covered ground as he went.

About halfway down he came upon an old post fence, two wires running its length about two feet and four feet off the ground. It must have been used at one time to keep in the cattle. He bent over and ducked between the two wires, noticing the posts were nothing more than stripped tree branches four or five inches in diameter.

Fenton stopped momentarily as the chain saw fell quiet. *Shit!* Was Jonah leaving? Had he finished for the day? Had Fenton gotten this close only to have the opportunity of a lifetime plucked from his grasp? His gait accelerated. He was hoping against hope that Jonah would busy himself with the fruits of his labors before heading in.

Fenton walked the remaining couple of acres with surprising speed. He had to duck through the post fence again at the far edge of the pasture where the line of trees began. No one had been in these woods for years. Tree stumps poked up through the snow, fallen trees and limbs lay everywhere. Slowly making his way through the maze, Fenton smiled as the sound of the chain saw started up again. *Must have stopped to tighten it, maybe fill it with gas.*

Like a fly to honey, Fenton homed in on its sound as it led him inexorably to his prey. The Maine woods are not easily tamed, and Fenton would find his mission today no exception. He grew ever more frustrated as he desperately tried to move with some degree of speed through the woods. There was no way he could force the issue.

The woods were what they were, and there wasn't a damn thing he could do about it.

Occasionally, he needed to stop. In the woods, the quickest way from point A to point B is not always a straight line. He occasionally came upon thickets of bushes or fallen trees that were easier to walk around than go through. He would stand, eyeing his options in all directions, always mindful of the direction of the chain saw's hum.

Fenton measured distances with his eyes, always opting for the path of least resistance. Every move, every detour was carefully reasoned, designed to save time, but simultaneously thought out so as to cost as little energy as possible.

He was making progress . . . slowly but steadily. He turned to look behind him now. He could barely make out the pastures behind. He was getting there. As he toiled through the woods he thought he saw a long thin opening through the trees. It reminded him of a long runway. Fenton concentrated on it, working his way unwaveringly in its direction. When he finally pushed through enough timber to make it out, he smiled and thanked God. It was a path of some sort. An omen, he thought.

Walking quickly now in the direction of the small engine, he worried that perhaps the path was taking him a little to its left. But still, it seemed to be keeping close enough. He could always backtrack if he had to. He was saving too much time this way to give it up so quickly.

He stopped in his tracks at the sound of a crunch to his left. Almost from instinct he knelt at the side of the path, quietly hugging the trunk of a tree. The chain saw was closer now, but it was still a distant noise—droning background filler. The crunch was much closer. There was clearly someone . . . or something . . . moving in the woods to his left. His eyes scanned the area like radar, registering everything he saw to the synapses of his brain.

He heard it again and pulled his revolver from his vest. He hugged the tree, motionless. Every muscle in his body constricted and shut down. As his eyes darted about the woods he saw a six-point buck walk out from behind a large fir, grazing in the snow. It pushed snow aside with its nose, nibbling on saplings and other ground flora.

Just what I need. Some hunter's going to miss the fucking deer and drop me, or worse yet, mistake me for a deer. The thought chilled him. The hunter's words came back to him. "I'd stay out of the woods if I was you." But this was private property. Surely there wouldn't be hunters out here.

He watched the buck for a while, fascinated with its majestic beauty and sleek lines. How could someone shoot something so beautiful? *People really are screwed up.* No wonder he hated them. *When will they realize they exist for the earth, not the other way around?*

The thought that grown men stalked these woods, hoping they could take a gorgeous animal like that home for bragging rights, only heightened his resolve to murder Jonah. He was scum like the rest of them. They were all scum. He wished he could murder every last one of them.

"I knew there was something about that boy," Mavis Fornier told the three cops when they visited her home midmorning on Saturday.

Harrison's town clerk relayed as best she could the events of Fenton's visit to the town offices on Friday, telling them of his interest in the town's tax map, and Jonah's properties in particular.

Halliway wanted to know if Fenton had mentioned anything about the Thompsons' place on Edes Falls.

"No, not a word," she answered.

She doubted Fenton ever went to McGilicutty's Realty, or the Thompsons' for that matter. Hill and Halliway doubted it too. "I'll tell you where I think you'll find him," she said. "The Roberts family farm. *That's* where that boy is."

"Nice woman," Halliway said after the three men left the Fornier home.

"So what do you want to do?" Boyd asked.

"I know what *I* want to do," Hill said from in back of the cruiser.

"Let me guess," Halliway said. "You want to visit the farm."

Hill smiled. "Great minds think alike."

It was almost 1:00 P.M. when Captain Boyd pulled his cruiser into the loop in front of the Roberts family farmhouse. The three men had stopped by McGilicutty's Realty in town and the Thompsons' on Edes Falls, just to be sure. Not surprisingly, Mavis Fornier's hunch had been correct. No one at either location had ever seen the man whose photos the police showed them. At least not in person. When they came up empty-handed both places, they made a beeline to the farm.

"Looks quiet," Boyd said, cutting the engine to his cruiser.

"Why am I not surprised?" Halliway said quietly, opening his door and stepping out of the car. "Where first?"

Boyd shrugged his shoulders, looking at Hill. "The barn?"

Halliway reached underneath the left side of his jacket and pulled his semiautomatic from its holster. Walking toward the barn he positioned himself on the left side of its doors. He held his gun, muzzle up, and motioned with his left hand for Hill to take a spot to the right. He pointed first to Boyd, then to the rear of the barn. No sense all three men entering from one side while the other remained unguarded.

Boyd scurried off down the side of the large, windworn building. When everyone was in place Halliway nodded to Hill, pointing to the barn's large doors. Hill quickly stepped in front of them, removed the two-by-four, and laboriously swung the right one open, leaping back out of the way.

Both men stood still . . . waiting. Nothing. Halliway stepped forward and grabbed the inside of the left door and pulled on it, he too taking cover behind it as it swung open. The two men stood on either side of the open barn doors now, peering out to one another from behind the ends of each. Halliway held up two fingers and the thumb of his left hand, Hill nodding acknowledgment. Slowly, one at a time, he brought down each digit. On the last drop they both whipped around the ends of the doors, guns drawn, kneeling in front of the huge open expanse. Fenton's Bonneville stared both of them in the face.

Their eyes scanned every crevice visible to the naked eye. When satisfied there was nothing moving in the barn, or at least nothing that could be seen from where they stood, Halliway rose and slowly walked inside the barn. He kept to the left of the Bonneville, feeling its slightly snow-covered hood with his hands for warmth. Hill followed suit, turning to look at the farmhouse, just to make sure they weren't blindsided.

Halliway took the left of the barn, Hill the right. They navigated their way through the old barn's dusty antique inventory, stepping over rotting piles of lumber, old bikes, lawn mowers, tools, crates and boxes. Both men held their weapons up, coming upon each opening and hidden space with cautious stealth.

In just over ten minutes the search was complete. Halliway and Hill hooked up at the far end of the barn.

"Nothing," Hill said.

"Anything?" Halliway asked Boyd, sticking his head out the opening to the rear.

Boyd shook his head.

"Come on around," Halliway said to him, looking up at the ancient timbers of the barn roof ten feet above. "Let's have a look upstairs."

He and Hill walked back toward the front as quickly as they could through the maze. Boyd beat them to it, watching them as they approached.

"Anything?" he asked quietly.

Both men shook their heads. Halliway pointed up to the hayloft. They'd already been stung this way once before. They weren't about to let it happen to them again. Before stepping on the wooden ladder up to the hay loft, Halliway leaned over and grabbed an old, rusty coffee can. Climbing headfirst into the loft made him

482

completely vulnerable. His stomach churned with anxiety. He stepped on the first rung and started up, followed by Hill.

He could just see it now: like the last soldier killed by the last bullet fired in a war that was effectively over, he could envision being this close to the end, on his last case, and buying a quick trip to a long dirt nap. Just before reaching the opening to the loft, he tossed the coffee can up through the hole, hoping he might scare whoever lay in wait to react. When nothing happened, he poked his head up, a few inches at first, looking in all directions. Hill stood on the ladder, his hands a rung below Halliway's feet.

Halliway scurried through the opening as fast as he could and took shelter behind an old mouse-ridden bale of hay. Hill came up right after him, doing the same with a bale opposite his partner. They didn't need to speak. They knew each other too well. They looked at each other, rose in unison, and began searching through the hayloft. Hill turned around, walking backwards slowly, looking up at the rafters. They climbed up piles of hay, seven or eight feet tall, occasionally startled by field mice hastily seeking shelter from the first humans they had no doubt ever seen.

When the search was complete, Halliway walked back to the opening, picked up his coffee can, and handed it to Hill. He pointed to the wooden ladder leading to the two-hundred-year-old cupola on top of the barn. It didn't need to be said. It was Hill's turn. He took the ladder first. Just before reaching the top, he tossed the can into the cupola, accidentally shattering one of its window panes.

He poked his head up slowly and crawled through the hole, standing on the small platform of hand-hewn wood. He was able to see in all directions. Too bad the weather was so poor.

"What do you see?" Halliway asked, a little louder now. It was obvious the barn was empty.

"Not much!" Hill shouted down. "Snow makes it kind of tough, but I think we got a nice set of prints heading down the pasture toward the woods in back!"

"Scott!" Halliway screamed up. "He's headed toward the woods. Let's go!"

The two men climbed down the ladder to the barn below, joining Boyd leaning against the side of the Bonneville.

"Tom, follow us. I think we got him," Halliway said, walking quickly out of the garage and around the side of the farmhouse. Approaching the back, they stood still for a moment, visually following the footprints down through the fields.

They were close now. They could feel it. The three men followed the tracks to the pastures below. The lower one was obviously a favorite trekking ground for hunters. As they traversed the slick and bumpy earth, it became obvious that Fenton's were not the only tracks. There were tracks everywhere, heading in all directions. Some more covered with snow than others, but still, it was impossible to know whose were whose. The only way they could follow him was to break up. A decision had to be made.

"Shit," Halliway said, standing in the trodden snow, trying to figure the best course of action. "That's it," he said, turning around. "Tom, we need a command post, ASAP." He walked back toward the farmhouse, passing the two men who had just been following him.

Boyd turned also, giving Hill a look as he passed. Hill shrugged his shoulders, as if to say, What can I say, he's a man on a mission. The two men followed Halliway to the barn and stood in a circle at the head of the Bonneville.

"He's in those woods, Tom," Halliway said. "And if I have anything to say about it, he isn't coming out unless he's either in a bag or shackled like an animal. I want every available man you have. Let's set up a command post here at the farm. How do you want to handle this?"

"Well," Boyd started, "first we contact my commanding officer at the barracks. We can't go sendin' a hundred men into those woods. It'd be a nightmare. We need bloodhounds."

"How soon can you get them?" Hill asked.

Boyd looked at his watch. "Well . . . let's see. It's after

three. I know the sheriff's got a couple. So do the game wardens. I know we've got at least two. I think we can have six to eight dogs out here in an hour. Two hours max."

Halliway clapped his hands twice. "Let's move. Time's a wastin'."

Boyd ran back to the cruiser, sitting in the front seat, legs hung over the side. "Dispatch, this is twenty-eight."

"Ten three, twenty-eight."

"We've located Montague in the woods outside Harrison."

"Ten four, twenty-eight. What's your ten twenty?" he asked.

"We're at the Roberts farm on Carsley Road. About halfway between Edes Falls and Maple Ridge. It's the only farmhouse on the north side of the road."

"Ten four."

"Spence, here's what we need," Boyd said, looking up at Halliway standing above him now. "Hold on, dispatch," he said, releasing the button on the mike. "It's your call, Lieutenant."

Halliway leaned with one hand on the open door and another on the roof. "Tell him we need to form a perimeter around the entire Roberts property. We'll need every free man he can shake loose, locals, sheriffs, game wardens, state police. Also tell him we need dogs. As many as he can find. And we need them here yesterday."

"Dispatch."

"Ten three, twenty-eight."

"We need every available man you can muster: sheriffs, game wardens, local police, as many of our boys as you can find. And Spence . . . no sirens. Repeat. No sirens. We also need trackers. Lots of 'em. Every one you can get your hands on. We need them now. Hold on, dispatch," Boyd said again, releasing the mike to hear what Halliway was trying to say to him.

"What's that?" he asked Halliway.

"Do you have a chopper?"

"Sort of," Boyd answered. "It's not really a chopper, it's a Cessna one thirty-five."

"On call?"

"State police," Boyd answered.

"State police pilot?" Halliway asked.

Boyd nodded his head.

"Good. Get it. We can use it to monitor the open end of the box. Hand me that map," he said, pointing to the US Geological Survey map lying on the cruiser's front seat.

Boyd turned and retrieved it. "It won't be long and it's going to start gettin' dark, Lieutenant" he said, handing it to Halliway.

"What time?"

Boyd kind of shook his head and shoulders back and forth. "Fivish. Either side. Much past then and a plane's gonna be pretty useless."

"Okay, we got approximately one and a half miles to cover between Maple Ridge and Edes Falls, on the north border of the property line," Halliway said, pointing to the map he'd laid out on the cruiser's hood. "The other three sides are bordered by road. Tell him to get a map. Show him the exact area we need the plane to watch."

"This should be fun over the radio," Boyd said smiling. "Dispatch, twenty-eight."

"Ten three, twenty-eight."

"Get ahold of Phil in South Portland. Tell him to get the Cessna out here. And Spence, grab a survey will ya? I need to show you the area we need him to cover."

"Hold on."

Boyd looked up at Halliway. Hill was busy studying the map on the hood. "I'm waiting. He's getting a map," Boyd said to them.

Halliway nodded his head in acknowledgment. "I can hear a chain saw out there," he said.

"I know. I hear it too."

"So do I," Hill added, looking up.

"You think it's Roberts?" Halliway asked.

"Could be."

"Get in touch with the detail at Roberts's place. Let them know what's going on. They've got to have a man with him. Get him out of there. Pronto."

Boyd held up a finger as dispatch came back. "Ten three, twenty-eight," the dispatcher said.

As best he could, Boyd walked the desk sergeant through the measurements of the area. It wasn't much trouble getting him to find the spot where they stood. The desk sergeant could easily see the lone black dot on his map. The touchier part for both men was trying to figure out just how far north of Carsley the plane should cover. They agreed on a distance which the dispatcher marked on his map with a pen, signing off to call the pilot. He lived less than five minutes from the Portland International Jetport. Not by coincidence.

A few minutes later the dispatcher was back. "Twenty-eight, this is dispatch."

"Ten three."

"Plane's on its way."

"Good," Halliway said. "Tell him we need a command post set up here at the farm. I assume you've got procedure to handle different agencies from a chain of command viewpoint?" he asked.

For the first time, Boyd was a little miffed. *No, we're not that smart up here.* "Of course," he said.

The dispatcher was waiting. "Hold on, Spence," Boyd said.

"Use it," Halliway said.

Maine has one of the most sophisticated cellular networks in the country—superior to New York's or Connecticut's. Hence, Maine law enforcement has state-wide car-to-car radio capabilities. Known as state-wide, it bypasses each department's frequency and allows vehicle-to-vehicle, intra-agency communication.

"Spence, get everyone involved to go state-wide. I got to be able to talk to them."

"Ten four."

Boyd was still seated. He stared into Halliway's face and thought he caught a wisp of worry in his eyes. He was out of his element and knew it. "There's a lot of road here, Tom. How do you suggest we cover it?"

"It's all a function of how many men we can get up here and how quickly. But I'm guessing we'll have forty, maybe fifty men in less than half an hour. With that many men we can set up a pretty good barrier around the perimeter. I'd place a unit every hundred, hundred and fifty yards, and tell them to stay put with their eyes peeled."

"Sounds good to me. Scott? Any problems with that?"

"It works in my book," Hill said.

"Do it," Halliway said.

"Spence, you with me?" Boyd asked.

"Ten three."

"Okay, listen hard. We need to set up a command post here at the farm, ten eighteen. It'd be best to have Walters in charge of the CP, but it'll take him too long to get here. We'll have forty cruisers here sooner than he can be here. Tell him what's up, and to get here ASAP. I'll run the CP until he arrives. Get the mobile command on its way. I'll make do with what I've got until it arrives. Also, get in touch with the detail at Roberts's place. Let them know what's going on. We can hear a chain saw in the woods out there. If that's Roberts, get him out of there now."

Dispatch responded. "Ten four. About the Roberts detail, Tom. Ahh . . . apparently you . . ."

There was a tension in the air, a thick and menacing feel that permeated everyone's actions and thoughts. The battle was about to begin, and though they were many and Fenton was just one, still there lingered in the recesses of their minds the worry that brains usually beat brawn.

"Hang on, Spence," Boyd said, interrupted yet again by Halliway's attempt at communication while he was on the radio. Boyd stretched his patience to keep Halliway's interruptions from getting the better of him.

"Ten four," dispatch responded.

I can only listen to one of you at once. "I'm sorry, I didn't catch that," he said, looking up at Halliway, taking a long, deep breath.

"What about firepower? Let's get some sniper rifles out here with night vision scopes."

Boyd depressed the mike, releasing it again as Halliway began. "Oh, and no Magnums. Have 'em bring

Savages or Winchesters. I want to take him out of there alive," Halliway added.

Not that Boyd could tell the difference. Sure, a Magnum's going to take someone's arm off if it hits right, but it's not like a direct hit with a Winchester or a Savage was going to work wonders for someone's pulse. Still, he was willing to let Halliway run the show. Boyd could sense there was a good deal of emotion wrapped up in this for both men. He was willing to play their game. To a point.

"Spence, let's be sure to get some sniper rifles out here with night vision scopes. Preferably Savages and/or Winchesters. No Magnums," Boyd added for Halliway's benefit. "We want the boy alive."

"Ten four."

"Any questions?"

"Negative. But about Roberts's detail . . . There's been some changes."

"Like what?" Boyd asked.

"Apparently, Spowart took deathly sick. We're not sure how, but he's almost dead, Tom. Fran and Bob ran him to Bridgton."

"Almost dead?" he asked, frowning, looking beyond Halliway at the barn.

Hill looked at Boyd through the windshield, then caught Halliway's eyes. A cop down anywhere is always a concern for another cop.

"It doesn't look good, Tom."

"Jesus. You hear anything from the hospital yet?" Boyd asked.

"Negative. Only that he's in emergency."

Damn. "Who's mindin' the store?"

"Stickney's still there. Hank's there also."

"Ten four. Hank's got the cruiser, right?"

"Affirmative."

"Reach him, Spence. If Roberts is in the woods, Stickney's with him. They wouldn't leave him out there alone, and Hank's not on the detail. Tell him to get Roberts out of those woods now."

"Ten four."

"Can you think of anything we left out, Spence?"

"Only that I think we should request every agency to bring as many night vision goggles as they can get."

Boyd looked up at Halliway. He was nodding his head vigorously. "Good one, Spence. Now get busy. You got work to do."

"Ten four."

Halliway chuckled and shook his head slightly. Hill glanced up from the map, looking at Boyd through the windshield. He was smiling.

"You boys are a touch more laid back here than where we come from," Halliway said.

"Maybe," Boyd said, rising from his seat. "But don't let it fool you. This asshole's gonna wish you caught him before he ever set eyes on this state."

Hill glanced at his partner. "Ouch," he said.

———————

Perspiration covered Jonah's face, mixing with the snow that had worked its way down through the trees. Jonah laid the idling chain saw on a large rock and removed his gloves. He bent over, curling his forefingers over his eyebrows, wiping away the moisture they had collected. He dabbed his forehead with the arm of his flannel shirt and ran his fingers through his hair.

Where the hell was Stickney? He'd been gone for some time now. Jonah wasn't sure just how long, but it sure seemed longer than he'd anticipated. He looked at his watch. It was after 2:00 P.M. Christ, Stickney had been gone well over half an hour. Jonah was so wrapped up in his project he hadn't even noticed the time flying by.

What is going on? Had Stickney finally decided that Jonah was right? Had he gotten too damn bored lifting trees from one spot to another and decided to hang back at the house? Certainly Cunningham would know that he'd come back to the house, if in fact he had. Jonah couldn't see Cunningham acquiescing and letting him stay there—not without replacing him with someone else.

Something didn't fit. Something was definitely wrong. These guys were too good. They were too professional to just all of a sudden slough off like this. For a fleeting instant Jonah worried that he was now alone in the woods. A wave of anxiety slowly embraced him, the uneasiness chilling his spine, like a spider crawling up his back.

Come on now, get a grip. There's some logical explanation. You just don't know what it is. He'll be back sooner than you think, no doubt with some ridiculous excuse. Maybe he got lost in the woods. Maybe he got a case of the runs. Yeah, but Cunningham would have replaced him with someone else if he'd taken ill. And certainly whoever that was would have followed the sound of the chain saw to Jonah's exact spot. Hell, a cow could find me out here. Don't be so paranoid. Shit, a couple of hours ago you were begging to be left alone, and now you're wishing the guy would come back. What's it gonna be, boy? You can't have it both ways.

Jonah leaned against a tree, watching the snow fall through its branches, blanketing everything with a pristine layer of sparkling white. As Jonah thought it through, he realized it wasn't the being alone that bothered him. Hell, he didn't care if Stickney came back just to tell him he was leaving. In fact, he thought he would like that. No, it wasn't that he was alone, it was that Stickney had just disappeared. It ran against everything he told Jonah at the entrance to the trail. It just didn't jibe. He tried to ignore it, but his mind wasn't bowing on this one. Something was wrong.

He smiled for some strange reason, picturing the robot on "Lost in Space" waving its arms madly, droning the words "Danger, Danger, Danger." He hadn't thought of that in decades. He shook his head and rubbed his hair back with his left hand. *The mind's a strange thing.*

The chain saw lay idling as he looked around the woods. There was no life anywhere to be seen. At least nothing mobile. Jonah decided to keep on cutting, more to convince himself he wasn't going to succumb to Fenton's game of terror than because he believed he was safer here than just about anywhere else on earth.

He put his gloves back on, leaned over, and picked up the chain saw, depressing the finger trigger a couple of times to see how much oil spurted out from the tip of the blurring blade. He let the blade stop, hung the saw at his side, and walked a few yards to an huge old fir that lay across the route he had chosen for the bridle path. He stood back for a moment, eyeing the tree. It had to be three feet in diameter. He wasn't sure he felt like tackling it. It had somehow uprooted, probably in the big storm that passed through back in October. The tree's dirt-covered roots stuck up and out, like a giant saucer with black spaghetti spilling over its sides.

He thought of moving the path farther to the left, around the tree's exposed roots. But even in the snow, Jonah could see the entire section to his left was swamp. It would require far more effort to make passable than removing the tree. The first ten feet or so from the roots up were bare. The branches didn't start until well past the point where he felt the path should go. Jonah wiped snow away from the massive trunk with his gloved left hand, clearing a space long and wide enough to get a good view of the chain's progress.

Holding the saw in front of him he pulled the handle trigger firmly, slowly at first, working up to a smooth pace. Placing the teeth of the saw on the trunk, he began what would no doubt be a lengthy and tiresome cut. The tree had not been dead long enough to dry. It was still green, and cutting green trees is like cutting chewing gum.

He worked the blade of the saw with precision, moving it back and forth, pushing forward with his left hand, then pulling down with his right—occasionally working the middle of the expanding incision with the very tip of his blade. The sound was deafening. Only Jonah's plugs would keep his eardrums from ringing for a week. Wood chips flew everywhere, covering the surrounding snow with a layer of yellowish-white, sappy fragments.

He'd been out here for a few hours now. His saw was getting dull, and he wished now he'd tackled this tree first, when the blade was still razor sharp. He had a file in the barn, but with all the bullshit taking place in his life, he'd forgotten to bring it. Jonah thought for a minute it might be worth taking the saw in to sharpen it, but this was clearly one of those times when it was six of one, half dozen of the other. In the time it would take to go back and sharpen the saw he could be nearly done. *Anyway, I've already started. I'm not stopping now.*

He depressed the trigger, walked around the expanse of the roots, wiping snow from the back side of the cut. He placed a foot on the tree for balance, working the sticky wound ever deeper. Jonah wanted to inspect how far he'd come and brush some of the chips away. He was giving the saw one last, deep push when the blade suddenly disengaged from its arm.

"Shit!"

A trip to the barn was inevitable now. It was just as well. It would give him the opportunity to replace the chain before finishing the tree—not to mention checking up on Stickney. It was good something had forced the issue. Stickney was taking longer than he liked.

He brushed the chips away with his gloved hands, blowing into the crevice to check for depth. Jonah took off his gloves and laid them on the tree. He was wiping perspiration off his forehead with the right arm of his flannel shirt when a movement through the trees twenty yards ahead of him caught his eye. It looked like a dark spider crawling on a whitewashed wall. The movement from tree to tree was unmistakable.

He smiled. *It's about fucking time. I was beginning to think you'd blown me off.* He stood, watching the trees, waiting for Stickney to become visible. Time passed. Nothing moved. He had seen something move in the trees, hadn't he? He knew he had. He'd spent the last six years of his life out here in these woods. He knew movement in them when he saw it. But there was nothing.

He slid down the end of the trunk, his mind subconsciously keeping the tree between himself and the spot in the distance at which he stared. *Maybe it was a deer.* His eyes penetrated into the woods beyond, darting from tree to tree. He kept his body still. Jonah realized he wasn't breathing and closed his eyes long enough to take a deep breath. Exhaling, he opened them just in time to see it again. This time, he thought he knew which tree whatever it was had dashed behind. It sure as hell wasn't any deer.

He thought for a moment that maybe the cops had decided to play a little joke on him—break up the monotony by ambushing him. Maybe these battle-hardened men thought it would be funny to see a grown man piss in his pants. *Very funny.*

"Hey, Stickney!" he called out. "Cut the shit! I can see you plain as day!"

There was no response. No movement. What the hell was going on? A sense of terror gripped him, his breath coming raw in his throat.

"Stickney! Come on, I'm serious! I'm not in the mood for fun and games! Don't fuck around! Get over here, will ya? I need your help!"

Oh, oh. This didn't feel right. First Stickney tells him he's got to keep his eyes on him whether he liked it or not. Then he leaves for the better part of an hour, and now someone was sneaking up on him through the woods, making every effort not to be seen.

Jonah screamed almost gutturally. "Hey, Stickney, you asshole! I'm serious! Cut the shit!" he yelled, realizing now he was wasting his breath.

His eyes were transfixed with horror as he peered through the woods in front of him. A face appeared from behind a tree, and not the tree he'd thought, either. Whoever it was, didn't pull back right away. The face seemed almost a surreal appendage to the tree as it just hung there smiling . . . not moving . . . just smiling.

"Holy shit," Jonah whispered to himself, ducking down behind the tree. "Holy shit," he said again, as the blood drained from his face. *Okay, okay, okay. Think. Think.*

He ran his fingers through his hair, his temples burning with heat. His heart was palpitating madly; Jonah thought it would pound out of his chest. *I can't believe I'm out here by myself, and all I've got is a dead chain saw and a fucking ax.* His back was to the tree trunk now. Suddenly he realized he couldn't see whoever it was, squatting as he was behind the fir. He scurried down the trunk to his right a bit, poking his head up through the still-green branches, hoping they would offer enough camouflage. But his quarry was gone.

Jonah scanned the woods before him, moving his body slightly from left to right in an effort to see. His eyes darted about maniacally, picking imaginary villains out of the snow. He was in deep shit now and he knew it. He was unarmed, in the woods, stalked by some as yet unknown man, and Jonah didn't even know where he was. *It had to be Fenton. Who else could it be? But how could that be? How the hell had Fenton gotten by three cops?* He strained his corneas to see, expanding his field of vision farther to the left and right. He felt naked.

Jonah jumped as he heard the sound of an owl come from somewhere in front of him. It sounded closer than he'd like. He pressed his chest against the massive cord of timber before him.

"Whooo. Whooo," came the sound floating through the snow.

"Fuck you!" Jonah screamed over the trunk.

"Whooo. Whooo."

Suddenly his mind-set changed. *It's time. At least we're going to get this nightmare over with. One way or another, it ends today.* Jonah thought back to his father sitting on the edge of his bed. He could hear his voice clearly now. "Jonah, son, what's the worst thing that can happen?" Jonah knew the answer today and didn't much like it. But still, he didn't care. After today, at least, it would be over.

He stood defiantly, cupping his mouth to be heard. "Montague! If that's you, stop hiding like some fucking mouse and show your face where I can see you, you son of a bitch! You want to get it on. Then let's get it on! Right here! Right now! Just you and me! May the best man win!"

"The best man's already won!" a voice cried back. "You're dead, friend, and you don't even know it!"

Who the hell was this? Jonah hadn't heard Montague's voice in twenty years. "I'm shaking now you little fuck!"

"Not yet, you're not! Not like you and David made me!"

It *was* Montague! Jonah was suddenly filled with

courage *and* rage. The enemy was known now. Somehow, with the mystery gone, the terror evaporated for him also. *Let go, let God.*

Jonah prayed quickly. "God," he said quietly. "I don't ask you for much, but I'm asking you now. Please give me the strength to escape this psycho. He killed my best friend. It's my turn now. I leave it in your hands."

At that, Jonah bolted to his left, hurtling himself with surprising speed toward the woods, in the direction of the family farmhouse. He could see the stone wall about twenty yards in front of him. Nothing would stop him from getting there. Nothing but God—or a bullet. He ducked low branches and jumped deadwood, falling on his face in a thicket of sharp, dry tree limbs.

"Shit!" he cried.

He didn't know it, but blood streamed down his forehead now.

—◆◆◆—

Trooper Henry Fairchild was standing at the entrance to the barn, inspecting a new dung rake. The end of it was plastic. When plastic dung rakes first came out, choruses of criticism from the old guard were unanimous. It was too light, they said. Now, almost everybody used one. He was turning it over in his hands, pretending to use it, when the call came in on his radio.

"Unit Twelve, this is dispatch. Acknowledge."

Fairchild dropped the rake where he stood. He didn't bother running to his cruiser. He grabbed the radio off his holster and responded.

"This is Twelve. Ten three, Spence."

"Hank, all hell's breakin' loose over at the Roberts farm."

"I'm at the Roberts farm, Spence. There's nothing doin' here."

"Negative, Hank. You're at Jonah's home. I mean the old family farm on the other end of the property. Over on Carsley."

"I copy. Ten three."

"Listen good, Hank. The two cops from Connecticut

are with Boyd over at the farm. They're bettin' the ranch Montague's in the woods someplace between their ten twenty and yours."

Fairchild walked toward his cruiser now. "Ten four. How far a distance is that?"

"A mile, give or take. Anyway, long story short, when Stick called me earlier, he said Roberts was in the woods. Is that his current ten twenty?"

Fairchild had already pieced it together. "Affirmative."

"Get him out of there now, Hank."

"Stick's with him," Fairchild said. "I can't reach him, Spence. Apparently his radio's out. He said something about his batteries being dead."

"All right then, you got to go get him. There's no other choice."

"That leaves the house and barn empty."

"That's not an issue now," Spencer said. "We got to get him out of those woods."

"Ten four. One problem, though. The chain saw's been runnin' since I got here. But it just stopped a few minutes ago. I haven't heard it since. I wouldn't have the slightest idea where to begin to look for them. And if Montague's in those woods, the last thing we want to be doin' is screaming back and forth to each other. Without the chain saw, I'll be like Helen Keller out there."

"How long ago did Stick go back out?"

"He just left."

"Can you follow his tracks?"

"Hope so. It's our only chance."

"Then get going. When you find Roberts, bring him back to the house, then drive him to the farm. They're setting up a CP there now. Everyone but the National Guard's gettin' called. We're ringing the perimeter with cruisers now."

"What about the north side?" Hank asked. "It's a mile of open woods."

"Phil's flyin' up now. He can cover it."

"Not for long, he can't. If we don't get him in the next couple o' hours, it's gonna be too dark for the plane to do any good."

"Right, so move. Oh, and Hank."

"Yeah."

"Command Post's in charge from here on out. Good luck."

"Ten four, Spence, I'll be back to you as soon as we get out."

"Negative. From now on you go directly to CP. Now go."

Fairchild threw his radio on the front seat, zipped up his leather jacket, put on his hat, and unlocked the shotgun from its holster on the dash. He filled his jacket pocket with extra shells, patted his 9mm Glock semiautomatic, and checked his extra ammo cartridge to make sure it was there. He was ready for battle if one came.

Without looking back, he jogged down the pasture toward the opening in the woods, following Stickney's footprints in the snow. He needed to move quickly and would have to call upon all his training to pull this off well. There were three men out there now. He could only shoot one. Fairchild's pulse quickened as his adrenal glands kicked in, sending nauseating spurts coursing through his veins.

He came upon the opening and stood motionless for a moment, trying to get a feel for the woods. He knew you can never take them lightly. Not in this state. Not in the snow. Every Mainer knows that. Fairchild stared down the open corridor, brushed thickly white with the falling snow. *This is where we separate the men from the boys.*

He followed the tracks down the path, stopping occasionally to look around. There was a certain clamor in the still quiet of the woods. He inhaled, held his breath, and listened. His own heart and the soft sound of falling snow were the only sounds disturbing the placid calm. He could hear the sound of a hundred million snowflakes settling lightly on the trees, like the powdered sugar his grandmother used to sprinkle on her morning cereal. Any other time he would have enjoyed the moment.

Fairchild continued, dreading the point at which the tracks would veer off toward the woods. Up until now everything had been easy. Nothing stood in his way, so he was able to focus entirely on the immediate area of the trees around him. He knew that once he stepped off the trail he would have to battle branches and fallen trees, swamp and rocks. His shotgun wouldn't make it any easier.

From that moment on, he'd need to pay attention to what stood immediately in front of him. Not that he felt he couldn't do it. After all, he'd hunted deer from the time he was ten. There was an art to navigating the denseness of the woods while keeping an eye on all that surrounded you. He felt confident no one could do it better. Still, deer don't carry guns.

Fairchild came upon the bridge Jonah had built, not giving it a second thought. A few yards past it, he noticed the tractor parked in the path and Stickney's tracks shift direction toward the left, into the woods. *Here we go.* He ducked a few yards into the thickness of the trees, stopping just long enough to check the woods behind him. He stood still, barely breathing, looking in all directions. It would be his last chance to check this flank.

You got to move, boy. You don't have much time. He ducked under a low-hanging branch, coming up on the other side, and began tracking the footsteps in the snow. He hunted like a predator one moment, scanning his keen eyes around him like prey the next. He followed the footprints sharply left, his bowels nearly letting loose as he walked right into Stickney's feet dangling in the air.

Fairchild looked up to see his colleague hanging from a limb, desperately gasping for breath, his hands digging into his bleeding throat in a futile effort to loosen the nylon rope's hold from his neck. He was nude. Someone had taken his uniform.

In a moment of paralyzing terror, Fairchild's mind registered a barrage of simultaneous thoughts, all of them tearing through his head with meteoric speed. In a fleeting second, his eyes told his brain that his fellow trooper was hanging from a tree, that Fenton had been here, that he might be here still, that Stickney was still alive, and that he had to get him down.

He didn't say a word. Fairchild's eyes followed the nylon rope over the limb and down the back side of the tree to a smaller tree a few feet beyond. On pure instinct, he ran to the tree to which the rope was tied, pulled out a pocket knife, and sliced it through with one quick, fluid motion. A second after his right hand yanked the knife nearly back to his shoulder he heard the thud of Stickney's body hitting the ground. He didn't give much thought to his drop. That was the least of both of their worries.

What kills victims of hanging, at least the official kind, is the snap of the neck. If the drop is long enough, the spine simply lacks the strength to counter the sheer weight of the body. But if someone is pulled up by the neck, there is no drop. They suffer instead the agonizingly slow death of asphyxiation.

Hank ran around the larger tree, hurrying to aid his friend. As he knelt, he reached for his radio. *Shit!* He'd left it in his cruiser.

Stickney was coughing uncontrollably. He lay on his back, rubbing his neck with the fingers of both hands. His face had turned blue.

Kneeling at his side, Fairchild whispered to his colleague, wrapping his jacket around him. "Jesus Christ, Stick. What the fuck happened?"

Stickney tried to talk. The pain was overpowering. He winced as he spoke. "He whacked me . . ." he said in a thick, raspy voice, barely able to move his lips.

Hank leaned down closer to hear him, eyeing the woods beyond. "What?" he asked.

"He whacked me on the . . ." was all Fairchild heard before his friend lost consciousness.

"Dammit," Fairchild said, leaning on one knee, scanning the woods around him.

What should he do now? Jonah was out here somewhere, no doubt with this psycho on his tail. For all he knew, he was already dead. That whole part of the equation was an enigma. What was clear was that a trooper was down . . . and hurting . . . possibly dying. He had to get him medical attention. That much was nonnegotiable. He thought for a moment. How should he handle this? His colleague had to come first, but his professionalism wouldn't let him just walk away from the target of the detail.

Jonah was in very serious danger, if he was alive at all. Hank knew it was quite possible he was the only person in the world who could still save him. But what if he left Stickney lying in the snow, and he didn't make it? Christ, he could freeze to death. How would he ever live with himself? How could he attend the funeral, look his wife and children in the eyes, knowing he alone could have saved his life? No tribunal in the world would fault him for tending to his colleague first. Every cop learns early in their training that they have to look out for each other. No one else gives a shit.

Fairchild hoisted Stickney over his right shoulder, stood for a moment to glance around the woods, and took off as quickly as he could in the direction of the bridle path. Jonah would have to fend for himself, at least for the time being. A cop was down.

With a level of strength only crisis breeds, Hank raced through the woods with surprising speed, and even faster once he reached the bridle path. He thought momentarily of using the tractor but knew he could run faster than that, even with Stickney on his back, and even in the snow. Anyway, tractors aren't exactly made for stealth.

Once out of the woods, Fairchild made it up the slight hill of the pasture in less than two minutes, and threw his colleague in the passenger seat of his cruiser. He turned the ignition, flipping the heat on as high as it would go, and ran to the trunk to get a blanket. He slid into the driver's seat, covered Stickney, and whipped his cruiser in reverse, grabbing the mike on his dash with his free hand.

"CP, this is Hank Fairchild at the Roberts's residence. We have a trooper down. Repeat. Trooper down. It's Stickney. I found him hanging from a tree. He's still alive, but hurting. I'm taking him to Bridgton now."

Jesus. "Ten four," Boyd said.

"One more thing," Fairchild said, racing down the

drive. "He's nude. Weapon and uniform nowhere to be found. Be advised, perp may be dressed as a police officer. Repeat. Perp may be dressed as a police officer."

"Ten four," Boyd said, replacing his mike, rubbing his temples with his thumb and forefinger. *This is unfucking believable.* He put both his hands on the steering wheel of his cruiser, staring out toward the barn. "This can't be happening," he said.

—⁓—

One by one, various law enforcement agency cruisers pulled up to the Roberts family homestead. They started as a trickle at first. A couple of state police cruisers and a Cumberland County sheriff were the first to respond. The two state police vehicles pulled into the opposite end of the loop, closest to the barn. The sheriff pulled up on the side of the road.

They approached Captain Boyd standing by the front door of his cruiser. Halliway and Hill stood with him. Hill took a drag from a Camel and exhaled, watching its gray smoke waft into the thick flakes of snow in front of him. Pleasantries were exchanged as the police officers introduced themselves to one another. Boyd described the situation, explaining the plan to ring the perimeter of the Roberts property.

"We'll have more cops here than we can handle in the next half hour," Boyd said to Halliway. "I was thinking we just start fanning them out from here and keep looping cruisers around the perimeter as they show. You got a better plan?" he asked.

Halliway shrugged his shoulders, looking at Hill. "Sounds good to me."

"Me too," Hill added.

"Okay, here's what we do, guys . . ." Boyd said, explaining the plan to the three officers standing in front of him. He sent the sheriff off to the right of the farmhouse, about a hundred yards down Carsley. The two state troopers he sent off to the left, spaced evenly apart.

"Go state-wide, gentlemen," he said, wrapping up his instructions. "And keep your eyes peeled. If you got night vision goggles, get 'em out. There's no telling where he'll emerge. You can assume he is armed and extremely dangerous. And . . . we have reason to believe he may be dressed as a police officer."

"You're joking, right?" someone asked.

"I'm dead serious."

On Halliway's advice he reported the same information to Phil in the plane. "We want to know if you see anyone crossing that northern boundary, Phil. Policeman or otherwise. Got it?"

"A chipmunk's not gettin' out of there," Phil replied.

The perimeter ring had begun. Like constructing a thousand-piece jigsaw puzzle, the hardest part was always the beginning. Once you have something to build on, it always seems to move quicker from there. Boyd got on his mike, going state-wide for the first time.

"Command Post to all responding officers. This is Captain Thomas Boyd of the Maine state police. I'm your CP contact until my CO arrives. We're going to break out in teams of two. If you are approaching from the east, you're now a member of team one. If you are approaching from the west, you're now on team two. Any questions?"

"If I'm coming from the east, what team is that again?" someone asked.

Boyd repeated his instructions, asking again if anyone had questions. "Okay, time's an issue guys, so let's move. All team one and team two members, listen up, please. Here's the plan. The idea is to set up a perimeter around the Roberts property. We're placing cruisers every hundred yards or so the entire length of Carsley Road, then north up Edes Falls and Maple Ridge. Team one, approach on Carsley until you see a cruiser, and set up camp a football field or so away from it. Whoever gets to Carsley last, stake out the corner. If you get to Carsley and there's a cruiser there, then continue north on Maple Ridge. Same routine, same distance. You should be able to plainly see the vehicle ahead of you. If you can't, then you are too far away. If there's a hill, then set up on the hill. No blind spots. As you settle in, radio your approximate ten twenty. Any questions?"

"How far up Maple Ridge do you want us to go?" someone asked.

"Stand by," Boyd said, looking at Halliway. "How far north did we tell Spence when he called Phil?" Boyd asked.

"What was it, Scott?" Halliway asked Hill. "A half mile, right?"

"Yeah. Half mile," Hill said, looking at Boyd.

"CP to team one. Cover Maple Ridge a little over a half mile north of Carsley. You may need to drive down to Carsley then watch the odometer on your way back. Questions, gentlemen?"

Silence.

"Team two. Same procedure. Ring Carsley spaced a hundred yards or so apart. Someone take the corner. Then north a little over half a mile on Edes Falls. No blind spots. Report ten twenties. Any questions?"

"What are our instructions if we spot the perp? A hundred yards is a long way. If he dashes between us, do we shoot?"

Good question. "Stand by," Boyd said. "Should we leave standing orders to shoot?" he asked Halliway.

"Damn it. There's no good answer here, I'm afraid," Halliway said to Boyd. "Scott, any words of wisdom?" Hill stubbed out his butt in the snow with the toe of his shoe. He stood facing his partner, his hands in his pockets. Halliway faced him, holding his right arm around his chest, his left elbow resting over his right arm, holding his jaw in the palm of his hand.

"It's your jurisdiction," Hill responded, looking at Boyd.

All three men knew these are the decisions that can come back to haunt you. An executive decision made in the heat of battle was always a possible career buster. Hill was willing to lose it all on this one. He didn't care anymore. He knew what he would order.

"I say if he tries to make a break for it, we drop him," Boyd finally said. "Identify ourselves, then shoot. Ask questions later. No way this asshole gets out of here tonight."

"Man after my own heart," Hill said.

"All right, I agree," Halliway said. "But follow me on this thought. Let's say he makes a run for it. It's conceivable he could be between two cruisers. You could have two cops shooting right at each other."

"That's just logistics, Ric," Hill said, shrugging his shoulders. "Make sure all the cruisers are parked on the inside of the road, closest to the property. Leave standing instructions to wait until he's in the road. The angles should work then."

"But we definitely shoot, right?" Halliway asked.

"That's my vote," Boyd said.

Halliway smiled faintly. "Shit, Captain, it's your show. Order it."

Boyd picked up the mike. "CP to teams one and two, you have standing instructions to shoot if necessary. Be sure you are parked on the inside of the road, closest to the property. The farther the better. Do not shoot unless he is in the road or farther. We want to avoid people firing at one another. Any questions?"

Silence.

"Good. If there's more cruisers than we need, then start filling in gaps. Space your vehicles accordingly. We got canines on the way. We're gonna start flushing him out shortly. I'll radio the general direction of the flush as the hounds' handlers report in. Stay put and *do not* go in the woods. Repeat. *Do not* go in the woods."

"What about lights?" someone asked.

"Stand by," Boyd said. "Shit, I hadn't thought about that. Ideas, gentlemen?"

"What do you suggest?" Halliway asked.

"I say we have all the cruisers face the same direction, lights on. Away from the farmhouse on Carsley, north on Edes Falls and Maple Ridge."

"Sounds like a plan," Halliway said.

Boyd was relaying instructions when he heard the wailing yelps of the first bloodhounds to arrive.

"About time," Hill said.

The light-blue K-9 unit station wagon pulled into the loop near the barn. Two men stepped out, dressed in fatigues and black army boots, with semiautomatic weapons strapped to their chests with shoulder holsters.

They walked to the rear of the car and began leashing two Irish wolfhounds in their metal cages.

The dogs jumped out of their skin, anxious to begin the chase. They were hungry for the hunt. When their handlers were satisfied they were properly secured, each man let his dog jump from the rear platform, holding his animal close on a short leash. They jumped and swirled, barking with earsplitting ferociousness. They were eager to perform the duties for which they were trained.

"Show 'em the car, will you, Lieutenant?" Boyd said.

Halliway approached the station wagon with Hill in tow. They could hear intermittent transmissions over the radio now as cruisers began reporting their locations back to the Command Post.

"Gentlemen," Halliway said, over the cacophony of screeching barks. "The perp's car is in here. Is that what you'd like to see?"

"That'll work just fine," one of the state police handlers said.

As they approached the barn, Boyd called out to Halliway. "Ric, I got the game wardens on the phone. Could you send one of those gentlemen over here, please?"

Halliway looked at them both. "Either one of you in charge?"

They looked at each other. "I'll go," one said.

The state police handler walked over to Boyd's cruiser. "Captain Thomas Boyd," he said, holding out a hand to the K-9 trooper.

"Sergeant Cal Berkshire, Captain. What 'ya need?"

"I got the wardens on the phone. They're looking for instructions. Should I bring 'em here?"

"There's no sense having more than one tracker from here. Can I talk to him?" Berkshire asked.

"Be my guest," Boyd said, handing Berkshire the mike.

"This is Sergeant Berkshire of the state police K-9 unit."

Most of the canine men in the state knew each other. "Hi, Cal. It's Matt."

"Hey, Matt. What's your ten twenty?"

"We're just looping around the lake now. We'll be there in ten minutes. If you're already there, it seems overkill."

"Roger that. Stand by, Matt," Berkshire said, looking at Boyd. "Captain, do you have maps of the property?"

Boyd called out to Hill toward the barn. "Scott! Where'd you put that survey?"

"It's on the floor in front. On the passenger side."

Boyd opened his door, reached in, and pulled it out, handing it to the state cop.

"Point out the perimeter to me, please, Captain," he said.

Boyd showed Berkshire where they were and outlined a rough triangle with the closed tip of his pen. "You got this whole length here, from Maple Ridge to Edes Falls, up about a half mile or so."

"Thanks," Berkshire said, depressing the mike. "Matt, you copy?"

"Ten three."

"You got Billy with you, right?"

"Always."

"Okay, take your dogs to the intersection of Carsley and Edes Falls. Measure half a mile up with your vehicle. See if you can place yourselves at equal distances from Carsley to the half mile marker. I'm following the tracks from here. I'll radio CP and let them know which direction we're heading once we get inside. Await further instructions from there."

"Ten four."

Contrary to the way they are depicted on TV, tracking dogs don't follow the scent they've been given. They can, and will, *if* it's the newest scent. If the tracks aren't virgin—that is, if there are different, newer tracks on top of the ones being followed, those are the ones the dogs lock on to. By definition, having more than one dog follow Fenton's tracks meant all but the lead dog would be following other scents. It simply wouldn't work. They'd need to ring the perimeter with the animals and slowly tighten the noose from different, and fresh, directions.

"You still want to see the car?" Halliway asked Berkshire as he approached the barn.

"We're here, might as well do it," he said.

Miraculously, abruptly, the dogs' yapping, which had so completely drowned out virtually every other noise, came to a halt as the handlers gave the orders for their respective dogs to heel. The two of them stood next to the car now, their dogs obediently sitting at their sides. They let them have free rein over the car. They jumped over the front seat and into the back and into the front seat again. Sniffing madly at every surface in the car. After a few minutes the dogs were leashed again and made to sit quietly next to their handlers.

Halliway and Hill stood by the car with the two men. Halliway filled the troopers in on the situation while they watched the dogs familiarize themselves with the smell of the interior of the car.

"What have we got?" one of them asked.

Halliway answered. "Perp's in his forties. Caucasian. Slight beard with short hair. May be dressed as a police officer."

"Yeah, we heard that on the way over," one of the men said, patting his dog on the side.

Halliway continued. "He's wanted in connection with five murders that we know of. One of them a police officer."

There was no better way to get a cop's attention. Hearing those words could make them take a great deal of interest in what could otherwise be a bitch of a detail.

"Is he armed?" one of them asked.

"We have to make that assumption," Halliway said. "I would say he is armed and extremely dangerous. If you find him, be very, very careful."

"Count on it," Berkshire said.

"I'd be concerned he'll kill your dogs," Halliway said.

The men stood, each one reflexively reaching down to pat his animal. "Ever seen a man tracked?" one of them asked.

"No," Halliway answered.

"Well, when you find him, you circle the dogs around

him. They'll be coming from every direction. He couldn't kill them all. No matter how hard he tries."

Berkshire chimed in. "He kills Lucky and it'll be the worst mistake he ever makes."

His partner nodded his head. Over the years these men form a bond with their animals that is very similar to the bond between human partners. Grown men have wept at the loss of their dog.

"How old are the tracks?" one of them asked Halliway.

He pursed his lips, shrugging his shoulders slightly. "Hard to say, really. Not that long. They were pretty fresh in the snow when we got here. An hour maybe."

The men looked at each other and smiled.

"Is that good?" Halliway asked.

"It'll work," one of them said.

"They're getting covered with snow," Halliway added.

"Not enough," one of them said.

His partner chimed in. "It's long enough to make me nervous. We need to move."

"Okay," Berkshire said. "Randy, take Soot to the Maple Ridge perimeter. CP will radio how to proceed."

"Roger," Berkshire's partner said, placing Soot in the front seat of the station wagon before driving away.

Halliway walked Berkshire and Lucky around the side of the house, Berkshire stopping at Boyd's cruiser just long enough to let him know he wanted to be informed the second another tracking team called in. He'd let him know where to place them.

They came to the expansive back pasture, Halliway showing Berkshire and his dog the footprints in the snow. They had begun to fade as they accumulated a new layer of snow. But that would be no obstacle. It would have to snow a hell of a lot more than this to keep these dogs from performing their task. Halliway explained that they believed those were Fenton's tracks and that he was somewhere in the woods between here and Edes Falls and Maple Ridge.

"I'm afraid it gets a little tangled with tracks further down," he said.

"Hunters?" Berkshire asked.

"Must be."

"If he's out there," Berkshire responded, "we'll find him."

"Good, because I'm gonna be right next to you," Halliway said.

"That makes two of us," Hill added.

Neither Halliway or Hill had planned on trekking in the Maine woods. Both wore slacks, tailored shirts, and street shoes. Halliway wore a sweater. Each wore a parka—their only accommodation to the Maine cold.

Berkshire looked at them both. "You guys aren't exactly dressed for this, you know?"

"Don't you worry about us," Halliway said. "Wild horses couldn't keep us out of those woods."

"Okay," Berkshire said, a bit skeptically. "Suit yourselves."

With that, they were gone. Berkshire's fatigue-clad body pulled mightily in an effort to keep his dog from dragging him face first into the woods.

Fenton stood behind a large maple, checking his .45. He was breathing deeply, his death instinct in full bloom. He peered from around the tree in the direction of the fallen fir where he'd last seen Jonah. There was nothing. He stood still for a moment thinking he'd see some movement.

After a short while he abandoned the vigil and began walking in a straight line toward his prey's last known location. He approached robotically, a maniacal smile pasted on his face. His time had come. The final moment of salvation was finally upon him. From this day forward it would be for fun—for lust of death. The inherent power and sensual beauty. But this . . . this was business. It was a job that had to be done. No matter what the cost or the consequences, Jonah Roberts would die today.

He walked along the snow-covered floor of the woods,

occasionally ducking beneath a hanging branch. He never looked down, not even once. Brushing against a tree or branch with his shin he would simply lift his foot, feeling his way with the heels of his boots. He eyed the fallen fir, his eyes locked on it like radar. Approaching closer, he switched his semiautomatic to his left hand and leaned down to pick up a medium-size rock with his right. He lobbed it grenade-like in the direction of the tree, watching with glee as it crashed down on the branches, falling on the opposite side of the trunk.

Fenton was disappointed. He felt sure that would have roused Jonah if he were still hiding there. He was only fifteen yards or so from the trunk of the fir. He picked up his pace, then slowed as he approached the upended roots. Crouching, he walked slowly now, one heel after the other. He crawled through the ditch left by the roots, peeking his head around the tree. Nothing.

"Shit," he whispered.

Fenton rose, walked to where Jonah had stood, and eyed the tracks leading off into the woods toward the rock wall. He followed them, not missing a beat. As he came upon the thicket of dead branches and tree limbs he was pleased to see tiny droplets of blood appear on the virgin white snow. The punishment had already begun. Fenton smiled.

"Jo-nah. I know you're out there," he crooned aloud, his voice a singsong rhythm.

Silence.

"Oh, Jo-nah. Come out, come out wherever you are."

There was a small clearing beyond the rock wall, clearly visible from his vantage point. There were no tracks through it. Fenton felt certain that Jonah lay somewhere behind the rock wall. What he did not know was how far down along the wall he had crawled. Was he directly in front of him? Had he scooted several yards beyond the spot where the tracks ended at the wall?

Fenton didn't want to risk scaling its three-foot height from the middle. He would be too vulnerable that way. After all, he thought it possible that Jonah could be armed. Not that it mattered. Fate was on his side. He

opted instead to approach the wall from fifteen or twenty
yards down. He figured he could walk its length from on
top, viewing both sides as he approached the spot where
the tracks had stopped in front.

As he began to make his way to his right he froze in
mid step, his right boot hovering above the snow. He
could hear it clearly now. *Was that a dog?* He stopped
and listened, holding his chin almost to his chest. That
was definitely a dog.

"Son of a bitch!" he cried.

So the newspaper story had been a ruse! The sons of
bitches were smarter than he gave them credit for.
Fleetingly, Fenton panicked, fearful now that they were
way ahead of him—that unwittingly he had walked right
into their trap. Above all else, he needed to escape
capture, at least long enough to ensure his final victory.

"Damn it!"

His mind raced with options as he tried to rethink his
movement through the woods. They'd be coming upon
the bridle path soon enough, eventually looping off to the
right and coming to the fir Jonah had tried to cut. He had
to move quickly now. There was no choice, no time for
calculations and experimentation. It was now or never.
Quite literally, do or die.

Fenton raced straight ahead, coming upon his own
tracks that he'd left in the middle of the bridle path. He
stopped, looked down and then up the path. He hoped
desperately to find a branch hanging low enough that he
might grab it and pull himself up. He would have no
such luck today. In an instant of cerebral brilliance, the
way out flashed into his brain. He walked quickly now,
back down the bridle path, making a reasonable attempt
to use the same prints he had left before. When he came
to the bridge, he stopped, glancing behind him. They
were getting closer now. He had to do it.

Fortuitously, when he had crossed the bridge the first
time he'd done so nearer the left side, close to its edge.
He stood in his tracks, kneeling slightly, flexing his
knees. Stuffing his gun in his belt at the small of his back,
he stood, hands out, like an Olympic diver preparing for

a jump. He leapt into the air, straining his thighs to bring his body over the edge of the small bridge.

He landed in the stream on all fours, the ice cold water splashing up against his stomach and torso. He remained still a moment, mentally checking his body for breaks or sprains. His left hand had landed at an odd angle on a rock, and winced in pain when he tried to move it. He thought perhaps he had broken his wrist. He had definitely sprained it anyway. Small price to pay for freedom.

Fenton backed his way underneath the bridge, keeping his body tight against the bank closest to the approaching hound. He held his left wrist with his right hand, massaging it slightly. It was beginning to swell. He was in pain.

Damn it!

He had precious little time to worry about his wound. He lay there like a contortionist, wedging his body between the bank and the bridge.

He could hear loud sniffing now, accompanied by an occasional whine. The dog sounded almost mad as it approached. He could hear it drawing nearer, the sound of its whines and demonic sniffing wrapping around the underside of the bridge. At any moment he expected it to come snooping wildly underneath the bridge. But his plan had worked! They continued on. The sound of the tracking team softened to his ears almost immediately after they passed the bridge. Still, Fenton didn't move. He waited until they had made the turn into the woods.

As the noise grew more distant he gained the courage to crawl out from under the bridge and began to work his way back up the bank of the stream. His ascent was slower than he would have liked, hampered by the fact he only had the use of one hand. He brought his head up even with the height of the bridge and looked in the direction of the tracking team. They were nearly out of sight now.

Fenton scurried to his feet, standing now at the far end of the bridge. He knew it would be only a few short minutes and they would be heading back in his direction, the dog dutifully following the loop Fenton had just taken. He could hear an occasional calamitous yelp off in the distance, heading away from him. He knew soon enough he'd hear it make the turn.

He had to find Jonah. "Don't lose him, Fenton!" his mother cried. "Don't lose him!"

———————

Just before Fenton heard the dog, when he was still in hot pursuit, Jonah had crawled on all fours several yards down the rock wall. He leaned his body against the massive trunk of an old oak tree that had spent the last century and a half growing around it.

He knew in his heart as he shimmied up against the tree, that someone was going to die today. He prayed to God it would not be he. Not that he was frightened of death. On the contrary, he was at peace with the prospect that we all must meet our maker. What drove him mad was the concept that he might die a meaningless death at the hands of such a deranged and psychotic loser. In his mind he simply could not bear the thought of losing this battle to *this* scumbag. He'd rather get taken out with friendly fire from one of the cops than from a bullet fired by this societal lowlife.

He leaned his back tightly to the tree, his mind quickly scrolling through what few options he had left. He tried desperately to ignore Fenton's haunting siren song. He could hear him calling his name. Jonah had just thought of the possibility of climbing the tree and was glancing up at the height of its first branches, when he, too, heard the dog. *Thank God. I thought you guys had forgotten me.*

Jonah could hear Fenton crunching through the snow a few yards beyond the wall—his fight or flight instinct invaded every cell of his body. An overwhelming sense of relief enveloped him as he heard Fenton's footsteps take him farther down the wall, away from his precarious and vulnerable position at the tree.

Jonah waited, listening intently as the dog approached. Standing with his back to the tree, he could tell it was somewhere off to his right. *They must be using the bridle path.* The sense of relief from his imminent rescue grew as he heard the hound approaching ever closer down the path. But it was soon replaced with a newer, deeper sense of dread as he heard it move away from him. He wanted desperately to scream out, but didn't dare. There was a madman between them.

His mind was screaming. *I'm over here! This way!* His body sighed heavy with relief as they approached again, this time from behind. They were working their way toward him. They were coming back! He realized now they were following the path Fenton had taken. *Of course. He came at me from that direction. It only makes sense.* He knew now it would only be a matter of minutes and they'd be at the rock wall. He was going to make it.

But where was Fenton? Jonah thought for sure he would be able to tell if they came upon him. Wouldn't he hear the dog go crazier still? Wouldn't he hear the cops screaming orders? "Don't move!" "On the ground. Now!" "Drop the gun!" "Put your hands in the air!" But there was none of that. Instead, the dog continued its obsessive pursuit, giving no sign that anyone had been found, much less caught.

There'd be plenty of time to worry about that later. What mattered now was that he was going to walk out of these woods alive. Jonah could hear them approaching the fallen fir. Any moment now and he'd be safe, able to hold . . . to make love to . . . Victoria once again. He thought he'd cry as the sense of relief shook his body. He almost hadn't lived to tell about this one.

As they approached the wall, he wondered now the best way of getting their attention without getting himself killed. He thought it safest to show himself early rather than risk being shot by leaping out from behind the tree. Throwing caution to the wind, he stepped out, waving his hands back and forth in the air.

Of the three men in the woods, none of them had ever laid eyes on Jonah Roberts before. Berkshire was the first to see him. He whipped his semiautomatic from his shoulder holster with his free right hand and laid his sights directly on Jonah's heart.

"Don't move, asshole!" he screamed.

REGAN ASHBAUGH

Halliway and Hill approached from different directions, both of them holding their weapons on Jonah.

"Freeze!" Hill said.

"I'm Jonah Roberts!" he yelled. "Montague slipped back in the woods that way!" he said, pointing to his left.

"Keep your hands where we can see them!" Berkshire yelled.

"I'm Jonah Roberts!" he yelled again.

Jonah was virtually surrounded by strange men holding weapons directly at him. He hadn't thought of this outcome when he envisioned his rescue just a few short moments ago.

Something didn't sit right with Halliway. This man had no beard and his hair seemed to long. Still, he thought it wisest to play it safe.

"Wait!" Halliway said, approaching Jonah, holding his free hand in the air. "Tell me what you told me when we last spoke on the phone," he said.

"Who the hell are you?" Jonah asked.

"I'm Lieutenant Halliway of the Connecticut state police."

"About what?" Jonah asked, his hands still in the air.

"About David's funeral."

"I told you I didn't give a shit what you thought. That David was my best friend and I was going to go."

"And what did I say? What made you change your mind?" Halliway asked.

"You told me you understood, but that my attending would put everyone else in danger."

"It's okay, gentlemen," Halliway said, replacing his gun in his shoulder holster. "This is Mr. Roberts."

"Montague went that way," Jonah said again, pointing. "I can't believe you guys missed him."

"We just came from there," Berkshire offered.

"I know. I could hear you. But I'm telling you, I heard him take off in that direction. I know he's down there."

"What do you want to do, Lieutenant?" Berkshire asked.

"Berkshire, you follow the trail. Scott, you take care of Mr. Roberts. I'll go with the team."

"Okay, where do you want me to take him?" Hill asked.

"Back to the CP. Get him an ambulance. It looks like he's bleeding."

"Done."

"Come on, let's move," Halliway said, making a circling motion with his left hand, pointing in the direction of the tracks.

The two men took off toward the bridle path, stopping at the point where Fenton's tracks connected with his originals. The dog was confused now. It yelped and spun, pulling Berkshire in all directions. Halliway and Berkshire looked at each other, somewhat perplexed.

"All right, now's where you earn your keep," Halliway said. "Can you read tracks?" he asked.

Berkshire wished one of the game wardens were here. Now *there* are some people who can read tracks. Part policeman, part Native American, part Maine guide— *no one* can work the Maine woods better than a game warden.

"Well, I'll do my best," Berkshire responded.

"Tell me you can do this," Halliway said, looking him in the eye.

Berkshire nodded acknowledgment. "I've been known to flush out a find or two," he answered with typical Yankee understatement.

"Good, take a look at what we've got here," Halliway said, waving his hands over the footprints. "See if you can figure it out."

It sounded easier than it was. Fenton's original tracks, as well as his subsequent secondary tracks, had been rendered almost unreadable, obliterated by the recent stampede of Berkshire, Halliway, Hill, and Lucky. The tracks in the snow were chewed up beyond any ability to translate them into usable information.

Halliway watched as Berkshire handed him Lucky's leash, ordering him to heel. Only the sound of labored breathing broke the silent dusk. Berkshire knelt at the intersection, picking at something with his right hand. Halliway pulled Lucky out of his way, moving him off to the side of the path. Berkshire frowned as he looked up toward the bridge, then turned his head and looked back down the path in the direction of the farm.

He walked alongside the tracks heading toward the farm, abruptly stopped, and walked back toward the bridge. He continued in that direction, eventually stopping just before the bridge. Halliway watched as he disappeared below the bank of the stream, under the bridge.

"Lieutenant!" Berkshire called. "Take a look at this!"

Halliway's mind played with a hundred possibilities. Maybe Fenton had shot himself and was lying in the stream. Maybe he'd broken down and was lying in a helpless fetal position, blubbering to himself. He ran to the bridge, Lucky jogging at his side.

"See these tracks here?" Berkshire asked, pointing up the riverbank from down below.

"Yes."

"Looks like he came to the tracks back there," he said, clambering back up the small incline, pointing to where they had just been standing. "Ran to this spot here and jumped into the stream. Probably was underneath us as we passed over the bridge. You see how these tracks here are climbing up?"

"Shit."

"I think he jumped into the stream, waited for us to pass, climbed back up, and backtracked the way we came."

"You mean to tell me you think he was under this bridge when we went over it?" Halliway asked incredulously, following Berkshire back down the path.

"Looks that way to me."

Jonah and Hill had joined the group. They stood listening to the conversation. When Berkshire came upon the intersection again he knelt, one knee up, one knee down, although neither touched the snow. "That explains these tracks here," he said, pointing. "You see how these tracks overlap ours? Heading back toward the pastures?"

"Sure do."

"He's a sly one, this boy, if I do say so myself. No

doubt in my mind. He waited for us to enter the woods there," Berkshire said, pointing to where they had veered off. "And hightailed it back toward the farm over our tracks as soon as we were out of sight."

"So, the bottom line is he's not here. He's back in that direction," Halliway said, pointing up the path.

"Right," Berkshire answered.

"Shit! He could be anywhere."

"Hey, not to worry, Lieutenant," Berkshire said, taking Lucky's leash back from Halliway. "That's what the dogs are for. He'll drop dead before Lucky even tires."

"Why do I have this uneasy feeling this time's gonna be different?" Halliway asked.

— ∞ —

Fenton Montague was running for his life, not that he particularly cared much about it at this point. He had come so close! He had Jonah right where he had dreamed, only to have those damn cops cause him to scuttle his plans. There was no way he would leave these woods today without killing Jonah. *No fucking way!* If he died in the process . . . *well, life just isn't fair.*

He followed the footprints in the snow, back in the direction of the farmhouse. The sky was beginning to darken. He had already fallen once on a limb he couldn't see, and was reluctantly forced to slow his pace somewhat to accommodate the rapidly diminishing sunlight. He thought he could see open pasture through the thickness of the trees and pushed forward with as much speed as he could.

Fenton stopped as he came to a tree he had leaned against on his initial trek in. Looking up, he realized it would be perfect for climbing. It was knotted, with an old split down the middle, probably from a lightning storm many years back. He scanned its branches, trying to get some sense of the distance of their reach beyond the trunk.

Without another moment's hesitation Fenton jumped onto the huge tree, grabbing the V in its trunk with his right hand, simultaneously pulling up a foot to rest on a knot. He struggled mightily just to climb a few feet, eventually wrapping his arms around one of the two trunks. Pulling himself up entirely with his right hand from a branch twisting out toward the middle, he turned his body so that only his left foot was stuck in the split.

Slowly, and yet with acrobatic precision, he began to shinny down the length of one of the lower, longer limbs. When he was about as far out as he figured he could comfortably go without risking snapping the branch, he eyed the ground below him and sat sidesaddle on the limb, grabbing it to his side with both hands. Sliding his rear off the branch, his body turned as he now swung freely from it, pumping his legs for speed on his jump. His left wrist screamed with pain. It slipped from the branch as he tried to use it to hold on.

He would have liked to land just far enough away so as not to make his footprints easily visible from the trail. However, the loss of the use of one hand left him hanging precariously at best. He simply wasn't strong enough to do this one-handed. His body fell to the ground ten to twelve feet from the trunk of the tree. He figured one of three things could happen. The dog would smell it and they would waste valuable time searching up in the trees. The dog wouldn't smell it and would continue on down the tracks toward the farmhouse from where it came. Or the dog would get confused and not know which track to follow.

Any one of these options offered him the precious time he needed. All he had to do was throw them off the trail, even if just for a short while. Fenton took off at an angle away from the tree, heading back in Jonah's direction in a zigzagging pattern away from the trail.

He could hear the dog sniffing its way through the woods, making its way toward the split maple. They were a good fifteen or twenty yards to his left. He stopped to kneel behind a thick fir just long enough to let them get comfortably by before he began to tack back in on his original tracks—the ones the tracking team had just followed toward the tree. He had closed the gap a good ten yards or so when he froze, thinking he heard voices. He stood motionless, holding his breath for quiet.

Those were voices! It had to be Jonah. Who was he with? He could only guess, but he didn't care. Fenton cut sharp left again now, heading almost back in the direction of the farmhouse, always cutting his angles closer back toward the trail. He could hear the two men plainly now.

Fenton knelt behind a tree, just beside the now mangled prints on the bridle trail he had made on his way in. He couldn't see the two men, but they had to be close. He could hear their conversation now. He waited until he could see Hill and Jonah, pulled out Stickney's semiautomatic, and stepped out onto the tracks. He smiled. *I may die tonight, but I won't be the only one. I got you now, you son of a bitch.*

—∿∿—

Berkshire and the dog had headed off back down the path in the direction of the farmhouse; Halliway was dutifully following right behind. Hill and Jonah walked slowly in their tracks.

"How ya feeling?" Hill asked him.

"I'll be all right. It's more of a scratch than anything else."

"I mean emotionally. You holdin' up okay?"

"Me? Yeah, sure. I thought I was going to buy it there for a minute. The troopers had someone with me, but he left to check in with his detail and I never saw him again. When I first saw Montague, I thought it was my escort."

Hill was surprised. "Which way did he go?" he asked.

"Who?" Jonah asked.

"Your escort."

"Well . . . I was trying to cut that big fir. He took off back toward the path."

"And you didn't see him after that?"

"Nope. If I almost bought it because that son of a bitch got bored . . . I don't even want to think about what I'll do."

It made sense to Hill now. "You know, Mr. Roberts, I think the reason is far bleaker than that."

"Oh, yeah?"

"When I was up at the Command Post back at the farmhouse, one of the troopers mentioned on the radio that he'd found a colleague hanging from a tree. He'd been stripped nude. They even think Fenton could be wearing a uniform. What 'ya wanna bet that was your detail man?"

"Son of a bitch!" Jonah exclaimed. "That explains why I thought Fenton was one of the cops. I must have caught a glimpse of his uniform. Subconsciously anyway."

"I'm afraid it sounded rather dire."

Jonah stopped and looked at Hill, suddenly full of guilt. "You think he could be dead?"

"I didn't say that," Hill responded. "But it sounded rather serious. I know his colleague was rushing him to the hospital."

Jonah stopped at the end of the path. It would be woods from here on out. "Damn. I hope he makes it. This Fenton guy is a fucking death machine."

Hill stopped to squint through the trees. "Yes he is, Mr. Roberts. That's why my partner and I are here."

The two men ducked into the woods, listening to the sounds of the tracking team growing more faint in front of them. They were in no rush. Wherever Fenton was, he wasn't here, and wasn't going to be here, either. Anyway, the team was between them and him.

Jonah's heart stopped beating at the sight of a strange man standing at the edge of the trail a few feet in front of them. It was getting much darker now. He had trouble making him out.

"What the—"

Hill pulled his gun from his shoulder holster. "Freeze! Don't move a muscle," he said.

It was then he noticed it was a cop. For a brief moment—a split second really—he relaxed his guard. "Oh," he said, beginning to replace his weapon. *What's wrong with this picture?* "Sorry about . . ." *Wait a min-*

ute. Pulling his gun back out of its holster again, he knew he was in trouble. "Stop!" he screamed, but it was too late.

"Not tonight," Fenton said, as a blinding flash lit up the crisp evening air.

Detective Hill's gun flew free from his hand, his body spinning around as the bullet from Stickney's weapon struck him with devastating brutality. He spun, falling backwards and on his right side, tripping over a fallen limb, crashing harshly to the ground.

Hill's gun lay practically at Jonah's feet. He didn't dare make a move to retrieve it. He was paralyzed, lost somewhere between stark terror and shock. He didn't remove his eyes from Fenton, glaring at him with tenacious concentration.

"So, Jonah. We finally meet again. I'm disappointed. You didn't think you were just going to walk out of here, did you?"

Jonah's mind swirled. A second ago he and Hill were having a calm conversation, and now . . . now his ears were ringing and there was a madman with a gun pointed at his face. Fenton held all the cards. Fifty-one of them, anyway. Would silence work better here? Should he attempt to taunt Fenton? Cause him to do something stupid, possibly make some kind of mistake?

Jonah tried to act calm. "Yep. As a matter of fact, I did."

"Well now, Jonah, as you can see, there's been a slight change in plans. I've spent many a long year planning for this night."

"Seems like wasted time to me," Jonah said, needling Fenton, attempting to keep him off guard. "I hope it's been worth it."

Fenton smiled. "Oh, it'll be worth it," he said, leveling his gun at Jonah's chest. "Now move."

———

Lucky had taken Berkshire and Halliway right to the old split maple. He acted perplexed, disoriented by the

newest scent of Fenton at the tree and those of himsel
and the team that had come this way only a short time
ago.

The dog sniffed wildly at the tree then pulled his
handler further down the now mangled tracks. Berkshire
stopped when Lucky stopped, the ten-foot leash stil
slack. Berkshire waited as his dog came sniffing back in
his direction, again toward the maple. This time Lucky
was sure. He sniffed madly about the tree, eventually
rising on his hind legs and scratching at its trunk
howling like a werewolf at the moon.

Many deer hunters never track their prey. Bow and
arrow hunters merely set up shop high in the branches of
a tree and wait. For the first time, Halliway was struck
with fear as he realized Fenton could easily be in the
trees above, lying in wait. He whipped out his semiautomatic, pointing it up at the dark intertwining branches.
Crouching, he turned slowly in all directions.

"What are you doing, Lieutenant?" Berkshire asked.

"The son of a bitch could be up there, just waiting for
us."

"Just figure that out, did you? I've been looking in the
trees since we got out here."

*All right, so you're more accustomed to the woods than
I am. I'd like to see you on the drug infested streets of the
slums of Stamford.* Like someone stopped at a red light
caught picking their nose, Halliway felt exposed—taken
aback by his false sense of self-assurance. *How could I
not have thought of that? How many other times has my
flank been so vulnerable and I haven't even noticed?* He
felt somewhat embarrassed, secretly glad Berkshire was
with him.

Berkshire shone his light in the branches of the maple.
"He's been here all right. See how the snow here is all
messed up?" he said, pointing to the split in the tree.

"Shit," Halliway said. "If he's in the trees, that's a
whole nother dimension, isn't it?"

"Yeah . . . kinda, but he's not a monkey, Ric. If he's in
the trees, one thing's for certain. He's stationary."

"But that means we could walk right under him."

Berkshire was unperturbed. "We'll see. It's gettin' dark. Just keep your eyes peeled."

"Jesus."

Berkshire got on his radio. "CP. This is Tracker One."

About damn time. "Ten three, One," Boyd said.

"Please relay to tracking teams to commence closing in. We're in the middle of the property. He's been here. We're close."

"Ten four, One."

Berkshire's transmission was interrupted by the deafening boom of a gunshot piercing the woods.

"Tracker One. Tracker One. Do you read me?"

Berkshire and Halliway both dropped to their knees. "Ten four, CP," Berkshire responded.

Halliway's only thought was his partner. He had left him somewhere behind with Jonah. Who had fired the shot?

"Scott!" he screamed.

"I just heard a shot. Are you involved?" Boyd asked.

"Negative, CP. We're in pursuit now."

"I'm sending people in."

"Negative!" Berkshire boomed. "It's too dark. We're acclimated now. You get people running around down here, it's gonna be a shootout. We're in pursuit. Will report. Ten twenty-three. *Repeat. Ten twenty-three."*

"Ten four, One. But if I don't hear from you in a few minutes, I'm sending in backup."

"Come on boy," Berkshire said to his dog, lightly patting him on the rear, indicating he wanted him to follow the trail back.

Berkshire held Lucky's leash with his left hand, his right pulling out his weapon. Halliway tagged directly behind. He'd never put his away.

"Stay alert, Ric," Berkshire said with his head turned halfway around. "You see anything out of the ordinary, holler. We got to watch our butts now."

Halliway stumbled over some fallen wood. "Oh, don't worry. I'm as alert as it gets."

Within a couple of minutes, they came upon Sergeant Hill stumbling through the woods, delirious from blood loss. He held his left hand to his wounded shoulder, collapsing in Halliway's arms as they approached.

"Scott," Halliway said softly. "Holy shit. He's been shot, Cal. Here, sit down."

"Lucky Heel," Berkshire said to his dog, leaning down to help.

Berkshire was already pulling his radio out when Halliway turned to him. "Radio CP, Cal. We got an officer down."

"CP. This is Tracker One. We have an officer down. Need immediate medical assistance. Repeat. Officer down!"

"Shit!" Boyd cried. "Tracker One, what's your ten twenty?"

"CP, do you have a tracking team there?"

"Affirmative, One."

"Send them down. If they can't follow the trail because of the snow, just tell them to visual whatever tracks they can make out once they get in the woods. The dog will pick us up from there. I'll be waving my flashlight in their direction. Follow the light."

"Ten four, One. Follow the light."

Boyd immediately rounded up the one tracking team he had on the premises, three other officers, and two EMTs. They were on their way in less than two minutes.

Halliway sat in the snow, oblivious to its wet cold on the seat of his slacks. Hill's head lay in his lap. He tried to apply some pressure to the wound, but Hill screamed in pain. Anyway, the hole was too large.

"Here," Berkshire said, offering Halliway a small towel from the first aid kit he wore around his waist.

"Thanks," Halliway said, attempting to stop his partner's bleeding.

Halliway looked down at Hill's head in his lap. "Jesus, Scott. I thought we might of lost you. Was it Fenton?" Hill coughed, trying to move. "Easy. Easy, buddy. Help's on the way," Halliway said, holding his partner tight.

Hill tried to speak, his voice weak. Halliway leaned down to hear him. "He's wearing a cop uniform, Ric. I wasn't thinking. I dropped my guard just for a second. I should've known better," he said, coughing through his frustration. "Just for one second, Ric. It's my fault."

"Shhh," Halliway said. "It's nobody's fault. I'd have done the same thing, Scott. It's instinct. You say he is dressed like a cop?"

"Yes," came the feeble response.

"Where's Roberts, Scott?" Halliway asked. "Does Fenton have him?"

Hill nodded his head, Halliway more able to feel it than see it.

Berkshire waved his flashlight in the direction of the farmhouse. He turned his head, catching a glimpse of Halliway's eyes staring directly at him in the thinning light.

"CP. Tracker One."

"Ten three, One."

"CP. We've just received word, suspect *is* wearing a policeman's uniform. Repeat. Suspect *is* dressed like a cop."

"Beautiful," Boyd said. "Ten four, One."

"Cal, I got it under control here," Halliway said. "Take the dog and follow the son of a bitch. Whatever it takes, find him and kill him!"

"Easy, Lieutenant. I'm not going anywhere. Not until help arrives. He's not gettin' out of here tonight."

"You don't know him like we do. You must find him, Cal. He'll find a way. Go find him."

"Negative, Lieutenant. Lucky and I stay right here until your partner gets help. I'm sorry."

Halliway looked down at Hill's face. "How ya doin', Scott? Hang in there."

"I'm not going anywhere," he whispered. "Ric?"

"What?" Halliway said, leaning down.

"Take him alive, Ric," Hill said, coughing. "I want to look in his eyes."

"I'll try. I promise."

"Do it for me, Ric. Don't try. Do it."

Some time passed as the three men and the dog huddled close together, Halliway tending to his partner. Berkshire waved the flashlight, keeping a keen eye on the forest around them. He tried to kill time.

"Reminds me of Nam," he said.

Halliway looked up at him. "How so? Scott was in Nam, weren't you, buddy?" he said, looking back down at Hill's head in his lap, wiping snow from his face.

Hill closed his eyes, nodding slightly. He squeezed Halliway's hand.

"I remember in the spring of sixty-nine. I was on a patrol up the Mekong River Delta. What a hell hole that place was. I still have nightmares about it. Anyway, some Charlies had taken out a command center near Can Tho, and our orders were to take them out. One night, we got ambushed. They came out of nowhere. Only three of us made it out. Somehow, we got back to the river and had to wait the whole next day to get picked up by a patrol. There was this corporal, I remember him like he was standin' here right now. Funniest guy I ever met. He lost a foot in the attack. I don't know how we kept him alive, but we did. By the time the patrol boat came, we had—"

"I hear them," Halliway said.

"Yep," Berkshire responded, standing so as to make the beam of his flashlight clearly visible. "Hey! Over here! Hurry!" he yelled, waving it furiously back and forth.

Hill squeezed his partner's hand. "You with us, buddy?" Halliway asked.

"What happened?" Hill whispered.

"What d'ya mean, Scott? What happened where?"

"The patrol," he said, coughing up blood now. "Did the corporal make it?"

"Ssshhhh. Don't talk, Scott. Save your strength. You're going to need it to get out of here."

"What happened?" he asked again, wincing as he strained to sit.

Halliway held him down. "Come on, buddy. Listen to me. Relax. Don't move. I mean it now."

Berkshire held his flashlight out, leaning down to speak to Hill. They were kindred souls. Halliway felt left out.

Berkshire hadn't heard Hill's question. "What's he want to know?" he asked Halliway.

"He wants to know if the corporal made it."

"Shit yeah. He's a congressman now."

The tracking team and back up officers were just yards away now. Halliway could feel his partner's grip weakening.

He knew how important it was to keep him alert. "Scott. Come on man. Stay awake for me," he said, lightly slapping his cheek. "Cavalry's here, Scott. Come on, stay with us."

The command post had an ambulance on call. The two EMTs immediately took control. Halliway stepped away, handing Hill's head to one of them. Like medics in battle, they set to work in an unfriendly environment, stabilizing Hill's blood pressure and body temperature.

Halliway was torn. He didn't know what to do. He wanted desperately to follow Montague, but felt he couldn't leave his partner.

"How can I help?" he asked one of the EMTs.

"Thank you, Lieutenant, but you can't," one of them said, as the newly arrived officers began carrying Hill away.

"I'm his partner," Halliway said. "I need to stay with him."

"That's fine," an EMT said, "but please stay to the side. We'll need some room."

The officers had Hill in a stretcher, hurriedly moving him through the trees. They stopped when Hill cried out.

"Ric!" he screamed.

Halliway ran to his side. "Yeah, Scott, I'm right here."

With what little strength he had left, Hill motioned for his partner to put his head close. Halliway leaned down. "I'm right here, Scott. Talk to me."

"Find him, Ric," he said, coughing profusely. "Don't stay with me. Find him. I need to know he'll get taken alive. I'll be okay now. Just find him, Ric."

"All right. I promise. I'll see ya at the hospital."

Hill smiled weakly as they yanked him away through the woods. One of the officers stayed with Berkshire and Halliway. They made introductions, Berkshire giving the new arrival some instructions. They prepared to set out on the tracks. Lucky would pick up right where he'd left off.

Halliway spoke to Berkshire before they began. "This congressman," he said.

"What congressman?"

"You know, the one you told Scott about. That corporal."

"Oh, him. Yeah, what about him?"

"What state's he from? I mean, what district's he serve?"

"He doesn't."

"I thought you said he was a congressman."

"I lied. He died on the boat."

———

Fenton had known Jonah would never eat the brownies he sent him. At least he hoped he wouldn't. They were designed to bring a little terror to the doorstep of the Roberts home, and beyond. Just a little wake up call. Something that says, I've got you on my mind.

"Keep your hands up where I can see them!" Fenton said, poking Jonah's back harshly with the muzzle of his gun.

"What are you going to do, Fenton?" Jonah asked defiantly. "Shoot me in the back? I thought even you had more balls than that."

"Shut up!"

Jonah walked slowly, trying to keep their pace as leisurely as possible. Both men knew the dogs were out. Jonah wanted to give them time to catch up, Fenton wanted to move as quickly as he could.

Jonah ducked under a branch, talking loudly ahead of him to be heard. "So, what was it like when you severed David's head, Fenton? Did you feel powerful? Did you come in your pants?"

"I'm telling you for the last time, asshole. *Shut up!*"

Jonah played the biggest poker hand of his life. He'd played some major bluffs before, but then there were only huge sums of money at stake. His downside here was a little more serious. Yet, somehow, the fear was gone. The boogey man was out of the closet now. The curtain had been pulled out from behind the Great Wizard. *He's just one man. He just happens to have a gun at your back.*

Jonah tried to think of what his father would tell him now. Would he think his son a fool for teasing this madman? Would he be proud? If there was ever a bully, this was him—deriving desperately needed confidence and self worth from the pleadings of his victims. Jonah knew one thing for sure. He would never plead for his life. Not with this scumbag. Not in a million years. He was at peace with the concept of death. But something inside him told him it would be okay. He hoped he could trust his gut.

Fenton eyed Jonah carefully, occasionally taking a few steps forward when the terrain allowed him to push his captive onward. But in his heart, he wasn't having the fun he'd imagined. *Why aren't you more scared, Jonah? I hold your life in my hands. You're supposed to be frightened, not bold. You should be pleading, not taunting.*

There was no bulge in Fenton's pants. In fact, there was nothing sensual about this moment at all. He felt drudgery, not excitement. *Cower, you son of a bitch! Don't you know who I am? What I can do to you?* Fenton was disillusioned and very disappointed. It wasn't supposed to be this way.

That's okay. Soon enough, you'll wish you'd treated me with a little more respect. He pushed Jonah again in a frenzied attempt to create the excitement he yearned for. He had the power! No two-bit little egotist was going to sap him of it with meaningless, defiant antics.

Jonah was determined to triumph. He thought he could begin to feel Fenton's frustration. He mocked Fenton subtly now, more with his actions than his words. He deliberately slowed his pace, certain he was causing Fenton to go quietly mad, as if he were driving behind an old man going ten miles under the speed limit on a one lane road. He could feel Fenton's blood start to boil.

Fenton had had enough. He needed to regain control. He switched his gun to his left hand, leaned down, and picked up a small branch, striking Jonah viciously across the right side of his head, splitting open his ear. Jonah was momentarily stunned, dropping to his knees. He brought his right hand down, holding it against the side of his head. Blood ran profusely through his fingers and down his neck.

"Don't fuck with me!" Fenton said. "You want to die here, that's okay with me. Now you got two choices, shithead. Either pick up the pace, or die right here, right now. Choose."

Jonah turned, still on his knees, looking at the black silhouette of Fenton's body against the bluish-black trees.

"I said *choose!*" Fenton boomed.

"What do you mean?" Jonah asked.

"I want to hear you tell me. What do you want it to be? *Say it!* Move faster or die. Your choice."

When you draw a line in the sand, you'd better be prepared to follow through with your threat if it's crossed. Secretly, Fenton hoped Jonah would succumb. He wasn't prepared to kill him here. He would live the rest of his life unfulfilled. It would be too quick, too painless. He was desperate to see him suffer. But he had served up the volley and the ball was in Jonah's court now.

Jonah's head reeled with pain as his mind scurried through what few choices he had. Fenton stood too far back for Jonah to have any chance of lunging at him, and he was loath to acquiesce to Fenton's demand. But he feared he might have just pushed him farther than was safe.

"Choose! Say it!" Fenton yelled, pointing the gun directly at Jonah's head. "I'm waiting, asshole."

Always look at your downside, Jonah's father had taught him. Was Fenton bluffing? Did Jonah dare take a stand? The man who had decapitated his best friend stood before him with a gun to his face. His heart beat out of his chest, his ear pulsating with pain. What could he do?

Fenton had his own plans. Inside he secretly pleaded. *Please don't cross the line. Please don't cross the line.*

"All right!" Jonah screamed. "You want to move faster. We'll move faster," he said, walking quickly away from his captor.

"Hey! Not so fast," Fenton said.

Jonah turned. "You're a pain in the ass, you know that? First, you're not happy with how slow I'm going. Now you're not happy with how fast I'm going. Why don't *you* take the lead and set a pace *you'll* be happy with."

"Fuck you. Move."

The two men continued down the bridle path, finally exiting the woods at Jonah's pastures. Jonah stopped.

"Where to?" he asked.

"The house."

Good. I'll gladly walk you into the mouth of the lion. You don't know what's sitting up there, Fenton. Lots of firepower and angry cops, and they've all been waiting for you. Jonah moved quickly. Whatever Fenton had in mind was going to happen soon. *Too bad it's all in your dreams.*

They moved at a brisk pace up the slight incline from the woods. The outline of the house was clearly visible. A light shone through the kitchen window. What Jonah couldn't know was that the premises were empty. The last remaining cop had been taken off the beat when Hank drove Stickney to the hospital. Jonah prayed someone would show. He could envision a sniper shot coming from the hayloft. He tried to keep his distance from Fenton in order to give them enough room.

The barn grew larger as he approached, but nothing happened. *Where the hell are you guys?* Maybe they were waiting for a clean shot. Waiting for the whites of his eyes. He brought Fenton circuitously by the wood chip pile, hoping he would be clearly visible to whoever was staked out in the barn. They passed the pile, Jonah slowing his gait.

Fenton stood about five yards back. He was all by himself. Jonah was going mad with anticipation. *Come on! Shoot! What the hell are you waiting for?* Jonah stopped and turned. *They're not here.* With cruel comprehension, Jonah realized he was alone with this madman. *God, give me strength. Of course, the police think I'm still out in the woods.* It was just as it had been when David died: the perimeter was tightly sealed while the virus attacked from within.

"You still have the brownies I sent you?" Fenton asked.

"What brownies?" Jonah asked, acting dumb.

"Inside," Fenton said, waving his gun toward the house.

Jonah tried to overcome his sense of being vanquished. A feeling of foreboding began tugging at his heart. Who was he to think that some Universal Power would look after him? *What makes me so special? David didn't make it . . . why should I?*

He climbed the stairs, frantically searching his mind for a way out. Like a driver spinning out of control on an ice-covered street, watching the tree approach the side of his car—he lost a dozen alternatives with every passing second. Eventually, all you can do is close your eyes and hope not to die.

Jonah put his hand on the door handle. *That's it! I'll whip myself inside, lock the door, and run to the other door and lock it.* He'd be inside with a phone, while Fenton would be locked out. His hand squeezed, adrenaline pumping through his veins. He was ready. *All right, now!*

"*Stop!*" Fenton screamed, Jonah freezing in his tracks.

"You think you're going to lock me out?" Fenton asked. "You think I'm a child? I got news for you, asshole. I may have been born at night, but I wasn't born last night. Now, get on your knees."

There was a moment of silence. "No," Jonah said. "You'll have to shoot me first. I will never get on my knees for you. Do you understand me? Never!"

"Really?" Fenton asked, wheeling his right foot back, crashing his heel into the back of Jonah's rib cage.

Jonah's torso arched backwards, his face slamming against the closed door. He crumpled to his knees. Fenton stood back a few feet. He had a trapped animal now. Those are the most dangerous kind.

"Funny how things change, isn't it, Jonah? Now, open the door before I decide to end this little game."

Jonah's nose was broken. It bled freely down his mouth, dripping off his chin. He reached up and turned the knob, opening the door just an inch. Fenton shoved his butt with his right boot, pushing Jonah through the opening, onto the rug beyond.

Now this is more like it. Fenton was beginning to feel the excitement now. The blood smeared the rug, staining Jonah's clothing. His captive lay helplessly bleeding on the floor in front of him. The only thing missing was the begging. Jonah was still a bit too irreverent for his liking. *We're going to change that right now.*

He was beginning to feel the control. The power began to overtake him. He was the director of his play again. Fenton's need for death pumped wildly through his veins. It was all coming together now, just as he had imagined.

He couldn't let Jonah achieve a sense of security. He had to maintain the upper hand. Fenton eyed the light switch on the wall to his left. He flipped it off, pouncing on Jonah's back with his right knee as the house went dark. He thrust his left arm under Jonah's chin and pulled his head up, holding the gun at Jonah's right temple. Blood oozed onto its muzzle. He pushed it into Jonah's head as hard as he could, feeling the beginnings of an erection as Jonah's face grimaced, turning partially to the left.

"Now, listen good, Jonah. You're gonna crawl to the living room. You even try to get up and I'll decorate the floor with your brains. Got it?"

Silence.

Fenton's broken wrist screamed with pain as he jerked Jonah's head up as far as he could. *"Got it?"* he asked again.

Jonah couldn't speak with his throat so stretched. He moved his head slightly up and down.

"That's a good boy."

Fenton raised himself off of Jonah, flipping the light switch back on. He tapped the soles of Jonah's boots occasionally with his own, just to let him know where he was. As they approached the corner to the kitchen, Fenton eyed the brownies on the kitchen table. A broad smile spread across his face. It would happen exactly as he'd planned after all. Jonah's answer to his earlier question had caused him to think he'd have to improvise. He took solace in the knowledge he would now watch Jonah die an agonizing death—just the way he'd planned.

Fenton picked up the tin container. "What brownies?" he mimicked. "Jonah, I'm surprised at you. You lied to me."

Fenton watched Jonah crawl on the linoleum floor toward the living room, smearing a trail of blood as he went. As he approached the carpeted floor by the wood-burning stove, Fenton ordered him to stop. He stepped on his back, taking one long stride over Jonah's head and turned, pointing his gun directly as his face. Fenton pulled the rocking chair in front of Jonah, safely out of reach, about five feet away.

He sat for a while in silence, his gun's muzzle staring menacingly at his life's nemesis. Jonah remained frozen, stone like, waiting patiently for his chance. In time Fenton removed the open container of brownies from his lap and placed them on the floor, shoving them in front of Jonah's face with a boot.

Some time passed as Fenton appeared to gather his thoughts. It was only a minute or so, but it seemed like a week to Jonah. Indeed, Fenton was thinking. *There is one loose end.* He began unbuttoning Trooper Stickney's pilfered shirt. He figured by now the cops would undoubtedly assume him to be wearing a policeman's uniform. If the heat came crashing in, a sixth sense told him they would shoot first and ask questions later. And if that happened, he sure as hell didn't want to be the one wearing that badge.

"Put this on," Fenton said, tossing Stickney's shirt over Jonah's bloodied face.

Jonah hesitated, but eventually acquiesced. For the moment at least, Fenton had all the power. But with emotions running this high, Jonah knew how quickly that could change. Like a shark sensing blood in the water, he would know when to strike. And when his chance came, it wouldn't matter what he was wearing.

Fenton wore a demented smile. "We're gonna have some fun now, Jonah."

———❦———

Lucky sniffed his way up the bridle path, the clearing's lack of trees or branches making for swift travel. They approached the bridge, Halliway feeling disappointment at how close they'd previously been. Lucky didn't hesitate, dragging his handler quickly over the bridge toward the opening to the pastures. As they exited the woods, the expanse of snow-covered grass stood before the two men, shining a translucent blue in their faces.

"Wait!" Halliway said, grabbing Berkshire by the shoulder.

"Whoa boy," Berkshire ordered Lucky, pulling firmly on his leash.

Halliway stared up at the light in the kitchen window. "He's taken him to the house. Do you still have anyone there?"

"I don't know," Berkshire said, getting on his radio. "CP, this is Tracker One. We have an possible ten eighty-nine in progress. Suspect has apparently taken Mr. Roberts back to the house. Do we still have anyone stationed at that location?"

Boyd made a face. *I don't have any idea.* "Stand by, One," Boyd said. He radioed Sergeant Spencer at the Gray Barracks.

"CP to Gray dispatch. Acknowledge."

Spence had been listening to every transmission since the search began. "Ten four, CP."

"Spence, we got a hostage situation at the Roberts home. Do we still have men at that location?" Boyd asked.

Spence was embarrassed to admit it, but no one had been redeployed after Hank left with Stickney for the hospital. There didn't seem any need. But there was no getting around this one. He answered directly, eschewing explanation. "Negative, CP."

537

"Shhhit," Boyd said in exasperation. "CP to Tracker One," he said, getting back on the radio.

"Ten three," Berkshire said.

"That's a negative. Repeat. Negative."

"Shit," Berkshire said, turning to look at Halliway as he tugged at Berkshire's jacket sleeve. "Stand by, CP."

"Cal, we need a SWAT team out here ASAP," Halliway said. "We need the best men they've got, and we need them absolutely quiet. We send cruisers up that driveway and Roberts is as good as dead."

"I agree. Any ideas on the best way to coordinate it?"

Halliway held his left hand in a fist, pointing his thumb up to begin the count. "First, make sure they've all got ear mikes. There can't be any audible radio transmission. Second, have them approach via the back of the house. We'll meet up in the barn."

"How many men?" Berkshire asked, answering his own question. Both men said six simultaneously. "Okay, anything else?"

"Yeah, have an ambulance ready at the end of the driveway. Two if possible."

Berkshire nodded his head. "Tracker One to CP."

"Ten three, One."

"CP, listen carefully. Request a SWAT team at the Roberts property. They need to proceed as follows. We need six men on the QT. They need ear mikes. There can be *no*, repeat, *no*, audible radio transmission. Send them via the back. We will meet them in the barn. Also, have two ambulances on call at the end of the driveway. No lights. No sirens. We're going dark now. All subsequent transmissions are to come via the team."

"Ten four, One. Give us ten minutes."

The first thing Boyd did was request one of his men to call in two ambulances, describing where they should wait and how they should approach. He had precious little time and could only do so much at once. That done, he started in.

Several of the men surrounding the perimeter were members of various departments' SWAT teams. Boyd went car-to-car on his radio. "CP to perimeter details. Tracking team reports a ten eighty-nine in progress at the Roberts home. We need six men experienced in hostage situations. Please respond."

Within a minute several men reported in, each identifying his department and current location. Eight men responded in all, necessitating that two be left back.

Boyd wanted teams already familiar with one another wherever possible. "How many of you are currently in a team?" he asked.

There were two teams. The others were solo. Boyd was now stuck with a diplomatic nightmare. Should he include the sheriff and local men along with his own? If he didn't, that was the kind of thing that could fester for a long time to come. For better or worse, Boyd made an executive decision. He knew state police procedure and knew his SWAT guys were well trained. He knew the sheriffs were capable as well. The two trained together. It had nothing to do with competence, everything to do with experience and familiarity.

"How many of you are state police?" he asked over the radio.

Four men responded.

"How many of you are sheriffs?"

Two men responded. That meant the other two were from local law enforcement. As good as they might be, he just couldn't risk it.

"Okay gentlemen. We only need six, so you all can't go. If you're one of the four state policemen or two sheriffs who responded, suit up and wait for a cruiser to come around."

There would be no doubt be some bruised departmental egos over this one.

Boyd had to think quickly. What was the most efficient way to do this? He couldn't very well have everyone take their cruiser and leave their partner just standing by the side of the road. He acted on instinct. "CP to SWAT team members. Listen up. Once you have your gear, wait by the side of the road. A cruiser will be by shortly."

Halliway and Berkshire didn't have the luxury of ear mikes. Consequently, they missed the entire series of transmissions. Not that it mattered. They knew that soon enough there would be six men dressed in black fatigues approaching the back of the barn, and they needed to get there. Now.

Boyd pulled in Lucky's leash, patting his dog vigorously around the neck and side. "Good boy, Lucky. Lucky. Quiet, boy," is all he said to his hound.

"That's it?" Halliway asked.

"That's it."

Halliway was not convinced. "You're not worried he'll forget or something?"

"Lieutenant, I'm more worried about you than him right now."

"Hmmm. He's that well trained?" Halliway asked with a look of concern.

"You bet."

"Who trained him?" Halliway asked.

"I did."

Halliway was impressed. "No shit?"

"No shit. Come on, let's go."

Boyd went state-wide again. "CP to last cruiser on Maple Ridge."

"Ten three, CP."

"Are you a SWAT team member?"

"Negative, CP."

"Good. Start down Maple Ridge. Pick up the SWAT members you see on the side of the road. Loop right on Carsley and stop here for a geological survey. You'll need one."

"Ten four. Rolling now."

The cruiser stopped at the corner of Maple Ridge and Carsley, picking up his first man, then stopped once more between Maple Ridge and the farm. As instructed, he pulled into the loop in front of the Roberts farm.

"Here," Boyd said, handing the driver the rolled up survey. "Anything else you need, gentlemen?" he asked the two men sitting in the back.

"All set," one of them said, the other one shaking his head.

"Okay. Good luck."

The cruiser pulled out, picking up two other men before reaching Edes Falls. They picked up the last two

540

men halfway up the road to Jonah's house. The men packed the car like sardines.

"CP, this is transport. Team intact. Approaching now."

"Stand by, transport. Stop until further instructions."

The men gave a collective sigh. They wanted to get out of the overcrowded car as much as they wanted to get on with the show.

"Ten four," the driver said, pulling to the side of the road.

"Jesus Christ," one of the men said. "What the hell are we waiting for?"

Boyd had a sudden thought. *Shit!* He didn't have the geological survey but thought now he remembered a black dot on the map not too far from Jonah's farm. He suddenly remembered there was another house relatively close and he hadn't ordered it evacuated.

Standard operating procedure dictates that during a barricade or hostage situation all surrounding dwellings be evacuated. Now, as he stood ready to order his men onto the property of the farmhouse next to Jonah's he realized he hadn't done it. If anything were to go wrong . . . now *that* would be a career ender.

The state-wide car-to-car channel was quiet now, virtually every man waiting for Boyd's instructions. The wait seemed interminable.

"CP, you with us?" someone asked.

"Ten four. CP to transport. Take a look at that survey map will you, please?"

"Ten four, CP. I got it here."

"Do you see a black dot near the Roberts residence?"

Within seconds, to a man, they knew what had happened.

"No one moved them?" someone from the transport car inquired.

"CP, this is Franklin from the sheriff's department. I'm closest to the property on Edes Falls. You want me to get them out?"

"Please, Sheriff. Thank you," Boyd said, feeling embarrassed. He was only one man and there was an awful lot going on. Yes, he told himself, he shouldn't have overlooked it but shit happens. "One moment, transport," Boyd said. "My apologies."

"Hey, we're all human," someone called back.

"Transport, while we're waiting, you are to hook up with a member of the K-9 unit of the Maine state police and a lieutenant from the Connecticut state police at the barn on Roberts's property. Once you meet up with them, it's their show. They will communicate through you to me. Any questions?"

"Any help with the terrain at all?" one of them asked.

"Just the geological survey. I suggest you familiarize yourselves with it before heading out."

"Do you want him alive?" another one asked.

"At this point, gentlemen, I don't think anyone gives a shit," Boyd said, his swearing breaking all the procedural rules in the book. But he was on a tactical channel now. Very few people could hear him. "Just get Roberts out of there in one piece and breathing. Do what you gotta do, but do it quickly."

There was silence for some time as everyone waited for Franklin to evacuate the Kirsten homestead. A few minutes later the call came out.

"CP, this is Franklin. The owners are with me. The property is empty. You're free to proceed."

"Ten four. Thank them for us," Boyd said.

"Will do."

"CP to transport. You're free to move, gentlemen. Sorry for the delay."

The cruiser pulled up old farmer Kirsten's driveway and darkly clad men poured out like so many clowns from a circus car. Each member of the team wore black fatigues, black boots, bulletproof vests, black ski masks, and fingerless tactical gloves. They were heavily armed and well trained in the art of self-defense. They each held black belts in karate and could take down and immobilize a man twice their size in a matter of seconds. If at all possible, you'd want to avoid them.

They circled around the hood of the cruiser. A couple of men held down the four corners of the map. The driver shone a flashlight on it. Black dots signified the Kirsten farm and the Roberts home. The men had chosen a team leader while they waited in the car. They went by rank, selecting a Lieutenant Polmeroy. He spoke first.

"Okay, we're here," he said, pointing to a black dot on the map. "We want to be here. No doubt there's wire fencing around the perimeter of the property so we'll need to be careful. I think if we can just get beyond this ridge here," he said, pointing, "we should be able to see the barn. From that moment on we communicate via the ear mikes. Let's go in single file. Any questions?"

No one responded.

"Good. Let's move."

Less than nine minutes had passed from the time Berkshire had made his first transmission. A lifetime in Jonah's eyes. The team leader brought his men over the crest of the ridge, holding up his hand, stopping the convoy. He spoke into the transmitter on his shoulder.

"There's the barn, gentlemen. There's a fence in front of me. I'll hold the wire up while you crawl underneath. One at a time. Move."

The last man ducked beneath the two-wire fence, turned and held it apart for Polmeroy to follow suit, passing his now stationary men. He took the front again as they made their way down the slight but slippery incline.

"Careful, gentlemen," he said. "There's ice here."

Halliway and Berkshire had quietly made their way past the wood chip pile and ducked into the barn a good five minutes earlier. They were surprised by the stirrings of the horses and decided to wait outside the rear of the barn so as not to spook them any further. They could apparently smell Lucky. He had to be removed as quickly as possible. The slightest noise now could serve as an alarm. Stealth was of paramount importance. They stood in silence, waiting, Berkshire rubbing the side of Lucky's neck.

"I see them," Berkshire said, whispering out of the side of his mouth, flipping his flashlight on and off three times, acting as a beacon for the team.

Halliway whispered back. "Good. Let's get this show on the road."

As the team approached, they came upon another wired fence, this one used by Jonah to keep his horses in. The men followed the same procedure. Discipline was their hallmark. *Nothing* pushed. *Everything* calculated. The men waited for Polmeroy to get in front and followed him quickly to the opening of the barn, forming a semicircle as they came upon their contacts. There was no time for pleasantries. None were expected, none were offered, though Berkshire did introduce himself and Halliway to Polmeroy simply for logistics.

"What ya got?" Polmeroy inquired.

"Don't know yet," Berkshire responded. "Didn't want to fuck it up. Figured we'd wait for you."

"Either one of you gentlemen work a SWAT detail before?"

Both men shook their heads.

"Okay, from here on out, I call the shots. These men are my responsibility."

Halliway and Berkshire nodded affirmation.

"Stay put," Polmeroy said, leaving to walk to the corner of the barn closest to the house. Halliway felt a pit in his stomach as he watched the man duck out of sight around the corner. He'd seen a lot in his thirty years, but he'd never done anything like this. The past twelve hours seemed almost like a sideshow to him. He was definitely out of his element.

No one spoke as the seven men stood still and silent at the rear of the barn. It wasn't an uncomfortable silence but rather an anticipatory one. Speech would be superfluous now. Each man wrestled with his own demons, wondering if this would be his last night on earth.

Halliway watched with impressed curiosity as the men tweaked their battle gear just right—tightening a belt here, twisting a vest there, checking weapons and mikes. They looked like deadly ninjas preparing for Armageddon. Halliway was the only man in slacks. He felt like an accountant at a Hell's Angels party.

Polmeroy came back around the side of the barn, moving closely toward his tightly packed crew. "Okay, here's the plan. The perp's got Roberts lying on the carpeting just inside the living room. The light's on. If we play this right we should be able to wrap this up quick. Lieutenant," he asked, looking at Halliway. "Do you care if we take him out?"

Halliway was almost embarrassed. All seven men looked at him now. How could he tell them what he'd promised his partner? This was hardly a warm and fuzzy lot. These men were not here for fun and games. They were deadly serious, had a job to do, and were going to get it done.

"Lieutenant?" Polmeroy asked again.

"Look, I don't know how to say this," Halliway started tentatively. "That son of a bitch just shot my partner, not to mention that he killed a cop in my home state. The last thing my partner asked me before they took him away was . . . well . . . he made me promise to take him alive. I told him I'd do everything in my power."

Polmeroy dropped his head slightly, scratching the top of his ski mask. *Couldn't be easy, could it?* "Christ," he said, sighing. "All right—"

"Listen, do what you've gotta do," Halliway interrupted. "My partner's a big boy. He'll understand. If you think your safest route is to take him out, then take him out."

"I'd like to see him spend the rest of his life rotting in some cell myself," Polmeroy said. "But I don't think we can take the chance. I'm sorry, Lieutenant, but as he is now, we can take him out with one shot between the eyes. I don't think we've got a choice."

"Did you get a look inside?" one of his men asked.

"Yeah."

"And?"

"He's sitting on a rocker facing the side kitchen window. He's got a gun at Roberts's face. We got two things going for us. First, Roberts is lyin' face down in front of the perp. Second, the lights are on so he can't see outside."

"Are you guys open to suggestions?" Halliway asked.

Polmeroy looked at him. "Always."

"Well, I don't know all there is to know about this, but

why can't we just blow his gun shoulder off? You zero in on his shoulder with one of these babies, and he'll never hold anything again."

"And if we miss? Just graze him?"

"Yes, but don't you run that same risk if you try to kill him?"

Polmeroy thought a minute. "Okay, who's the best sniper among us?" he asked.

"That's got to be Jackson," one of the two sheriffs said. "Shit, he can knock a penny off the top of a bottle from a half mile, and you'd still be able to drink from it when he's done."

"Which one's Jackson?" Polmeroy asked.

Jackson stepped forward.

"Is that true?" Polmeroy wanted to know.

"I've been known to hit a target or two in my day," Jackson said, almost embarrassed.

"Come on, son. No bullshit now. This isn't the time for humility. Can you take this job or not?"

Jackson looked Polmeroy in the eye. "Shit, yeah."

Polmeroy wanted to follow procedure. Normally that required some type of forced entry, usually aided by the use of concussion grenades, smoke bombs, and the like. Snipers are always used as a last resort. But when and if they're called, every SWAT team sniper will tell you they're trained for one thing and one thing only. And it's not to ensure their target keeps breathing.

The risks here were so great, Polmeroy couldn't believe the words he heard himself speak. "Can you take out his shoulder?" he asked Jackson.

"I don't know. You said he was in a rocking chair, right?" Jackson asked.

"Yes."

"Is he rocking?"

"Yes."

"Fast?" Jackson asked.

"Fast enough."

It was hard to make out his facial expression with the poor lighting and the ski mask, but Halliway thought he saw a frown between his eyes.

"It's hard to say," Jackson said. His voice having lost

some of its previous confidence. "I can try. What if I think I can't do it? Do I have orders to take him out?"

Polmeroy looked at Halliway. Halliway shrugged, holding his hands open. "You gotta do what you gotta do," he said. "Just stop him before he kills Roberts."

"All right," Polmeroy said. "I saw a tractor out there not too far from the window. See if you can get a clear shot from on top of it. I think it's your best bet. Take the cleanest shot you can. But, Jackson—"

"What?"

"Just end it, okay?"

"Oh, don't worry, sir. I'll end it."

———⁓———

"What's the matter, Jonah? Lost your appetite?" Fenton asked.

He was firmly in control now. He rocked slowly back and forth, laughing at Jonah. How sweet this revenge would finally be. He had his doubts there for a while, but he knew deep down that he'd win. He always did. Fenton was lost in his delusional world; the thought of cops never entered his mind. What he cared about—in fact, the only thing he could think of—lay directly in front of him. Nothing else mattered. And anyway, he was Fenton Montague. No one could catch him. He was unstoppable.

"What did I just tell you to do?" Fenton asked.

Jonah lay silent.

"A little defiance at the end. Isn't that quaint. You know, Jonah, David cried at the end. He begged me for his life. I didn't know a grown man could carry on that way. It was really kind of pitiful watching him piss his pants. You're so much the bigger man."

"Fuck you!"

"Tch, tch, tch," Fenton said, clicking his tongue. "You really do need to do something about that anger, you know that?"

"If it's the last thing I do. I swear—"

"The last thing *you* do?" Fenton boomed from his belly. He turned, suddenly serious, leaning forward, staring into Jonah's eyes. "I'll tell you the *last* thing you're going to do, Jonah Roberts. *You*, my friend, are going to eat those brownies. And you're not going to leave a crumb."

"Says who?"

"Says a little voice in the back of my head."

If Jonah was going to die, he was determined to go out with style. If he was going to see David again, albeit on a higher plane, he couldn't look him in the eye knowing he'd turned coward when it counted most. "Oh, I bet you got plenty of those, don't you, Fenton? Those voices of yours . . . they're probably yapping at you all the time. How can you sleep at night with all that chitter chatter going on up there?"

"Enough!"

"Doesn't it ever get old? Don't you wish you could just be alone, by yourself, with your own thoughts now and then?"

"I said, *enough!* I'll blow your brains out right now."

Go ahead. Kill me. "Oh, I'm shaking in my boots. Can't you see how scared I am?"

"I said eat!"

"No!"

"Eat!"

"No!"

"All right, then I'm going to make you eat."

That's right, asshole, come to pappa. Just a little closer.

Fenton sprang out of the chair and was upon Jonah in an instant, sticking the muzzle of his bloodstained gun deep inside Jonah's mouth. He shoved hard, and Jonah's gag reflex took over. The gun seemed past his tonsils now, like a tube being shoved down his throat. Jonah tried desperately to pull his head back, but his back could only arch so far. The farther he arched, the harder Fenton pushed.

If I'm going to die, it's going to be fighting. Almost unconscious, Jonah whipped his right hand up from his side, jabbing two fingers into Fenton's eyes. Fenton recoiled with pain. *Now!* Jonah dropped his right hand down from Fenton's face onto the gun in a fluid motion, whipping it out of his mouth, the metal sight guard ripping the roof of his mouth as it exited.

In a single motion he jumped to his knees, jabbing the four knuckles of his right fingers into Fenton's Adam's apple. Not the knuckles of his hand, but the knuckles of his fingers, which felt more like the point of a boot than its heel. Fenton grabbed his throat with both hands, releasing the gun.

Yes! Jonah grabbed the gun and swung it as hard as he could across Fenton's right temple, a deep gash spurting blood almost immediately. Fenton knelt on his knees, holding various parts of his head and neck. Fury raged now in Jonah.

"You son of a bitch!" he yelled, kicking Fenton in the groin with the full strength of his right foot.

Fenton vomited.

"You son of a bitch!" Jonah screamed again, spit and blood spewing from his mouth. "Who the *fuck* do you think you are, you goddamned, cocksucking bastard?"

Jonah stepped behind him now, driving his foot directly at Fenton's kidney.

"Die! You yellow-bellied little shit!"

Jonah whipped Fenton's head around, his body turning pathetically in its wake. Jonah kneed him squarely in the nose, driving cartilage up his sinus cavity, blinding Fenton's brain with flashes of white. Jonah hit him two more times across the top of the head with the gun, breaking Fenton's skin deeply with each thrash. He threw Fenton's head to the floor, smashing his nose on the carpet. Fenton lay on his left side now, his face lying toward the wood stove.

"Get on your stomach!" Jonah boomed. *"Now!"*

Fenton began to cry, doing as he was told. "Don't hurt me, Mother," he moaned. "Please don't hurt me."

In the ultimate irony, Jonah felt a twinge of sympathy float momentarily across his heart. *The guy's crying for his mother?* "You're nothing but a stinking, lowlife coward, you know that?"

Fenton blubbered before him now, as Jonah sat in the rocking chair, pointing Stickney's gun directly at his

He rocked slowly back and forth, smiling at his guest.

"Funny how things change, isn't it, Fenton? Now eat."

Fenton's words were nearly indistinguishable. He was choking on the blood in his mouth. "Oh, Mommy. *Please?* I'll be a good boy. I promise I won't do it again."

"Shut up!" Jonah boomed. *"Fuck* you and this mommy crap. You think you can fool me with your little act, you prick? Now pick up a brownie and eat."

Fenton grabbed a brownie. He wanted to die, but he was afraid to go out this way. "Shoot me! Please. Just shoot me!" he begged.

"Shoot you?" Jonah said, leaning over to stare at the blubbering captive before him. *"Shoot* you? I wouldn't shoot you if you just killed my mother. You're going to suffer, asshole. Just like David."

"But I don't want—"

"You don't want?" Jonah interrupted almost maniacally. "Like I give a *shit* what you want. I'll tell you what *I* want. I want to know how David really died. He didn't cry, did he?"

Silence.

"Did he?"

Fenton shook his head as he lay on the carpet, blood covering his face.

"He didn't beg you for his life, did he, Fenton? *Did he?"*

Fenton shook his head back and forth on the carpet.

"But *you* can beg, can't you, Fenton? *You* can beg for *your* life, right?"

Fenton was defeated. His play was over. The critics had panned it. He would be relegated to nothingness again for the rest of his life.

"I said *beg!"* Jonah yelled. "Beg for your life, you little fuck!"

Fenton collapsed emotionally, his body heaving in gulps of tears. He could hardly breathe as the sobs poured from his soul. His whole little world was crashing down on him with ferocious finality. He was nobody. Jonah had won yet again.

Fenton reached for the brownies and began shoving

them in his mouth. As fast as he could, he shoved . . . pushing until there wasn't room to push any more, chewing the dry mush as best he could, the blood in his mouth his only moisture. He lay with his head on the floor, chewing quietly, like a cow masticating its cud.

Jonah sat there watching him. It was finally over. Whatever was in those brownies, Fenton had just finished them off. Jonah didn't know what to expect. He sat and waited, watching Fenton's mouth move. An odd sense of loss tugged at him. He couldn't explain it. He leaned his head back, motionless in the chair, watching Fenton eat his last meal.

—✥—

Lieutenant Polmeroy was thinking of the best way to handle the situation. Roberts was stuck inside his home with a madman pointing a gun at his face. Fenton was open for a clear shot. Polmeroy's only desire was to stop him. Dead or alive, he had to be stopped.

On the one hand Polmeroy wanted to take him alive. It always looks better when police don't have to kill someone, no matter how heinous the individual or the crimes he has committed. A part of him also wanted to see the bastard rot in jail for the rest of his life. A guilty verdict, and the family's opportunity to face their loved one's killer always provides some relief and closure. The forces of good and evil, battling toe to toe, with good the final victor.

On the other hand he was loath to give in to sentiment. Polmeroy understood all too well Halliway's request and the importance it held for him. But too much could go wrong. There was too much at stake, not least of which was his job. If for some reason, the shot only grazed Fenton, or if he was left able to finish Jonah in some other fashion, how could Polmeroy ever explain it—to himself, much less everyone else? It was nonnegotiable. There was only one option. He felt confident he could handle this to everyone's satisfaction.

He told his troops to wait. He wanted to reconnoiter the layout of the house one last time. Polmeroy walked quickly down the near side of the barn, stopping at the corner closest to the house. Ducking as far down as his forty-three-year-old body would allow, he made his way to the front corner, eyeing distances, window heights, and door placement. He made his way back in the same fashion . . . quiet as a cat.

There were seven men awaiting his instructions at the back of the barn, their breath drifting off in the snowy, damp night air. Polmeroy thought of deploying them around the house but was hesitant to cause unnecessary noise. Fenton was still wearing Stickney's shirt when Polmeroy had eyed him, and from what he saw, with him sitting still in the rocker like that . . . well . . . Fenton certainly qualified as the perfect target. In fact, Polmeroy couldn't have set him on a pedestal any clearer. If half a dozen men started mucking around the house, who knew what could happen.

But the men felt the urgency to move. They could hear intermittent yelling originating from the house. It was difficult to tell who was who, but the two men inside were obviously having words.

"Hurry, Lieutenant," Halliway said. "Every second counts."

"Jackson," Polmeroy whispered, motioning for the sheriff to come forward.

"Yes, sir."

Polmeroy put his arm around Jackson's shoulder, turning him to face the other men in the semicircle. He wanted Halliway to hear this.

"Walk around the far side of the barn. I don't want to spook the horses more than we have to. Make tracks to that tractor and report back when you're in position. You'll see 'im. He's wearing a cop uniform. If he's stationary, take out his gun shoulder. If he's not, then go straight for the head. Got it?"

"Pretty simple."

"Wait for my order."

"Roger."

"And, Jackson."

"Yeah?"

"You got exactly one shot. Make it count."

"Thanks for the reminder," Jackson responded, taking off around the side of the barn.

With Jackson gone and Polmeroy in command, only four men remained available for action. Polmeroy hated to create movement where he didn't have to, but he'd have to have his men in a position to storm the house once the shot was fired. For better or worse, they would need to make an immediate entrance to secure the safety of the hostage and make certain of Fenton's neutralization.

"Follow me," he said, motioning to two of the team. When they came to the near corner at the back of the barn, he put up an arm indicating for them to stop. "You see the corner of the house there?" he whispered.

The two men nodded.

"Take positions there and wait. The side door to the house is immediately to your right. There's a large kitchen window on the side. You can get through it from the steps. If the door is locked, then smash in the side window and enter that way. I want you in that house one second after that shot is fired. Understand? Report to me when you're in. Remember, you're Team Red. Now, quiet as a mouse . . . go."

The two men left down the side of the barn, kneeling where they were told, motioning among themselves who would do what once they heard the shot.

Polmeroy quietly made his way back to the rear of the barn. He had no sooner arrived then Jackson reported he was in position. "I'm set," he whispered into his mike.

"Good. Stand by," Polmeroy whispered into his mike.

"You two," Polmeroy said, meeting back up with the other two state policemen. "From here out, you're Team Blue. Make your way along the back of the house, here," he said, motioning with his extended arm. "Quietly but quickly, see if you can get in position by the side door. I want one of you at the base of the steps, the other at the base of the far window. When you hear that shot, I want you both in that house before we hear the echo. If the door's locked, then follow your partner through the window. Report when you're in. All right, gentlemen, go . . . and don't make a peep."

"Wait here a moment, please," he ordered Halliway and Berkshire. "I'll be right back." He passed them and made his way around the far end of the barn.

Polmeroy walked approximately halfway down its length, then jogged to the end. He wished he could speak to Jackson on the tac channel, but that would make everyone else on the detail privy to the conversation he knew they needed to have. This was something best left to just the two of them. He walked around the corner of the barn, easily spying Jackson atop the tractor in the illumination of the kitchen light.

"Pssst," he whispered as he approached.

Jackson turned his head, watching his team leader approach. Polmeroy stepped up on the foot rail, Jackson leaning down to hear him.

"Jackson. Listen son," Polmeroy whispered. "I know what I said back there. But I'd feel a hell of a lot better if you just took him out," he whispered. "We just can't fuck around for these Connecticut boys, no matter how much I want to. There's too much at stake."

"You want me to take him out?" Jackson asked.

"Yes."

"With pleasure, sir."

"Good man," Polmeroy whispered, patting Jackson's rear before stepping down. "Oh . . . and Jackson," he said, taking one step back up.

"Yes, sir?"

"Let's just keep this between ourselves. I think that's best, don't you?"

"Yes, sir."

Polmeroy lightly grasped his shoulder. "Good luck," he whispered into Jackson's ear, leaving to make his way back to the rear of the barn.

"Gentlemen," he said, meeting up with Berkshire and Halliway in the back. "You can stay here or you can follow me. As long as the dog is quiet," he said, looking at Berkshire.

"Have you heard him yet?" Berkshire asked.

Polmeroy started toward the far side of the barn. "This way, gents," he said, leading the pack.

As they walked around the corner of the barn, the two men reported back from the far side of the house. "Team Blue in position," one of them whispered into Polmeroy's earplug.

"Copy that," Polmeroy said, holding up his unlikely entourage by raising a hand in back of him.

"Team Red. You ready?"

"Ten four," came the hushed response.

"Jackson. You got him lined up?"

"Roger."

"He's all yours. Fire at will."

Polmeroy and his two observers stepped quietly around the side of the barn, the light from the kitchen throwing Jackson's shadow twenty feet beyond. Halliway felt butterflies fluttering in his stomach, an internal voice repeating his one true wish. *Don't kill him. Just don't kill him.* In his thirty years on the force he couldn't think of anything he'd wanted more than to slap cuffs on this son of a bitch.

Halliway stood with Polmeroy, Lucky, and Berkshire by the near side of the wood chip pile. He wanted to see this. He deserved it. So did Bennett and Scott. He took a couple of steps over to the spreader and quietly placed a foot on a tire, hoisting himself up for a better view. *Your ass is grass, mister.*

Polmeroy held up his right hand for quiet, whispering into his mike. "Be ready, gentlemen. It's time."

There was hushed silence. Every man waiting for the thunder to arrive. No one breathed. In a second, it would all be over.

Halliway was a good twelve yards away. He squinted his eyes, fixing them like lasers on Fenton's face. It's odd how you see what you expect to see. Fenton looked different than he remembered. *Oh my God!* Halliway looked hard again, straining to clarify what he saw in his mind's eye. *Wait a minute. That's not Fenton! That's Roberts! You're shooting an innocent man!*

"*Wait!*" he boomed.

"Jesus Christ!" Polmeroy screamed, turning toward Halliway with murderous eyes. "What the fuck are—"

"Jackson! Don't shoot!" Halliway screamed, scurrying down the spreader. "That's not Fenton! The man in the rocking chair is Roberts. Don't shoot!" he pleaded, sprinting toward Jackson and the tractor.

Polmeroy hesitated for a split second, thundering instructions as Halliway's words registered. "Teams Red . . . Blue . . . Go! Go! Go!" he yelled, bolting toward the house.

———※———

The cavalry had yet to arrive as Jonah sat calmly, watching his hapless captive melt before his eyes. *What a poor excuse for a human being.* He softly patted the gaping wound on his ear, glancing at his fingers to check the blood. He wiped his upper lip with the back of his hand.

"Hungry, Fenton? What's in those things anyway? It can't be that bad."

Fenton mumbled something to the floor.

"What?" Jonah asked.

Fenton swallowed, clearing his mouth somewhat. He moved his face slightly off the carpet. Jonah heard the word from Fenton's partially-full mouth but didn't believe it. *What person in their right mind would shove a container of brownies full of strychnine in their mouth?* He laughed at the stupidity of his question. Fenton was hardly in his right mind.

"Strychnine?" he asked, raising an eyebrow in a questioning slant. "Right. And I'm Santa Claus."

"Whatever," Fenton said, rolling on his side.

"Then how come you're not dying on me?" Jonah asked, pointing his gun right at him.

"It takes time to work," Fenton whispered, his spirit broken.

"What?"

"I said, it takes time to work," Fenton said louder, staring at the stove.

Jonah was full of contempt. "You're full of shit, you know that? How much time?"

"Ten minutes, give or take."

Jonah didn't believe him, although he had to ask himself why Fenton was so adamant that *he* eat the brownies before the tables had turned. "Then we'll just wait, won't we? I could use some entertainment."

"You'll wish you hadn't."

"Why?"

"You'll see."

"You going to shit your pants? I could use a laugh."

Jonah nearly did just that when he heard Halliway's scream from outside, his eyes momentarily glancing at the far kitchen window he now faced. *What the hell?* He stood, taking a step toward Fenton, realizing where he stood at exactly the same instant his brain registered that Fenton's firm grip was around his ankle. The moment was upon him and moved in surreal slow motion.

Fenton was a dead man, but his body didn't know it yet. He'd be damned if he was going to meet God having failed in his mission. There was time yet to see *his* will through. With surprising strength, Fenton yanked Jonah's foot forward, sending him flying backwards to the ground. Jonah's head bounced as it hit the floor, blood spurting onto the carpeting from the wound to his ear.

Fenton leapt on top of Jonah, the two men locked now in a Herculean fight for life. Only two or three seconds had passed since they'd both heard Halliway yell from outside. It seemed like an hour. Fenton was by far the more dangerous one, at least for a short while. After all, of the two, *he* had very little left to lose. He straddled Jonah, butting his forehead into his enemy's broken nose, searing Jonah's brain with blistering waves of pain to his cerebellum.

Jonah's scream was rooted in his DNA—a primordial cry, rising from deep within his genes. *"AAAAAGGGH!"*

His scream was almost loud enough and long enough to drown out the sound of the SWAT team crashing through various means of entrances to the house. Fenton struggled with Jonah's right hand, trying to wrest control of the gun. His broken left wrist writhed in pain as the two grappled on the floor.

The SWAT team members converged on them, one of them stepping on Jonah's right wrist, holding down the gun. They'd never seen either Jonah or Fenton before, and they weren't sure who was who. Not that it would have mattered if they had seen them. All the blood and sweat covering their faces had rendered both men nearly unrecognizable.

Halliway ran into the kitchen, slowing his pace as he approached Fenton lying on the floor. One of the SWAT men held a boot to the side of his head, while another sat on his rear, bringing his hands around to cuff him.

Halliway frowned when he saw a team preparing Jonah the same way. "Careful. Careful," he said, standing over Fenton. *"This* is our boy." He tapped the shoulder of the cop on Fenton's back. "You mind?" he asked.

"Be my guest," the man said, scooting down Fenton's legs, allowing room for Halliway to sit.

Halliway smiled broadly as he straddled Fenton, plopping his weight down on the small of his back. "Hello, Fenton," he said, pulling Fenton's left arm back. "I'm Lieutenant Halliway. It's a pleasure to finally make your acquaintance."

Halliway could plainly see that Fenton's left wrist was broken, and slapped the cuffs on forcefully, snapping them tightly around his shattered bone. Fenton screamed from the shooting pain.

"This one's for Scott," he said, pulling Fenton's right arm back, doing likewise with it. Fenton screamed again—this time at the realization that he'd been caught—that he would spend his remaining years caged like some animal at the zoo.

"Somebody get shackles," Halliway said. "I've been waiting for this moment."

Jonah mumbled something about strychnine, but no one seemed to hear.

Fenton lay on his stomach, while Halliway sat on his back. Someone else was sitting on his calves while another cop's boot pushed squarely down on his jaw.

DOWNTICK

Tears streamed from Fenton's eyes. *Defeat!* "I'm sorry, Mommy," he sobbed. "I'm so sorry."

Halliway leaned down, placing his lips to his captive's ear, his cheek resting on the trooper's boot pushing at Fenton's jaw. "Your mommy can't help you now," he whispered.

EPILOGUE

—⟋⟍—

Bridgton Hospital
Bridgton, Maine
Monday, November 6

Resembling a boxer after a fifteen-round title fight, Jonah Roberts stood at the foot of Scott Hill's hospital bed holding Victoria by the hand. His eyes were black and blue and his ear was bandaged, but all things considered, he still looked remarkably healthy. There was a twinkle in his eyes, the natural result of the weight of the world having been lifted from his shoulders.

Halliway sat in a chair, the morning's *Portland Press Herald* folded in his lap. He looked fit and rested. He wore blue corduroys and cordovan loafers and his shirt sleeves were rolled up to the middle of his forearms.

Jonah and Victoria had spent the last twenty minutes speaking with the two detectives. They were both thankful but were also anxious to put this all behind them. They wanted to enjoy the farm . . . alone . . . together.

"Well . . . I guess we should get going," Jonah said. "We just wanted to come by and thank you both for all you've done. There's no way we can ever repay you."

Scott Hill was jovial, the narcotics flowing through his bloodstream helping to numb his body to the otherwise unbearable pain. "Nonsense," he said, a wide grin across his face. "All you have to do is let me and the family use your place for our vacation this summer and we'll call it even."

"Careful, Scott," Halliway said, looking up at his partner.

560

"Oh, relax, Ric. I'm only joking."

"You know, Sergeant, that's a great idea," Jonah said, looking at his wife. "Vickie and I are going to Australia this July. Why don't you consider the place yours? That'd be okay, huh, hon?"

"I think it's a great idea," Vickie said.

Hill spoke softly. "No, Mr. Roberts, I couldn't. But thank you just the same."

"Why not?" Jonah asked. "You think your partner here couldn't live with the graft?"

Hill grimaced as he laughed.

"Now wait just a minute," Halliway chimed in. "I don't have a problem with you giving your house away."

"Then what's the problem?"

"The only problem I've got is that *I* want to use it."

Hill thought he would vomit, but couldn't help himself. He laughed right through narcotized pain. "Yeah, that will be the day," he said.

"I'm serious. Chief doesn't know it yet," Halliway said, looking at his partner, "but I just worked my last case. I don't have to worry about accepting gifts if I'm not on the force."

Hill turned somber for a moment. "You serious, Ric?"

"As a matter of fact, I am. You know I've been thinking a lot about it the last few years, Scott, and I know Rose is just dying to get on with the rest of our lives. I can't think of a better exit point than now. It can only be downhill from here."

"Quit while you're on top, right Lieutenant?" Jonah added.

"Well, I can't say I blame you," Hill said. "I just wish I had another fifteen years under my belt."

"No you don't, Scott. It stinks growing old."

"Yeah, I was surprised to see you left your walker at the hotel."

Everyone laughed.

"Funny. Very funny."

"I hear Trooper Spowart's in the room next door," Jonah said. "Have you seen him yet?"

Halliway nodded. "I popped in this morning. Now

there's one lucky man. I guess they got him here fast enough for the docs to work their magic."

"I didn't know there were antidotes to strychnine," Jonah said.

Halliway crossed his arms. "Neither did I. As luck would have it, the doc on duty happened to be a trained toxicologist. I guess they gave him some intravenous Valium and some other stuff. Starts with an S, I think. Still, it was touch and go for a while."

"Man," Jonah said, shaking his head. "How about the other cop? The one they found hanging from the tree?"

"He's fine," Halliway said. "Just lucky his buddy found him when he did."

"So much mayhem for one man," Jonah said. "So . . . the same doctor works on Montague, and he pulls through. What do you think they'll do with him?"

"I know what I'd *like* to see," Halliway said. "But he'll be found incompetent to stand trial. Probably spend the rest of his miserable life in some cell in a psych hospital for the criminally insane."

"They should fry him for what he did to that poor boy," Hill said, contorting his face as he tried to find a comfortable position.

"They found the boy?" Victoria asked. "Was he alive?"

"No," Halliway said, staring down at his paper. "He wasn't as lucky as Montague. I spoke to our people this morning. New York found him in some ravine yesterday after the cops here spent a few hours grilling Montague. It looks like he bled to death. A cryin' shame."

"He won't ever get out, will he?" Victoria asked.

"No, don't worry about that, Mrs. Roberts. You'll be in real estate before the chance of that ever happens," Halliway said, as Hill nodded his head.

Vickie looked at Jonah. "Real estate?" she asked.

"Yeah, you know? Pushing daisies?"

"Oh . . . I get it," she said with a smile. "That's funny."

"How was the funeral?" Hill asked, his eyes growing groggy now.

Victoria took a deep breath. "Oh, you know how it goes. It was sad. Everyone cried."

DOWNTICK

The room fell silent for a bit.

Halliway broke it. "How are the boys?"

"I'm very proud of those kids," she said. "They've been through hell and back and they've held up like troopers."

"I like that phrase," Hill added, beginning to nod off.

"What are they going to do?" Halliway asked.

"Well, I'm not sure Becky knows. Money won't be a problem. They're back at the farm now. I think they'll stay for a month or so and then start to look around up here. I thought maybe the kids wouldn't want to, but she says they're excited. You know? Starting fresh and all."

"So they're moving to Maine, huh?" Halliway asked.

"Yep," Vickie said. *"You* should retire here, Lieutenant. It's a nice place to live."

Halliway smiled. "Yeah, I've kinda noticed that."

*"Hell is oneself; Hell is alone,
the other figures in it merely projections.
There is nothing to escape from
and nothing to escape to.
One is always alone."*

George Eliot